The Jøssing Affair

J.L. Oakley

ISBN 13: 978-0-9973237-0-2

Cover Design: j. allen fielder
Photo: Shutterstock

Published in the United States of America

1 3 5 7 9 10 8 6 4 2

DEDICATION

The Jøssing Affair is a piece of fiction set in German-occupied Norway during WW II. I almost stopped writing it after my second interview. The man's story of danger and hard choices that could bring tragedy to his family was beyond belief. How could I write fiction? Many thanks to those who told me to continue because I appreciated and understood the impact of the occupation on their generation.

I dedicate this work to all those ordinary citizens of the five year-long occupation of Norway and to those who resisted, some losing their lives. Jøssings all..

ACKNOWLEDGMENTS

Tusen takk to Martine Kalhovtd who explained fishing and fishing boats during the German occupation to me, a total landlubber; Jens Olaussen who told me about rationing and how the wood-burning funaces worked on their cars; Per Sorum who shared his life in occupied Trondheim; John and Lillian Froyen for their stories of life in Bergen, including the restaurant above the bowling alley used by the Nazis. Lillian skimmed the fat from the soup when no one was looking.

I would also like to thank Ivar Karglund at the *Norges Hjemmefrontmuseum* in Oslo for answering my questions about the resistance; Anders Krus, head priest at the *Hovedpresten for Norges Døve* in 1989. Many thanks to Hilde Meadow and her aunt Ellen Kastler for help with Norwegian words and phrases. Ellen was a girl when Norway was invaded and has stories of her own.

Tusen takk to Andrew S. McBride for editing and to Sara Stamey and Stephanie Cheng for their willingness to be a typo-hunter on such a big work.

Finally, a mention to Donna Marcontonio, my first ever reader of *The Jøssing Affair*, who listened to my crazy dream of a man in the snow and told me to write it down.

PROLOGUE

He found the young man lying in the snow, his battered body pushed deep under the brambles at the bottom of a ravine. If it had not been for the sound of the car door slamming, Hans Gunnerson would never have found him. Already the blanket wrapped around him was covered with snowflakes, partially hiding the bloodstains stiffening on the shoulders and back. Soon he would be lost forever to frost and mold.

A snowstorm that had threatened all day had finally come off the fjord. In record time, the snow had gathered strength and was hissing and whirling with a vengeance. It filled up the snow-laden woods with a dull silence. All for a car door.

Like a ghost, Gunnerson pressed back against the rock and stood still. Faintly, he heard a second and third metallic thud. Far off, two more doors had been opened and shut. There was a car on the logging road.

Torn between curiosity and caution, Gunnerson stayed where he was. The trail was well hidden from the road. Eight yards beyond, it switched back sharply to the right, away from the road and landslide. He crept forward in a cautious crouch. Obscured by the drooping spruce boughs, he was able to see the car, confirming his worst fears.

It was a black limousine, the kind favored by the Gestapo. Two officers dressed in the uniforms of the all-Norwegian SD stood beside it. One of them stomped and slapped his arms through his greatcoat while the other appeared to be talking to someone at the back of the car.

Gunnerson swallowed, trying to rid the taste of bile in his mouth. A feeling of dread and extreme danger started to seize him. All his senses were alert now.

And then Gunnerson saw him. Despite the cold, a sweat broke out on Gunnerson's brow. His mouth went dry.

A small, slim man with coarse black hair stepped away from the car and walked over to a nearby ravine. He pointed down into the gully, then turned back, his face looking in Gunnerson's direction. The narrow face with high cheekbones and thin lips in a wry smile left no doubt. It was Henry Oliver Rinnan.

Gunnerson's stomach tightened. Rinnan's presence could only mean one thing: an execution. His gaze stayed riveted to the uniformed men who were now gathered around the back door of the car. The little Norwegian was a Gestapo unit unto himself with a maniacal lust for brutal punishment of patriotic Norwegians. Gunnerson knew of him too well, but he could do nothing.

In dreamlike slowness, the door opened and what appeared to be a man was half-dragged, half-carried out onto the snow. Gunnerson could see bare shoulders before the blanket in which he was wrapped was pulled tighter around his head. He looked dead. The SD men maneuvered the body into the ravine. At a word from Rinnan, one of the men pulled out a gun, aimed and fired into the brambles. As Gunnerson expected, there was no sound from the long silencer.

The snow was falling steadily now. The men seemed anxious to leave, hunkering down against the wind or wiping snowflakes off their shoulders as they walked back to the car. Rinnan got in. After brushing the windshield, the other two followed. The car roared to life. For a brief moment, the wheels spun in the wet snow. Then it rocked and slipped its way back down the road and out of Gunnerson's line of sight. The woods became silent again.

Cautiously, Gunnerson stood up. Snowflakes covered his cap and gray beard like wet stickers. His hands were cold. *God help me*, he thought. *When will it ever end?*

He readjusted his rucksack and stepped back up on the trail. The snow hissed about his grim face. He felt weak, a hollow emptiness gurgling in his stomach, but he knew he would have to go down to that terrible place and see for himself. He feared and hated Rinnan, but it was terrible to die by *Nacht-und-Nebel* orders, laid in an unmarked grave.

He set off down through the trees and undergrowth. After some scrambling, he finally came out by the pile of earth and trees blocking the road. All that was left of the car was a rectangular patch of fuzzy new snow on the old. Gunnerson looked down the road and felt sure that it was deserted. There was no reason for them to suspect that they had been watched. They were too sure of themselves. Besides, the snowstorm was picking up.

At the bottom of the ravine, he stopped. His heart beat heavily, his bowels growled. The brambles were already piling up with snow. It was hard to see, so removing his rucksack, Gunnerson began to knock the snow off the tangle of bare branches at the deepest point of the ravine.

The body lay in the blanket like a mummy. A light veneer of snow already clung to it, but Gunnerson still could see a neat hole near the top, where the blanket was stiff with blood. He crouched in closer, and then, taking a deep breath, pulled the blanket away.

The young man was lying face down on his right cheek. He had been badly beaten. His eyes were shut tight and his lips were swollen. The skin beneath the cuts and bruises was a ghoulish pale gray, a haunted mask in the failing light. Was he an illegal worker or some innocent caught in Rinnan's net?

Gunnerson pulled the blanket away further to reveal heavily bruised shoulders and a flailed and savagely beaten upper back. The man's hands were tied. His right shoulder was covered with fresh blood where the bullet had nicked the flesh on top of the collarbone. The gunman had nearly missed his target altogether.

No matter. Nothing could be done for him now.

Gunnerson sighed. He knew there would be no identification. *Nach-und-Nebel* prisoners were generally stripped for that very reason. He looked at the black-haired head and in a moment of pity stroked it. *Just like Nils. My son...* The old grief returned. He closed his watery eyes. A slight gust of wind rose and sighed amid the falling snow. And then again—

Gunnerson's eyes sprung open and abruptly he took his hand away from the head.

You are imagining things, old fool, he thought. It's time to go.

He gathered the edge of the blanket and looked at the face again. The battered lips were parted, something he hadn't noticed before. Was it possible?

He searched for a pulse on the man's neck, cursing himself for not doing this sooner. Dead men did not bleed. His rough hand trembled. Nothing. Higher on the throat, he found a weak but fairly steady pulse. The young man was still alive! Alive! The old man was filled with a savage joy. Perhaps Rinnan had been cheated after all.

If Gunerson was to save the battered man, he had to work quickly. It might be dangerous to move him, but the cold was a greater danger. Kneeling down beside him, Gunnerson removed the bloody blanket from the man's lacerated back and cut the ropes that bound him. Only the man's shoes and socks were gone.

Gunnerson rolled him onto his back. A faint strangled moan escaped from the swollen lips, but the old man hardened himself to dressing the man with a shirt and socks from his rucksack. He stanched the wound with his scarf, then tightly wrapped him back in the blanket and put his own wool ski cap on the man's head.

There was a lull in the storm, but Gunnerson continued to work furiously. He decided to return to his hut by the logging road, the long-disused portion above the landslide. He chopped and limbed two small trees, then dragged and tossed them up on the road. He hoisted the blanketed bundle on his shoulder and put him on a travois from his own zipped-up coat with the newly-made poles pushed through and out the neck. He lashed them together with rope from the pack.

The woods were in almost total darkness when he started up the frozen hill. It took all of his strength to climb the gradually rising road. For nearly thirty minutes, he pulled and dragged his device, its precious cargo often slipping down under the rope as the coat sagged to the ground and skimmed the snow. He had to stop frequently to catch his breath, but the young man's faint heartbeat urged him on.

The one-room cabin, built for holiday hunters, was situated in a small tree-filled bowl. Gunnerson had improved it with bookshelves and more comfortable furniture. After lighting a lantern inside, he picked the young man up like a babe in arms and carried him inside. A large gray cat stretched on a bed near the corner of the room. He blinked his yellow eyes and yawned.

"Company, Samers." Gunnerson laid the young man on the bed.

He stoked the woodstove to a roar and completely removed the wet clothes from the unconscious man. In the bright light of the lantern, the full extent of his torture became apparent. In addition to his face and back—slashed, beaten, and caked with filth and dried blood from shoulders to buttocks—two fingers on his left hand were broken, the nails removed. An obscene two-inch swastika mark had been branded into his side.

"You bastard, Rinnan," he spat.

After checking for frostbite on the feet, and placing a new pad on the shoulder wound, Gunnerson gently piled covers over him. "Must warm him up gradually," he said to the cat. "Then I can fix him up."

Satisfied he had done enough, he changed his own clothes and made a cup of bouillon for himself. Pulling over a chair by the bed, he settled down to wait.

It was a long afternoon, and an even longer black night. The snow increased, piling up drifts on the windows and all around the bowl. Inside, it was warm, the only sounds the crack of the fire and the hissing lantern. His patient was so still. Nevertheless, he dripped warm water onto his lips to slake any thirst. It dribbled down the man's chin onto the pillow.

At some point he drifted off to sleep. When he woke, Samers was nestled in his lap. The snow had shrunk to smaller and less frequent flakes. The room was cooler. There was some semblance of color under the bruises on the swollen face. He felt the pulse and found it stronger. The skin tone looked better, too.

He got up and put more wood in the stove. He carefully dripped a teaspoonful of bouillon between the young man's teeth, then stopped, fearful he might choke him. The broth bubbled on the young man's lips, going down when he swallowed. Gunnerson decided to leave it at that. He searched for his pipe and settled back down in the chair.

Past dawn and through the rest of the day, he helped his patient fight a battle between chills and fever, bringing Gunnerson to the point of exhaustion. Through it all, he marveled that someone with so few reserves could exert so much will to not cry out. The few times he did, the sounds were mauled and flat, not the voice of anyone Gunnerson had ever heard. Sometimes, too, his good hand would jerk, the fingers moving in shapes and patterns as if they had meaning. God knew what he had been through—and only God knew where he was going. The old man took the hand and held it, thinking of his own dead son.

The fever abated on the second day along with the snowstorm. The sun was shining wanly through a gray January sky when Gunnerson came into the cabin with a load of wood. He had been thinking about his patient. Several things about him were intriguing. It was obvious that he had been in excellent shape before his ordeal. His hands showed that he was accustomed to work, but careful scrutiny of his right hand suggested telegraph or radio work. That fit into Gunnerson's theory that Rinnan had tortured him for information.

Samers was hunched down on the chair directly in front of the bed. The young man was awake. His one good eye was open. A gray color, it was full of fever and pain. He was on his side, looking at the cat.

"Well, *God morgen* to you. I hope you like cats," Gunnerson said. No response.

He carried the wood over to the stove and dropped it in a box while watching his patient on the bed. Still no response. He walked back over to the bed and picked up the cat. This time, the eye moved and looked at him. With some difficulty, the young man tried to move his head, but Gunnerson stayed him.

He sat down in the chair. "*Nei. Nei.* Rest. Don't trouble yourself. I am a friend and you are safe. Do you understand me?"

Slowly, the eye closed and opened again. The fingers on the good hand came together and made a series of weak motions.

Gunerson cleared his throat. "Do you have a name?"

The young man moved his hand to his throat and tapped it.

"Can't talk?" Of course, you can't, poor devil. Gunnerson lumbered up and returned with a pencil and a pad. "Can you write it?"

His patient paused, knitting his brows together. Finally he stabbed a name out: Jens Hans—

The young man shuddered. He dropped the pencil.

"Jens Hanstad? Hansen? Jens Hansen? Is that it?" Gunnerson wondered out loud, but the patient gave no answer. As he sank into his pillow, his fevered eye fluttered and closed. He let out a haunted sigh, then lay motionless upon the bed. The effort of writing seemed to have exhausted him.

Damn. Gunnerson turned the sheet of paper over in his hands, wondering what he should do next. Circumstances decided for him.

The fever returned that afternoon, far worse than before. But this time, there were no sounds. Only the man's fingers weakly moving in shapes and patterns, over and over again, telling some story he could only see.

BOOK 1

"Cod and herring all go the same way."

– *Old Norwegian saying*

CHAPTER 1

Central Norway, April 1944, Seven months earlier

"*Dumkopf!*"

Kjell Arneson looked up from his paperwork and froze. From the other side of the open fishhold, a German seaman had his man Hansen pressed up against the sloping shape of the scuttle.

"I said to show me what you have in the barrels." Taking his cap, the seaman slapped Hansen's face, making him recoil in shock and rub his cheek.

Only moments before the patrol boat had surprised them and ordered him to give way to come aboard. A slim officer in an oversized naval greatcoat and captain's cap too large for his head appeared and issued orders for inspection. His voice singing out above the tonk-tonk of the *Otta*'s engine, the German declared in broken Norwegian that he'd take charge of paperwork while the ordinary seamen inspected the hold and crew's cabin down below. Lines were thrown from the patrol boat. Uniformed German seamen came out from hiding and swarmed all over his luckless boat. The Devil take them, he thought.

"Oh, dear," Kjell said to the officer holding his passes. "I'm afraid my man can't..." His heart dropped a couple of beats.

"What's going on?" the German officer shouted.

"He won't comply, *Kapitänleutnant* Weissman, sir." The seaman grabbed Hansen by his coat front and jammed him against the scuttle. "*Dumkopf!*"

Like sharks, the other sailors waited impatiently for Hansen to obey.

"He can't hear. He's —" Kjell protested, but the officer cut him off.

"Bring him here," he bellowed. "We'll see if he'll comply."

Rough hands seized Hansen and pushed him alongside the edge of the fishhold to the wheelhouse where he was abruptly deposited in front of Weissman. At the officer's nod, they released him.

"You giving trouble?" Weissman barked.

Hansen shook his head, looking in Kjell's direction.

"Don't look at him. I'm talking to you."

"*Vær så snill,*" Kjell said. "He's a deaf-mute. He means no harm."

Hansen swallowed. He took out a battered little notebook and a pencil. Like a mime, he showed it to the officer, scribbling something on it before handing it over.

Kjell quickly made some signs to him. The young man's eyes lit up. He wrote again on the pad. The officer grabbed it before Hansen was able to finish. It read:

My name Jens Hansen. Write what you want me to do. I—

Weissman tossed the pad back. "Where are his papers?" he asked the seaman.

"All in order, sir. He has a medical card."

Weissman sneered, doing little to conceal his disdain, but Kjell felt more hopeful they would get through the search in one piece.

The second-in-command came up from the crew's quarters and signaled that nothing unusual had been found. The fishhold held no secrets beyond the stink of the night's catch, but fortunately they hadn't discovered the false wall in the galley. Weissman gave the cards back to Hansen, then dismissed him with a wave of his hand. "Where are you bound?" he asked Kjell.

"To the *landhandel* on that skerry over there, then home to Fjellstad. Should be in by three." Weissman looked in the direction Kjell pointed, but the mist had closed in again. "I have bills of lading, if you wish to see."

"*Nein*, it won't be necessary. You will observe the fifty mile fishing limit." He barked orders to return to the boat. He handed back Kjell's papers. "Be sure you register with the harbor masters at all times and keep that posted up." Weissman pointed to the required posters in the wheelhouse announcing the death penalty for anyone trying to flee the country by boat.

Bowing, Kjell put the papers back into his wallet. He signed "Get ready" to the deaf-mute. Hansen took off for the stern. He stood by the anchor, waiting for additional orders. When the Germans were back on the patrol boat, they released the lines. Seconds later, the vessel pulled away, its motor a hollow roar in the seeping mist. The inspection had taken less than twenty minutes.

Kjell waited until the boat disappeared behind the curtain of fog. Signing "All's well" to Hansen, he breathed a loud sigh of relief. When he arrived home, he'd remove the contraband.

***

The *Otta* returned to Fjellstad just before lunch. As they came up the long, narrow fjord, the little fishing village greeted them. A small hamlet scattered around the head of the fjord, its docks and attendant marine buildings were set below a ridge. The rest of the village sat on top: the main tourist hotel, *landhandel* and other businesses, a church, a school and brightly-colored square houses with high-pitched roofs. Beyond, the land gave way to farms and forests of pine and spruce clambering over rugged hills that swept back sharply to the barren *fjell* and towering mountains. Cold and unyielding, still heavy with winter snow, the mountains dwarfed everything spread below.

Fishing boats were everywhere, but tied up in an orderly manner, like keys on a piano. To the right, on the rocky shore, cod dried on tall racks by the hundreds. Split in half and hung over the rails, the fish looked like hand towels neatly placed on gigantic laundry racks.

The *Otta* docked at the small wharf next to a large red warehouse. An old ramshackle building on ancient pilings, it was visible from some distance even in the worst of weather, as was the painted sign on its top: *ARNESON OG SONN.* The warehouse and its sign had been there for many years, as familiar as the church and schoolyard. Unlike his father and grandfather, Kjell had no sons. While he fished, his two daughters kept the books and the home. It was an arrangement come to them by hardship after their mother died six years ago. While he had been in the maritime trades most of his life, he had never regretted his return to fishing local waters nor worried being seen as a stay-at-home man. In wartime, it gave him cover.

Now as Hansen made ready to weigh anchor, Kjell's throat tightened. The girls were there to assist. Kitty, a sixteen-year-old saved from plainness by a lively spirit and expressive blue eyes, led the way. "*Hei*, Pappa! How are you?"

"Fine!" Except for the last couple of nerve-wracking hours.

"And Jens?" She craned her neck to find him.

Kjell shook his head and laughed. What a case of puppy love. As soon as Hansen showed his face, she joined him in securing the small catch of cod in its barrels of brine.

"*Hei*, Pappa." Rika, his nineteen-year-old daughter, came dressed for work in her overalls, rubber boots, and a heavy wool sweater. She had the same flaxen hair as Kitty and a clear, almost transparent complexion, touched by a blush of pink on her flat cheeks, but the features in her oval face were more focused, making her quite pretty. A reflection of his wife Christine. Kjell sighed. Her talk of going to Trondheim to do bookkeeping and other office work made him fear he was losing her.

"Looks like you've been deserted. Can I help?"

Kjell handed her a rope to coil and caught up with news.

"There's mail inside the office, Pappa. Ella has several phone orders for you and a plate of *kake* from the *konditori*. Oh, the Germans are leaving."

Kjell quickly looked over to the edge of the wharf. The bulky shape of Frederick Fasting, the Nazi sheriff in their district, was mingling with the soldiers. Their distinctive steel helmets and field-gray greatcoats seemed out of place here. Local governments might run under the direction of the *Nasjional*

Samling, Norway's own Nazi party, but it was the administration of Joseph Terboven, the German *Reichcommissar* appointed by Hitler himself who ran the country, not Minister-President Vikdun Quisling. Nothing could change the fact that Norway was occupied.

Kjell layered the rope in a neat circle. "They clear out of the schoolhouse?"

"*Ja*, and their officer has checked out of the Tourist Hotel."

Kjell frowned, keeping his feelings of relief to himself. He didn't want to further worry his girls. He knew the drill: the soldiers came to make a house-to-house search for radios and other illegal contraband, a process that took several days. According to Rika, like many such operations done by bored soldiers in a rural community, they had run it sloppily. Sometimes they seemed more interested in eating and taking their breaks, but they were well armed and trained. The villagers were careful to observe the curfew and other restrictions.

Kjell was glad to see the Germans heavily laden with rifles, rucksacks, and other field equipment, a sure sign that they were going. Then Fjellstad could return to normal—if being occupied was normal.

"We've got soup on the stove and bread," Rika said.

"Sounds good." Kjell whistled to get Kitty's attention. "Let Jens know we're going in. We'll clean out the hold later." He gave Rika a hug when they were down.

Inside the chilly warehouse, he washed up at the faucet. The space was sparse, but neatly organized with nets, barrels for brining and fishing gear. He mentally made note of their last haul, including the materials of a more illegal nature, then went back into the warmth of the wood-paneled office. While Rika laid out soup bowls, Kjell took his place at the little table, stacking his mail by his plate. Kitty and Jens joined them last.

"Sit, sit," Kjell said. He always enjoyed this time. Kitty chattered on in her half-woman way and trying her best to please Hansen. Hansen drew a map and pictures in his notebook, signing and writing the story of their trip in the islands, but leaving out the patrol boat. It was typical of Rika to eat quietly while her sister monopolized Jens.

After a time, Hansen tapped Kjell on his wrist. What next job? he signed. He watched Kjell's lips intently.

"Why don't we finish unloading on top, then take the rest of the day off? You can catch up on your sleep then." He nodded toward the little room behind the office. It served as Hansen's bedroom. There had been a place for him at the house, but he preferred living alone.

Hansen nodded, making a sound in his throat, about as much as they ever heard from him.

"You could do me a favor, though," Kjell went on. "Kitty's going to the *landhandel* for canned goods. You wouldn't mind helping her to carry the stuff back, would you?"

Kitty stopped talking to her sister in mid-sentence, her cheeks flushing.

Hansen grinned at the girl. You, me, he signed. Ready, go, now?

"Oh, *ja* sure, Jens." She scrambled away from her chair and got her coat off the coat tree.

***

Outside, the air was crisp. By the edge of the warehouse, Hansen put his coat on while Kitty adjusted her wool headscarf. A woman with a little girl tugging on her hand behind her was coming down the dock toward them. Hansen watched her with interest. She was beautiful. About his age, she was tall and blonde with a slender figure that moved gracefully. Her red wool coat was open. The soft dark wool dress underneath seemed to flow over her body, caressing it in an unconscious way, giving accent to average but full breasts and hips. Slender legs disappeared into rugged high leather boots. She gave him a wary smile.

Her daughter broke out of her grasp, trotting along the open side of the wharf trying to kick a small rock down the icy boards. "Lisel!" the woman scolded.

Kitty pulled Hansen's coat sleeve, making him twist away. "*Tyskertøs*, Jens. A quisling. Didn't Pappa tell you? She's the Woman."

What?

"She's bad." Bad, Kitty signed for emphasis. She dragged him away, then suddenly froze. She stared past Hansen, her mouth half-opened.

What wrong?

Kitty's eyes widened, her hands gripping his coat lapels. It caused him to turn.

At the side of the wharf, the Woman was down on her knees. In her hands she held a long-handled fish net with which she desperately slapped at the water down below. The little girl was nowhere in sight. The Woman turned back toward him to plead for help, her eyes full of tears.

Hansen felt like he had been punched. An image of the little girl floating face down in the freezing water flashed across his mind. He moved instantly. Dashing over to the edge of the wharf, he followed the direction the Woman's hands pointed out into the cold gray water. To his relief, the girl was upright, weakly thrashing her arms. Hansen threw off his boots and jumped down into the water, hitting it feet first.

As the bitter cold water closed over him, he felt a wave of shock searing through his body, sucking his breath away and making it difficult to think. He oriented himself toward the little girl, concentrating on pulling her toward him. Once he had her, he put a hand under her chin, trying to ease her onto his hip, but she panicked, failing her hands and scratching him. He secured her and swam back to the side of the wharf. Kjell and several other men were hanging from a ladder there with their arms stretched out.

The little girl was leaf-light, her tow-colored hair plastered to her head, but when she went limp, Hansen felt his own body becoming numb, too. The weight of his bulky sweater and wool pants pulled him down. Kicking out once more, he grabbed onto the bottom rung and with Kjell's help lifted the girl out of the water. He was relieved when she began to whimper and cry.

After she was passed up, he pulled himself out and climbed up on his own power. His stocking feet were numb and slippery, but he still managed to scale the wood ladder.

Kitty and Rika threw blankets over him, leading him shivering toward the warehouse with large puddles of water in his wake. People were talking around him and at him, but he took no notice. He sought out the little blanketed bundle now being rushed up to Ella Bjornson's place. Someone from the village was carrying her, while alongside her the young mother gave words of encouragement. The Woman turned back toward him. Her lips formed "*Tusen takk.*" And then she was gone. For all his effort, he hoped it would be his first and only encounter with her. He knew more about the Woman than he had let on to Kitty.

Hansen spent most of the afternoon in front of the woodstove. The short time in the water had sucked all the warmth out of his body. The change of clothes and a cup of hot tea improved his disposition, but after the shivering stopped, he felt ridiculously sleepy for the next hour or so.

Finally, throwing on an extra sweater and coat, he headed up to the Bjornson store. Kjell had said the little girl was fine, but he wanted to see for himself. As he approached the tawny stucco storefront, he noticed once again that a blind in the window on the far right side had been pulled down.

The Bjornson store and its *konditori* was the heart of the waterfront, but it was going through hard times. Ella had lost a good deal during the summer of 1940. First, she lost her husband weeks after he was badly wounded during the fighting against the invading Germans in May. Then she lost the post office contract to the *landhandel* on top. Its owners were more correctly aligned to the new administrators of the land. It hurt her business, but many still came to the *konditori* because it was one place in the district boasting such fine pastries. Despite rationing, Ella had a way with baking.

The shop bell jangled when he stepped in. He peered over the tops of the half-filled shelves of merchandise, but no one was there. To his right, the *konditori* was deserted, too, so he headed directly to the back of the store, to Ella's living quarters upstairs.

He was about to knock when she came out, nearly crashing into him. She was a plump, generous woman. "Jens. Why on earth are you out? Why don't you rest?" Rest, she signed.

I fine. Where girl? She all right? He made soft sounds in his throat.

"She's gone." Ella's face grew hard. "Dr. Grimstad said she just needed to keep warm and watched."

She stopped talking as if to see if he was getting it all. Satisfied, she continued, "I'll not begrudge the little girl, sweet thing, but I can't understand why the Woman stays. We're supposed to tolerate the Germans so they'll actually think we like them and kowtow to all the quislings, but I will never. Especially that one." A fierce pride came to her eyes as she turned away.

Hansen reassured her with a clap on her plump shoulder. He signed he was leaving.

Outside, he stood on the steps for a moment. Kjell was down by his office.

I have news, he signed to Hansen. They walked off together.

CHAPTER 2

The night was deep and moonless, the village shut up tight and asleep. A man emerged from the shadows. Dressed in dark clothing, he negotiated with stealth the space between the last building and the open fields, sticking to the cover of the roadside ditch. After several hundred yards, he went off to the right along a narrow road running toward some scattered farms.

He moved quickly, staying down in the center of the road to avoid sky-lining himself on the shadowed hills. When he approached a farmhouse, its ochre-painted sides weird and ghostlike in the dark, he went to the opposite side of the road to avoid the possibility of dogs. The patches of old snow dotting the lane he dodged confidently. He had come this way several times before.

Soon, he cut off again, heading up into the pines that flowed down the flanks of the sharply rising hills. Half-groping his way, he came to a steep path nearly rising straight up along the incline. Now he encountered pockets of snow he could not avoid, but using their faint glow, he scrambled on up, grabbing onto the spindly trunks of pines lining the path. Eventually he came out on top of a wide sloping area several acres in size.

He stopped briefly to catch his breath and get his bearings. Partially covered with snow, the area once had been used for a *seter*—a place to graze cows and other livestock during the summer to free up the precious land below for crops.

Black objects, poorly defined, stood out against the charcoal-colored fields, but the man moved easily toward a leaning shape that seemed to rise out of rock. His hands moved over the rough stone and wood surface, locating a door. Seconds later, he was stepping down onto the musky dirt floor of an ancient hut. He closed the door, leaving himself in pitch darkness.

For the first time since leaving the village he risked using a light. He took a flashlight from his coat pocket and sprayed light on the back stone wall, illuminating a pile of old milk cans. He selected a battered can from the haphazard arrangement, lifting it carefully into the center of the room. The flashlight now illuminated a shelf protruding from the stones with a kerosene lamp upon it. After lighting it, he put it down on the floor beside the can and began searching for a hidden finger grip on the can's bottom. One pull on the metal and wood plug, and he exposed a British-made wireless transmitter receiver.

He quickly put the W/T in order on the steps. After checking the glowing dials on his watch, he laid out some cheese and bread and ate. He would have to wait in the cold.

He watched the lamplight make weird designs on the walls, illuminating his breath floating like puffs of fog before him. It reminded him of the time he had hidden from his brothers in their grandmother's dairy and got locked in. He nearly froze.

He checked his watch again. It was time. He wiped his hands on his pants and blew on them to warm them as best he could. He opened the door, making sure the lantern was covered. He adjusted the aerial. Placing the earphones on his head, he began sending his message.

First, he gave a series of signals to identify himself, then rapidly fired off his report to England. It was short and compact to avoid being tracked and ended almost as soon as it began. He closed down the W/T, carefully put it back into the milk can and placed it back within the pile. This might be the last time that he could transmit here. The long days of endless sun were coming and it would be too hard to make the trek up here without being observed. He would have to move it in closer—how to do that without risk to the villagers? He had taken a chance already, sending so soon after the soldiers left, but he had his orders.

He removed all signs of his presence in the hut and left, closing the door behind him. A flick of his flashlight around the door and he was off.

***

A few days after the incident at the wharf, Hansen received a note from Henrik Foss, the Fjellstad Tourist Hotel's manager. Since the first of April, Hansen had been doing odd jobs for Foss there. The hotel was a large two-story building commanding an excellent view of the fjord and its high walls looking out to its mouth. It had a comfortable sitting room as well as a dining room that boasted a fine *gravlaks*— dish salmon cured in brandy and fresh dill—and several other similar delicacies from the sea when in season.

Coming into the kitchen, Hansen slipped under the sink with his plumbing tools. It was a messy task. Hansen lay on his back, his undershirt sleeves rolled up, exposing his muscular arms. His long legs stuck out into the room. The kitchen staff was careful not to step on him as they got the lunch menu out to the tables, but from the dim space under the sink there appeared to be a lot of jostling. He suspected some of it was directed at him.

Eventually he stood up to turn on the now-working water faucet. Some staff seemed startled, as if he had reentered their presence a little too soon. One of the girls blushed. Marthe Larsen, the head cook, shooed them away with floured hands. Hansen cleaned up around the sink and put away the tools in the hotel's workroom.

When he emerged again, with clean shirt and hair combed, Marthe was waiting for him with a piece of *bløt kake*. "Come and sit, *Herr* Hansen," she said, pulling out the chair. "*Vær så snill*." She pantomimed eating and sitting.

Smiling, Hansen signed it wasn't necessary. When she insisted, he sat down. He didn't want to offend her. He bit into the sponge cake, savoring the cream and strawberries preserved from last summer. It was light and fruity, like the ones *Tante* Sophie made long ago.

Tante Sophie. Onkel Kris. Telavåg. An image of slaughtered cows and burning houses hit him. People screaming with no sound coming out of their mouths. He turned his face away from the cook, forcing the vision down.

She tapped his wrist and he turned back. "*Herr* Hansen. Don't you like it?"

Takk. Very nice. When he was finished, he wrote in his notebook: Where Foss?

"I haven't seen him since this morning." The cook took his empty plate.

Working at the hotel was often difficult. The female kitchen staff was kind and fun-loving and he knew he did good work, but that didn't prevent Foss from cheating him and treating him like an idiot. "Watch out for Foss," Kjell had warned him not long after he arrived in the village. "He's an outspoken supporter of German and Quisling policies and hates any civil resistance. He actually cheered when the Germans closed down Oslo University last winter and arrested a thousand students after they rioted. Don't cross him."

Hansen promised he would be careful, though it was hard when most of his dealings were with Foss. It was Foss who sent down messages to have him come to do an odd job, Foss who wrote down the instructions and Foss who paid him. He often showed his superiority toward Hansen by ordering him to do a job, canceling it, then complaining that he was lazy. He sensed Foss talked about him behind his back in his presence, but there wasn't much Hansen could do.

He thanked Marthe again and started for the back door. Suddenly, she caught him by the arm, giving him a warning look. He turned to see Foss standing just inside the swinging doors to the dining room. He was immaculate as ever, his tiny blond mustache carefully combed over his thin lips, his silk handkerchief in the proper jacket pocket.

"Come here," he said to Hansen.

What?

"Enough of that finger wagging. There is someone to see you in the sitting room."

Hansen's eyes widened. Who?

Foss didn't explain. He took two leaps and, grabbing Hansen by the coat sleeve, drew him out of the kitchen into a servant's corridor. "Now look, you idiot, I will not tolerate any disrespect. I know what many think of her, but you—you will be polite. Do you understand?"

Foss took off through the dim corridor lined with linens, coffee urns and other serving materials. Catching up, Hansen came around to the entrance to a hallway. Directly to the left French doors opened into a large room known as the sitting room. Well-appointed with rugs and floral drapes at the windows in the corner that looked out onto the fjord, the walls were paneled in pine and hung with prints of various scenes of rural life. Plump, comfortable chairs and a sofa were arranged in front of a stone fireplace removed from an ancient Norwegian farmhouse.

Foss led the way in. Hansen's curiosity was up now. Somehow it didn't surprise him that the beautiful young woman rising from the wing-backed chair was the distraught mother, the German whore. Foss introduced her in an almost self-effacing way. He obviously held her in high esteem.

"*Fru* Anna Fromme, this is our handyman, *Herr* Hansen."

"*God aften*." She smiled shyly, then turned to Foss. "Would you mind leaving us alone?" When Foss protested, she said it would be all right and walked him to the door.

After Foss left, Hansen watched her with a renewed interest. Up close, she was even lovelier. If she were in Germany, they'd probably be singing songs about her, yet he was struck by a gentle, sincere modesty as intriguing as the rosewater scent she wore.

"Shall I talk slowly? I understand that you read lips... Or write. Would you like to write?" Hansen flipped open his worn notebook. Me sit? He pointed to a chair.

She sat down on the sofa. "I won't keep you," she continued, speaking slowly, "but when I heard you were here..." Hansen wondered who told her. "…I wanted to come and thank you for saving my child. I can never repay you. The water was so cold. I was afraid for both of you."

Hansen grunted. He rocked his arms, the sign for "baby."

She understood! "Oh, Lisel is much better, *tusen takk*. She got a terrible cold, but today she wanted to play. She is only four, you know."

Anna rummaged in her worn leather purse, bringing out a book wrapped in paper and string. "*Vær så snill*, take this. I was told you enjoyed reading. It was one of my husband's favorites." She paused, frowning slightly. "He loved Lisel so and would thank you himself…"

Anna swallowed. Hansen was surprised to see her eyes glisten. "Vær så snill, you can open it later. That is all."

Hansen didn't know how to answer, but took the package. She stood up, struggling into her coat. On impulse he reached over to help her. She smiled softly. "Takk." They started for the door, but before they reached it, Hansen stopped and although he knew it would be cruel, he wrote down: You said "Was." Where is your husband?

Anna gave him a startled look. "*Mein Gott...* You don't know, do you? Then truly you can be my only friend and not judge me like the others. But then I will tell you that he is dead and now I lose you. Anyone can tell you the rest gladly. Good-bye, friend."

She opened the glass doors and slipped out down the wood paneled hallway to the left.

When he went after her, she was walking across the small lobby. People turned their backs on her—his countrymen's small act of civil resistance against Germans—but she held her head high and stepped through the doors to the outside.

Damn! he thought.

CHAPTER 3

A week after the soldiers left, Kjell and Hansen rose before dawn for a trip to Trondheim, the major city in the district. Borrowing Ella's wood-burning American Packard, they loaded the backseat with a basket of bread, cheese, and reindeer sausage for *spekemat* and extra bags of charcoal for the *knottgenerator*, a tall, unwieldy metal furnace mounted on the back of the car.

"Bye, Ella." Kjell stood at the *konditori's* threshold. The single bulb in the store made a dripping yellow patch of light on the steps.

"See you in a couple of days. *Takk* for watching the girls."

"Be good." Ella followed him down the stairs and waved good-bye to Hansen.

The car chugged out the long winding trek through the gray mountainous valleys east of the fjord. The sun was up and already the snow on the highest peak was tinged with pink. Here the mountains dove down to the edge of neat little farms with red barns and clusters of lowland birch, maple, and oak. The trees' small leaves were out in full force, a riot of spring greens against the pines on the hills and mountains. The single lane cut several times across the small river that in a month would bring the salmon fishermen out in droves, always climbing a little bit toward the deep wooded valley that led out of the fjord.

There was little communication. Kjell knew Hansen was tired. Hansen had been up most of the night preparing for this trip and the one they planned next week to the islands, so Kjell wasn't surprised when Hansen fell asleep. Still, after two and a half months, Kjell felt he had come to know the younger man's shifts of mood quite well. Lately, he had sensed a buildup of tension, like the slight tightening of a spring. Kjell knew the risks he took for himself and especially his daughters, but sometimes he wondered what drove Hansen to put himself in such a terrible, lonely position?

Sometimes he wondered who the hell Jens Hansen really was.

***

An hour later, Kjell pulled onto a muddy road screened by woods of birch, alders and a few large pines. After a few hundred yards they came to rest in front of an old moss-covered, deserted cabin. Kjell got out to check the *knottgenerator*. The slamming door woke Hansen and he sat up. "This it?" he called out in a clear masculine voice.

"*Ja*," Kjell answered.

As if a whole new person had stepped out of his skin, Hansen got out and stretched his legs. Gone was the fisherman's slouch and bland expression on his face. When he leaned his elbows on the hood of the car to run his fingers through his thick dark hair, he moved with the grace of a cat stretching from its rest.

"*God morgen,* Jens. Wondered when you'd wake up." Using elbow-length gloves, Kjell wedged a paper bag of charcoal into the furnace. "Just fueling up. Two bags should do it."

Hansen grinned. "Then I think I'll let you tangle with that. I'm going to change."

"How long will that take?"

"Not long. We'll be on time for the train." Hansen smiled an infectious grin.

Kjell closed up the furnace and put his gear on the back seat. When they were alone like this, they could finally let down their guard. No one knew, not even Kjell's daughters. Talking was forbidden except in the most secret places. Kjell could talk all he wanted, but if he forgot to face Hansen or tap him on his shoulder or pound on the table before speaking, Hansen ignored him.

"You just can't walk into a room and expect a deaf person to respond," Hansen had said.

Kjell learned that the hard way. The first day he brought Hansen to Fjellstad, Nazi Sheriff Fasting had demanded to see his papers. Hansen pretended not to hear and was beaten up for not complying. Kjell intervened, terrified that Hansen would be found out. Hansen was more than a new hand hired to help him with the fishing. He worked for the Shetland Bus.

Special Operations Executive (SOE), which had been created in Britain to train English agents for secret work, directed the Shetland Bus organization. Norway had its own section, and a part of it was a collection of Norwegian fishing boats and their skippers who had been going back and forth to the Shetland Islands northeast of Scotland since the invasion. The runs carried arms and agents. The runs were so regular they were dubbed the "Shetland Bus," but by fall of 1943 the Germans had become suspicious of the larger fishing boats. Some were attacked, a crew captured at least once. Recognizing the value of the Bus to the Allied war effort, Admiral Nimitz of the American Navy stepped in and offered SOE-Norway three submarine chasers: the *Hitra*, *Hessa*, and *Vigra*.

When he was asked to meet Hansen, Kjell had been working for export, a branch of the resistance that helped people in trouble to get out of Norway. Kjell was to house him and provide him a cover while Hansen established an operational group on the Central Norway coast. Hansen and Kjell had done this over the past eleven weeks. Working on their own, the two of them had operated the line undermanned and in utter secrecy.

"How late were you up?" Kjell closed the car door and came around to the front.

"Too late, but when we meet the *Hitra* next week I need all my hard intelligence ready."

Without further word, Hansen retrieved a rucksack from his seat and walked around to the back of the cabin. Kjell went off to relieve himself. Coming back to the car, he opened the door and took a piece of smoked reindeer meat from Ella's food basket. He was a bit nervous about all this. Hansen was going to travel south, and he didn't like the risk that it imposed even if it was necessary. Maybe he just didn't like changes.

They had become friends, as close as could be allowed because "Know only what you need to know" was the dictum in this line of work. The only thing Kjell's superiors had told him about Hansen was that despite his age he was an experienced intelligence agent. Kjell guessed he was from Oslo, from his accent, and probably highly educated, from the conversations they had out in the boat. Hansen did share that he had been working closely with XU, the intelligence service of the Norwegian resistance, and Britain's SIS since the spring of 1941 and that he had survived several "roll ups.' Kjell liked him for his quick mind tempered with a dry sense of humor.

Once Hansen was settled in at the warehouse, Kjell began to train him in all aspects of fishing. The cod were running and they spent cold, dark nights out with the longlines. Hansen had sailing experience, but hadn't done much sea fishing. Under Kjell, Hansen blossomed. Fuel shortages were common so there were no trips to the Lofoten Islands this time.

The "game" as they called it, went on. It was very dangerous, but Kjell learned to trust Hansen's ability to be the person he chose to be. Hansen taught him how to sign and communicate with him, finally involving Rika and Kitty, though they were not told of his true identity. He had a card showing how to finger spell the ABC's and wrote words down in a notebook before showing the sign. It took practice, but it became a part of their daily routine. Only when they were absolutely alone—totally unobserved—could they talk quietly.

Kjell once asked Hansen how he had come to know how to sign and finger spell. "It's unusual, you know, around here. The only deaf person I ever knew was a boy from a village down the coast. He was sent away to Trondheim to the *Hjemmet for Døve*, the Home for the Deaf, years ago. I think they taught only speech and lip-reading."

"I learned as a boy," was all Hansen said.

Hansen came out a few minutes later, wearing a threadbare suit and vest with a white shirt and stiff high collar. A pair of round tortoise shell spectacles made him looked pinched. The thick, sometimes unruly hair had been tamed, plastered with hair grease, and parted down the middle. There was a suggestion of gray at the temples. He looked like a formidable *Herr* Professor. Kjell squirmed when he saw him. Hansen tugged at the collar and grinned.

"Didn't you go to *gymnasium*, Kjell?'

"*Nei*. I went to sea, but cod and coalfish all go the same way, *jo*?"

"That's what they say. And so do men. Everything ends up in the same net." Hansen's eyes twinkled, but removing the spectacles to rub the bridge of his nose, he became more serious.

"Don't worry, Kjell. I promise you, things'll be fine. After you drop me off, you can go immediately to Trondheim. We'll meet as planned at Nidaros." He clapped Kjell reassuringly on the shoulder and put his spectacles back on. "Let's go."

Back in the car Hansen sorted through the large number of documents he piled on his lap. "Was everything there?" Kjell asked.

"*Ja*, tickets, ration cards, clothes. I've put away my coastal permit with my medical card."

Both men sat silent. They knew the risks. Once before in 1942, the Gestapo had "rolled up" a great number of underground organizations, especially Milorg, the military organization, and after brutal interrogations shot their leaders. A huge sweep came, first in the south, then in the north. British-trained agents had been exposed then, captured and executed. It didn't make it any more palatable to know that even the mere suspicion of being an "illegal" worker could mean disappearing in the "night fog"—*Nacht-und-Nebel.*

Kjell said nothing as he started the car and moved out to the roadway. Somehow, Hansen had caught his apprehension. Not that Kjell was worried about him. The hard life at sea created a few axeioms of his own, such as: "If a squall comes up, the boat will rock."

Someone could fall overboard, but not Hansen. He'd adjust and ride out the storm.

For himself, Kjell hoped when the storm came, he would have a port to run home to.

CHAPTER 4

The train was late, but Hansen took the news in stride. Inside the little brick station he bought a copy of *Fritt Folk*, the quisling newspaper. He found a wood bench opposite the main entrance in case there was trouble and sat down. On the other end a woman sat breastfeeding her infant under a woven shawl. She had her round back to him, but she turned when he put his suitcase on the bench. He nodded, then looked at the newspaper.

"Big News," the headline said, but it was the usual tripe about Quisling addressing some NS function in Oslo. Hansen didn't recognize all the names. He read it anyway, holding the paper over his knees like a map. Around him the room ebbed and flowed with the comings and goings of farm folk loaded down with baskets and overstuffed luggage, and loudmouthed German soldiers on leave. When the big Dovregubben engine finally chugged in, he put the newspaper under his arm and quietly joined the line forming at the gate.

"Papers," a uniformed train guard commanded wearily at one of the little card tables inside the gate.

"*Ja*, of course." *Poor bastard*, Hansen thought as he pulled out his ticket and passes. Another Norwegian pressed into service.

"*Herr* Professor Smolen?"

"*Ja*." And a million other names. Today, Smolen, this morning Hansen. When was the last time he had been himself, Tore Haugland?

He did not even watch the proceedings of flipping and stamping the pages, trusting that his papers made in a rabbit warren of offices in London would pass the test. Behind the tables a number of soldiers attached to the SD watched like observant field-gray hawks on a telephone line, ready to pounce at the slightest nervousness in their prey. The train guard pored over the booklet then gave it back.

"Enjoy your holiday."

"*Takk*," Haugland said. He dipped his head and moved on. He was not out of danger yet, but he had passed this test. Ever conscious of being watched, he calmly put his papers inside his coat and began walking toward one of the third class cars where a group of soldiers from the Wehrmacht were chatting with a young woman leaning out of a window. A puff of steam drifted up from the car's undercarriage. She batted it away. A soldier offered her a pencil and notebook, another his cigarette lighter as she leaned low and exposed cleavage and a lacy pink slip under her dress.

"Halt!" someone yelled.

The hairs on the back of his neck prickled, but Haugland didn't halt. He kept moving, breathing easier as soldiers brushed past him. Haugland did not look back, not even at sounds of scuffling, the clatter of falling chairs, and the voice of a man shouting as he was subdued.

Inside one of the crowded compartments, Haugland stuffed his gear into the overhead shelf, then found a seat next to an elderly *fru* who regarded him with the respect offered teachers. Moments later, they were off with a hesitant jerk. Soon scenery was whipping by the window.

Haugland began to relax. After the train made its short run across the river valley dotted with neat farms, it would head toward the high mountains of the Dovrefjell, a steady climb of over seventy miles. The valley walls narrowed there, becoming forested and steep with hints of snow in the upper regions. He didn't believe snow conditions at the 3,300-foot summit at Hjerkinn would be difficult. The rest of the way would be literally downhill. It would take about ten hours to get to Oslo, but his point of departure was the station in Kvam, where he was to make contact with the local underground, roughly half way from the end of the line.

At first, the trip went smoothly. Sitting on the cushioned wood bench, he engaged in small talk with his companion, *Fru* Brun, who spoke of her farm and life in Lillehammer, in the Gudbrandsdal Valley in southern Norway where fertile farmlands undulated alongside its length.

"Of course, things have changed," she said in a low voice, "but we do our best."

Haugland offered his condolences. During the campaign of April 1940, many of the villages were bombed. There had been heavy fighting between the Germans and the vastly outclassed Norwegians and British and French troops sent in to help them. He wondered if she had lost someone. They didn't speak of this. Only the life that went on now despite deprivations and the threats of hostage-taking.

"This is my favorite time of year," she said.

It had been his once, too, but for the last four years April and May had meant personal loss from betrayal or executions.

"It's a good farm," she said. "And you, *Herr* Professor, are you on holiday?"

"I am," he replied. "I've taken leave of my *gymnasium* to write a book on door mantels in old farmhouses. It's a passion of mine." He gave her some examples meant to reinforce her opinion that he was a learned and interesting person. Although if she really considered it, he thought, I've told her absolutely nothing about myself.

Eventually, the conversation slackened. *Fru* Brun took out some knitting. He excused himself and went off in search of the men's room in the second-class cars.

The train was now deep into its ascent to the summit at Hjerkin. Following the Driva River, the line went through a pine and birch forested valley that had become very narrow and precipitous. It continued on, more and more gorge-like, until snowsheds, stone screens, and tunnels appeared, erected to protect against avalanches and rockfall. The mountain walls here were almost perpendicular and the passing train seemed dwarfed beneath them. In fact, it noticeably struggled up the incline.

Haugland lurched through the swaying corridors of the second-class cars. Here the compartments were not much different from third class. The train spread out. From the long windows in the passage it seemed to bend back on itself. He found the rest room and stepped in.

Minutes later, opening the door to go back out, he heard voices speaking in German down the corridor. He stood perfectly still. With the door slightly ajar, he could see one of the men from a reflection on the window. When the train plunged into darkness as it entered a long tunnel, it created a mirror along the length of the car in the eerie overhead light. Haugland saw a heavy-set man with short-cropped red hair.

"Was hast du herausgefunden?"

"Ja, ganz gewiss gibt es mit dem Motor Probleme. Ich meine, wir müssen eine Stunde in Hjerkinn warten. Der Schaffner ist schon befragt worden."

So there was something wrong with the train's engine.

Haugland listened carefully as they made plans to have everyone disembark one car at a time once they reached Hjerkinn. They would check papers. It would be for an extended period. The other man he couldn't see, but before the train emerged from the tunnel in an explosion of light, the man moved and Haugland saw that it was a Gestapo agent from the spot check. His stomach tightened. Trouble was brewing.

The voices broke off as someone entered the corridor from the opposite end. He carefully closed and locked the door, then turned on the tap. He looked at himself in the mirror over the sink. He looked grim and tired. This was not the easy trip he has planned, but he knew what he had to do. Giving the toilet another flush, he combed his hair flat and unlocked the door.

Except for a well-dressed gentleman who waited, there was no one else in the corridor. Haugland nodded to him stiffly, then headed off in the opposite direction from his coach. Somewhere ahead was the dining car and if he guessed right, another special car. There was more than the usual security on board.

This railroad was a major link between Oslo and Trondheim. More importantly, he knew it connected in Trondheim to the only rail route into the northern part of the country where the Germans maintained troops and equipment.

Haugland continued along through the next two cars, finally arriving at the door to the diner car. Standing in the cold entryway, he peered through the window into the room. It was partially filled. Squaring his shoulders, he opened the door, stepping into the warm room where the clink of glass and utensils and the hum of conversation drowsily mingled with that of the train. He pretended to seek out a table, but looked back at the end of the car and saw what he knew he'd see—a soldier stationed outside the door leading to the next car. In addition, agents occupied the last two tables— their haircuts gave them away. Someone special was on board.

"May I help you, *Herr* Professor?" an approaching waiter asked.

"A menu, *tusen takk*." Haugland looked at it quickly while he stood near the door. "I should like to reserve a table for two." He made a decision. The train was going to stop for some time in Hjerkinn, and they would be asked to disembark. He would at least be comfortable and boldly sit in the most closely watched spot.

Sometime later he came back, escorting a beaming *Fru* Brun.

He got the attention of the waiter, who sat them at a table near the center of the car by a window. Haugland couldn't have picked a better place himself. As for *Fru* Brun, it wasn't his intention in any way to put her in danger, but she aided his cover. If questioned, their acquaintance had evolved naturally as it happens when traveling and he was only being courteous. He felt she wouldn't be harmed.

The train moved higher toward the summit and the wild fjell. There was snow on the ridges and sullen clouds clung to the bare rocks at odd angles, like hoary feather boas drifting in the wind. As they came closer to the vast mountain plateau, it seemed to him, though, that there was a noticeable change in the way the train was moving, as if it were straining to reach its goal. This side of the summit was steep, but much more gradual than the approach from Dombås on the other side; yet the train seemed to move slower and slower. He began to suspect sabotage, but not of a lethal nature because this was a passenger train and his countrymen frowned on hurting innocent citizens.

Perhaps some local group wanted to delay the train because someone important was on board. For that they could use abrasive grease, a specialty of SOE. It looked ordinary except it wore out the parts in the engine it was supposed to lubricate. Given the strain the engine was under, it could have been applied and cause damage since they left Trondheim. No one could pinpoint the exact place of application.

Whatever the motive or method, the diner car seemed to strain and pull back. Haugland began to wonder if they would even make it to Kongsvoll, the next stop on the line, but more importantly he wondered what would happen when they got there. It would be ironic that after all his careful planning and precautions, he'd be caught in the aftermath of some other resistance group's activities. It wouldn't be the first time, he thought grimly, that an agent had been exposed in such a fashion.

"Is anything wrong?" *Fru* Brun asked.

"I believe the train is under some stress," he said as he wiped his mouth carefully with his napkin. He was annoyed with himself for being uncommonly transparent, but he was worried. If he was delayed, he could miss his contact in Kvam. If they were all carted off to a detention camp, he could be found out. He thought of his suitcase above his seat and prayed it wouldn't be searched.

"Is it serious?"

"I believe so. Are your papers in order? We may be stopping for some time. We'll wait here. It will be more comfortable."

Not long after, a conductor stuck his head into the diner, announcing Kongsvoll. Only one person got up to leave, but watching the door to the other car, Haugland noticed activity behind it. The soldier had stepped aside, and the heavyset man he had seen earlier came out and briefly talked to the two men at the far table before leaving for the passenger cars.

It was drizzling when the train came limping into Kongsvoll. Pulling up to the station, it seemed to shudder, letting out a blast of steam in one long gasp. Some train personnel got off, but Kongsvoll was only a winter sports station and there would be little here. Only a few miles up the line was the vast Dovrefjell. Hjerkinn, the summit, wasn't far beyond. For a long time nothing happened. The rain beaded upon the window with little pinpricks of water, distorting the buildings and people outside. It looked chilly and miserable.

Inside it was warm. The clink of dishes and murmur of conversation continued around them, belying any suspicion of trouble. Haugland ordered two more coffees and some dessert for *Fru* Brun and was about to sip the steaming liquid when there was a shout outside. From out of the gray gloom came the stamp and scrape of jackbooted German soldiers. They lined up alongside the train in formation, their rifles at their sides. Several people at the tables stood up and craned their necks for a better view, looking in disbelief as a large group of men and boys were herded in front of the soldiers, their backs to the train. They ranged in age from a youth to several elderly men.

So it's begun, Haugland thought as he watched them spread out in a line and stand there, confused, but silent. They were unloading car by car like the German said. Some of the hostages stiffened when an officer from the *Wehrmacht*, accompanied by the two plain-clothes men Haugland had met earlier, walked along in front of them, occasionally stopping to address someone in the line. The trolls were having a field day.

"There is no reason for alarm," a voice boomed from the back of the car. One of the SD men seated at the back stood up and addressed the diners. There was dead silence.

"I suggest that you all sit down. There has been some problem with the engine. It will be necessary to bring up a new one."

There was a gasp of dismay.

The agent continued in fluent Norwegian, "In the meantime, you will wait. We find it necessary, however, to ask men and boys to leave the car and wait outside with the others. This you will do now. I regret the inconvenience."

Everyone who was standing sat. Someone began to weep.

"Why are they doing this?" *Fru* Brun whispered.

"Just as he says, to inconvenience us."

"But the weather..."

"I don't think it worries them at all." He shrugged. He gave her a reassuring smile though his mouth was dry and his legs felt weak. He straightened his shoulders. He would do what he was trained to do and concentrate on that. Grateful he had brought his hat, Haugland stood and bowed to *Fru* Brun. "May we meet again." Then he joined the exodus to the dismal world outside.

CHAPTER 5

Having made the last ten miles of winding road on the remaining bag of *knott*, Kjell steeled himself for a new kind of ordeal—finding a parking space in the city of Trondheim. He had arrived just in time for the late morning jam of bicycles and German motor vehicles. As a result, he made a left to avoid the snarl, bringing him onto the bridge that crossed the river Nid into the city itself.

"The Devil." He squeezed behind a truck and a bevy of bicycles and crawled into Trondheim.

Trondheim was the third largest city in Norway—with 56,000 souls. It was founded almost nine hundred years before at the mouth of the river Nid. It had once been the capital of Norway in the Middle Ages. In modern times, because it was a major port, the Germans included it in their attack on Norway. It fell to them readily after ships brought troops into the harbor. But you're still beautiful, Kjell thought. Germans or no.

Kjell loved coming here, making the trip at least once a year. He wondered if Hansen felt the same way about the city as he did. Hansen had shown his knowledge of the city's importance as a rich agricultural and industrial region, its seaport with shipbuilding facilities and busy quays. But what of its heart should he look down on it from the forested hills outside the city? Hansen probably would only see the German marine traffic and airfields of the Luftwaffe as they sortied out to harass and destroy the Allied convoys going far north to Murmansk. He certainly was interested in the specially built pens for German U-boats.

"Forget Hansen, you lovely old girl," Kjell said. "We'll get you back. I promise."

Kjell intended to check on some marine supply houses for the remainder of the morning, but as he drove up the broad Prinsensgata, he decided to go by the ancient Nidros Cathedral. He would meet Jens there in two days. As he drove along he could see its single spire soaring above all the other buildings. At its back, near the ambulatory, there were trees that went down to the river flowing alongside the large grounds. Kjell parked the car and decided to go visit.

The cathedral was an imposing, bluish gray structure with a single spire in the middle of its roof. It was set well back from the road, but the church's full length paralleled it. Composed of several styles, the western end of the ancient structure had been restored in a Gothic style after fire had ravaged it three times. The original transept and chapter house were late Romanesque. Nidaros Cathedral was the pride of the nation.

The day was sunny and warm. Families, young lovers, and workers crowded the grounds. After the long, dark winter, everyone wanted to be in the sunshine. Kjell smiled, but dropped it when a group of uniformed German soldiers, some with Norwegian girlfriends on their arms, threaded their way past him. The sunshine that touched them was cold. Instinctively, he removed his fisherman's cap as they went by.

"Kjell!"

He turned to face two young men dressed in ill-fitting suits and ties. They were fishermen from the island of Frøya some distance from the coast and Fjellstad.

"Bent," Kjell said. "I thought you couldn't leave your girl longer than five minutes."

"*Ja, ja.*" Bent Kjelstrup beamed a broad, boyish smile. He was a slim young man in his early twenties. Kjell was his godfather. The other man was Odd Sorting, a strong and compactly built man with clean, sharp features and a robust complexion. He had recently returned to the islands after an absence of five years. He had a pleasant, ingratiating manner most found acceptable, but Kjell thought him a bit loose with his lips.

"We're on holiday," Sorting said. "We've had good two days of it already. Say, where's your man, Hansen?" Sorting looked around. "I thought he always went with you."

"Doing some sightseeing." Kjell hid rising irritation. "He can handle himself."

Bent turned to Kjell. "Why are you here?"

"Shopping for a net, if I can find one."

"We're thinking of finding a *bakeri* and getting something to eat. Can you come?"

"I never turn down *kake*, but only for a little bit. You're not going to Frøya next week?"

Bent hesitated, shooting a glance at Sorting. The other nodded slightly. Bent looked cautiously at the people moving around them before he turned back to Kjell.

"Can I answer you at the *bakeri*? There's something I want to tell you."

Ten minutes later they were seated in a booth away from the bustle of the other customers. They ordered coffee and pastry. Kjell and Bent caught up on family news until they were served. Sorting leaned back against the dark wooden paneling and stroked the handle of his coffee mug with his index finger like he was stroking a cat.

Bent shifted uncomfortably. "There's a boat being made available to us on Frøya, for about thirty in all, so we can go to the Shetland Islands. It's being outfitted now and a pilot looked for. Imagine me in Scotland! In a few days I'll be free!"

This was news to Kjell. The export section of the resistance provided means of escape for those being hunted by the Gestapo or wishing to join the Norwegian forces in England. Kjell had been involved with the regional cell for some time, but he hadn't heard about this action.

"Who's organizing it? This is risky, Bent."

"A loyal Norwegian I know." Sorting put his elbows on the table, clasping his hands like he was going to arm wrestle them. "They hope to leave the middle of May."

"Are you going too?" Kjell felt hot and uneasy.

"*Nei*, I'm going to stay back. There's important work to do."

Kjell understood what kind of work the man was hinting at, but he didn't take Sorting's bait. He wanted people to believe he was not a political man.

Kjell looked at Bent. He understood Bent's desire to leave Norway. There had been talk of conscripting young men for the labor service (AT) again, but under a new plan of Quisling's some feared they would be sent to Germany to meet the rising demand for workers as more German men were sent to the front. Worse, they could be forced into the *Wehrmacht*.

Kjell put his hands together as in prayer. "I wish you well, Bent. But *vær så snill, vær så snill*, be cautious. Remember Ålesund and Lillehavn."

"I do."

Kjell was looking at Bent, but he detected just the slightest twitch on Sorting's lips. Maybe I've scored a point, Kjell thought. *Razzias* had struck both places with deadly force.

"I know your parents will think it worth the risk for you and their own lives," Kjell continued. "Don't forget Frøya has been gun-shy since last fall. There were arrests."

Bent shivered. "I won't. I know that there could be reprisals against my family. I'm sorry that Odd isn't going, though, but I understand." He smiled at his friend. Kjell smiled too.

"Well, at least I will have someone to look up when I go to the islands. Perhaps we can talk again, *Herr* Sorting. I'll treat you to lunch." Kjell's voice was congenial and warm as always.

"*Takk.*" Sorting nodded his pleasure. With that, they finished up and made ready to go. Bent got up first, his mouth in a frown. "Kjell, tell no one. Just that I've gone south."

"Of course."

There was a final good-bye, then the two took off, leaving Kjell standing alone by the entrance. He suddenly felt tired and prayed that all would go well. Escapes by boat had been happening since the early days of the occupation, but somehow, this one felt different.

Look for a common thread. That's what Hansen had warned. Sorting had given it away with his eyes because in both incidents at Ålesund and Lillehavn there was a common thread, a man named Henry Oliver Rinnan.

Kjell pulled his coat closer. Hansen should be here, he thought. After all the weeks they had been working side-by-side, he felt he found their first break.

And for the first time, he was afraid.

CHAPTER 6

Anna Fromme quietly moved to the edge of the bed and swung her bare feet onto the pine wood floor. Behind her Lisel slept, her stuffy nose a gentle snore. Since falling into the water she had been fighting a cold. Worse, her nightmares had returned. She couldn't sleep.

Anna sat for a while listening to the sounds of the house as her feet sought a pair of worn slippers placed by the bed, then picking up a shawl hanging on the headboard went out to the dim living area. At a large window covered by a thick blind of painted black cloth, she tugged at the cord and the curtain snapped up readily, allowing not only the daylight to pour into the room, but a spectacular view of the fjord.

"Oh, Einar." She snuffled back sudden tears. "Sweetheart. It's so beautiful today."

Einar Fromme's great-grandfather, Jarle Fromme, had built the house on a hill. Loving the inland sea that flowed to the rocky shore of the fjord's wide head, he had built the kitchen and the living room or *stue* as one so he could always look at it. To the right, the roofs of Fjellstad and the masts of many boats could be seen a mile away. Anna could almost smell the cod, split, and drying on wood racks.

Directly in front of the window were four fruit trees. Dwarfed by the wind, their delicate pink blossoms rustled slightly in the breeze. From there the grassy hill rolled gently away from the house and down. A driveway followed it. To the left, the land curved around for another mile until it came up against the steep forested flanks of the mountains. There were other farms like hers, connected by a gravel road that followed the shore, but only a few fisher huts were next to the water. It was quite uninhabited, with stands of pine trees separating the little farms.

Anna stared at the fjord, lost in thoughts of her husband Einar trudging up their gravel road in Lilllehavn, Einar in rubber boots over his schoolteacher pants. A cat meowed and the image popped. Padding over from the kitchen table was a large black and white cat.

"*Gut morgen*, Gretel," Anna said in German. "Where's Gubben?" Her kitten had to be somewhere about. Five weeks old and already as big as a troll, she thought.

She rolled up the blackout curtain on the window in the kitchen area, then set about making breakfast and coffee. With Lisel coming to her bed, Anna had slept little herself.

A thud from the bedroom made her turn in time to see a white kitten with a black nose scurry out of the hallway. Barely keeping its footing on the polished wood floor, the kitten charged by her, but Anna scooped it up. "Come on, you little rascal. Let's go see the damage."

Anna tiptoed into the room and stopped. On the floor a silver picture frame lay facedown.

Putting the kitten on the bed, she tenderly picked up the frame. It wasn't broken, but it still caused tears to come unbidden for the second time that morning.

It was picture of Einar she had taken six years ago when there was love and hope in the world—their world—and nothing could shake it.

He wore a Nordic sweater and wool pants and leaned against one of the canal bridges in Amsterdam. The black and white photo couldn't show the depth of his dark blue eyes, nor the softness of his hair the color of flax, but Anna could see the warmth in his eyes and mouth. He held his favorite pipe in his hands and he was laughing. Except when Lisel was born, it had been one of the happiest times of her life.

She had met Einar by accident. He had come over from neutral Norway to Amsterdam for a holiday. She had gone to Amsterdam as a guide for a "Strength Through Joy" group, a popular vacation program set up for workers and their families in the Nazi Party. In 1938, it was still easy to travel.

Each holding a ticket for the same seat at a concert, they stood in the middle of the row and tried several languages before they discovered they both could speak English.

"Everyone learns it in school in Norway," he said. Anna spoke it quite well because of her mother.

Their conversation plowed on until they both started laughing. "I thought you were Dutch," he said. She thought him Swedish. Their nationalities surprised them both.

"I can come back another time," Anna said.

"No, you must stay. I insist."

"Only if you will consent to meeting me tomorrow. I have passes to see the Rembrandts."

Einar smiled. "I agree."

Anna put the picture on her breast and cradled it in her arms, a faint smile on her lips. Tears rolled down her cheeks and caressed the edges of her mouth.

He was older by almost eight years, but they not only spent a wonderful day together, but the entire week. Making sure she was not followed, they would meet at a prearranged spot and slip away to hours of discovery and open discussions of books and ideas. In her own household, it was difficult discussing events without arguing or feeling intense disapproval since her father remarried.

"I love you," she said to the picture, though she couldn't remember if it was love at first sight or their first week together or his talk of Norway. He often spoke of his country and his life here. It sounded beautiful, but there were more people in Berlin than in all of Norway. It was the most sparsely populated country in Europe, its people living in tiny hamlets isolated by mountains or fjords. She wondered if she'd like that and kept imagining herself in the places he talked about and being there with him.

Whatever it was, they became more relaxed and increasingly so conscious of each other that the brief brush of fingers on hand or walking too close disturbed them both. They felt alive and deliciously happy.

On the fifth day they took the train out to Rotterdam and spent the day there.

Anna put a finger on her lips. "You kissed me and then you said, 'Come to Norway. We'll get married. It's neutral. You'll be safe.'"

It had been love, dizzy love. They had gone to Copenhagen for a couple of days after that. They secured the necessary paperwork and took off immediately. It was a time of great happiness and growth. Although he didn't press her, they finally made love in a tiny room, she making the decision herself after weighing the consequences. Before parting, he promised to write and make arrangements to get her out.

Lisel sighed in her sleep and pulled her pillow close to her little chest. Anna backed away from the bed, the picture clutched in her arm. She began to weep silently again.

"I want Lisel to be safe, Einar, but I have no idea whom to turn to. *I* want to be safe. And I miss you so." She kissed the frame. "You kept your promises. We were so happy. Why did you change? Why didn't you trust me anymore?

CHAPTER 7

Fog drifted across the rails like a frozen stray cloud, graying the station and outbuildings, the train and a lone truck. For over an hour, Haugland and the group of men and boys braved oppressive cold and mist as they stood along the tracks under heavy guard. The fog seeped into their clothing and splattered their faces. Like Haugland, some had managed to grab coats, but many had none. When he adjusted the collar of his soaked wool overcoat, he bumped into a youth standing next to him.

"Sorry," he murmured.

"It's all right." The boy hunched his shoulders. "Are you a schoolteacher?"

Haugland nodded yes. His damned spectacles were fogged up, but he didn't dare move.

"I was in *gymnasium* until the Nazis closed it. No one wanted to follow the new Nazi rules."

"Where's your home?"

"Kvam."

"Ah." Haugland's own destination, except meeting his contact, was blown to hell now. Too dangerous to expect them to wait, it was equally dangerous to check into a *pensionat* if the village had one. His papers would be checked. "I'm going there too," he said.

"Then I can give you a ride on my motorbike to your place when we get in."

Three hours later, a train appeared. There was a terrible tension, born of fear and hope as the train's single light pierced the lightly drifting rain. Immediately, four black-uniformed SS officers came out of the two curtained railcars with luggage and walked to the waiting train.

Definitely someone important onboard.

"Maybe we'll be getting onboard soon," the boy whispered.

Others around them seemed to agree, but an officer in the gray uniform of the Intelligence Service (*Sicherheitsdienst*) soon dashed that prospect.

"I have good news," the SD officer announced in excellent Norwegian. "An engine has been located and will arrive in the next hour. In the meantime, prepare to present your cards for inspection."

The group groaned in unison, but the officer ignored them, shouting orders to the soldiers to prod the men into five lines in front of the station.

The boy was terrified. "What shall I answer?" he whispered.

"As little as possible. Keep your answers simple. Don't draw attention to yourself."

There was so much activity Haugland almost missed the reason for the whole debacle: stepping down off the metal steps of the mysterious railcar was General Marthinsen, Chief of the Stapo, the secret police in Norway. Haugland wondered what might have brought him to Trondheim. Perhaps a visit to the slave camps further north where Polish and Russian POW's languished. Once onboard, the train pulled away from the station.

The replacement locomotive appeared an hour later. The men and boys were marched back to their compartments. Haugland found a prim *Fru* Brun sitting in her seat.

"Poor dear Professor," she said.

"I'm all right. A little damp." He took a quick glance up at his suitcase.

"It's fine. They looked at everything only briefly. Nothing was taken."

They left not long after, but Haugland's troubles continued as the train strained to maintain some sense of schedule and got further behind. Worse, when he finally did arrive in Kvam and had said his good-byes to *Fru* Brun, he discovered to his shock a Gestapo agent detaining the boy. As Haugland passed the pair, his heart at an elevated thump, the angular-faced troll was going through a rucksack the boy held in front of him. There was nothing Haugland could do for him. Haugland had problems of his own. He would have to walk through the village.

Kvam was deserted, the dinner hour long over. Some of the houses cast in pink by the sinking sun already had their blinds drawn. Others stood in shadow like the shattered empty vessels that they were—victims of the 1940 bombing raids. He did not linger and no one followed.

Once out on the forested valley road, Haugland removed his spectacles and high collar. He continued a couple of miles on his own through rolling fields dotted with pine trees. He tucked his copy of the newspaper he had bought earlier in the day under his arm. As dark approached, a truck came up on him. The truck stopped. Warily, its middle-aged occupants began a carefully guarded conversation about his newspaper.

"Today's *Fritt Folk*? What do you think of the article on page three?" the woman asked.

"I'm always for ski jumping." Haugland began to relax. They were his contacts.

"We've been worried." The driver idled the truck. "There's been trouble at the depot."

As they talked, Haugland soon realized that the boy had been carrying something illegal.

It was nearly dark now. After he climbed in, the headlights were turned on, illuminating weird shapes as they passed by fences close to the single lane. The pines became taller and thicker. He was glad the couple had caught up with him. He would have ended up sleeping in the bushes. The moon came out, its light languishing on an increasingly wilder landscape. Finally, in a deeply forested area, they stopped. "The cabin's right up that dirt road," the woman said.

Haugland got out with his suitcase. "*Tusen takk*. Be careful."

They wished him well, then turned around on the narrow road and dashed off, the taillights disappearing like red cat's eyes in the dark.

As soon as the truck disappeared, Haugland slipped up into the forest and opened his suitcase. Inside his shaving kit, he felt for his razor. Twisting off its head, his fingers rubbed the handle. and in an instant, a tiny light came on. He traded his hat for a dark wool watch cap and closed the suitcase. Looking through the gloom he decided to take a side route. He wasn't about to go waltzing up the road. If there had been trouble, it could have come up here.

Locating a game trail paralleling the road, he worked his way up the hill through the trees. A thick layer of pine needles provided a quiet buffer to noise, but he stopped every now and then to rest, listening for sounds in the night. He knew the cabin was close, but he had no idea what the layout would be like. He moved silently along, cold and tired, until the trail abruptly turned back on him. As his foot stepped off into thin air, he frantically grabbed at the black shape of an overhanging limb, his feet kicking pebbles and dirt out into nothing. The suitcase fell down the embankment.

"Damn." He barely regained his footing on firmer ground.

Thunk! To his left, farther up, there came the sound of someone chopping wood. The cabin was close, but pines obscured his line of vision. There were no lights anyway; the blackout was observed even up here. He knelt, listening for voices, but heard none. Carefully, he pulled the suitcase back up and set it next to a large fir. He would get it later.

Twenty yards ahead, the road began to widen until he could make out the black form of a cabin in a clearing. A porch ran the whole side of the building, and where the moonlight reached down, he could spot smoke coming out of a chimney on the steep roof. There were no signs of vehicles. He stood watching for a time, when suddenly the door opened, sending a rectangular patch of light across the stone porch. A screen door screeched and a tall man stepped into the light. Haugland smiled. He knew that figure.

He began to make his way closer to the cabin, still in the trees, when a slight sound came from behind him, followed by a metallic click. Without hesitating, he turned, throwing himself directly at the darkest shadow, and knocked it down. The shadow was a man, and he bellowed when Haugland fell on him seeking control of the gun.

For several moments they wrestled, their breath coming in short grunts, and shoes digging muddy furrows into the earth. The man finally laid a solid punch on Haugland's cheek. He blocked a second punch only to have his wrist seized. Suddenly the attacker twisted to Haugland's left and rolled free. Haugland rolled too and was on his feet in an instant. It was dark, but he could see his adversary's face floating like a ghostly circle, the gun coming up. Haugland charged again, slamming him against a thin pine tree, sending down a shower of needles on their heads. Using the gun as club, the stocky opponent struck Haugland's head, but it only glanced off the thick fold on his watch cap. Haugland increased his hold, using his longs legs to trip his opponent but the man evaded him and in one great rush rammed his head into Haugland's chest.

Pain searing through him, Haugland lost his balance and fell back, but not without taking the man with him. At the last instant he flipped him over his head, sending him flying off the embankment onto the road four feet below. The gun soared off into the darkness.

"Bloody hell!" the man roared in English as he hit the ground with a thud and rolled over.

"Renvik. What's going on?" The tall shape from the cabin loomed up, approaching cautiously. Another followed behind him.

Haugland cleared his throat. "Is that really you, Tommy? I thought you were in bonny Scotland."

"Haugland? I could have killed you. I definitely tried to."

"Thanks." Haugland got up and dusted some needles off his coat for the want of anything else to do. He was exhausted, the whole day a blur. "Sorry, you surprised me. I didn't know who the hell was out here. There was trouble in Kvam." He pulled Tommy Renvik up. The two stood there as the others approached in the pale moonlight, heavily armed.

"Renvik! What happened?" the tall man called out in the dark.

"Nothing serious. Your baby brother just tried to take my head off. He's decided to give up, though."

"Tore?"

Haugland stepped out from behind Tommy. "Hello, Lars. Nice place you have here." They spoke in English, although Lars had a noticeable Norwegian accent. They embraced with affection.

"Good God. You're soaked." Lars turned to the man behind him. "Torstein. Could you get that wood inside?" He looked back at Haugland. "How on earth did you get wet? And what took you so long?"

"Long story. The whole day's been an adventure. Next time, I go by car."

"You didn't like third class?" They all started toward the cabin when Haugland stopped. "Shit. My suitcase is back there."

"Look, no problem," Tommy said. "I'll get it. Where's your torch, Lars?"

"Thanks. It's back about eighty feet to the right. Under a fir. Except they're all fir."

Inside what turned out to be a well-appointed cabin, Lars led Haugland into the main room where a cozy fire crackled in a large stone fireplace. At the back, there was a tall, wide window completely covered with a dark drape. A comfortable sofa and two overstuffed chairs were placed around the low table by the fire.

"Whose place is this?"

"It belongs to a man who was a judge before the war. Of course, he has other work these days. Come on, Tore, I have some clothes for you. You look like you'll float."

Down a hallway, Lars turned on the lights in a pine-paneled bedroom and showed Haugland some clothes on an iron bed. "I have good news," Lars said. "They located Alex. Our brother's in Little Norway, Toronto." He spoke in the Telemark dialect of their youth.

"Canada?" Haugland threw his jacket on the bed. "Incredible. I thought he was dead."

"He's alive and well with the Free Forces. Got there about two months ago after going through Russia. Took him that long."

"Alex." His second oldest brother had left Norway in 1942.

Haugland stripped while Lars went off in search of socks. He surveyed the damage from the fight in a mirror on the wall. His left cheek was tight and shiny, and there a nasty bruise forming on his chest where Tommy had butted him.

"Ouch." Lars threw him a towel and, while Haugland dried off, began to stuff a pipe. "The pants should fit all right. There are dry socks there somewhere."

Haugland smiled. It had been three months since they'd been together in London. "It's damn good to see you, Lars."

Lars leaned against the doorframe. "Are you hungry? There's *lapskaus* in the kitchen."

"*Takk*. I could use it."

"Just how much trouble were you in?"

Haugland shrugged. "Some of the local lads did a bit of sabotage on the train. The Germans unloaded the entire male population and made us wait. Marthinsen was on board."

"The Devil, you say." Lars came away from the door. "Anything else I should know?"

"Had my papers checked twice. A Gestapo agent wanted to show the SD officer what a Norwegian *legitimasjonskor*t was supposed to look like. I got called back. The SD officer is apparently new to the country. He looked it over. Forgot to ask if it was made in London."

Lars grinned behind his pipe. Haugland laughed.

As brothers went, they were exact opposites. "Salt and Pepper" they had been called as boys and no wonder. Where Haugland was dark, Lars was blonde with light blue eyes. He was as tall, but more robust and fuller in the face. He had powerful shoulders that filled his rugged sweater and he walked with military bearing. He was Haugland's eldest brother by eight years and in resistance affairs, his superior. When Haugland told him about the boy at the train station Lars straightened up, his mouth frowning.

"I'll have someone watch the road for the rest of the night. Just in case there is unexpected company." He affectionately clapped Haugland on his shoulder. "Come on, Tore. Finish up. I'll get that *lapkaus*. It has horsemeat."

While Lars went into the kitchen and dished up the promised stew, Haugland stood in front of the fire, soaking in its warmth. Despite being back on the train for several hours, he felt cold. The dry sweater fed his drowsiness. Everything began to feel distant and unreal. Lars laid the food down on the low table in front of the sofa and invited him to sit down. Outside there was the scrape of boots on the gravel, then low voices rising above the dull sound of footsteps on the stone porch. Tommy and Torstein were back. Lars went out to meet them, the screen door whining. Haugland sat down heavily on the sofa. He was exhausted. He was aware of Tommy coming into the room, exhibiting a few interesting bruises of his own of his face, of his brother's voice floating and fading. He looked at them like an observer at a play, totally disconnected. Then with eyes too heavy to keep open, he gave in and fell sound asleep.

CHAPTER 8

"Go to sleep, Munchkin," Anna said gently, rocking her daughter in the chair. Ever since her grandmother had sent her *The Wizard of Oz* as a girl, she had loved the sound and the image of the word. She stroked Lisel's silky head, holding her safe in her arms, just as her own mother had when she had been sick. She spoke to Lisel in English, and remembered *Mutti*.

They sat in the living room portion of the house by the woodstove, the blackout curtains pulled down for the night. On the hand-woven rug by the fire, the two cats curled up like a furry Ying and Yang. She had been reading some old folk tales to Lisel. Now Lisel was fast asleep.

The day had been very nice, light and airy as the days rushed toward summer and the endless light. She never got used to it, feeling the same driving urge to be outdoors in whatever sun or daylight like everyone else. It was as if her life depended on it: soak up all you can so you can survive the endless dark of winter. The Norwegians called the dark *Morketiden*—the Murky Time—and it certainly was that.

From October to April, autumn and spring merged with winter so closely that winter came in three parts. First there was fall-winter, October and November— not too dark until after the first of November, but depressing because it was going to get darker and stay dark through high winter. High winter was from December to February. So dark that even in Oslo, the city lights turned on at 3:00 p.m. and didn't go off until 9:00 a.m. . When winter-spring finally came, people were so glad to see it they braved the roads awash with mud and slush, waiting for the light. Anna embraced it, trying to make sense of what was a nightmare.

She had always thought the expression, "I'm living in a nightmare," trite. In a nightmare odd things happened such as turning on the tap in the kitchen and the handle breaks off and the water floods the room up past the clock on the wall. In a nightmare, things were absurdly out of proportion or worse, and the deepest fears really happened. A nightmare was dark, as dark as *Morketiden*, but it wasn't real. Or so she had thought.

Her nightmare began with Einar's arrest. The Gestapo came into their kitchen and pounced on him when he returned from the school. All he had time for was to kiss her and whisper, "I'm sorry. Be brave. Take care of Lisel," before he was pushed out the door. He gave her such a look of sorrow and regret that it burned into her like a terrible fever, staying with her long after he was gone. That was a nightmare, but it was real.

In the deepest dark of winter the Gestapo took Einar away along with the shopkeeper, the pharmacist, and the man who sailed the mailboat from village to village. She never saw him again. She was told of his death a week later, but there was no body, no funeral. She had no idea he was connected with the resistance. He had never told her, leaving her with terrible doubts.

People at first were very sympathetic and supportive, but that changed by the second week. Friends began to excuse themselves, and those who only knew her by sight became hostile. Anna decided to take Lisel and go to Fjellstad where Einar had inherited a farm. Thinking she would return after the shock of the arrests (which continued as more people up and down the *fjord* were exposed), she settled into the farmhouse, exhausted. Exhaustion gave way to illness, illness to a miscarriage that left her alone and frightened. And that was a nightmare. A woman with keys to the house found her and went for the doctor. Anna was ill for weeks. She had wanted this new baby very much, but had delayed telling Einar because they had been arguing about him being away so often. A day of waiting meant a lifetime of sorrow for the little boy she lost.

Anna looked down at her daughter and smiled. Lisel was sound asleep, her pinky finger in her mouth. She was all Anna had left of Einar. Anna put her to bed and made some tea. Though nine at night, it was still light. Opening the door leading out to the little porch between the living room and kitchen, she stepped out. The air was chilly. There could be frost even as late as the second week in May. She looked down to Fjellstad where the windows were blacked-out for fear of RAF or American bombing raids. *Fru* Andersson at the *landhandel* said planes had bombed Oslo a month ago and that Trondheim had some important targets too. Out in front, the twilight deepened the air sweet with smells of fruit blossoms and the damp earth. She was glad she came here even if she was isolated and cut off.

The Fromme farm had promise, twenty hectares with some good arable land. She knew Norwegian farms tended to be small, but she had enough fields for hay and potatoes. Farther up, there were stands of birch in the pine forest. She was low on wood fuel for winter. She might have to resort to burning peat unless she could cut up some of the wood downed by last winter's storms. She wondered if she might be able to trade her hay for several cords of wood.

Anna laughed. A farmwife. What would her stepmother say if she saw Anna grubbing around in the muck and putting in potatoes? The woman was a great proponent of the virtue of the farming peasant, but she would have been appalled to see Anna in boots and Einar's overalls actually doing it. So much for Nazi metaphysics.

"Now I must do something about me, Einar," she said out loud. "I left Lillehavn too soon. Ugly rumors followed me." She sniffed, holding back a sudden bubble of grief. She put the hot cup to her cheek. "I know. I should have gone to Scotland when you said I could. But I was afraid to be apart from you. Now I am apart from you forever and—accused."

The tears came suddenly as they often did and burned her eyes. The sobs came next. She had to hold them back in her hands before she regained composure and went back inside.

Over by the kitchen several boxes peeked out from the stairs. In a small room across from it, there were more of them, all filled with books. She had spent a good part of the day sorting through them. Some of the books were banned, but Einar didn't want to destroy them and had given them new covers that read "Chemistry" or "Nordic Legends," keeping the most dangerous hidden in the bottom of a trunk. To think Hemingway or *Emile and the Detectives* dangerous.

She thought of the book she had given Jens Hansen. It had been a favorite of Einar's, a tale of medieval knights in a Nordic setting. She had been surprised to learn Hansen was deaf, but she still wanted to thank him for saving Lisel. She thought a book would do and had Foss arrange the meeting, but it was all so embarrassing. She went through with her little speech and surprised Hansen with the book, but it hurt her deeply when he asked in his neat handwriting where her husband was. It was not only rude; it shattered her illusion that there was still one person who hadn't heard the vicious talk. It seemed that it had reached the ears of the deaf as well.

CHAPTER 9

The fire burned cheerfully in its grate, flinging shadows across the dark room. The cabin was still. The only person stirring was Lars Haugland, sitting by the fire in an overstuffed chair. Tommy was asleep, Torstein out in the woods keeping watch. On the sofa his brother Tore, lately "*Herr* Professor Smolen" and "Jens Hansen," stretched out. He slept deeply, making no sound at all. Lars laid a blanket over him.

Lars watched Tore for a while, his pipe glowing in the dark. It was funny how a sleeping person could look so much younger, with cares and time wiped away. Light softened his face even more. Tore's dark hair had fallen down on his forehead, giving him a boyish look. Lars remembered the boy affectionately, but a man was sleeping there now, hardened by the past three and a half years of secret work, hardened by the memory of Ålesund and Telavåg. Lars watched Tore and was afraid for a moment he saw a stranger there.

Of his brothers, Tore was his favorite. Lars had almost a father's pride in watching Tore grow up, but hadn't hesitated to push Tore into the kind of work he now excelled in. At the end of 1940, he urged Tore to escape to England and train with the Secret Intelligence Service (SIS). The organization needed English speakers to assist British advisors and Norwegian resistance groups. Tore spoke English, German and Russian flawlessly. Graduate studies in history and languages at Cambridge were a plus.

I got you into this, Lars thought. *I had the authority and still do.*

He closed his eyes, listening to the crack and pop of the fire. He was an engineer by profession, but was in the army reserves when the Germans invaded on April 9, 1940. He had been out late with friends and had returned to Oslo only to discover all the lights off and wild rumors about German warships in Oslo Fjord and soldiers advancing on Oslo. By 8:00 in the morning, King Haakon VII, his government, the members of the *Storting*, Norway's Parliament, and the Norwegian High Command had fled, leaving the city's residents on their own.

Lars drew on his pipe. He had wasted no time in skiing north of the city. He saw action at Lillehammer when the Germans launched their attack north of Oslo five days later. When the war was over for Norway by June, he returned home and began quietly working with some people he knew. Today, he had an important position in the Home Front. He was high up in Milorg, the military organization of the Resistance, working closely with J. C. Hauge, its leader, but he also worked with Sivorg, the civilian branch of the Resistance.

A piece of coal exploded in the fireplace like a tiny gunshot. Strangely, Tore didn't sir. Lars shifted in his chair and took a puff on his pipe. He wasn't sure why he continued to smoke. Sometimes the tobacco he got with the ration card, if he got it, was awful.

He picked up a manila envelope by his chair and laid it on his lap. Inside there were snapshots and papers. He chose two five-by-seven photographs and by the light of the fireplace, examined them.

The first was of two men and a boy. It was himself at age twenty-two, blond hair, sun-streaked and windblown, dressed in a dark two-piece swimming suit. He was leaner then, less serious. Next to him was a boy with dark hair, about fourteen, laughing and attempting to put a blanket over him and another man next to him. The boy was unmistakably Tore. Even in the black and white photo, the gray eyes seemed to sparkle, full of the devil. The young man pushing back on Tore was a tall blond Lars's age. It was Einar Fromme, his best boyhood friend.

He remembered the day. Escaping the summer heat and humidity, they had gone to the lake. Tore tagged along with their sister Solveig. Lars and Einar had tried to pick up girls, but Tore had kept butting in. Not a successful outing in that respect, but fun in other ways.

Lars chuckled. He and Einar met when they were eight, the summer Tore was born. Father, a noted geology professor at the University of Oslo, was in Cambridge, England, delivering a geological address on disharmonic folding in some far-off mountain range. Mother had taken the four children Lars, Alex, Per and Solveig to Bergen to be with their grandmother. She was a week overdue, but decided to risk the train trip rather than be alone. Father had been invited to give his paper some time ago, so he went, but the baby still hadn't come when he got back a week later.

"It was the only time Tore was late for anything," his mother used to stay after that.

Tore was born the day after Father returned. The family decided to stay in Bergen for the rest of the summer. It was 1920. The Great War was over. Norway—barely getting by as a neutral country—was enjoying their second year of peace. On a musical outing, Lars met Einar, the son of a friend of Mother's.

It was a friendship associated with hiking, riding *fjordling* ponies, and the midnight sun, for most often they were together in the summertime. It became a friendship that grew with time, remaining constant, even if months and years separated them. The Hauglands came to Bergen for three weeks every summer before the older boys began to follow Father on his many field trips around the country and abroad.

Einar, dear friend, Lars thought. The last time he had seen Einar was in early 1938. A year later he received a letter from him.

"I've gotten married. She's a wonderful girl from Denmark. We're in a little place called Lillehavn. I have a teaching position here. Hope you can come sometime."

Lars wanted to visit, but the German invasion of Norway changed everything, not only for the country. As with so many Norwegian families, the invasion tore the Haugland family apart.

Lars sighed, holding hard to the edge of the photograph. Father's sudden, fatal heart attack in September 1940 following his brief arrest seemed to signal the worst to come. It was hard enough to look after the family, let alone friendships. Lars had no contact with Einar after that and had learned of his friend's arrest from an investigation of Milorg's collapse in Lillehavn last winter. Einar had been in Rinnan's hands. Lars couldn't believe Einar was gone, moldering in some unmarked grave. He didn't deserve it.

Lars put down the photograph and picked up the other one. It was taken much later—August 1939 was scrawled on the back— and Einar looked older and very much the *gymnasium* schoolteacher he was. He looked quite content. In his arms was Anna, his new wife. They were both smiling, the woman looking toward the camera, the gold hair in ringlets around her face. She looked bemused, as if Einar had just nibbled her ear and whispered something suggestive. Whatever it was, they were obviously a happy couple. She was beautiful, and he could see why Einar had been taken with her. But what had happened?

From a room down the hall, Tommy coughed. The steel bed's springs creaked as he turned over. The rest of the house was quiet, and as soon as Tommy settled down, silent. Lars laid the photographs down side by side near his chair. He had requested information on Anna Fromme from the Norwegian Legation in Stockholm, Sweden, and received it a few days ago. What he had been given both surprised and worried him. She was much more complicated than he thought. Lars was aware she had moved to Fjellstad only a short time after Einar's death. Lars had warned Tore in London of this complication before Tore was sent to the fishing village. If she recognized him in any way, the whole operation could be compromised. Worse, if there were truth to the rumor that she had betrayed Einar and the others to Rinnan, then Tore would be in grave danger. And now, this new information from Stockholm. Lars rubbed his unshaven chin. The problem was how much danger? Einar, after all, had been his friend.

Lars leaned over and looked at the picture of the three of them in a forgotten life long ago. Here were two people he loved and cared about. To Einar, he vowed he would find the one who betrayed him. For Tore, he prayed Godspeed.

CHAPTER 10

Tore Haugland woke to the sound of clinking dishes and the smell of coffee, but not remembering where he was, he stayed mute and feigned sleep on what seemed to be a lumpy, musty sofa.

"Tore. Wake up. Come on, lad." A strong hand gently shook his shoulder. Tore opened his eyes. Lars was sitting next to him on a low table, stuffing his pipe. Behind him a low fire burned in a stone fireplace. *The judge's cabin.*

"Are you feeling all right, Tore? You've been out cold. I was getting worried."

"I'll let you know in a minute. What time is it?"

"You don't want to know. You've slept about twelve hours."

"Twelve hours? The Devil." Tore sat up, then wished he hadn't. His head ached and his chest was tender. Disgusted with himself, Tore rubbed his temples with his palms.

Lars chuckled. "Have some coffee. There's not much to eat, but you can still have your *lapskaus.* You never touched it." Lars waved his hand at a cup of steaming coffee on the table.

"*Takk.*" Grumbling, Haugland reached for the cup. "Where is everyone?"

"Tommy's out chopping wood. Torstein went into the village to see his brother and to make sure everything's all right."

"Any problems?"

"I don't think so." Lars went to the kitchen and came back with a steaming bowl in his hands. "Torstein was just going to have a look, but I did keep a watch for a while last night."

Haugland ran his fingers through his hair. "Sorry about last night."

Lars chuckled. "You were nodding off before you sat down. Tommy never got a chance to show off his bruises." He grew serious. "Why don't you eat and tell me about Fjellstad, then I'll show you what I have on Anna Fromme. It's surprising. Tommy can fill you in on his schedule for the coming month. How's your new W/T?"

"My W/T's fine. I send if only there's something to say. Don't want to get tied down."

"No trouble with parts?"

"*Nei*." Haugland went on to describe his months in Fjellstad. From the first hair-raising encounter with Sheriff Fasting to fishing or visiting the islands with Kjell, he presented it as in a report, but succeeded in making it more. By the time he got around to describing the silly and sometimes embarrassing exchanges around him in the hotel kitchen with the kitchen girls, Lars was in tears from laughing.

"They treat you like a bloody wall."

Haugland tapped his ear. "This one hears. I've done pretty well with the contacts too."

"Including girls?"

Haugland jabbed his spoon at his brother. "Don't get me started. I said contacts. I've been exploring sites for future drops and storage." He gave him a final summation on German counterintelligence and Rinnan.

"Very good." Lars drew on his pipe. "I was worried you'd stick out, but it seems you've settled into the community with no suspicion. No inquiries into your forged medical records in Molde." Lars got up and opened up the drapes, letting light into the room. "The two agents before you were exposed by Rinnan and executed. I can't help but be nervous."

Haugland looked outside the window. A thick stand of pine mixed with birch was all around them. Clumps of snow lay on the forested hill rising sharply behind the cabin. "Then forget I'm your brother. I asked for this." From outside came the sound of wood being chopped. "What's Tommy doing? Getting an early start on next year's pile?"

"Why don't you find out for yourself?" Lars answered. "He's been wanting to talk to you. Want any more *lapskaus*?"

Haugland shook his head no, but took his coffee with him. "Be back in a minute."

Outside, the morning air was cool and crisp. Except for the occasional twitter of some small bird and the steady chop of Tommy's axee, the forest was remarkably quiet. Tommy had his back to him. and when Haugland saw the red-gold hair, he smiled. *Renvik the Red.*

"Good morning, Tommy. Need some help?" Haugland spoke in English, because after spending so much time in Scotland between commando assignments, Tommy was almost more comfortable with it than his own Norwegian. Besides, Tommy got his name from a grandfather who had come from the Shetlands.

Tommy stopped the axe in mid-air and turned around, a wry grin on his face. One of his lips was cut, and there was a large bruise under his left eye and on one of his flat, pink cheeks. He was a couple of inches shorter than Haugland and stockier. His gray-blue eyes looked out under pale reddish eyebrows and eyelashes.

"The top of the day to you and about time. Jesus, you surprise a guy, he beats on you, and before you get in a word edgewise, he falls asleep."

"Sorry about that."

"Hmph." Tommy balanced a piece of wood on the chopping block and split it single-handedly with one stroke. "Lars said you had a rough day yesterday. Bastards." He flipped another onto the block and split it. "Still, sleep seems to have done wonders. You're looking your wonderful self. Haven't aged a bit."

Haugland burst out laughing. There was no animosity between them. They had known each other for three and half years and would laugh about the fight long after. Their friendship went back to the early days of the occupation when they both escaped to Scotland on the same boat. Tommy was already an old hand at escaping by sea because it was his second attempt.

His first had been from a place near Bergen, a popular jumping-off point because it was so close to the Shetlands. Someone "allowed" his boat to be stolen by a group of young and inexperienced men. They made it to within forty miles of the coast of Scotland when they ran out of fuel and drifted back to Norway where Tommy's group had scattered, cold and dejected. He lay low for a while watching helplessly as friends were arrested. When another chance came, he took it. Haugland was on that second boat. "Take a seat," Tommy said.

"Thanks." Haugland sat down on the edge of the porch, careful not to jolt his head.

Their friendship was strong despite the fact they hardly saw each other for any length of time. In the beginning, they were at a Patriot School in Scotland, essentially a detention center where refugees were vigorously screened, then selected for programs that would put them back in Norway.

They went through the same basic conditioning program learning fieldcraft before they were separated. With his education and language ability, Haugland was channeled toward pure intelligence and was back in Norway almost immediately. Tommy ended up as a sergeant in the Linge Company, a part of SOE-Norway. He stayed in Glenmore, Scotland, waiting for an assignment.

Tommy split another piece of wood. "Let's see. Was it February I saw you in London?"

"You know damn well it was," Haugland said. "You got me drunk at some godforsaken flat. Nearly missed my plane ride back, let alone time to check to see if my 'chute worked." He chuckled. "Still, you're the only one I want for my SOE contact."

Tommy gave Haugland a half grin. "Your confidence is dazzling."

"We'll see."

"I won't disappoint. I get tired of twiddling my thumbs in Scotland. I'll be able to pick up my social life, though come to think about it, it's lonelier hanging around you."

Haugland grinned, feeling a sudden rush of weightlessness. After weeks of tension of always being "Jens Hansen," he was free.

"I was dropped here three weeks ago," Tommy continued. "But I was sent here to tell you that I probably can't start with you until after Midsummers Eve in June, possibly not until July."

Haugland straightened up at that. It wasn't what he wanted to hear, but it reinforced the last message he had received from London. "Why?"

"The Allies are softening up the Germans," Tommy said. "The invasion's anytime now on the French coast, not here—but then we've always known that, haven't we?"

Haugland nodded. Invasion talk about Norway had gone on for so long that Milorg had even received arms and prepared for it, but all that came were the terrible roll-ups in 1942 that wiped out Milorg units nationwide. After that it was just talk.

"So it's coming?" Haugland said.

"Yes, but any action on the part of SOE and Milorg is on hold. Sorry."

Haugland stared at his cup. "Oh, well. Don't worry about me. It'll give me a chance to do some salmon fishing and if things continue to screw up, there's always that red deer hunting season in September."

Tommy grinned and pretended to throw a piece of wood at him. "You're nuts."

"Here, let me do that," Haugland said. "You're going to hurt someone."

Haugland took Tommy's place and began splitting the remaining wood. Tommy sat on the porch steps. He took out a penknife and, picking up a birch branch in the mud near his boots, began to whittle at it, making smooth strokes with his broad, red hands.

For the next fifteen minutes they chatted, each centered on their particular task. While Haugland enjoyed the monotony of his chore, Tommy concentrated on the piece of wood in his hands, carving it with a surprising delicacy.

Like splicing electrical wires, Haugland thought. His friend had been an electrician before the war and probably put that to good use in the Linge Company, blowing up train tracks, aluminum processing plants or whatever. Anything to trip up the Germans.

All around them were the trees, close and immutable, except for the birches sending out their new leaves. Haugland breathed in the tangy scent of pine trees and wood smoke. It was good to be with people who knew him as himself. Despite his friendship with Kjell, whom he genuinely liked, he would never burden Kjell with his true identity. He would always be Jens Hansen to put off the day of sorrow if either should ever be arrested.

"You get any news in Fjellstad?" Tommy asked.

"Sure. I've seen uncensored information—legal press material like *London*

Nytt and *Krigens Gang*. 'Course the press raids in Oslo last February stopped that, but new mimeographed papers are coming in. Someone apparently has a radio for the BBC broadcasts, but that source was hidden two weeks ago. There was a house check. How's Scotland?"

"Full of heather and tweeds. Did find the latest French thrillers."

"Always in taste."

Haugland laughed. Tommy's preferences in books and motion pictures weren't always the same as his, but Tommy's choices were still the latest news and fads. "Ever hear of *The Moon Is Down* by the American, John Steinbeck?" A story about the Norwegian resistance, it was banned by the Germans in Norway and in other occupied countries, but Haugland had seen some mimeographed copies in Bergen and Stavanger.

"Yeah. They're talking about making it into a play in New York."

"You're kidding."

They were still discussing that when Lars came out and called them in to work.

CHAPTER 11

Back in the cabin, Lars briefed Haugland and Tommy on resistance activities and the German-NS political scene.

"The evidence is all there," he said. "Norwegian boys just called up for the AT are going to be mobilized to fight with German Forces on the continent, so the Home Front will encourage them not to report and go directly to the forests and mountains. But if the directive is totally heeded, such a concentration of men could cause problems. Getting them food, especially. The ration cards are, of course, strictly controlled."

Haugland thought of the boys he knew in Fjellstad. Would they flee? They were all fishermen. Norway needed to eat. He watched his brother put some photographs on the already cluttered table. Lars seemed anxious to get the session over.

"Now the other matter. This is what I got from the Norwegian Legation in Stockholm."

Haugland leaned over the small coffee table to look. It was Einar with the Woman.

"Her name is Anna Howard von Schauffer Fromme. She is the daughter of Heinrick von Schauffer. Von Schauffer is an old moneyed German family. Before the turn of the century, the elder von Schauffer invested in chemical and petroleum concerns. He made millions, then lost most of it just before the Depression."

Tommy whistled. Haugland said nothing but he wondered how Einar met her. What had led her to a simple schoolmaster?

"What are his politics?" Tommy asked.

"Von Schauffer joined the Nazi Party in 1935, but our agent hinted he may be involved in some clandestine work for the small anti-Nazi resistance there, possibly a cover. His wife, though, is very active in the Nazi Party and according to reports, rabid."

Haugland turned the second picture around. It was a woman in her late forties. A blond, she was a Nazi *frau* with a veneer of beauty, somewhat overripe and vain. She was standing with a mustachioed, older man. He looked like a well-dressed businessman.

"That's Elsa von Schauffer. Von Schauffer's second wife. The man is von Schauffer."

"This is not Anna Fromme's mother?" Haugland took his hand away.

"*Nei*, and that's the interesting part," Lars answered. "Her real mother died in a car crash in 1933. Her name was Margaret Howard and she was an American."

"How did that happen?" Haugland couldn't believe it.

"Von Schauffer met Margaret Howard in 1914 while visiting the United States. They fell in love and married. Anna was born in Oxford, Maryland, in 1919. They lived in the U.S. until 1930. They moved to London where von Schauffer patented some of his chemical processes. He returned to Germany with the family in 1932."

"Her mother's family, by the way, is well-off, even has military connections. Her uncle's been on Eisenhower's staff. "

"You're kidding." Haugland stared at his brother in disbelief. "What's she doing here? Haugland suppressed the image of her at the hotel as he grappled with this new information. Those blue eyes and curly blond hair. Not a Nazi poster model. An American. "Did she ever go back?"

"*Ja*. Her mother made at least two boat trips to visit her parents. Took the children with her."

"Why did he stay in Germany after she died? Not go back to London?"

Lars frowned. "I don't know. Could have something to do with his work. He could have been coerced."

"Did Einar ever tell you this?"

"*Nei*. Einar wrote he'd gone to Copenhagen before they married. He implied that she was well-off, but beyond that, he never said anything, except that she was Danish of German extraction. Never even hinted of America."

Lars took a sip from his mug of coffee. "From the comments this agent made," he went on, "the children never joined the Nazi youth organizations, but it must have been difficult to sit on the fence without censure. I can't speak for von Schauffer, but I think he helped to get his daughter over here and disappear."

"How could you know?" Haugland asked

"The maiden name on her passport is false. It took a lucky break to trace her back."

Lars collected himself before continuing. "They lived in Bergen where Einar taught, and she studied at the university branch there, then in Lillehavn at the start of '41. So I've been told... They stayed there until...." Lars stopped talking and swallowed.

Haugland knew what Lars was thinking. After three and a half years, his brother had seen it all: friends or colleagues forced to go into hiding or over the export routes to Sweden or worse, arrested, imprisoned, tortured, shot and executed. It numbed him to the drama repeated again and again. Haugland felt that way too, but the loss of Einar had been especially hard for Lars.

"What do you think, Tore? Did she implicate Einar and cause him to be delivered to Rinnan?"

"Honestly, I don't know." Haugland looked up. "I've heard every rumor: that she informed on Einar or said something that led to his arrest; that she was working with someone. Rinnan most likely *had* an agent in Lillehavn. Is she the one?" He shrugged. "I don't know. I've only met her once. She did seem genuinely grieved over Einar."

He absentmindedly moved the pictures on the table. "An American. Something's not right. The truth, I suppose, is somewhere between rumor and reality."

"Perhaps," Lars said. "Just don't get close to her until security figures it out."

"All right." Haugland didn't know what else to say to his brother. Einar was a lifelong friend, and he felt the same grief. Haugland looked at his hands. Lars stared out the window.

Tommy got up and excused himself. "I think I'll just leave you two alone for a bit and go check on Torstein. He's late. It's afternoon."

Haugland heard him go out on the porch, the door whining shut behind him. It broke his mood. "Did they ever find Einar's body?"

"*Nei,*" Lars said. "He was probably dumped out in the *Trondheimsleia* or in the forests."

Haugland shook his head. His headache was back. It worsened when a car tore up into the clearing and boots pounded on the porch.

"Got to get out now," Tommy yelled. "There's been trouble in Kvam again."

"Where's Torstein?" Lars rose calmly from his chair.

"Right here." Torstein came through the door, his glasses askew, and out of breath. "The boy detained last evening was arrested. He was carrying plastique in his pack, packed in bars of soap. I've been trying to slip out all night."

"Where is he now?" Lars asked.

"I think the Gestapo is taking him to Oslo," Torstein answered.

"Did anyone see you?"

"*Nei,* but my brother did say soldiers were asking about a stranger who came through last evening." Torstein looked at Haugland. "Sorry, someone saw you."

"What about *my* contacts?" A familiar queasy feeling of fright or flight grew in Haugland's stomach. "The couple? Have they been questioned?"

"I heard nothing about that." Torstein motioned to Lars. "We must go. There's a back road out that skirts the valley down toward Lillehammer."

Haugland got up. "Good. You take my brother. Tommy'll come with me."

"And how will you get out?" Lars asked.

"Don't worry. Saw a trail behind the cabin. I assume it connects with something heading north. Tommy and I'll take it. Keep to the hills for a while."

"An excellent plan," Torstein said when Lars protested. "Stay on that trail. It will bring to you an old farmstead five miles from here. I have a friend there. He can get you out by car."

"What do you think, Tommy? Want to hike?" Haugland asked.

"Sure. Could use the exercise." Tommy's red face was beaming.

"It sounds like everything's arranged," Lars said dryly. "I guess I'll pack."

They worked hurriedly clearing out their gear. While Torstein put the rooms down the hall back in order, Tommy went out and checked the grounds. Lars gave Haugland a rucksack for stuffing his old papers from the lining of the suitcase. "It has a hidden seam. I'll take your suitcase with me." Lars added some baked potatoes and dried fish.

"Take these jars for water."

Once packed, Lars gathered all his papers and pictures from the table and began feeding them into the fire. Haugland teased it with a poker. "How's Mother?" he asked.

"She saw our sister a couple of weeks ago at the camp."

He closed his eyes to an image of his sister being hauled away with the other women from Telavåg. Lars put his hand on Haugland's shoulder.

"It'll be all right. She's strong." Lars picked up the remaining photographs and tossed them one by one onto the coals. "Remember this?" He was holding the picture of them at the lake.

"Sure. My idols."

Lars chuckled. He looked at the picture fondly, then leaned over and laid it on the fire reverently, like an offering. They stood watching it on the coals. In seconds it began to burn, first around Einar, a searing hole exploding in his face and head, then around the boy Tore, his torso puckering before the edges curled and turned brown. The portrait of Lars broke off untouched. He pushed it back into the coals with his boot where it finally was consumed. They stood there for a moment, sober and restrained. Haugland felt a chill go down his back. Einar was gone. Would this be the last time he'd see his brother?

"How should I contact you?" Lars shut the curtains and headed for the door.

"Why not send me that fishing catalogue we used to get? It's apparently the favorite of the discriminating *Wehrmacht* angler. Write your usual gibberish. I'll figure it out."

Out on the porch, Lars locked the door behind them. In all, it had taken only fifteen minutes to get organized. Torstein had the car running, anxious to go. Haugland followed Lars to the passenger side. Lars got into the car and rolled down the window.

"Watch out for the trolls, big brother." Haugland leaned on the door. "They're not going to like the Home Front's action on the AT call up. I'm sure we'll hear about it in a few days."

"I'm sure we will," Lars said. "And promise me you'll watch *your* back. Rinnan's gang is all around you." He started to say something else, then seemed to think better of it. "If you need help."

Haugland patted his hand. "*Takk*."

Torstein revved up the motor and started to roll away. Lars waved and they were off.

CHAPTER 12

Kjell entered the cathedral and a hush fell over him as it always did. It was like stepping into a different world, a vast timeless space. Even in the restored Gothic section where he entered, there was a sense of otherworldliness that was oppressive and weightless at the same time. The diffused light coming from the clearstory so high up was natural. It illuminated the ancient pillars and capitals of bluish-gray soapstone. The rose window was fractured with vermilion light.

This is a place where history breathes, he thought.

The cathedral was a holy place and a place of tradition. Kings were crowned and buried here—even after the Reformation. In the Middle Ages, pilgrims came to Nidros Cathedral from all over Norway and abroad to see the tomb of the Viking king-saint, Olav Haraldson. Haraldson brought Christianity to Norway by force and was canonized after his death. Kjell was only seven years old when his father put him up on his shoulders to see King Haakon VII, now exiled in London, go by on his way to his coronation in 1906.

And the Nazis wanted to bring that bastard Quisling here, he muttered.

Kjell remembered how the Nazis wanted to use the cathedral to install Vidkun Quisling as Minister-President and celebrate the event with a special service. One of the few Norwegian ministers with Nasjonal Samling (NS) leaning led it, but no one showed up on that bitter cold February morning in 1942 to hear the fascist minister.

Later that afternoon, however, 10,000 showed up to hear Reverend Fjellbu, dean of the cathedral, preach his postponed service. The police arrived to close the crowd off, but no one left. For a half-hour they stood silent. Then someone began to sing "A Mighty Fortress Is Our God."

Kjell loved that story. It was a wonderful moment, one savored over the long years of occupation. The crowd sang a few more hymn, then finished with the national anthem before dispersing as silently as they had come.

Kjell walked down the center of the aisle toward the altar and the ambulatory behind it. The stone floor dipped under his feet, the tread of ages under him. Somewhere back there, Jens waited for him, a day late. They were supposed to meet yesterday, but a woman called him at his friend Thomas Nissen's place, informing him that his package was late being shipped and would he mind picking it up tomorrow? Olav would have it for him by one o'clock.

"*Nei*, no problem," he said. He could wait. He thanked her and hung up. Now what was that all about? What kind of trouble had there been? At least the meeting place was the same: St. Olav's Spring.

Kjell didn't find Hansen immediately, but going through the high-pointed Gothic entrance to the ambulatory behind the altar, he went more than a quarter of the way around to St. Olav's Spring. He picked out a tall man with a shabby coat and glasses consulting a *Baedeker*. It was Hansen. Barely. With puffy cheeks and dark mustache, Kjell almost missed him.

Without looking at him, Hansen said, "Nice to see you, Kjell. Have a nice visit?"

"*Ja*, very pleasant, but I was worried about you."

Hansen kept his nose in the travel book. "Believe me, I would have warned you if there had been a real problem." He flipped his *Baedeker* closed. "Let's go look at the grounds."

Outside the south entrance, the overcast day was spring-sweet scent with a hint of pine. In front of them, the cathedral's green lawns fanned out to the curving River Nid bordering the grounds, passing between newly leafed trees and the gray stone buildings of the medieval *Erkebispegarden*. Across the river were the roofs of houses in the suburbs. Beyond were the green and forested hills outside the town.

"I almost didn't recognize you," Kjell said. "What did you do? It's not just the mustache."

Hansen tapped his cheek. "Rubber pads. Makes a lemming look like a heavy weight. Let's walk. I want to get clear of the crowds."

They headed down to the old stone buildings. They were several stories high with orange-pitched roofs that were in sharp contrast to the sea green of the cathedral's roof. There were a few people about. Only a farmer and his wife, a trio of office workers in spring dresses and opened coats, and a group of young girls dressed in the yellow shirt and blue tie, tunic and skirt of the *Gjentehird*, the NS youth organization based on its German counterpart. The girls streamed toward them. Their uniformed adult leader opened her mouth to apologize, but at the last moment, Hansen veered off to the left toward a grove of tall trees.

"I think we can talk here," Hansen said. "I take it you had no trouble staying an extra day."

"*Nei*, but what happened?"

Hansen gave him an account of the train trip and an equally crazy story of a hike and car trip back up the Osterdal Valley yesterday.

"The Devil," Kjell said, both appalled and amused by Hansen's misadventures. "Were you followed?"

"*Nei*. I'm sure of it."

They wandered down to the edge of the grounds where the river curved north like an open "U." They talked quietly at the wall, mindful of the naval buildings nearby.

"How was your stay?" Hansen asked.

"I got a net."

"I won't ask where you got it. Thought you said it's impossible to get them."

"And I won't tell." Kjell cleared his throat. "Do have a bit of concern." He told Hansen about his chance meeting with Bent Kjelstrup and Odd Sorting at the cathedral, how they went to *bakeri* and Kjell told of the mysterious boat being sent to the Shetlands.

"How long have you known Sorting?" Hansen asked.

"Personally, not long. He started showing up in the islands this past February, just a short time before I met you." Kjell frowned. "He gets along with everyone, but I think he's too chatty. When I mentioned Lillehavn and Ålesund, he got real quiet. He knew something. I saw it in his mouth. I don't like him. He's either a quisling or worse." He spat out his last sentence.

"When's the boat leaving?"

"He didn't say, but I'd guess around the fifteenth. Bent said about thirty could go."

Hansen picked up a pebble and skipped it across the water. It managed three hops before it sank. He fingered another pebble in his hand.

"Well, 'worse' could be Rinnan, out to gain the confidence of the local resistance. He always works a negative line and all he needs is one person. First, we'll watch Sorting."

"You'll get your chance soon. I promised him lunch." Kjell stuffed his hands in his pockets. "We can go home any time. Ella's not expecting us until after curfew."

"Great. When we get back, I want to look at that place you told me about. I think it's time I distanced myself a bit from the village."

"All right, I'll take you tomorrow. Oh, by the way, my old friend Thomas Nissen has invited Rika to come here and live with him and his wife. It's something she has always wanted so I think I'll do it. It'll keep her out of our hair. Ella can keep Kitty preoccupied."

Hansen tossed the pebble in his hand then flicked it across the water. "They're good girls, Kjell, but it's best to have Rika away. The next months will be critical."

"*Ja*, for sure. The Allies are in Italy. Victories reported all the time..."

Hansen removed his cap and ran his fingers through his hair. "Many people want to believe we'll be liberated by August. That's dangerous because they'll become bold and careless—move too soon against the NS and Germans. There aren't enough arms, let alone trained men." He smiled wanly. "My orders changed again. I'm staying longer than I thought. That's why I want to move out."

Kjell clammed up. The thought of having to wait a few more months for freedom meant more danger for his daughters.

They walked along the water's edge away from the naval buildings and arsenal behind them and back up to the trees. The group of uniformed girls passed them heading for the river wall. Their leader gave them a hurried smile. Kjell and Hansen stopped in the grove.

"*Tusen takk* for helping me these past few days," Hansen said. "You've done well."

Kjell dipped his head. "Your meeting was important?"

"*Ja*, very important. Met with our Milorg contact."

They walked up the path back toward the cathedral's south side. At the path's end, Hansen turned to Kjell.

"Do we have enough *knott* to go back?" Hansen asked.

"I bought four bags," Kjell said. "I think we're safe."

CHAPTER 13

"Give me a kiss, Freyda," Sorting said.

The young woman complied, long and slow, a promise of more to come. Pulling her down by her masculine tie, he tried to put his hand up her skirt. She giggled and jerked the tie away. "Odd. Wait. I'm hungry." She twirled out of his grasp and went to the kitchen.

Sorting got up from the sofa and followed her. The apartment was fairly up-to-date, built just before the war. The kitchen was small, but modern. A couple of years ago, he had secured the place for her after its original owner had been arrested and the contents confiscated.

"You're always hungry. Good thing you don't have to wait in line for anything."

"*Nei*, I don't, but I did have to wait to get back into my apartment. You and your young friend Bent. I hope he got his ticket back." She stabbed a fork at some tender pieces of veal frying in a pan on the tiny stove. The aroma of their juicy sizzle made his stomach growl.

When he came to press his cause, she thrust an unopened bottle of wine into his hands.

"Here, open this." Her green eyes sparkled.

She was playing with him, but he didn't mind. Resigned, he took the bottle and corkscrew and went back into the living room. He watched her move about. Freyda was a real beauty, just twenty-one, with white-blond hair and a full figure whose every nuance he knew. He had missed her, something that continued to surprise him. He was actually in love, an emotion he wasn't quite sure what to do with. He even entertained the idea of marrying her. As long as the Chief approved.

The Chief. It had been a busy two days. Yesterday he saw Bent Kjelstrup off on a steamer back to Frøya and spent the rest of the day helping to outfit a boat chosen to take the islanders to the Shetlands. Though Flesch, head of the Gestapo in Trondheim, approved the project, it was being done in secrecy without the knowledge of local State Police and other authorities. In a few days, the Chief would take the boat over and hide it. They hoped to be gone by the night of the sixteenth.

The wine cork came off with a pop. He strolled to the kitchen searching for wine glasses and passing her, came back and pressed his aching groin up against her hips. He lifted her hair and kissed her on the neck, then pushed the collar of her suit jacket down and rubbed the top of her shoulder. "Odd..."

"All right, I'm leaving." He took the glasses to the low table in front of the sofa and sat down heavily. He poured a glass for himself. They bantered back and forth while she took the meat out of the pan. Finally she complained about his leaving again. "Must you go?"

"*Ja*."

She set two china plates out on a small, cloth-covered table decorated with flowers in a blue glass vase. From the kitchen she came back with steaming dishes. "I wish you wouldn't."

"I'll be there for a week or so, then I'm to go to Fjellstad. I should be back by the month's end." He sat down at the table and attacked the veal.

She pouted, but he knew she was only acting. She understood the rules. In the return for the place and its furnishings and fashionable clothes not made from cellulose, she was asked to do certain things. Often her apartment was used for special meetings, including those led by the Chief.

Sorting had encountered Freyda while she was standing in a ration line for bread near the *Torvet*, the marketplace in the center of Trondheim. At the end of the first winter of the occupation, she was warding off the cold under an ample pile of woolens and thick fur coat.

"You want some coffee?" he had asked. She paused for a moment, probably because she had been waiting a long time in the line and didn't want to miss her item. She finally went with him to a *bakeri*. There it had taken an effort for him to look at his coffee and not her chest. She was gorgeous, but surprisingly, very naive. After a week of meetings she went home with him, but before he could get her into the sack, she had passed out from the wine he had supplied her. He ended up taking a cold shower. When she woke up in the morning, she called him a gentleman for not taking advantage of her.

"Odd, are you listening?" Freyda put her fork down. "Must you go to Fjellstad?"

Sorting answered by rubbing a shoeless foot against her ankle. She moved her foot, but not too far. "I won't be away long."

Actually, he wasn't sure how long he would be gone. Using a piece of bread to wipe up the gravy on his plate, he recalled how readily the Chief had approved his idea. Surveillance was going to be picked up this summer—in part due to invasion talk in France. The Germans were pressing for action. They needed the Chief's organization.

"I'm going to hang around the islands for a few days." He put the bread into his mouth. "Then I'll go over to Fjellstad." He gave the girl a wink, then went back to his food and thoughts.

Once he arrived in the fishing village he'd go see Bugge Grande, a fisherman he'd met, and ask for work. Then he'd just watch and listen. Check out rumors of new activity out in the islands and along the coast, including transmitters.

A sweep a couple of weeks ago produced a complete list of residents in the Fjellstad district. He found Kjell Arneson on the list. No suspicion there. He kept his licenses up to date and bought his fuel legally. He owned a boat, home, and some *seter* land. He had two daughters and a hired man of questionable intelligence who was a deaf-mute to boot.

Finally, he had come across a name that was very familiar to him, but couldn't place. It was an unusual name, not typical Norwegian. *Anna Fromme.* The Fromme name gave him a chill.

It had taken him all day to figure it out. He finally remembered it was the name of a schoolteacher he had met in a little coastal village south of here. After several months of infiltration, the Chief himself had been able to work his way into a sizeable Milorg organization and expose it. Arrests were made in December. Einar Fromme was one of them.

Weren't you lucky. The Chief didn't bother to turn Fromme over to Gestapo headquarters, but took him straight to the Cloister. Worked Fromme over good, too, but he didn't talk.

Sorting paused, mindful of Freyda across the table from him. He gave her an indulgent smile, stirring listlessly at the remnants of his food. He shivered. Somehow Fromme had managed to find a piece of glass and slit his own throat. They found him lying dead in a pool of blood. But that still wasn't the reason Sorting recalled Fromme's name. As hardened as he was…

"Odd, what's wrong?" He gradually became aware that Freyda was looking at him. He must have been staring off into space, the horror on his face.

"Nothing." He drained his wineglass and looked at her greedily. "Nothing a roll in the hay won't cure." He reached for her small hand and rubbed his thumb in her palm. She giggled. Parting her lips, she leaned across the table to kiss him deeply, her full breasts brushing the tops of the flowers on the table. Dinner was over.

Later on in bed with Freyda asleep against his naked thigh, he thought nothing could cure what he had been ordered to do to Fromme. Maybe it was time to get out, take Freyda with him. The Germans weren't doing so well. He had only been in it for the money and his friendship with the Chief's brother Rolf, although he felt a thrill to work undercover and worm his way into some group of farmers or islanders. God, sometimes his countrymen were so stupid. Like at Telavåg.

He stroked the girl's hair, reaching over for a pack of cigarettes. Settling back on the pile of pillows, he lit a cigarette. Leaving would be tricky. He had discovered a deadly secret about the Chief. He knew his boss collected information on everyone, including the Germans. What he hadn't realized was that the Chief also had been in touch with the Soviet KGB. That his boss would think about leaving was unsettling. It meant he didn't think much of the Germans' future either.

He drew in on the cigarette. What to do? He couldn't leave until autumn, though the expected Allied invasion of France could change everything. I'll have to stay low, then go.

He thought of the salmon running now on the river near Fjellstad. He could get a permit right there at the little *pensionat*. They had fishing rights. Suddenly things looked brighter. The long white nights were coming. It would be good to be out of the city in the light and sun. Just as he did as a kid. Hike in the hills, look for strawberries. Good memories, not reeking of death.

The girl stirred, her full lips making mewing sounds. Her heavy breasts pushed against his skin. Her flesh felt cool against his, arousing him. He took one last drag and smashed the butt in a plate by the bed. He'd have all summer to make plans. In the meantime, he'd enjoy himself. As if to prove it, he slid down and, thrusting his fingers between her legs, woke her with his hands and mouth.

Book 2

The tender grass, the buds turning green
The young girls with leaves in their arms
And mothers smiling at children's eyes

All is Hope!—Nordahl Grieg

CHAPTER 14

Summer 1944

"Do you see anything?" Kjell asked.

Haugland looked at Kjell. "*Nei*,"

It was near the end of the long twilight, the *Otta* anchored west of the islands of Smøla and Hitra. The sea was flat, though the boat rose slightly from time to time on a swell. Occasional sun breaks broke up the dark blue gray water with shimmering streaks of platinum and gold at the horizon, then disappeared. From the southwest came the promise of rain. Haugland wondered if the weather would hold.

After instructing Kjell to take the *Otta* out as far as he dared, Haugland had set out a couple of poles on the starboard side for catching late cod. He sat with Kjell waiting for the results. This was the last Shetland run for a while. Too little darkness in summer.

He flipped his notebook to a fresh page. A hollow feeling in his gut was getting worse. They were carrying hard intelligence he had collected. He had the documents wrapped in an oilcloth pouch and sealed tight in a metal box. The box now hung on a rope inside an oil drum full of brine and fish and secured below the surface by a ring. A scrap of netting tied around some rocks weighed the box down. Until it was placed in the right hands, it was a danger to them.

"Think I'll wait out there." Haugland pointed with his notebook. "Watch for air patrols."

Kjell nodded and took a book off a shelf next to his chair.

Outside, Haugland sat on the fish hold and, keeping an eye on the fishing lines, made sketches in his notebook. He sketched the deck of the boat from the varioius perspectives while there was light, coming into the wheelhouse once it was too dim.

"Those are very good," Kjell said of the sketches. "Want some of that coffee?"

"That coffee" was real coffee Haugland had found yesterday in a box on a deserted skerry. It had been dropped during the last Christmas season. Inside was English chocolate, coffee, and tobacco. Wrapped around each item were greetings from the Nygaardsvoll government, the Norwegian government in exile in London.

Kjell disappeared into the tiny galley while Haugland kept watch in the wheelhouse. Behind him, the skerries appeared a deep black-blue against the evening sky. These small islands were low-lying and treeless, but people lived on them. They heated their simple homes with peat, which was found on many of the islands, going by boat once a week to get supplies at some village *landhandel.* Out here, though, these particular islands were uninhabited.

Haugland put on his jacket and sat down on a stool in the small space. Through the open door, he gazed across the water. It was peaceful, except for the night sounds of the shore and far off an occasional snort from a brown seal disturbed in its sleep. He had always loved the sea, cherishing the summer trips to his grandparents' home in Bergen where he could explore the shore, but in the months he had been in Fjellstad, the wildness of the coast and the beauty of the fjords and islands had become his standard. More and more he thought of it as a place he might return to after the war. *If I live that long.*

"Here you go. Watch it. It's hot." Kjell handed Haugland a cup of steaming coffee and sat down in his pilot's chair. In the dark, they sipped the strong brew and looked out to the west. Behind them, there was the promise of the moon.

"Once we make our delivery, I want you to meet Sig Haraldsen." Kjell's voice was quiet in the dark. "He lives near Hitra and is an old friend—known me since I was born. Totally trustworthy. I know you want to expand our cell. I think he would be an excellent resource. He knows many people and acts as a screen for those who came looking for more than a bolt to repair an engine. Sig is a good Norwegian—a *jøssing*—and can be counted on. Besides tomorrow is Constitution Day. His wife makes good *sandbakkels*."

"All right," Haugland said. "Don't think we should go to Frøya, though. Not with Bent Kjelstrups's boat leaving. Too dangerous to be nosing about."

A seal muttered and they both looked to see what had disturbed it, but heard nothing.

"Here." Kjell broke a bar of chocolate in half. "Too bad I can't save it for the girls," Kjell said.

"Well, you know you can't. It's English chocolate," Haugland replied. "And the only way you get it is by parachute drop. When we're done, we'll burn the wrapper."

"You're serious about this"

"*Ja*, sure. Last year, a similar candy bar wrapper tipped the Germans to the whereabouts of SOE commandos just after sabotage action in the south. The men got away, but after 10,000 soldiers went looking for them."

Haugland popped a piece into his mouth. "Hear anything else about the boys?"

"The boys" were three nineteen-year-olds from the village who had run off after Quisling began ranting and raving on the controlled radio about the Bolsheviks and the need to fight them on their soil. Just as Lars said, young men eighteen to twenty-five were urged to join up so the war's end would be speeded up, at last giving Norway its own government. The *Hjemmefronten* told these same young men to refuse the mobilization. Go to the forests, mountains or Sweden.

"No word." Kjell tapped the side of his cup. "How will they get food? They'll starve. The BBC said the response has been tremendous."

"In the thousands. Tell me the boys' names again."

"Petter Stagg, Karl Olavsen, and Arne Berg."

"Your village will find a way to get them food, I'm sure. They should take care, though, about the next quarter's ration cards. Individuals, not families, must have their own cards now. It will be hard to supply those boys gone *pa skauen*."

Outside, a cloak of deep blue enfolding most of the sky headed down toward the last light on the horizon. Haugland looked for any speck of light that might signal a patrol boat. He relaxed when he saw none. "Who painted the H-7 on the rocks? Sheriff Fasting was pissed off."

They both knew the H-7, a symbol of Haakon VII, Norway's king, was also a sign of resistance.

"I don't know. Hopefully not the boys' friends. I've had enough of soldiers snooping around." Kjell shook his head. "I thought I'd seen it all, but this mobilization to send our boys over to fight on the Eastern Front is bullshit! We're just cannon fodder."

"We always were, Kjell," Haugland said quietly, "despite that pure racist crap we are true Nordic brothers. It's just going to get worse. The food situation is already bad and I expect reprisals to increase. It's been worse since the beginning of the year."

Kjell said nothing else. Not wanting to upset him further, Haugland let the matter lie. Absentmindedly he spelled words with his fingers.

"Where did you ever learn to do that?" Kjell asked.

"This?" Haugland wiggled his fingers. He weighed the consequence of sharing this bit of personal information, decided it would be okay. "My *Onkel* Kris. He was deaf, but one of the most remarkable men I ever knew. He was a painter and a marine biologist."

"Really? What did he paint?"

"Birds, seashore life. He sold his paintings in galleries and had prints in publications several times. Many didn't know he was deaf because he could read lips. When he was a little boy he got scarlet fever. He lost his hearing.

My grandparents couldn't bear to send him away, so they hired a teacher to save his speech and teach him how to sign. He was stone deaf. You'd have to bang on the table to get his attention." As he talked he made signs in the air.

"That sounds vaguely like your cover story."

Haugland smiled softly. "A germ of truth. My uncle was lucky to have good speech for the hearing world, but it has no value in the deaf world. So he signed too."

"That's why you don't speak, isn't it? People wouldn't believe you were deaf."

"Sad, isn't it? To be deaf somehow implies you are stupid, just as being able to speak is equated with intelligence. It's worse in Germany. The Nazi sterilize deaf girls. All because deaf girls are unable to hear the full beauty of the New Order." Haugland's voice hardened. His fingers clutched the handle of his cup. This subject always angered him. He cleared his throat to resume.

"As for myself—my lack of speech is more for self-preservation. People tend to misunderstand deaf speech. It's dangerous-sounding. It's better to stay quiet and act dumb. There's enough danger just getting my notebook out. It could be mistaken for a gun."

"I know," Kjell said. "I worry about that."

"Because it's a very real possibility. I heard of a man in Oslo being shot dead by the Stapo for the very thing just a year ago. He was a parishioner at the Deaf Church there."

"I've heard of the Deaf Church. Did your uncle go there?"

"*Ja*. I know the head pastor, Conrad Bonnevie-Svendsen." Haugland knew the pastor all right. He was not only Norway's minister to the deaf, but also a highly placed member of Sivorg, the civilian branch of the resistance. Unfortunately, Haugland couldn't share that with Kjell.

"I hear he gives his sermons in sign language," Kjell said. "That true?"

"*Ja*, true. Conrad's a wonderful man. His father was the Deaf Church's first pastor back in the 1890s. My uncle knew both men. In fact, Conrad senior encouraged my uncle to study art."

Haugland slapped his thighs with his hands. "Well, haven't I've been the *Herr* Professor. Forgive me." He knew Kjell was burning with curiosity, but he would say no more about his uncle nor the Deaf Church. Besides, it was almost time. Toward the southwest through the vertical windows of the wheelhouse, a pearly gray streak still lingered at the horizon bright in the inky blue sky. He tugged at his oilskin jacket and went outside into the moist, cool air. The hollow pit in his stomach bordered on gurgling. This was not only the last run. It was one of the latest in the season. Beginning in mid-August, the runs usually ran through winter until the first week in May. After that, it was too risky, due to the long periods of light.

Thank God for the new submarine chasers, he thought.

In the past, when the Bus consisted only of fishing boats, they had to come over, blend into the local marine traffic, and return to the Shetlands when their mission was done. After the introduction of the submarine chasers, the runs became normal naval operations, even though their crews of independent-minded fishermen made them unique in the service. Casualties dropped to zero, with no boat lost.

Before Haugland did anything further, he took out a pair of wire spectacles from inside his jacket and plopped them on his nose, then put rubber pads between his cheeks and teeth. He hated disguises, not always trusting them, but wanted to alter his appearance for the two men he would be transporting. He especially disliked the rubber pads. They had a flat taste.

Haugland worked his way to the front of the boat, crossing over to the starboard side where the large poles were set into holders. Reeling a line in, he landed a couple of bottom fish and let them flop on the deck once they were released. A second pole produced another large fish, chomped off behind the gills, leaving only the head. Seals. He threw it back.

He cleaned the gear and put the fish into the barrel full of brine. It was very still, the only sound the faint tapping of the ropes against the masts and the soft creak of wood as the boat gently rose and fell, tethered to its anchor. The streak at the horizon was gone, but as his eyes adjusted the sea looked oily. Totally deserted.

Yet Haugland knew before he heard or saw it the submarine chaser was there, coming close. His stomach tightened in anticipation. Restless, he got up.

Suddenly, like a gray ghost one hundred and ten feet long, the boat appeared, skimming smoothly on the oily black sea. On its narrow deck, uniformed crew members moved back and forth. The *Hitra* was on time.

The boat reversed its engines, the water churning from under its long wooden hull. The *Hitra* dwarfed the *Otta*, yet its deck was just above Haugland's ear. Kjell joined him by the fish hold. A headline secured his boat, while a welcoming committee on top leaned over.

On top there were no lights, but to his left he could see the dull shape of an antiaircraft gun in the dark. He shook the hand of a crewman who helped him over. The deckhouse door opened and an officer emerged wearing an oilskin coat. "*Velkommen*. I'm Eidsheim."

The skipper shook Haugland's hand warmly. Once Kjell was on deck, Eidsheim introduced his second in command, and invited them to come belowdecks out of the cool night air.

"I'll give you a tour."

Haugland ducked under the scuttle. A subtle glow at the bottom of the ladder came from a door he knew led into the galley. He climbed down. Like the other two boats he'd been on, the Hitra had electricity, refrigerated water, and speeds to over fifteen knots. A crew of twenty-four enlisted men and three officers were crammed into spaces as narrow as horse stalls.

Haugland listened with interest as the skipper discussed the boat's features, its variable speed propellers, its firepower, but the little group of young men waiting for them in the tight, low-ceilinged galley interested him more. They looked up when Haugland stepped over the knife-edge behind Eidsheim and faced them.

The introductions were brief. Hot coffee served immediately. Introduced as "Frode" for security reasons, Haugland sat down at the metal table and drank his coffee thoughtfully. The whole scene was a bit unreal: the electric light seemed too bright and unnatural after nightfall outside, and under the conversations there was a low hum from the boat's inner workings. Kjell discovered an old acquaintance he hadn't seen in over two years. The two others were the men he was to deliver— "Kaare" and "Robert."

Haugland took their introductions at face value. Like him, they probably had more than one *deknavn* or code name. For this operation, Haugland was Frode, but he had a more secret name that only a few knew—"Ryper."

"How do you want the goods loaded?" Eidsheim asked.

Haugland nodded at Kjell, who was deeply involved in conversation with his friend. "He's the boss. Do you want to start now?"

"As soon as possible. *Vær så snil.* You, take your time. By the way, I have the things you ordered. They put them together as fast as they could. Don't know about the books, though."

Haugland chuckled. "I thought you kept a regular library. Fines must be outrageous."

"Oh, we try. Did you get the extra radio crystals you needed and another supply of iron rations and medicine. SOE sent some money too." Eidsheim took out a long brown envelope. "Two final things. Your orders for now—and a letter from London for your light reading later on."

"*Takk.*" Haugland spent the next few minutes talking with Robert across the narrow table. He had been born in Norway, but had immigrated to the United States when he was a boy.

"I'm from Conway, Washington," Robert said. He talked for a bit about his adopted country, speaking in a Norwegian that had lost its place of origin. Haugland asked many questions, including where was Oxford, Maryland, Anna Fromme's birthplace.

An enlisted man served ham along with boiled potatoes and a can of fruit. Everyone was under pressure. Kjell wolfed his food down, but Haugland used his time to read his orders and then explain to Robert and Kaare how they would meet their contact on the mainland. He hoped to have them over by five o'clock in the morning.

Eventually, Kjell went up to start the loading. Haugland stayed back to talk to Eidsheim.

"You've got five crates of Sten guns, two Bren guns, Mills hand grenades and an assortment of ammunition. The man you're meeting is reliable, but there was a serious sweep of a Milorg group over five months ago. Did you hear about Lillehavn?"

"*Ja*," Haugland said quietly. *Einar Fromme.*

He handed Eidsheim the oilskin pouch along with the metal box. It contained materials and hard data that couldn't be transmitted, such as maps showing the locations of new mines and photos or sketches of certain vessels.

"There's a list of names of collaborators in there," Haugland said. "FO IV in London will know what to do with it." Haugland stood up. "Guess we better get moving."

Everyone filed toward the door. As they crowded at the entrance, Haugland studied the men he was to deliver later in the morning. They had an authentic Norwegian look about them, even the tobacco Robert used in his pipe. All out of the stores kept at Lunna Voe in the Shetlands, Haugland thought, but they're still nervous.

Their tension was something Haugland could appreciate. The boat ride over had only been an artificial lull before a different sort of storm.

Back on top, the loading was nearly complete. Boxes filled the fish hold, and covered with canvas and fish netting, looked no different from the legitimate supplies Kjell carried. Eidsheim gave Haugland a bill of lading for lead weights and other fishing gear, which partially filled the boxes. "Time to shove off. Better get the men on board. It's been good talking to you."

Haugland nodded in agreement. He had enough news about the war to mull over for several days. It was even encouraging. As he prepared to go, the second officer brought over a heavy duffel bag for Haugland.

"Here you are, sir. Compliments of the best bus service around. The lieutenant thought you might like some tinned meat, fruit and other food. I believe the books are on top."

"*Takk*. Tell your lieutenant thanks. See you in a few months," he said to Eidsheim.

"Good luck to you. Godspeed."

A few minutes later, the boats separated. Then the *Hitra* was gone as silently as it had come.

CHAPTER 15

Unmarked cove. Rocky walls flushed with the first pink of dawn. Abandoned boathouse on the shore. Behind it, scrubby pine and more rock on a hill rising up at an alarming angle.

Haugland eyed it all as Kjell brought the *Otta* in and cut the motor eighty feet out from shore. To the right of the boathouse where the land was more forgiving, a road ambled down to a suspiciously unstable dock. The abrupt silencing of the boat's tonk-a-tonk left an eerie void on the water and in the light morning breeze. Haugland put down the anchor.

"I'll go over alone," he said when Kjell joined him at the gunwale. "It shouldn't take long. They'll want to get over the mountains early so they can make the ferry across the fjord."

"You really expecting trouble?" Kjell stared at the empty shore.

"*Nei*," Haugland said. "London said my contact is reliable." Haugland patted his pocket where his pistol was hidden. "Still, I won't go without backup. We were sent here because of a *razzia* in another district last December. A Milorg group was destroyed." He didn't add that the district had been Einar Fromme's. "You never know. If there's trouble, take my Sten gun and shoot them. I'll do what I need to do. For now, keep Kaare and Robert below."

With that he untied the ropes to the *Otta*'s dinghy and lowered it to cold clear water of the cove. Then he waited.

Around four-thirty, a black Chevrolet sedan came racing down the gravel road. The bits of rocks it stirred up made sparks against its chassis. A sign on top said "Taxi." It had the familiar furnace on its back, but from the way the car was traveling, Haugland suspected it was using gasoline. Enterprising folks, he thought. It slowed down the last few turns, paused briefly by the boathouse, and then came to rest at the dock.

Haugland checked the license plate with his binoculars. It matched his instructions. "We're on."

He watched two men get out of the car, an older man in his fifties, the other a young man Haugland's age. The latter cupped his hand to his mouth and shouted over.

"Catch anything?" the man said.

"*Nei*," Haugland yelled back.

"Then wait for the west wind."

"Good idea. You want some?"

"I only need two. Trollheim sent me." The man put his hands down.

"Well, that's that, Kjell," Haugland said. "See you in fifteen minutes. Get Robert and Kaare ready. We'll move the crates at the appropriate time." He climbed over the side and down the ladder into the dinghy. He set the oars and pulled himself over to the shore.

"You are not Ivar," Haugland said when he was on top of the dock. Up by the boathouse a third man appeared, leaning against the weathered boards. He was a grizzled, tough-looking blond in his thirties and dressed like a fisherman. "That's Ivar."

Haugland knew he was right. Something was wrong, and the men weren't taking any chances. He ignored the men and headed up to the old building. As he predicted, they hurried on past him, protesting all the way. The fisherman came away from the wall, where he had watched everything with detached amusement.

"Ryper, I take it. I apologize for the dramatics. You're right. I'm Ivar. You just can't be sure about the hired help these days."

Haugland smiled wryly. "Depends on who's doing the hiring. References and all that."

"Do you care to see mine?" Ivar's deep voice sounded like he was used to giving orders.

"*Nei*," Haugland answered. "'Trollheim' is reference enough. I would like to know what's spooked you, though." He kept his hand on the pistol in his pocket and was careful how he faced Ivar and the other men. He wanted the merchandise to be safely delivered. "Were you followed?"

"I was going to ask the same of you." Ivar looked at Haugland thoughtfully. "Olav, get the car ready for the trip back. Fritz, be ready to move when I say."

Olav drove the taxi around into the boathouse. Fritz leaned against the wall. When they were set, Ivar beckoned for Haugland to follow him back onto the dock. They walked a short ways down on the slimy green boards. Haugland kept his back to the *Otta*. Ivar squinted when he looked toward the boat. Sun must be hitting the wheelhouse windows, blinding him, Haugland thought. It would be hard to see who was onboard.

"No offense, you know. Have to be cautious," Ivar said. "A group was compromised."

"I heard. What happened?" Haugland kept his face still, but he was listening intently.

"Two arrests were made. Everyone laid low for a while, until the interrogations were finished. One man was released, the other one's in a hospital in Kristiansund N. No one said anything." Ivar spoke softly but his jaw was set. His hand clenched and unclenched. "Four days ago Fritz found the man hidden in a private room. He was in pretty bad shape. Broken bones, lacerations and massive bruising. Beaten with a *totenschlager*. He's been crippled."

Haugland looked away, thinking of his brother Per. A *totenschlager* was a steel spiral spring with a steel ball or spike at the tip. It not only beat a person viciously, it inflicted open wounds. The Gestapo and the Stapo favored it.

Ivar took out a pipe. After lighting it, he took a couple of puffs before he continued. "Fritz didn't speak to him," Ivar continued, "but an hour after he got home, someone from the Stapo came knocking at the front door. He went out the back while his mother explained he had gone fishing. He still hasn't been home."

"Do you feel things are jeopardized now?" Haugland removed his hand from his pocket.

"We think it's a coincidence. They haven't come back to ask questions. We're splitting up, though. Fritz and Olav will take the taxi. I'll drive the others to the proper drop off."

"Security says the district has been shaky for some time."

"Not my group. South of here. But you're right. People are afraid. The *razzia* in Lillehavn shook people up. I knew the school master, Einar Fromme."

Haugland felt like he had been hit. "You knew him?"

"*Ja,* we played chess frequently at his home. Still can't believe he's gone. He was a damn good Milorg leader."

"My condolences." Haugland cleared his throat. "We need to move now."

Haugland rowed them over to the *Otta*. Onboard, Kjell called up Robert and Kaare from the crew's quarters. Names were given around, even though everyone knew they were using *deknavns*. Haugland and Kjell removed the fish hold cover and brought up two crates. Kjell carefully opened the lid on one of them. Inside were lead weights and other fishing equipment. Underneath, in a hidden false bottom, were the unassembled pieces to several Sten guns. Ivar blew his breath out heavily.

"You've been dreaming about these?" Haugland asked.

"You bet."

He picked up the three pieces to a gun and quickly assembled it. "They're brand new, which means you should check for burrs inside their barrels. Have them smoothed down or else they'll blow up on you. And be careful about dropping a loaded one. The trigger mechanism's light."

He tossed it to Ivar, who caught it mid-air and turned it over in his hands. He lined up the sight and grunted with pleasure. It was an odd-looking piece with its T-shaped metal tube for a stock, but it was robust—and cheap.

"There are twenty guns total and ammunition for them. More will come early fall."

"Fall," Ivar remarked. "Where are we all going to be this fall?"

On shore, the guns were put into cloth sacks unassembled. The taxi's backseat was removed, exposing a hidden storage space. After the guns were laid in, the seat was set back in.

"Nice work," Haugland said.

"*Takk*. Fritz was in auto bodywork before the war."

Haugland put his hand on the furnace. It felt warm. "Fan?"

Ivar grinned. "*Ja*. Gasoline is so much better, but we don't want to get caught on that."

Haugland laughed. "I heard a German once call the furnace Norwegian ingenuity. Little did he know that the car was really running on gas. Good luck with it."

The farewells were brief, both groups anxious to get off. The taxi was loaded and ready to go, its exhaust making thick clouds of smoke along the ground. Out in the cove, Kjell waited.

"If I don't hear about you, I'll assume everything is all right," Haugland said to Ivar.

"*Ja*. That will be the best way. The same for you."

"Then it's good-bye and good luck."

They shook hands and departed. Rowing back to the *Otta*, Haugland watched Ivar walk back to the car and get in. Haugland gave him a wave and the car took off.

Ten minutes later Kjell and Haugland pulled anchor, leaving the cove deserted in the early morning light.

CHAPTER 16

Kjell and Haugland arrived at Haraldsen's store shortly before noon. Located on a low, rocky island north of the much larger island of Hitra and the *Trondheimsleia*, the two-storied wood building sat on a flat, barren rise. It was a combination of *landhandel*, home, and marine repair shop. Behind it stood a barn peeling blue paint, the only other major building in sight. There were a few birch trees and a long narrow field of grass for putting up hay, but mostly it was all rocks, like the countless other small, flat islands that were scattered throughout the waterway here. To the east where the mainland was steep and bare, rising more than a two thousand feet from sea level, Haugland saw various gulls and terns reeling along the shore. A few fishing boats bobbed in the distance. The clouds had cleared away and the sky was clear and blue.

"*God dag*!" a man called from the dock as the *Otta* eased against the old tires hanging from pilings. He was dressed in traditional attire of dark vest and white collarless linen shirt, but Haugland saw right away that it would be a mistake to consign Sig Haraldsen to a rocking chair. Despite his white hair and mustache and a slight stoop, he appeared quite robust. Once they were off the boat, Sig greeted Kjell with a rough pat on the back, then turned to Haugland.

"So. You are Jens Hansen," he said in a loud, deliberate voice. "It's good to meet you. Welcome."

He shook his hand, then turned to Kjell. "Dark Norwegian, isn't he? You said he was from Molde? So many lost there." His head was slightly turned away so Haugland acted like he hadn't understood and signed to Kjell, What say?

"Sig," Kjell said. "You must speak directly to my young friend."

"Of course. Forgive me." Sig repeated everything.

This will be exhausting, Haugland thought. But it had to be done.

The country store was old and cluttered with foodstuffs, gear, and repair materials for fishing boats. Lanterns, ropes in neat coils, and nets dangled from the beams. At the back there was a heavy wood counter. Near the left corner, a stove burned peat, next to which the wall had been punched out to hold bay windows hung with bright cafe curtains. In the space a cloth-draped table, benches, and chairs had been set up. The low ceiling, rubbed with linseed oil, sagged slightly, creaking from the footsteps in the living quarters overhead. He felt very comfortable here. It reminded him of his *Onkel* Kris's place at Telavåg.

"Come in, come in. Oh, Kjell. You look so fine." A slim woman in her mid-forties with reddish blond hair came forward, wiping her hands on her apron. She kissed Kjell on each cheek, then stepped aside so the couple behind her could greet him. "You're going to stay for supper, aren't you? It's Constitution Day." The woman laughed. "We'll celebrate and remember. See?" She moved aside her apron bib. Underneath, there was a chain of paper clips hanging off the button on her dress. A symbol of solidarity. "We'll hang together against the Germans."

"Hang?" Kjell laughed. "I was promised *sandbakkels*, Andrina Paal."

Andrina Paal patted Kjell's midsection. "Mother made them just for you." Suddenly she was aware of Haugland, standing to the back. "Is this Jens?"

Haugland looked at the group and smiled wryly.

CHAPTER 17

Anna Fromme sat at the dining table and stared at the manila envelope before her. On its front was the familiar handwriting. She had gone with Lisel to the village *landhandel* to get a couple of items that she needed with her ration card. She was surprised there was a package for her, but didn't give the quisling proprietress, *Fru* Andersson, any satisfaction in discovering who had sent it.

She knew it would contain letters, which were never mailed directly, but passed to a special friend in the *Wehrmacht* here in Norway. So Pappa had found her.

"Let's go to go to the Tourist Hotel and have a sweet. Won't that be fun?" Anna said as she led Lisel out the door.

As she hoped, the dining room was half-filled. Foss greeted her at the entrance and found her a quiet spot in a corner. She ordered pastries and tea. While Lisel sat in her chair, legs dangling, Anna talked about the wool she had found in the barn.

"You can help me wash it, Lisel. We'll dry clouds of it all over the yard." Anna had discovered the bags the other day while cleaning out the barn. The fleeces were old, but usable. "I'll spin it up and make socks and sweaters for each of us."

Another skill I've learned since arriving here, she thought. Einar's mother had welcomed her and had taught her how to spin early on. Anna was sorry that she had passed away two years ago.

"Can I have some wool too, Mama?" Lisel looked at her with huge eyes, her shoulders barely clearing the linen-draped table.

"Of course, Munchkin. When it's washed. It's very dirty." They spoke in Norwegian.

The pastries arrived with cups of tea. Lisel ate her piece. Anna opened up the envelope and took out the first letter. It was dated 30 Nov 1943, just a week before Einar was arrested.

"My dear Anna," the letter went on in German, "I hope you, Einar, and my sweet granddaughter are well, for it gives me strength in this dark time."

He wrote fairly freely without censure because he had once told her that he believed in the security of its posting through a trusted friend. Known to her only as "Uncle Felix" this friend arranged for her father's mail to get to her. It was dangerous work. If they were found out, they would be shot.

"I am no longer living in Berlin. Our house is safe, but heavy bombing has forced me to work in the countryside." He didn't say where, but Anna wondered if factories had been moved to rural areas. Her father's work in synthetic fuels was crucial.

"It makes for an uneasy ride. We are occasionally strafed by Allied aircraft, but I am all right, I assure you. Willy is fine, but I must warn you that he has been drafted out of the Labor Service and is being sent to France with the *Wehrmacht.* It won't be a dangerous job—he's in some sort of information corps— and might be stationed in Paris. I can't help but think it is a way to watch him, so I will cooperate with the research. How I regret not getting Willy out to the west as well! I'll always be grateful to Einar for arranging your safe departure from Germany. After the war, I hope to get to know him better."

Anna folded the letter against her breast, tears welling up. *Pappa, you'll never be able to thank him.* She sniffed and opened the second letter dated, 22 Feb 1944. Her father was worried about her, not having heard from her for some time. Was she all right?

"I heard the food situation continues to grow worse in Norway," he wrote, "and only emergency help from Denmark and Sweden keeps many from starving. Are the rural places as bad as the cities? I wish you would write."

Anna rested the letter on the edge of the table. Actually, she had been afraid to write. After Einar's death, the Gestapo and the State Police had questioned her. To her relief, they seemed to believe her innocence concerning Einar's underground activities. Yet, she was not naïve enough to think they would not continue to be suspicious. She had married a Norwegian citizen who suddenly had come under the scrutiny of the security police.

She glanced furtively at the people in the dining room and swallowed.

I'll never feel safe, she thought. *My papers are forged. What if someone finds out I'm an American? Worse, what if the Gestapo finds Pappa out?*

She touched the edge of the stationery. After Einar's arrest she hadn't dared send anything through "Uncle Felix." In the end, Uncle Felix located her.

Anna stopped reading. She put down the letters and sampled the pastry. Lisel was nearly done. There were crumbs at the corner of her mouth.

"Please wipe your mouth, Munchkin. Crumbs." She showed Lisel how to do it by wiping the corner of her own mouth with her napkin. "It's good, isn't it?"

"Uh-huh." Lisel reached for her cup of tea and sipped it noisily.

"Lisel. Shh." Anna stopped. Lisel was leaning back, frozen in her chair and eyes wide.

Cautiously, Anna turned toward the door out to the lobby. Just entering were *Wehrmacht* soldiers and officers. Their field-gray uniforms were immaculate. With them were two attractive Norwegian women, dressed in fashionable spring dresses and coats, arms intimately linked. They looked out of place.

Foss showed them where to sit, but they chose their own places according to rank. The soldiers sat at one table, officers at another, chattering in German. It was strange listening to them. Anna seldom heard German on the coast, and it sounded more and more like a foreign language. She didn't even dream in it any more. She dreamed in Norwegian and English. "It's all right, Sweetie."

Ever since Einar's arrest, Lisel had been afraid of German uniforms and helmets. Back in late April, when the soldiers made house-to-house searches, their lieutenant, a stocky Bavarian, had attempted to speak with her, knowing that she was part German. Lisel had hidden her face in the folds of Anna's dress. Anna was polite, but she realized for the first time that her speaking German confused Lisel. Soldiers had been present when Einar was arrested.

Behind her, the small party continued to chatter. She was no prude, but the young women's shameless behavior bothered her. One girl was already drunk, practically making love in public. Anna had noticed that increasingly German soldiers were showing up at the hotel on leave. Foss said they came for the summer run of salmon. She looked down at the letters and decided to put them away.

"Lisel, don't be afraid." She took one last bite, placed the remainder in a clean handkerchief, and folded it up. She set the correct *kroner* and *ore* for the pastries and tea by her plate.

She helped Lisel down and, shouldering the rucksack, shepherded her toward the door. As she went by, she brushed against the chair of one of the officers. He turned and admired her.

"Ah, *Fraulein... Frau*," he corrected when he saw her ring.

She pretended not to understand them and went out the door, laughter following.

CHAPTER 18

The promise of *sandbakkels* was nice, but Haugland was partaking of something more substantial and thoroughly enjoying himself. From the beginning the family had fussed over him. After only a few minutes, a cup of *ersatz* coffee was in his hands. They spoke to him in deliberate, sometimes loud voices and were always careful to face him. He enjoyed listening to them. They spoke in a dialect typical of the area. Soon he was seated at the table and with his notebook engaged in a lopsided communication with Andrina Paal. When Kjell went off with one of her brothers, Andrina Paal moved closer to Haugland.

"Do you remember the *Alta,* the fishing boat?" she asked. "Finn Thorsen?"

Haugland remembered. The *Alta* fished for cod. Last February, it rolled while he and some others were helping unload its catch. Haugland and Finn Thorsen were thrown into the water. They had dived deep to avoid the weight of the nets, but an edge still caught Thorsen. Haugland freed him and pulled him to safety. Fortunately, all they got were nicks and bad colds. *Ja,* Haugland's face and hands said. Friend?

"My husband's cousin. You saved his life. Look, I have something for you, Jens." She turned to an elderly woman working behind the counter. "Mother, could you bring the package?"

She turned back. "When Father said you were coming this time, Finn Thorsen's wife found out. It's something she made."

Fru Haraldsen came to the table with a cardboard shirt box. She was a beautiful, vibrant woman, her white hair pulled back off her pink face.

"Open it. *Vær så god, Herr* Hansen."

Haugland complied. Inside was sweater made of handspun white and dark gray wool knit in a traditional Nordic pattern. He looked at the women.

It beautiful, his hands said. *Tusen takk.* He held it up to show it would fit.

The shop bell jingled. Haugland kept his eyes on the women, but heard the footsteps of at least three people.

"Are you still bothering him? Women." Sig shooed his wife away, but not before kissing her snowy head. "You too, *datter*. The men will visit."

Andrina Paal shook her finger at her father and laughed. "Come, Mother. Dinner waits."

Sig sat down stiffly and invited Kjell to do the same. A son introduced as Manus sat down and slapped a deck of cards on the table.

"Who'll start?" he said.

The rest of the day passed pleasantly. The men sat and played cards for the most part, sitting by the window drinking *ersatz* coffee or raspberry tea. Kjell and the Haraldsens joked and laughed as they shuffled cards and played, sharing family news or arguing over past adventures. When discussion became serious, it was about the fishing season or the state of equipment, or when the women were upstairs, some incident they had heard of out in the islands. Haugland could see why Kjell wanted him to meet them. They were as solid as they came and could be trusted to work secretly. As they trusted Kjell, they accepted him as their own.

When Haugland showed he could play cards with a devious hand, Sig laughed. "You must be keeping track of the cards in your notebook."

Not me, Haugland signed and grinned.

During the late afternoon, Sig led Kjell and Haugland up the rocky hill behind the store. Tufts of grass grew between the rocks sometimes causing their boots to slip. The old man negotiated the climb like a goat. When they reached the top they could look out over the store and the barn, seeing beyond in all directions. The area was dotted with small islands, many uninhabited. It took a skilled pilot navigator like Kjell to go through them. A few boats were out, some with sails. The tonk-a-tonk of one echoed faintly across the blue water.

Haugland pointed out the boats and signed, How many boats there you know?

Kjell told Sig what he had signed. The old man looked at Haugland.

"That noisy one out there is Remy Karlsson's."

Jøssing? Haugland motioned.

"*Ja*, but he doesn't have a head on his shoulders."

Haugland looked at Kjell and swallowed. He was about to expose himself to someone he had only Kjell's word on. *This is the riskiest part of this work*, he thought.

Can anyone keep a secret? Haugland wrote in his notebook.

"I wouldn't ask Remy Karlsson, not that he's bad. But I could," Sig answered. "Why?"

Haugland scribbled, If you wanted to hide potatoes, where would you put them?

Sig looked at Kjell. "What are you up to, Kjell Arneson? Should I trust this young man? Are we talking about contraband?" Sig answered his own question. "*Nei*, we're not talking about potatoes or black market food. We are talking about something more serious."

"*Ja*, we are," Kjell answered, "but you can trust him. We're together."

"My dear friend."

Sig studied Haugland's face intently as if he was seeking the full measure of his character. His eyes rested on Haugland's eyes. Haugland looked back with equal interest, but Sig did not blink. Haugland nodded.

I know what you ask, Haugland signed.

Kjell started to interpret, but Sig stayed him. "I understand him. You forget I have a nephew like him up near Vikna. Deaf since infancy. He lives a full and useful life." He looked at Haugland. "I suppose you do too."

I try, Haugland signed.

"All right," Sig said turning to Kjell. "I'll help you as I've helped before, but I suspect this is new, more dangerous work. When the time comes, we'll talk. I can get the men if you want. Now supper will be ready soon. We'd better wash or the women will fuss. They want us to work hard, but they don't like dirty nails."

They headed down the hill, Sig leading. Haugland looked over at Kjell going carefully because of his knee. Kjell grinned at him.

He fine, Haugland signed. After supper, he would personally tell Sig who he was. Then two people would know his identity.

***

The meal was excellent, fish caught that day and, of course, potatoes. Haugland knew that people in the remote rural areas sometimes ate well enough. Rationing didn't make sense when they could catch or raise food away from inquiring eyes if they had arable land. Not everything went to the German army.

They were squeezed around the dining room in the apartment above the store. Three of Sig's middle-aged children were there and a few of his teenage grandchildren. It was a happy gathering. *Fru* Haraldsen had brought up a bottle of fine wine from her 'royal' stock, which she was saving for the day the king returned. There were many toasts to the sound of "*Skoal.*" May seventeenth was an important day to Norwegians, the day in 1814 when the country received its own constitution. In peacetime, Norwegians had celebrated Constitution Day with flags and children's parades. During the last dreary four years it was celebrated indoors with a spark of defiance.

Haugland began to relax a little, but was careful to nurse the wine. Getting drunk on a holiday was sometimes a national tradition too.

Sig's oldest son Holger, a dark Norwegian like Haugland, stood up to recite patriotic poetry in a rich, earthy voice. Soon he began the poem written on the king's seventieth birthday. Warmed by the wine, Holger began to recite, glass in hand. It was a poem often read on the BBC and printed in the illegal papers. Everyone at the table listened intently. Haugland watched his face.

"To King Haakon..."

"To King Haakon," everyone repeated.
Haugland cocked his head, but was quiet.

"...my all for Norway, truly
You kept the pledge you vowed
Even when with ones unruly
Our rebel tongues were loud..."

Haugland's mind wandered as the poem went on. Where had he been on this day last year? Hiding in a forest hut after a black propaganda effort against the Germans got too hot. Where was he on any of those days the past four years? Never with family.

He looked over at *Fru* Haraldsen. She came from peasant stock, and although his mother came from an old well-to-do family in Bergen, they seemed very much alike. Suddenly, he felt lonely and wished he could see his mother and let her know he was alive. But it was not allowed. Instead, when the summer was over, he would put that hurt aside and go to Sweden for a month's break. He'd find his friend Brita. She never was averse to sleeping with him. Maybe they'd—

Suddenly Haugland realized someone was staring at him and he looked up. It was one of Sig's granddaughters. She was fair, buxom, and very pretty. Her mind was wandering too. He smiled at her, then looked back at Holger, who was on the last stanza.

"The paltry treason spurning
Of dastard hireling bands
In hopes of your returning
Your realm united stands.
Though now disarmed and feeble
Uncowed we still remain;
Here waits your land, your people
To greet you home again!"

When Holger finished, everyone stood up and said, "To the king" then sat down again, breaking into small talk. Haugland got up and down out of order. *Fru* Haraldsen went into the kitchen. Haugland got Kjell's attention.

What's up? he signed.

"*Sandbakkels*."

Andrina Paal laughed, her hand on Kjell's arm. "Whenever Kjell comes, Mother makes *sandbakkels*. It is an old story."

Kjell and Andrina Paal looked at each other warmly. Haugland now knew that her husband was abroad. He had been away on a merchant ship when the invasion came, so headed straight to the first Allied port, which happened to be New York City. He was with *Nordship*, Norway's greatest contribution to the war effort. Kjell seemed to be enjoying all the attention.

"Are you staying with *Onkel* Kjell?"

The granddaughter was back again. Haugland didn't answer her because he was looking across the table at Kjell. He picked up his wineglass and took a long sip. There was a technique to all this. He continued to ignore her. When she asked again, to everyone's astonishment, Kjell pounded the table so the dishes rattled. Then Haugland looked at Kjell. Definitely a science.

"Sorry," Kjell apologized. He pointed to Haugland then over to the girl. "She wants to say something." His eyes were sparkling as if to say, "See if you can get out of this."

Not very well. Until dessert was served, Haugland had the undivided attention of eighteen-year-old Astrid Haraldsen who acted like she had never seen a man before. While Sig and his sons talked about flyfishing for trout and what flies should be used down at their end of the table, Haugland had to concentrate on what Astrid was saying and responded the best he could with his notebook. He was torn with being polite or feigning total incomprehension and ignoring her, but her lively attention to him was also a bittersweet counterpoint to the fact that his sister was in a detention camp.

In the end, the *sandbakkels* saved him. With a flourish, *Fru* Haraldsen brought the little brown fluted cakes to the table to the accompaniment of many compliments. Haugland marveled at how she had put them together. Where had she found the nuts and cream?

After the dessert, the blackout curtains were drawn, blotting out a beautiful sunset and peaceful twilight. In time, the families prepared to go. Holger and his family had a half-hour boat ride to their home on another island. Everyone said his or her good-byes, then they all went downstairs, leaving Haugland alone.

It was quiet except for the ticking of a clock and the muffled sound of voices as they passed under him and went outside. Haugland sat down on a long sofa beneath the drawn floral curtains and picked up a fishing catalogue laying on it. He had brought it along to share, but it no longer contained the message from Lars written with invisible ink on the return envelope.

"Be careful," Lars warned him. "I returned to Oslo with no trouble, but the fate of the boy is bad. He's been taken down to Lillehammer for more questioning and will likely be sent to Møllergata 19. The couple who picked you up in Kvam has gone into hiding."

Møllergata 19, Haugland thought. The dreaded Gestapo prison in Oslo. Father was sent there.

He closed his eyes and pushed away the image of his father the last time he saw him. Worn and haggard. Haugland was wanted by the Gestapo and had already gone into hiding at the Deaf Church in Oslo. He was surprised when Father showed up to see Conrad Bonnevie-Svendson. Behind the rectory door, Haugland listened to the men talk about his father's treatment at Møllergata 19. It broke his heart to hear his father mourn his supposed death in a shootout with soldiers. Two days later, Father was dead. He looked at the table where the Haraldsens had gathered earlier. I'll remember. I promise.

Not long after, Kjell and Haugland returned to the *Otta*. The night was sharp and clear, the stars close and heavy. Kjell turned off the hooded flashlight once they were by the boat, leaving them in total darkness. All that was left was the sound of the water against the pilings.

"Did you have a good day?" Kjell asked. They stood at the edge of the dock, a night breeze gently tugging at their dark clothes.

Haugland stood with his arms folded across his chest. "*Ja*. Very much. Unexpected, actually."

"They are good friends. I've known them a long time." Kjell cleared his throat. "I was even going to marry Andrina Paal."

"Really?"

"*Ja*, but I wanted to be at sea. She was a schoolteacher and wanted me home. Then she married someone who loved the sea too. She was still a schoolteacher, but now someone else was away. It has been hard, but the marriage worked, even with him gone. We're friends now."

Kjell stopped briefly. "My wife Kristine understood me. I was in the merchant marine. I was a pilot—although I don't let the Nazis know so they will force me to work for them. I went all over the world. I only stopped my traveling when she got the cancer. She was born to be a mariner's wife. Let that be a lesson to you." In the dark his face seemed to glow a pale ghost light. "Sometimes things, like love, happen when you are not looking for them. I always wanted Andrina Paal, but I loved the sea. I found Kristine by accident. From the very beginning it was right. I loved Kristine very much from the start."

Haugland wondered what had started Kjell on this. Maybe he felt the need to explain himself and the handsome daughter of Sig Haraldsen.

"So, you liked my friends? They liked you. Especially *Fru* Haraldsen."

Haugland noticed that even Kjell called her "*Fru*."

"And of course, Astrid. You are quite the ladies' man, *jo*?"

"Uh." Haugland grew serious. He looked out across the black water, looking for the dark shapes of the islands. There was almost enough starlight to make them out. The breeze caressed his face. His voice was soft when he spoke.

"I liked them very much, Kjell. Sig will be a valuable asset, but even more I think they made it clear to me why I'm doing this. Somehow it'll come out all right."

CHAPTER 19

After leaving Sig, Kjell and Haugland spent two days on the small island of Frøya, then headed down to see another friend of Kjell's. The morning sky was gray and overcast. The sea was slightly choppy, but the *Otta* made good time. Inside the wheelhouse, Haugland and Kjell talked about their coming visit.

"I've known the family for many years," Kjell said. "Andrew Kjelstrup is Bent's big brother. We call him A.C. He makes his living fishing and collecting peat even though he's lame."

"How's that?" Haugland asked.

"German bullet. Got hit near the knee while fighting them during the invasion. He's lucky to have kept his leg." Kjell slowed the *Otta* down as they approached A.C.'s little dock sticking off a rocky, barren island. A small ochre-painted house and a large warehouse where nets hung off hooks under the eaves loomed up in the back. "But on the bright side," he said over the engine, "his limp has made him unfit for the AT. There he is now."

A young man dressed in a wool sweater and pants and rubber boots walked down to the dock with a halting limp. He was tall with broad shoulders and curly hair the color of a newborn fawn. A large, heavy-coated Norwegian elkhound flitted close to his master's heels with a dainty little trot.

"Kjell!" A.C. came alongside the boat, catching the rope Kjell threw him. "Wondered when you'd get here."

"I'm on time and you know it. Meet my new man, Jens Hansen. You'll have to talk slow. He's deaf." Haugland came forward on Kjell's signal and signed to A.C. The young man nodded, then turning away, ignored him. Doesn't know what to do with me, Haugland thought.

Once Kjell was on the dock, the friends started up for the house. Haugland followed behind. The dog wagged his tail, circling Haugland before bounding ahead to the house.

"Have any word on Bent?" Haugland heard as he arrived at A.C.'s little house. It consisted of a large whitewashed room and what appeared to be a bedroom and a larder behind two doors. A peat fire popped in the stove. A coffee pot was on a cloth-draped table.

"The boat left for the Shetland Islands on May fifteenth. There were thirty onboard." A.C. leaned over to stir his cup of *ersatz* coffee. "They arrived safely a few days later."

"How do you know that, A.C?" Kjell asked.

"A friend came around to see me. Odd Sorting. I'm very grateful to him."

"You should be careful," Kjell said. "There's something peculiar about him and the escape."

"Bent wasn't worried." A.C.'s voice had a tinge of emotion.

"Bent is an open-faced boy, A.C.," Kjell's voice rose.

"All right, I'll be careful, but I think you're wrong."

Haugland sat down. Except for a series of motions and sputtering sounds, he just petted the dog and was silent. That did not prevent him from thinking. A.C. was part of a group of people who were active against the Germans on Frøya. Many of their members had left on that boat, but they would regroup. For security reasons, Haugland didn't know who was in that cell, but secret work often became dangerously interconnected. Haugland was prepared to drop Kjelstrup if he persisted in associating with Sorting and not show care.

***

The day they returned, Haugland loaded a trunk full of clothes, books, and a box of fishing tackle into the back seat of Ella's car. He was moving up to a cabin along the fjord road. As Kjell helped him load the car, several people came out of the *konditori* to watch him.

"You going on a vacation, Jens?" a fisherman asked.

Boats noisy, he pantomimed. Someone caught the joke and laughed.

Two nights later, just before midnight, Haugland climbed up to the *seter* hut to get the W/T. His two-week silence was nearly over. London would be expecting a call from him soon.

He grinned wryly at the stakes in running a W/T as he hiked up through the dark woods of birch and pine. If he didn't send at the specific time, they would expect trouble. If he sent late, they would think the W/T had been compromised. If the keystrokes were different, they would think someone who shouldn't be was using it. Only a series of security check questions at the end of an exchange between a radio operator and London could defuse such a crisis or confirm it.

Haugland clenched the straps of his rucksack, his boots stepping lightly along a trail thawed recently into mud. The sky had just let go of its twilight glow, descending into dark. Under the trees his path was a pungent black ribbon.

He wore half gloves on his fingers to keep them warm. Once his hands got freezing cold while huddled in a sleeping bag waiting to send his message. His stiff fingers sounded different to the person on the other end—most likely a girl Rika's age—and he was asked to identify himself by answering the question, "Do you like cheese?" He didn't answer yes or no, because that meant someone who shouldn't was using the W/T. The correct answer was supposed to be absurd. Like Aunt Maude wears size 10 shoes or something like that. Hastily blowing on his hands to coaxe them to warmth, he sent the answer and all was well.

At the *seter* hut, Haugland put the W/T in his rucksack. Following a line of trees that moved seaward from the *seter*, he headed back down to his cabin. The forest grew close to the walls of the fjord valley here. In the dark, he could smell the new growth of spring.

Change was coming. It made him restless. In round-the-clock light, he would have to send more messages than he had the past winter. That meant more chance of exposure. Increasingly his name would go out in secret code: *Ryper*. In Norwegian, that meant "ptarmigan," a quiet game bird capable of changing colors. An unusual name for a radio operator in Norway. Many Norwegian radio operators were named after rodents like "Mouse" and "Lemming." At least I'm not in Holland. I'd be a vegetable.

He was nearly down to his woods when he stopped to adjust his load. He walked to the edge of the trees to get better lighting. There a nearly full moon tried to push through the clouds, against the bare stirrings of predawn. Barely discernible, he could make out the woods on the next hill and an old farmhouse below the woods. How ironic to find it had belonged to Einar Fromme's own grandfather. Haugland had been told he had a neighbor, but he didn't expect Anna Fromme. Suddenly a light appeared at the back of the house. It was bright enough to make out the form of the woman as she stepped through the door. She stood, lantern high, and seemed to be wearing a man's coat over her long nightgown, but distance distorted the image into a long flame of light. After a time, she went back in.

Now what was that all about? He still couldn't believe she was an American.

Haugland returned to the cabin. A simple log hut with an old-fashioned grass roof, it sat on a hill, surrounded on three sides by woods. If he walked out to the edge of the hill. there was a clear view of the fjord and the road below. Out the back door a small building served as a log splitting station. It was big enough for him and the W/T. Behind it a thick stand of pine and some birch. It gave him the privacy he needed.

He lit a lantern and stoked the fire. Under the low ceiling with its peeled and burnished birch log rafters, the lantern flickered, sending light and shadow around the walls and birch-planked floor. Unloading the rucksack, he placed the W/T on his bed, keeping the components together. He had been given a newer model this time: a Mark IV that fit into a suitcase and weighed about nine kilograms. By the stove, he kept a large chopping block. Removing the axe sticking out of it, he wrestled the gnarly oak stump to his bed. Gently working his fingers on its bottom, he exposed a hollowed out box many inches deep. Attached by two hinges to the thick lower section of the stump, the lid was secured by wire at its top. Haugland placed the W/T inside. Some hook-eye screws and wire secured it. He closed the lid and the seam disappeared. He set it aright at the stove, chopped the axe home into the top, and prepared for bed.

He decided to get a few hours' sleep, then give Kjell a hand painting the *Otta*. Later, he'd like to take a couple days off to fish. The salmon were starting to run.

***

As it turned out, Haugland would do more than fish.

A few nights later, Foss summoned him to the Tourist Hotel to do some odd jobs. He had just finished replacing the cord and plug on a sitting room lamp, when he remembered he had left a tool there. It was nearly ten-thirty. The kitchen was dark, closed down for the night. The pots and pans hung up clean and shiny in the gloom. He passed through, going down the narrow corridor Foss had taken him over a month ago. As he prepared go into the darkened sitting room, the door to Foss's office opened slightly, voices and light spilling into the dim hall.

He recognized the oily voice of Foss immediately, but there were others in the room. Eventually, he discerned the voices of sheriff Fasting and Victor Pedersen, the hotel's owner. A fourth man he couldn't identify. It was an odd time for an NS meeting.

"...but according to reports, it began this morning," Foss was saying. "Very heavy fighting. The *Wehrmacht*, of course, has responded forcefully. The Americans and British are taking heavy losses on the beaches. They'll see how strong we are when they try to move inland."

Haugland strained to listen. So the Allies had landed on the beaches at last. Exciting news, but it also increased the danger for him. He hoped the villagers would not substitute euphoria for caution. The voices grew louder in the office. For the first time Haugland heard the voice speaking German. Its owner seemed to be less concerned with the immediate news than locating and arresting the three boys who had slipped away. Gestapo?

Haugland carefully slipped through the open French doors. Without turning on lights he found the pair of wire cutters about the same time voices and footsteps came out into the hall. He made himself busy, preparing for the attack, because Foss was out there, full of vitriol and bad humor. The approaching footsteps on the wood floor sounded angry.

The doors swung open behind him. Someone came in and slamming his hand on the light switch, jiggled it on and off, making the light flicker. Haugland turned.

"What are you doing here?" Foss barked.

Haugland pointed to the lamp and held up the pliers in his hand.

Foss's eyes suddenly narrowed. "How long have you been here?"

Some time, Haugland motioned, then wrote hurriedly in his notebook: Fix lamp. Clean up tools. Left one here. Go now.

"You'll go when I tell you, you idiot!" Foss's face was red, angry enough to strike.

"Good heavens, Frederick. Leave the poor boy alone." Victor Pedersen stood at the door. He was a tall, handsome blond man in his fifties who smoked pipes and favored tweeds. In a calm, cultured voice he dismissed Foss. He sighed. "You mustn't let him treat you that way. He hasn't the right."

Haugland shrugged, turning the wire cutters in his hands.

"I have some business to finish. Will you wait for me in your workshop? I want to talk to you." Pedersen went back to Foss's office. Fasting and a thin, angular man in a long leather coat stood in the doorway. *He's definitely Gestapo*, Haugland thought. He watched them leave for the lobby from the security of the glass doors before heading back to the kitchen.

It was after eleven o'clock when Pedersen finally got back to him. "Sorry to keep you waiting. I have a special job for you down in the basement. It doesn't concern Foss. It will only take a moment, then I'll write you a night pass." Haugland hesitated, as he knew he should.

"Please. It will take only a few minutes."

Haugland relented, but only for show. Kjell had not only warned him about Foss when he first arrived in Fjellstad. Pedersen had a story too. "He's a *jøssing*. A patriot. He's part of a secret group here. I trust him completely."

Through his position, Pederson gathered information on the members of the *Wehrmacht* and SS *Waffen* as well as the *Hird* and other Norwegian Nazi organizations who came for good food and fishing. He was a *jøssing*, but in declaring his quisling affiliation had lost his family and many of his friends.

In the musty basement smelling of old concrete and damp stone, they passed through a doorway leading into a room with an immense furnace. Once the hotel had been heated with oil. Due to the fuel shortage, the furnace had been converted to burning wood. Huge logs were stacked against the wall. On the other side of the furnace was another room with a wall made of river stone. Seated at a long wooden table were Ella Bjornson, the parish priest, and the schoolmaster.

So this is the little group, he thought. Kjell was a liaison to the group and had given Haugland some particulars, but it was interesting to see them together in secret.

Ella smiled at him, signing him a welcome. *God kveld*, Jens. I glad you come. You know everyone? She was the only one besides Kjell and the girls who had learned to sign. "I think you know *Herr* Ola Stagg, our school master, Pastor Helvig," she voiced.

Haugland dipped his head to both of them. This job? He signed to her.

"*God kveld, Herr* Hansen," Stagg said. Helvig gave Haugland a shy smile.

Pedersen patted his shoulder. "Sit down, if you would be so kind."

Stagg, a thin, bald-headed man in his sixties, began to talk to him in a slow, deliberate voice. Bjornson signed. Haugland watched his lips and her hands. "Do you remember our village boys gone *pa skauen*? They left right after Quisling ordered all young men across the country to sign up for the AT. They took food with them, but we think they're extremely low by now. They could starve. Now we hear the State Police and Gestapo are renewing their efforts to locate them."

"Kjell said you are taking some time off to fish the river," Ella said. "We wondered if you would consider fishing further out on the road, then take some food to our boys."

Me? Haugland signed. He stared at her, startled at their request.

Stagg tapped his hand. "You can move freely. You'd be gone a few days and not missed."

Pedersen leaned over the table. He conveyed an energy shared by the others. "*Vær så snil.* You're strong and resourceful, yet no one would suspect you. We'll help you get ready."

"It means much to many." Stagg's eyes glistened. "Petter Stagg is my grandson."

What could he say? He couldn't jeopardize his mission. He had worked so hard to establish his cover. Yet their asking him to do this was confirmation he had succeeded extremely well. Who would suspect Jens Hansen?

He studied them for a moment. He knew that they were all *jøssings*. If he helped the boys, it might prevent any troops from returning to the village. It was just the complications of it all, the juggling of a dangerous set of balls in the air as it often was in resistance matters. All right, he indicated. I go. Hopefully, he would find them in good condition.

The little group gave a collective sigh of relief.

He wrote a few sentences in his notebook:

What do I take? When should I go? My fishing permit is for five days. Start tomorrow?

He showed them the notebook, then added that he wanted to know about Fasting's visit. He didn't mention the fourth man, the Gestapo agent.

At that, it dawned on them that he wouldn't know, of course, the news about the invasion.

They began to talk all at once, but it was Ella who signed the news:

Invasion start. Norway free by end summer.

Haugland beamed. Good news. He stood up, bringing the meeting to a close.

Pedersen waited for him at the narrow door to the room. The overhead light threw down shadows on all of them and marked them. Haugland would remember the scene a long time later. He was in even deeper now, and there would be no backing away.

CHAPTER 20

The second morning after meeting the secret group, Haugland went out to the river to fish. At a spot suggested by Kjell, he cast out his line and let it drift. Here the riverbed lined the rushing water like a bumpy gray carpet of smooth stones. Up on the bank, birch trees shimmered in sharp morning light. He took a deep breath of the cool, sweet air and pulled his line in. He was not alone. Local men from the village and a few German soldiers were already casting their lines from the riverbank. They bunched up by nationality, the Norwegians giving the soldiers the silent treatment.

Bloody Germans, he thought. *Recreating at our expense.*

Ten minutes later he got a big strike. Up and down the river he walked, fighting to bring the big salmon in. The men encouraged him, moving aside or patting him on his shoulder as he passed. Finally, he yanked the fish on shore, its long silver body writhing and flopping. Haugland killed it with a well-placed blow with a rock and lifted it up with his hands in its gills. The men around him applauded. As he gutted it on the rocks, he was pleased with himself. He hadn't fished since the war started.

"What weight think be?" a German voice said in Norwegian behind him.

Haugland continued to work on the fish, pushing its rosy guts onto the stony beach. Polished boots came next to his side. He heard the group of Norwegians grow silent, the rush of the water the only sound. He knew he was in danger, but he could not respond until the right moment.

"I say you, what big fish weight?" The voice was harsher, disturbed.

Suddenly, a hand touched his shoulder. "He means no harm, *Unterfeldwebel*. He is a simple boy. He's deaf." It was the schoolmaster Stagg, just in time. Haugland turned. What?

"He… likes… your… fish, Jens. Wants… to… know… how much… it weighs."

Haugland stood up. He wiped his bloody hands on his pants and gave the soldier the respect he expected. He dipped his head. In his shirtsleeves and suspenders, the soldier looked like he was fresh out of *gymnasium*, with ears that stuck out from under his cap. *Unterfeldwebel*—Sergeant, Stagg had said. Haugland pretended to weigh his answer. He flashed his hands twice for twenty pounds.

"*Gut.*" The tension broke. Some of the soldier's companions joined him to admire the fish, then left. Stagg offered to help Haugland with his fishing gear. When no one was looking, he slipped a note into his coat pocket. Haugland put his catch into a cloth sack. As he gathered his gear, he noticed a stranger watching from up by the trees. He was a stocky man with a clean-shaven face, dressed in knickers and a vest. A cap perched cockeyed on top of his straw blonde head. He held a pole and a wooden box with a handle in one hand and cigarette in the other.

Must be Sorting. He certainly matched Kjell's description. Haugland wondered how long he had been standing there. Had he seen the note?

"Come, Jens." Together Stagg and Haugland climbed up the sandy riverbank to the trees, the schoolmaster going first. As they passed, Sorting stepped aside to give the older man more room on the trail, but he stepped back when Haugland came up.

Sorting took a drag on his cigarette. "Good job. Big fish." Smoke blew off from the side of his mouth. He pointed to the fish.

Haugland cocked his head at him, then acted like he finally understood.

Takk, he signed and stepped around him. He felt Sorting's eyes on his back all the way to the road and wondered if it was from curiosity or ridicule because he did not speak.

***

Two hours later, Haugland slipped past the fishing crowd on Kjell's bike and rode on a couple more miles. Here the river had cut back to the right side of the valley. When he was sure he was unobserved, he slipped into the woods. He hid the bike and fishing pole and forded the river at calf height. Once across, he hiked to a prearranged spot where he picked up a pack heavy with food and medicine. Using a map sketched on the note, he followed a trail deep into the forested mountains. It was silent, broken only by the sound of birds flitting in the understory.

It took Haugland three hours to hike in and find the boys. He heard them before he saw them. They had set up camp in a small, swampy area, which afforded good hiding cover, but not from constant rain. Under the trees their tent looked disheveled. It sagged in the middle. Two of the boys were sitting outside around a small fire. Neither looked happy.

Where's the third? Haugland wondered. Taking a deep breath, he sauntered in. Instantly, the boys were on their feet, their mouths open in disbelief.

"Jens Hansen?" the shorter of the two asked.

Haugland nodded, *Ja*, Who you?

"Petter Stagg."

Haugland gave the boy an expansive grin. He flipped open his notebook and jabbed the air with his finger. 1-2-3. He scribbled it down. Where third?

Petter gave the note a quick glance. "Arne's sick. In the tent."

Haugland frowned. Petter and the other boy, Karl, looked thin and drawn, but Haugland had food for them. He put down his rucksack and handed Petter a folded note from his notebook. While Petter read, he crawled into the tent.

In the sepia light of the canvas sides, Arne's face looked pale and full of bug bites. His eyes were closed, but opened when Haugland touched his forehead. "Jens?"

"He's brought food, Arne," Petter said he scrambled into the tent.

The boy sighed. He touched Haugland's arm weakly. Haugland patted his shoulder and set to work.

Outside he unloaded some of his British-issued stores of vacuumed-dried mutton and dehydrated potatoes wrapped in tarpaper packages. It was a risk showing them this, but he had to trust them just as he knew it was the only way.

I'll make you stew, he wrote, but first Arne. He has fever. Could be lack of food or bug bites. We'll work on that.

Pulling out a Primus stove and paraffin from his sixty-pound pack, he boiled water in a small pot and added dried apricots for a thin broth for the boy. When it was ready, he put on another pot of water and added two squares of dried mutton and dehydrated potatoes.

Not smart make fire, he motioned.

"What should we do?" Petter asked as he refolded his grandfather's note and put it into his pocket. He was an athletic blonde nineteen-year-old.

Haugland hurriedly scribbled: Keep the stove, but hide it or throw it into a lake if you are discovered. It's foreign. Bury wrappers.

Once they were fed and Arne Berg attended to, he gave them messages from their families and informed them by writing and by gesture that the Allies had invaded Normandy.

"That's wonderful," Karl Olavsen said as they sat under the thick branches of pine and birch. His brown hair stuck up from his cowlick like a series of hatpins. His sweater was dirty and covered with flecks of fern and leaves.

"Sure it is," Petter grumbled, "but I want to join up and fight now, instead of hiding out in the woods."

Haugland considered him for future reference to Tommy Renvik, who might be looking for recruits for Milorg.

Hear, see anyone?

"There were poachers here a week ago. They weren't from around here. Carried shotguns. We moved down here after that."

Haugland didn't like that. You move again.

For the next two days Haugland scouted around with Petter, but never heard or saw anyone. Eventually he moved them to a drier and more remote site. Finding a small kidney-shaped lake filled with trout, Haugland gave them a net and some hooks. He encouraged them to find a backup place—maybe a cave. When he left, Arne was moving on his own.

Someone else will come, he wrote. You should be good for the next few weeks. Privately, he hoped he'd never see them again.

CHAPTER 21

Kjell put the last touch of linseed oil on the interior of the *Otta*'s wheelhouse, then went to the warehouse to clean up his brushes. Since their return from Trondheim, he had painted and treated every inch of the boat with the precious linseed oil he had bought with *kroner* Jens had given him. Finally, it was done. The *Otta* looked shipshape and he was happy.

Like other boats of its type, the *Otta* was made almost entirely of softwood, mainly fir. The keel, frames and planking were all fir, and the six-inch square frames were doubled and spaced so close together that they almost formed a solid block of timber. The outer planking so beautifully laid along the sloping lines of the boat was nearly three inches thick. Both the skin and frames were fastened with trenails, wooden pegs driven through and tightened with wooden wedges. It was an ancient art for which Norwegians were celebrated.

Kjell went into the office and changed his clothes in Jens's old room, stopping at the mirror over the washstand to give his hair a quick brushing. He paused. The rest of the day was his, but he felt a bit guilty. Rika was leaving in the morning for Trondheim, and it was Ella who was preparing a special dinner for her, not him. But Ella had insisted, saying Rika's going away dinner needed a woman's touch.

"She'll be missing her mother tonight, you know," Ella had said. "This is a coming of age party, too. Moving to Trondheim is going to be a high point of her life, and her mother's not here."

Ella's right, he thought as he resumed brushing his hair. He only hoped the excitement of being in the country's third largest city wouldn't blind her to reality. There was a dark underside.

It was good Rika was staying with his friend Thomas and his wife. Rika would work in an insurance office during the day and come home in the evening.

"Just hope you aren't bored, *lille gjente*," Kjell said out loud. "There really isn't much to do in the evenings. All they've got are either AUF films or German-produced plays. Sports are out."

Kjell looked into the mirror and imagined his wife Kristine standing behind him. "We protected her," he said. "I went to sea at fourteen. You went to live with *Tante* Turid to do housework at fifteen." Kjell touched the mirror with his forefinger. "Rika stayed in school. Went further than we ever did, didn't she? She's a lovely young lady, Kristine."

Kjell stopped. Sadness he hadn't in felt in a long time overcame him. He looked back at the mirror and only saw himself, his mouth turned down and tears in his eyes.

A few minutes later, Kjell was in the shop looking for Ella, but found only Bette Gudderson, her young, heavyset helper serving in the *konditori*. He waved to her, then froze. A young man with stocky shoulders and neck and straw-colored hair sat at a table with a local fisherman, Bugg Grande, talking with hands that cupped the air.

Odd Sorting.

So he had made it here after all. Quietly, Kjell backed out. He climbed the stairs to Ella's apartment, knocking on a second door at the top. When he got no answer, he opened the door.

"Ella?"

It was quiet in the apartment, but the smell of baked cinnamon bread filled the room. As he passed through the living room to the kitchen, he heard a door close in the back.

"There you are," he said as Ella came through the porch door.

"*Hei*, Kjell," she said, her eyes full of warmth. "Just washing up some herbs. Help yourself to coffee." She worked at the sink under the only window in the long narrow kitchen. It looked out to the rugged cliffs and mountains alongside the fjord wall. Bright colored curtains framed the window, the inevitable blackout curtain ready to be rolled at the top of a rod underneath.

They talked for a while as she worked around the counter and stove.

One thing about Ella, he thought, she can make shoe leather taste good. Dried fish in her hands was a wonder.

"No sign of Jens?" Ella asked. "He's been gone over two days."

"*Nei*," Kjell replied.

"We shouldn't have asked him," Ella said. "He can't possibly do it. He'll get lost."

"Because he's deaf? You're forgetting Dag Sorenson, the boy from Tustna. He went to school and now he's a clerk in Kristiansund N. Jens can take care of himself. He's a man, not a boy. Jens went skiing alone all winter, and had no difficulties. I trust him on the boat. Look what happened on the *Alta*. People still thank him."

"Well, I worry." Ella pulled some bread out of the oven. She gently knocked the loaves out of their pans and placed them on a breadboard. When she wasn't looking, Kjell took a pinch. He leaned against the sink and cleared his throat.

"Have you been downstairs lately?" he asked. "There's a man with Bugge."

"Oh, that nice young man," Ella said. She closed the oven and put a linen towel over the loaves. "He's staying out at *Fru* Holve's place. He's been fishing on the river."

"Really?"

"*Ja.* Said he saw Jens catch a huge fish." She looked up. "Something wrong?"

Kjell held up his hands. "Just hope Jens got out safely to the boys without everyone noticing where he went. When's dinner?"

"We'll eat at five. Bette will close up."

He patted her arm. "I'll be back." He went the backstairs, avoiding Sorting altogether.

***

Rika looked into the long mirror in Ella Bjornson's bedroom and smoothed her dress down one last time. She had only finished making it today, copying a pattern she had seen in a four-year-old ladies magazine. It was a light blue color and made from real cotton cloth Ella had given her, not the wrinkly cloth made with a high portion of cellulose available now with the ration card and very, very expensive.

"Bless you, Ella," Rika said out loud. She was, on the whole, feeling confident, but as the sound of company gathering out in the dining area came to her, she experienced a growing, nervous excitement. She pinched her cheeks.

"In a few hours, I'll be leaving. Twelve hours after that, I'll be in Trondheim!" It was something she had always dreamed of doing.

"Rika, dear." Ella knocked lightly on the door, then peeked in. "Everyone's here. Are you ready?"

"*Ja, takk.*" Rika took a deep breath and turned around. Her father was standing in the door behind Ella. He smiled softly and offered her his arm.

***

Kjell woke her at five in the morning. There was a special breakfast, then a subdued walk to the wharf where a handful of people were already gathered for the motorboat getting ready to take her and other passengers to the coastal steamer anchored in the fjord. The sun had already been up for some time, but the morning air was still cool.

"It's going to be a nice day," Rika said as she pulled her coat around her.

"*Ja,*" Kjell said. He wondered if she was having as much trouble with words as he was.

Coming alongside the motorboat, he ignored the two German soldiers guarding it and handed down her suitcase to the boatman, then turned and gave her a mighty hug.

"Don't look so sad, Pappa," Rika soothed. "I'll be fine."

Kjell had trouble with his voice. It had become gummed up with emotion. He cleared it too nosily, flushed with embarrassment at the sound.

"*Ja, ja*. I know. You behave yourself," he finally said. "Remember the things your Mama taught you." He kept his big arm around her to keep him steady. This is much harder than he thought.

"And you." Rika replied. "Oh, Pappa, thank you for making this happen."

She kissed him gently on his cheek, then turned away suddenly when a tear ran down her cheek. Kjell pretended he didn't see. He gave her a kiss, then promptly left. Stepping back behind the little crowd, he watched the boatman complete some last minute adjustments of luggage and people. He almost missed seeing the last passenger get on before it left.

It was Odd Sorting.

CHAPTER 22

Anna Fromme took a deep breath and stepped up into the *konditori*, causing the little bell over the door to jangle. It sounded too loud, like a town crier announcing who she was.

Everyone take appropriate action.

She closed the door behind her and walked over to the display case where a cold buffet was displayed as well as pastries. The room was clean and correct with its little tables and lace curtains. Ignoring the elderly couple and fisherman who stared at her, she asked for Ella Bjornson.

A woman came through the curtains behind the case. There was no softness in her eyes the color of a midsummer's sky. "I'm *Fru* Bjornson." Her voice was cold.

"I wish some *spekemat*," Anna said then waited with dread for the expected response.

The chairs in the room behind Anna scraped followed, by the sound of shoes and boots scuffing en masse as everyone got up and left, grabbing their lunch from the plates.

Anna stood rigidly in place. It was so humiliating. When the room cleared, she pointed out what she wanted, paid for it, and then went into her little speech.

It was a simple proposition: the use of her fields and pasture in exchange for winter wood and milk for Lisel. "I heard that in the past this had been done," she said.

For what seemed an eternity, *Fru* Bjornson stared at Anna. "Why should I help you?" she finally hissed. "Why not ask *Herr* Foss?"

"I do not like *Herr* Foss..."

"I can't help you."

"Why? Am I so awful? Aren't I a woman like you? Alone?"

Ella hit the counter with her hand. "*Nei*, you are not," Ella said. "German soldiers caused my husband's death, but you... you brought your own husband's death and those of the others. You shouldn't have come. You should leave Fjellstad."

Anna's face flushed.

"And who has told you this?" Anna's voice cracked at this new humiliation. "I loved my husband. Einar was a fine man, a good man, the father of my Lisel." Anna felt like she was talking to a stone. "How can you speak when you do not know me or care to know the truth? In all the time I've been here, no one has asked. Why? Because you are afraid it might not be what you want to believe?"

When Ella said nothing, Anna stiffened. "*God dag, Fru* Bjornson." Her cheeks burning, she stepped down to the door, hoping to escape further insult.

"And what is the truth?"

Anna paused. She wished she could tell the woman she was an American trapped here because of the war, but after her treatment when Einar died she trusted no one. They could report her to the Gestapo, and the Gestapo threw Americans into jail. They might think her a spy. And her father could be found out.

She put her hand on the lace-curtained door and whispered. "The truth is that I have lived nearly six years in Norway. It is my home. The truth is that I hate the Nazis. I always have. And the truth *is* that I never knew… I *never* knew he was in the Resistance." She yanked open the door. "If I had known, maybe I could have helped him." She left with tears stinging her eyes.

After collecting Lisel from the cook at the Tourist Hotel, she headed out the fjord road to her farm. She felt close to tears again, but anger won out. Anger at the townspeople, anger at Einar for taking such risks unknown to her, anger at him for dying.

Her heart sank. That wasn't true. Maybe anger at the empty space he left, but not anger at him when he must have suffered so. There was another feeling for that: guilt.

She closed her eyes to a creeping exhaustion. How tired I am.

She trudged along the gravel road that meandered up and down along the low, grassy ridge. The numbness she experienced after Einar's death came over her again. She felt dead inside, and soon she fell behind her little daughter skipping ahead of her. The fjord on her right looked gray today, but the pinewoods and rolling fields on her left looked no less inviting. She suddenly thought of Berlin as she had last seen it, the wide avenues and cafes, the busyness of it. Her father's house. Or better still, *Grossmutter's* villa in Hamburg.

So far away. And dying.

The bombing would increase with the invasion. She stopped climbing the rise and put her hands over her eyes and wept.

What will become of us? And Lisel? The war will be over soon. What if I'm arrested? She wiped her eyes on her coat sleeve. The depression passed. The anger returned.

She'd survive. What did Einar always say? *Det vil helst ga godt.* It will come out all right.

Dear Einar. Always optimistic.

Composing herself, she looked around for Lisel, but she wasn't in sight. Panicking, Anna ran up the road, afraid Lisel might have fallen down on the scree that lay between the ridge and the beach below. At the top, the road curved sharply to the left. Hurrying, she came around the bend and found her. Lisel wasn't alone.

A fisherman hunkered down at the side of the road, working intently on his bicycle. Lisel was beside him, chattering away while he worked on the chain. As Anna came closer, she realized that it was Jens Hansen, the deaf man who saved her daughter. Her shoulders stiffened. She didn't want to deal with him. Too embarrassing.

Anna placed her hands on Lisel's shoulders. "Come, Munchkin. You went too far ahead. Leave him alone."

"But, Mama…" Lisel patted the fisherman on his shoulder. He turned and smiled at her.

"Can you help my kitty?"

He looked puzzled.

"Shh... Lisel," Anna said behind him. "He doesn't understand you. Come, *vær så snil.* Now!" She reached for Lisel's hand, pulling her away. The movement caught the man's attention and he swung around.

Jens Hansen looked straight at her as he had at the Tourist Hotel, but this time he was looking at her eyes. Suddenly, she remembered that she had been weeping. Anna quickly put a hand to her cheek and then blushed.

The man got up and stood next to the bike. He seemed taller than she remembered, and despite several days' growth of dark beard looked quite handsome. The gray eyes seemed alive, changing color at the will of their owner. He made some motion around his eyes, then pointed to her.

"Oh, I'm all right," she lied. "What happened to your bike?" She pointed to it. Broke, his hands said. She nodded understanding. The gesture was so obvious.

Anna started to say something when Lisel began to weave in and out between them singing a song. Wrapping an arm around her mother's leg, she went around her and then crossed over to him, like they were two poles. She showed no fear of him. It annoyed Anna, but the man grinned at the little imp. Anna watched his eyes flare up and sparkle. She began to be less wary. She still felt a strain from her talk with *Fru* Bjornson, but his quiet calmness was reassuring.

Lisel came swinging around toward him again, and very gently he took her hand and turned her around toward Anna. The gesture was friendly, but firm. He leaned down to retrieve a small screwdriver and moved away, loading up the rucksack around a sizable fish. Its tail flopped over when the fisherman set the rucksack upright.

Lisel squatted down beside him. "Are you going to eat that?"

Hansen nodded. *Ja.*

"My Gubben loves fish, but he can't eat. Can you fix my kitty?"

He turned and, pointing to Lisel, made a gesture, but Anna didn't understand. He took out a small notebook and wrote: Cat. Something wrong?

Once again she was reminded of their meeting in the sitting room. He had been formal, but polite. Pleasant toward her, then humiliated her with his question about Einar. She wasn't going to let that happen again, but suddenly she was explaining.

"It's really very silly. Lisel has a kitten that she loves very much. Somehow a fishhook has become caught in one of her kitten's lips, but I don't know how to get it out." Anna hung a finger off her mouth to show how it looked. "It just hangs there like a Christmas ornament."

He made a sound like laughter. He drew furiously. Next to a picture of a small cat it said, "I fix."

Anna read the words, not believing. I can't trade my fields for help, she thought, but someone will take a fishhook out of my daughter's wayward kitten. Anna laughed bitterly. It didn't make sense, but he was offering.

He waited for her to answer. Lisel's oval face was so expectant.

"You'd do this?"

Ja, he nodded. Hansen took the notebook back and wrote: I'll come this afternoon.

Anna's face crumpled. She turned her face away, trying to get a grip on herself. Just one small gesture of friendliness from someone other than Foss, she thought. She cleared her throat, and brushed back a telltale tear. "Would four o'clock be all right?" Her voice was thick. When he signed yes, for the first time since coming here, she felt a glimmer of hope.

***

Back at his cabin Haugland put down the rucksack and built a fire to boil water. He felt dirty and tired, but things had gone well. The young men were hidden for now until measures were set in place. Seeing them, however, had touched him in an unexpected way. They had reminded him of his brother Per because like those three boys he had wanted to escape.

Per Haugland had been in school doing some advanced work in geology when the invasion came. He had looked after Mother and their sister Solveig after their father died of a heart attack, eventually moving to Bergen.

But you wanted to go, Per. I wished you had waited.

Haugland rubbed his lips with his thumb like he was wiping away beer froth. This sudden flame of raw emotion surprised him sometimes. Like it was the first time he heard the news.

Per had contacted an export group in Ålesund up the coast from Bergen, and was to leave on the night of February 23, 1942. The fishing boat never left. Posing as an anti-Nazi, Rinnan had infiltrated the group. On the night of departure, the Gestapo struck, and Per was arrested along with twenty-two others. He was thrown into prison, beaten, then sent to the Grini concentration camp near Oslo. There he languished until April, when the incident at Telavåg occurred. For that, *Reichcommisorit* Terboven himself ordered Per and eighteen others shot.

They took you to the woods and shot you down like a dog.

Haugland closed his eyes and saw red under his eyelids. Like the red morning sun on the day Per died.

While the water heated, Haugland checked the chopping block set by the small woodshed. Satisfied the W/T was secured secretly inside, he returned to his cabin where he stripped off his clothes and bathed. He checked his hair in the mirror, looking again along the cowlick at the back of his head. Before he had gone to London last February, he had been a blond. It had been dyed black for his trip back to Norway. Now his natural brown-black colored hair was coming in. *Good*, he thought.

After shaving, Haugland prepared a small meal. While he ate, he thought of the encounter on the road. It couldn't have worked out better. For weeks he had been thinking of a way to get into Anna Fromme's house. She didn't go away very often, so time was limited as when he could break into the house if need be. Now he would be able to see at least some portion of the house freely. He could decide when to go in on his own later.

There were several things he was searching for, but most importantly, any pictures she might have that could link Einar to himself and Lars. Something that could compromise his cover. Surely, Einar had told her about Lars. There could be letters or some childhood or adolescent picture of Einar Fromme and Lars Haugland together in a scrapbook. *Or me*, Haugland thought. So much time growing up together.

He cut up the fish into a roast, then made some steaks. He'd share with Kjell again and Leif Sorenson, a recently injured fisherman. For a brief moment, he thought of taking some to Anna Fromme, but vetoed the idea. It wouldn't do to be too friendly. Keep a distance. He was on delicate ground. People were used to him being different, but this he'd have to keep on the quiet. He'd take care of the kitten, have a look around. That's all.

He wondered about her, though. She had been crying, and the little girl looked thin. Lisel? Was that her name? She definitely favored Einar. She had his eyes and smile and a sweetness that touched Haugland. Poor thing. He hoped folks didn't single her out, as happened so often with the children of quislings. He felt a twinge of remorse. Maybe he could watch out for her—for Einar's sake. After checking the cabin over carefully, he grabbed a pair of wire cutters and cautiously approached Anna Fromme's farmhouse.

***

"His name is Gubben, and he's my best friend." Lisel held the kitten in her hands. It looked comfortable as if it was used to having its hind legs dangle out in space. Hugging Gubben, she sat down on the sagging wooden step at the back of the old weatherworn farmhouse.

Gubben meant "old man" in Norwegian, but Haugland thought the kitten looked more like a troll. The black nose on its white face looked bulbous. It meowed at him, a ridiculous action, for hanging out of its upper lip was a small hook with some line still attached.

"Can you fix it?" Anna asked.

Haugland examined the kitten's mouth. The hook went inside the mouth and up and out of the upper lip. He wrote: I need a towel and disinfectant.

Anna got up and went inside and returned with the needed items. Haugland indicated that she should wrap the towel around the kitten up to its neck. She sat down next to him, holding it while he operated. Lisel put her hands over her eyes.

The operation took less than a minute. Gently but firmly taking the kitten's head in his hand, he clipped the hook above the barb in one swift cut of his wire cutters. The kitten wiggled. Next, he lifted the lip with his fingers and drew the pointless hook down through the lip. The kitten hissed and spat, twisting its neck.

He picked up the bottle of disinfectant and poured it on the wound. With a howl of displeasure, the kitten struggled in the towel. Haugland put out his left hand, but wiggling violently, the kitten got its forepaws loose and sank its sharp claws into the palm of his hand, then bit him before bolting away.

Haugland grunted and shook his hand, but didn't cry out—he didn't dare break character. Three circles of blood welled up and began to drip.

"Auch, you are hurt," Anna cried. She pressed the towel on the long, deep scratches.

And it stings like hell, but I'll survive.

"*Vær så snill.*"

"Come inside. I'll patch you up."

The door opened into an entryway where coats hung and boots were stored. A room on his right. On his left, stairs leading from the kitchen to… an attic? Beneath them was a trapdoor in the floor, leading probably to a dairy room and cellar down below. At a table next to the kitchen window, she bade him sit down, then disappeared down another hallway.

He remained standing. The view from the windows was spectacular. Like a hawk perched on a nest, the house looked west, skimming over the grassy hill and trees in front of it and over the fjord waters that flowed in from the *Trondheimsleia*. Steep forests flanked the fjord's sides, coveting the village and its wharf to the right. The view ran the length of the house and seemed to fill up the room.

A pot of soup warmed on top of an old-fashioned cookstove. On the wall between the two hallways, a walnut wood bookcase held books and knickknacks. Photographs hung above. The *stue* held a small wood-burning stove, a sofa, and a couple of overstuffed chairs. Beside one of them sat an old Norwegian spinning wheel with a half-filled bobbin of wool yarn. He hadn't seen one in use since his grandmother's house in Telemark long ago.

His eyes returned to the pictures, an odd assortment of frames and photographs, some old, some recent. Two stood out: one of a young woman with a bobbed, permed hairdo who looked strikingly like Anna Fromme, and another of an elderly couple standing in front of an American-made car in a field of stubble grain. The man was holding a brace of large geese, a dog sitting in front of him. They looked decidedly non-European. American relatives? Again, he had the feeling Anna Fromme was more complex than she appeared.

When she came back into the room, Haugland was sitting at the table, looking down at the fjord. She took off the towel he had held obediently in place. The bleeding had pretty much stopped, except for one deep cut that welled up again as soon as the pressure was off. No worse than some nasty cuts he had received from hooks in the course of fishing with Kjell. He let her cluck over it and clean it out with a hot, wet cloth.

She worked quietly, her golden head bent, as if it was the most natural thing in the world to tend him. She held his hand gently, as she patted dry it and smoothed on some salve. She made a pad of gauze and soon had his hand firmly wrapped.

"There. Finished." She looked at him. "I'm so sorry."

He took his hand away, shrugging.

"But I feel so terrible about this. Please. *Bitte*, *vær så snill*, let me do something for you. Can I make you at least a cup of coffee or tea? To have climbed all the way up here and then this..." Her voice trailed off, as if she was rethinking the impact of her suggestion.

Tusen takk. Haugland took out his notebook. Coffee fine, he wrote.

She cleared the table, then busied herself at the stove. Haugland watched her slim figure as she worked with her back to him. Her hair was pulled back with a clip. The sun had streaked it into bands of gold and wheat. From time to time, she looked down the hall as if she were listening for her daughter. Once she began to ask him something, her face turned away, but she must have remembered that he couldn't hear, so stopped. Finally, she brought two cups and an enamel coffeepot over, followed by a plate with cheese and homemade flat bread.

"*Vær så snil.* Drink."

Real coffee. Now where did she get that? He sipped it slowly, indicating that it was good. She smiled shyly at him, hiding behind her cup. They were quiet for a while, both looking out the window, where far-off gulls and terns circled about the gray sky.

There was an explosion of noise in the outer hall, followed by scampering padded feet on a dead run. The kitten skidded sharply through the kitchen and down the other hall. Lisel was close behind.

Haugland sat silently, ignoring the commotion, turning only when Anna Fromme stiffened at the sound of a crash.

She excused herself, muttering, "Not Einar's picture again."

She returned shortly thereafter. "Sorry," she said as she sat down. The perpetrators came into the room, making their way over to Haugland. Lisel lifted her dangling kitten high above her waist and plopped it into his lap.

"Gubben wants to say *Tusen takk*," she said breathlessly. "Me, too." She climbed up his ladder-back chair and kissed his cheek. The kitten was affectionate too, kneading its sharp claws into his thighs. Kindness was going to kill him.

As she hugged him, without thinking, he hugged her back, bandaged hand and all. It was so comical, so poignantly silly, but it touched him deeply. *Einar's little girl.* Haugland looked over at Anna Fromme and smiled helplessly. He was trapped.

She slapped a hand over her mouth and began to laugh. "Oh, I'm sorry, *Herr* Hansen. I'm afraid it's been a hard day for me. It is good to laugh at something so innocent, so spontaneous. Do you understand?"

He did.

"Lisel, *Vær så snill*, don't bother *Herr* Hansen. He likes Gubben"—she shot an amused look at him—"but he would rather you took him somewhere else. Please go outside."

With a small protest, the little girl ran off with the kitten tight in her arms, her shoes clacking on the wood floor. The door slammed behind her.

Anna offered to replenish his cup of coffee and pushed the plate of cheese and flat bread toward him. He quietly ate some, although he wasn't really hungry.

"Did you read the book I gave you?"

Ja, he lied. He had looked at it only once. *Takk*. You like read? He placed his hands together palms up for the sign for "book."

"*Ja*, I do." She leaned over like a conspirator. "Though I hate having to choose from what books I'm told I can and cannot read."

Cautiously, they began to talk about books, gradually they moved from guarded to open speaking. They talked about fishing and the farm, sheep, and potatoes. And Lisel.

It wasn't easy to do. Sometimes he signed. Some of his gestures seemed obvious to her, but many were not, so he used the notebook, too. It was a laborious process and confusing, but confusion was exactly what he intended. She had to believe who he was.

Lisel came in. "I'm hungry, Mama."

Haugland stopped writing. His hand was cramped, and the paper in his notebook was almost gone. It had been a long day. He pointed to his wrist. Time to go.

"Are you going home?" Lisel asked, taking his hand in hers.

Ja, he nodded, smiling gently at her. He patted his pants pockets. He had the wire cutters.

"Are you coming back?" Lisel asked, grabbing his arm lightly. Light as a leaf.

Haugland shrugged, then looked at her mother. Maybe.

He took off shortly thereafter, walking down the steep road. It was only when he was halfway up his own wooded hill that he realized something. He liked Anna Fromme.

CHAPTER 23

Lars Haugland looked at the report one last time and closed it with a decisive toss on the desk. He leaned back in his wooden swivel chair. Not good.

He jammed his pipe into his mouth, then froze when someone knocked on the outer door to his engineering office. He was on the second floor of a building that some NS organizations also used. Though a good setup for *Hjemmefronten*, it was often nerve-wracking. Someone came into the waiting room, but he had no secretary there. Hiding the report under his ink blotter, he pulled open a drawer and slipped a handgun into his jacket pocket. On the other side of his opaque glass office door, a distorted shadow moved.

"Come in." Lars relaxed his grip on the gun when Torstein Kaaland appeared.

"Sorry." Torstein sat down with a rumpled thud. "Those stairs are going to kill me."

"What are you doing here? I thought you'd gone to Hamar."

"Not yet. There was something for you. I thought you should get right away. It's from Sieve."

Sieve. Lars's heart sagged. His love. His wife. His ex-wife.

Lars had met Sieve seven years ago on an outing near Lake Mosja. She was a bright and witty woman. They married and within a year had their first child. They had been very much in love. He still was. "What do you have?"

"A letter." Torstein handed it over. "I'll make myself scarce."

"*Nei*, wait. It's all right." Lars hadn't heard from Sieve in six months. Hadn't lived with her for three long years since he began his illegal work. To protect her and their young son, he had gone to a lawyer, arranged for a letter of separation and moved out. It was the hardest thing he'd ever done. At least they would be protected with those papers in hand.

Torstein went over to the window while Lars opened the letter. Eventually, Lars stirred at his desk. "It's my son, Trygve. He's going to have an operation on his leg."

Two winters ago, Sieve's car skidded on ice. Trygve was thrown out of the vehicle, causing a compound fracture in his right leg. There had been an operation then, but Lars couldn't see him. He had to send a present through a friend of Lars's mother-in-law, who never understood why they broke up. Trygve was sent home, but his leg healed improperty.

"You can't possibly think of going there and seeing them."

"I'm not," Lars grumbled. "It's tempting, but I know it's too dangerous."

Torstein took his glasses off and wiped them on a handkerchief. "You read the file?"

Lars frowned. "The Kvam boy's dead. He died last week at Møllergata 19 after being questioned." Lars sighed. "He's fingered Tore. Said a schoolteacher gave him soap bars with plastique in them. The Gestapo apparently believes him."

Lars bit on his pipe, mentally brushing away the fear growing in him. He kept thinking of the two agents sent into Tore's district ten months before. British-trained in Scotland, they had been exposed one after the other, their networks destroyed.

After Torstein left, Lars put the papers into the register below the room's sole window. Tomorrow he would destroy them. He looked down on the street. It was busy with people on the go. A trolley came by, its bell clanging. If it weren't for the helmeted and jack-booted soldiers on the street corners, it would look just like a typical sunny June afternoon with hours of daylight to go. Some June.

Lars put his hands over his growling stomach. He was hungry, like most people of Oslo. People got in lines at six in the morning, only to find by ten all the fish were gone. The evening paper's ad section was full of items for exchange with a hundred-pound bag of seed potatoes: a gramophone, feather beds, bicycles. Even hen canaries were offered because potatoes were life itself: fried, boiled, broiled, baked, souped. Every four months, veal or horsemeat might be available.

Without the Danish relief effort, the population in this area would starve. If it weren't for the Church of the Deaf, the men and women in the underground could not function. Thanks to the church, some of the Danish relief was hidden, then delivered to the safe houses around the city.

There was an example of Christian charity. Crates of food were stored behind the altar, then transported to half of Milorg's population and other members of Oslo's illegal citizenry. Conrad Bonnevie-Svendsen, Norway's minister to the deaf, made it all possible.

I must see Conrad, Lars thought. He could get a message to Tore via the Deaf Church in Trondheim. Conrad was an old family friend. He was not only a major leader in the *Hjemmefronten*, but someone who knew the exact nature of Tore's disappearance over three years ago.

Lars transferred his handgun to the holster strapped under his arm. He never went without it, walking through the city streets as normal as possible, the weight of the gun against him.

He locked the office door. After getting something to eat, he might go look for something for Trygve. Even if the gift was anonymous, it was one thing he could do for him. Then again, maybe surviving the war was. Lars patted his holster one more time and took off.

***

Haugland opened up the message from Lars and then decoded it.

There was news from the outside. Two weeks after the invasion, the Allies now controlled seven miles of beach, five to fifteen miles deep. Europe was hopeful for an early liberation. "But," Lars wrote, "General Eisenhower, Supreme Commander of the Allied Forces, has issued a directive stating that under no circumstances is Milorg to undertake any action."

Haugland knew why. Neither the British nor the Americans would be able to help if Milorg started military action against the Germans. Norway would have to wait for the Germans to capitulate. The thought didn't make Haugland feel particularly secure. That could take months, and the longer he stayed here, the greater his chance of exposure.

Haugland read on. "An action group blew up the last of the punch card machines. The call order is back in the Quisling government's hands. The response to the call up has been very successful, though there are still several thousand young men *pa skauen* in the *fjell* and forests. We expect to see that figure drop rapidly as they get jobs in the country or 'go east' to Sweden."

Haugland wondered how the three boys were doing.

The final part of Lars' message was the news about the Kvam boy. Dead at sixteen years. Haugland remembered him standing in the mist and rain wondering how to answer questions. There were no answers, only luck. He made a wad of the message and deciphered note and put it into his mouth. Made of rice paper, it tasted sweet and swallowed easily.

***

A few days later he broke into Anna Fromme's house. After watching the farm for several days, Haugland noticed she regularly took her daughter on walks down on the low-lying beach.

One afternoon, after they had left, he explored around the front of the house by its ancient stone foundation. Under the high porch, an old wooden door led into the old dairy, but its rusted Yale lock was jammed, so he went up to the back. As he prepared to use a thin piece of celluloid to open the door, he found it unlocked.

It took him about twenty minutes to make an initial sweep. He found few surprises except for a box in a room off the stairs containing some books in English. In one of them, *The Return to Oz*, he found dedicated in English:

> *"To my sweet Anna*
> *From Grandmother Howard*
> *For the trip home." May 1928*

Damn. Anna Fromme continued to baffle him. How well did she speak English? How strong were her American connections? He put the books back the way he found them.

Something fell down upstairs. He froze, listening carefully. Padded feet came down the stairs halfway and stopped. It was the mama cat. Hearing no signs of Anna Fromme outside, he continued his search in the other part of the house where there were bedrooms. After looking in the hall closets, a bathroom, the little girl's room, all he had left was Anna's room.

He located the light switch, plunging the cool, dim room into light. She hadn't bothered to put up the blackout curtain. From the way the room looked, she hadn't bothered to do anything at all. Unlike the rest of the house—which would have won approval from the most critical Norwegian *hus fru*—this room was cluttered. Books were stacked on the floor, and the maple wood vanity was cluttered with papers. A nightgown lay across the half-made bed. It was as though she couldn't bear to be in the room. *Sleep, if you can, but leave at first light.*

He surveyed the disorder, searching for a place to start, and came to rest on the picture of Einar by the bed. It was the first sign he had seen of Einar's presence in this house. More notably, any depth of feeling for him. In the midst of the storm around the room, this was a place of calm and order. The picture was set on a round table draped with a floor-length cloth that was both elegant and tidy. In front of it was laid a recently picked bouquet of flowers.

Flowers for his grave, wherever that was. Only Rinnan would know. It hurt Haugland thinking of Einar destroyed like that, and this intimate display of affection made him feel like an intruder. He hardened himself. There was no room for sentimentality.

Haugland moved indifferently through several albums stacked on the floor. They covered various stages of their married life: wedding pictures, a trip to the Fantoft Stave Church, skiing on some *fjell*, the birth of the little girl. Sitting on the floor, he flipped through them, stopping only when one revealed pictures of the west coast village of Lillehavn where they had spent their last years together. Barren, it was more exposed then Fjellstad, but Einar still kept a garden.

There were two final albums, each wrapped in brown paper. The first one yielded nothing. Easing off the strings and paper of the second, he found an album with a black cardboard cover mottled to look like leather. Its pages were heavy black papers laced together with a black satin cord. Haugland had found what he was looking for.

It was Einar's family album, but its pages were pages out of Haugland's own past, scenes so clearly etched in memory: the house in Bergen he ran through with Solveig and Per; Einar's secret hiding place in the Fromme raspberry bushes. Haugland slowed down to look and remember, putting himself in each scene. He was so absorbed that he was totally unprepared for the picture on the next page. It brought him back to reality in one sobering flash.

It was Telavåg. Haugland's uncle's house. Long before it had been destroyed. He'd forgotten they'd taken Einar there. His *Onkel* Kris had started going down for the summer when Haugland was about seven years old. The rustic fishing village appealed to his uncle's aesthetics. He could paint and watch the sea roll and play silently before him. I not hear sea, his uncle once signed, but I know moods by color and by salt taste in air. You see.

Later on in 1930, *Onkel* Kris moved there permanently and expanded his studio. He had become known worldwide for his scientific drawings of birds and nature. *Tante* Sophie was his secretary and bridge to the hearing world, running a household both artistic and traditional.

Haugland could still smell the mixture of oil paints and baked goods that permeated the house, see the birch-paneled wall and low-raftered ceilings, and the long window that looked out on the sea. Telavåg with its white houses perched on the bare rocks of the island.

Remember! his mind shouted. And never forget the brown-as-a-nut days climbing rocks in bare feet, searching tidal pools under high summer clouds. Or sitting by the fire while his uncle painted with gray rain slashing the windows. *Onkel* Kris with the sparkle in his gray eyes, painting images with his hands on canvas and in the air.

Haugland put his hands on his forehead. His mouth felt dry. Telavåg was all gone. Ashes. God, he thought. Why? Where was the justification for its cruel destruction?

It was only a peaceful little fishing village on the island of Sotra near Bergen. No more than 400 people. But in late April, 1942, just weeks after Per's arrest, there had been fighting on the island between some SOE agents and the SS. In reprisal for the death of two Germans, an enraged Terboven ordered the village destroyed. The area had long been a popular dropping point for agents coming back and forth between the Shetlands. Brutal interrogations exposed the resistance organizations there and all around the Bergen area. As final payment for the death of the Germans, Per and seventeen of the Ålesund men were shot.

Onkel Kris had been there when the troops attached to the SD descended upon Telavåg like avenging locusts, spreading out among the scattered houses, systematically driving the luckless inhabitants out. What did he feel when he saw the fishing boats cut loose and burned? The livestock slaughtered—seventy for each German—and the houses burned to the ground? His life's work crushed and wasted away in the smoke?

What sound does a flame make? What is the timbre of exploding wood?

Perhaps the sobs and cries his uncle couldn't hear were burned upon his eyes as he and all male inhabitants between the ages of sixteen and sixty-five were marched away and sent on a prison boat to a concentration camp in Germany.

Haugland put the album down and composed himself, his arms resting on his drawn-up knees. Per was gone, his sister Solveig taken away from her children and sent to a prison camp near Bergen. The children and baby sent off to be "re-educated." And what of his sixty-two-year-old uncle who was deaf? How could he possibly survive?

Odd, how something so tragic on a personal scale could become a part of the national conscience. The whole country had recoiled in horror. The world called it "The Lidice of the North He wiped his mouth with the back of his hand then resumed his search. There was no room for sentimentality.

Ever. He turned another page and his quest was over.

Precariously placed in the album with brackets were several pictures of Einar, Lars and Haugland's other brothers, Alex and Per. They were various scenes of their growing up years: swimming at the lake, picking cloud berries, riding the little fjord ponies at a cousin's farm. There were banal, sometimes funny captions in white ink, but he read them with little feeling. His mood was sour.

He decided to leave them since only first names were used. He took out a picture with him in the background of a group of youngsters holding a snake. Then, quite suddenly, the pictures came to an end, the remaining pages blank. Instead, he found stacks of pictures stuffed haphazardly between them. He drew them out carefully and shuffled through them. His luck turned. He found five of himself immediately, one as recent as five years ago with his mother's handwriting on its back. *"Torrey Cambridge University 1939."* There was a corny line underneath in English: "What a good show." Wistfully, he ran his finger over the words.

He pocketed this and the others in his jacket, gingerly laying the remaining pictures back in the album. He wrapped the paper carefully back in place. No worse for wear.

He checked his watch. He'd been here a lot longer than he realized. He stood still listening. Had he heard something? His hand strayed to his pocket where he kept his pistol.

There was a slight creak. Suddenly the kitten charged across the rug, wildly attacking the *dyne* close to the floor, his sharp little claws strafing his imagined prey. His antics increased as he maneuvered upside down along the *dyne's* edge, a ferocious killer of featherbeds. His black mood broken, Haugland chuckled, careful not to become a victim himself. Once was enough.

He gave the room one last look over. Under the long lace curtain, the rag rug didn't lay right. On inspection, he discovered a loose floorboard. He lifted it up, exposing a gray metal box. Inside was a collection of letters written in German, though one was in English. Dated March 1940, it was postmarked Oxford, Maryland, USA. The rest were from her father. He read a couple, then put the box back in the hole. When it wouldn't fit, he discovered a muslin bag with several thousand *kroner*. The discovery made him uneasy.

A shoe scraped in the gravel path. Laughter rang like a bell. He turned off the light. Lifting the blackout curtain, he caught a glimpse of Anna Fromme dressed in a dark bathing suit as she stopped near the barn.

Haugland put everything back in order and left. There was only one way out: the balcony door. As he slipped through, he could hear the little girl calling for the kitten in the entryway. He closed the door. Climbing over the ornate wooden railing, he hang-dropped to the ground. He stayed under the porch, waiting. As he anticipated, the door opened and the woman came out. "Try the bedroom, Lisel," she was saying. "He might be there." She laid something on top of the railing and went back in.

Haugland waited before working his way to the kitchen side of the house, keeping close to the wall. Back at the barn, he bolted for the trees between the barn and the hill. Only when he was safely in the cover of the trees, did he stop and turn around.

"Damn," he swore, a sinking feeling growing inside him. Where was that damn kitten? Had it gone into the hole or something? He turned and climbed up higher, heading for home. Down below, the little girl came out into the backyard and called, her voice high and plaintive.

"Gub... ben...Gub...ben… Here, Kitty...Gub...ben...."

Her calls hung like mist in the late summer afternoon, drifting up to the wooded hill.

But Haugland was gone.

CHAPTER 24

"Kjell Arneson, Fjellstad, Sord-Trøndelag," Rika wrote on the envelope. From where she sat outside, she could look down across the sloping sun-touched fields to Trondheim, spreading out on the low-lying plain between the fjord and the bending river Nid. It had been a warm enough day to wear short sleeves, and she relished it.

"Rika." A smiling *Fru* Nissen stood by the side of the red painted house. She was a pert, efficient woman in her mid-forties, the wife of Rika's host Thomas Nissen. "You have company."

"Why, A.C. Kjelstrup!" Rika jumped up spilling her pen and writing pad on the grass.

"*God kveld*, Rika." A.C. was dressed in a light summer suit that bagged at his ankles. His hair was combed, his hands and nails scrubbed to a raw pink.

But he's clean. Rika tried hard not to giggle. "*God kveld*, A.C. What are you doing here?"

A.C. laughed. "Always to the point. To see you, of course." He nodded to *Fru* Nissen, then limped over to Rika. "It took awhile, but I finally found the place. It was the flowers." He looked around the flower garden trembling with white, pink and blue flowers next to the two-story house. "Confusing, you know. You're the prettiest one here."

"Don't be silly." Rika laughed, but underneath she felt a giddy bubble of excitement. She had always liked A. C., and now he was saying she was pretty. The last time she had seen him, she was wearing rubber boots and stacking crates on the *Otta*. She felt a sudden flush of shyness.

Fru Nissen picked up the conversation. "Why don't you stay for drinks, *Herr* Kjelstrup?"

"*Tusen takk*." Kjelstrup bowed to her. "It's been hot today."

Rika walked over to the flowerbeds. "Now, A.C., why did you really come?"

"Well, I did see your father, but I would have come anyway." He spoke to her like an equal, saluting her newfound womanhood.

"And how is Pappa?"

"Kjell—your father—is fine. Working on the *Otta*, of course, with his new helper Jens Hansen." He eased into a lawn chair opposite her. "They came to my house. Interesting fellow, rather odd. Haven't a clue how you know what he's saying."

Rika laughed. "With his notebook. He writes oodles. We've all learned some signs too. He's very nice. Kitty's in love with him."

A.C. snorted. "How's Trondheim? Do you like it?"

"*Ja.*" Rika told him of all the things she'd done in her first two weeks, her job, her new friend Freyda Olsen, who worked in the office. She gave him a cheery account and hoped he would believe most of what she said, but he apparently wasn't fooled.

"Now tell me what's really going. Fjellstad's a bit provincial, after all," he said. "And Trondheim's not Oslo, but it's still a big town."

Rika swallowed. "*Vær så snill*, don't tell Pappa. Yesterday, two young men wearing the uniform of the *Hird* got on my trolley. Two workers sitting near them went to find new seats. I know this is the Ice Front we use against the Germans and NS, but the men were arrested and beaten right in front of me." Rika leaned over, her voice whispering. "I know such things go on. It's just upsetting to be helpless and unable to do anything. I've always wanted to do something about it."

"How would you propose to do that, Rika?" A.C. sat up straight. "Thinking about something and doing it are two different things. And one is definitely more dangerous. It's something that must be expressed very carefully to people you know you can trust."

"I know." She looked at him and didn't waver. "I couldn't say anything to the Nissens, but I could say it to you because I trust you, A.C. I've known you all my life, and because you were in the war. You have a realistic idea about things. About Germans."

A.C. shifted in the hard chair, easing his bad leg. "So you want to do something."

"*Ja*. In Fjellstad, I'd watch how Sheriff Fasting or Foss cowed people. And the stories I heard from the men coming into the warehouse about fishing conditions, the confiscation of their catches. I always wanted to do something."

She twisted her fingers. "In a way I already have. Back in May, a bunch of us were upset over Petter Stagg having to go into hiding, so we painted an H-7 on the rocks on cliffs past the harbor. I helped row them over."

"Rika!" A.C. shook his head. "Pretty reckless."

"Oh, I was scared, but it seems funny now. I want to do something more important." Her hands clenched tightly in her lap, Rika was close to tears.

A.C. leaned over and placed his hand on hers. "All right. But promise me something. Don't do anything without talking to me, all right? You mustn't say anything to any one. Not what we just talked about. Promise?"

"I promise," she muttered, then said more forcibly, "And?"

"Maybe I can find something for you to do. I might know someone."

A.C. left at ten. Rika went to bed by eleven, but it was hard to sleep. It was light as afternoon outside. Finally, slipping into a skirt and pullover, she went outside.

The sky was bright with pink clouds. To the west the sun was above the horizon. It cast a pinkish gold light all around the fields and houses. There was a slight breeze off the fjord that teased her cheeks with a warm, moist caress. She walked over to the edge of the house to where she could see the town. It lay like an island in a sea of gold, seemingly untouched by the events of the last four years. Like submarine pens and murder. "I'm going to do something. I am."

CHAPTER 25

In a suburb northeast of the Nissen home, Odd Sorting stood outside a house smoking a cigarette. The midnight sun shone on his face and hair too, lighting the one-story house behind.

As houses went, it wasn't different from other houses in the suburb. Built on a stone foundation, it was a roomy dwelling made of wood and shaped like a thick letter `L'. A walkway and cement steps led up to a partially enclosed patio nestling against the front door. It had large, shuttered windows all around and a handsomely shingled roof. Once it had belonged to a Jewish family, but it had a different purpose now.

Sorting took a long drag on his cigarette and leaned against the lamppost next to the stairs. He'd been making his arrangements for his trip back to Fjellstad. He had also taken some time to see Freyda and when he wasn't in the sack with her, checked on the process of his little project.

The idea had come to him on the long coastal boat trip from Fjellstad to Trondheim. Sorting had overheard Rika Arneson the girl talking to another passenger. From the way she spoke, she had strong *jøssing* feelings. She would be the perfect dupe. Sorting decided to follow her and located her new residence. He eventually found her place of work, and then laid his plan out to the Chief. He'd get her connected to what she thought a legitimate group but in reality exposing her community to his boss.

The Chief always worked the negative line. "Do it," the Chief said, but Sorting needed Freyda's help. After a few presents and a night of lovemaking that made him ache thinking about it, she readily agreed.

Sorting took another drag. So far it was going well. In one day, he had found Freyda a part-time position in the same office building as Rika's. Before long the young women met and became friends. That's my Freyda, he thought. She's lively and fun. People are naturally attracted to her. Just like me.

Her ripe breasts and flat belly with its teardrop button flashed before him, making him wish he were with her back at the flat. Too bad work came first.

He had been in Trondheim for over two weeks, laying the groundwork for the new operation around Fjellstad. He was to find any resistance organization, whether military, export or intelligence by gaining the confidence of the local community through his friendship with several men he already knew and work his way in. He would manipulate it to the Germans' advantage before exposing it. The Chief called the operation '*Albatross,*' implying the resistance would soon find his organization cruelly hanging around their necks.

A large man opened the door and called out to him. "Sorting? Chief's ready to see you."

"*Takk.* Tell him I'm coming right in." He took one last drag, then went inside.

The house was quiet. There were no sounds coming from the radio room used for contacting field agents. Whoever manned it around the clock had temporarily left. The other rooms used for living quarters were deserted. He looked over to the door leading to the basement. Quiet. No guests down there tonight. The tension in his neck eased.

"How are you, Odd?" Sorting turned. The Chief stood in the doorway to the parlor.

"Fine." Sorting followed the man in.

"Help yourself to a drink." The Chief sat down with his tumbler on an overstuffed chair.

The bottles on the side table were stacked two deep, all excellent quality. Sorting chose Scotch, an ironic touch since its place of origin was definitely on the enemies' list. Adding ice, he settled down on the sofa opposite his boss. "So, Odd, you're ready to go? Have everything you need?"

"I'm all set. I leave at six. I'll get there by evening." Sorting cleared his throat. "The village's a little shy since the sweep for radios and other contraband last April, but I'll take things as they go. There's the islander Kjelstrup who's grateful for his brother's escape, and Kjell Arneson, long-time friend of Kjelstrup's family. He was active in the Fisherman's Association."

The Chief looked at Odd with his piercing eyes. His usual half-smirk made long lines in his narrow face. He lifted his glass and toasted him. "Well, here's to success."

"To success." Odd downed a healthy portion of his drink. Over the top of his glass he watched the Chief settle into his chair. He seemed to sink into it, for he was a very small man, his feet dangling just off the floor. He wore child-size clothes because he was so stunted, but his looks were deceiving. The Chief was a cunning and dangerous man, not only to illegal groups, but to anyone he suspected of double-dealing. The Chief was Henry Oliver Rinnan.

"How's our girl?" Rinnan asked.

"Freyda's doing all right. She can type, so her boss won't be disappointed. She's made friends with the Arneson kid. Hear they have lunch together every day." Sorting took a long sip and studied Rinnan. *I can keep a secret too*, he thought. I can leave when I want and I can keep your damn postwar plans to myself. I don't care.

Well, he did care. Rinnan was dangerous, but they were friends of sorts. Sorting had known him now for three and half years. He had known his brother Rolf Rinnan even longer.

The Rinnans were from Levanger, a small port and timber town located north of Trondheim on the Trondheimfjord. Sorting met Rolf Rinnan there while visiting his uncle. When Trondheim fell to the Germans, Sorting had volunteered to work on some of the German projects around the Trøndelag area, including the building of the huge U-boat base in Trondheim. The pay was good as well as the food rations. But Rinnan paid better. He never regretted joining *Rinnan Banden,* and while the going was still good, he would stay. It had become so easy.

"When you have your transmitter set up, call," Rinnan was saying. "We can arrange for any hard materials to go out on the coastal steamer." Rinnan spoke in a low, vibrant voice.

"Fine."

Eventually, Rinnan dismissed him. Sorting wandered off to the sleeping quarters and found a cot. He wearily took off his shoes and rolled up in a blanket with his clothes still on. He fell asleep instantly and slept soundly through most of the night. Only once did he wake up when there was a commotion in the hallway as someone was brought into the house, then manhandled down the stairs to the basement. Sorting woke briefly, looked at the glowing face of an alarm clock across the room, then settled back. He didn't bother to investigate. Instead, he punched his pillow into shape and changed position, going back to sleep immediately. He didn't even wake when a muffled cry of despair shot up from the Cloister below shortly after. It had become too easy.

CHAPTER 26

It was a summons of sorts, so Anna took care to be on time. What she had asked for had been granted—at least the typewritten note signed by Ella Bjornson appeared to say so. Anna was to come to the church at eleven and sit near the back and wait.

Rising early, she did some chores, then throwing on a scarf and sweater, hurried toward the village. It was a hard walk. Lisel kept dawdling, wanting to stop and look at things, something Anna was in no mood to do. She became impatient and finally snapped at Lisel, scooting her ahead. They arrived at the little wooden church both in sour moods.

The whitewashed building was set on a gentle knoll that rose above the few homes about it. Around the back was a little graveyard where a lone wind-bent birch stood, a sentinel among the lichen-covered headstones. As they were early, Anna led Lisel there to a large stone slab and asked her to sit down.

"Mama's sorry she got angry." She cupped Lisel's face in her hands and kissed her softly on her forehead. "I have something important to do."

It was pleasant where they sat. A light breeze brought the smells of the inland sea and the sounds of children playing not far away. Lisel stood up on the slab and looked in the direction of the schoolhouse a long field away to the east. Boys were playing soccer on the playground, girls on swings or skipping rope. It was mid-June, but school was still in session. The soldiers in April had done that. Anna felt a pang of guilt Lisel did not have friends here.

"Come, let's look at the headstones. Find one with the letter B." Reluctantly, Lisel got down and walked among the stones. They found three right away, all Bjornsons. One of them read:

Haakon Bjornson
Beloved husband,
Died July 28, 1940.

Ella Bjornson's husband. What could she say?

There was no one inside the church when Anna stepped in. She followed Ella Bjornson's instructions and sat down on one of the wooden pews in the back. The church was an old structure with a tall, carved pulpit made of maple rising up to the heavens on the side. In front was a heavy table draped with a white linen altar cloth. A simple brass cross kept vigil.

Anna gave Lisel a piece of paper and a pencil, then opened a hymnal in front of her, but barely read it. Instead, she listened to the building creak gently as the wind blew past it. She stiffened when the door opened. Someone stepped in and slid into the pew behind her.

It was Ella Bjornson. "I'll will come to the point," the woman said.

Anna turned around. She had heard people say the woman had a sweet reputation, but there was nothing sweet about the face regarding her. *Fru* Bjornson's eyes were hard and her mouth was turned down as if she had tasted something bitter.

"Leif Sornenson wants to use your fields," Ella Bjornson said, "and though late, might put in some potatoes and other crops. He was badly injured a month ago."

"Who will help me?" Anna asked. She should have looked down, acted more differential, but it was so humiliating asking for help from someone who obviously hated her, so she returned the woman's penetrating look with a solid one of her own.

"Kjell Arneson has agreed to let his man Jens Hansen come. Things are slow right now and he can spare him. He will cut wood for you in exchange for the fields as you asked."

Bjornson shifted her position on her hardwood seat, gripping the back of Anna's pew. "He's a good young man, but deaf. He can read lips very well and isn't difficult to talk to. He can write what he needs."

Anna said nothing, but something like hope rose within her at the thought of seeing Hansen again. The women negotiated, and in the end, Anna got what she wanted: help with her farm and milk for Lisel in exchange for use of the fields.

A silence grew between them. Anna watched at the dust motes drifting down over the wood railing in front of the altar. The stillness grew heavy and profound. Finally she couldn't stand it anymore and turned around. "Why did you change your mind about helping me?"

"Not out of love. I want to keep Foss from taking the farm. Didn't you know?" Ella stood up. "He's always wanted the farm. He almost succeeded when Jarle Fromme died, but the good mayor believes in the *oder* even if he is a Nazi."

"The *oder*?"

"The law of inheritance. The farm stays with the descendant—Jarle's great-granddaughter, Lisel." Ella stepped out onto the aisle and passed Anna going toward the altar. Suddenly, she turned. She looked at Anna dispassionately. "There was a time we feared they would blow up the farm after Einar was arrested. It wouldn't be the first time the Germans did that. We thought it odd they didn't. Then you came. Suddenly it was clear why."

If Ella had struck her, the words couldn't have hurt more. Humiliated, Anna grabbed Lisel's hand."Come, Lisel. We're leaving now."

She hurrried down the creaky wooden aisle as quickly as possible. Standing outside, she let go Lisel's hand and took a deep breath. The air was sweet and moist with a hint of the low tide. She let it soothe the sting of embarrassment and shame.

Yet, I've done it, she thought. At least, things for now will be taken care of. She would be more prepared for winter when it came, and the long dark days that accompanied it. Last year had been one of the coldest in memory. Who knew what this year would bring?

Anna looked up at the gray sky veiled by layers of rolling clouds and pulled her sweater tightly around her body. Her happiness at her little victory slipped away. Ella Bjornson's chilling words returned. It didn't matter that she'd offered the valuable land to those who were *jøssings.*

I should start looking out for myself, she thought. Things are going to get worse. Liberation is coming, perhaps by the end of August. She had no idea how she would be treated.

She would contact "Uncle Felix" and ask for his help. Perhaps he could get her out of the country to Sweden. That would be the safest place for her and Lisel. And then...

Anna often thought of her grandparents in America. Her grandfather was dead, but her grandma had still been alive in 1940. She had an uncle there too. She had no idea if she would ever see her father and brother again. If she could get passage to America after the war.

"Mama, can we go?"

"*Ja,* we can go."

CHAPTER 27

"Mama! The funny man is here."

"Funny man? Who are you talking about?"

"The man who fixed Gubben." Lisel climbed onto the banister at the kitchen's edge and swung on it. Her blue overalls were powdered with dust and her scruffy shoes untied. Her fine hair was in disarray and had hay in it.

"You mean *Herr* Hansen? Is he outside?"

"U-huh. Is he mad?" Lisel asked as she swung the opposite direction.

"I don't think so." Anna reached for a piece of hay on Lisel's head.

"Then why doesn't he come see us?"

Why indeed? When she learned that Hansen would cut wood for her, she hoped they would visit again. She had been greatly disappointed when he came up to gather tools in the barn on the first day. He came with a teenage boy named Per Sorenson. "Would you like to come in?" she had asked.

Nei, he signed. He wrote: Barn. Tools. Then he and the boy spent nearly an hour sharpening the saw and axees they had found. Hansen was so standoffish, showing none of his earlier friendliness, that she stayed away. And now he was at her backdoor again after a week and a half's absence.

Anna sighed. Taking off her apron, she sent Lisel off to find her hairbrush, then straightening her blue farm dress, went out to the entryway.

Hansen stood at the backdoor with his cap in hand. He wore old dungarees and a short-sleeved jersey shirt opened at the breast. His face and muscular arms were tanned from the day's work. He smelled of sweat and dirt. Unaware of her, he looked toward the driveway, the expression on his face remote. Then the expression changed to weariness. He hunched his shoulders to relieve some stiffness.

It's not fair to watch him, she thought. He doesn't know I'm here. But it was something comfortable and familiar seeing him standing there. *Einar.* Home from their haying field, hot and tired. Only last summer. So long ago. Her eyes began to sting. She wiped them clean.

She pushed against the screen door she had put on herself a few days ago, causing it to screech, but it was movement that made him turn.

He raised a hand in recognition and smiled faintly at her, a smile that didn't quite go to his eyes, but was still friendly enough. Tucking his cap under his arm, he reached into his pants pocket and took out his notebook. Quickly, he wrote a couple of lines.

"You need to sharpen your saw? Of course. You don't need to ask." She looked behind him. "Where is your friend?"

Gone, his hands said. Then he walked away.

The next hour passed slowly. It was sunny and warm. Sitting on the back step, Anna brushed Lisel's silky hair into obedience. Hansen sat on a bench at the edge of the barn's wide door patiently sharpening each set of the saw's teeth with a special file. The small barnyard was a vast ocean between them.

"*Herr* Hansen, *Herr* Hansen," Lisel called, but Anna reminded her that he couldn't hear her. "He can't hear because he's not watching us." Lisel ran over and tapped his knee. Hansen stopped. "Are your ears working now?" she asked.

For the second time since she met him, Anna watched the light gray eyes flare up as Hansen's mouth broke into a warm grin. He made a dull sound in his mouth and motioned with his hand. *Nei.* He tapped his ear with his hand and shook his head.

Lisel stood back, her eyes wide, but he motioned she could sit down near him and watch. Then he resumed his work. After a while, Anna went inside, returning with some potatoes to peel. They were still apart, but somehow there was a line stretching between them as Lisel jabbered on, sometimes tapping his knee so he would look. He didn't seem to mind her.

Anna took her bowl inside and returned with a pitcher of cold milk. Stopping at the screen door, she watched them wistfully for a long time. Einar and Lisel had often visited like this while he worked on projects around the house, although in the last four months before he died, he had seemed preoccupied. Still, Einar would read to her when he could.

"What's your real name?" Lisel asked.

Hansen took a stick and scratched his name into the dirt. Lisel read the letters out loud. "J-E-N-S." She was very precocious. He took her little hand, and pointing to the first letter, he formed her fingers into a shape. He made a throaty sound, pointed to the next one, and repeated the process over again. When he was done with all four letters, he formed them in order. This little game amused her and Lisel giggled as she leaned against his knees. She picked up the stick and wrote her own name in a childish scrawl. He fingerspelled it. L-I-S-E-L.

"Show me another," Lisel said, but he begged off. It was time to go.

He took the tools into the barn. While he was gone, Anna went over to look at the writing in the dirt. When he came out, the fisherman nodded at her, giving her only a ghost of a smile, but at least this time it touched his eyes.

"Would you care for some milk, *Herr* Hansen?" Anna lifted the pitcher in front of him. Hesitating, he finally signed, *Ja* and took the cup from her when it was filled.

"You're working too hard. You should rest," she said. He stopped drinking and looked at her questioningly. "I said, you work too hard. It's not necessary. You should rest more often."

He raised the cup, indicating that this was his rest. When she offered seconds, he made a sign she thought might mean "thanks." She poured again and in doing so looked at his hands.

They are quite beautiful, she thought, in a masculine way. Long fingered, but strong. Not what she expected in a fisherman.

"Would you like to see my Gubben?" Lisel tugged his shirt. Taking his hand, she leaned back to take in his face high above her. "*Vær så snill.*"

"Oh, Munchkin, I think *Herr* Hansen is very tired. He wants to go home." Anna expected a weary nod of agreement, but instead he crouched down in front of Lisel. He looked at her very seriously.

L-I-S-E-L, he finger spelled, then he pantomimed: You get kitten. I stay here.

Before Anna could protest, Lisel was off like a shot, leaving them alone at the barn door. Anna felt foolish standing there with the pitcher and cup. He regarded her in his usual detached way. She wondered what he was thinking about. "Would you like to go in?" she asked.

Hansen tugged at his shirtfront to indicate that he wasn't very presentable and stood up.

"You know, you can use the water in the springhouse," she went on, trying to make small talk. "There is a pipe with flowing water. You can clean up there anytime. Even now."

Takk, he signed. He took out his mangled notebook and a pencil stub. He wrote: Tomorrow, get cart. Bring wood here. Where?

Lisel came out with Gubben. Hansen sat down on the low ramp leading into the barn and took the kitten in his hands. Lisel leaned against him and stroked the growing kitten's soft fur.

What a pair, Anna thought, and how extraordinary. Except for the cook, Lisel hadn't responded to anyone, especially to a man. It's Einar. She misses him. Thinking of him, Anna felt a lump in her throat

After awhile, Hansen gave Gubben back to Lisel, but it wiggled out of her arms, and bounded off in a funny staggering lope. What happened? he signed.

"Oh, the silly thing got lost in the subflooring. We heard it meowing, but couldn't find it. It was weak when we did."

"Silly Gubben," Lisel took the fisherman's hands and played with his fingers, trying to shape them the way he had shown her. Impulsively she put her arms around his neck and laid against his grimy shirt front. "J-E-N-S. I love you," she whispered.

Anna was startled to see he had been deeply moved. His mouth set hard, his lips were close to trembling, but she couldn't guess why and by the time she took Lisel back, his neutral mask was back in place.

***

Hansen came up the next morning with a two-wheel cart drawn by a *fjording*, a plump Norwegian fjord pony. Anna went out with Lisel to pet the animal. Though it was six years since she'd seen her first, the ponies continued to amuse her. They weren't at all like the sleek horses her uncle kept on an estate outside of Berlin. Not like the huge workhorses still found on many German farms despite the arsenal of farm machinery available before the war. Instead, they were their own creation: sturdy dun-colored ponies of medium height with fine dark manes that stood up like brooms on their necks and forelocks. They had stripes on their legs like zebras and had a stripe on the spine. They were well suited to the rough environment of Norway's west coast and had become priceless with the advent of rationing and fuel.

Per Sorenson sat in the driver's seat while Hansen adjusted the traces on the pony. Eventually, they left, Hansen leading the pony by the reins up through the pine forest. All morning they hauled the wood. At four, they came down for the last time. Anna was outside taking down laundry when they came down. As she laid the fresh-smelling clothes into a wicker basket, she watched them unload the wood into the shed, then separate. While the boy led the pony away, Hansen went to the back of the barn. The boy left.

Anna surveyed her small universe and sighed. The house needed paint and the barn needed some boards hammered down. Some of the other outbuildings looked almost derelict. She needed help for that. In a very few weeks the first crop of hay could be harvested. The rows of drying fences had been repaired and ready to be draped with sweet-smelling grass. Later there would be rye.

She picked up the load of clothes and carried the basket over to the back door. She looked around for Lisel.

"Munchkin." There was no response there or in the house. She headed over to the driveway and the garden. Nothing. Only the grazing pony in the field. *Where was the imp?*

"Lisel!" At the back of the barn came the sound of movement in the springhouse. Anna took off immediately. The springhouse was a new construction made of concrete blocks. It had replaced the old log structure just before the war. The pump was fairly recent, too. "Lisel?"

There were no voices, only a bucket scraping on the concrete floor. She pushed the wooden door open.

It was the fisherman. He was stripped to the waist and washing off the grime from his arms and chest with an old piece of toweling. As he leaned over the bucket of cold water to rinse the rag, the strong firm muscles in his upper back and broad shoulders rippled. Like a sleek lion. She backed down. He didn't know she was there, and she would have to go in to get his attention. She flushed with embarrassment and retreated to the barn wall.

Oh, where was Lisel? Anna contemplated going up to the forest edge when she heard the scrape of Hansen's boots in the springhouse. A few seconds later, he was at the door, bucket in hand. At the last moment he saw her. The look on his face was so comical she laughed. He looked down at the bucket and back at her.

Smiling wryly, he poured the water out at the side of the doorway. He was still shirtless, his suspenders dangling at his sides. The muscles in his arms and smooth chest were clearly defined. He's so lean and tough-looking, she thought, and it surprised her. It wasn't the gentle impression he generally gave. He looked formidable.

"Have you seen Lisel?" she asked.

Nei. He tapped his wrist for time. How long? You… want...me… look? Me look?

When she said yes, he went back inside, coming out again, pulling a clean knit shirt over his head. He tucked the ends into his pants, then pulled up his suspenders. Which way?

They split up, going around the barn in opposite directions. Hansen headed up the hill, while she went down the driveway, but they couldn't find Lisel. Discouraged, she wrung her hands. Hansen was calm. He pointed to the house. You look?

"Not really, but I did call inside earlier. She didn't answer."

He reached out and waved his hand in front of her. You look inside. His hands were very deliberate. It was almost an order. She went inside and found Lisel curled up on her bed with her kitten. When she came out, Hansen was waiting by the steps with his hands in his pockets.

"I found her," she said after getting his attention. "I'm sorry. All for nothing."

He shrugged. It's all right. I happy to help.

"You won't stay for coffee?"

He shook his head and left.

***

Haugland worked three more days. It hadn't been his idea to work for Ann Fromme. The little committee had approved his services after she had approached Ella Bjornson. Thinking it in the best interest of the village, Kjell told him to accept, promising him not to involve him in any more work of this nature again. It would be good for Haugland to work as a farmhand while he waited for the Shetland Bus. It was a summer tradition and it would keep him out of the village. Haugland agreed as long as he didn't have much contact with Anna Fromme. But he had, and now things were changing.

It had begun with Lisel. If she had been someone else's child, perhaps his wall of aloofness might have worked, but she was Einar's daughter and he genuinely cared for her.

Every day after they were done, Lisel would be waiting in the barn, bubbling with enthusiasm and questions. Per, who had younger sisters, played with her, but it was Haugland she always went back to. He began to soften his attitude toward being at the farm altogether and looked forward to the encounters that often took place when Anna came out to snag Lisel away. He knew that familiarity created new danger. This was shown clearly to him during the second week of logging.

It had drizzled Monday, but the next morning it was dry, so they put away their oilskins. As they came down in the late afternoon the rain came back with a vengeance. The cart slipped in the mud and spilled its load of split wood across the rugged forest track. Halfway through restacking the wood, a cloudburst thundered down on them. There was no time to run for cover under the tall pines. Soon, they were soaked.

In the barn, Haugland and Per hurriedly unhitched the pony, then waited at the barn door, cold and waterlogged. The rain was falling down in silver gray sheets. Per stamped his feet. Haugland put his hands in his wet coat pockets and hunched his shoulders. Across the puddles growing in the barnyard he noticed Lisel standing at the farmhouse door. She waved at him, then disappeared. Moments later she was back with Anna wearing an oilskin hat and coat. She came over, stepping carefully around the huge puddles. "*Herr* Hansen, you are soaked. You must come in at once."

He looked at the boy and shrugged. They would come.

In the entryway, they took off their boots and socks, padding down to the parlor where she gave them towels. She disappeared upstairs and returned with an armful of clothing.

"These were my husband's," she said. "Perhaps they'll fit." Anna closed the door.

When they were dressed, Haugland stepped out in Einar's pants and flannel shirt. It made him feel young again, like he had slipped into one of Einar's forbidden possessions.

"*Herr* Hansen. Come." Anna was standing near the table stuffing newspaper into one of his boots. On the table were steaming bowls of pottage sharp with the smell of rutabagas and potatoes. A plate of herring sandwiches was in the middle. Nothing more was said. Once they were seated, she put the boots by the woodstove and returned to a spinning wheel nearby and began to spin.

Outside the steamy windows, the fjord was socked in with low clouds, its waters chilling to the color of slate. The wind and rain slashed at the glass in irregular time, further limiting visibility. It was more like April than the last days of June, but inside it was warm and homey, the room mellowed by the kitchen smells and the lyric music of Edvard Grieg playing softly on a gramophone. In the center of it, Anna sat.

She had her head slightly bent over her work as she drew wool out and spun it into a fine yarn before it was swiftly wound up on the bobbin. Her lips were parted, and she moved occasionally to the rhythm of the wheel and treadle.

God, she's lovely, Haugland thought, admiring her complexion and the fine line of her throat down to the full swell of her breasts. He watched her work, and it struck him that this and the other farm tasks he had seen her do were all new skills learned here in Norway. What commitments she had made coming here. With her background, she should've been spoiled, but then she had been Einar's wife. *Einar.*

Einar wouldn't have been blinded by love, even if he were struck by it. He wasn't the sort. He had married late, but he would have chosen wisely, even if some arrangement had been involved. He looked at her and for the moment forgot she was part German, making peace with her in his mind.

"Jens, look." Per tapped Haugland's wrist and pointed. "Lights on the road. I think it's my uncle. He said he might come if the weather turned."

An elderly Ford truck with bug-eyed lights, one of the few private vehicles in the area, growled up the driveway, its voice nearly lost in the rain's clatter. Haugland went out to the entryway while Per hurriedly gathered up his half-dried clothes and put on the dry socks Anna offered. Out in the lighted entryway, the uncle dripped water from his oilskins and greeted Haugland in the loud voice just to make him understand.

"Get your things, Per. You'll be staying with us tonight. You won't be rowing over to your parents like last week. The fjord water's too rough. How was the German woman?"

"Maybe she's not the troll-wife everyone's made her out to be," the boy answered in a low voice.

"You be careful," the uncle hissed. "Maybe that's how she got those people into trouble with the Germans. Are you coming, Jens?"

Haugland shook his head. *Nei.*

"Well, *God veldt.*" He paused. "Tell the woman, *tusen takk* anyway."

Anna was carding wool when Haugland came back into the room. She got up when he came to the table to get his plate. He wondered if she had heard the uncle's talk.

"I forgot to give you coffee. I have cream, too."

Haugland ignored her and cleared his place.

Anna came over and touched his sleeve gently. "*Vær så snill*, I will do that. If you wish, I have coffee made."

Haugland hesitated. He shouldn't. There would be gossip enough after today's mishap. A sudden blast of rain hit the window that caused her to turn.

"You aren't really planning to go? It's terrible out."

He shrugged. *Nei*, he didn't really want to. Stay a little bit, he motioned.

She brought him *ersatz* coffee, then sat down opposite him with a cup of her own. He drank in silence for a while until she knocked on the table near his hand and asked him when he would be done with the logging. He answered in his notbook.

"*Tusen takk*." she murmured. "You cannot know you helped me. Not just the wood, but the feeling you are a friend. I know no one and I have not been welcomed. It is very hard to be left out and have people think things about you that are not true. I think, though, that of all the people here, you understand that feeling most of all."

Haugland didn't answer, letting her think what she wanted, but he often did feel left out. It was his fault, though. For the first time since the occupation, he had allowed himself a sense of place, but it was not his right to enjoy in it and the friendships he had made. He had come for a purpose and for that reason couldn't step outside the cover he had created for himself. Why, then, did it bother him that she took note of him being lonely?

"Can you read this to me?" Lisel shoved a large open book at him, then climbed into his lap.

"Lisel, he can't," Anna leaned over the table. "Not like Pappa. Please get down."

"Not like Pappa?"

"*Nei*, Munchkin. Not like Pappa."

Lisel was surprised. "Don't you know what a troll is?" She pointed to a line drawing in the book and tapped his arm. "See? That's a troll and that's —a troll hag."

I know trolls, Haugland signed, and he made a horrible face to prove it. He pointed to the picture and made the sign for troll. Excited, Lisel flipped to other pictures in the story. Each time she pointed, he signed or pantomimed. She giggled and leaned against him.

"See, Mama, he can read!"

"So he can. It's time for bed." The little girl complied reluctantly, but not before giving him a hug. *God kveld*, Jens," she whispered then climbed into her mother's arms.

Haugland left not long after, bundled up in his oilskins. Back at his cold cabin, he got his woodstove going and attempted to get some planning done, but he couldn't concentrate. The whole episode with Anna Fromme had been unsettling. He had come on a hired man basis, but he didn't see his relationship with her or the child that way anymore.

He was no fool. He was walking on dangerous ground. It was no good being drawn into their lives. It would have to end. He was glad the job was almost over. He wouldn't go back. The end of June was in days, and Tommy Renvik would be coming. It was time to implement what he had been sent to do.

CHAPTER 28

The sound was just the delicate snapping of a twig, but Tore Haugland was instantly awake. Grabbing his gun from under his pillow, he slipped silently to the cabin floor and glanced at his watch. It glowed one-fifteen in the morning. Cocking his head in the pitch-black space, he listened for further sounds outside, then crept to the back door where the intruder had moved. He listened again, then determining there was only one person, moved stealthily to the front to escape. A voice whispering in English stopped him.

"Scarlett, it's Rhett. You awake?" It was Tommy Renvik.

Scowling, Haugland came back and opened the back door. Tommy burst out laughing when he saw Haugland in his underwear with a handgun casually pointed at him.

"Action stations!" Tommy commanded as he came into the room, swinging his arms back and forth like a parading sergeant. He wore ordinary wool knickers and boots but under his long overcoat the jacket of a lieutenant in the British Army showed conspicuously.

"Sir!" Haugland gave him a stiff salute, then laughed. "Lucky bastard. I was going to take you out. Sir."

Once the kerosene lamp was lit, Haugland pulled into his pants while Tommy rustled up coffee from his rucksack. Eventually, they sat down at Haugland's rickety table.

"Nice place, Tore, but could you change the climb up from the road?"

"You came from the village?"

"No. From the *fjell.* I got turned around. Had to go down the road to orient myself."

"I'll draw you a map. There's no need to stumble around and show yourself." The coffeepot overflowed on the woodstove. Haugland jumped up and pulled it from the stove. He collected two heavy camp mugs from nails on the wall.

"How've you been, Tore? Not fishing now, are you?"

"No. I've been logging and doing an occasional job at the Tourist Hotel." He filled the mugs with steaming coffee and brought them to the table. "We'll probably resume fishing in the next week or so. First I'm meeting with a man named Sig Haraldsen and his sons to set up larger shipments of arms on the Bus. They're fishermen, and we'll work under that cover."

"You're really serious about this."

"No sense in being idle."

The two friends sat with legs stretched out, picking up their conversation from two months ago when they had waited for their ride out of the Kvam area. They had been running from the Germans then, but now they acted as if nothing had happened.

Haugland briefed Tommy on the Shetland Bus runs, the arms storage he had set up, and his general reconnaissance of the area. "It's taken me five months, but everything's in place, waiting for the next stage. I move fairly easily now. They don't expect much from me."

"As long as you don't blab in your sleep. Scares the shit out of me every time I think about it." Tommy reached into his rucksack and brought out a small flask. "Allow me." He poured a bit of whiskey into each of the mugs. Haugland took his and skoaled him.

"That isn't all I brought," Tommy went on. "I've got vitamins, iron rations, and a pair of decent boots for you. Got to keep you healthy and properly attired. Why the hell were you logging?"

"Because I *wasn't* fishing." Haugland told him about Anna Fromme.

"That's devilish business. Isn't it bizarre working for the very woman you're to avoid?"

"Not any more than some other things I'd had to do in the name of intelligence. Like collecting rubber scraps door to door. I'm done now anyway and won't be going back. Kjell has seen to that." Haugland reached for the flask. Even though Tommy had a right to be concerned, Haugland felt a rising irritation. "Where did you get the iron rations? Was there a drop?"

"No." Tommy flushed. "I was in Sweden."

"God Almighty, Renvik, you do more traveling than a *Baedeker* rep! How was it?"

"Stockholm's friendlier since the Normandy invasion, though Swedish platitudes about how the Germans treat us irritates the hell out of me. They think we're complaining about nothing. Saw a couple of American movies with Swedish subtitles. *Mrs. Miniver* is still around, but I saw Humphrey Bogart in *Action in the Atlantic.* Pretty decent."

"Anything for me?" Haugland picked up one of the bottles of pills and studied the label.

"The Major at MI IV I gave me your orders concerning Milorg Districts 21 and 22. He sends his greetings. From now on, he's your contact outside of the country. Call him 'Uncle.'"

Haugland took the news soberly. No more trips to London. "Was it all business?"

"No. I met someone at the British legation, a real pretty girl from Ålesund. She went over a year ago. Works with the Norwegian agents associated with SOE. I hope to see her again."

"Lucky you."

"On that, yes, but hell, Stockholm's bewildering." Tommy shook his head. "Neon lights all over the place. Sometimes I felt I was on a different planet. It was overwhelming to read uncensored newspapers, or to listen to news on the radio."

"Well, at least someone's still able to keep a social calendar."

Tommy laughed. "Yeah, sure, but London said you were ready, so I came back."

"I am ready. If we get started now, you could see your sweetheart by potato digging time."

Haugland rose early the next day and walked into the village to do a prearranged job at the Tourist Hotel, leaving Tommy curled up on the floor in his SOE-issued down bag. He returned at ten in the bright morning sun with Kjell. After he knocked the V for Victory signal of three shorts and a long, Tommy opened the door. He was still dressed in his uniform jacket with its Norwegian flag on the shoulder, armed with a Sten gun. Kjell was very moved to see him.

"It's the first time in four years that a free Norwegian soldier has been in Fjellstad."

Tommy shook his hand warmly and invited him in. He had set out a tin of biscuits and jam and pot of real coffee. The men settled down at the table.

"Any news on the war?" Kjell asked. "I'm getting tired of the 'official' news. The Germans are always winning."

"How do you get your news?" Tommy asked.

"Rumor." Kjell took a biscuit from the tin. "And sometimes information coming off the BBC, but that has to be spread slowly so the quislings don't know who has the radio. Is it true the Allied push to Paris is on?"

"Not entirely," Tommy went on to tell him about the Germans mounting a heavy counterattack near Caen where the British landed. "The weather's been rough. Wiped out two artificial harbors in the American section. The Allies had to push for Cherbourg and its harbor, but the Germans wrecked it. The Allies want all of Normandy. Paris will have to wait."

"What about the U-boats?" Haugland asked. It was an area of military intelligence he had been concerned with. "Brittany must be under a lot of pressure."

"XU believes the U-boats will be moved here. There are strong indications that the U-boat base at Bergen will be enlarged. They just don't know when."

Haugland shot Tommy a look of regret. He'd give his eyeteeth to be down there, but Bergen had become too hot for him eighteen months ago when a meeting had turned murderous.

"What do you mean?" Kjell asked.

"It means," Tommy paused, "that the Germans are digging in."

"We'll be last, Kjell," Haugland said softly. "Norway will be liberated last."

For a few moments, no one spoke. The Normandy invasion had been four weeks ago. The average Norwegian felt that liberation would come in August. Tommy broke the silence. "My friend says you'll start fishing soon."

"That's the plan," Kjell said, "but to be honest, I'm not sure if it's worth it, other than to provide cover for our work. The Germans take fifty percent of the catch now."

"We've money for that," Tommy said. "We can slip you what we can, some food as well."

"*Nei*, I'm in this as much as you. It's a matter of pride. There's been an Arneson fishing here for nearly two hundred years, and nothing's stopped us before."

The morning went on. They emptied the biscuit tin. Haugland made another pot of coffee. Suddenly, Haugland sat up. "Damn. I've got to finish up a paint job at the Hotel. Got to get in Foss's good graces if it's possible. He's pretty sore after I worked at the Fromme farm."

"Who's this Foss?" Tommy asked.

"A Norwegian Nazi and a quisling of the deepest kind," Kjell said. "Works at the Hotel."

Haugland stood up. "Look, I've got to go in. You two stay here. Tommy will fill you in on anything you need to know. Kjell, I'm borrowing your bike. Be back around four."

He grabbed a light canvas jacket off a nail on the door and started outside, but Tommy excused himself and followed him out. They walked to the deep green edge of the woods overlooking the fjord road. Haugland stopped. Tommy kept to the shadows.

"Ask Kjell anything you want to know," Haugland said, putting on his jacket. "For a fisherman, he knows the mountains really well. He's tromped through every swamp up there."

"A good man..."

"A very good man. That's why I want you to start to look for a way to get his youngest daughter out of here. The Shetland Bus can take refugees, but she'd be over in England with no relations. I know some people in Sweden. Might be better there for the duration of the war."

"You sound worried about something."

"Oh, just say that my feelers for keeping my skin intact have been activated. Be prepared. I was a pretty good Boy Scout, you know, although

I've probably broken half the oath in the last three and a half years. Except the loyalty part."

"I don't think Jack would mind. SOE is full of boy scouts."

Haugland chuckled. Colonel Jack Wilson, an Englishman, led SOE-Norway. He had been the international head of the Boy Scouts for fifteen years before the war. Many a European agent had learned the art of fieldwork in the scouting movement.

Haugland grew more serious and picked up the bike. "That train trip caused a bit of a problem. The Gestapo has been asking questions about me around Kvam. Remember the boy I told you about? They beat him to death, but not before he talked. Now they're looking for me, the schoolteacher. They will surmise I got on the train before Kongsvoll. The Gestapo will look north."

"So you want me to look into an export group for his daughter."

"Yes. I have a name. If we have to hightail it, I don't want him worrying about his daughter. I promised him that from the beginning. Get her to Sweden, I'll feel a lot safer."

"Anything else?"

Haugland mounted the bike and straddled it. "He's suspicious about a man named Odd Sorting. He's connected with a boat going from Frøya to the Shetlands. I've seen him a few times here. He's curious about me, but I think he's more interested in Kjell. His chance meeting with Bent Kjelstrup in Trondheim two months ago upset something. I'm going to ask London."

"I'd suggest our Uncle in Stockholm. I'll send along your request."

"Thanks. It may be nothing, but Kjell's an old hand in the fishing community, and if he feels Sorting is not quite right, I have to go along. Look, I've got to go."

***

Back inside, Kjell provided Tommy with a pair of dungarees and shirt.

"Jens thought you'd need them. No one comes up to talk to him, but just in case, you'll look like everyone else around here."

"*Takk.*" Tommy spoke in Norwegian.

He undressed, carefully folding his uniform jacket on the bed. When he was changed, the two men sat back down at the table. They talked for nearly an hour about the area and its people, the movements of German soldiers, and the known and suspected quislings before the conversation changed. It became more relaxed and personal. Tommy asked about Kjell and his family and was rewarded with anecdotes about them and village life.

"How about you?" Kjell asked. "How long have you been in the service of the king?"

"Since the beginning of `41," Tommy answered. "I was in the reserves during the invasion and saw action during the short war. I was wounded and captured during the fighting around Namsos, then a POW for a while, but I was released along with many others on Hitler's birthday. I was allowed to return home, but I got involved early on with other ex-servicemen trying to reach British advisors on what to do. When things got too—ah—difficult, I went over. That's when I met Jens. We trained together in Scotland. He hasn't told you much, has he?"

"*Nei.*"

"Does that bother you? You mustn't take offense, you know. He does it out of regard for you. He's very disciplined that way."

Kjell shrugged. "It's all right. Jens is always urging security, insisting we practice all the time so it will be natural and easy to carry off under the duress of any serious action."

"He's right, you know. He knows what the lack of security or carelessness in security can do. I probably shouldn't tell you, but twice there were serious actions against members of his family from such breaches. A relation was executed. It's hurt him deeply."

"That's terrible. Poor Jens. I'm so very sorry to hear that. Very sorry. I know he's right," Kjell went on, "yet I've wondered about him. I think I know him better than he realizes."

"Oh?"

"*Ja*, sure. I know he's educated, in speech and by the things we've talked about. He's no ordinary agent out of Oslo. He is a highly disciplined young man. Like yourself."

"Except he walks a much thinner line than I do," Tommy said. "Him being always in civilian dress, a firing squad is a heartbeat away, but you know that from the risks you take yourself."

Kjell looked down at his rough hands. "It's something that must be done. So many hardships: food and fuel shortages, fish quotas, and regulations. It's terrible seeing little children so thin, people's homes confiscated, schools closed, but these things one can bear because I think the worst hardship is the fear to trust anyone. Trust is such a delicate thing, but maybe it's the truest freedom."

Kjell sighed. "I'm just a simple fisherman. I don't really understand politics. I just want to be able to say and think what I want again. I want to be able to say these things without looking over my shoulder or judging whether I should speak to anyone at all. It's a freedom to be able to truly trust someone like I trust Jens. And for those of us who resist, sometimes it's the only thing we have."

Tommy nodded. "The truest freedom. I can't say I disagree."

CHAPTER 29

On the first Sunday in July, the fishermen of Fjellstad held a meeting after service. The issue was fishing. Many were undecided whether to go.

Haugland arrived late and sat down in a corner of the old wood church. Immediately, he felt Sorting's eyes on him so he feigned difficulty in following the talk and finally put his cap over his eyes. It was bad enough having Sorting listen to men speak freely, but he had troubles of his own. Let Sorting think him dozing in the pew, unable to understand.

"The fuel shortage's worse since the Normandy Allied invasion," Bugge Grande was saying. "As if the Germans aren't already restricting oil to a day's supply so we won't take off."

"Sail's fine, but sometimes it takes power to get out to the fishing grounds," Kjell said.

"I don't like the new fishing quotas," growled a fisherman in a voice Haugland didn't recognize. "They take too much. I wonder why we fish at all, especially for herring."

"I know, Helmer. We've got to eat," Bugge said, "but where do you draw the line?"

Haugland shifted in his seat, adjusting his cap so he could see. He mulled over what they were talking about. Fish was used to make margarine for families, their only source of fat. The Germans just took it for glycerin, which was used for war.

"That isn't all they get," another man said, making a sour face. "How much herring do they need for the *Wehrmacht* and naval stations here? That's a couple hundred thousand men."

"What do you think, Helmer?" Bugge asked.

"I say we shouldn't let them take the damn fish." Haugland wondered if the fisherman remembered it was in a church.

After the meeting, Haugland and a small group followed Kjell into his warehouse where they discussed fishing conditions some more. Sorting squeezed his way in with Bugge Grande.

"I have to go," said Kjell. "I need the money."

He started to say something else, when someone poked his head in the warehouse door.

"Sheriff Fasting's back." With that the group broke up, wishing all "*God fiske*." Around Fjellstad that was said almost as frequently as "*God dag*." A good catch was as important as a good day. Haugland hoped Sorting would get lost.

***

The next day Kjell and Haugland met Sig Haraldsen and his sons off the bare coast of the island of Hitra. In tandem their three boats proceeded further north to fish. The weather was good and the visibility excellent. In the golden morning light the large island looked sharp-edged and lavender. To the northwest the horizon was clear, with no signs of patrol planes. Haugland helped Kjell with his net, then went below. He was in the crew's quarters when he heard Sig and his sons come on board. "All the nets are down," the old man said. "Where's Jens?"

Haugland was waiting for them at the little table. Sitting against the pine-paneled wall of the quarters, he gave them the most formidable and commanding stance he could muster.

"*Væ så snill*" Haugland said.

Holger, who had entertained them all on Constitution Day with his poetry. gasped.

The other brother, Sverre, just frowned, though he too had been shocked by the look of his pale lips. He was a lean, fair-headed man in his late thirties. A chair was drawn up for Sig, but the brothers chose to sit on the bunk. Haugland sensed both a polite wariness and suspicion.

"I apologize for the ruse, gentlemen," Haugland said, "but it's been necessary all these months. And for security reasons it will, of course, continue when you return to your boats."

"Who are you?" Sverre disregarded his elderly father's scowl of disapproval.

"Jens Hansen will do. I was sent out several months ago to prepare for liberation."

"Liberation," Sverre spat. "The last time this happened, whole operations were exposed."

"I know. Up to now, Kjell and I have worked alone. Everything has been secret."

Sverre shrugged, but to show he was open to what Haugland had to say, took out his pipe and began stuffing it. The fisherman studied him over his pipe.

"You have hidden yourself well—Jens," Sverre said, "but how do we know you are who you say you are?"

"Only my word and Kjell's. I have nothing to impress you, which I think is the honest thing." Haugland eased back in his chair. "If you are uncomfortable, then go back to your boat and we'll say nothing."

Haugland looked straight at Sverre. After a moment, the older man had to lower his eyes.

"That won't be necessary," the fisherman said. "We have thought for a long time that something should be done. We are in this together."

"My son, despite his advanced years of thirty-six," Sig interrupted, "is still a hothead. He asks too many questions and shows no respect."

"I'm not offended," Haugland said. "So you'll stay?"

"*Ja*, I'll stay, but I want to know who you are with." He poked his pipe at Haugland.

"With the British, our true government's allies." Haugland went on to explain his role in working with the Shetland Bus. "We have been inactive during the white nights, but the time is coming when the mission will expand and we need your help."

"What do you want us to do?" Holger asked.

"Help us receive and store materials. You'll be required to move up and down the *Trondheimsleia*. We realize you'll need fuel beyond your ration. It's already stored in a secret place and I can get more."

"This material," Sverre asked, "is arms and munitions, isn't it? Who is it intended for?"

"I can't tell you that, although it will benefit the new Home Forces in some way...."

Their questions came fast and heated. Haugland calmly answered with what he could tell them letting the discussion drift over to Sig's corner, as he hoped it would. The old man might not be physically up to actually moving the arms, but he had a fine head for details. Soon a plan developed. With Kjell's probing, the group came up with some new sites for arms plus a place where extra fuel could be collected and stored. Haugland told them of another task: housing a radio operator.

"There hasn't been a radio operator in the islands for a long time, but we need to increase surveillance of German traffic in and out of Trondheimfjord. The Allies want their convoys to Altafjord and Tromsø to the north disrupted, as well as continue to track U-boat and destroyer traffic in the North Sea. One is being sent. He'll need to be housed."

"I can look into that." Sverre seemed more interested and involved. "Tell me," he asked, "when do you think the Germans will capitulate? This August? September?"

Haugland hesitated, not wanting to break their confidence. "Look, even though the Germans are taking a beating on the Eastern front they will fight like the Devil once the Allies break out from the coast of France, and the Rhine is in sight."

"But we will win. The Allies will win," Holger said.

"On the continent," Haugland answered. "But there are Nazi fanatics who will not give up. They will look to Norway because we have become *Festung Norwegan.* While German troops in the east are exhausted, their troops here are rested. They have always been the best disciplined of the troops in the occupied countries." He inclined his head at Sverre. "Hitler himself has seen to that. Capitulation will be hard for them and their naval counterparts."

"So you think it'll take longer, Jens?" Holger asked.

"A lot of it hinges on Allied advances, but *ja*, I think so." Haugland knew his thoughts were often in contrast to the opinions of higher ups in the resistance, but it was what he believed. He decided to soften his words. "All I am asking of you is to plan for the worst scenario—that of a longer, drawn out occupation. It will be a devilish time, but we will succeed."

"What about you, Jens?" Sig asked. "What do you want?"

He said the first thing that came to mind. "I want to go home." Wherever that was.

CHAPTER 30

A few days later, Anna went on an equally important rendezvous. She had sent a letter requesting to see "Uncle Felix" three weeks ago, not long after her meeting with Ella at the church. Now she had his answer. She was to book passage to Trondheim on the coastal steamer on the eleventh of July. She would take a stateroom, requesting a certain number.

That part was easy, but she had to swallow her pride again and find a place for Lisel down in the village. After hard persuasion, she was able to get Marthe Larsen, the head cook at the hotel, to watch Lisel for the three days she would be gone. She promised her money, but also knew the cook had once been a housekeeper for Einar's grandfather, Jarle Fromme. She played on that connection. Lisel was still sleepy, wrapped in blankets when Anna handed her over.

Now Anna was on the steamer, a large, comfortable ship that had seen a lot of service up and down the coast long before the Germans came. Anna knew it was part of the highway that went the long length of the Norwegian West Coast. Dressed in a warm coat over a floral printed dress and a much-treasured pair of stockings and shoes she had bought over a year ago at great cost, she was as nervous as a schoolgirl.

Anna leaned against the rail. Even in July, there were spots of snow in the very high reaches above the coastline. Along the blue-gray shore, isolated farmhouses and fishing huts painted red or yellow sat on rocky, micro-sized acreage. Some fishing boats were out. Around their fishholds swarms of gulls dipped and swooned across the choppy blue waters, searching for easy pickings. Their cries were so joyful that Anna was soon caught up in their play. For the first time in months, she felt truly lighthearted, a terrible weight lifting from her shoulders.

Picking up her valise, she went in search of a steward to get her key and settle into her stateroom belowdecks. Down the nearly deserted hall, she found it. Closing the door behind her, she laid the valise on the single bunk bed next to an ancient porcelain sink. She sat down on the only chair, but she didn't have to wait long. A knock startled her. "*Ja?*" She rose quickly.

"*Zu Ihren Diensten, gnädige Frau,*" a man's voice answered in German on the other side of the door. "At your service." He asked her to open the door, repeating the phrase. Cautiously, she unlocked the door. Outside was a soldier in the *Wehrmacht.*

"*Bitte...*" he continued in German, "Please follow me. Your uncle wishes to see you."

He led her down the dimly lit passage and along another corridor. He stopped in front of a door, snapping his heels together.

For the briefest moment she hesitated. Up to now, her trip had been an adventure, a much-needed change in her narrow life, but the enemy was there in that room, no matter how friendly to her. It was the *Wehrmacht* that occupied the country, manned the batteries, and garrisons, and sent commandos into the countryside to raid dairy farms and potato fields. It was the soldiers who came and took Einar away. She felt suddenly very uneasy.

The officer was not much older than she was. He seemed anxious to get her into the room. She stepped into a short hallway. The soldier closed the door, leading the way into a generous room where a man in his late fifties sat at a large desk. He was a colonel and a soldier of the old Prussian school, his gray hair cut short, his field-gray uniform immaculate. He had a handsome Aryan face with clear blue eyes. When he saw Anna, he stood up and smiled warmly at her.

"Anna. *Spatz. Du bist aber sehr hübsch geworden.*" He held his arms out to her.

"You are 'Uncle Felix'? *Mein Gott*, how wonderful!" Anna flew into his arms and embraced him affectionately. Joachim von Weber was not only a family friend, but a distant cousin of her father's. To her, he was a beloved uncle.

"So," he continued in German, "you are surprised? You didn't guess?" He motioned for her to sit down at a comfortable chair near the desk, then ordered his aide to bring some tea.

"*Nein*, I had no idea." Anna spoke German with some difficulty, as she used it infrequently now.

Von Weber smiled. "If you wish, we can speak in Norwegian, although mine is quite pitiful. Or English, which is worse."

"Oh, I don't care," Anna said. "I'm so happy. How is Pappa?"

"He's well. He has written again, but it is very dangerous to do so."

The aide brought a teapot to the table and poured cups for each of them. Von Weber sat back down at his desk. "Ah, thank you, Horst. Anna, this my aide, O*berleutnant* Klein."

The young man bowed to her, his brown forelock falling near his eyebrow. After he left, von Weber said, "He's a good young man. Totally trustworthy."

Anna sipped her tea. The paneled room was well-appointed with many fine pieces of furniture. She wondered if other traveling members of the *Wehrmacht* used the room.

"Now let us talk, as there is little time." Von Weber clasped his hands in front of him on the desk like he was a schoolmaster. "Your father and I have always been like brothers, even sharing the same political views, but wisely he let me think you had died in a car crash like your dear mother, Margaret. Then in the fall of 1940 when I was on leave, we met secretly in Berlin. He heard that I was assigned to southern Norway at Lillehammer and asked that I help him. Imagine my joy to hear you were alive. By then, of course, his plan to keep you safe had been upset by Norway being brought into the political sphere of the Reich."

Anna wasn't sure how to answer that. Norway wasn't exactly a willing participant in a pan-Germanic state. It had been seized so underhandedly.

"Now you are in difficulty again, I understand," von Weber continued. "How unfortunate that your husband chose to become involved in illegal activities. Very unwise. It has made the Gestapo look at you very closely. It has also stirred the interest of another unexpected source—the Norwegian resistance."

Anna gasped. "The resistance? But why?" She stopped. Of course, she knew why. The rumors. "Do you know this for sure?"

"I know that inquiries were made. This is a strange war, Anna. I am a soldier and I do my duty as a soldier, but I am not altogether unsympathetic to the protestations of the people in this country. I detest the Nazi machine and what it has done to Germany—I have come into contact with strange bedfellows. I can say no more— except to say that I have been made aware of an inquiry about you by the resistance."

Anna blanched, frightened by his words. "And the Gestapo?"

"No one is safe from the Gestapo, not even myself. It is difficult to make inquiries without becoming the object of an inquiry in turn. And I'm afraid your husband's actions have upset the balance of things and have put you in danger. Your father as well."

Anna sat very still in her chair and gripped its arms. Tears spilled down her cheeks. "I'm sorry. It has been very hard for me. I loved him very much." She sniffed, then looked directly at him. "Please do not speak of him as though he were a pariah, someone separate from me. I respect his decision to resist. Dear God! I wish I had known! Over and over I felt I let him down." She stopped talking and wept.

"Anna. You must stop now." The old Prussian got up and came around the desk. He put his arms around her and kissed the top of her head. After a while, he gave her a handkerchief. At a small table where some bottles of liquor were arranged, he poured some whiskey into a crystal shot glass and ordered her to drink it. She did so with a sputter.

He sat on the edge of the desk. "*Herzle*... my dear Anna. I'm so sorry. I didn't mean to be callous, but I have to protect you and your father. I just can't ignore your husband hiding arms. As an officer, I would have been bound to assist in his arrest, although I would have loathed turning him over to the Gestapo. I deeply regret his death
and the grief it has caused you. Why don't you tell me about Einar and your life in Norway?"

Anna talked for a long time. Morning stretched into lunchtime, so von Weber summoned Klein. Klein brought sandwiches and soup. They continued until their passage to Trondheim was nearly over.

"Now," he finally said, "the matter of getting you and your daughter out of Norway to Sweden. I believe that it can be arranged, the proper visas and papers made up and approved, but it could take a couple of weeks. Once there, if you were able to contact relatives in America through the Red Cross, it would be doubly better. I'll let you know how we will do it as soon as I can. Perhaps in a few days."

Anna thanked him. "If Einar hadn't died, I would stay. I do love Norway very much, but I must do what is best for my daughter."

"I agree." The old soldier stood up and went over to the little table. As he poured wine into two glasses for them he said, "Let us drink to safe passages for all of us. You see, this may be the last time I can help you. Your father is heavily guarded, his position quite impossible. He can't write any more. It's too dangerous, and I... well, there is a strong chance I may be called over to Germany. That is why I wish to do this now. There may never be another chance."

Anna returned to her room not long after, feeling strangely purged of grief. There was a future to look forward to. She went back unaccompanied. There was no one in the passageway except for a bespectacled man who bumped into her as she left von Weber's suite.

She stayed in her room until the boat was well into Trondheimfjord, then went up to watch the approach into the harbor. She looked for "Uncle Felix," but she never saw him again.

Once in Trondheim, Anna walked from her *pensionat* to the marketplace. It was a warm, fine day. At all the corners were stalls filled with flowers and fish and anything else the Germans permitted during these times. There was a mix of local townspeople and people from the farmlands and the *Bymarka*, the countryside east of the town, as well as soldiers and sailors from the German occupation forces. What a pretty town, she thought. She purchased some *kolbrot* at a stall and headed south to the cathedral, unaware she was being followed.

***

Torstein had noticed her as she came out of the quarters of *Oberst* von Weber, and out of curiosity, purposely bumped into her to confirm his suspicion. It didn't make him feel any better to know he was right. It was Anna Fromme, the one he had seen in the pictures at the cabin with Lars and Tore Haugland.

Torsein had been sent by S-G, the security branch of the resistance, to tail the German colonel and check on his activities. In the five weeks since the Normandy invasion, important information continued to be sent by von Weber to the resistance in Oslo. The information was reliable, but they were cautious about him. Von Weber was very useful, but there were several who trusted him only so far. He wasn't tainted by Nazi doctrines, but he was a professional soldier, and that counted for something. He would act ultimately in the best interests of his own country.

Discovering Anna Fromme on board, Torstein decided he would follow her if she disembarked in Trondheim. Lars Haugland, he felt, would want to know. When she did get off, he shadowed her as she wandered about the city. Torstein hoped to discover some intrigue about her, but after a while it was apparent that she was on holiday. Torstein decided to follow her for the rest of her stay anyway.

At one point, after purchasing a newspaper, Anna Fromme sat in a *konditori* and pored over what Torstein thought were ads. From across the street, he watched her make circles on a page, then pay her bill and head north. A few blocks later, she knocked on a door and was let in. Five minutes later, she emerged with a small child's scooter. She took off again, at one point coming directly back at him before she went west. For a moment he lost her, but found her going into a large residence that turned out to the *Hjemme for Døve*—Home for the Deaf. She stayed inside for some time, coming out only when a taxi showed up.

"Damn," Torstein muttered when she climbed in and took off with the scooter beside her. He was left flat footed in the street. He prayed she was returning to her *pensionat* and was relieved when she did. The next day she continued to visit the few tourist attractions and out to lunch. Finally, she returned to her *pensionat* and at one o'clock, on her last day, took the trolley back out to the steamship landing, carrying her valise and the scooter. Forty minutes later she was gone on the southbound coastal steamer.

At the train station, he bought a ticket for the southbound Oslo train and settled down for the long trip home. Nothing may have happened in Trondheim, but she was from Fjellstad, and the meeting with von Weber could affect the one who had the most to lose.— Tore Haugland.

CHAPTER 31

Not long after meeting the Haraldsens, Haugland slipped away to the *fjell* to see Tommy. His cabin was in a place so wild and barren that only heather, moss, grasses, and the occasional dwarf birch grew there. In winter, deep snow made it totally inhospitable except to a certain sort of men like Tommy who could take advantage of its frozen desolation, men who could live with its moods and be comfortable skiing many miles for wood and substenance. It was also in a restricted zone, so few hiked in to admire mountains that rolled on and on, leaving foot pads of little swamps and bigger lakes in their wakes and occasionally bumping into the long fingers of fjords.

Between making plans and exploring the area, the two friends unwound. Haugland had some of the books the *Hitra* had brought over. Tommy had a receiver. They spent their quiet times reading C.S. Forester and P.G. Wodehouse or listening to music and news from the BBC. Or they would take a net and go to one of the little lakes to fish for trout and lie half-naked on the rocks taking in the sun. They could have been on a different planet for all they cared —the Nazis far away. The only reminder of the war was the W/T. Haugland was on unrestricted call.

Upon his return to Fjellstad, Haugland stopped first at the *landhandel* to pick up Kjell's mail. He was surprised to find a package and a fishing catalogue addressed to him, but was even more surprised to find the store completely deserted except for *Fru* Andersson who greeted him in her usual overbearing way of mistress to a simpleton. It wasn't until he headed down to Kjell's warehouse that he understood why the *landhandel* was empty.

Outside of the *konditori,* a group of fishermen stood under the watchful eye of Sheriff Fasting. Another group was outside Kjell's office. Haugland nodded at them and went inside.

"Jens." Kjell sat at the table with two fishermen from the village. One of them was a fair-haired, wiry man in his mid-twenties. Haugland remembered him from the meeting at the church.

Trouble? he signed.

"You remember Helmer Stagg. He's Petter Stagg's cousin." Kjell wanted him to know just what the trouble was about. The *på skauen* boys.

"Fasting arrested my uncle," Helmer said, "because Petter ran away."

"There's a patrol out looking for Per and Karl. Arne's been taken." Kjell spoke deliberately for their charade, and Haugland quickly responded with his hands and fingers.

Tell more. He sat down quietly by the warehouse door.

Helmer turned to him. "We thought they were secure, but Arne was still sick and thought he'd do better if he turned himself in. Only Fasting made him tell them where they were hiding." His tortured look softened briefly. "I'm told you helped the boys."

Haugland found his notebook. He wrote Uncle?

"They took him to Trondheim with Arne yesterday afternoon. My grandfather, the schoolmaster, is under house arrest." He tapped Haugland's arm to make him look at him. "But don't you worry, Jens. I'll vouch for your whereabouts these past weeks. Hopefully, the other two boys took off as soon as they found Arne missing."

Haugland hoped they did too. If they moved up to a cave or packed out with their essentials, they might have a chance. He wished he could warn Tommy. He didn't like the idea of a patrol heading south to his hideout, although if it was an all-German patrol, they might not go too far in. Writing quickly, he asked if they had a Norwegian guide.

"I think so," Helmer said.

When they were gone, Kjell said, "Welcome back."

Walking into his former room, Haugland said in a low voice, "Gone three days, and all hell breaks loose." He sat down on his old bed facing the outside door. "What's this patrol?"

"They're tough. *Wehrmacht* from Kristiansund N. Fifteen in all." Kjell came in and sat down on a stool. "Fishing's allowed, but there's a nine o'clock curfew."

"Anything said about me? Any inquiries to where I was?"

"*Nei*, but then I don't know if Arne said anything about you."

Haugland picked up the fishing catalogue and looked at the cover. "I think Fasting would have arrested more than the boy and his father if he talked."

"I should have never gotten you involved with the boys."

"Never mind. What's done is done." He felt tired, aching like he was getting a cold.

Kjell went into the office. "You look bushed. Are you going to stay down here?" He reached for his coffeepot, dropping it on the stove when someone knocked on the door. It was Bugge Grande asking for Kjell. Kjell grabbed his coat and went outside.

When Haugland was sure they were gone, he picked up the package. It was a small box, wrapped in brown paper and mailed from Trondheim the day before he left for Tommy's cabin. Inside were two delicate, hand-tied fish flies. Underneath, he found a card with the words: "Thank you for your help. Your friend, Anna Fromme."

He didn't know quite what to think. He didn't want anyone getting any ideas, so he crumpled up the card and wrapping paper and put them into the woodstove.

Back in the room, he picked up the box. He hadn't been at her farm in almost two weeks, staying away purposefully, but now with the box in his hand, he thought of her the evening of the downpour. He put the box in his pocket.

Kjell came back in. "The fishing association has put together a fund for Ingrid Stagg so she can go to Trondheim to be near her husband. She'll go out on the next coastal steamer."

Haugland clapped him on his shoulder. Be strong, he signed. He drew Kjell deeper into the room. "We have to keep a normal routine," he said under his breath. "Only I can't be down here on the nineteenth." He made the sign for phone call. "London. I'm getting a new time frame for the Shetland Bus when they resume."

He craned his neck, listening for sounds. "It's not safe to talk here. Come up and we'll firm up plans if everything collapses."

CHAPTER 32

Anna put the last sweater and pair of socks into the valise and closed it shut. It had been very difficult to decide what to leave and what to take. She wasn't only leaving the country, she was leaving five and a half years of her life with the only man she had ever loved. She decided to take things that would be important to Lisel. She chose an album from their married years, Einar's picture from the bedroom, his pipe, and a selection of uncensored books. She also took one of his bulky sweaters, both for its warmth and the comfort it gave knowing it was his.

Uncle Felix had come through sooner than she'd ever dreamed. Two days after she got back, she received word that she was to once again book passage to Trondheim where his aide, Klein, would meet her and Lisel. They would cross over by train into Sweden some sixty miles away, she as the Norwegian dependent of a soldier. Once there she would disappear, resurfacing with a different identity. She would be spared the refugee camps for Norwegians and placed in a Swedish home for the duration of the war. She had to go in eight days. Since the Normandy invasion, Sweden was less neutral.

She stood by the kitchen window. On the little porch, wooden boxes overflowed with an assortment of flowers and one lonely potato plant put in by Lisel. Who will water my gardens? What would happen to the farm for that matter? The cats? She hadn't told Lisel anything. They would just go and not come back. No one must know.

A knock at the back door startled her. She wasn't expecting anyone. Checking on the parlor door as she passed, she went out to the entryway. It was the deaf fisherman.

"*Herr* Hansen. *God aften.*" She pushed open the screen door, stepping down to the ground. "Did you come to see Lisel?"

I see you, he motioned. See you. He made sounds in his throat, the clearest she had ever heard. His eyes were tired but friendly.

Suddenly, she felt ashamed leaving without seeing him again. Had he not been a friend? And the exhausting work he had done. All for nothing.

She wondered if guilt was written all over her face because he looked at her curiously. She stepped out and closed the screen door.

He reached into his pants pocket and took out a little box. *Takk.*

You're welcome, Anna signed. She beamed when he started. "Did you understand me?"

He quickly signed back.

"No fair. I don't know that one." She laughed at his confusion, then put out her hand. "I'm sorry. I wasn't making fun of you. Do you like them?" She pointed to the box.

He signed a few motions close to his heart. Then he wrote: Where you get them?

She hesitated, feeling quite afraid. Sitting down on the top stair, she tucked her farm dress under her. "I was in Trondheim."

He wrote: You know someone there?

"*Nei.* I've never been there before. It was the first time I traveled without my husband. It was so lonely. You see, I used to travel a lot with him."

Hansen sat down on a crate by the steps and scribbled quickly. Do you miss him?

Anna should've been startled at his great leap in subject, but she was used to him now. He didn't mean to be rude. He was just honest and direct and said what he thought. He was deaf.

The rules of convention, she thought, *must be difficult to understand because they are either spoken or implied.* If they weren't written down, how would he know? It would be the same if he were to ask if boiling water made noise, why didn't a sunbeam?

Suddenly, she found herself telling Hansen about Einar's arrest and the week of terror that followed. She told it simply, much like the way she had told her uncle, but she also told of the darker things and suspicions she had, something she had never been able to do with anyone before. When she finished, she began to weep. Quiet tears rolled down her cheeks.

"Excuse me," she said, swiping them away with her fingers. "I didn't mean to impose on you." She sniffed and dabbed her eyes with her apron. "You are so kind."

Hansen remained unusually quiet, but his eyes seemed to be summing her up. Finally, he picked up his pencil and wrote: Strangers come to your house?

"*Nei.* Only friends or maybe some of Einar's students. Why do you ask?"

Hansen's face gave no answer.

"I'm getting cold," Anna finally said. "Would you like to come in? There's something I would like to show you. Say yes, Herr Hansen."

He wrote: If you call me Jens.

"I'd like that… Jens. Please call me Anna." She offered her hand and he shook it.

***

Haugland waited in the *stue*, but as soon as he was sure she was down the bedroom hallway, he stepped back to the parlor door and opened it. Quickly, he looked behind the door.

In the shadows were two suitcases and a book box apparently packed. He closed the door, wiping the doorknob with a handkerchief. At the edge of the kitchen, he looked at the bookcase between the hallways. The wedding picture was missing.

He tapped the knuckles of his left hand. His insides were about as calm as a minor squall. Only two hours ago he had decoded Lars's message inside the fishing catalogue. His brother had summed up Torstein Kaaland's report and warned him of Anna Fromme's meeting with a *Wehrmacht* colonel on the coastal ferry. Torstein had followed her in Trondheim. "Be careful around her," Lars wrote.

Like hell. It had taken all the effort in the world to hide the emotions of grief and hatred that tore through him. He felt her grief and fears were genuine, but why then, did she lie about not meeting anyone on her trip? And where was she going now?

"Jens?" She was back in the room. She put her hand lightly on his arm. He decided her smile annoyed him because he liked it. She said his name in a such a charming way—"Yins."

"See what I have?" She held out a card and book to him. He took the small book and turned it over in his hands. A book of signs. He knew it well.

Point to the dog. Make the sign. Touch the table. Make the sign. The dog is on the table. How am I doing, uncle?

"I stumbled across a *Hjemme for Døve.* They gave me this card and book when I said I had a friend I wanted to talk to."

Haugland took the card showing the signs for the twenty-nine letters in the Norwegian alphabet. *Who is she?* he thought: the warm considerate woman that buys him hand-tied flies and wants to talk to him, to make him part of the human race or—agent provocateur?

Haugland stayed for an hour. Anna genuinely wanted him to be there, but Haugland also sensed ambivalence. The suitcases worried him. Did her contact with the *Wehrmacht* officer have something to do with them? When she said good-bye and somehow he felt that she meant it beyond its casual use. He was never going to see her again.

CHAPTER 33

As it turned out, Haugland had other things to worry about. Back home, he tried to eat a light supper of potatoes and some tinned meat Tommy had given him, but the need to sleep after his long hike was too strong. Lying down with the pistol under his pillow, he slept until eight, waking up as stiff as dried cod. His throat felt scratchy.

Had he heard a sound? He rolled heavily to the edge of the bed and listened. It was still light out as it would be until after ten. The sounds of pine trees stirring outside the one glass window in the cabin now opened, but above them came the thud of boots on the pine needle-covered path. Aching, he felt for his gun, then relaxed when Kjell knocked the V-for-Victory— da-da-da-daw. He had come after all.

On the doorstep at the back of the cabin, the two men sat down. "Nothing's changed in the village," Kjell said. "It's still very tense."

"I think it's time we talk about getting Kitty out. Tommy's been working on this. We'll send her south for a while, then over to Sweden. She'll be with a family and treated well."

Kjell picked at a scab on his hand. "When do you want this to happen?"

"As soon as possible. No later than the end of August."

"What about my Rika?"

"Rika's in Trondheim and hardly connected to the resistance. She knows nothing of our activities. That should at least keep her safe. I will be sure export is aware of her, though."

Kjell looked down at his big hands. "This matter of the boys has worried you, hasn't it?"

"I'd hate to be mentioned as an afterthought. It all depends on if Arne talks. Those aren't terribly good odds. As for Kitty, for now, the *seter* will be the safest place for her. I…"

Suddenly, Haugland put out his hand. He pointed to a place above the woodshed. Something there, he signed. He gripped the pistol in his pocket. With his left hand, he signed, Talk more. Fish talk.

While Kjell talked, Haugland slipped behind the shed and up into the pine forest. Haugland ducked and slipped between thin trees full of long, soft needles boasting new rubbery growth. At a clearing at the top of a rise he stopped to listen. There was a slight creak and suddenly something heavy slammed against him from behind. He instinctively reached at the arm going around his throat and shifting his weight threw the intruder over his shoulder to the ground.

"Ayeeh," the ragged figure cried as he landed hard on the ground.

Still moving, Haugland swung around with his gun drawn, aiming it point blank at a second intruder. It was Petter Stagg, one of the missing *på skauen* boys. By the time Kjell came bursting onto the scene brandishing an axee, Haugland had everyone on their feet and was roughly half-pushing, half-hauling the two dirty, ill-clad figures toward the trail.

"Well, well," Kjell said to them. "What happened?"

"Karl thought Jens was Gestapo so he jumped him," Petter said. "Not such a good idea."

"Jens, didn't you hit him too hard?" A welt on Karl's face was rising.

"Jens didn't hit him. He flipped him." Petter stumbled down and stopped to catch his breath. Haugland gave Karl needed support.

"What in the hell are you doing here anyway?" Kjell asked Petter, taking a cue from Haugland's stern face. "There's a patrol out looking for you."

"We know. We saw it yesterday. We only meant to get some food, then head on south. Jens helped us before. I thought..." Petter's voice dropped to a whisper. "It's Arne, isn't it?"

"*Ja*," Kjell said. "He was arrested yesterday."

Karl groaned. "We won't stay long. I..." The boy began to waiver on his feet. Haugland held him tighter and motioned Kjell to return to the cabin.

Inside the cabin, Haugland heated up leftovers while Kjell went back and located their rucksacks in the trees. The boys sat on the bunk leaning up against the log wall. Both looked thin and tired, and in need of a bath. Especially Karl. His face was haggard and pale, like an old man. Haugland suspected vitamin deficiency.

By the time Kjell got back, the food was on the table. All this time, Haugland said nothing, but he was aware of Petter's eyes on him. The boy was no fool. He knew something was going on, yet at the same time had the common sense not to ask questions.

"Have you seen my mother?" Karl asked as he stabbed his potatoes with a fork. "I wish I could get a message to her tonight."

"You can't," Kjell answered. "There's a curfew."

"Curfew?" Petter looked up. "Why?"

"There have been arrests. Your father for one, Petter" Kjell said gently as he could.

"Father! I've got to turn myself in." Petter rose from the table, knocking his plate awry.

"Don't be stupid," Haugland said a harsh voice.

Karl's fork clattered to his metal plate. Petter sat back down in his chair with a thud.

"This is not a game," Haugland continued, exasperated and bone-tired. "There are no rules, no legal system. You resisted the mobilization. You'll be arrested. What would that prove? You can't help your father and now we can't let you go back. Not after what you've seen and heard."

He stood up and checked his pistol. The silence that followed was thunderous. The *på skauen* boys stared at each other then at Kjell who sat stony-faced and unmoving.

"You can't stay here," Haugland said. "In no way can we be associated with you. Already there's danger that Arne might say something about me helping you."

"Can't we at least stay the night?" Karl asked. "We're tired."

"I know you are," Haugland answered more gently, "but you must go at once. I have a friend I'll take you to, but I must have your word of honor that you'll say nothing about this afterwards. Our lives and the lives of your families will depend on it, as well as this man here and myself." He gave the boys a sharp look, anger barely contained in his voice, but he softened again. "You can rest for a bit, then we'll go fast. I can't be too long from the village." With that he got up and went outside.

***

They were up on the barren *fjell* in an hour after leaving, carefully concealing their flight as much as possible in the mid-summer light. There was no talking. Haugland was in little mood for it. His cover had been blown. All because of a couple of lost boys. At four in the morning, they reached Tommy's cabin. Standing in the chilly morning air, Haugland whistled the "V" for Victory" before the door opened to them.

"Scarlett," Tommy said. He stepped back like he had been hit, his Sten gun out to his side. "Jesus, who the hell are they? You look as bad as they do. What happened?"

"Evading *på skauen* boys from the village." Haugland pushed past him, the boys following. Sinking to the floor, he was asleep as soon as introductions were over.

He woke to Tommy shaking him on the shoulder. The rough plank floor under him was hard and unforgiving. He had been covered with a blanket. "Scarlett."

Haugland opened his eyes and sat up groggily, feeling worse than when he first lay down. Tommy thrust a tin cup of real coffee into his hands. The flavorful steam woke him. "Nine in the morning," Tommy said in English. "What the hell is going on?"

The two boys were still asleep on the floor in their coats. Haugland struggled to his feet and stretching his back, limped outside into a misty gray morning that prickled with cold moist air.

"Jesus Christ," Tommy said after Haugland explained. "What do you want me to do?"

Sitting on lichen-covered boulders behind the cabin, Haugland fought to stay awake. "Get them to your contact and find a place for them, then export Karl out to Sweden. Petter, I'd keep. He needs fattening up, but he's still fit and a good recruit. Knows how to keep his trap shut."

"What about the boy arrested? Will he keep quiet?"

Haugland shrugged. "I honestly don't know."

"Maybe it's time to get out."

"And not finish? I'd rather stay. Besides, it might be bad to bolt during this turmoil. Create more problems for me and trouble for Kjell."

"Well, I guess you know what you're doing." Tommy put his reddening hands in his knickers pockets.

Haugland sipped the hot liquid. Neither spoke, watching instead the clouds creep down the gray-blue sides of a neighboring mountain. The spare, flat *fjell* spread around them dotted with twiggy heather and rock. A small stand of dwarf birch squashed down by wind provided some cover for them, but a chilly breeze, hinting of moisture, tugged at their clothes.

"Do you have one of these?" Tommy took a pill out of his pocket. The size of an American ten-cent piece, covered with a thin coat of rubber and full of potassium cyainide, it killed in a few seconds.

"Yes," Haugland said. "Usually in my collar. It's supposed to be easy to bite it that way."

Tommy sat down on Haugland's boulder. As long as they had known each other, they seldom talked about suicide. In fact, Haugland found it pretty much universally so throughout the resistance. Everyone knew the Gestapo used torture, so there was an underlying fear of capture. No one added that there was also the fear of not keeping silent.

"I think of being treated so terribly," someone once told him, "like a deep personal humiliation."

Haugland could only imagine, but knowing how his brother had been treated and the rumors of how Einar had died added special torment to his wondering.

Tommy rolled the pill around in his fingers. "I guess you could call this a friend. A guy in Linge Company once said you could swallow it and it would pass through safely. I never heard of anyone volunteering, though. One bite… I almost did once... a pretty tight spot."

"I've been there," was all Haugland said.

They were sitting shoulder to shoulder. Tommy studied Haugland for a moment. "Are you all right? You look lousy."

Haugland cleared his scratchy throat. "I'll be all right. I barely got back from here when *they* showed up. I'll catch up on my beauty sleep when I get back. Gotta go soon."

"Hope you have rain gear. It's going to get wet."

"I've got a poncho." Haugland said nothing about the new boots bothering his feet. He stood up and stretched. "Any more of this?"

"Coffee? Sure. Crumpets too."

"Just send for my taxi... I'm going to wake our young friends up."

Haugland went back inside. Petter was sitting up. "Coffee?" He spoke in Norwegian.

"*Ja, vær så snill.*"

Haugland poured a cup from a pot on the Primus stove then refilled his own. "Here." He leaned against a table set along the wall of the nearly barren cabin.

"Who are you?" Petter asked.

"A friend."

"Can you help my father?"

"*Nei*. I'm sorry."

The boy became silent, his disappointment painfully transparent. "You and Kjell have been in this from the beginning, haven't you? God! You must've thought I was pretty stupid going on about fighting when you were at our camp. I treated you like some dumb moron, but I meant what I said... about wanting to do something."

"I know." Haugland pushed down off from the table. "Why don't you wake Karl. We need to talk."

***

They separated at ten that morning. Hiding all signs of habitation, Tommy headed south with the boys. Haugland went northwest, keeping himself concealed as possible in the barren terrain. The patrol could still be out. The rain eventually hit in one violent blast, socking in the mountains around him, turning everything on the *fjell* slick and gray. As time went on, it became difficult to keep a steady pace. Grasses growing between the rocks became as slippery as ice. Occasionally, he stumbled. The drab poncho covered his torso, but rain soaked his knickers and long wool socks. Finally, he stopped, seeking shelter under a dwarf birch along the trail on the open *fjell*. As he gathered his breath and cooled down, he realized he was in trouble. He wasn't just tired. He was sick and running a fever.

Haugland checked his compass. He was heading due west now, the drop to the tree line less than an hour's hike due to the weather conditions, which he could expect not to change here above this eighteen hundred foot level.

He ate some dried fruit from Tommy's store. The rain had changed to a soft splatter, but he knew that if he stopped for much longer, he would stiffen up again. Already, the backs of his legs were sore and his arms and chest ached. He adjusted his rucksack and stepping out from under the tree, immediately discovered why else he couldn't stay. To the north, he detected movement out in the gray landscape where the clouds were hanging low like a pillowy canopy over the rocky *fjell.*

His cold fingers fumbled in his pocket for his binoculars. He focused on the line. It was the patrol or part of it. He counted nine. They looked like regular troops, not an SS or SD group. He supposed that would be in his favor, but they were well-armed, dressed for the weather, and at this point not too concerned about their comfort. Some appeared engaged in conversation, which he almost could make out. If they continued on in his direction, they could be upon him within fifteen minutes.

Trouble. He had no reason to be up here. This particular area was zoned frontier and though he had a pass to be in the coastal area, he would have some explaining to do about being up here. Right now, due to a pounding head, he didn't feel his mental skills were up to par.

Haugland pulled back from the trail, seeking cover among a line of dwarf birch trees and rubble, then headed west around a low hill. It was rough work for he had to invent his way, sometimes finding old trails which further exhausted him. Each time he stopped his face felt hot and tight. His eyes burned. The air felt unnaturally cool. Eventually at a safe distance, he took out his binoculars again. The party had stopped around someone holding a map. They seemed to be having a heated debate. As he studied them, the other half of the patrol came into view and to his surprise, he discovered they had two prisoners. He didn't recognize them.

Enough, he thought as his body broke into a wave of chills. He withdrew quietly and continued his journey toward the forest edge on the west, reaching it nearly forty minutes later than he should have. When he, at last, arrived at his cabin, he stumbled in to find it deserted.

Of course, Kjell was gone. But Haugland could care less. All he wanted to do was rest. He grabbed a bucket of water from the spring and after taking a long drink, set it by his bed. He removed his oilskins and his boots, then fell into an exhausted, fevered sleep.

CHAPTER 34

When Hansen didn't show up the next day, Kjell got a pass to go out to find him. With the Germans on alert since a patrol came back with some poachers in their midst, it was dangerous to be absent. Worried that Hansen had run into trouble up on the *fjell* with the boys, Kjell drove out in Ella's car and confirmed his worst fears. Stepping into the bone-chilling gloom of Hansen's cabin, Kjell found the blackout curtains shut and Hansen wrapped up in blankets on his bed.

"Jens?"

From the covers, Hansen made a muffled groan.

"What's wrong?" Kjell cried. "You're not hurt, are you?"

"Sick." Hansen whispered. "Too sick to move." There was a spasm of moist, congested coughing, then panting when it ended.

Kjell went over to the table and felt around for the matches and lit the lamp. Sharp light blossomed around the rough room and on Hansen's face. It looked pale and strained. His dark hair, glistening with sweat, lay plastered on his forehead. His eyes were fever bright.

"Good God," Kjell said under his breath, "You're soaked." Hiding his alarm, he went in search of some dry clothes. When he returned to the bed, Hansen had rolled part way out of the blankets. Kjell got him to a sitting position, helping him remove his knit shirt and undershirt. "When did you come down?" Kjell asked as he dried him off.

Hansen mumbled his answer, his head drooping like it was too heavy for him to hold up. Kjell's mouth suddenly went dry. "You've got to let Doctor Grimstad look at you."

"Can't go." Hansen collapsed back on his bed. He moved like every muscle hurt.

"There's been more trouble," Kjell said. "Everyone has to be accounted for tonight. The patrol caught two poachers."

"I know. I saw them on top." Hansen licked his lips. "I can't go. London's calling." Shivering, he looked up at Kjell. "What time is it?"

"It's after five in the afternoon."

"Have to send at nine." Hansen closed his eyes. His breathing was short and shallow. He seemed to shrink into the pillow.

"All right. Curfew's at eight but I've got a pass. How're the boys?"

"With a contact of Leif's," Hansen answered. "It'll be hard having family in prison." He stopped talking. "Sorry. So hot." Screwing up his face, he closed his eyes. Kjell saw tears.

Kjell found a scrap of clean shirting and made a cold compress for Hansen. "Rest, Jens. Go to sleep. I'll wake you up in time. I won't leave you."

Hansen nodded slightly, then went limp. He was soon sound asleep. Kjell got a fire going. He watched Hansen sleep fitfully.

What a fix this is. And with no help for miles around. Kjell felt a depressing weight of danger fall on his shoulders and was glad that the girls were out of the village. They could be counted elsewhere if needed. He pulled the blankets higher up on Hansen's shoulder.

It'll be hard having family in prison. Hansen was talking about himself.

Was Hansen's deaf uncle in prison? Someone else in his family? Once again, Kjell wondered, *Who are you? What sort of private hell are you running from?*

***

A half hour before Hansen was to send his message, Kjell woke Hansen up. Putting on a coat over his feverish body, Hansen plodded outside. Leaning precariously against the shed, he gave Kjell instructions on how to pull the W/T out of the chopping block and open it up. While Kjell got the codebook out of its hiding place, Hansen set up the aerial and got the W/T ready to go. He could barely keep his eyes open and twice, Kjell thought he would pass out.

"Jens, when this is done, I'm taking you down. No arguments. I have Ella's car."

Hansen smiled at him weakly. "None possible." He sat down on a log and coughed.

Just before nine, he put on the headphones and fiddled with the dials. Soon, the transmission from London began and he was busy writing. He decoded his message, made up his answer and sent it back all in the space of a few minutes. After that he seemed to drift.

"Are you done?" Kjell felt awe and respect.

Hansen started with a jerk. "*Ja.* Can you help me put the W/T away?" Once it was secured, he shakily went back into the cabin to close everything up.

Kjell led the way down. Hansen refused support, but halfway down, he abruptly stopped and threw up. Kjell ended up helping him anyway. Once he was resting in the car with a blanket wrapped around him, Kjell fired up the *knottgenerator* and headed back to the village.

They made it as far as the schoolhouse road before German soldiers stopped them. While one of the helmeted soldiers looked over Kjell's pass, the other opened the passenger door and shined his flashlight in Hansen's face even though it was still light out. Hansen winced.

"Who man this?" the soldier asked in broken Norwegian.

"My man," Kjell said. "Jens Hansen. No need talking to him. He's deaf." After a soldier consulted a list, they were allowed to go on to Kjell's house.

Docktor Grimstad came over and examined Hansen in the back room. When he was done, he washed his hands at the kitchen sink. "He'll live. It's not pneumonia—yet." He scrubbed his hands meticulously.

Grimstad was a lean, gray-haired man who was all business on call. "It's some sort of influenza, complicated, I should add, by sheer exhaustion. The fever doesn't help."

"Exhaustion?"

"The man's beat." Grimstad wiped his neatly manicured hands on a clean towel. "I'm not surprised—with all the hiking he's done. His feet are a mess."

Kjell said nothing, but Grimstad was too close to the truth. How soon until he found out? Hans was his best friend, but this was war. At the kitchen table, Kjell poured whiskey into some small glasses. They skoaled each other and savored their first sip.

Grimstad spoke first. "How long have we known each other?"

"Oh, probably since I punched you in *Herr* Thorsen's elementary class. I think it was about marbles."

"Did you take mine or did I take yours?" Grimstad smiled behind his glass.

Kjell chuckled "Maybe. Of course, it could have been about Hetta Martinson. She was pretty even then."

They each took another sip. Outside the kitchen window, the mountain peaks lining the valley were gold and pink. It was nearly ten, but bright as day.

"I gave him something for his fever," Grimstad said. "He should turn around in the next twenty hours, but that congestion. It's worrisome. I haven't ruled out pneumonia yet. Still, he's a tough young man, isn't he? A lot tougher than people realize."

This was more than a comment. Kjell knew he had to be careful.

"It's none of my business, of course," Grimstad continued. "Respiratory illness is common enough around here given the rain, the cold, and the mountains. So are blistered feet. I'm just a little curious about his blisters occurring during the search for our boys. In fact, I was rather hoping that somehow it had something to do with it."

Kjell looked down at his glass and ran his forefinger around its rim. Grimstad went on.

"It's interesting being a country doctor. Even more being *stadslege*_for our area. As County Health Officer and because of my oath, I must treat *jøssing* and quisling alike. Thus, I hear and see many things, have stimulating discussions. Take nutrition. Can a country feed itself solely on a diet of fish, potatoes and bread, especially when that bread is adulterated with chalk? Will the lack of fats cause further harm? How do you feed those in hospital when the Germans confiscate lifesaving items such as eggs? How do you feed those starving boys in the woods?"

"I don't know," Kjell said. "I'm only a fisherman."

"Did I tell you I spoke with Arne when he was brought here for questioning? They asked me to look at him. When we were alone, I asked how they managed to get food. He said he couldn't say, but they did all right."

"Interesting." Kjell stroked the rim of his glass. "What are you trying to say, Hans?"

"Nothing really." Grimstad took a sip of his whiskey. Kjell did the same. It was a forgotten taste because he bought the bottle before the war. It would be costly on the black market.

From the other room, Hansen stirred and coughed fitfully but to Kjell's great relief didn't make any other sound. Instead, the bed creaked as he rolled over on his side and then there was silence.

Kjell closed his eyes and took a drink, hoping Grimstad didn't notice his unease.

"You know, I've always been intrigued by him. He's a lot more intelligent than people think. Works hard in a quiet, unobtrusive way. Keeps to himself. You knew his family?"

"*Ja*." Kjell hated lying to his good friend. "He's a good young man to have around."

"I'm sure he is." Grimstad reached into his coat pocket and took out a prescription pad. "The Germans are going house to house. They could come here at this late hour. They'll ask questions. I don't know how thorough they'll be, but I'd keep his feet covered with socks. My medical report will explain his condition and why he may not have been here yesterday."

"You continue to worry about his feet, Hans."

"I hope to God that Petter and Karl are far from here. Then all this will have been worth it."

Grimstad left a few minutes later. Kjell locked the door and went back to the kitchen deep in thought. His friend had guessed something, but how much did he really figure out? He must have caught onto the food deliveries and perhaps Jens' initial role, but most certainly he suspected Jens's involvement in something concerning the two boys.

Kjell prepared a pitcher of warm water and took it into the room along with a bowl and toweling. Next to the night table, Jens was facing away, curled up in his blankets and shaking. Kjell pushed aside some of Jens' papers on the little stand and in doing so, uncovered his medical card. In one awful moment, he realized what Grimstad really knew or suspected.

The card was a fake.

***

As Grimstad predicted, sometime after eleven, there was banging on the door. Outside in the summer light, Mayor Pederson stood with three German soldiers, one of whom was an officer, who introduced himself as *Oberleutnant* Schiller. Kjell let them into his *stue* where he showed his own papers. He had been dreading this moment since Grimstad left. He had never counted on having a sick man on his hands. Jens was always in control of himself. Now he was not.

The lieutenant was an efficient, but pleasant man. Like some of the regular troops in Norway, Kjell thought he was trying to be as helpful as possible. He was still a young man and with his full red cheeks and limp blonde hair he looked like a baker's son. It didn't change Kjell's distaste or fear of him.

Schiller handed back his papers. "And now your man."

Kjell pointed toward the kitchen and with a pounding heart led the way. At the doorway to the little room, Kjell stopped. "My man is ill and asleep."

"Wake him," Schiller ordered.

Kjell tiptoed over to the bed. The light from the kitchen fell near Hansen's pillows. He was sleeping propped up and with his mouth slightly opened, his breathing sounded shallow and labored. Even in the gloom, his face appeared flushed and tight over his cheekbones. When Kjell picked up Hansen's papers, he stirred and groaned slightly. Kjell prayed he wouldn't open his mouth and start talking.

"He lives with you?"

"*Nei*. He has a place on the fjord road. I brought him here to take care of him."

Schiller shuffled through the papers. "What is wrong with him?" His accent was thick. He used a pencil to note items in the papers and didn't look up as he asked questions.

"He has a high fever. Influenza. You can ask Dr. Grimstad for his report."

Kjell eased onto the side of the bed, turning on the lamp. Hansen started and rolled his head listlessly way from the light. His eyes fluttered and opened. Disoriented, he gradually moved his head like it was a fragile glass ball. Breathing noisily through his mouth, he moved his lips to form words.

Pay attention! Kjell signed, then made the sign for troll, their code for Germans and Nazis. Trolls. Pay attention to me. Trolls!

Hansen furrowed his brow. His parched lips trembled, but he looked straight at Kjell and in a flash of understanding, he inclined his head. Then he signed for water.

Kjell patted his hand, relieved he understood the danger, but it alarmed him that Hansen's hand was hot and the skin dry. "*Ja.*" Kjell reached for the pitcher of water.

"He is awake?" Schiller asked. The German came alongside the bed and looked down at Hansen, then at the photo on the pass. "You are Jens Hansen?"

Hansen didn't respond. Kjell tapped his left shoulder and pointed to the German standing next to the bed, honestly not sure if he was clearheaded enough to follow along. The danger was so overwhelming at that moment of him speaking that Kjell was surprised that everyone else there didn't smell his fear. Your name, he signed.

Hansen listlessly signed it.

"This man is truly deaf?"

"*Ja.*" Kjell gently lifted Hansen's head and gave him a drink of water. Hansen laid back deep in his pillows, his eyes and mouth half closed. He resumed his tortured breathing. Kjell kept a hand on Hansen's arm to keep him focused, gently rubbing it from time to time.

The German looked at the medical card. "He is from Molde?"

"*Ja.*" Kjell put his hands in his pockets to hide their urge to shake.

"Then his card should be updated and certified for this area. See that it is done. That is all." He turned to Pederson. "We are done now. You can join my men outside."

After the soldiers and mayor were gone, Schiller stood by Hansen's bed. "My uncle was a doctor in Leipzig. They had a famous school for the deaf there. Several of my uncle's patients were deaf. Tell me, how does your man get along?"

"Fine." Kjell watched Hansen slowly drift to sleep again, but suddenly was alert to what the German had just said. Did he know sign language? Had he seen him sign a warning to Jens?

"I apologize for your time. Make sure he gets rest. Perhaps I can talk to him sometime. Been fascinated with the subject."

Kjell was surprised Schiller showed any compassion for someone who might easily been branded a defective and destroyed in some camp as rumored. He showed the German out the front door and after an appropriate pause, locked it. Back to the sick room, Hansen was still awake. His half-closed eyes followed Kjell's entry into the room. He lay wearily, his hands on top of the covers. His breathing sounded too loud in the little room.

"Did I say... anything… while they… were here?" he whispered.

"*Nei,* Jens. You did fine. Go to sleep now. I don't believe they will come back."

"What was he saying about the card? Some... thing...about the card…" Hansen licked his lips and after swallowing hard, coughed.

"Don't worry about it, Jens. We'll talk about everything later." Kjell unbuttoned Hansen's borrowed pajama front. He was sweating again, the beads of perspiration pooling in the hollow of his neck. Kjell dried him off, pulling the top blanket off the pile and folded it at the end of the bed.

Hansen said nothing. His throat rattling, he slowly closed his eyes and fell asleep.

CHAPTER 35

Sorting's motorboat fought the small swells at the mouth of the forested cove, then shot its way to the empty landing. From appearances, the place looked deserted, but he knew Rinnan's boat was inside. He whistled low and the door opened.

"Ah, Odd. Join us for a small supper. Are you hungry?" Rinnan was seated at a small folding table covered with a tablecloth. On the narrow dock two other men, not including the crew, sat on folding chairs near him. A squatty kerosene heater provided heat.

Of course, I'm hungry, Sorting thought. His stomach growled with anticipation.

"So. How does it go?" He invited Sorting to sit down. "You said you had a problem."

"The whole village's in an uproar over the arrests. It's interfering with my plans."

"What do you want to do?" Rinnan showed him a platter of meats and cheese.

Sorting reached over. "I want the prisoners smuggled out, and the search called off."

"You can't do that," a dark-haired man sitting on one of the chairs said. "*Obersturmführer* Flesch won't allow it." Like the Chief, he was dressed like a fisherman, but Sorting knew he did his fishing closer to Hamburg or Kiel. He was Gestapo.

"Come now, Werner," Rinnan answered. "Where is your imagination?" He dismissed the German with a flash of his intense eyes, his voice as smooth as silk. "Why, Sorting?"

"To gain the trust of the community's leaders. Arrange a transfer of the prisoners from Falstad Prison to say, Mission Hotel, intercept them with the usual guns and theatrics and get them over the border. I'll claim credit."

Sorting assembled a sandwich. It had been quite awhile since he had meat and he didn't pinch on it. "As for a secret group here, the fishermen's association met. There was leadership. It's a matter of time." He slapped a piece of bread on top and took a big bite.

"Good," Rinnan said. "Our DRTs picked up a signal from around Fjellstad. Might tie in with a report about an arms delivery in mid-May." The Chief poured himself some wine, offering the bottle to Sorting. "I think we can arrange for an 'escape.'"

Sorting watched Werner protest then quiet under Rinnan's gaze. He felt a certain glee, but kept to the matter at hand. "About the patrol. It upsets the village. I can't do anything until they are gone. They found only two poachers and the boys' camp. It hadn't been used for days."

"Again, I'll see what I can do. I'm sure Werner will see the merit of it." The German winced, but said nothing. "Make another sandwich, Odd. The rest of you can get onboard," he said to the others.

After they left, Rinnan continued. "Berlin wants some of our operations wrapped up. Things have changed since the Allied invasion in France. Berlin is especially vocal about Vikna."

"Vikna's a hundred miles north of here. A bunch of amateurs playing hero."

Rinnan grinned. His mouth pulled back like a grimacing skull. "*Ja*, Sorting, and we're just playing along. Berlin wants us to close the trap."

"Do you want me to go?" Sorting cut his new sandwich in half.

"*Nei*. Stay in Fjellstad. Sabotage and other activity is up in the south. It's sure to increase around Trondheimfjord." The Chief lowered his voice. "There's been some disturbing news from Finland. There's convincing intelligence the Finns will settle with the Russians. The Germans, the Finn's present ally, will withdraw into Northern Norway."

Sorting's heart pounded. He washed his sandwich down with wine.

"August, September," Rinnan said. "You know what that means. The Bolsheviks will liberate northern Norway. Our worst nightmare."

Sorting knew what it meant, but wasn't solely convinced by his comments since Rinnan was working both sides of the fence. Sorting had collected sizable amounts of intelligence on the Germans for Rinnan. It would be used as a bargaining chip with the Russians when the Chief defected to them as Sorting felt he would. Sorting felt vulnerable, like he was the last rat on a sinking ship with no way off. "Sure, Chief," Sorting said, taking a final bite.

CHAPTER 36

Anna stood outside the hotel dining room and waited for the soldier to open the French doors. Through the glass panels she saw tables neatly stacked with napkins folded like red bishop hats at each place, but the rest of the hotel looked deserted and strangely shut down.

Was it the curfew? Her insides tightened. A half-hour before, a trio of young German soldiers had appeared at her door. The nearest soldier spoke in schoolboy Norwegian, his foul weather gear dripping on the back steps. "Headquarters is asking for you. We've come to escort you."

"Why?"

"It's orders. We go by truck. You won't be gone long."

Anna hadn't asked further questions. She had heard of the arrests, but had stayed away from the village to avoid the villagers' animosity. But what did this all have to do with her?

Inside the dining room, Anna helped Lisel out of her wet coat. After Anna took hers off, she sat down at one of the nearest tables, pulling Lisel into her lap.

"Just a little wait, Munchkin, then we can go. Lisel snuggled up against her and Anna felt again the wild fluttering of her daughter's heart. Like a little trapped bird. The soldiers, no matter how friendly, had frightened her again.

"Pappa," she whimpered softly. "I want Pappa."

"Shh. Look." Anna showed her how to play a finger game. They were playing when she heard the doors open and someone crossed the carpeted floor with heavy boots. Lisel stiffened, burying herself on Anna's breast. Anna looked up. A tall soldier in a well-kept green-gray uniform that seemed to match the color of his eyes stood by her table. His fresh, open face reminded her of her brother. Though wary, she liked him instantly in spite of Lisel's shrinking fear.

"*Fru* Fromme," he said in thick Norwegian. "I apologize for keeping you waiting. May I sit down?" Taking off his gloves, he indicated the chair opposite her. He removed his hat and swept his lank blonde hair off his forehead with one stroke of his hand.

"Allow me to introduce myself. I am *Oberleutnant* Maxine Schiller. I—What is wrong with her? " He nodded at Lisel.

"She is afraid of you. I'm sorry." She didn't know why she said sorry, but he looked sorry.

Schiller sat down. "I never want to scare small children. What is her name?" When she told him, he said, "Very nice. But then her mother is German, is she not?" He switched to German. "Did my sergeant tell you why you're here?"

"You are accounting for everyone," she answered back in Norwegian.

If he noticed this little act of defiance, he appeared not to care. "*Ja*. I must include you, though the mayor said you were of German extraction," he said in German. "Where are you from?"

"From a small town in Denmark." She spoke in Norwegian. "My parents were German."

"That is a language I don't know, Danish."

Neither do I, thought Anna, *although I have practiced.*

He cleared his throat and asked for her papers. She pushed Lisel off her lap to reach her purse. While he read, she watched him under lowered eyelashes. She decided she must not be lulled by his casual charm. She was as worse off as everyone else under the occupation.

As if on cue, Foss swept in with coffee and set it down with precision at the table, then asked Schiller if he would like some. Foss's German was very good.

"Actually," Schilller said, "I'd like to get something to eat. The cook's still about, isn't she? No reason the place should be all gloom and doom just because the news from the *Vaterland* is bad." He looked at her.

"Would you care for something to eat? No, forget that. Just bring what you have for both of us." When Anna protested, fearful of village talk, he continued. "I am not quite done. You will stay. I'll not ask anything else at this point, except that you speak in German. This conversation is quite one-sided. Try as I might, my Norwegian's not very good."

Schiller signaled to Foss and flashed two fingers at him. He nodded at the little girl.

Foss came over to Anna's chair. She leaned away from him "Anna," he said, his voice all velvety. "Marthe's in the kitchen. Perhaps Lisel would like to visit." Foss smiled at Lisel. "Would you like to see *Tante* Marthe?"

"Mama? Can I?"

Anna knew she was being manipulated, but common sense held sway over her revulsion. "*Ja*, Lisel."

Once they were alone, she pulled the front of her cardigan together. She held her breath while Schiller read her papers.

"I'm sorry restrictions and curfew had to be imposed," he said when he was done. "Order and discipline must be maintained, even if the Quisling government's labor mobilization plan is a dismal failure. The boys ran away. I must bring them back. I suppose two poachers will do."

Anna didn't know if he would be a friend or foe. "Will the restrictions be on for long?" she asked carefully.

"Travel restrictions will be lifted in the next couple of days. We'll go out for the escapees one more time." Changing the subject, he said, "You know, I've always wanted to come to Norway," he said. "The Viking lore always thrilled me as a boy and the pictures of the fjords—truly wonderful. But it's quite different from wanting something than actually getting it and not being able to have it as your own. Despite the propaganda, the people don't like us very much. The Gestapo ruined it."

It's not like you came bearing flowers, Anna thought. There was a trail of destruction from Lillehammer through Molde to Namsos and Steinkjer. Hospitals had been bombed.

Schiller went on. "But maybe it won't matter in the end. Tell me, aren't you a bit curious why the hotel's shut down at this time of night? On a Thursday?"

"I did think it odd."

"It's Foss. Out of reverence for the *Führer*. There was an assassination attempt on his life today. Some of his aides were killed, but most got away with moderate injuries."

Anna gripped the arms of her chair. "Was Hitler killed?"

"*Nein*. Injured. He was well enough to go on the radio." Schiller's voice had a hint of sarcasm which shocked her. She feared nationwide restrictions would make her escape impossible. She put a hand over her thumping heart.

Schiller slammed back in his chair. "Where's that dinner? It's past eight and I'm starved." He started to get up, when on the other side of the glass doors his aide beckoned to him. Schiller waved him in. The soldier walked in and snapped to attention. "What is it? I'm having dinner right now."

"The mayor's outside. He says there's an emergency."

"Very well, send him in." Schiller sighed. "This will take only a moment," he said to Anna.

Pederson was ushered in, taking his time to shake out his umbrella before he came close.

"It's for Grimstad," he explained in German. "The doctor needs to get out to a woman in labor. The midwife sent for help. He'll leave as soon as he's able."

"Will he be going by boat?"

"*Ja*, of course. Odd Sorting will take him. I'll need a pass for him too." Pederson saw Anna, and inclined his head at her.

She sat still, dreading what he might be thinking even if he was a Nazi.

Schiller wrote out two passes. "Did the doctor see the deaf-mute?"

"*Ja*, he's seriously ill. Grimstad was called back early this morning. The young man has pneumonia and a raging fever, but he rallied, I heard, sometime this afternoon. The fever broke."

Anna gasped and turned around in her chair. "*Vær så snill.* Please… he will not die?"

"You know this man?" Schiller asked her in Norwegian.

"*Ja.* He has done work for me. He's very kind, so helpful. He will be all right?"

"I think he'll pull through," Pederson replied. He bowed to Schiller and left.

Dinner came. Fresh trout, potatoes, some vegetables. A bottle of wine. The inn still got food on the table, despite the increasing odds, but Anna had no appetite.

She ate listlessly, her mind on her only friend struggling for his breath a couple of blocks away. It was hard imagining him so ill, the gray eyes dull, his strong body burning with fever. She prayed for his recovery.

Schiller cleared his throat. "You don't like your dinner?"

"I'm sorry. It's very nice, but it's my daughter's bedtime." To her relief, Schiller called for Foss's car. Anna escaped to the kitchen where Lisel was drawing pictures with the cook.

As she put on Lisel's coat, on impulse, Anna asked the cook, "Could I write on one of the pictures? I'd like to make a card for Jens Hansen. He's very sick." The woman glared at her, then handed her a crayon picture of a fishing boat with fish jumping into it. When Anna was finished, the woman took the card, her fingers just holding its edge like the rest was poisoned.

To her relief, Schiller said good-bye at the dining room door. His aide would drive them back in one of the patrol's *Kübelwagens*. But he indicated that he would like to see her again. She didn't encourage him.

Foss came out with her. "Are you all right? Was Schiller a gentleman?"

"*Ja*." They stood on the broad stone steps of the hotel facing the fjord. It was getting late. The drizzling had stopped, but the wind was chilly. She pulled her coat around her. Lisel squeezed her hand and swung it gently back and forth.

Down toward the main street where the road dipped down to the boats and *konditori* below, two men stood in conversation. One wore a long coat and hat. The other one was a stocky fisherman with straw-colored hair. As if he sensed that he was being watched, he turned toward her, showing his face fully, but he was looking at something else and turned back.

"*Herr* Foss." Anna said. "Who is that man? The fisherman." A feeling of suffocating fear rose in her. She fought to keep it off her face and out of her voice.

"That's Odd Sorting. He's taking Grimstad out to the Eriksen home. That'll be a rough ride by the looks of the water."

She watched the man move like someone in a dream or a movie with no soundtrack, but she saw him more clearly than a memory or camera could. Only ten months ago, she'd seen him talking with Einar and another man. They never saw her and she never asked. But four weeks later Einar was arrested. In five he was dead. That man was there. But his name wasn't Sorting.

"The car's here." Foss's voice sounded far away.

She got into the back with Lisel and left without a word. When she got to the farmhouse she locked the back door.

Anna never left. Two days later she received a telegram. It said:

> *Illness in family. STOP. Uncle Felix called home. STOP.*
> *Impossible to keep appointment. STOP. Godspeed.*
> *Cordially, Cousin H.*

She was trapped. Something had gone wrong and von Weber had been called back to Germany. She could never leave and would have to continue to bear the villagers' insults. But worse, for the first time, she was in danger.

CHAPTER 37

Jens was dozing when Kitty came in. She thought he looked much better than the first time she'd seen him two days ago. The dark spots under his eyes had nearly faded, gone with the ragged breath and cold sweats that had soaked his bedclothes and bedding. He'd been far sicker than they realized, his body fever-racked. The doctor had been summoned around six that first morning using what little medicine was available. Over the next five hours, her father and Dr. Grimstad brought him out of danger. It was pneumonia after all, on top of the influenza.

Yet he was awake and propped up on pillows late that night and the following afternoon felt well enough to eat broth and have visitors. She was one of the first having come down from Ekberg *seter* as soon as she was able.

She set the tray down on the bedside table, straightening up around the bed. He was sleeping on his side, his pajama front unbuttoned and she saw again now tough and lean-muscular he was. How could he have been so ill? She walked around to the end of the bed and removed the extra *dyne* at his feet. It must have disturbed him, for he slowly opened his eyes and looked down at her. Turning over, he smoothed his dark hair with his fingers, then signed, What time?

"It's noon, Jens." Time to eat, she motioned.

Ah. He straightened up with a slow weariness, fiddling with the pillows behind him while she waited with the tray. When she set it down on his lap he looked at it like he was a starving teenage boy. Nice, he motioned. This lunch?

"*Ja*. Someone gave us eggs, which I poached, and there is light rye toast. The berries in the bowl are from the *seter* where I work in the mountains. There's milk and coffee."

She sat on the chair next to him and watched him eat, but after a time tapped him on his arm. "If you wish, I can give you a shave. Unless you want to look like Olav Sorensen who has had a beard since eighteen and never cut it off. And he's ninety-two."

You... want... shave... me? he motioned. He suddenly looked terrified, making the international sign of slit throat across his neck.

"Jens!" she giggled. "I'm not that bad." She threw a napkin at him.

CHAPTER 38

For the next few days, Haugland stayed on Kjell's sofa. A restless patient, he obeyed orders to stay put. When Grimstad came to check on him, he was strong enough for the doctor reluctantly to give his approval for him to go out. Grimstad tucked his stethoscope into his worn leather bag. "I know your secret. I've told Kjell so. He is my good friend, you see."

Haugland stifled a cough. He wasn't pleased at this turn of events.

"Don't be alarmed. Your secret is safe. I assure you that no one else knows. You fooled me for quite a while with the medical card—which is very good, by way, except the person who signed it was away on the day it was supposed to be signed." Grimstad snapped the bag shut.

"How did you figure it out?"

"We were both at a medical meeting. There are other things. You're a very convincing deaf-mute, but Kjell's behavior the night I came, the disappearance of the boys and your feet—I put everything together." He put on his coat. "Allow me to help you."

Haugland folded his arms across his chest, weighing options. "Too dangerous."

"I insist. I have free access to many people and places. I want to do my part."

"Well, I could use a cutout. That's someone who takes messages to a drop point."

"I could do that," Grimstad answered, "but first, more rest. No boats for a while."

Gradually, Haugland resumed his activities. He was well enough to inventory crates, mend nets sitting down. Eventually he did tasks on the *Otta*. On August first, two weeks after leaving the boys with Tommy, he went up to the Tourist Hotel. He felt tired, but had to press on.

The little room was stuffy and forlorn. No one had used it since he'd been ill. He pulled the string to the light and cleared the workbench of a forgotten project. He found two letters pinned to his bulletin board.

One had a hastily made envelope, the other some sort of pale blue stationery. He opened the homey one first. Inside it said, "Get well soon" in Anna Fromme's handwriting and "I LOV YOU, JENS" in the little girl's hand. He wondered when it had been made. He set it on the worktable and opened the other. "JENS" was written on the front. It read:

So glad to hear you are doing well.
Terrible to be so sick. Could you see me?
I have another job for you if you are able.
Three o'clock at blue fisher hut on road.
Cordially, Anna

A shadow fell across the wall. It was Marthe. "I see you found the notes."

Haugland tapped his wrist for time.

"When? Lisel made the card the day you were so sick. The woman wanted me to take it to you, but I didn't know how you felt about her, so I pinned it up. The note came this morning"

The heavyset cook looked around the dingy room. "I don't think Foss has anything for you, dear. Someone can let you know. No one was sure when or if you would be back."

Me same, he signed.

She squeezed his arm affectionately. "You're a good man, Jens, I'm so glad you're better." Marthe would have mothered him to death, if she could.

She left him alone to mull over the intricacies of life. She didn't have to say a word about her feelings for "the Woman."

He prepared to leave when one of the waitresses, a buxom farm girl, ran up and pulled on his shirtsleeve. "Jens. Come. Pastor Helvig is in the lobby asking for you."

Me? Why? he signed. He hardly ever dealt with Pastor Helvig, seldom going to church with the excuse he would only understand less than half of what was said.

Helvig was waiting by the desk where Foss stood with *Fritt Folk* in his hand. With the middle-aged cleric was a man not much older than Haugland. He was of medium height with brown hair cut short save for a thick thatch on top. He was dressed in the dark jacket and white collar of a clergyman. "There you are," said Helvig. The stranger signed *God dag*.

Haugland signed *God dag* back, but he was instantly wary, looking for a trick. The man signed like an expert. A conversation of hands and fingers followed.

I H-A-R-O-L-D S-O-L-H-E-I-M, the man fingerspelled. I new to T-R-O-N-D-H-E-I-M. I go work with deaf folk in S-O-R T-R-Ø-N-D-E-L-A-G. Pastor Helvig invite me stay day or two. I hear of you.

"Is there some place we can talk?" Solheim asked Helvig after signing a few more comments to Haugland. "I'm afraid this is embarrassing the young man." He nodded at the clusters of hotel staff and soldiers in the dining room leaning out over the backs of chairs regarding Haugland with unveiled curiosity.

"But, of course. My rectory. The housekeeper will be gone until late afternoon. You can be alone as long as you like. I'll come over later."

***

As soon as the door to the rectory's library closed behind them, Haugland turned and looked at the man carefully. What Solheim had said so eloquently to Helvig about Haugland's need for privacy was a cover for what he had really signed to Haugland.

We have a mutual friend, he had signed—Boy Scout. Oslo sent me.

The rest was cautious maneuvering to establish each other's identity. "Boy Scout" was a *deknavn* only Haugland's brother Lars used.

Solheim took out a letter from a small prayer book. "I had orders to make contact with 'Jens' in Fjellstad. Any details about why I'm here, I'm to answer verbally."

Haugland scanned it quickly. It was written on church letterhead by Lars, introducing Solheim as a pastor who desired outreach ministry with Jens Hansen. It listed services and special help in Trondheim if he desired. "Special help" was underlined. Haugland wondered if Solheim was a genuine cleric.

"That letter's in case some snoops see it too. If you need final verification, you can contact the Nidaros diocese in Trondheim. I believe I'll be either living on the grounds of the *Hjemme for Døve* or at a flat near the Deaf Church. I'm to give you this as well." Solheim gave him an order form for the fishing catalogue Haugland and Lars used for messages.

Haugland took it, then signed, You real priest?

Solheim chuckled. "I was ordained in 1940 two months after the invasion. I joined the resistance a week later." He signed as well as spoke, a style Haugland knew well.

Where learn sign?

"My mother is deaf."

Haugland nodded understanding. You know C-B-S?

"*Ja*, I know Conrad Bonnevie-Svendsen. I've been working with him since 1941. He promises to stay in touch."

I'm sure he will, Haugland thought. Solheim appeared to be in Conrad's inner circle of pastors serving the deaf while serving their country. After signing a few quick questions to be sure of Solheim's authenticity for teaching the deaf, he began to relax. The man was genuine both in vocation and secret work.

"How about you?" Solheim asked.

Haugland signed, He old family friend, then voiced, "He saved my life once."

"Ah, that. Boy Scout said I was to repeat it to you as final confirmation."

Solheim began to rattle off facts of what had been a nightmare for Haugland: the arrest of his father for his anti-Nazi activities at the university; the massive search for Haugland and his brothers by the Gestapo; his flight to a mountain cabin with some school chums and their discovery by the Germans. The shoot-out in which he had been seriously wounded, but managed to escape to the only person he could trust—Bonnevie-Svendsen—who hid and cared for him at the *Hjemme for Dove* near Oslo for two weeks. The others had not been so lucky.

When Solheim finished, Haugland discovered that he had crushed the letter into a ball. Haugland smoothed it out and folded it into quarters. "My brother has prompted you well."

"He was insistent," Solheim said. "I'm only staying through tomorrow. Once I'm settled in Trondheim, my orders are to help you in any way I can. I've been in contact with some of the local resistance people already. We can use the *Hjemme for Døve* as a place to meet."

"All right. Sounds fine." He put the letter in his notebook. "I'm expecting a delivery somewhere around the fifteenth. It will be heavier than usual. I need to check with the local Resistance group in Trondheim on the feasibility of moving some of it into Trondheimfjord."

"It'll be risky, but we have no choice, *jo*? Not until the Allied air drops resume again."

Haugland grinned. For a pastor, Solheim had an ease with resistance matters. "I suppose you're anxious to get settled in."

"I've come to help people cope. God willing."

CHAPTER 39

Haugland approached the faded blue fishing hut cautiously, looking for any signs of life. He was taking a risk doing this, even though the hut was well past the path to his own cabin and isolated. What remained of the gravel road petered out a hundred yards beyond it, coming up against a wall of solid rock rising back dramatically to steep hills carpeted with pine. Once a holiday hut, it now appeared to be used as a storage area for lobster pots and other fishing materials. He looked up and down the road and out on the water before he pushed on the weathered door.

It was dim inside. Most of the windows had been painted with blackout paint, but on the west side, hastily applied paper had been ripped away from one of the windows. Sunshine streamed through the panes. It fell on Anna Fromme's face. For a moment she seemed to brace herself for what he didn't know. When she recognized him, her face blossomed into relief.

"Jens, I'm so glad you came." She studied him. "You are well? When I heard you were so sick, I felt very bad. You worked too hard. It was too much work for one man and a boy."

He shrugged. Logging not hurt me, he signed, although it wasn't such a farfetched idea. He laid his illness to exhaustion, the influenza, and working on a meager diet. They stood close, so close he smelled the fresh scent of her newly washed hair.

You want talk me? he motioned. When she said yes, he thought, She understands me. That really pleased him. He pointed to the window where the light was better and brought out his mangled notebook.:You have job for me? he wrote.

"I'm sorry, Jens. I don't—But I didn't think you would come." She signed sorry.

He cocked his head at her, then signed, You friend.

My dear friend, she signed back. "I didn't want to cause gossip. To get you in trouble."

He wrote: You afraid of talk?

"They always talk, but now they think I love the German officer. I had no choice. I was escorted to the hotel the night of the arrests. He made me eat with him." Her voice trailed off.

Nervously stroking her fingers, she looked out the window to the rocky beach down below. Haugland followed her line of sight. The tide was out, exposing gray boulders speckled with blobs of orange lichen-like growth and strands of seaweed. Two seagulls flew about in aerial combat, fighting over some marine debris. It was a beautiful, warm day.

What wrong?

She settled on a crate below the window. "Do you remember when we talked about Einar? You asked if I had seen any strangers in our village. I said no, but then I remembered."

She had his attention now as she told him about the man she had seen at the Tourist Hotel. Six weeks before Einar was arrested she'd seen the same man with her husband in Lillehavn. Haugland stopped her and motioned for her to write the name down on his notebook. She scribbled down ODD SORTING in capital letters.

Haugland's mouth went suddenly dry. He felt like he was walking barefoot on the edge of a knife. One false move and he'd lose his footing and—his foot.

"But," she said, "that was not the name I heard! I think you spell it this way." She took the pencil from his hand and wrote on the notebook page: AKE MORKDAL.

He turned the notebook around. The name meant nothing to him, but he would get it sent out as soon as possible. Kjell's fears were correct.

"I was in the trees when I saw them talking in the meadow."

You hear talk? Haugland felt like he had been punched.

"Not very well. But three weeks later he returned with someone new. I had gone to the schoolhouse to take dinner to Einar. I was in the cloakroom when they arrived. I hid again."

Haugland stopped her. He was frustrated. Having to motion and write was getting him nowhere. He put out his hands to slow her down. What did he look like?

"He was a very odd. Like Sorting, he was dressed like a fisherman, but he was, you see, a very small man. His body was so small, like a boy. His face was narrow, like this." Anne drew her hand down her cheek. "And his eyes—very hard, light eyes. His hair was black."

Haugland kept his face blank, but he had no control over the lump of ice forming in his gut and spreading like killer frost throughout his whole body. He knew the answer to his next question whether she did or not. Did you hear name?

She took the pencil from him and wrote: WHIST. "I didn't hear his first name. I'm sorry. I just felt foolish. Like a schoolgirl listening in."

Haugland didn't hear her. He was looking at the names wavering on the paper. He closed his eyes, trying to block the image of Einar Fromme speaking to the two men and Einar Fromme broken in their hands a scant three weeks later.

`Whist' was Rinnan, a *deknavn* SOE-Norway had sent Haugland recently from London. There was no doubt now. She had described and named Rinnan, putting Sorting-Morkdal in league with him.

Haugland felt sick. Lars had wanted Einar's betrayers exposed. Now they were, but Haugland thought it was a hollow victory. It wouldn't bring Einar back. It couldn't bring justice.

Anna was still talking and he slowly drifted back to what she was saying. "… never saw Sorting again until now, but I saw the little one the evening Einar was arrested at the house. He was dressed in a SD uniform, smaller than everyone else."

She stopped. Tears glistened on her cheeks. She wiped them with her fingers. "*Vær så snill*, don't wait on this. This man is a danger to everyone." She stopped. "God, I hope you understand me. *Vær så snill*, say you do, Jens."

He signed he did.

"Thank God." He watched her whole body relax with relief. She got up and looked out the flyspecked window. He was tempted to leave her alone, but he had other questions. What she had told him was extraordinary. And for the first time since they met, he truly trusted her.

He touched her on her shoulder. To his surprise, she began to tremble and leaned her face into his shoulder, laying her tightly clenched fist on his chest. At first he held her awkwardly, putting his arms around her like a sibling. At least he tried to make it awkward. It had been a long time since he had held a woman in his arms, but like jolt of electricity, he knew that he didn't mind holding her. He drew her closer.

Nothing was said. To hold and be held was enough. An act of friendship and trust. She turned and laid her cheek on his chest, remaining that way for some time. Eventually, the trembling stopped. Smiling faintly at him, she pushed away. He let her go, careful to act more embarrassed than reluctant.

"I'm sorry."

It's all right, he motioned. You all right? He pointed to her.

"*Ja*." She swept her curly hair off her face, then wiped her eyes again. "It's been a long two weeks. I haven't quite decided what to do, but I know that I am no longer going to just let things happen to me. I will say yes or no to whatever I feel is best for Lisel and me. I will not let others dictate or slander me, just because they feel that they should. That includes Herr Schiller."

She took a breath before going on.

"There was a time when I thought that I could go away, but now I can't. I will have to stay until the whole thing is over, despised by everyone. They call me "The Woman," the "German Whore'." She shook her head. "Nothing will change. Even after you warn them about Odd Sorting because you won't be able to tell them who told you. They wouldn't believe you."

She backed away from him. "It's all right. I can manage as long as Lisel is not harmed by the gossip. She's not a part of their dirty little war." Slowly tears rolled down over her cheeks, gathering at the edges of her mouth.

Haugland looked at her gently, his respect for her growing all the time. He wrote: Be careful about Sorting. He may not have seen you, but could connect your name.

"I will. I promise." She sniffed, then returned his quiet smile.

Anna, he wrote, after Einar died, were people good to you?

"*Ja*," she answered looking surprised. She wiped her tears away. "Strange you should ask. I have always been hurt by that. People were at first very supportive, but after word came that Einar...died...there was a change. It was subtle at first, then came accusations. By the end of the second week, no one was talking to me, not even after the Gestapo questioned me and rifled our house." She pursed her lips. "It was a very bad time. I panicked and came here." She leaned against the wall and played with a net dangling from a nail.

Her eyes are clear now, he thought. She seems beyond breaking down again. She is, he thought, a strong woman.

He looked at his watch. It had been an emotionally draining hour for him. He wanted to get out into the fresh air, to breathe it deeply into his healing lungs. The hut had become as stifling as his old sick room.

I'm leaving, he motioned. He tapped his watch.

"Must you go?"

Ja.

"Will I see you again?" Her face was full of hope.

Nei.

It had to be "no" He would be breaking his own rules if he allowed this to continue. Even if he wanted to help her, give her support.

I can't, he wrote. Fishing. Work all the time.

She nodded her head dismally, but said she understood. Then she brightened.

"It doesn't matter, Jens. I'll be all right. You've done enough for me already and for that I'll always be grateful. Just warn your friends. You be careful too."

He signed that he would. He picked up the pencil and notebook one last time and wrote: Thank Lisel for the card.

He couldn't think of any other way to end it, but when he left cautiously a few minutes later, he felt like he had let her and Einar down.

Book 3

"It's this darkness.
It came while the house was asleep, settled over it, and will not go away. It sprang up like a seething spring, so that the windows were blinded, mouths became dumb, and from out of the darkness came people who held power. They lit up corridors with their bright shining arrows. Then they sat about making their own house within the house and at once the silent storm began wearing it down."

~Terjei Vesaas, 1945
The House in the Dark

Heroism consists of hanging on one minute longer.

~Norwegian saying

CHAPTER 40

Fall, 1944

The Shetland Bus resumed the seventeenth of August with a run to Southern Norway. The *Vigra* went first. Five days later, Haugland was ordered to meet the *Hessa.* He was to expect a large delivery of arms and two agents and would be responsible for their dispersion in the Trondheim area. Physically and mentally, he felt he was ready.

He had made a rapid recovery since his illness, spending several days out in the *Trondheimsleia* laying nets for salmon with Kjell. He tired less and no longer coughed as he worked about the *Otta.* If there was any residue of illness, it was his appetite. Not wanting him ill again, Grimstad made sure Haugland stayed healthy by supplying him with nourishing food from a source set aside for hospital patients. It was Grimstad's way, Haugland felt, to show he could be trusted. Soon he would test the doctor with his first assignment as a cutout.

A few days before they were to meet the *Hessa*, the *Otta* slipped away to Sig Haraldsen's home. The cover for the trip was the birthday of Sig's granddaughter, Astrid, who was turning eighteen. When they arrived at the barren island, they found the family grieving.

"What's going on?" Kjell asked as they secured the boat at the dock.

"It's my son-in-law, Johann," Sig said. "The Swedish Red Cross just told us he was killed in May during a convoy run to Murmansk. My Andrina's taking it hard. Where shall we meet?"

"Jens says in the barn, but first we'll pay our respects to you and your granddaughter."

A while later, the men went to the barn. Haugland quickly laid out the details.

"The *Hessa's* arriving on August 22 at about eleven p.m. We've only got a brief curtain of darkness to unload. We're taking three boats, but only one will carry the material. It's been hauling peat and cellulose from Frøya to Trondheim most of the summer and has all the permits. Inspection boat knows it well." Haugland looked at Sig and then Holger, an emerging leader within the group. "I expect forty to fifty crates. Two agents are coming as well. One's bringing a W/T and will report on ship movement to London. Did you get that place for him, Sig?"

"*Ja*, with Anson. He has a small woodworking business."

"Good." Haugland asked about restrictions. Down around Edoy there was an important lighthouse. Though not in use due to wartime, it was German controlled and prone to patrols.

Holger puffed on his pipe. "I've heard nothing new."

"Excellent." Haugland went on to talk about the materiel. "A portion's being transported either in peat or cellulose. SOE likes peat because the Shetland Islands have peat bogs. They can package and disguise the arms over there. I like cellulose because you can stuff explosives and similar armaments in any center you hollow-out in the flat sheet bundles."

"I like cellulose too," Sverre said. "With molasses poured over it, our farmers can feed it to their cows."

"Both items are common enough around here and in Trondheim," Sig added, "so whatever you choose, Jens, would work." At that, everyone voiced his opinion all at once.

Later, they sat on crates and barrels smoking pipes and cigarettes, a gift from Haugland. Sitting off quietly to the side, he listened to the talk flow from the weather, fishing and Andrina Paal to their brother-in-law, Johann.

"He was good, Johann," Sverre said.

"*Ja*. Easy-going, hardworking," Holger said. "He'll be missed. Pity no children."

"Poor sister." Another brother turned to Haugland. "Johann was already gone four months when we got invaded. Stranded him in New York City."

"Did you ever hear of the *Kys Mig i Reva* Club, Jens?" Sverre asked.

"Sure."

"Stupid Germans. They planned the invasion during the fishing season! Almost all our whaling boats were up in Iceland and many boats were fishing in the Lofotens. Ships from our merchant marine were out too, scattered all over the world."

"I remember what Quisling did," Haugland said. "Requested all the captains of merchant ships proceed to Norwegian, German or neutral ports. Supposed to wait for further orders."

"But not a one complied." Holger's face beamed with pride. "Instead they sent telegrams that read: "To Vidkun Quisling-Norway—*Kys Mig i Reva*—Kiss My Ass." He gave a broad grin before putting his pipe back into his mouth. He drew on it thoughtfully.

"Johann Paal was in that club." There were tears in Sverre's eyes. "He reported to Allied authorities in New York City. Because of him and the others only a sixth of our fleet fell into German hands. He made us all very proud of him."

Haugland watched Kjell out of the corner of his eye. The big blonde man had been silent during this time, hunched over a crate next to Sig. Haugland wondered if he still cared for Andrina Paal after all the years, but no one would want this. And Kjell, with his sense of propriety, would do nothing to press his case.

***

The next day they arrived at A.C. Kjelstrup's after a slow run by sail. He limped down to the boat, his dog Balder following him like his shadow. While Hansen made things shipshape, A.C. stood on the dock with his hands in his trousers and chatted with Kjell. "Why don't you come on up? I've got some herring and cheese. How's Jens feeling?"

"You can ask him yourself. Did well for his first big trip out since he was ill." Kjell got down. He petted the dog, roughing up the dark fur around its thick neck. "He'll be along."

Red and white flowers burst from a single blue flower box hung in front of a multi-paned window. The flowers were the only signs of vegetation on the rocky, low-lying island. Kjell knew it was so low-lying that every ten years or so the high tide came halfway up the path to the door. The forty-foot fishing boat that was his pride and livelihood was kept in a small but deep cove away from the house for that reason.

"Come in, Kjell." Limping over to his peat-burning stove, A.C. removed an enameled coffeepot from it. While he went in into his larder in the back, Kjell looked around the little room. He discovered a photo of Rika tacked onto the wood-paneled wall.

"Andrew Christian, I didn't know you had a picture of Rika. When was this one taken?"

"Oh, early this August," he answered. "I developed it myself."

My *lille gjente*, where are you? Where's the little girl who used to romp around the docks in rubber boots too large for her feet? She was wearing a new dress and with her hair pulled back from her face, she looked like a beautiful, sophisticated young woman. He suddenly felt a stab of suspicion, and glanced at A.C. He was a bit too quiet as he laid out the cups on the table. Kjell watched him with new interest. "I didn't know you saw Rika very often."

"You wouldn't mind, would you?" A.C. said suddenly. "I like her very much." He gave Kjell a cup of steaming *ersatz* coffe, easing down onto his chair. "Sit, *Vær så snill*."

"*Ja*, it's fine," Kjell said, but he was surprised. Rika never wrote anything about this. A.C. appeared nervous. Was this more serious than A.C. was letting on?

They caught up with news. Finally, A.C. brought up the subject of his boat.

"We're going to load it," Kjell said. "You'll take it into Trondheimfjord. We'll be onboard, of course—as crew. We'll get our own paperwork, but we'll tell you where to go."

"I understand it's sensitive stuff."

"It is. It's all arranged. We'll bring the shipment to you. You take it in."

A.C. pointed out the window. "Why's he involved? How can he possibly understand?"

"He does understand and more, he wants to do it. He knows the lay of things. Jens is not dumb." Kjell pointed to his temple and tapped it.

"I didn't say he was dumb."

"I know. I just want you to understand him, A.C. He's very astute. His silence is an asset. People often dismiss him, but they don't know how much he observes. He's very clever and he knows the risks. He's a *jøssing*—just like you and me."

"I never said otherwise. He's just sort of... innocent. Like he's not a part of the war."

"Oh, but he is. He lost his whole family in Molde when it was bombed. Terrible loss." Having made his speech, Kjell took a sip out of his coffee. It tasted bitter like roasted split peas. He drank it anyway, watching the young man guiltily. He hated lying to A.C.

"When do you want it?" A.C. came away from the window.

"Around the twenty-second. I'll have an exact date soon."

A.C. sighed. "I'm glad my friends on Frøya aren't involved. Thirty people escaped to Scotland on my brother's boat. Many more were arrested in reprisal. People are wary."

Kjell watched Hansen walk up the dock toward land. Balder leaped around him like a puppy. Kjell saw him throw something. The dog took off. Kjell took another sip of coffee, trying not to grimace. "Have you seen Sorting recently?"

"*Nei*, not here, although I have seen him out fishing. Still don't trust him, do you?"

"*Nei*, and you shouldn't either."

"Don't worry. I took your advice and I see him less, though I thought he might be suspicious if I dropped him suddenly. In time, I'll stop seeing him completely. I promise."

A shadow appeared in the open doorway. It was Hansen. He had to squeeze in against the doorframe competing with the dog for space as it slipped through.

"*Hei.* How are you, Jens?" A.C. asked.

Me fine, the hands said, then he took a place at the table.

The *Otta* left that evening for Fjellstad and points south in the Trondheimsleia where Kjell said they might fish. It had been a pleasant afternoon. A.C. always looked forward to his friend's visits and since he got to know Hansen, him as well. A.C. was always surprised how well they worked together.

It's a solid friendship, he thought. Kjell has always wanted a son. He briefly felt a pang of jealousy, forgetting Kjell's long-standing affection for him. It was just lately he had discovered how much he valued the older man's opinion. All because of her.

He looked at the photograph. It captured all the things he saw in Rika: her warmth, her wit, and intelligence. He had fallen in love and took every opportunity to see her. They met in parks, at the cathedral of Nidros, or some of the few open museums.

It had begun innocently. True to his word, he had found some resistance work for her, delivering ration coupon books. Every Monday she went to a stall in the women's room in her office building. There she would find a package of the little paper books wrapped in newspaper.

"It's very easy, A.C.," she told once him. "When I am able—usually during lunchtime—I go to the fish stalls near the marketplace and buy fish from our friend. If the lines are long, I invent a way to see him. Just like you trained me. Other times, I just lay down the package and leave with my order of fish, which you know, is also wrapped in newspaper. I am not afraid."

He had been pleased. She had done so well she had been given the added responsibility of delivering stencils to the illegal press across the river in the suburb of Mollenberg.

He was coming into Trondheim regularly, sometimes twice a week, bringing in peat and taking back bales of cellulose to the islands. He saw her whenever he could, but they kept their visits and her illegal work separate. Whatever she did was best left unsaid unless she needed advice. "Never say anything to your father. In fact, you must not say anything to *any* family members or friends."

Rika complied. It was the most important rule in illegal work.

A.C. shot a glance at her photo again. He had kissed that face, tasted her lips. He wanted to marry her. He wondered if Kjell guessed how he much loved her. He'd have to be careful with his old friend. Kjell would not approve of his involving Rika in illegal work. He could get angry enough to separate them.

A.C. scrunched up his shoulders like he was warding off a chill. He knew some day it would come to this—taking on more dangerous work. But now he wanted to be more careful, take fewer risks. Because of Rika.

The only trouble was that when he looked that far ahead, all he saw was a void, a dark curtain across his mind. Like he wasn't there at all.

CHAPTER 41

They needed another Milorg man, so Lars Haugland went along at the last minute.

"Thank God," he told Torstein Kaaland as they stood at the window in the little engineering office and watched the empty Oslo street below. It was five o'clock in the morning. Already the midsummer light had reached the tops of the buildings. "One more day of inaction and I'll go nuts. Waiting out Allied action in France and not being allowed to do anything in our own country gives me fits. Pity Milorg's forbidden to act."

Torstein took off his spectacles and wiped them on a handkerchief from his suit pocket.

"Sabotage action is up since the Normandy invasion," he said.

"That's the 'Oslo Gang' from Linge Company—all trained by SOE and acting on orders out of Stockholm and London. Not necessarily locally generated." Lars put his hands behind his back. "About time I did something, even if it's stealing a truckload of ration cards. I'm glad we were invited to join them on this."

Torstein put his spectacles back on. "From the printing plant on the day of delivery. I mean no offense, Lars, but anything could go wrong. It's risky for you to go."

Lars smiled at his friend. "They just need a backup, that's all. We've got thousands of nineteen and twenty-year-old boys in hiding with relatives or friends, in agricultural districts, in the mountains. Keeping the places secret and feeding so many people is becoming impossible. It all comes down to ration cards."

Torstein sighed. "Well, that's true. When the police showed up to arrest my nephew in Kvam, his ration card was canceled in his absence. Without it, he can't get food."

Lars straightened up. "There's the car and the signal. I've got to go." He brushed down the workman coveralls he was wearing. "Take care. I'll see you later."

By eight, Lars was in the backseat of a gray, nondescript Ford with a machine gun across his lap. The driver had discreetly parked the car near the printing office. The required charcoal burner was on its back, but it was revved up to go on a full tank of gas. It might be overkill, but they feared the truck carrying the ration cards was heavily armed. The Gestapo had been edgy with the recent sabotage actions. That part he hadn't told Torstein.

He leaned back against the felt-covered seat and checked his watch. The sun made pale yellow patches on the buildings' stone walls and sidewalks. The Oslo traffic was still light. Additional men would be here soon, probably on bikes. They would do the actual hijacking. He stretched his legs then warily settled back to wait. Nobody talked. His two companions in front were frozen in their places. It gave him time to think and ignore his fluttering stomach.

He had been busy, going to Sweden twice in the past five weeks to check on the police camps approved by the Swedish government. He had also met with SOE and government representatives from London on Milorg matters. When he found the time, there were personal problems to tend to as well. One concerned his son, the other, his mother.

Trygve had come through his surgery all right, but had developed an infection. He was readmitted almost immediately. Lars heard about it while he was in Stockholm. He was so upset by it that he asked everywhere for medical advice. Friends at the British Legation were able to obtain some medicine, including penicillin, a new wonder drug recently available in the west. He arranged for resistance contacts at the hospital to give it to Trygve's doctor. He was relieved to hear the young Viking was now out in a heavy cast playing with the family dog.

The other thing that occupied Lars's attention was his mother.

You dear, grand woman. You not only lost Father, but our home.

Lars closed his eyes and saw the study with its books and French doors opening onto a patio with Italian stone pavers. Flower gardens and pine trees around the grounds. He had grown up there in the suburbs of Oslo. It was home until the Germans confiscated it in the fall of 1940 and sent Mother packing with only personal belongings. She went to her parents' stately home in Bergen where she continued to be harassed by the State Police. Because of his illegal work, however, Lars was unable to help her. He gripped his gun tighter thinking about it.

He couldn't help again when, two years later, his brother Per was arrested in February 1942 after trying to escape to the west from Ålesund. The family thought it was just another thing they'd have to bear, but they weren't prepared for his execution. After Telavåg, it seemed wretchedly heartless.

"Erling, they're here."

Lars looked up sharply at the sound of his *deknavn*. A little way up the road stood three men with their bicycles. Their wait wasn't long. A few minutes ahead of time, the truck came out of the printing plant, moving slowly toward the crossing. One of the men on the bicycles signaled to the Ford. The driver started up, coming quickly to the intersection where they turned in front of the truck. Because the car had the right of way, the truck stopped and immediately one of the hijackers opened the cab door and ordered the two men inside to move over. The other hijackers climbed into the canvassed back, then they were off.

"So far so good," one of Lars's companions said.

"Stay alert." Lars cleared his throat. His mouth had become dry.

The truck rumbled down to the Post Office, its intended destination, then took off in totally different direction. Lars's car followed behind keeping a discreet distance. A few minutes later, the truck stopped and parked. Here a contact would be waiting with a password.

"Pull over here," Lars said.

The Ford slowed down and parked some distance away. There was an agonizing wait. A few minutes later a car drove up behind the truck and a group of men got out and began to unload the ration cards and transfer the boxes. From their car, Lars and his companions kept their eyes peeled for any signs of trouble, but nothing happened.

"Incredible," one of the companions said. "A ton of cards and they aren't guarded."

"A lucky break indeed," Lars said. "We could destroy Quisling's whole supply system."

"Won't he be pissed. The Germans will be furious." It was hard to not to smile.

Two days after the ration card heist, Lars learned that all the Rationing Offices in Norway received orders to issue ration cards to everyone without exception, including evaders of the AT. The *Hjemmefronten* had won and returned some 70,000 ration cards plus 30,000 tobacco and supplement cards. Norway always had to import foodstuffs from before the war, and rationing was supposed to preserve the stores, even though the Germans took the best. The bastard Quisling couldn't have the Germans stepping into the chaos resulting from such a disruption of the rationing system.

"They're going to dock us five days' worth of alcohol and tobacco rations," Torstein said when the news broke in the paper that Monday.

Lars shrugged. "The Quisling government is just trying to save face. People won't complain too much when the truth gets out about the resistance's intent."

CHAPTER 42

On the 18th of August, Haugland was hidden onboard a coastal steamer for Trondheim and smuggled into the city. There on the other side of the canal near the ferry dock, he found a bicycle waiting for him. Like a young man on no particular mission, taking the day off at his employer's expense, he made his way through the town's center of old two-story stone buildings and wide streets over to Elgeseter Bru, one of the main bridges over the river Nid.

It was a beautiful day, but arriving in the suburbs of Elgeseter and Oya he was careful, since there had been a *razzia* by the Gestapo at the Technical Institute only days before. Nothing escaped his notice as he approached his meeting point.

That man standing on the street. The car parked on the road; it had no furnace.

He couldn't forget that this beautiful, ancient town was Rinnan's headquarters and that the notorious Cloister was only blocks away. He was supposed to be meeting an XU contact by the Deaf Church, but had no idea with whom.

He rode past the car and came opposite a church. Putting down the kickstand he fiddled with the chain. A man and woman came out of a building, got into the car, and drove off. The man in the summer suit had crossed the street and was heading away from him. It was peaceful, but when his contact didn't show he became restless and decided to leave.

"You weren't having bike trouble were you?" a woman's lilting voice asked.

"My chain." He put his tools back into his pocket

"If it's loose, I know a place where it can be mended."

"It's fine now." Haugland turned. She was young, pretty, with soft brown hair and china blue eyes. She was wearing sport trousers and a blouse. She had a bike too.

"You're late," he said.

"Sorry. The Stapo showed up at your contact's flat looking for someone else in the building. He decided to take no chances. I'm to take you to his new location."

Haugland sized the girl up. She had given the correct exchange for their meeting although one word wasn't quite right. He had no choice but to take a chance and go with her.

"I'm ready," he said.

"Really?" The girl laughed. "You don't look ready. We have to go several blocks." She leaned over and kissed him lightly on the lips. "And, you're my sweetheart." She kissed him again. This time she put her arms around his neck.

"Then do it like you mean it," he said, giving her a hard kiss back. He stroked her cheek and grinned. "Sweetheart."

"Okay, smart aleck." She tore off toward the bridge where there were some apartments. Down a side street, she stopped and leaned toward him. "There's an old woman in the first floor apartment," she whispered. "Her son's in the *Hird*. Since you like it so much, kiss me again. Then we can go on up."

Haugland obliged with a much slower, tender kiss.

She stopped on the second floor landing while he continued up to the fourth. He found the green painted door easily. It opened to a tall and angular man with an easily forgotten blonde face. He was an old colleague from XU, the resistance intelligence group. Haugland knew him only as Harry.

"*God dag*, Harry. Where did you find that one?"

"Who?"

"My escort. Does she kiss everyone she meets? Or am I just special?"

Harry chuckled. "Ryper."

"Just wondering. She's not a Communist? Their groups are a little more action oriented."

Harry slapped his thigh. "*Nei*, but is there something I should be telling her boyfriend?"

"Keep an eye on her. She's frisky." Haugland swung off his rucksack and put it on the bare wood floor. "When did you get in from Sweden, Harry?"

"Two weeks ago. Uncle sent me. We came down by Lake Selbu."

"Ah." Haugland looked around the little two-room apartment. It was sparsely furnished with three kitchen chairs, a sagging and tattered cat-scratched brown sofa, and a card table. Just a place to meet. From habit, he stole a glance out the Venetian blinds halfway up the curtained window.

They sat on the sofa that nearly sagged to the floor. Haugland wondered if it had fleas too. He took out a radio part hidden in a secret lining at the bottom of his pack. Harry gave it a quick inspection, his eye close to the part. "Well, there's a piece damaged here. I can see that. Tell you what, I'll just get you a whole new part. How's that?"

"Great," Haugland said.

"You'll need it. Hear the latest? Finland's about to settle with Russia."

"The Germans won't like that. They'll have to withdraw from the Petsamo mines and retreat into Finnmark." Haugland shifted his position on the sofa as it seemed to be sinking lower as he sat. "Lose all that nickel." Finnmark was the northernmost county in Norway.

Harry turned the piece over. "London wants information on carrier movement out of Trondheim and any other vital marine traffic. We're putting in a coastal radio station. I'll be back and forth."

"Heard there was a *razzia* at the Technical Institute a few days ago. What happened?"

"They arrested some students. They're at Falstad concentration camp now. I wasn't affected, but a man who's very good at fixing radios and W/Ts was detained for twenty-four hours then released." Harry put the radio piece into a wooden fish tackle box and set it next to the sofa. "It'll take a day to get the piece."

Haugland looked thoughtful. "All right. I'll pick it up tomorrow. In the meantime can you do another favor for me?"

"*Ja* sure."

"A couple of people from Fjellstad were smuggled out to Sweden by Rinnan's group. I want to find their camp and keep them isolated from another refugee who went over just before them. He's an AT evader and knows I'm doing illegal work. Name's Karl Olavsen."

"All right, I'll see what Uncle can do. One more problem. There's an island community called Vikna about two hundred miles north of here. They have a large resistance group there. Storing arms, observing marine traffic. Their leader has been meeting with a resistance contact from Trondheim for over fourteen months. Then the quisling sheriff arrested their leader and brought him here. The contact intervened and helped him escape to Sweden."

"And?"

"SOE-Norway in London identified this contact as Rinnan. Uses the name Olav Whist."

"Jesus." Haugland felt queasy. Whist... Just as in Lillehavn.

"Know anyone up there?" Harry asked. "It could collapse anytime. The damn people refuse to believe that Whist is Rinnan. Think he's a hero getting their leader out. Took all of FO-IV and SOE in London to convince the leader, but Vikna folk won't listen to the couriers we've sent to warn them. What a mess."

Haugland started to say he didn't know anyone, then remembered Arne Finn, Sig's nephew.

He left an hour later promising to meet the following day. On the next landing, the girl was waiting. She smiled wryly when he came down beside her.

"Can't live without me, can you?" Haugland grinned.

She laughed. "I'm supposed to see you off."

"Tell you what. If you know of a safe *konditori*, I'll take you out. It's been a while since I went out with a sweetheart."

She demurely gave him her arm. The snoop in the first floor flat got quite a show.

***

For the rest of the day, Haugland stayed hidden at a small apartment over a tailor's shop near the Marketplace. It was the flat of a contact's parents, but they showed no fear for a stranger in their home and more importantly, didn't ask questions. At eight o'clock, about two hours before curfew, Haugland picked up his bike in the back of the store and left for his next meeting.

The evening had turned cool and overcast as he rode again down through the market center. In the overcast light, the statue of the old Viking Olav, the main feature of the area, looked unusually austere. Haugland eyed him as he passed by his high pedestal, heading down to his destination, the *Hjemme for Døve.*

Haugland arrived there not long after. It was an imposing old building set right on the street. Ignoring the front door, he sought out the service entrance on the side, walking the bike back with him. It was quiet, the blackout curtains already drawn in the windows. Coming to the side steps, he leaned the bike against the wall and mounted the stairs. After knocking, he waited patiently. There was the sound of movement on the other side of the door, then a click as the door was unlocked. A matronly woman with short dark hair peered out. "*Ja?*" she asked.

My name H-A-N-S-E-N, Haugland fingerspelled.

"Do come in. You've been expected." She glanced out into the walkway. Satisfied he hadn't been followed, she closed the door, leading the way through a big institutional kitchen. It was neat and tidy, the big pots and pans carefully stored away for the night. Open shelves revealed heavy white plates stacked under cups hanging on hooks. Colorful curtains in the windows and a picture of Jesus tending His flock completed the decor.

Come, she signed. I take you to room.

The room was down a hall and after pointing out the WC, she left him. He shut the door, turning on a small light on the nightstand. The room was simple. There was another door on the other side of the bed. Perhaps this had been an examining room. He took off the rucksack and took out his gun from a secret compartment. He placed it under the bolster, and then lay down. All he had to do was wait for three steady knocks.

He folded his arms across his chest and stared at the fir-paneled ceiling. Blocking everything else out except for the sounds of the building, he listened until he could distinguish what belonged to the Home and what did not. He hadn't stayed in one of these homes since he'd been wounded after his father's arrest in 1940. He remembered the silence, though. He fought the urge to sleep.

Suddenly, he heard the tread of feet on the other side of the wall, then three knocks on the other door. Instantly awake, he sat up sharply, his fingers brushing the gun. He knocked two short raps on the wall behind him. A voice called through the door, giving him the password.

It was Solheim. Haugland opened the door. Behind him was a dark blonde.

"Axel," Solheim said to his companion, "This is Ryper."

"*God kveld.*" Axel extended his hand. It was rough and callused. He was short, but had a commanding presence. He had to be. He was Milorg head for Trondheim and Sor-Trøndelag areas. "Welcome, Ryper. The Ptarmigan. I like that, although flounder might be more appropriate for a fisherman. They camouflage themselves pretty well too."

Haugland grinned. "As long as I stay camouflaged. Fin or feather, I don't really care."

"I've brought someone else." Solheim stepped aside. Behind him was a man in his forties, with smooth graying hair swept off his forehead. He had high cheeks leaning toward jowls and wore simple wire-rimmed glasses. A clerical collar graced his neck. It was Conrad Bonnevie-Svendsen, priest for the deaf. Haugland hadn't seen him in nearly two years.

"Conrad, what on earth are you doing here?" He shook his hand vigorously, feeling a burst of joy to see someone from his old life before the war. Someone who knew him.

"Making the rounds of the deaf churches and schools and doing a little illegal work. Have to keep things going on the civilian side of life despite the occupation. Accommodations all right?"

Haugland laughed. Very good, he signed. "Shall we sit, gentlemen?"

He laid out the mission. "There are forty to fifty crates containing five hundred machine pistols and ammunition. A third will be brought into Trondheimfjord. This is risky but with Allied attention directed toward Paris, air drops between here and Sweden are out."

"Let's get to work." Solheim rubbed his hands together like an enthusiastic schoolboy. Haugland soon learned that for a pastor, Solheim had an uncanny knowledge of guns and grenades.

Sometime after two in the morning, Axel and Solheim left, slipping out into the dim light that was night. It had been an intense six hours of discussion on how to organize the shipment of arms into the Trondheim area. Conrad stayed afterwards and they talked about the war and family news.

"I've seen your mother, Tore. She's doing well. A very strong woman."

Haugland sighed. "It hurts she thinks I was killed in that shoot-out four years ago. It's hard enough for her to lose Father and Per. And my uncle?"

"No word out of the camps in Poland. Which right now is a good thing." Conrad put a hand on his shoulder. "Why don't we say a little prayer on that?"

After Conrad left, Haugland lay down in the dark, but sleep wouldn't come. He stared at the wall, thinking about all the things he had to do and the increasing odds against getting them accomplished. Vikna was unsettling. It could pose an additional danger to him. He decided to bring Sig's nephew, Arne Finn, down as soon as possible. He'd invent a job and pay him.

Haugland tucked his arms under his head. Tomorrow he'd get the radio part from Harry, then board a fishing boat to the island of Hitra. He continued to stare through the dark and was able to make out shapes on the wall in front of him. Pictures. What were they?

Cows grazing around some mountain *seter*, boats sailing in the Trondheimfjord. The third was a little girl herding goats. As he tried to recall her face, the sweet features of Lisel Fromme took hold, her silky flaxen hair in braids on top of her head. Why he thought of her, he couldn't guess, but there was a power in that pixie-like face. Maybe it was obligation to Einar, or genuine love for her, something missing from his life. He closed his eyes and she was nestling in his arms, clutching her half-grown cat. He could almost hear her giggling. He drifted off, then scowled. Unbidden, another face came. Beautiful, fresh as the morning sun.

Was it obligation? Or what? The thought never finished. He fell asleep.

CHAPTER 43

Haugland quietly returned to Fjellstad, confident everything was now in place for the biggest shipment of arms he would ever receive. The next day, he and Kjell rendezvoused with the Haraldsens on Hitra, using new information from Trondheim to finalize their plans. "Find some way for Arne Finn to come down to Hitra," he said to Sig just before the *Otta* took off for home. He didn't explain.

When they returned to Fjellstad later that evening, Haugland excused himself.

"Going so soon?" Kjell asked. "Didn't Holger bring the best poetry from the BBC? Better yet the news the Americans are so close to Paris?"

"It was good news."

"Then we should celebrate. I have that stash Hans and I can't drink up. Surely, the Germans are going to negotiate."

Haugland clapped his shoulder. "Will you forgive me? Another time. Sorry, I'm just tired."

Haugland went on up on the ridge, but instead of going home, he sought out Grimstad.

The doctor's house wasn't much different than the other two-story houses along the graveled lane except he had two front doors—the main door and one that led into his office. Knocking, Haugland waited on the wood steps, looking at the pots of flowering geraniums pooling around the walk. When the screen door opened carefully against his shoulder, an elderly woman whose dress suggested the self-efficiency and cleanliness of a doctor's housekeeper greeted him.

While he studied the prints in the waiting room she went off to get Grimstad, returning to tell him with motions and a loud voice that the doctor had invited him into the house. She led the way down to a private study and left him. "*God aften. Herr Doktor* will be down shortly."

Haugland looked around the room. It reminded him of his father's study with its floor to ceiling shelves of books covering two walls. They flowed around the occasional print hung here and there. Closer examination, however, revealed display areas neatly organized with a wide variety of crystals: lustrous galena, vibrant azurite and quartz crystals among some of them. Haugland named them without thinking, finally resting his eyes on a collection of books behind a comfortable, leather chair in the corner of the room. His heart thumping, he walked over and turned on a floor lamp next to the chair. He had recognized the titles on the spines.

The first one he pulled out was a small book written by his father in the late 1920s, detailing his ideas about various aspects of disharmonic folding, a special interest of his. Opening the cover, he found it autographed. Surprised, he wondered if there were other books by him in Grimstad's collection. He put it back and pulled out the other book that had caused him to start.

It was much larger than his father's, a heavy tome with a red leather cover, titled *The Birds of Coastal Norway.* He had forgotten the name of the author, but he knew who had done the artist's plates. "Illustrated by Kristian Oldsgaard" was printed neatly beneath the author's name on the title page inside. Wistfully, he turned the pages looking for a particular favorite, a watercolor of a puffin.

He remembered the day he had gone to his uncle's house in Telavåg and had seen the painting in progress on the special table in his uncle's studio. He had been working in watercolor and Haugland had watched the bird evolve the whole weeklong period he had stayed there. He had loved the comical face of the bird as it emerged from the paper. Noting this, *Onkel* Kris told him that the bird could always be his. On his birthday late that summer, true to his word, the completed painting was presented as a gift, its print already at the publishers. It was the most wonderful thing he had, he told his uncle in sign and after that he had kept it framed in his room, taking it with him when he went off to the university. It had gone back to his parents's home for safekeeping when he went to Cambridge, but he wasn't sure where it was now. Like his family, everything had become lost or scattered, even a painting of a puffin.

How old had he been? Ten, going on eleven and old enough to know his beloved uncle was different from other people. Not just from the way he communicated—but also different in the great gift he had in his artist's eye of seeing nature and the wonderful world around him. It made him unique yet at the same time connected him with everyone else because he expressed what they saw too but couldn't explain. From the time Haugland was a boy, he had followed his uncle's career as his reputation grew.

The last time he had seen *Onkel* Kris had been in March of 1940 when he had traveled to Telavåg for his sixtieth birthday. Everyone had gone for what would be the last time the family would ever be together. Perhaps they sensed that the war—already six months old—would soon engulf their world.

It had been a cold, blustery day, but Haugland and his uncle had bundled up and gone off along the shore as they often did when he was much younger. They talked, their hands moving with words and emotions. His uncle seemed much older than he had remembered. He had complained of arthritis in his hands. His hair, once as dark as Haugland's, had gray in it.

Holding the pages open to the puffin, Haugland remembered guiltily how he had thought then that he loved this man in some ways more than his own father. He was afraid he might die before he could tell him how he felt. Sadly, that had come true. They had been distracted by the flight of some bird in their path and the moment slipped away. Haugland never saw him again.

"Find anything interesting?"

Haugland held the book too tight as he put it back. "Where did you find the pyrite?" Haugland picked up a shiny egg-sized piece of fool's gold and turned it in his hand.

"A friend at the local Orkdal mine. Before its occupation by the Germans."

"Have you ever been there?"

"I got a tour once. The world's first electric train's there, you know. Of course, the Germans want the ore to make sulfur."

"It's more important than you know. The Allies have cut them off from their sources in Sicily." Haugland nodded at the rocks. "I didn't know you were a collector."

"A little hobby. I fancy myself an amateur geologist. I go to the Museum of Natural History in Oslo when I can."

They talked about the collection for a bit. Grimstad seemed genuinely delighted he knew something of geology. Haugland became relaxed, especially after being offered some brandy.

"I acquired a case of this brandy after a German, grateful to me for saving his frostbitten foot."

Haugland chuckled. He could get used to drinking brandy here. He hadn't talked to anyone about geology in a long time, a subject he had inhaled since he was a very little boy. Kjell was interested in the formations of the coast and islands too, but was more concerned about how he would get around them if there was a low tide between the skerries.

"What's on your mind?" Grimstad put a crystal back on a shelf.

Haugland came quickly to the point. "I want you to get in touch with the *stadsleges* for Frøya and the west side of the Trondheimfjord near Leksvik. People who are completely trustworthy because I want them to search the records for Odd Sorting."

Grimstad wrinkled his eyebrows. "Is he in some sort of trouble?"

"I consider him to be very dangerous. He's not to be trusted."

The doctor looked shocked. "He's a Nazi?" He took a hard sip of his brandy.

"Sorting? I doubt he has any political motive, but he is an agent provocateur. Kjell has always suspected him. I just got the proof." He didn't say it was on Anna Fromme's word.

"God. Bugge. He's so solid with Bugge." He sagged down on a chair.

"It's a problem. People like Bugge think Sorting arranged the escape of schoolmaster Ola Stagg and Arne Berg. They won't believe anything against him. All our work could backfire."

"Why the paperwork?"

"Sorting said he was born in Leksvik. I want any medical information about the Sorting family there. Check the name Morkdal too."

"You have medical records. They're fake."

"Mine disappeared in the bombing of Molde. No one's bombed Frøya."

Grimstad took a swift drink. "All right. I'll get on it."

"Be careful. Despite appearances, Sorting is assuredly responsible for the death of ten men and the arrest of about thirty more south of here. Who knows where else he has worked."

"He works for the Germans?"

"*Nei*. He works for Rinnan."

"The Devil you say." The color drained from Grimstad's his face.

"Do you want to back out? You can, you know. It's not too late. There are no cases of brandy in this. And if you're caught, only a prayer for a quick bullet in the back of the head. Don't mention glory. There's not much in it when you know the enemy's capable of prying the very bones out of you. I wouldn't blame you."

"*Nei*. I'm staying. I want to help."

Haugland put down his drink. "Good. For now, be friendly. Don't alter your rounds. But be careful. There could be a second person in the community involved in this."

Grimstad took a last sip of the brandy. "Is there anything else you wanted to talk about?"

Haugland straightened up. He wasn't sure how to initiate the next subject but felt something should be said. He wished that he could talk about it to Kjell, but sensed that right now, it wouldn't work. He wouldn't understand. "What do you know about Anna Fromme?"

"Oh, not much more than what folks know and say, but local opinion has been pretty strong."

"What's your opinion?"

Grimstad shrugged. "Well, Anna Fromme's never struck me as being a Nazi. She's well-mannered and seems educated. Totally out of place here. I find that intriguing."

"Do you think she betrayed her husband?"

Grimstad was silent for a moment. "*Nei*. The rumors didn't start here. People knew about Lillehavn because it involved Jarle's grandson, Einar. The gossip must have followed her. I became suspicious last February when a colleague made a comment that one of the men arrested, then released, was a secret Nazi. Worked with the Germans. He wouldn't elaborate. Was afraid to. He also thought that this man introduced Fromme to a Rinnan agent."

Sorting. Haugland stood up. "What did this friend of yours think about Anna Fromme?"

Grimstad pursed his lips. "He said he thought she'd been slandered. Mind telling me your interest?"

Haugland made a face. "Believe me, I have no love for Germans, but I think she is innocent." *Her word,* he thought, and would have left it at that except Grimstad, noticeably interested in his statement, expressed his relief that Haugland found her blameless.

"Can you help her?" he asked.

"*Nei*. Not until capitulation."

"Poor woman. I sometimes feel quite ashamed."

Haugland shrugged. He wanted to be noncommittal, but didn't have the heart. "Maybe you could look at her little girl. She looks thin."

"I think I can do that. I can see her on the sly. And the woman?"

"I don't know. Be a friend. At arms' length if you have to."

Haugland stood up. It was time to go. He gave Grimstad final instructions on the search for Sorting's medical papers. The answer might come while he was gone. "We're going to try brisling again and will be gone for a couple of days."

Giving Haugland the useless platitude to get some rest, Grimstad saw him off. After shaking hands, Haugland departed solemnly. His words hung in the air.

"*They can pry the very bones out of you.*"

CHAPTER 44

Sorting made his way into the mouth of the fjord leading back to Fjellstad, steering his motorboat across the dark waves kicked up by the wind. The tide was out, exposing tangled green ribbons of seaweed as well as dead fish and other marine debris. As he tied up, a pair of terns tore off, speeding over the water, their cries echoing off the steep forested hills behind him. It was a beautiful lonely place and it suited him.

His hut was small, suitable for no more than three people on holiday. Through its three big windows he could observe traffic going in and out of the fjord. He took a quick look around the room to check for forced entry, and then took off his damp outer clothes. He had been out all night.

The day before, he had received a radio message to meet with Birger Strom, currently one of Rinnan's favorites. Strom was intelligent, athletic with a good sense of humor and a diabolical lust for helping human beings disintegrate under interrogation at the Cloister. Sorting liked the ex-policeman, but he had no moral compass—something he couldn't ignore. He was careful around him.

They met at eleven last night inside the mouth of the fjord. Strom brought materials, a bottle of wine and news that a signal had once again been picked up near Fjellstad by DRTs in both Trondheim and southwestern Norway. The Chief suspected some action.

Sorting lit a fire for coffee in his little stove and waited. The sun was up, but none of the fishing boats were out because it was Sunday. People were sleeping in. He debated whether to do that himself. His body ached.

You're working your tail off, Sorting, he thought. Like the rest of the fishing community he worked long hours with Bugge Grande, making connections with other fishermen out in their boats as they took brisling. He ate, slept and played cards with them, joining in on the occasional song. But unknown to them, bit by bit, he looked for news of any strange boats or the movement of men. Because he was Bugge's friend, no one doubted his loyalty.

Despite these friendships, however, Sorting hadn't come any closer to locating the W/T. *Who's hiding you? And where did you keep it?* The signals started five months ago—a long time to keep such a person hidden—but Sorting couldn't find it.

The W/T wasn't the only failure. Sorting, try as he might, couldn't win a friendship with Kjell Arneson. To learn anything now from him, his only hope was stupid Hansen. Or perhaps Rika, Kjell's daughter. Rika and Freyda had become fast friends in Trondheim. Freyda. She had been able to glean that Rika was involved with some sort of illegal work.

He learned something else: A.C. Kjelstrup was seeing her. Now that was something. He decided to make an appearance at the *konditori* then come back and sleep the day away. After securing the cabin, he went down to his motorboat.

***

The lights were on in the Arneson warehouse. As he approached, Sorting realized that the warehouse door was open. Hansen was inside working on some nets. From the side of the door, he watched him put on rubber gloves and pull a net out of a large wooden vat where it had been soaking. Sorting thought the solution looked blue and wondered if it had copper sulfate, a chemical that was scarce. Fishermen soaked their nets in boiled birch bark to prevent the build-up of algae. Sorting wondered where Arneson had acquired the chemical. His question was answered when he saw a battered box up on a shelf clearly marked. It looked pre-war.

Hansen set the wet net on a frame, then went back to mending. His hands were quick and strong as he worked his ball of cotton seine and mending shuttle with precision. Sorting finally stepped inside and tapped on Hansen's shoulder. The deaf-mute seemed startled to see him.

"You're up early," Sorting said. "Going fishing. Tomorrow isn't it?"

Hansen made a sound in his mouth, nodded yes, then went back to work. As he worked, they carried on a lopsided conversation, Hansen often writing a quick word or two in his notebook. Sorting soon learned they would be gone for several days fishing.

Sorting watched him for a bit longer, then announced that he was going to the *konditori.* Would Jens like to come?

Ja. First finish hole, Hansen motioned.

Sorting smiled. He was making great progress with Arneson's man—someone he felt he could easily trick. He didn't see Hansen's scowl when he left.

There were five people inside. One was Bette, Ella's young assistant. A heavyset girl with gray cow eyes and straight light brown hair, she was so good-natured and simple even the craggiest fisherman was cheered by her. She regularly flirted with Sorting. She was the perfect sort of female friend:

prone to gossip which was useful to him and living life based on juicy romance magazines. So lonely, so needy. She blushed when he winked at her.

Sorting sat down by one of the lace-curtained windows. Outside at the seawall, was a young woman with a soft peasant scarf over her head. A sweater covered a cotton print dress. Her legs were bare, but he knew without looking further she was slim and graceful. Beside her was a little girl. She clutched the woman's hand as though deathly afraid of something. The woman bent to soothe her and as she did, the scarf slipped off, freeing the woman's hair. She was beautiful with the Nordic mystique the Nazi posters were always trying to capture, but could only produce in stilted replication. Suddenly, Sorting realized he knew her. She was "The Woman," the schoolmaster's wife in Lillehavn.

Lighting a cigarette, he sat by the window and watched her with a gnawing flick of lust.

When did she come here? He had left Lillehavn before the arrests, but had been around for some of the interrogations in Trondheim. She must've come here after that.

He took a drag and watched her slim body move under the thin dress that flowed over her. He eyed on her full breasts, the space at the top of her legs where the cloth dipped in below her flat belly, then back to her face. It was disturbing thinking of her naked, lying in the arms of Fromme, making love. *When he still had arms.*

The image of Fromme's body slashed across his mind and he closed his eyes. It was something he didn't want to remember. The bloody image faded away and he opened his eyes.

Does she know? If she looks at me will she guess? No one knew, really. The coffin had been bored with holes and disposed of in the usual way. No one had seen the body. It was his secret.

He stopped smoking and looked at his hands. They were trembling. Damn her for making him remember. He was glad Bette came over with his usual order. He dove into it, trying to keep his fingers from shaking.

The shop bell jangled as the woman and girl stepped into the store. Her eyes met briefly with his as she came up the wide step into the tearoom. She looked down shyly as she passed, the little girl staying close to her dress skirt. At the counter she asked for *Fru* Bjornson.

"She's not here," Sorting heard Bette say.

"Then I'll leave a message."

"*Herr* Sorting?"

Sorting looked up with jolt. Bette was staring at him from behind the counter, her face a mix of fear and uncertainty. Everyone in the *konditori* was looking at her. He worried they would look at him and make some conclusions.

"What am I to do?" the girl said in a trembling voice.

"Just take the message. It wouldn't hurt."

The Woman turned and said, "*Takk.*" Her eyes showed appreciation. Sorting nodded back at her. *Nei,* she hadn't guessed his secret. She didn't know who he was.

Bette shoved a piece of paper and a pencil in front of her.

The shop bell rang again. Hansen came in. He had put on his dark Sunday coat. He came directly into the tearoom before he noticed any trouble.

"Jens!" The little girl broke away from her mother and skipped up to Hansen. He stared at her, his face puzzled so she began to move her fingers in some sort of sign.

"Lisel! Oh, do forgive her, *vær så snill*,." the woman scolded her. Firmly grasping her hand, she led Lisel away and out the door, practically walking into Ella Bjornson, dressed in her Sunday best. Outside she continued to scold the little girl, now in tears.

Sorting turned back. Hansen had slipped into a chair next to him and was watching too. Sorting tapped him.

"That the woman you worked for?"

Hansen nodded yes, then signing, made a face.

"*Ja*, too bad. She's pretty. Might be nice to get to know her under the covers." Sorting looked at Hansen and wondered if he ever thought of women. Or was he some eunuch?

Breakfast came and went. Sorting was sleepy and told Hansen he'd been out late playing cards. He asked about their trip tomorrow. "You've been out a lot too."

Hansen flipped over a page in the notebook. Fish runs good, he wrote, but fuel supplies low. Use sail all the time to return. Get stuck. Better to stay out.

"*Ja*, I know what you mean. Bugge wanted to go out but he's discovered an electrical failure in his relay switch. The fuel gauge was way off. Used up the rest of his ration for the month. He'll do sail, but can't go out as far. We'll just put net down and leave. Damn pity."

Sorry, Hansen motioned.

Around nine the *konditori* began to empty. It would be closed during church service, opening briefly before it was closed for the day. Hansen stood up. He signed thanks for the meal and indicated he would see Sorting around. Sorting wished him "*God fiske.*"

CHAPTER 45

Out of Sorting's sight, after leaving the *konditori*, Haugland went directly to see Kjell. His friend sat dejected at the kitchen table in his work clothes. No church today.

You all right? Haugland signed.

Kjell shifted in his chair and grimaced. "I'm all right. Just my knee acting up."

"Maybe Grimstad should look at it," Haugland voiced.

"Now that's the last thing I need. It's nothing... Better than some things around here."

Haugland looked at him and wondered what he meant. "Is Kitty packing?" he asked.

"She'll be ready by tomorrow," Kjell sighed. "Wants to be sure that her boyfriend Gram will write. If only it wasn't so far."

"She'll be all right. I know it's a hard decision, but the school will be good for her. I got the nets fixed. The *Otta*'s ready to go. We can leave at three as planned." He walked over to the sink. "Where's your whiskey stash? I know you've been hiding one."

"It's in the bottom cupboard. What the devil for?"

"Purely medicinal, though I can't decide whether to pour it down your throat or on you."

Haugland poured some into two small glass jars and set one down in front of the older man. Drink, he signed. He sat down opposite him and put the bottle on the table.

Kjell sipped, then gave Haugland a troubled look. He cleared his throat. "You've been in my house for five months now. You've eaten my food; you've gotten to know my family and friends. To your credit and my benefit, you've worked hard—far beyond what I had expected in this arrangement. You are a wonderful companion—a good friend. Maybe you're like a son.— I realized that when you were so sick."

Haugland's eyes didn't flinch, but he was surprised.

"But you have hurt me."

"Hurt you? How have I hurt you?" He leaned over his glass, his hands clasping its sides.

"It's something I heard about Bugge's boat. He lost the rest of his gas ration. I don't know how, but I know you did it."

"*Ja*. two nights ago. I monkeyed around with the relay switch."

Kjell's voice shook. "Do you know what this did to him? He got out in the channel. That's when he discovered the loss of fuel. They had to come in early."

"I know, but it had to be done. I can't allow Sorting to be out with him for this coming action. Sorting must be in Fjellstad."

Kjell picked up the jar and after tossing down the remaining whiskey held it out for more.

Haugland complied, pouring some more for himself. "Believe me," he said, "It was the only kind of sabotage I could think of that wouldn't be obvious. If he were with us, I'm sure he would've done it himself."

"You could have told me."

"Would you have stopped me?" Kjell didn't answer. "Sorting came down to the warehouse this morning. He watched me for a bit, then invited me to breakfast up to the *konditori*. Said he was up late, but I think he was out."

Kjell blanched.

"He may know of my signal to London two nights ago. If he met someone like I believe, he could have been told. There are DRTs in Trondheim and Kristiansund N tracking signals. I'm sorry," he said, "but it had to be done."

Kjell cleared his throat and shifted in his place. "You think Sorting figured it out?"

"*Nei*. Look, we're stuck. Sorting's here. The *Hessa*'s coming. The main thing is keeping people quiet. Our security is as good as the people Sig has chosen to help hide the crates."

Haugland stopped and looked down at the whiskey in his glass jar. He didn't really want to finish it. Too much to think about. It wasn't just Sorting. It was Anna Fromme. Her sudden appearance at the *konditori* had surprised him. Sorting didn't appear to recognize her, but Haugland had seen the dull look of lust in his eyes.

"Jens? Rika wants to see Kitty when we get back. Can I tell her the truth about her sister going to Kongsvinger?"

"*Nei*, Kjell. You can't tell her. It's for the best. In the meantime, I want Sorting watched."

Haugland rode back to his cabin on Kjell's bike. The day was warm and full of seaweed smell on the light breeze puffing off the fjord. At the last bend, he dismounted. Ahead the pine forest flowing around the fields of the Fromme farm came into view. He couldn't see the farmhouse, but as he came closer he saw to his surprise Anna Fromme sitting on the bank near the gravel driveway rising steeply back to it.

"*God dag*, Jens," she said shyly. "I heard someone say you were coming back. I hope you don't mind I waited. I was worried you got into trouble. Did Sorting notice anything?"

He shook his head no. He looked up and down the road and out to the fjord before writing in his notebook: You did fine. Sorting didn't recognize you. I warned my friends.

"I'm so glad. You must be careful. You shouldn't be friends with him."

I careful, he signed. Where Lisel? He circled his chin with his fingers. *Sweet.*

"Home," Anna replied, "I'm afraid I upset her. She didn't understand." She paused. "She's very fond of you. She thinks you are angry with her."

Haugland looked away. *Dammit!* Why did he feel this obligation to them? It was suicide getting involved, but every time he took steps to stay away, something happened. That they are Einar's family he could rationalize. *Nei*, he knew he didn't need the excuse. He wanted to be with them, to sit in the long *stue,* and watch the fjord from the windows.

He wanted to be with her.

It was all so crazy. Just one slip and he would blow everything. Worse, none of the people who depended on him would understand. A German woman. God... he didn't understand himself.

He felt his resolve drain away. He wrote: If you want to see me, we can meet in the woods behind your barn.

"But how will I let you know?"

Haugland thought for a moment then took out a medium-sized fishhook used for salmon fishing from his jacket pocket.

You want talk me. He walked over to an old wooden post by the driveway and pulling back the clump of grass and wildflowers around it hooked the barb near the base. Taking the dull steel hook back to her, he put it in her hand.

She held it like a treasure. "*Takk*. Once again you are my friend. How can I thank you?"

Haugland shrugged. No need.

She brushed her dress. "Well, I'm going back to the farmhouse. Lisel and I are going to have a picnic. Will you come? I have food and some books I'd like to give you. We'll meet in the woods, so we'd always know where to find each other. Please say yes."

Haugland signed yes, knowing whatever he did now, he could not turn back.

CHAPTER 46

Anna climbed the steep hill behind her barn and passed through the row of birch into the pine forest beyond. Lisel was not far behind, swishing her way through the tall grass and vibrant blue and orange flowers that were as high as her waist. She wore blue overalls and carried a little leather rucksack on her back. When she broke through the grass into the trees with little leaps, she came up to her mother flushed with excitement.

"Did you see the bunny, Mama? I almost caught it."

"*Ja*, Munchkin." Anna said she had seen it, a fuzzy brown blur.

Near the edge of the woods Anna put down an old wool blanket. She opened up the basket while Lisel undid her rucksack. Anna brought out a thermos and tins. Lisel brought out a rag doll and a child's china tea set. Anna chuckled, then looked up.

Coming down along the edge of the field was Jens Hansen. He was in his shirtsleeves with the arms rolled up and wore dark trousers held up by suspenders. He stopped and looked down in the direction of the barn, quite a ways below, then further down to the back of the house.

He doesn't know we're here, she thought, wondering how she would get his attention. He stood with his hands on his hips, lost in thought, perhaps watching the birds on the barn roof rise up and catch ants flying in the air as she had done a few hours ago. The light breeze caressed the dark hair on his brow, lifting it up. She thought again what a handsome, nice-looking man he was, made even nicer because he was a decent person. She knew she could trust him.

He walked away from the birches and into the steep meadow. He moved with ease and confidence that was spellbinding. This is how he was that day in the springhouse when I couldn't find Lisel. Strong and self-assured. Not the way he usually presents himself.

Who are you? she wondered. He tapped his hands together, then made some motions near his face and chest. She realized that he was talking to himself with his hands. It was so unexpected and unusual that she laughed. Could you sign swear words with your hands?

"Lisel, go tell Jens where we are. He doesn't see us. Quickly." When Lisel balked, Anna said, her voice close to laughing. "He's not angry with you. Nor am I. Go Munchkin. Then we'll have tea with Dolly. Remember to go close so he sees you."

If days could be measured, Anna thought later, this one would be one of the very best. She brought food she had acquired under her agreement with Ella. Together, they served their guest. Anna poured raspberry tea from her thermos into Lisel's little teapot. Lisel poured cups for them both. Hansen's was two fingers deep.

Takk he signed then drank it very daintily, crooking his pinky finger.

The day improved. It was almost hot, but the sky stayed overcast with periodic sun breaks that created kidney-shaped shadows on the mountains above the valley. The afternoon stretched out and Lisel fell asleep in Anna's lap. She laid her down on the blanket. Hansen cleaned up.

"*Takk,*" she said, remembering the sign then settled back against a slim birch tree. From her rucksack she took out a bundle wrapped in a dishtowel and laid it in front of him. "These are for you. There are four. Einar and I enjoyed reading them."

Hansen leaned over and undid the dishtowel. Inside was a stack of books. He turned them over, then looked at her. He seemed surprised. Slowly he fingerspelled: A-M-E-R-I-C-A-N.

"*Ja,* three of them are American. Do you know them? That one is Faulkner, the other is Hemmingway. They are all translations, part of the Yellow Series from ten years ago. There is a Sinclair Lewis. The fourth is Norwegian—Vesaas. I like him very much, but I'd never seen so much American writing as I have here in Norway."

Hansen made a slit throat sign on his neck.

"I know. They're all banned—though I'm not sure about Vesaas. Einar had many such books but we couldn't bear throwing them away, so we hid them."

Takk. He smiled clear to his eyes.

He started to put them aside, but Anna touched his hand. He stopped and looked at her. She withdrew her hand, struck hard at how much his friendship meant to her.

Anna glanced at Lisel. She was curled up, her fists against her mouth. Anna put her shawl on her shoulders and tucked it around her neck. When she was finished, she discovered Hansen had written in his notebook: Do you read *englesk*? it said.

"*Ja,* I can read English," she replied. "I learned a long time ago, but I do not tell this to just anyone. Only a special friend like you."

And? His fingers pulled the word across the air.

She swallowed, her heart thumping. "I was born in America and lived there until my family moved to London. My mother was American. My father is German. I have been hiding here in Norway."

Hansen looked stunned.

Secret, he signed.

Ja, secret, Anna signed back, a great sense of relief flowing through her. No one except Einar knew she was American.

Hansen waved his hand at her. Mother?

"My mother died in a car accident some years before."

Sorry.

Hansen wrapped the towel tighter around the books and stood up.

"Is Jens going, Mama?" Lisel rubbed her eyes.

"*Ja*, Munchkin. He has to go."

He wrote in the notebook and handed it to her. *Takk*, it said, giving instructions about the hook and him meeting her. Only for emergencies. The writing was cold and impersonal.

Lisel got up and took his hand. He smiled at her and gave her hand a squeeze.

Good-bye, he signed to them.

Good-bye, Anna signed back, no longer feeling alone.

CHAPTER 47

The *Otta* left at three in the morning, slipping past Sorting's spit as quietly as possible. Once out of earshot of Sorting's hut, Kjell brought the engine up to speed. The Otta moved forward with a steady *tonka, tonka, tonka,* the mist-shrouded hills and walls of the fjord muffling the motor.

They reached the Trondheimsleia about forty minutes later under a cold, dark sky. Chugging over to one of Kjell's favorite fishing grounds where he had rights, they put down net and set it high in the water for salmon. Back in the wheelhouse, Kjell lit a lantern and pulled down the blackout curtains. There, gently rocking on a calm sea, they waited for the Haraldsen men.

"Do you have all the papers, Jens?"

"Right here." Haugland eased them out of his pocket. They were manifest papers made up in Trondheim by the resistance. For the last two days he had been aging them in his jacket as he worked around the diesel engine on the *Otta*.

At five, they went out in the dinghy to haul in the net. Rowing along the length of the net in the lavender morning light, they brought up sections to check for fish. It was very heavy as big stones were fastened to it to hold it down in the water. Working quickly, Haugland pulled fish from the eyes in the net, bashing their heads on the dinghy's side to kill them.

"Damned good catch," Kjell threw one onto the bottom of the sturdy little boat. "The school hit the net just right."

Not long after, Sverre's boat appeared. Weighing anchor close by, he hailed them. With him were his oldest boy, Kolbjorn, a youth of seventeen and a cousin. Rowing over, they helped bring up the last of the net. Kjell set it back in after fixing one of the cork disks keeping it afloat.

Back on the *Otta*, they waited for Sig and Holger. It was light now, visibility out on the channel clear to about a half mile off of Hitra which was still misty along its long shore. Moderate traffic appeared—trawlers, fishing boats and occasionally a German naval vessel of dubious purpose. To the south, it looked busy.

"Would you look at that," Kjell said.

A large convoy was moving into view, most likely on a run to Tromsø several hundred miles to the north. Important German naval bases were there as well as the battleship *Tirpitz*, Haugland thought. The *Bismarck*'s sister ship continued to threaten despite damage from sabotage last year.

He quickly identified them. One was a heavy cruiser accompanied by several Narvik class destroyers, bristling with guns under the Nazi flag. He spotted an oiler, supply ships and and various other types of vessels accompanied by escorts that included torpedo boats, the so-called E-boats. Moving in the convoy like gray ghosts they all made up Germany's "fleet of being" in Norway since the early 40's. The convoy was long and spread out. Haugland decided that it was worth a picture and went to get his camera.

"Might be a good idea to have Sverre check on his net," Haugland said. "Our boats together might look suspicious."

While they were gone, Haugland set up the camera near the wheelhouse where he could be partially hidden. He screwed on the long-range lens and waited. While the cruiser had been in the north before, these destroyers were generally down in naval yards in Bergen, an area he knew intimately. If his hunch was right, their movement was another sign of an impending crisis in Finnmark.

A couple of hours later, Sig Haraldsen showed up. "I had a devilish time," he said as he came onboard. "First it was the convoy. Then I got stopped by a patrol boat looking for contraband food."

"What happened?" Kjell looked worried.

"They didn't find anything so they took the lobsters I just got out of my pots. All for vegetables," he grumbled. "The damn *Veg-stapo* is at it again."

CHAPTER 48

"This the man?"

"*Jawohl, Sturbannmführer*. We located the picture last week." The young assistant, Krischen Gebhardt, snapped his heels at attention. Sweat stains discolored his gray uniform. "His name is Torstein Kaaland. His family lives in Kvam. Related to half the people there."

Sturbannmführer Martin Koeller straightened up in his desk chair. The picture was of a blonde man with a long face, high forehead, and dark eyes behind spectacles.

"This isn't the schoolteacher. The hair color's wrong."

"*Ja*, but he was in the village the day the boy was arrested."

He loosened his uniform collar "Why should I be concerned about him?"

"His name was discovered on a list of known criminals involved in XU."

Koeller pushed his arms against his desk and stretched. Out of the country for nearly three weeks, he had come back to Oslo for briefings and several hours at the prison interrogating a man involved in so-called export. He had only just returned to his office in the ornate Victoria Terrace, Gestapo headquarters for Norway. So much to do. He had the investigation of the train sabotage to finish, but the new, more serious investigation of *Oberst* Joachim von Weber's role in the Hitler Plot was pressing. Von Weber was one of several officers stationed in Norway involved in it.

"So what do you have?"

"I think he met the schoolteacher at that cabin we searched last month. He was seen walking through the village going out that way early in the evening."

"Ah. So the boy was right. The schoolteacher is up to something." Koeller sat up. He remembered the man, the one who had been called back at Hjerkinn so that his papers could be reviewed. Dark hair, spectacles.

Gebhardt laid an envelope on the desk. "We have at least two sets of fingerprints at the cabin and some photograph fragments taken from the fireplace. They're fragile."

"*Danke,* Franz. You've been most thorough. I couldn't have done it better." He leaned back in his chair and rubbed his eyes.

The aide beamed. "*Danke*, sir. Will you be going out? I can have your dress uniform pressed." He went behind Koeller to close the heavy curtains on the tall narrow windows. It was past six, well into the dinner hour.

"*Nein.* Not tonight. Just leave the files. We can discuss them in the morning."

After his aide left, Koeller pulled off his tall, shiny boots, massaging his stocking toes into the thick Oriental carpet for a moment. He lit a cigarette from a gold case and after savoring the first drag, he went through a pile of materials on his desk.

There were a variety of records, most of them gathered after von Weber's arrest in Berlin. He had been lured over only a few days after the plot failed and was now imprisoned under the sentence of death. His aide, *Feldwebel* Horst Klein, had been interrogated here, initially in Lillehammer. He was out on restricted duty.

Koeller separated the photos into four piles, then spread one in a line. These had been taken from von Weber's villa in Prussia maintained by a small staff during his long assignment in Norway. Seized, the property belonged to the SS now.

In the pile was a haunting black and white photograph of a beautiful teenage girl dressed for a party. Sweet and on the verge of womanhood, she had fascinated him right off with her magnetic beauty and nagging familiarity, but the middle-aged von Weber had no known children.

Who is she then? Why did her face nag at him? Had she been at some party in Berlin? Like an unquiet ghost, she had grown on him, slipping into his thoughts unbidden. The puzzle had deepened when a second photograph of her—obviously taken in Norway—was discovered in a safe in von Weber's office near Lillehammer. She was looking straight into the camera and was laughing. She was several years older and leaned against a handsome blonde man. Their bodies melded together as the man's arms encircled her. They were obviously in love. Koeller felt a sense of betrayal.

Koeller pulled the materials together when he remembered the envelope. Gently opening its flap, he exposed two badly burned photograph fragments. He pulled them out with tweezers and froze. On top was the woman, this time standing alone in the badly scorched remnant. The rest had burned off. Too bad, he thought, feeling vast disappointment. Another traitor. He rubbed her image across her breasts with a finger, then swore at his stupidity. The fragment instantly shattered into brittle pieces, destroying the other image. He never saw the boy with the dancing eyes.

CHAPTER 49

It was still light when *Doktor* Grimstad drove his black Chevrolet coupe into Anna Fromme's barnyard. Totally devoid of any chickens or livestock, the old buildings looked rundown and forlorn. Two cats jumped down off the back porch step when he approached the screen door.

"*God aften*," he called. A few moments later, the little girl came into the entryway. "Is your mother here?" he asked. Tell her the *stadsledge* is here. She'll understand."

"Mama!" Lisel ran off into the house, her voice trailing behind.

Anna came to the door, wearing a shapeless farm dress.

"*Fru* Fromme, I apologize for coming so late, but I need to update my records. I have to keep track of respiratory illness. It will only take a little while." Grimstad wasn't sure if she would be receptive to any of this. Jens had asked him to check on the girl, to be a friend to the woman. This was the only way he could think of doing it. He was relieved when she let him in.

At the window in the *stue*, Grimstad paused to admire the view on the fjord. The evening was cool and heavily overcast, but the water was shimmery silver. "I used to come here as boy, you know. I did work for the elder Fromme, Jarle."

"My husband's grandfather." Anna looked uncomfortable. "Did you want to see Lisel?"

"*Vær så snill.* Just a peek. We can do it over at the sofa."

"I'm sorry the house is so cool. I haven't lit a fire."

When he was finished examining Lisel, Anna took her into the bathroom and started the water for a bath. She came out with a towel. "Would you like tea, *Herr Doktor*?"

"*Takk*." Grimstad felt he was repeating himself, but was pleased at this turn.

She put a pot of water on to boil. He announced he would start her fire. He laid kindling in the stove. "How are the two of you getting by?"

"We get by as well as the others. I buy at the *landhandel* and have a garden. I have been collecting berries all summer for preserves even though sugar is hard to come by. I get meat, butter and milk in exchange for the pasture." She handed him a box of matches. "How is Lisel?"

"She's fine. People have a tendency to get bronchitis again once they'd had it. I brought her vitamins and cod-liver oil. I can get eggs for her using a special ration for children. "

The teakettle sang. The fire took hold. Anna put a pot of steeping tea on the table, then went to check on Lisel. There were splashing sounds in the bathroom, then water gargling down the drain. Lisel came into the hallway wrapped in a large blue towel, her light hair dripping.

"Get dressed, Munchkin." Anna herded her into a room across the hall. Eventually she returned to the *stue*.

"Do you have children, *Herr Doktor*?"

"I had a son. A little older than your daughter is now. He drowned along with his mother in a boating accident many years ago."

"Oh, I am so sorry about your wife and boy. Life can be so hard on the coast. One of my husband's most promising students was lost at sea while fishing with his father."

"*Tusen takk*." It still hurt. He took solace in the scene outside. The sun had broken through, sending down three long rays of light.

"Do you like our fjord?" he asked.

"*Ja*, it is very beautiful. I love the forests that ring the ridges above the water and how the little farms are tucked in along the inlets. It was very barren in Lillehavn. Not so protected."

"I'm not sure if I've ever been there."

"Ah, it's such a little place. You'd miss it if you took the coastal steamer. We moved there about five years ago. As fond as he was of Bergen, Einar wanted to teach in a rural setting. It had its own beauty, but that was deceptive like here."

"I think I met Einar once. He was a little boy. Visiting his grandparents."

"You would have liked him," Anna said. "A warm, caring man and very smart."

Lisel came into the *stue* wearing a pink nightgown, still flushed from the hot bath water. "If you don't mind, I'm going to put her to bed now. Say *God natt*, Lisel."

While she was gone, Grimstad counted out pills from a large bottle and wrote some instructions on a tablet. Eventually, Anna joined him at the table. "Why are you being so kind to my daughter and me? You know what the others think."

Grimstad cleared his throat. "I'm a doctor and it's my duty." But this wasn't a very satisfactory answer, so he finally added, "It's a matter of justice." When she looked at him puzzled, he explained. "I think it's indecent that Jarle Fromme's great-granddaughter should be ostracized. It isn't right. Not for her mother either."

Her puzzled look gave way to confusion.

"It's something I heard, *Fru* Fromme," he said quietly. "Something that I take very seriously. You may have been slandered. I'd like to help you."

Anna became very still, her face frozen. She's looking for a trick, he thought. Eventually she brightened. *My God*, he thought. *You're beautiful.*

"You already have," Anna said. "I thank you for my Lisel and for what you have said."

She looked out the window, out toward the mouth of the fjord where pinks and lavender sunset was gathering. When she turned back, it framed her face, creating a halo of light behind her. A tear glistened on her cheek. "And my dear Einar thanks you."

He suddenly felt ashamed for not saying more on her behalf. Hansen said to be a friend—at "arm's length" if he had to. He wished he could do more. *We're the guilty ones*, he thought. We've shut her out before letting her in. Her story hasn't been told. The thought stuck in his mind all the way home and for the rest of the night.

CHAPTER 50

"You must have seen a pig." Sverre's cousin, Ole, threw down his card on the table. "Did you know, Jens that seeing a pig before going out fishing causes a bad catch?"

"I didn't know," Haugland answered honestly.

Everyone burst out laughing, some making ribald comments about local lore. Which led to ghost stories.

It was nine-thirty at night and the *Otta* was out as far as she could legally go, but in sight of skerries if she had to run. Kjell and Haugland were crammed inside the crew's quarters with Sverre Haraldsen, his father Sig, and some of his brothers and nephews. As they waited for the arrival of the *Hessa* bringing them the arms shipment from the Shetland Islands, they found space at the table, on the bunks or on the floor while Holger the poet told ghost stories.

"Did you ever hear of the *Draugen*, Jens?"

"Don't remember." The ship's lantern cast a deep shadow on Haugland's face. "Does the *Draugen* eat humans? Or is that the name of the new German fish buyer?"

Sverre banged the little galley table with the flat of his hand and laughed. He turned to Kjell. "Obviously, this man's education is lacking. Jens, you don't want to see the *Draugen*. He's a horrible being."

Just hours before they were to leave the island of Hitra for their meeting with the *Hessa*, Kjell was approached by someone he knew from export down near Kristiansund N.

"I need your help," the man said. "I have some people who need to get to England tonight. The Gestapo's looking for them. I radioed London and learned the *Hessa* was coming."

Now six adults and two small children hid on Sverre's fishing boat, the *Marje*, drifting not too far away and deliberately kept dark.

Somehow ghost stories seemed appropriate as they waited—hoping to avoid being sighted by an air patrol at this late hour.

"The *Draugen*'s a being very unfriendly to humans," Sverre said. "He's an evil-looking man—terrible to behold." He leaned out from the bunk where he was sitting and spreading his fingers, framed his face with his hands. His teenage son, Tel, was all bug-eyed, but Holger sat on the other end of the bunk and chuckled. His pipe filled the cramped space with sweet tobacco smoke.

"In a terrible storm, you can hear him laughing," Sverre shook his voice, swaying as he spoke. "He sits on the keel of half a boat, sailing close to fishermen. Back and forth, back and forth as the boat rocks. Any fisherman who sees the *Draugen* knows his hour has come. He will never see his home again."

When Sverre finished, there was dead silence. It's like that American bogeyman, Haugland thought. No one quite believed in it, but if you talked about it long enough, it got to you. The tension in here is enough to break glass.

Kjell looked up from a chart. "Our *Draugen*'s not a *jøssing* these days, is he? After all, he is Norwegian. Maybe he goes after only Germans now."

Sverre shook his head. "*Nei.* The *Draugen*'s the *Draugen.* He comes to every fisherman."

"Maybe he comes around the convoys up north, too," Tel said, his voice cracking. "Maybe the *Draugen* sits on half a U-boat."

An even weirder thought. Haugland nodded to Kjell. Maybe it was time to stop and get back to business. Haugland was ready, wearing his spectacles and the cheek pads again.

"Let me see that list of refugees again, Kjell," he said.

Haugland looked at the list Kjell had scribbled hastily. There were eight. Fjellbu and Jorgeson were two young illegal workers in genuine trouble—their arrest imminent if they hadn't left. Fjellbu had a wife and two small kids he was bringing along. There was a fifty-year old *Fru* Torvik whose husband had been in Grini Concentration Camp before he disappeared. Severson was a boat mechanic in trouble with an NS party member at work.

Buland, the final man, was a mystery. Haugland disliked him immediately. He was supposed to be from Brattvag, and had some connection to illegal work. His papers were in order, but when Haugland said he didn't like him, Kjell and Sig agreed too.

"I don't like his bragging," Sig said, "I don't like loudmouths. If you ask me, I'd say he'd been drinking 'though I didn't get close enough to check."

Kjell frowned. "There were supposed to be only seven. Buland was added at the last minute. It seemed all right because Fjellbu knew him."

Haugland tapped Buland's name with his finger. There was enough danger. If they were caught meeting with the *Hessa,* they would all be tortured, then shot. If his identity was discovered, his own death would be particularly ugly, but there could also be terrible consequences for Sig's entire family and his friends. He didn't begrudge taking the men and their women and children. The Shetland Bus did it all the time, but not having Buland checked out was unacceptable.

Haugland stood up. "Think I'll go look at Buland's paperwork. The *Hessa*'s still —"

When something bumped against the *Otta*, Haugland's hand dropped to his pistol.

"Father!" Kolbjorn, Sverre's son, practically jumped down the entryway to the crew's quarters. "We need Jens. Come quick!"

"Hold on," Sverre said. "What's wrong?"

"Buland's drunk and threatening to take our boat and go back! Quick!"

Haugland was already to the ladder. He mashed down Kolbjorn's cap as he came by him. "Good work. Stay here with your grandfather. You coming Sverre?"

Sverre and Kjell both came.

Outside, the sky was black, with a hint of fading silver on the horizon. In the gloom, the *Marje* bobbed like a bulky gray shadow. They slipped cautiously over to her side, their oars already silenced with rags for the coming night's work with the *Hessa*. The boat was completely dark except for a glow near the scuttle.

Dammit, Haugland thought. The *Marje* is leaking light. On deck, the men crept across the deck to the companionway to the crew's quarters. Down below, it appeared to be quiet, but on closer inspection, they could hear a baby crying.

Two voices argued. "I said," a voice growled, "I want to go back." The words slurred.

"You're not very smart about it. How will you pilot the boat, Gregers? No one can take you back at this point." The voice trailed away into the interior of the room.

Haugland tapped Kjell. Pay attention, he signed. You stay on top. I send up boy.

Creeping down the steep ladder, Haugland landed at the bottom. The door to the crew's quarters was partially open. To the left, huddling under the top bunk, were the women, the young mother dismally holding a baby. He couldn't see the other child. The two young resistance workers were at the table. Fjellbu, he guessed, was talking to Buland somewhere out of view. Ulstein was off to the right side of the door, his shoulder partially covering it. The room stunk like a spilled bottle of aquavit.

"Don't move" Haugland whispered. "I want to get the women and children out, but not with Buland there. Make an excuse to go up. I'll come in after you go."

Ulstein made his excuse, the oldest in all of nature. Buland, after some grumbling, let him go. Haugland patted Ulstein's shoulder as he slipped by. Now if Haugland could keep their voices down. Sound traveled far on water.

"Gregers, have some coffee," Fjellbu said. "You're upsetting the women and children."

"Go to the Devil." Buland paced to the door and back.

Haugland got Fjellbu's attention. Without missing a beat, he talked Buland over to the table. Haugland could now see that Buland had a bottle in one hand and a knife in the other.

"Mind if I join you?"

Buland swung around jerkily. He was a big, sloppy middle-aged man with powerful shoulders and chest. His blue eyes looked raw and he was unshaven. He swayed slightly, but something in Haugland must have threatened him. He advanced on one of the women.

Haugland ignored him. "*Fru* Torvik, why don't you grab that blanket behind you and go on up? Take *Fru* Fjellbu with you. No lights."

"Stop." Buland pointed his knife at the women. They shrank back under the bunk.

Haugland flicked his eyes about the room. Severson was on the other end of the bunk. On the top, a little boy slept. "We've got about twenty minutes to go, Buland. Let them take a break. There's no need to bully women and young boys."

"I want to go back."

"Impossible. This is a one-way operation. Besides, alcohol is not allowed. You knew the rule before you came. And if you were to go, you might say something."

Buland glowered at him, then took a swig of aquavit.

Haugland came in further, careful not to threaten. Behind him, someone climbed carefully down. Sverre, probably. He was glad for the backup.

"I just want to go back." Buland's voice trailed off, but his eyes were on Haugland like a malevolent pig's.

"Why? I would think a man in your position would be happy to get out." He nodded to Jorgeson, the other resistance worker. "Take his seat. We'll talk."

"Don't!" Buland shouted.

"It's all right, Jorgeson." Haugland motioned for the man to sit by the woman. "Look, Gregers, there's no sense in being uncooperative. You can't go back. I can't guarantee your safety."

"What do you mean 'guarantee' my safety?" Buland lowered his knife slightly.

"I don't think the resistance councils would trust you anymore. If they decide you've informed on them, they will betray you to the Gestapo on trumped-up charges or rub you out themselves." Haugland was making everything up as fast as he could go, a bit of truth as well as gibberish, but Buland seemed to believe him.

Buland licked his lips, then took a step back. His face lightened a shade.

"People make bad decisions when they feel hungry. No one will blame you if you just put down the knife and relax. Enjoy the trip over." Haugland didn't add that he'd recommend the brig and questioning by intelligence when they arrived.

"Come, Gregers," Fjellbu was saying. "Have a cup of coffee. It's going to be all right."

Buland lowered the knife and the bottle. Suddenly, the little boy woke up in his perch and let a sob of fear. Everyone turned, except Haugland from old practice. Buland bolted, and swung the bottle at Haugland's throat.

"Jens!" Sverre jumped forward and pushed Haugland to his left.

The bottle deflected and smashed into Haugland's right shoulder and chest, knocking him back onto the floor. The bottle flew out of Buland's hand and exploded, sending shards and liquid back at Buland and around the room.

Before Sverre could regain his footing, Buland plunged the knife into his left shoulder. Sverre's cry was sharp as he slipped to the floor.

On his back, Haugland rolled forward and tackled Buland's legs, fending off Buland's second blow. The knife jabbed full force into the sliding door.

"You devil," Buland roared, twisting and turning as he tried to dislodge both his knife in the wood and Haugland's grip on his feet. He made one last desperate lunge through the door and ran into Kjell's .38.

Hanging from the ladder, Kjell put it to his forehead. "I think you should stop now."

Buland groaned as Fjellbu and Jorgeson seized his arms, flattening him against the wall.

Jorgeson turned out Buland's pockets. "Well, look at this. Ration and fuel cards. Multiple fuel cards. What are you doing with fuel cards?"

Haugland didn't wait for Buland's answer. He stared at the boy screaming in terror for his mother as she reached up to him. The cabin was a shambles, a chaotic nightmare. The room reeked of sweat and alcohol. There was blood and glass everywhere. Avoiding shards, Haugland walked on his knees to Sverre who half-sat against the wall near the door. The fisherman's face was gray, his lips white, but he was conscious. Sverre smiled weakly.

Haugland pulled some rope out of Sverre's coat and tossed it to Kjell. "Tie Buland up good," he spat. "Feet too. Get the kids and women out of here." He turned back to Sverre and began to remove his bloody jacket. Behind him, Buland foamed and swore invoking the Devil's name. "Put a sock in his mouth while you're at it. Yesterday's pair."

The women scrambled past him. Kjell crouched beside Sverre.

"How is he?" Kjell asked.

"Bad," Haugland said. "We'll have to send one of the boats back."

He tore Sverre's bloody shirt open further, working to stop the bleeding.

Sverre rolled his eyes at Haugland. "*Nei*, Jens, the *Hessa*. We've got to be here for the arms. We've got to take everything. We must."

Haugland pressed a clean handkerchief against the seeping wound. "I know. I'm sorry. We need both boats."

They lifted Sverre onto the lower bunk. Jorgeson took Haugland's place and sat on the bed, holding the hankerchief on the wound.

"What time is it?" Haugland asked, getting out of the way.

"The *Hessa* is close," someone said. "I'll get the first aid kit."

"May I help?" It was *Fru* Torvik. Stepping gingerly over the bits of glass, she headed toward Sverre.

Haugland motioned her away. "Not now. Go up with the other women. *Vær så snill*."

She rolled up her sleeves. "I think not. I'm a surgical nurse."

"Thank God," said Kjell.

***

A subdued group met the *Hessa*, its appearance anti-climactic. Haugland was the first to get up on the submarine chaser's deck with Holger and Sig close behind. The crew was already in action, some unloading, others manning the large antiaircraft guns.

"Good God," said Petter Salen, the boat's skipper, when he saw Haugland's face. "Looks you hit a wall."

"Bloody quisling," Haugland spat. "Nearly killed my friend." Even though he had a new knit shirt on, dried splats of blood remained on his neck. His ear ached.

"How is he?" Salen frowned while Haugland described the fight and ensuing emergency.

"Holding on. We lucked out. One of the refugees is a damn good nurse. Took eighteen stitches." Haugland shook his head. The night was just beginning and he was tired already.

"Want us to take him? He'd get good care in the Shetlands."

"*Nei*," Sig said. "If Sverre went missing, it would cause problems."

"He's badly hurt, Father," Holger said.

"I know, but I don't want to jeopardize the operation's secrecy. Anyone wondering where Sverre was could uncover our operation here. More than one life would be at stake." The old man turned to Haugland. "My son is strong. I leave him in God's hands."

"Well, then. He stays." Haugland was relieved he didn't have to change plans.

On the *Hessa*, Kjell and the subchaser's crew organized the crates and large bales of cellulose and peat. In addition to the five hundred machine gun pistols, there were two hundred gallons of gasoline and forty thousand *kroner*. The *Otta* would be loaded first, taking all the bales of cellulose and peat bags as well as all the money. Eventually, Holger and Ole Haraldsen rowed over to assist with the transfer while the three strongest seamen from the *Hessa* were sent back to the *Marje* to bring over Buland.

Haugland stoode at the safety wire next to Salen. "Looks like there's a leak in that Kristiansund N. export group. Buland had a large collection of ration books and fuel cards on him and this."He took out a folded typewritten list. "Fjellbu's troubled by a couple of the names on this."

Salen grunted. "I'll get on it and see that London starts an investigation."

Down in the mess of the *Hessa*, Haugland briefed the incoming agent and radioman. They would be going to separate destinations. Back on top again he spoke to Salen about his film and the papers from the Trondheim group. The crew had moved efficiently, and was finishing loading of the crates on *Marje*.

"If you're wondering, Buland's onboard," Salen said.

"Throw the book at him."

***

Thirty minutes after the *Hessa*'s arrival, the *Otta* and *Marje* were ready to go. The crates of arms bound for hiding on Hitra had been loaded in the *Marje*'s hold. On the *Otta*, the arms-laden bales of cellulose and peat bound for Trondheim were secured and covered. Salen and Haugland stood on the *Hessa* and reviewed the list one last time.

"Got something for your little group," Salen said. He pointed at a boat being lowered over the side, a graceful seventeen-foot dinghy. It was double-ended and like all Norwegian dinghies, a miniature Viking boat, only the boat builders in the Shetlands had made it.

"It should fit into local traffic just fine. See that plywood box?" Salen pointed to the boat's stern. "We've mounted a 1 ½ horsepower Stuart Turner engine in it. Lid's tight and dry."

"*Tusen takk*. We have need of one."

"One other thing." Salen turned to his second in command who came forward with a small package. "We brought this for field agents in your area, but use it on your friend. It's penicillin. For fighting infection, it's amazing. If you're not squeamish about syringes, you can administer it yourself. Instructions are inside the case. Be careful, though. Sometimes, there's a reaction. I'd say, however, that it's worth the risk."

Haugland accepted the package. "*Takk*. I'm not squeamish. Believe me. I'll do it."

"Good luck, Ryper. You've got an efficient group. Hope to see you again."

Haugland got down into the new dinghy and putted over to the *Marje* where he would direct the unloading of the crates with a waiting party at another location. Kjell went back to the *Otta* to meet up with A.C. Kjelstrup. The boats separated a few minutes later. The *Hessa* disappeared into the night going west to the Shetlands and freedom.

***

Haugland meant to sleep, but instead, sat quietly by Sverre, letting Holger take charge. A wind had picked up, making the water choppy and the fishing boat roll uncomfortably side-to-side as it ran toward its destination. He checked Sverre's wound. As he suspected, it was red and swollen around the dark stitches. He laid the bandage back in place and pulled the wool blanket over Sverre's bare chest. The fisherman's eyelids fluttered. It didn't take much to see where he was heading.

Haugland went to the gear shelf and carried his shaving kit back to the bunk. Inside was the long skinny box Salen had given him. Similar to a necklace case, he forced the jaws open, revealing a stainless steel syringe and two small bottles. Instructions in English were stuck to the top. He read them so intently he didn't hear Holger come down.

"How's my brother, Jens?" he whispered.

"Not good. There's some swelling, possible infection. I've got some medicine the skipper gave me. Only I don't know how Sverre will react. It's supposed to be strong stuff."

"Do it, Jens," Holger replied. "Can I help?"

Haugland boiled some water on the stove then threw in the needle and the syringe. When they were sterile, he set up the hypodermic needle, filling the syringe according to instructions. Holger uncovered his brother's hip and winced when Haugland shot it home.

Haugland didn't tell him he'd never done it before.

***

The *Marje* was in place around 1:30 a.m., a bit later than planned. A light signal was set up and soon their call was answered. For the next few hours, three dinghies went back and forth, transferring their special cargo. Once on shore the boxes were loaded on a two-wheel cart hooked up to a sleepy *fjordling*. When filled, two men led the pony back through the woods. Others carried the crates on stretchers or their shoulders. A procession as solemn as a funeral took off through the woods, one of the few forested areas on the island. High above, a waiting committee was ready to put the crates into the ground. Under Haugland's orders everyone wore dark clothes and stocking caps with holes for their eyes. No one spoke except when necessary.

Haugland stayed on the beach. The site had been chosen long before and it was only on the last trip did he shoulder a small crate and follow them up into the woods for the long, arduous climb. It was difficult in the dark, but dawn wasn't far off. Finally, the last crate was in the ground and covered. The soil was smoothed out, pine needles spread over the newly dug earth and dead tree limbs laid down to Haugland's satisfaction. One of the men brushed all tracks away. It was an isolated place, close to the *fjell.* It would be safe as long as they kept quiet. He trusted the twenty men Sverre and Sig had handpicked. When the area was secured, the men quietly split up and disappeared into the pre-dawn gloom.

Holger and Haugland descended the mountain behind a local man, speaking very little. Now that this second stage was over, Haugland began to relax but he felt like he hadn't slept in ages.

The wind had continued to increase. Rain moved cross the water. Above the rocky beach, their guide left them and they descended carefully down to their dinghy. It was light out now and on the *Marje* a lantern was lit in the wheelhouse, a hazy glow in the grey rain. Haugland pulled the stocking cap up off his face, gingerly avoiding his ear and let the cold rain splatter on his face. They pushed the new dinghy out into the water then climbed in. The motor started up immediately and they were off.

Onboard, Magnus Haraldsen greeted them. He was a taciturn dark blonde. "How did it go?" he asked.

"Well, enough," Haugland said. "The men did fine."

"Glad to hear. Now look at Sverre. He's pretty sick. He's been out of his head the last half-hour."

Down in the warmth of the crew's quarters, Sverre was on his back, stirring restlessly. His eyes were closed and he was muttering. Haugland was disappointed the medicine hadn't worked and worried he was reacting to the penicillin, but they couldn't wait. They had to disperse now.

Haugland gently lifted the blanket to examine Sverre's hip. To his relief, he found no unusual swelling or redness where he had given the shot. Sverre stirred and moaned lightly as Haugland laid the blanket back in place, then was still. "Where can we take him?"

"I know a woman. She can be trusted," Magnus answered.

"Good." Haugland tried to look reassuring, but they all knew Sverre's wound was one more thing they had to hide. With this grim thought on their minds, the boats took off and headed along the east coast of Hitra.

CHAPTER 51

Not long after the boats separated, the *Marje's* engine went out. While Holger coaxeed the engine back to life in the hold, the men put up sail and kept moving. Haugland stayed with Sverre and watched him slip in and out of consciousness. Haugland could only let the medicine take its course and trust in its "magic." Discouraged, he lay down and tried to get some sleep.

The *Marje* set anchor some time later near a barren windswept island. While the dinghy was prepared, Haugland and Holger struggled to get Sverre awake. They partially dressed him and with his coat about his shoulders, helped him onto his feet. He was weak, but awake.

"What's happening?" he asked. "Where are… the boxes?"

"In the ground. We're taking you to *Fru* Jensen's house," Holger said as they walked him to the ladder. They struggled to get him up the rungs. On deck, Sverre passed out. They laid him gently on sailcloth, tied the ends, and lowered him into the dinghy.

"We'll be back, shortly," Holger said. "I'll explain the instructions for the medicine."

"Hurry." Haugland tapped his watch.

***

Kjell and Sig were waiting for them in a remote cove. Next to the *Otta*, was A.C. Kjelstrup's larger boat, the *Trøndelag*.

"You made it," Kjell said to Haugland when he came onboard the *Otta*.

Haugland didn't answer. Gone were his cheek pads and glasses. He was Jens Hansen again. Load now, he signed to Sig, then, Sverre safe.

They spent the next forty minutes transferring the bales of cellulose and peat and the two agents from the *Otta* into the hold of the *Trøndelag*. The *Otta* was moved, anchored and closed up. With the *Marje* following, the *Trøndelag* left, heading north.

They made good time despite choppy seas. Eventually, the *Marje* left them and dropped off the radioman along with Ole, Sig and Sverre's son

Tel in a three-dwelling village. For security reasons, Haugland didn't go with them, but stayed aboard the *Trøndelag* with Kjell, A.C., and the remaining Haraldsen men. The Haraldsens knew that they must treat Jens differently now in A.C.'s presence, reverting to the game of signals and notebook. They were to use his *deknavn,* "Frode."

Haugland, for his part, was quiet and unassuming, but he was aware of Haraldsen men's smoldering, growing dislike for A.C. Since they came aboard the *Trøndelag,* A.C. had said only one word to him, then completely ignored him.

They are thinking about their deaf cousin, Arne Finn, he thought. Same lack of consideration. It was odd, but he had become used to it, yet hard feelings would not work here. He was relieved when Kjell drew all into an account of their journey, using sign and writing to help things along.

A while later, Ole and Holger returned in the new dinghy and joined them on the *Trøndelag*. Now they could proceed to the final stage.

Once the *Trøndelag* got under way again, Kjell took charge. While A.C. piloted the trek across the Trondheimsleia to the mouth of the Trondheimfjord and all its minefields, the rest of the men met down below. There Kjell described what they could expect going into the area based on A.C.'s accounts of dealing with the inspection ship.

"The arms and ammunition are safely sandwiched in bales of cellulose or bags of peat labelled 'Edoy,' so if the Germans ask where that is, you can say it's an island down near Smøla where there's a lot of commerce in peat and not tell a lie. The inspection officer will scrutinize us closely once we're boarded. There's no need to go topside, but I'd like two or three men up anyway to make things look natural. We could be detained for as long as twenty minutes."

"Then what?" asked one of the men.

"After we're done," Kjell said, "we'll go to a place above Trondheim. It's very sensitive militarily, so we can expect to be stopped and boarded any time on the whim of any patrol boat in the area. I think if we keep our appearance low, we should be able to meet our contact safely. We're going to unload in broad daylight and have it hauled off. Any other questions?" There were none.

At two in the afternoon, the *Trøndelag* came within sight of a rocky island off the mouth of Trondheimfjord. A few miles ahead were the minefields and the patrol boats. Everyone made a last minute check for any incriminating food or guns and carefully stowed the itms away behind a false wall in the galley area. Once settled, they returned to their duties as a crew on a fishing boat.

As the *Trondelag* made the approach to the entrance, Haugland came up on topside to watch. Walking to the starboard side, he leaned against the rail. The air was very cool and moist, the threat of rain imminent. Despite the low blue-gray clouds and choppy water, visibility, was good. The hills on both sides of the passage were low-lying and bare. From repeated practice, A.C. made his way smoothly through the minefields, passing underneath the formidable fortifications on both sides of the narrow neck of the fjord. On the other side was a large trawler that served as a patrol boat and beyond, the inspection boat.

Kjell came up beside Haugland as A.C. joined a line of boats waiting for inspection.

Too busy, Haugland signed.

"*Ja*, for sure," Kjell answered. "Not what I expected."

Overhead, planes buzzed low over them on their way out from the airfield north of the town that lay miles to the east. A floatplane landed on the water. Ahead, there was a lot of patrol boat activity. Even a small fishing boat had been pressed into service. A half-hour later, it was their turn alongside the inspection boat.

"Heads up," A.C said. "The inspection officer is new."

Once they were secured to the other boat, the Germans wasted no time in boarding.

"Papers!" A humorless, over-efficient officer barked at A.C. Behind him, teams of seaman spread throughout the *Trøndelag*, some going down to the crew's quarters, others into the hold and pilot house. But the cellulose and bags of peat held their secrets.

"Why all the caution?" A.C asked when his papers were returned.

"There was an explosion at Thamshavn yesterday," the German said. "Some criminals damaged one of the electric trains. We're looking for them now. If you deliver in Trondheim, you'll find a curfew and tight security getting in and out. I wouldn't stay long if I were you."

He waved his men back over to the inspection boat, then brought out his stamp pad and made up a pass for their entry into the fjord. He snapped his heels when he handed it over, then stepped back onto his own boat. A minute later the *Trøndelag* took off.

The trip through the narrow neck of Trondheimfjord was uneventful. Protected by the forested hills on either side, the water was less rough. The men began to relax as they got further away from the inspection boat. The agent stayed on topside with Kjell and A.C. The Haraldsens went down below to sleep. Haugland sat quietly in a corner of the wheelhouse while the men talked, their excitement growing now that they had passed safely into the restricted zone. A few miles later, the boat broke through the neck and into the wider part of the fjord. Ahead and all about them were merchant ships, fishing boats, and a German warship heading out to sea.

"It hasn't changed much," the agent commented as they passed a lone house and boat by the forested shore. "In fact, it looks quite peaceful."

"Looks are deceiving," A.C. answered. "The inspector said there's a curfew. I wonder how it'll affect our reception committee."

Haugland wondered too. He was supposed to meet with Axel at the Deaf Church in town to finalize plans. Once the arms shipment was out of their hands, it was no longer their problem, but security would continue to be. It added to their worries about the large cache on Hitra and the other small ones he and Kjell had handled.

He leaned against the wall and rubbed his aching shoulder. The agent went on about the situation in Trondheim, but Haugland worried about events happening elsewhere in Norway. Salen said a zealous Gestapo agent down near Oslo had executed four people all because of news about the Allies closing on Paris. In another incident, the *Hjemmefronten* warned all the sheriffs about harassing young men who fled the mobilization. When a Nazi sheriff did not stop, he was assassinated as an example.

Some good that did, he thought. The Germans were overwhelmingly in control. They responded to the sheriff's execution by rounding up hostages, continuing the grim cycle of reprisals.

Kjell and A.C. continued to talk in the cramped quarters of the wheelhouse, but Haugland grew distant. He finally tapped Kjell's arm. He motioned he would go down and get some much needed sleep. He would heed Grimstad's advice not to become overtired.

Wake me, he signed and plodded down to the crew's quarters.

CHAPTER 52

"How many did you say?" Rika sat frozen, her fork poised over her plate of roast pork.

"Ten." Freyda wiggled in her chair. "Almost two years ago, our most prominent citizens were taken hostage, then shot. Their deaths were announced even before it happened."

"How awful." Rika stared at the piece of pork roast. Only Freyda scared up such treats.

"It was frightening. A zoo. All the German hotshots came here to see the executions. Even Terboven came, then gave a dinner party in his rail coach. And they weren't satisfied with ten. They killed some twenty young men for trying to escape to England. It was an awful time. It still gives me the shivers." Freyda shook her shoulders like she had a chill then cut her piece of pork roast into dainty pieces.

"I've never seen a *razzia* before. Not 'til today." Rika frowned. She had come to her friend's apartment because she had been shaken. She had just left work when she heard the squeal of tires on the wide street. Immediately, she began walking the other direction. Over her shoulder she saw soldiers leap out of the black vans—the ones people called "Black Marias,"—and throw whoever was closest to them into the vehicles. Panicking, she slipped down the nearest alley and ran only to fall and cut her bare knees. Rising in pain, she limped to the main street and took the trolley to Freyda's apartment.

"I heard about that, Rika. There was sabotage at Thamshavn. Something got blown up—a train, I think. Now there will be reprisals. They'll just round up people and throw them into Falstad Prison—worse at the Mission Hotel. But that's not a true *razzia*. A *razzia* is when a whole village is raided for illegal work." Freyda helped herself to some wine. "You haven't seen the real face of the enemy until you see that."

"I've seen quite a bit, actually." Rika stirred her meat with her fork. "I was at the train station the other day. A troop train filled with POWs pulled in and unloaded."

"Russians?"

"Someone said Poles, shipped over from the Eastern Front. Poor fellows. Some were nearly naked. They looked like ghosts."

Freyda patted the edges of her mouth leaving red lipstick marks on her napkin. "Bound for Falstad concentration camp just outside Trondheim or north to the slave camps for a road the Germans want open year round."

Rika sighed. "There was a scuffle when a woman tried to give them packages with socks and food. She was beaten down, then hauled away. No one looked. No one protested. I had to slip away from that one too, but… but it's so shameful. It doesn't seem like anyone cares."

"Oh, but they do care, Rika, they're just afraid. I know *you* care and want to do something about it. I'm so glad you're meeting my friend tonight. Olav has been looking for a dedicated *jøssing* with ties to the coast. Someone who's not afraid of illegal work."

Rika gave her a weak smile. "I… I'm glad too, but I just want to listen first, then decide."

She became silent, not knowing why she had blurted out to Freyda a couple of weeks ago that with the coming liberation, she wanted to help to prepare for that day. She had never said anything to Freyda about her activities in the city. One thing A.C. had taught her was to never say anything to *anyone* until she was really sure about that person. At the office, people were quiet, going about their daily duties displaying just the subtleties of resistance such as wearing paperclips or sharing the latest jokes about quislings and Germans. There, however, she was assured of their loyalty because her father's friend Thomas Nissen had placed her with the job. He personally knew them all. Yet she had never told them what she was doing. She had not expected such a response from Freyda. Her friend was almost overjoyed.

"Is Ragnar coming back?" Freyda asked.

"He's supposed to bring another load of peat any day. He said he'd call."

"He's crazy about you, you know. I think he's in love with you."

Rika flushed. "Do you think so?" She wished she didn't have to hold secrets from Freyda. She would have liked to tell her all about A.C.—how kind he was, the secret work he did. He had chosen the code name "Ragnar" himself. Just to be safe.

"*Ja*." Freyda giggled. "He's kind of sweet and very funny. Has he made love to you?"

"Freyda," Rika gasped, putting her hands over her mouth to cover up a nervous giggle.

Freyda took another sip of wine. "Rika, you are so good, but I think you like him more than you are saying." She squeezed Rika's hand in a sisterly gesture. Rika flushed again. "It doesn't matter. Whatever happens, I'm sure you'll be happy. Finish your meat. I had to smuggle two pork roasts in from the countryside under my dress. It made me look like I was nursing two calves."

At nine o'clock at night, there was a knock on the door. Outside a man beckoned them to come with him. They silently followed him downstairs to a waiting black car. Freyda got in next to the man in the front, instructing Rika to get into the back. It wasn't until the car took off, that Rika realized someone was sitting in the corner opposite her, hidden by shadows.

With no streetlights, the streets were dark. Even the car had hoods over its headlamps for the blackout, but as she sat in her corner, she began to make out the features of a man. He was small, the size of a boy, with a wide high forehead and jet black hair. His face was narrow. He wore a suit, but it could have come from the juvenile department. If she didn't sense he was important, she would have laughed. She expected the leader of this secret group to be tall and stalwart, not some shrunken half-pint. His heart-shaped face floated in the shadowy gloom.

Freyda turned around. "Rika, this is Olav Whist. He's the group leader of a special group here in Trondheim that has ties to London."

"*God kveld.*" The man spoke in a low resonant voice. "How do you like our little town?"

"I like it very much. It's such a pretty place."

The car drove to the Elgeseter Bridge, but instead of crossing over the river into Trondheim, turned right and began to drive through the hills. Eventually, the car came into a residential area and stopped at a one-story house.

Rika froze in her seat. Up to this point, she had stayed calm, but she was beginning to have grave misgivings. She rubbed her bruised knees. "Are you coming in, Freyda?"

"*Ja*, for sure."

They followed Whist into the house. A matronly woman greeted them in the hall and invited them into a small, cozy parlor. Standing over at an ornate fireplace, was a brown-haired young man in his mid-twenties. Rika recognized him immediately. A.C. had introduced her to him some time ago. Paul Larsen. She began to relax.

After coffee was ordered from the woman, Whist wasted no time in laying out his intentions. "I don't know what Freya has told you, but my organization's a secret, independent group working closely with Oslo and London. Our purpose is to prepare for liberation, but because of arrests and reprisals on Frøya and other islands, people in the underground there are scattered. We need new contacts out on the coast and islands. Freyda says you grew up there. You will remain in Trondheim, but you can make contacts when you go home."

"How will I do this?"

"Talk to people you trust in Fjellstad and on Hitra. Realize that you are a conduit, a way for people to recieve advice and materials, if necessary, a way to export out people in danger. We can do it. But be careful. Choose wisely."

Whist put a tin of Scottish shortbread on the coffee table between them. "Have some. Got it on our last drop." There was a map of the coast around Sor-Trøndelag and some papers and pictures out on the table next to him. A reel tape on top of a box written with the words, "Speeches of King Haakon" lay next to them. "Why don't you show me where you are from?"

Rika helped herself to shortbread and pointed out Fjellstad on the map.

"Good stalwart people out there," Whist said. "*Jøssings* all."

Paul cleared his throat and said that they would be able to pay for travel expenses or any materials she needed. That included the weekly steamer to the islands.

"By the way, export is an important part of our work," Paul said as he sipped his coffee. "Have you heard of the boat that went from Frøya early this spring? That was our boat." He showed her a typed list of names lying on the coffee table. One of the names was Bent Kjelstrup.

"I know him," she said breathlessly. *I know his brother too*, she thought, but decided not to say that. The more she thought about this group, the more excited she was about joining it. A group with national connections. But she would say nothing about her other work. "He is well?"

"He's in England," Whist said.

"Wonderful." She couldn't keep her excitement out of her voice. Her friend grinned when she caught her eye. For one brief moment she wondered if she should ask A.C. about this, but instinctively she knew she must do this alone and not mix the purposes of each illegal organization. "That was the way of things," he had once cautioned.

"I think I might know some people on the island," Rika said at last.

"Excellent! So, are there any questions? Will you join us?"

This is what I had hoped for, Rika thought. A way to help my village and bring the occupation to an end. The prospect of joining with this man frightened her, but it also made her feel proud. "*Ja*," she said.

Coffee was served. "It's a gift from England," Whist said.

And it tastes good with shortbread, she thought. A.C. had never brought her that.

At ten-thirty, they were done. Paul escorted Rika and Freyda out to the waiting car. There was a brief good-bye, then the car slinked off with Rika's head full of patriotic dreams.

CHAPTER 53

The *Trøndelag* made its way through the busy fjord in just a few hours and turned northeast. It chugged past Trondheim where the green-blue spire of Nidaros rose above the other buildings in the city. The rounded hills behind it were green and vibrant.

The day stayed overcast and a wind swept out of the valley south of the city, but the *Trøndelag* continued to make good time. It passed by the harbor and shipyards and the omnipresent pens of the U-boats and eventually beyond to a more rural area where farms spread out along the Trondheim depression. Holger woke Haugland three hours after he lay down.

"Where's Kjell?" he mouthed after looking for signs of A.C.

"Sleeping over there. He came down an hour ago."

Haugland rolled off the bunk. Everyone looked haggard from the lack of sleep. As they crowded around the table eating canned ham and potatoes donated from the *Hessa*, Haugland gave some last minute instructions. When he was done, he sent Ole up with ham sandwiches and coffee for A.C. All they could do now was wait.

A half-hour later, Ole came down to say they were approaching the cove where they would unload the bales of cellulose and bags of peat. Haugland woke Kjell and all went up.

The men stood at the rails looking out over the bow. The *Trøndelag* had gone some ways along the east side of the fjord. Not far off was a pine-forested cove cutting deep into the rocky shore. At its head was a large dock with a small warehouse. Parked near by was a large truck. Its canvas top was suitably weathered and the name of the company painted on the cab. No one was about, but Haugland suspected everyone was ready as they were.

A.C. brought his fishing boat into the cove, easing up to the dock. Haugland and the others, including the agent, uncovered the fish hold and prepared the crane on the boat for lifting the bales. As soon as the boat was secured, several men materialized out of the truck and warehouse. Kjell greeted them with the proper passwords, then got down to business.

The cellulose was unloaded first. As soon as A.C. lifted each full pallet onto the dock, everyone loaded the bales into the truck. The bags of peat went over last. When they were done, Kjelstrup and the group leader, a sallow-looking man in his thirties named Nass, exchanged paperwork proving delivery and transport. That they were all forgeries didn't matter.

"I need you to go with me," Nass said to Kjell. "And someone strong." He pointed to Haugland. "I'll take your man, too,. He can cram in with us."

They got into the truck's cab, while the rest of waiting party got into a vehicle hidden among the trees. They took off, immediately climbing out of the cove and onto the forested road above. When they had gone a little further, the group leader stopped the truck, letting the engine idle.

"Well, Ryper," he said to Haugland. "Axel has a message for you. It's too dangerous to come into Trondheim. He'll meet you tomorrow outside the city."

"We heard train lines near the pyrite mines were taken out."

"*Ja.* There are checkpoints everywhere." He gave the name of the place and instructions on how they would pick him up. "You're not spending the night down there are you?"

"*Nei,*" said Haugland. "We're moving to another spot for the night."

"Good. Here's some material for you to read. Destroy it when you're done." He gave him an envelope containing sheets made of rice paper.

"*Takk.*" Haugland reached into his jacket pocket and brought out a small paper bag of coffee beans. "Picked this is up on our travels. Thought your men might like it."

"*Takk.*" The man beamed. "Now, I've got to go. See that crooked pine over there? There's a trail right beside it. It'll take you right back to the cove. Sleep well, but be careful."

"I don't think anyone will have trouble doing that."

They moved the *Trøndelag* a mile up the coast and spent the night there. On the pretense of helping to finalize the settlement of the agent into place, the following morning Kjell took off with Haugland where they were picked up by Nass. They were driven to an old wood frame country church out in the rolling countryside. Waiting on the steps was Solheim, a little harried since the last time Haugland saw him at the *Hjemme for Døve.*

He was wearing the black, floor-length vestment of a Lutheran priest with its tall circular collar around his neck. He led them into the empty, high-ceilinged sanctuary. "We'll meet back in the spare room." He pointed toward a door to the right of the altar railing. "Don't mind the floor. It creaks."

"*Hei,*" Axel said from a long closet full of choir robes and hymnals. "Find yourself a spot." He beckoned them to some hardback chairs and putting a pile of books on the floor, sat down. Next to him sat a dour-looking man. "This is Lasse Vang, a group leader here in Trondheim."

They talked for the next two hours. Haugland received pertinent information from headquarters in Sweden. He already knew that it could be a month before the next Shetland Bus returned to the area, but now he had orders to be on call if the "waiting" organizations should need access to the caches in the event of capitulation.

"We're waiting for the fall of Paris," Torholm said. "Then the Allies will drive to the Rhine. Berlin will fall. It's a matter of time. We'll need those arms."

Haugland listened with rising irritation and restlessness. It was too soon.

"Is there anything else?"

"*Nei*," Solheim answered. "Not at this moment."

Haugland shifted in his seat.

"Anything wrong?" Axel asked.

"Not really. I know men need live ammunition to practice, but I prefer not moving the caches as yet. Wait for the RAF and American drops this fall near Sweden. It makes more sense."

"If we wait," Torholm said, "we won't be ready for the Germans when they surrender."

"You must be patient," Haugland answered. "The coming fall of Paris has gone to everyone's head, but the Germans aren't finished. They may be drawing back now and seem weak, but they'll fight hard once the Allies cross the Rhine. This war isn't remote, something that we can follow by placing a pin on a map. The Germans still fear an Allied invasion along our long coast. Any suggestions of resistance mobilization or shipment of arms of any size, the Gestapo will pounce. They must protect their northern flank. In this district, that means Rinnan."

"No one is suggesting mobilization," Axel said. "Milorg's orders are to wait."

"I know that, but our civilian friends in Sivorg are under enormous pressure to act. With Communist groups pushing for strikes as they have done in Denmark and carrying out acts of sabotage, it's becoming difficult to justify the lack of sabotage action on the part of Milorg. It may become necessary to act just to keep morale up. On top of that, the Finns appear to be settling with the Russians. They'll no longer need to be allied with the Germans. How the Germans will respond is anyone's guess. The Finns are sure to kick them out."

"I never thought of you as overly cautious, Ryper," Axel commented.

"I follow my instincts, but I'm no hothead. Two years ago we built up our arms and forces for an Allied invasion that never happened. The rollups that followed were terrible, not to mention the reprisals. It could happen again if we aren't cautious. We mustn't be lulled into a false hope that capitulation will come in two weeks. We must be prepared to act alone, without aid from anyone." Haugland paused. "One of the alarming bits of news I just received from Scotland is that the Allied force set up there for dispatch during the liberation phase of our country is being drained of British troops for the continent. It leaves us further isolated..."

"So we do nothing," Torholm said.

"Of course not. Milorg has its specific orders to carry out sabotage on German gas and oil supplies. SOE's advising in some other actions, but with the rush for Berlin, the *Hjemmefronten* will become more open. Then both the civilian and military organizations could be exposed."

"This goes against what the leadership says," Torholm went on. "Are you a fence-sitter?"

"Torholm," Axel warned.

Haugland didn't answer. He looked directly at Axel. "If I'm ordered to do it, I'll move the caches, but it'll be done under the tightest security measures. No one should ever relax just because of Allied gains on the continent." Haugland looked at his watch. "Who's going first?"

"We will," Axel said. "It takes a bit of ingenuity getting in and out of the city these days."

Haugland calmed his voice. "How long do you think the precautions will go on?"

"Hard to say." Axel stood up. The others followed him. "The Germans are furioius about the train. The engine will be out of service for weeks. They have to ship it down to Oslo to repair it, adding more time, something they can't afford. Our pyrites are essential to Germany now."

"Was the sabotage a local effort?" Haugland put a stack of hymnals back on his chair.

"Combined."

Which meant outside help had come from SOE-trained specialists in Sweden. Probably some of Tommy's friends.

Axel and Torholm shook hands with Haugland and Kjell, then left. Kjell went out to locate their ride. Solheim and Haugland stayed back, strolling out into the deserted sanctuary. It was a pretty church with white-washed walls and stained glass windows with blackout curtains rolled up. People still came to worship despite the actions against the State Church two years ago. Haugland stood by one of the pews and looked down on one of the hard maple benches. A hymnal was opened and he glanced at the title—"A Mighty Fortress"—possibly for the coming service. Its number was posted on the hymn board on one of the dark wooden pillars.

Solheim came up beside him and picked up the hymnal. "When's the last time you had communion, Ryper? Went to church?"

Long time, he signed.

Haugland looked about the church, a forgotten memory from his childhood stirring in him. He glanced at Solheim's tall circular collar. When he was a boy, the ruff had reminded him of a white, lacy doughnut. It still did.

"Once I felt comfortable here, secure in the strength and love of my family and God."

"What happened?"

Telavåg, Ålesund, he thought bitterly. My father's harassment. "I don't know," he shrugged. "The occupation. I simply drifted away...."

"God keep you," Solheim said. "And give you luck."

CHAPTER 54

"Pretty isn't it?" the accented voice said. "It never ceases to inspire me."

Anna jumped, the hair on the nape of her neck standing up like a cat startled from its sleep. Turning with as much poise as she could muster, she faced a soldier out of uniform and dressed in less formal attire.

"Lieutenant Schiller. I didn't hear you come in." She had not seen him since the rainy night she had been brought to the hotel to show her papers to him. Not since the night Jens Hansen had been so ill.

"I'm back on leave. You are well? Your little girl, Lisel?"

He remembered her name. "She's with the cook."

Anna moved out into the center of the room, then over to the fireplace. Her path was like that of a slow moving billiard ball playing off the rails, an English game Einar sometimes had indulged in. She stared into the grate where logs had been stacked for a future fire.

She didn't want to say more. Now that her plans to go to Sweden had been dashed, it was imperative she not upset anyone in the village in any way. At stake was Lisel's welfare. I can be humiliated but not my daughter. She had taken Jens's advice and stayed out of the village as much as possible. "Please excuse me."

"You are going?"

"*Vær så snill*," she said. "You know it makes things very difficult for me when you talk to me. People do not understand. They'll blame me if there's a poor potato crop."

"I'm sorry." He sat down on the arm of a large flower-patterned chair and smiled half-heartedly. "I just wanted to chat," he said.

Anna sighed in exasperation. "All right. Just this once. Tell me, what did you do before the war?"

"Would you believe second chair violinist in the Leipzig Symphony? I also worked in an insurance company part-time. Pretty domestic stuff. Not exactly a warrior. But I got caught up in the war like so many others. Snagged, is more like it and here I am, trying to make the best of it."

Anna didn't know how to answer. Her parents had tried hard to keep her from getting her "snagged." She wasn't allowed to go with friends on the hikes or singing fests, not to be apart of the BMD when it was considered the thing to do by her female peers. Her mother had been frightened by the huge paramilitary rallies and the Nazi view of women and race, which ran against her mother's American ideals of equality. Anna had made the best of it too, and was grateful for the courage of her parents in the face of increasing disapproval by neighbors and politicos.

Schiller lit his pipe, letting the smoke puff back into the room.

"And you? Are you going to stay in Norway after the war?"

"*Ja*. I'm a citizen," Anna answered with pride.

"Might be better to go back. I don't think the months following capitulation will be pleasant. Especially for civilians suspected of crimes."

His words gave her a chill. "You speak as though it will happen soon."

"It may be happening now." He leaned over to her. "Our troops are withdrawing from Finland to northern Norway. It began a few days ago."

Anna stiffened.

"It's the 20th Mountain—a massive retreat. The Finns broke relations with Berlin four days ago. Our troops began moving immediately out of Finland into Finnmark. I don't think it will make for a clean retreat. There could be harsh consequences for the inhabitants there. "

"How awful," Anna gasped. "Are you sure?"

"*Nein*, but I know some of the officers. They'll carry out their orders with no remorse. They could totally level the countryside and leave it uninhabitable for survival in winter."

Anna got up. "Why are you telling me this? It's dangerous talking this way. Aren't you afraid I would tell someone?"

"I don't know. It's your lack of Nazi fervor. Your breath of sanity. Maybe it's your face. It's very beautiful, you know."

"Stop. *Vær så snill*."

"Sorry." He stood in her way, blocking her. She was conscious of his breathing and his scent. She wasn't sure if she was in trouble or not, but relied on instinct that said he had a moral code that meant her no harm.

"It's all right." He gave her room, then asked, "May I pick you up in my motorcar?"

"*Nei*." She stepped past him and started toward the door.

"What if I ordered you to come? I can, you know. I have the authority."

Startled, she turned back to him. "I'm sure you can, but it doesn't sound like the second chair in the Leipzig Symphony. Unless you really are a warrior."

Schiller laughed. "All right, I won't press you. Not now. A patrol is going to be set up permanently here in Fjellstad. I would return as its officer."

Anna was shocked. "Why?"

"Officially, I don't know, but I don't think it's a request from *Wehrmacht* headquarters. I think it comes from the Gestapo. There has been an increase in criminal activity around here."

Unsettled, Anna slipped out, knowing it was not the ending he wanted.

CHAPTER 55

Haugland and Kjell quietly returned to Fjellstad and for a couple of weeks resumed their normal routine around the docks, repairing nets and preparing the *Otta* for the rapidly approaching fall-winter. Already the sky had a grayer tone and the leaves on the birches and maples were turning burnished golds and reds. The taut air clicked with energy as vibrant as the news out of Paris and Sweden. Paris, to the thrill of the free and occupied world, was liberated on August 25th, the day after Haugland had gone to see Axel and Solheim at the country church. The liberation of Brussels and Antwerp followed in early September.

Haugland kept in close touch with the Haraldsens. No authority in the islands talked of any unusual action and the arms caches were secure. Sverre was out of danger but Haugland had Grimstad go over and look at him anyway.

"The wound is healing nicely," the doctor said when he came back, "but it will be some time before he can return to work. The shoulder needs to stay immobilized a bit longer."

"What does his wife think?"

"Well, she's scolded him good, but she thinks he impaled himself on some fishing equipment. She believes the lie."

Liberation news was received at the *konditori* with silent exaltation, only to be crushed with news of the sinking of the transport boat, *Westphalen,* a boat that regularly carried prisoners culled out of Grini and other Norwegian prisons to Germany.

"Did you know," Ella said in a hushed voice to Kjell in her apartment, "the radio says it was struck by a British torpedo? Some eighty Norwegian prisoners died."

"I heard. And only four survivors out of hundreds, soldiers and all."

Behind them, Haugland listened sullenly. His uncle went that way some two years before.

"I see that German officer is back." Kjell picked up his empty plate on the coffee table.

"Oh, *ja*. Heard he checked in at the Tourist Hotel in civilian clothes."

"I wonder why he comes."

"I know why," Ella said as she started for the kitchen with her tray. "It's the Woman. He's come to see her. Marthe saw her there this morning."

Haugland stepped out of her way as she came through. He avoided looking at Kjell.

***

On September 9, there was a going away party for Kitty. Close family friends attended. Rika was home briefly from Trondheim. It was an emotional time for Kjell and his girls and Haugland was touched to have been included when he was responsible for her leaving. Just before Kitty departed for the train station for Oslo, Kitty cut Haugland's hair for the last time. Sitting on a stool in the Arneson kitchen they laughed and gossiped in sign. As Kitty finished his haircut, she suddenly burst into tears.

"I'll miss you, Jens." She hugged him, and ran from the room.

So will I, Haugland thought. Stranded on the stool with a towel over his naked shoulders, he looked up to see Rika standing in the kitchen doorway. Lowering a bunch of flowers in her hands, she smiled wistfully at him. Haugland hoped she would forgive him when it was all over.

***

Ella Bjornson stood stock-still in her shop. As she feared, Sorting was in his usual spot in the *konditori*, away from the door and facing the shop. He was talking to Bette. Ella frowned. The girl was sweet, but she talked too much, a habit too dangerous in the increasingly unfriendly atmosphere around the village. Sorting's presence made it so.

Outside the shop window a boat came into moor. Its linseed oil stained hull looked rich and glossy in the sun. Most of the boats had gone out early and were coming in now. Ella turned back when Sorting laughed. No longer indecisive, she took off through the shop toward the tables just in time to hear Bette ask him a question.

"When are you going, Odd? It should be fun."

"Going where, *Herr* Sorting?" Ella asked warmly. "Is Bugge going out again? Such a shame about his boat."

"I'm going to Trondheim. An old friend's getting married."

"How nice," Ella said. "A wedding's always fine. Do you mind?" She eased down onto a chair next to him. "Bette, why don't you see to *Herr* Farren? His tea is getting cold."

"*Ja*, sure, ma'am."

"Busy morning?" Sorting asked Ella.

"*Ja.* And you?" Kjell had asked her to keep an eye on Sorting and report where he went. If he was going to Trondheim she would let Kjell know. She had found it easy to continue to feign friendship with Sorting, even after Kjell warned her of Sorting's true nature a month ago. A viper in the nest. She disliked him more than the German officer who was staying at the Tourist Hotel. Being sensible, Ella feared him. If only she could get Bette to stop flirting with him. He was using her.

They talked pleasantly for several minutes but she was relieved to see Jens standing in front of the seawall with Bugge Grande. They were talking and Jens had taken out his notebook, waiting to write something. Two minutes later, he came into the *konditori* and after acknowledging Sorting, looked at Ella. She greeted him with sign.

I need see you.

"You don't mind, *Herr* Sorting? I have a problem with one of my drains upstairs. Jens is very good at fixing things." She adjusted the cardigan on her shoulders. "*God dag,* to you."

Upstairs she turned on the kitchen faucet and let it run. Haugland watched her curiously from the door. Her face was so serious. "I just wanted an excuse to get out of there. Do you understand?"

Ja. What wrong?

"It's Sorting. He has been asking Bette a lot of questions. She's quite taken with him, you know. I'm afraid she will say something about the boys. He's been asking about them. There was something else. The mailboat brought news about a terrible *razzia* in Vikna. Some of us have friends there. Sorting has been very quiet about it."

Haugland came away from the door. This is what Harry had feared.

"Will Kjell be back tonight?" When Haugland nodded yes, Ella sighed. "It's going to be hard on him with both girls gone."

Haugland pointed to her, then, signed, You fix.

"Me?" Ella burst out laughing. "Why, Jens, are you trying to be a matchmaker?"

Haugland grinned, making Ella laugh again. "I think you need a sweet so you can explain this to me."

He didn't object.

After saying good-bye, Haugland rode Kjell's bike out to the cabin. At the bottom of Anna's driveway he stopped at the post. Since coming back from Trondheimfjord, he had looked for the hook several times. At first, he was disappointed never finding the hook, but he was pleased she heeded his caution about meeting him only for emergencies. Now as he moved the dry grass back, the hook was there, stuck into the wood like a question mark. He stuffed it into his pocket and caressed it, thinking of her.

CHAPTER 56

Slipping out of the trees between the cabin and her farm, Haugland watched Anna in the garden putting up the wash. Her mouth full of clothespins, she pinned a pair of Lisel's little socks on the line. Such a small thing, but he smiled at its normalcy.

And I've worked so hard to keep you out of my thoughts. He met her at the edge of the driveway and put the hook into her hand.

"Oh, Jens," Anna said. "It works, doesn't it?" She waved at the barn, holding her empty basket on her hip. "I'll be over in a minute."

Inside the old structure, Haugland found the two-man saw still hanging along with other logging tools. It was hard to believe it was almost two months since he had logged. Out of habit he found himself straightening up her equipment. The stout barn was in need of repair, but so well made it could stand another winter. He found some missing battens and studied how they might be fixed then stopped. He had never planned to be in Fjellstad past summer.

The ramp into the barn reverberated with the clunk of wooden shoes, but he continued working until Anna came up and touched his arm.

"*Hei*," she said when he turned, then thanked him in sign when she saw what he'd done.

Her signing was a little consideration, but it touched him. You sign well, he signed.

Encouraged, she attempted to talk to him this way until they both laughed at the game. Still, he was frustrated. Suddenly, he wanted to be himself. You want see me?

"*Ja*. I heard something," Anna said. "I thought it was important. Schiller was at the hotel—you know the German officer who led the patrol last July. He's come back."

He nodded, wondering why. What he say?

"Something terrible. He said the Finns broke diplomatic relations with Berlin four days ago. That the Germans are now evacuating Finland into northern Norway. He predicts widespread destruction as they pull back from the Soviet army, leaving the countryside uninhabitable."

To be sure he understood, she took his pencil and notebook and wrote the words "Finns," "Russians," "German Army," "20th Mountain."

Haugland appeared to read thoughtfully, but his mind was racing ahead at this news.

A settlement between the Russians and Finns was expected, speculation had been rampant for weeks about what the Germans would do. It had been discussed on the *Hessa* as he caught up on news from the free world. Intelligence had been murky.

The 20th, he knew, consisted of seven divisions—175,000 men—and they occupied the part of northern Norway and Finland known as Nordmarka. Their primary objective would be protecting the Karesuando-Fualo line carrying nickel from the Petsamo mines. The Soviets would be expected to engage in combat against the Germans as soon as the settlement went through.

What else say?

"A patrol may be permanently set up in Fjellstad. Schiller hoped to be sent here."

He tapped his notebook, then wrote: Why he tell this?

"I have no idea and that frightens me. It's dangerous talk."

Haugland moved away, knowing she was watching him, but he had to be careful with his response. He finally turned back to her and wrote in his notebook: Beware of friends easily made. The Germans may still want your husband's papers.

"I have tried to avoid him, Jens, but he's very persistent. How will I keep him away?"

Haugland shrugged. What could he say? He wondered if she knew of von Weber's arrest in Germany, something he had learned of only a few short days ago. She could be in more trouble than just her being the wife of Einar Fromme. But he couldn't tell her. It'd give himself away, yet in his heart he couldn't just leave her on her own.

Haugland made a sound in his mouth to get her attention. You fine?

"*Ja*. I'm fine. No hysterics," she said smiling. "I promised."

He wrote: I'll tell friends about patrol. Be careful. Dangerous.

"I know." She leaned against the wall, absentmindedly toying with a strap from a harness hanging on a hook. The leather end fell between her breasts. Lovely, he thought. The slight tension he had felt between them eased and to his relief harmony was restored. More than anything he must not give his cover away, but at the same time he wanted her friendship. It was a delicate line that was becoming increasingly hard not to cross.

How Lisel? he motioned.

"She's fine. We have a new friend—*Doktor* Grimstad." She went on to tell him of the visit, the vitamins. "I see a change already. It's wonderful." She signed, happy, her face aglow.

Happy, he thought. To see your face full of light, your cheeks flushed with pleasure makes me happy. He signed, Good. Now I work. Where hammer?

For a time he mended boards and replaced battens on the barn wall. Hauling nails and boards for him, Anna talked, and once again he found himself enjoying the company of a smart woman. It made him curious about her upbringing. Very liberal no doubt and an outcrop of sanity during the turbulent years in Germany following the Great War. He wondered about the influence of her American mother, but von Schauffer, her father, must have influenced her, too. To have grown up unscathed from all the Nazi youth propaganda.

Lisel found them a little later putting up a batten and joined the work party.

It will be difficult to continue doing this, he thought, because Lisel was sure to talk. When they finished, to his surprise Anna took the little girl aside and reminded her that she mustn't say anything about Jens being here, not even to *Tante* Marthe. It would get him into trouble. He was their secret friend and no one talked about secrets. When she was finished she looked back over to him. Friend, she signed as Lisel nestled against her.

Making a fist, he tapped his chin twice with his thumb. Secret, he signed back.

The words were as potent as their bond of trust. They each had secrets.

***

Torstein pulled his jacket tight around him and stepping down from the bus braced himself for the light rain that was falling across the twilight-lit park. A short walk and he'd be back at his apartment and in bed, hopefully before curfew. He was bushed. The day had been long, beginning at five in the morning when he rose to catch the first bus to the country south of the city. There he had spent most of the day meeting with contacts in the security branch in the Oslo area and beyond, just as he had for the past week or so. Allied movement on the continent had brought on a rush of meetings in the civilian section of the underground that went as high as the Coordinating Committee (KK) and the Circle itself.

One of the most important was the National Conference that had taken place a week ago on September 4 and 5 at the *Hjemme for Døve* in the Oslo suburbs. Nearly forty attended on the second day, a security logistics nightmare to say the least. Torstein's job was to provide security and keep knowledge of the flurry of activity secret. It was a heady time, preparing for liberation, but the meetings were premature.

Torstein stopped halfway up the darkened block. Further up on the right he saw movement and realized that there were several dark cars parked in front of his building. The movement was the unmistakable leather coat of a Gestapo agent going into the building. Three more quickly followed. His hand straying to his pistol, he stood stock-still until he was sure where everyone was placed, then carefully withdrew. When he reached the end of the block, he took off.

Ten minutes later, he was on the phone to Lars Haugland. There was silence on the other end of the line as he talked, but as soon as he was finished, Lars broke in.

"Get as low as possible for a while. A list of names has fallen into German hands. Your name was on it."

"Jesus," Torstein said. "All right, I'm off. I've got some clothes stashed at another flat. I'll contact you in a few days."

"Better use the cutout. We can let you know how things are. If it gets too hot, you better consider leaving. Sweden's nice this time of year—I think."

"Who cares, Listen, you keep your head low too, Lars. The buzz word is capitulation not decapitation."

Lars laughed. "I'll take that on advisement. See you around."

Torstein said good-bye. There was a click on the other end. He wondered if it was the last time he would ever talk to Torstein.

***

The week after Kjell returned from seeing Kitty off, Haugland announced they were to meet the *Hessa* in the islands to the west side of Hitra in two days.

"We might as well take a couple of days to fish. Maybe we'll catch something worth selling." He made some simple preparations and when Kjell wasn't looking, went to see Anna.

He had gone on the pretense of returning books, but frankly he just wanted to see her. He ended up helping Anna clear out a space down in the dairy for the potatoes she was harvesting. There in a small storage room with shelves. When he explored it, he discovered a natural cave hidden behind a wall.

Look, he signed.

Anna crept closer with a lantern. Pushing on the wall, he showed her its spring-loaded latch. Behind it, the space was high enough for two people to move around without too much discomfort.

"Why do you think it's there?" Anna asked.

Haugland shrugged. He had no idea why it had been built, but he was glad that he found it.

When they were done, they went back up into the warmth of the *stue* where Anna made sandwiches. Lisel settled in Haugland's lap for a story, dripping her herring pieces on the table as she pored over a book. Anna was appalled.

"She's taking advantage of you, Jens," she said after Lisel left to play with her dolls. "You are like family." For a while they watched the boats out on the fjord. The day was overcast and the waters a slate gray, making a counterpoint to the yellow and gold autumn colors.

"Beautiful," she murmured.

Haugland, looking at her, signed yes.

CHAPTER 57

The light pierced the dark closet. A soldier dragged Torstein Kaaland out into the hallway and propelled him down to a shadowy room. He felt weak from being in the heat box, but he had no idea how long he had been there. He had been brought to Victoria Terrasse in the morning straight from his hospital bed. Was it afternoon or night? He couldn't tell. Loss of blood, complicated by an appalling thirst left him weak.

A soldier threw him onto a stool. "Sit down, *swinen*." He licked his lips and swallowed, trying to get some moisture into his throat, but his mouth was like a sandpit.

"Are you thirsty?" a voice asked in flawless Norwegian.

He lifted his head to face a new German officer. Torstein had a flicker of hope until he saw the man's eyes. They were cold and dead as yesterday's catch. His badge read Koeller.

"*Ja*," he nodded and was surprised to hear the order to have water brought to him.

Now he'll play with me, he thought.

For the next few minutes they asked about his movements in the last six months, which he had the mental clarity to answer. The raid at the apartment wasn't mentioned. Was that three days ago? He was aware of several men standing back behind the blinding lights set above and in front of him. As the grilling continued, the activity behind the lights increased around a side table with surgical tools and wires laid out like silverware on a white cloth. Torstein felt his courage drain into his shoeless feet.

"Why did you go to Kvam last May?"

"To visit my brother."

The German shoved a crude drawing under Torstein's nose. It was of a man wearing spectacles and dark hair, He wondered if it was supposed to be Tore Haugland. "Know him? We suspect him of sabotage on a train carrying an important official. I believe he met you in Kvam."

"*Nei*. I've never seen him before in my life."

"A boy from there says otherwise. Said this man passed dangerous explosives to him. Did you receive materiel as well?"

"I don't know this man."

Two men came into the lights. While one man seized him, the other calmly broke one of his toes. Torstein hit the floor before he knew what was happening. When he came to, Koeller was leaning against a table smoking a cigarette. Koeller reached over and lifted up his chin.

"Look up," the German said.

Weakly, Torstein obeyed, trying to focus his eyes behind his crooked and dripping glasses. In front of him was a photograph of Joachim von Weber. When he saw it, his heart sank. There was no hope for him now. "Do you know this man?"

"*Nei.*" He felt ridiculously light-headed. The pain in his foot was intolerable.

"You are lying, *swinen*. You followed this man last summer. You boarded a coastal ferry and got off in Trondheim."

Torstein blanched. How could they have found out? "I was never on a steamer this summer. I've never seen him before."

"All lies," he said. "You've told me all lies. You are protecting this schoolteacher and you followed the traitor von Weber. One last thing." Koeller showed him a picture of Anna and Einar Fromme. "Know them?"

Torstein shook his head no, then marshaled his battered brain to think. Koeller's words had registered. It explained the attack on the apartment. The Gestapo had already been looking for him, before his name appeared on the captured list of XU and security agents. Von Weber and the Hitler Plot... Anna von Schauffer Fromme.

Koeller picked up another paper. "You're in the security branch of your illegal organization. Your job is to provide security for meetings, communication between groups. You also do intelligence gathering and occasionally— sabotage. The schoolteacher, he is your leader?"

"*Nei.*" He felt absurdly weak.

"No matter. We'll find him." Koeller paced back and forth in front, causing the bright lights to flicker like an old silent movie.

Torstein lifted his head. "I don't... know him." He never saw the signal. Three heavy blows fell across his back. He felt himself slip and then blacked out.

Torstein woke up on the floor of a dark, dank, room smelling of urine. He was too weak to move and lay staring into the pitch blackness. In his pain his mind began to wander and he saw snow—cool, refreshing snow. He saw his sister and brother. They were all kids, rushing down the hill behind their Kvam farm on their sleds. Someone made a snowman and set up sheaves of wheat for the birds. Christmas, he thought. I'll never see it.

The idea revived him, but as tears rolled down his battered face he knew what he must do. He shifted his broken body and touched his side. I've got at least two broken ribs, possible shoulder damage, but I can walk—despite the foot now swollen like a club. It was enough.

He slept. Sometime later, he heard footsteps in the hall. He groaned. He couldn't go through it again. The door was unbolted and light poured into the small room. A man in civilian work clothes was standing there.

"You all right?" he asked in Norwegian.

Torstein said nothing.

"I'm to take you to clean up. *Vær så snill*, let me help you."

Torstein wondered if he was a prisoner too. He let the man get him into a sitting position, and eventually standing. He could barely put weight on his mangled foot but he tried. He had to.

He was taken down a hall to a washroom where he relieved himself in private and cleaned up at the sink. There was a mirror. He was shocked to see his face and torn bloody shirt.

The man did little talking, except to ask after his injuries. He gave him news from outside, speaking in a whisper. There were guards just outside the opened door. Torstein wasn't sure if he should completely trust him. It was an old Gestapo trick. Yet the man seemed genuine.

"Hurry up," one of the guards barked. They started back when a soldier told them to halt. They were led down another way and up a flight of stairs he could only take one at a time.

Torstein's heart sank. All his remaining strength was leaving him but he had to hold on. Finally they arrived in an area where he could hear a typewriter and a woman's voice. A short walk and they were ushered into a large, spacious room with fine carpets and tall, elegant windows. He was surprised to see one of the curtains drawn and a bright rosy morning developing outside. He'd thought he'd never see dawn again. He had made it through the night.

"Over there," one of the uniformed guards yelled. Torstein limped his way to the spot indicated by the guard, vaguely wondering if the other Norwegian was here to witness his torture. There was a bustle at a door and the guards snapped to attention.

"*Heil*, Hitler!"

"*Heil*, Hitler!" Koeller came around to his desk and tossed his gloves on it. A young uniformed aide stood off to the right, his arms folded behind his back. Koeller began talking and spreading out papers, but Torstein looked over at the window and watched the lightening pink sky. It looked so beautiful that his eyes began to sting but he ordered his body to desist. He needed to see. Koeller wanted him to sign a confession to his crimes of working against the Reich then he would be left alone. All they needed was a signature.

Torstein began to tremble, but it wasn't from fear, only the exertion of pulling all his reserves of strength together. It was very effective though, covering his intention. He approached the desk on the side as though to pick up the pen and sign. With a speed fired by determination, he picked up a brass lamp on the desk. Torstein shouted, "My all for Norway!" then charging, Torstein threw himself against the long window. There was brief resistance from the glass, then a silvery shattering sound as the lamp did its damage and he was through.

The Germans were stunned.

The air was cool and crisp and Torstein was thinking of snow when he smashed into the pavement four stories below.

CHAPTER 58

Anna was in the barn when she heard an unfamiliar voice. Never having company, she went out to investigate. A stranger with vaguely familiar face was talking to Lisel. He dressed like a Norwegian laborer, spoke idiomatic Norwegian, but he wasn't Norwegian. But there wasn't any way she could say it was so.

"Anna Mueller," the stranger said in German.

Anna froze, the strange sensation of her knees locking and holding her in place killing any notion of flight even when the stranger had spoken a name only her father and uncle knew.

"*Können Sie sich noch an mich erinnern*?" he asked.

"*Nein*." The word tumbled out. She couldn't control her tongue anymore then she could control her pounding heart. Instinctively, she held out her hand to Lisel.

"I didn't mean to alarm you, *Fru* Fromme," he said switching to Norwegian. "I'm *Feldwebel* Horst Klein, your uncle's aide—Uncle Felix."

"Of course." The fear she felt softened, but she still sensed danger. Somehow she got her nerves under control. "I thought you looked familiar despite the change of clothes."

He looked down at his garb and laughed. "It's a bit provincial, isn't it?"

She drew Lisel closer to her. "I didn't know you spoke Norwegian."

"I came here frequently as a boy. My father worked on a merchant ship out of Hamburg. Sailed back and forth between Oslo and Stavanger all the time." He cleared his throat. "*Fru* Fromme. Can we talk? It concerns you and your uncle. I have risked a good deal coming here."

Inside Anna invited him to sit at the table while she made tea. Klein couldn't wait.

"Your uncle was arrested in Germany. After the attempt on Hitler's life, he was lured over. I can't tell you much, only that he was among a group of officers here in Norway opposed the Nazi machine and the direction of the war for some time."

Anna sucked her breath in, feeling the same sickening way she had when Einar died.

"Is he dead?"

"*Nein*. He was sentenced to death, but it was recently commuted to life. The Swedes have been very active on his behalf."

Anna made the tea, but it took all her concentration to do it without spilling, her hands were trembling so. When Klein reached for his cup, the sleeves on his simple shirt pulled back, exposing ugly red sores the size of *ore* on the underside of his wrist. Half-healed, they were barely scabbed over. Klein pulled the sleeves back. Anna sat down at the table with a thunk.

"You've been hurt." On his face, there were signs of healing amid cuts and faint traces of bruising around his eyes and mouth. His nose could have been broken.

"No one's safe from the Gestapo." He looked at her gently. "I was questioned, but your secret is safe. I would die for von Weber. Knowing he cares for you, I give myself to you."

Anna was deeply moved. She put a hand on his arm. "How did you find me?"

"He told me once. I came by the mailboat and asked for directions at the *landhandel* on how to get out to the fjord road. I didn't say whom I was seeing. Wasn't sure which farmstead."

"You weren't afraid to come?"

"Do you mean, have I been watched?" When she nodded, Klein shrugged. "My movements were initially restricted, but I got permission to go on this trip. I dumped a tail on the train before Dombas. He's probably ranting and raving in Trondheim by now, never knowing I went to Åndalsnes on the coast. There's no danger to you."

"Won't they arrest you if you don't go back?"

"I'll be all right…" He looked uncomfortable and cleared his throat. "You realize, I hope by now, that *Oberst* von Weber confided in me about your family and how you came here. In fact, I often was the one who arranged the mails. Since his arrest, I have felt a new responsibility for you. I came here because I thought you should be warned." He hesitated slightly. "There have been inquiries about you."

Anna put a hand to her throat. Despite her treatment by the villagers, she had at least felt safe and thought herself secure for duration of war as long as she didn't antagonize anyone. "Why? My husband is dead. Why after all this time?"

"The Gestapo seized von Weber's property in Prussia. I just learned they found his secret safe in Lillehammer. I thought it secure. I'm afraid there were photographs."

Anna turned away. Out on the water rain moved toward the shore like a dark, gray curtain. A chill settled on her shoulders, spreading down her arms. Neither of them spoke, not even when the rain came up and slapped at the windows with little taps.

"I'm sorry to alarm you. It's hard to say what the Gestapo wants. I think you're safe for now because they don't have a name. It's been over six years since you were smuggled over here." Klein drank the last of the tea. "Try to be strong. Time, I think, is on your side. The prospects for a German surrender in the next month still look good. It's a matter of time. Since there'll be no further communication between you or your father, the trail will be dead."

Anna smiled as though his words had calmed her, but she felt the utmost dread.

***

Klein returned to the village where he rented a small boat with a motor. He intended to fish for the rest of the day, weather permitting, before meeting his contact. If all went well, he'd be on the final step of his planned departure to Sweden. Several weeks before he had met with someone from a group he had been told about—a group that helped German soldiers to desert. It was very risky work. Often only safe havens were provided while paperwork could be made up. The soldier was passed onto some place in the countryside where he might live low-key. Other times, arrangements were made to actually smuggle them out, but they weren't passed along regular export lines. Trust only went so far. Klein had been lucky. Someone from this group would see him through the controls at Trondheimfjord and into Sweden.

He took his time going out the fjord, letting the little motor idle so he could fish, using line and hook attached to a block of wood. The rain had held off since its first outburst, but it was cold and blustery now, the wind kicking up the waves into choppy swells. Traffic on the *Trondheimsleia* had nearly vanished.

Eventually Klein saw a rundown hut perched on a high rocky shore. As he motored in, he spied someone standing in the door of the hut. By the time he tied up, a man was on the mossy path. Dressed like a fisherman, Klein thought him an unsavory sort, ill-kept and shifty-eyed. It shouldn't have affected him, but Klein distrusted him, even when the Norwegian offered him some tinned herring and bread. They ate quietly, but the Norwegian kept asking Klein questions that further increased his uneasiness. Adept at interrogation himself, this man was not. When he was asked what unit he was from in the *Wehrmacht*, he politely refused.

"Of course, I shouldn't ask. Shall we go?"

At the dock's edge, Klein saw for the first time the boat that would lead him to freedom. Tied to a long narrow floating platform, it was not much more than a large dinghy with a sail. The water around it was dark, matching the approach of thick weather and night. In just a few short weeks, the days had shortened dramatically. In the encroaching evening, the island of Hitra took on a distant look across the channel, a hazy contrast to the rugged, bare mainland.

"Want to secure your boat? We can leave as soon as you are ready."

Klein climbed down. The Norwegian followed him, walking past him to the floating dock. Klein knelt to test his line. Out of the corner of his eye, he watched the Norwegian put down his rucksack and fiddle with the tether. He started to turn back to his own work when he saw the Norwegian slip a gun into his pocket.

I shouldn't be so on edge, he thought. It's the man's business, but the gun was a Walther PPK, a Gestapo favorite for plainclothesmen. Alarmed, he weighed the choices he had: confront the man and disarm him or let him move him along the export line. Heartsick, he realized he should assume the worst. Too much was at stake. Carefully, he took out his gun. "Turn around."

"What?" the Norwegian said.

"I want to see the gun. Just turn around and ease it out." Klein cocked his.

"All right. I'm turning, but you are sadly mistaken my friend. Just give me a second. I'm stiff." The Norwegian straightened up, wobbling to get his balance. Too late Klein realized the trick. He fired but he was off his mark. The Norwegian wasn't. Klein fell down onto the slippery, wet boards of the dock, clasping his shoulder. Instantly, the Norwegian was on him, clawing at his weapon. Klein began to feel woozy. He couldn't get his breath. The gun slipped away from his fingers. I am dead. *Mutti*, I love you.

Seconds later there was exploding white light and then nothing.

When he came to, Klein was lying on his side in the bottom of his motorboat. He lifted his aching head. *Whack!* The boat shook as the man bashed a slit in its side just above the water line. With great effort, Klein moved his right hand down to his pants and patted his pocket. His envelope of money was gone, but to his relief, his knife was still there.

The man turned. "You're just in time, hagfish bait. Then I'll get my bounty." The poacher waddled over and knelt over him.

"You want more?" Klein garbled in his throat. The Norwegian strained to listen. Klein drove the blade deep into the soft spot below the man's sternum as all his remaining strength could allow, then twisted it up and down. Blood splurged around the knife onto his cold hands.

The Norwegian tried to say something, his mouth a round "o," but fell back into the slowly rising water in the bottom of the boat. He died as he drowned.

Panting, Klein struggled to a sitting position. The water was bloody, but so was he. He ripped the watch cap off the Norwegian's head to staunch his wound.

A gull cried out. Klein imagined for a moment it was someone calling to him, but there was no one on the Trondheimsleia, not even a fishing boat heading home before the fall of night and the barometer. To the west, Hitra was gone, lost in haze. All he could see were the towering, naked cliffs behind him and the beckoning entrance to Fjellstad's fjord to the south. Sick at heart, he thought about going back to the village and getting help from Anna, but he had to go on. Spying some rope under the seat, he began to lash the body to it and painfully prepared to leave.

CHAPTER 59

On the day Anna talked to Klein, the *Otta* met with the submariner chaser *Hessa*. It transferred an agent and Haugland passed along hard material. Everything had gone smoothly, but there was tension in the air that had less to do with the season change as to conditions.

"Didn't say earlier," the captain said as they stood outside the pilot house, "but the *Hitra* was attacked a few days ago at Jossundfjord. They managed to get away."

"Damn. Will that affect the Bus?"

"*Nei*, just a sign things are heating up. We've done a bit of action too. There was another Allied attack on the *Tirpitz* in Alta Fjord. She won't be threatening our actions for a while."

"Not if she's always in repair." Haugland looked over at Kjell waiting on the *Otta*. He looked anxious to go. *We're all feeling it. Something's coming.*

***

They got back into Fjellstad the following day, just before dinnertime. While they secured the boat and catch, Ella came down to see them.

"*Hei*, Kjell. We missed you." Missed you, she signed to Haugland. "You boys were gone some time. Any trouble?"

"*Nei*," Kjell said. "Nothing more unusual than a patrol boat and a little squall. Neither bothered us, don't you worry."

"Well, I'm sure you're tired." She put her hands into her coat pockets. She seemed nervous.

What? Haugland signed.

She acknowledged him, but spoke to Kjell. "I was wondering if you and Jens would like to come for dinner."

Kjell stood up straight. "Well, don't mind if I do. I miss the company of ladies. I'm sure Jens feels the same way. As soon as we clean up and look presentable."

Haugland kept his head down as he put the boat's lines in order so not to betray his grin, but "matchmaker" ran through his head.

Ella served them a simple meal of fish hash with bread and cheese Kjell brought. Haugland was tired, but enjoyed their lively evening. As he sat, listening to the banter between Kjell and Ella, he thought, *How lucky I am to be here with these wonderful people.* Yet, he knew things were changing and he should be thinking about leaving. He'd been here too long.

When they were done, they went into the living room for *ersatz* coffee.

"Are you staying down for the night, Jens?" Ella asked as she set down the tea tray.

Yes, he signed.

She was about to pour the coffee, when the shop bell down below jangled. "Surely, they must know the shop is closed." The bell jangled again, a little more urgent this time.

"I'll go, Ella," Kjell volunteered. "I'll see what the fuss is all about." He signed. Be back.

He left them sitting there and went down to investigate. Seconds later, there were footsteps on the wood stairs, at first slow, then hurried. "Get Jens's attention," Kjell said as he came into the living room. Trouble, he signed. "Will you excuse us, Ella?"

"Why?"

Kjell hesitated. "Helmer Stagg found a boat adrift near the mouth of the fjord. There's a dead man in it. I'm going to take Jens over to help hide it."

"Hide it? Why?" Ella asked.

"Helmer thinks he's German, although he has no papers."

"Where is he now?" Ella asked, preparing to come.

"On the floor of my warehouse." Kjell watched her reach for her sweater. "Ella, I'm not sure you should come. I don't want you involved."

"And what does that mean, involved?"

"It could be real trouble, Ella. The man was shot." Kjell signed: Man dead. Shot.

Ella snorted. "I *am* involved. Always have been." And with that, she led the way down.

They joined Helmer around the bedraggled figure wrapped in a canvas shroud. When Kjell set down his hooded lantern, the large dark space of the warehouse blossomed into sharp shadows and angular light exposing the rafters, the windows covered with blackout paper, and stacked equipment. He knelt beside the corpse. On Kjell's signal Haugland opened the canvas.

The young man in death looked oddly at peace, except for his bloody shirt and coat. Trying not to look too expert, Haugland carefully examined the body. The man had been shot near the neck. Haugland went through his coat pockets and finding nothing, opened the jacket. He found a couple of Norwegian *ore,* and a soggy train ticket in the pockets.

Haugland patted the dead man's pants, undoing the fly and pants buttons.

Pulling out his shirt he found bruises on the belly and chest, signs of some struggle. He discovered a flat, bloodstained wallet inside a cotton pouch secured to his thigh.

"I'll be damned," said Helmer. "Why'd he put them in his shorts?"

While Kjell examined the leather wallet's contents, Haugland turned the cold, stiffening body over. Finding nothing on his body, he checked the back of his head. There was a wet, sticky spot. Saying nothing, he straightened the man's clothes as decently as possible and got up.

"Norwegian *legitmasjonskort* here, ration cards," Kjell was saying. "Says Bakken. Jorge. Why did you think him German, Helmer?"

"I saw him at the *landhandel.* He spoke very good Norwegian. Haircut was funny."

Kjell gave the wallet to Haugland. He took it apart. Out of a secret lining, he pulled out a photo showing an older couple with the man. He was wearing the uniform of a lieutenant in the *Wehrmacht,* his arm was lovingly around the woman. His mother?

"Now what?" Helmer grumbled. "A dirty German and we are stuck with him."

"Not if we stick with the identification he carries," Kjell answered. "What we don't need is the State Police sniffing around. As soon as Grimstad gets here, we'll take care of him."

Standing to the side, Ella wrapped her sweater tight against her body. Haugland looked up at her. In just the past few weeks she had lost weight. The softness had gone out of her face. He noticed she couldn't take her eyes off the German.

"Poor boy," she finally said. "I feel sorry for him. He should be given a proper burial."

"And he shall," Kjell said. "As soon as we can get him out of these clothes."

Grimstad came down and began a thorough examination. Everyone was on edge while they waited, but Haugland kept his emotions to himself and stayed sitting next to the body.

"What if he is a deserter?" he heard Helmer ask. Haugland couldn't tell if he was afraid or angry. "How will we explain the gunshot wound? We could be accused of murdering him. There could be reprisals against all of us here."

Grimstad finished his examination. "I think he was shot, then fought off his attacker or the other way around, but ultimately couldn't save himself against the elements. He lost a lot of blood, but the cold got him."

"Can you make up a death certificate, Hans?" Kjell asked.

"*Ja*. I'll take care of Fasting too if he asks to see the body. How about a box made for him?"

"I'll see to it," Helmer put the canvas back over the German's face.

"Good," Kjell said, "The sooner buried, the better off we'll be. One thing I would like to know. Does anyone have any idea whom he went to see?"

"The Fromme woman, I think" Helmer volunteered.

"I was afraid of that," Kjell said.

Haugland stayed quiet, but felt a wicked headache coming on.

CHAPTER 60

Rising early, Anna went into the village, carrying all her hopes and fears with her. After Horst Klein left her, she realized how tenuous her position was. If the Gestapo was looking for her then she must do everything to keep herself hidden until capitulation. On the other hand, when liberation did come, whatever authority was in place could still arrest her. In their eyes, she was a quisling. She wasn't naive to think she would be treated with a gentle hand. What about the French women who had collaborated or had relations with German soldiers? Taunted and hair shorn by the resistance, they had been paraded through the liberated streets of Paris, and countless other towns, their shame for all to see. Anna didn't know if the whispered stories were true, but they frightened her for one simple reason—Lisel. What would happen to her? Who would care?

The doctor had hinted at helping and there was Jens, but she wasn't sure what they could do. What she needed was a woman. Women— the silent sisterhood that kept things going despite deprivation and the terrors of living under occupation—saw to the welfare and moral justice of a community. If she could gain a protector for Lisel, Anna could be at peace about the future. So far, she had cultivated the friendship of Marthe, the cook.

From the beginning, when Lisel tagged along with Anna to the Tourist Hotel, Marthe had taken an interest in Lisel. She often invited Lisel to the kitchen for sweets.

"Why is she so kind?" Anna asked Foss one day.

"She was Jarle Fromme's housekeeper many years ago. I believe she knew your husband when he was a boy. There is a natural affinity, I supposed," Foss said. "She's a sentimental bag of lard."

Sensing the growing attachment, Anna went to see Marthe and proposed having Marthe's daughter Ingrid take Lisel a few times a week. "I know that you despise me, but it is wrong to ostracize my daughter. She is innocent and, after all, Jarle Fromme's great-granddaughter. I'll pay you for it."

"Why me? Why should I do that?" Marthe grumbled.

"Because you love my Lisel and because you are not afraid of what the others will say. What you say behind my back is your business."

To Anna's relief, Marthe said yes. It wasn't long before the cook asked Anna if she could take Lisel to church on Sunday. Anna agreed, but later decided she would go see Pastor Helvig first.

It was early, a cool overcast day. The mist still bobbed along the shore of the fjord, the sun trapped behind the high wall of mountains and clouds. No one was in the village lane. The church seemed deserted. At the top of the steps she tried the double doors. They were locked.

"Is Auntie there?" Lisel asked. Dressed in her red wool coat, she clutched her doll.

"*Nei*, Munchin. We'll go to the hotel to see her. Then you can play with Ingrid." Anna pulled her coat around her. A breeze gently stroked the dry grass near the steps and rustled the scarves about their heads. There was an edge to mornings every day.

From the back of the church and its old weathered cemetery, came the sound of shovels breaking up earth. "Wait here." Anna tiptoed around to the side of the building, stopping when she saw the old caretaker from the village and his son digging a grave. The younger man was in the hole up to his waist while the other appeared to be taking a break.

"Should be done in another twenty minutes. Pastor Helvig will coming then."

"Has Fasting seen him?"

"He'll want to, even if Grimstad said accidental death."

The men talked on. Anna stepped back. A side door stood ajar. On an impulse, she stepped in to look for Pastor Helvig. A single light blazed in the sanctuary. To the right of the altar rail was a little organ. By the pulpit, a simple pine coffin rested on wood sawhorses.

Was this the man they were talking about? She felt a sudden chill as a childhood memory flashed before her. *Mutti*. Her mother lying dead in her coffin at the family estate. *Mutti*. So beautiful and young; everyone in black with pale, weeping faces. She closed her eyes. She had been thirteen when *Mutti* died. What did a young girl know about death when she barely knew about life? Her heart in her mouth, she stepped forward, the memory of her mother so vivid. She had been afraid to touch her, afraid to feel the coldness of her body, but she had stayed by her to talk.

Looking at the plain, forlorn box, Anna covered her mouth as a wave of nausea swept over her.

Einar. She never saw him again after the Gestapo took him away. She never had a body to claim, to touch, or say good-bye to. Only the rumor he had died by his own hand. An image of him beaten and bloody, his handsome face contorted in pain welled up in front of her. Against her instincts, she walked across the creaky wood floor toward the coffin. If she saw the man, maybe the vision would go away. Maybe she would see Einar as he should have lain, his suffering over.

The lid was ajar so the head, upper chest and shoulders of the man were exposed. She tried to be detached and objective. His eyes were closed and the expression on his gray face peaceful. His arms were folded. Nothing frightening, no terrible nightmare here. Except...the stranger was *Feldwebel* Horst Klein.

As realization set in, something inside of her collapsed and she felt her skin prickle. The hair rose all around the edge of her scalp. She grabbed the side of the coffin and tried to collect herself. What had they said? Accidental death? His face might seem like he was asleep, but she knew it was not true. Klein had been murdered.

Someone is looking for you. The lieutenant had been so sure that he hadn't been followed. So confident things would be all right. Now he was dead.

She glanced around the church. She had to know. Swallowing her fear and the bile in her mouth, she reached into the coffin. Klein had been laid out with respect. He was wearing an old white linen shirt. Her hands trembling, she undid his buttons, appalled by her nerve and the heavy chill of the dead man's skin.

There were no signs on his face of any injury except the faint marks she remembered from his visit. Had the cold and a night out on the water really killed him? Where were the signs of the accident? When she opened the shirt she found her answer. The lieutenant had been shot. He had a ghastly bullet wound in the neck.

Her hands gripped the edge of the coffin, but they were trembling uncontrollably now. Her whole body trembled. Only her brain seemed on hold.

"Ma-ma!" Lisel's little voice revived her. No longer squeamish, she redid his buttons, straightening the shirt into order and left. "Lisel!" She whispered as she came down the steps with shaky knees.

"Ma-ma? I thought you got lost and left me."

"*Nei*, Lisel. I wasn't lost and I won't leave you—ever. Look, your shoelace is untied, sweetie."

Anna knelt down and retied the shoelace, the small action steadying her. "There, you're all set." She was directly eye level with her girl. Brushing her cheek, she said, "I love you."

Lisel nodded solemnly. "I love you too, Mama," she whispered.

Anna hugged her. Lisel was so thin that her arms could have gone around a second time, but she felt immediate calm. We're alive. This little moment is all we have that means anything.

At the back of the church came men's voices again as they approached the building. One voice sounded familiar. Anna cautioned Lisel and sat down on the steps. "What did Fasting say?"

"The sheriff can't make it back, so he said go ahead and bury him. What a stroke of luck that is. I'm to present his papers when he gets back." The men stopped and there was silence for a moment as if they were looking at something, then the familiar voice spoke again.

"You're going to say some words?"

"*Ja*. Jerry or *Nordman*, he's God's son. Can you can help us get him out here?"

Anna heard the men approach and braced herself.

"*Fru* Fromme." It was *Doktor* Grimstad and the pastor. Grimstad's eyes were wide with surprise. He exchanged a glance with Helvig. "What brings you here?"

She rose awkwardly. "*God dag*. I dropped by to see you, Pastor Helvig. Marthe Larsen wants to bring my daughter to church school."

"Is this the man who lives in the church?" Lisel asked.

Anna smiled but it was hard thinking of Klein dead inside the church and these men relieved he was to be buried as soon as possible. "*Ja, herze*." Anna squeezed Lisel's hand, an effort to calm her nerves and avoid Grimstad. *He knows Klein came to see me. Was he her friend anymore?* The pastor obviously wasn't.

"Are you going to the Hotel now?" The doctor asked unexpectedly. "If so, come to my office and I'll give you more vitamins for Lisel. It will only take a moment." Grimstad turned back to the pastor. "I'll only be gone for a while. I'll send someone if I'm delayed longer."

Anna said nothing. He had decided for her.

***

After settling Lisel in his kitchen with the housekeeper, Grimstad took Anna to his study and asked her to sit down near his desk. He came right to the point.

"Yesterday, a fisherman from another *fylke* was killed in an accident. He is being buried this morning at the churchyard."

"Will you say something over him?" When Grimstad said yes, Anna sighed. "I'm glad. It's very sad to die so far from home."

"Was he far from home? Germany?"

Anna's looked at him sharply. "Are you asking me?"

"*Ja,* I'm asking," Grimstad said. "You were in the church today, weren't you? Did you see him in the coffin? Just answer yes or no."

Anna twisted her hands in her lap. "*Ja,* I saw him."

"*Takk*. I'm glad you said you were there, because it means you trust me. We must trust one another." He shifted in his chair. "Very difficult times are ahead. Every day there is talk of liberation, but September is nearly over and Norway is not free. The Gestapo grows stronger every day. Tell me, did you know him well?"

Anna's eyes were suddenly moist. "*Nei*, but I can tell you he was a good man. Not a Nazi."

"When he was found, he was carrying papers showing that he was a Norwegian from Nord-Trøndelag. Do you have any idea how he got them? Do you think he was a deserter?"

Anna was shocked. She hadn't thought about Klein deserting. He said he was going to be all right. Maybe he *was* escaping.

"He was shot," Grimstad said. "Officially, he died from exposure after sustaining a blow to his head. You can see why we are uneasy and why I must ask you if he had an interest in Fjellstad."

Though she felt Grimstad was being friendly, his clenched jaw betrayed his worry.

"*Nei*. He came only to see me—to see if I was all right."

"Deserter or not, the village is in trouble. His murderer is still at large."

"I will say nothing," Anna said.

"Good." He smiled, but his lips were tense. "You should go now. Helvig knows I have been treating your daughter but he knows nothing about me talking to you. He wouldn't understand." He stood up and pushed in his chair. "Will you excuse me? I'll get Lisel."

Left alone in the study Anna sat staring out the window. In the distance, she could see mountains with a powdering of snow.

Winter's coming, she thought with a chill. Was the Gestapo close behind?

CHAPTER 61

Haugland was upstairs when Anna and Lisel came to the front of the Tourist Hotel. Standing at the long window over the main entrance, he watched them with detached curiosity. Since finding the dead man, his feelings of trust had been shaken. After all, even if Anna was totally innocent of any wrongdoing, as he believed, who was she anyway? Only Einar had known her thoroughly. There would be associates only they would know about. He thought of the money under the floor of her bedroom. As if he didn't have enough to worry about.

Still, this whole incident touched him in a way he hadn't calculated. He saw for the first time how terribly isolated she was and this bothered him to the point of distraction. He wished she trusted him enough to tell him who she really was, how she met Einar, what brought her here.

Anna and Lisel came up to the stone steps of the main entrance. She took off Lisel's scarf and then untied her own, releasing her golden hair. Haugland felt an odd sensation of discomfort. It was as if she had, in an intimate way, done it for his eyes only. The thought struck him so hard that he pulled back from the window. When he looked back she was gone.

A light flashed on the water as the window on a boat's wheelhouse caught the sun filtering through. Haugland looked toward the spit where Sorting's hut was located and saw a mid-sized fishing boat going out. He hoped it was Helmer Stagg's boat. Word had come they had located Sorenson's boat. The mystery about the dead German might be solved soon.

In the little harbor below he could see friends on the seawall as they prepared nets and dried gear for the coming cod season. Forgetting who he was for a moment, he looked forward to that time with a high anticipation—as any fisherman would do—then remembered the dismal state of fishing and his own agenda. As much as he enjoyed being on the boats, he had other business.

Another Bus was coming, this time to the west of Frøya. According to orders, he was to meet and disperse the material to the south. It would be even more dangerous work. The authorities by now must be on full alert since the clash near Lillehavn. It was up to him to meet the boat and use his own people. Winter was a month away.

From out in the hall, a door opened and shut. Footsteps came down the wooden floorboards. "Hurry," a young girl said. "Foss said to be ready. They'll be coming any time."

"Oh, Foss. His mustache has grown into his brain. I can't make sense of him anymore."

"I think he's crazy. My Stigmar says he's been getting threatening notes since the end of August." They passed by the door. Haugland felt their eyes on him when they paused.

He wondered if what they said was true. The staff was always passing rumors since they had no access to real information. They no longer cared if he was in the room. They talked behind his back all the time. He listened to the housemaids as they went down the service stairs. He gathered up his cloths and bucket of tools and headed down too. He had one more job to do.

In the sitting room, he laid a fire in the fireplace. He was down on his knees with kindling and logs from a bin when he heard the French doors open and someone come in. The door closed and the person came in further. "Jens?"

His heart thumped at her voice, but he waited until she put a hand on his shoulder.

"Jens, I didn't think you'd be working today." Her voice was strained and high strung. She could barely keep her hands still. Did she know about the German?

What wrong? he signed.

"Nothing really. The season, I suspect." She smiled softly at him. "I'm all right."

If you have a problem, he wrote, tell me. You need help at farm?

When she finished reading the words, her eyes were shimmering. She took his hand and squeezing it, briefly held it. Suddenly she stiffened. "Oh, Jens. There are soldiers in the hall. *Vær så snill.* I don't want them to see me. I want to go away. Could I leave a message with Marthe? Have Ingrid bring Lisel up to the turn in the road?"

She put her hand on his chest. He was suddenly aware how grimy his clothing was, but even more how her light touch affected him. She withdrew it carefully. Friend, she signed.

He hustled her down to the service passageway and out to the back of the hotel. He opened a door into a grassy area dotted with wood furniture and a garden. The wood structures of homes and other buildings of Fjellstad were beyond a fence. He pointed to a gate on the far side.

"All right." She pulled her wool coat around her and smiled faintly at him. She didn't say anything more, but it was enough for him.

After she left, Haugland stood at the opened door, ignoring the cold wind and threat of rain. *What had Kjell said?* Love comes unexpectedly.

This was unexpected, but it made no sense. It was against his principles and training and contrary to his strong personal feelings against those who had taken his country away. But the fact was that he had fallen in love with Anna Fromme.

CHAPTER 62

Early the next day, Helmer Stagg sent word for Kjell and Haugland to come and look at the dead man he had found in the missing boat. Drifting below the surface not too far in from the lip of the fjord, the body had been tied to the seat. "Come see before it is buried," he wrote. Helmer, by now, was part of Haugland's little cell in Fjellstad.

"Any complaints about his joining?" Haugland asked Kjell as the *Otta* slipped out past Sorting's spit to a little skerry outside the fjord. The morning mist was floating like a skirt's hem above the feet of the green gray walls of the fjord.

"*Nei*. He's overjoyed. Been itching to do something since the last patrol. The dead German was the final straw. He'll be discreet, though. I can guarantee that."

"Sorting back?"

"*Nei*, but Bugge did get a postcard from him, but no date when he would be returning. What about Lillehavn?" Kjell asked.

"I'm taking your advice. There's too much to do. I'll wait for the cutout."

"When's the next Bus coming?"

"The *Hitra*'s due on the 28th out near Frøya. Holger Haraldsen will take me out. I'll be back by Saturday. That'll give you two days to putter around."

Kjell sighed. "Where did September go? When's the next Bus after that?"

"Second week in October. First we need to get this business behind us."

The `business' was wrapped up in a tarp because it was all that was available. A powerful stench of stale vinegar and seaweed hit them as they entered the fisher hut. Taking a deep breath away from it, Helmer opened up the tarp for Haugland and Kjell to see. The body was bloated and torn from where sea life had fed on it. After a brief look with a handkerchief to his nose, Haugland had him shut it up.

"He's a mess," Kjell said, "but I think he's one of the poachers arrested last summer."

"You sure?" Haugland asked. "I was too sick to really make them out."

"Reasonably sure. He may have turned informer. He could have bargained with them to avoid the death penalty."

Kjell looked like he wanted to spit. "It would certainly fit into our scenario about the German deserting. I heard desertions are up. If this man infiltrated a group helping soldiers, then our dead German was another victim."

"That's a sizeable slash in his shirt," Haugland said. "Was there a knife?"

"*Ja,"* Helmer said. "It was sticking out of him when I found him."

"Any other signs of a struggle?"

"In his condition, it's a bit hard to tell, but I did find this." Helmer handed over a Walther PKK. "Found it stuffed in his pants."

"Gestapo." Haugland checked to see if it had been fired. It had. "Maybe you ought to warn your export people about it, Kjell. Could be Rinnan too. He's been very active in trying to penetrate export groups this summer. He may have a negative agent in place somewhere." He handed the gun back to Helmer and gave him a wry smile. He knew the fisherman had a lot of questions because it was the first time he had ever heard Haugland speak.

"Well, let's bury him," Kjell said. "No sense in dragging this out. You got a shovel?"

They buried the poacher in the only stretch of soil in the woods behind the hut. Kjell went out and checked on some lobster pots near the mouth of the fjord while Haugland stayed back and talked to Helmer. Telling him only what he needed to know, Haugland outlined some of the things they would be expected to do in the next few weeks and what part Helmer would play.

"We need another man because of Sorting. We're being watched and he has to be kept away. You'll pick up some of our work. It's enormously important to me that you do this, but I also want you to understand the risk."

"There's no need to explain, Jens. I'd do anything for you. You saved my cousin's life."

***

At dusk, Kjell was back. Bidding goodbye to Helmer, they left for the opposite side of the fjord where Sorting's spit stuck out like pointing finger. Going by sail, they quietly entered a little forested inlet behind it. Here Kjell was able to put down an anchor. Climbing over the stern, Hansen lowered himself into the dinghy and rowed over to the rocky beach. He dragged the boat up and disappeared into the pine trees.

Hansen was gone a long time. As the minutes lengthened, Kjell became nervous. Looking out toward the front of the spit, he could see the hut's roof sticking up behind the ridge. In the fading light, it looked dark and sinister. Walking to the bow of the boat, he peered into the dark looking for any sign. Finally, he caught a guarded light as Hansen came down to the dinghy. He saw the beam rise and fall three times, then turn off as the dinghy moved across the water.

"Sorry, Kjell," Hansen said when he came onboard. "Took longer than I thought, but I had to be careful. I checked everywhere for traps and security measures, but dammit, Sorting's pretty sure of himself. I found none of the standard precautions nor anything sophisticated. Still, it took a while with just the flashlight."

"What did you find?"

"What I feared—a W/T. It's Gestapo issued. There's no doubt where he's connected."

Kjell sucked his breath in. Everything he had suspected was true. Now here was the proof. "God. How much do you think he knows?"

"I have no idea but we'll assume he's aware of illegal work. I've got to leave Fjellstad."

"Oh," Kjell said. His shoulders sagged at this news.

Hansen smiled softly. "We've known it could come to this. Strangely, I wouldn't mind staying around Fjellstad."

"And not go back to the university?"

Hansen laughed. "Funny, isn't it? Pursue academia, then fall for a boat. I could be on a boat like this. Fish 'til the *Draugen* finds me."

"Don't talk so loud," Kjell cautioned. "He might hear you."

CHAPTER 63

After the second knock, Anna knew it was Jens. He had found the hook. She took a deep breath, knowing what she was about to do would change everything. He came late, after she had put Lisel to bed. In the fading twilight, he waited patiently for her to open the door, removing his fisherman's cap when he entered.

At the table, he carefully hung his coat on the back of his chair. The blinds had been drawn for the night, so the room felt closed in and snug but she still felt chilled.

"*Takk* for the other day," she began. "I was unnerved by the soldiers." She kept her hands under the table and twisted them. He regarded her with his usual unreadable face, except for his eyes. There was a glimmer of interest.

It all right, he signed. He laid a hand in front of her, but suddenly took it away. "Jens...." Her heart went out to him.

He took out his notebook. You talk. Why hook?

"Oh, Jens, do you know about the dead fisherman?"

Ja.

"Did you know he came to see me?"

Nei. Why man come? he signed.

"Because he is an associate of someone I love and trust. He came to warn me." She began the speech she had practiced over and over. "Do you remember when I told you I was born in America?" Slowly she told him her most guarded secret, using a sheet of paper to clarify things for him: how her parents had met in America, how she had lived there as a little girl. She told him of her mother's death, what she knew of her father's important research, and the dangerous political environment and the fear of being held hostage by the Gestapo. "My father was afraid we wouldn't be allowed to go. The last time he traveled abroad he couldn't get exit visas for us."

She checked his face for any response. He seemed to be taking the information in the same way he had taken the news about Sorting—calmly.

"I met Einar in Amsterdam. We fell in love immediately. Getting me out was very difficult. Some friends of my father helped me escape. My death was faked. I was hidden and then smuggled out of Germany through Denmark to Sweden. Einar met me there and for a couple of years we lived quite safely. No one dreamed Norway would be invaded. No one."

Hansen looked as if he were sizing her up. Who knows this? he wrote.

"No one. Not even Einar's closest friends." She went on to describe their decision to move to Lillehavn when the Gestapo began arresting Americans and other foreigners. "Even though no one knew I was born in America, it was still risky. Then Einar was arrested for his resistance activities. Oh, the look on his face when they took him away. It broke my heart."

Hansen leaned over the table. Despite his silence, he conveyed a strong masculine presence crackling with energy. She wondered why she had never felt it before. It was oddly disturbing and comforting at the same time. She wondered what had made it possible for him to come to work for her and become her friend. Three months ago she would have thought it impossible. Now she didn't know what she'd do without him.

Why man warn you?

"The SD has found out that I am alive in this country. They don't know my new name but they know I have a connection to someone who is being investigated by the Gestapo for the plot against Hitler. Someone found pictures of me. That is why Horst Klein came to see me."

Hansen tapped her arm, then wrote: Was dead man running away?

"He did tell me the Gestapo questioned him. Now he is dead." She hugged her arms.

Hansen wrote: Friends think he met man from black market. A bad Norwegian. He's dead too.

"Won't someone come looking for this Norwegian?"

Maybe. Hansen's hands and shrug were so clear.

"Then I'm lost. They'll find me. They'll take Lisel."

Hansen touched her arm. Again a presence so strong and protective. He tried to reassure her in sign, making a sound in his throat, but grew embarrassed again. He grabbed his pencil. Do nothing, he wrote. Live quietly like now. Avoid contact with people. Wait out the war.

He leaned back in his chair. His face had a curious, bemused look on it. It became serious again as he leaned forward and picked up his pencil. You have pictures of family in Germany?

"*Nei*, but I have pictures of my American grandparents." She pointed out to the wall. "My mother. My grandfather, John Howard, is the one who tied fish flies. Remember?"

He pointed to the stove. Burn them. Papers too.

Anna swallowed. She knew he was right, but it was hard to burn up what little she had left of her old life. She fetched the cigar box from her bedroom. Hansen was stoking the fire. She touched his arm and gave him a batch of letters written in German. She lifted out another batch, stopping briefly to read one, then relinquished it to the flames. She added pictures. When he was finished, he closed up the woodstove. Sorry, he signed.

He stood beside her and she felt the crackle of energy again. Feeling sad, she leaned against him. She had done the right thing in telling him. She didn't mind his arm around her.

I go now, he signed. Fish tomorrow early. He looked straight at her, his eyes blazing at her in a way she had never seen before. His mouth was tense as though he was struggling with something. On his chest his fingers thumped out A-N-N-A. I watch for you. He placed the hook on the table. You need me, I find.

"*Takk*. I couldn't do it alone anymore." She kissed him lightly on his cheek. "I'll never be able to repay you, but I hope to God we'll always be friends. Let me help you with your coat."

Hansen protested, but she was quicker. In her haste to get the jacket off the back of the chair, it snagged and one side of it jerked forward when she tugged on it. To their mutual astonishment, the contents of his coat pocket spilled onto the floor: a set of keys, a pair of nail clippers and a Colt .38 that spun across the wood surface. When it slammed up against the bookcase, there was a deafening silence as they both stared at it.

Anna put her hands on her chest. "Who are you?" Anna shrank back as an image flashed before her eyes.

The lion in the springhouse last summer. Lean and tough. Not the gentleman she had become accustomed to. Not her helpful friend. Someone different.

A sense of real danger seized her. He wasn't who he said he was. She thought of Klein lying in the coffin. He had trusted and now he was dead. Jens knew about Klein. *How did he know so much?* She looked at his eyes. They flashed like the color of steel before they shut down. His jaw was set in anger. He was found out!

She moved away from the table, her hands groping behind her as she backed toward the kitchen stove and cupboards. Stop! When he signed, his fingers were firm and angry.

"I want to know who you are."

Friend. He made a puffing sound as he signed it, but there was urgency in his fingers.

"*Nei*." Anna's voice went hoarse. She felt her way to the knife drawer as he advanced.

Who… you… think me? His hands were sharp, his fingers slicing the air.

"I don't know. You're pretending. I trusted you." She found the round drawer pull. He advanced cautiously, but kept his distance. "Are you really deaf?"

A-N-N-A. He watched with alert eyes, but came no further.

Every motive she could think of ran through her mind. Were people seeking justice for Lillehavn? Why of all people did he become her friend? He had befriended Lisel first.

Hansen sighed, stepping closer. He wrote furiously in the notebook. When he finished, he ripped the page off and held it out to her. Friend. Trust me.

Anna snatched the paper and crumpled it. "You lied to me. You have a gun. Are you doing illegal work?" She threw the wad at him. She opened the drawer just enough to reach in for a knife. When he took a step, she whipped a boning knife around in front of her.

Respectfully, he raised his hands for peace. You cut me?

"I don't want to," Anna fought to keep her voice steady and fear out of it.

Good. I happy. Give to me. Hansen jabbed the paper with his pencil as he wrote, then showed it to her. I never hurt you or Lisel, the hurried words said. Hansen signed: secret.

"Secret?"

Ja, he nodded. Same you. He kept his distance and wrote in the notebook. Ripping out the sheet he held out it to her. I'm from Molde, it said. I came last winter to help my friend, Kjell. I watch for things for him and our friends. No one knows. People think I'm stupid.

Anna didn't ask what those things might be. She lost focus. Without warning, his hand was on the knife handle. She briefly resisted, but he was too strong. She let him take it. Feeling defeated, she backed into the corner by the window. He didn't approach her any further.

Eventually he backed off, setting the knife back in the drawer. She watched numbly as he picked the gun up off the floor and checked the clip. He put his jumbled coat on, his back to her.

"Jens." He didn't answer so she said his name louder. No answer. She took a heavy ladle from the stove and tapped the side of one of the pots. It made a sharp metallic sound. But he didn't turn. So, he *was* deaf. She began to feel lightheaded. His movements became dream-like. She was aware of tears rolling down her face, of him coming to her, but she couldn't move.

Beauty, he signed. Was that his name sign for her? No weep.

She felt the crackle of energy as he gently brushed a tear away. She leaned into his hand crying, all her fears about Klein and the Gestapo overwhelming her, all her doubts about him completely open. He signed A-N-N-A, then brushed his lips against her mouth. He kissed her, slow and gentle. No fear. I get help. He pulled her into his arms. You be fine.

She was, but not until she had cried hard. She cried for herself and for Einar. When she was done she felt drained. He held her close but he must have sensed her emotional exhaustion. He picked her up and carried her to the couch. He laid her down, covering her with an afghan from the rocking chair.

He sat down in the chair. The last thing she saw was Hansen sitting there. It was only later when she awoke and found him gone that she remembered something.

He had kissed her.

CHAPTER 64

On September 28th Haugland met the *Hitra* at Lyingvaer, a scattering of small islands to the west of Frøya. He passed on materials he had received, acquiring in turn an agent to send along the line to Trondheim and instructions on a possible run in mid-October.

"*God kveld*, Ryper." The *Hitra*'s commander, Ingvald Eidsheim, greeted him as Haugland climbed up. "How's fishing?"

"Ridiculous. Too many controls. What's the news on the Front?"

"On the good news side, the Allies launched attacks in the Scheldt estuary in Belgium. Antwerp is liberated," Eisheim said as they talked in the wheelhouse. "Then they attacked Aachen too, but at what cost! Thousands of American, British, and Canadian soldiers. The bad news—they're bogged down."

"What happened to our old friend, Buland?"

"Quite the talker. Gave us some useful information. How's the fellow who got knifed?"

"Back in action, but he's likely not to forget Buland."

"I'm sure. Well, good luck to you all. How about some coffee and biscuits?"

"*Takk*," Kjell said, poking his head in.

***

October began with sun, turning to rain that drove across the fjord in icy sheets and churned its waters into black. For several days, the boats couldn't go out, so they sat forlorn and idle in the little harbor, bobbing up and down at their moorings.

There was frost on the ground that touched the dying grasses and nipped the summer flowers in the fields, going deep and erratic. It clawed the potatoes still left in the ground and rotted them. As the month unfolded with high hopes and equally deflated despair, Haugland thought the world as surly and confused as the weather. He stayed land-bound at the warehouse, watching for a change.

One day Haugland received a notice Trondheim was dispatching an agent to him. "Meet him on out on the valley road," his decoded message said.

Grabbing his bike, Haugland rode four miles out to a wooded spot close to the river. He pulled into the trees and waited. Not long after, an old black Opel came along. When it slowed down, Haugland came out just enough to be spotted. The driver pulled over.

"How's fishing?" It was Harry, his contact in Trondheim.

"The sea trout is late but you'll find something."

Harry parked the car close to the trees and got out with a pole in hand. "Good to see you, Frode," The XU agent cheerily pumped Haugland's hand. "Trondheim's been dull since you left. Sabotage's down, not much action. Not even an Allied bomb drop."

"How's my sweetheart?" Haugland had continued their flirtation after they left Harry.

"She's dumped you. She got married last week. Nice little ceremony outside of Trondheim. I'd say a good number of the illegal community showed up to wish them well."

"Tell her I'm heartbroken. Think she'll stay home?"

"Not this one. She can lead her own group."

They went down to the river lined by trees. The gusty, chilly breeze rustled the leaves. On the riverbank, Harry gave Haugland a letter, then took out a pipe and smoked. Haugland got out his codebook and deciphered the first sheet.

"Bad news. Torstein is dead at Victoria Terrasse," Lars wrote.

Haugland kept his back to Harry, not wanting him to see the shock on his face. *Torstein. Dead.*

"I'm greatly concerned for you, brother," the note went on. "A witness has been located at Grini who spoke to him before he died. Torstein wanted him to warn someone named 'Ryper' about a connection to von Weber. That was all the witness could convey. Martin Koeller—the officer leading the train sabotage investigation—has been investigating von Weber's connections in Norway. What worries me is that he's made some connection between von Weber and Torstein following Anna Fromme in Trondheim and you, the schoolteacher."

Haugland closed his eyes. He felt tired. The long years of secret work weighed on him.

"Trouble?"

"Unfortunately, yes."

"Any reply?" Harry asked.

"*Ja, takk.*" Haugland took a sheet of thin rice paper from a small envelope in his inside coat pocket and quickly composed a response, then encoded it. When he was done, he took the sheet Lars had sent him and put it into his mouth. He chewed quickly and swallowed.

"U-boat and troop carriers are moving out of Trondheim," Harry said as he pocketed Haugland's note, "Transports too. Some say for Tromsø. The details are murky, but headquarters thinks the Russians launched an attack up north near Finland. Milorg thought the Germans would hold with 220,000 of their troops still controlling Petsamo and its nickel mines, but they've retreated."

"When did this start?" Haugland asked.

"Beginning of October. A contact in the *Wehrmacht* headquarters in Trondheim shows an interest in finding extra accommodations for an expected influx of soldiers and train schedules from up north to Trondheim. There's a rumor that Hitler has given an order to raze the province."

"Christ," Haugland said. "How about here?"

Harry took a long drag on his pipe. "Well, it's not all bad. The *Hjemmefronten* has formalized its governing plans between capitulation and the arrival of the elected government. Better yet, three permanent military bases have been set up for training in country."

"And air drops? We need those supplies."

"They're increasing. In addition more trained specialists are coming to the various Milorg districts, some of which you know have only been on paper."

"Well, that is good news," Haugland said. He pulled his jacket closed. There was more to the chill in the air than from the autumn wind.

"So, when are you coming back to Trondheim, Frode?" Harry asked.

"Don't know. I'm waiting on orders."

Harry shook his head. "I know what you mean. Despite the good news, I still wonder if we'll still be doing this at Christmas. Honest to God, I don't know if we can hold out too much longer. There were raids down in Stavanger and Vestfold just the other day. Good chunk of the leadership in Sivorg taken. The Gestapo's after Milorg, but they want civilian planners too."

After Harry left, Haugland rode back to Kjell's house, cutting through the schoolhouse yard. There, he encountered a lively game of soccer among some boys. Stopping by the stone fence, he watched quietly for a moment until the ball rolled against his foot. He started to kick it back, but when a boy came running in to get it, he went around him and began to dribble it across the schoolyard with the clever footwork of a champion. Shouting their excitement, the boys tried to trick him, but he evaded them to the other side.

"Jens, Jens!" the boys laughed and yelled as they tried to retrieve their ball.

He twisted and turned and eventually kicked it into their makeshift goal.

Only then did he realize his mistake. Sorting had been watching.

CHAPTER 65

"Are you sure?" Koeller glared at his aide. "Klein has disappeared?"

"*Jawohl, Strumbannführer.* As you ordered, we've checked at Åndalsnes and other coastal towns as well as around the Swedish border. There was rumor he was deserting."

"Impossible. He can't be gone."

Koeller jabbed his pen into the leather-edged blotter on his desk, then stomped over to the remaining window in the room. The other window was still not repaired after two and half weeks. A large board covered it, keeping the room in somber light all the time. Lack of glass in country, he was told. Outside Victoria Terrasse it was raining. The Oslo sky was cold and gray. He watched the rain splash on the glass and slide down the sill. Far below, figures dashed with umbrellas and newspapers on their heads.

Gebhardt cringed. "Sorry, sir. Under the circumstances, I've done my best."

Circumstances. The suicide of the criminal Torstein Kaaland had completely thrown him off. He had died before giving him any information he didn't already know about the cabin at Kvam and the schoolteacher. *Feldweber* Horst Klein was the only other connection, but that had gone to ground too. He slapped his hands behind his back and frowned.

"May I make a suggestion, sir?"

Koeller turned around. Sometimes he felt a certain delight in making the young man sweat —stains showed on his uniform under his arms—but he was a useful sort. In the last few months, he was one of his few friends. "Go on."

"I was thinking we should stop looking for him in *gymnasiums*. We should look for him at the University."

"Why? We've no real proof that he was a teacher. It could easily have been a cover."

"What if he was at the university?"

Koeller came back to his desk and opened a decanter. "Then he wouldn't be here. He'd been sent over to Germany with the rest of the rioters last November."

"Perhaps he's only associated with it. A student posing. There should be records somewhere. In particular, photographs—student passes, clubs, faculty gatherings, sports teams."

Koeller poured whiskey into a glass. He nodded at Gebhardt. "All right. I'll let you run with that." He raised his glass to the young man and downed his drink in one motion. "In meantime, you may take the rest of the afternoon off for a job well-done."

"*Danke.*" The young man snapped his heels and left.

As soon as he was gone, Koeller took his drink over to his file cabinet and pulled out an envelope. In it were photographs seized at von Weber's estate. He looked at the one of a woman. He knew who she was now: Anna von Schauffer. He had met her at a party eight years before in Berlin. A young womanl shy of sixteen, she was sweet and virginal. He had been drinking and seeking a WC he left the ballroom full of SS officers, Nazi politicos and their women and wandered down a deserted hall. He discovered her in a study reading a book.

Koeller felt a stirring in his groin.

He had staggered in. Being a well-trained young lady, she had been polite until he tried to kiss and grope her. She had hit him with her book and fled with her dress disheveled. Only later did he learn that she was the host's stepdaughter. So why was she in Norway? Why in the cabin with the schoolteacher and Kaaland? He had not asked Gebhardt to investigate this, but had remembered one detail. She was supposed to be dead.

CHAPTER 66

By mid-October, night came early and cold. There was frost on the grass in the mornings. Out on the water, little flakes of snow zigzaged down. Bundled up in their sweaters and oilskins, Haugland and Kjell worked the long lines for the cod beginning to run. They slept when they could.

One moonless night, they slipped away south to Smøla where they met the *Hitra* in the shelter of the many skerries around the island. It was a dangerous place for the *Otta* even in the daytime but Kjell was familiar with its waters. Once onboard the submarine chaser under a moonless sky, Haugland delivered the hard intelligence Harry had given him just days before and in return received fuel, arms, kroner, and several packages to be distributed to agents in Trondheim and Kristiansund N.

"Take a couple for yourself," he was told.

Curious, Haugland opened one and found everything from socks and underwear to soap and condoms. What could he say? He needed the socks.

They returned to Fjellstad on the evening of the eighteenth, sore and tired. Once the *Otta* was secured they retreated to their own homes. Agitated, Haugland trudged along in the dark. Despite the success of his group, instinct warned him to leave. The arrests in Trondheim had been troubling. He needed to leave, direct his line from another location. He would find a new place on the coast near Hitra with access to the *fjell.* During the dark winter months he would need access to a village for re-supply and a good spot for radio transmission. If they were still at war. It all hung on Allied success action and Germany's willingness to surrender.

What he required, though, was a motive to leave because Sheriff Fasting and other quislings would report his disappearance. He decided on economics.

Fishing was dismal. The catches were generally good, but the financial gain pitiful. He stopped at the bottom of the trail to his cabin and looked out toward the fjord.

The Germans were confiscating over ninety percent of the fish. Although the boards governing the distribution of the catch didn't want to antagonize the fishermen or disrupt the movement of the fish on the markets, the system was falling apart. There was no fuel for the boats and no fuel for trucks to deliver the catch. Fearful of labor strikes, the Germans took the catches directly. Kjell could let him go.

He put a load of wood into his stove then selected some potatoes from his shelf. On the table was a fish he had brought up from the Otta. A medium-sized cod, it was too much for him. He had no way of keeping it. There was someone else who could. He wondered about seeing her, then made a decision.

***

"All right, handsome," Anna said as Gubben meowed to go out and moved toward the hallway. "This is the last time you go out. In and out, in and out. That's all you've done today."

She followed him into the barnyard. It was late but a new moon had risen. She could easily make out the features of the barn and nearby buildings. The cat disappeared into the shadow of the old structure, slinking along its edge to the right. At the end, sat down, its tail twitching.

"Are you waiting for a girlfriend, Gubben?" Anna wrapped her sweater tighter to ward off the heavy chill. *Silly cat.* She gave him one last scolding and turned to go when he suddenly bolted back toward her. "Gubben?" She shielded her eyes from the moonlight. Out toward the chicken coop where shadows laid deep, there was a presence, a semblance of a shape.

"Who's there?" Fear rising in her, she motioned for whoever it was to come forward.

In the darkest spot between the barn and the old hen house, a tall shadow separated and came out into the moonlight. The moonlight caused an eerie aura around his head and broad shoulders. She knew instantly it was Jens, yet he might as well have been a stranger.

After her emotional confrontation with him, the trusting, easy-going friendship they had developed had been shattered. He had not come back to the farm and she had only glimpsed him once as he worked on the wharf. She had no idea of what to do now.

I came last winter to help my friend, Kjell. I watch for things for him and our friends.

Jens was doing illegal work. Incredibly, he was involved, hiding behind an innocuous personality everyone believed. She saw him quite differently. Anna put her fingers on her lips. He had kissed her. What should she do now? What would he want?

Hansen came forward, in the dim light, clutching his right side with his left hand.

"Jens," she said. "You scared me." Troll, she signed, unable to remember any other sign.

Hansen made a chuckling sound, sending a cloud of frigid breath into the light. Sorry, he motioned.

"I didn't leave the hook," Anna said. Hook, she signed.

I know. I come see you. *Jo*? The aura glowed around the motioning hands too.

Inside, the *stue* was dim, lit only by a lamp over the table and muffled by the blackout curtains. Self-consciously, she led him to the covered window and discovered that he was uneasy too. He clutched his side and stiffly waited for permission to sit. Where L-I-S-E-L?

"She's sleeping. I didn't expect to see you. I wasn't sure anymore."

Silence. Stretching into a great distance between them. Finally, he reached inside his coat and pulled out a large wrapped package and handed it to her. She laid it on the table and opened it up. Inside was a cod cleaned and waiting to be cut.

"Oh, Jens. *Tusen takk*." She signed thanks. He shrugged. He looked toward her sink and made the sign for knife. "In the drawer... but you know that," she said when he looked back.

Ja. He was grinning ear to ear now and the tension broke.

He prepared the fish according to her wishes, arranging it in an enamel pan for her icebox. When he was finished, he cleaned up the blood around the sink and after washing the knife, wiped his hands on a towel.

When he was done, he leaned against the counter. He was dressed simply in wool pants, boots and sweater, but Anna thought that no matter what he wore, it would never again hide his strength and vitality. Her vision of him as being lean and tough would never go away. Glancing at his handsome face, she was acutely aware of him for the first time as a man she was attracted to. Uncomfortable, she lowered her eyes. She was Einar's widow. It was too soon to feel this way.

He took out his notebook. You burn pictures?

"*Ja*, I burned them all. Did you hear anything more about the dead man?" Anna asked.

Nei, he shook his head. He smiled faintly at her. His dark hair fell over his brow.

"I'm glad you've come, Jens. I've missed you."

He straightened up. Me too. I come you like. He made an aspirant sound with each sign.

"I would like that."

***

So Haugland came, usually after Lisel was asleep. He knew now he was truly in love with her. He wasn't sure whether he had any right to such feelings.

It went against his principles as an agent for his country and for England, but he couldn't help himself anymore. As yet, there was nothing physical, just a deepening friendship he realized she needed as much as he did. He nurtured it because it would become only more convoluted if he acted on his own feelings.

Once on a moonlit November night when a soft, warm *foehn* wind was blowing down the side of the mountains, he persuaded her to go for a walk up to the *seter*. They slipped up the logging road, heading up through the dark trees where the waning moonlight came through. It lay shiny patches on the forest floor, like rungs on a ladder. As they passed they sometimes stepped from light to light. The forest was still. The leaves had long dropped from the birches and maples, but the pines were dense, draping the sides of the path like gigantic curtains. When they reached the *seter*, he set out flat bread, a small sausage and cheese on the steps. The old milk cans were still there leaning into each other. The lantern blossomed with a match.

"Jens. Like our summer picnic."

They stayed for a short time, then headed down. "*Takk*," she said at her door.

He took her hand and held it. The urge to hold and kiss her was so strong, but he dared not act on it. She withdrew her hand. This is enough, he thought.

He knew she must never know his identity, but he had no idea how long or how far he could go with meeting her without giving away his feelings. So, as he prepared to withdraw from the village and put duty above need, he fell deeper in love.

CHAPTER 67

"Damn," Lars murmured. "What I got you into, Tore." He rapped his razor on the side of the porcelain sink, knocking shaving soap foam into it. His stomach felt sour. It made him sick thinking of his brother.

Just nine days ago, the Gestapo had struck. Infiltrating an export group running a route to Sweden, Rinnan's agents uncovered the head of Sivorg in Trondheim. He was arrested along with his contacts with the export group. The Sor-Trøndelag region was now paralyzed both in the interior and on the coast. It was only a matter of time before Rinnan found Tore.

Nine days. The poor wretch still hadn't spoken despite beatings and torture, but he couldn't hold out much longer. When he did break, the damage would be considerable. Lars prayed Tore could get out of Fjellstad soon because Rinnan's organization was insidious.

"You need something?" Sieverson stood in the hallway with a rolled newspaper under his arm.

"*Nei*. Thought I nicked myself."

"No pink on your chin."

Lars laughed and wiped his face with a towel.

Things were hard after Torstein died. Sieverson, his new aide and bodyguard, had kept him focused and safe. What really saved him, though, was a major reorganization of the *Hjemmefronten* leadership. Both Sivorg and Milorg had come together last spring, but it wasn't until recently the Home Front Command was formally reorganized with twelve representatives from the old Circle and KK in Sivorg, Milorg, and representatives from groups such as the police. It would govern until the government in exile returned.

A chairman was selected and a steering committee of four created. J.C. Hauge, Lars's superior and inspector general for Milorg since 1942, was one of them. Lars was involved because Hauge had invited him to work with him. They promoted a close working relationship between the civilian and military branches of the resistance.

Lars picked up a sweater hanging over the claw-foot tub. Many in the exiled government in London and the resistance leadership believed the war would be over in the matter of weeks and they had to be prepared. The Milorg districts in southern Norway were part of this preparation, but while the east was quite active, some areas were non-existent, giving new meaning to the term "waiting organization."

But we got "*Våg,*" our first military base to be established in the mountains. Now if only we knew what was going on in northern Norway. The Russians had advanced into northern Norway pushing back the retreating Germans. For the first time in nearly four and a half years a part of Norway was free. Rumors were troubling, however, about the Germans blowing up fishing villages, killing animals, and throwing people out in sub freezing weather.

On a table near the sofa, the phone rang. Lars and Sieverson both stared at it. It rang three times, then stopped. Lars waited and in a few moments it rang again.

Sieverson picked up the receiver and said, "*Tante* Torsk. *Ja*, we would like some." Lars watched him listen to the voice on the other line, his mouth going from a wry smile at the code word game they always had to play to a down-turned frown. "*Takk*," Sieverson said into the phone then hung up.

"So?" Lars asked.

"That was headquarters. Bad news from Trondheim. The Sivorg leader killed himself."

Lars took the loss almost personally. Hadn't Einar died the same horrific way?

CHAPTER 68

Sorting heard the same news about the Sivorg leader committing suicide, but knew the real truth. The man was alive, a ruse meant to encourage illegal workers to come out of hiding prematurely. Rinnan had done it before with wicked results. This man was a big fish and would be kept alive. His meeting with Birger Strom just a short while ago confirmed it.

Sorting stood at his window and looked back toward Fjellstad. The days were running short now, the dark descending close to four thirty in the afternoon, but the weather had improved, producing cool but piercing bright days. Sorting sometimes borrowed a bike from Bugge and stopped to visit the widow *Fru* Holve at her *pensionat*. He continued the friendship long after he had left her place and was glad because she continued to be a source of information.

He shouldn't have gone away. Village opinion of him had changed. While not quite unfriendly, it was more reserved. He still occasionally fished with Bugge, still talked with the fishermen as they repaired their equipment. When patriotic talk came up, people became silent.

"They're afraid," Bugge said. "Vikna's too strong in their minds. Men and boys were tortured, some murdered. People just want to keep their heads low. It's best not to say anything."

Sorting wondered if it was all right to say anything in private either.

So it was with great interest when on his weekly visit to see *Fru* Holve at her *pensionat* she mentioned Arne, Karl and Petter and how they had to hide in the mountains.

"Good thing someone was able to get food to them. To set them up."

"Oh?" Sorting said. "Someone contacted them?"

"Now I don't know for sure, mind you, but it was a young man from the village. Would you like more tea, *Herr* Sorting?"

"*Ja*, sure," he said. "It must have been difficult."

"I'm sure it was, but not as difficult as getting Arne, Karl and Petter away from the patrol."

Sorting was alert now, his spoon poised over his cup.

"Red Cross sent another letter to Ingrid Stagg from her son in Sweden," *Fru* Holve said. "Petter's logging in the north." She leaned across her cloth-draped table and smiled conspiratorially at him. "But then you should know. I've heard you helped too."

"I don't know what you mean. I was in the village during the search like everyone."

The widow pushed a sweet toward him. "Oh, I think that you are one. You're too modest. I think you helped the boys in the first place."

Sorting stepped away from the window. The widow had it wrong. No one could leave the village the night the patrol was out—but Jens Hansen?

Hansen had been gone at the beginning of the troubles. What if he was gone for a reason? What if he was the one who took the food to the boys? What if Hansen was the "young man"? He certainly was physically fit. Sorting had seen him work the boats countless times. That day in the schoolyard. Hansen had moved with surprising speed among the school boys, his feet carrying the leather ball forward with sophisticated maneuvers. Could some deaf-mute from Molde do that? People were used to Hansen being unobtrusive. He could move around in plain sight and not be suspect. He would the perfect courier.

Sorting put his mug down. All this speculation was getting him nowhere. The Chief wanted results. Sorting had nothing to show except his suspicions—yet, Vikna wasn't destroyed by suspicions. It was disemboweled by negative agents and Rinnan's own people posing as agents of the patriot Olav Whist. Fjellstad was no different. He would let Rika Arneson do her damage.

A man arrested recently in Trondheim named A.C. Kjelstrup during his interrogation. A large delivery of arms had been made last August in Trondheim. The boat may have come from Frøya. Kjelstrup was from Frøya and he knew Kjell Arneson. The missing boys. Hansen and Arneson and boats in the night. You didn't catch herring with a salmon net.

CHAPTER 69

A.C. Kjelstrup came into the great space of Nidaros and found a seat halfway up the center of the cathedral. Easing down onto a wood chair, he picked up a hymnal on the seat beside him, trying to look inconspicuous. The Sivorg leader arrested two weeks ago had committed suicide. It didn't threaten him, but the arrest of a friend in export did. As a result, both men *were* connected to him and he was becoming uneasy.

Up to now, things had gone well. After the arms had been dispersed, he had resumed his weekly "excursion" into Trondheim, delivering peat and picking up goods to take back to the islands. The regular inspector was back at the control boat to the fjord and he went through with no problem. His layovers varied, but he stayed if he could. Then he would be free to visit a cafe or *bakeri* with Rika. They were in love, but now with the stormy autumn weather, the early descent of dark and, curfews it was hard to meet.

A.C. leaned back in the creaky folding chair and looked up at the vaulted stone ceiling high above him. He sat back self-consciously when an elderly woman in a worn, black coat passed by him on the other side of the pillar. She found a seat in the field of chairs some rows ahead of him, making a hollow scraping sound as she sat down. He rubbed his hands together. It was chilly in the space, enough to make his fingers ache, a reflection of stormy November days since the first of the month. Above him the light fell rapidly outside the ancient windows. He wished Rika Arneson would come. He had been waiting for this for some time.

Feet scraped next to him by the heavy pillar. Brown leather heels with straps and white anklet socks. Guardedly, his eyes followed the legs up to a plaid skirt and dark blue coat and eventually, Rika's beautiful face. "What did Freyda say?"

"She says we can have her apartment." She sat down shyly next to him. "For the night."

A.C. ignored where he was and kissed her tenderly. Her lips felt soft and yielding. Her skin smelled of lavender water.

"I love you." he said, his heart pounding. What would Kjell think of this?

***

They dined at a little restaurant popular with German soldiers and their women. He found a place in a less noisy corner where they enjoyed a modest, overpriced meal. Too much in love to care, they rode partway to the apartment by trolley, walking the last few blocks in the cloudy dark night holding hands.

They walked close together, sometimes stopping to whisper and exchange heated embraces against some wall until they had to flee at the clattering of hobnailed boots on the icy streets. They climbed the stairs to the flat slowly and stealthily, not wishing to call attention to themselves and arrived in the apartment to find flowers and a bottle of wine on the table.

"Freyda." Rika picked up a note.

"Anything of interest?" he asked, putting his arms around her.

"Just girl talk." She reached out for the bottle and stroked its long neck, then reached up behind her and touched his curly head.

He kissed her on her neck, tension starting to grow in his groin. "Are you sure you want to do this?"

"I'm sure." She stroked his cheek. "It's what I want. I'm not afraid. I love you."

He kissed her hand, hoping she didn't see how nervous he was. Why was he nervous? It wasn't lust that drove him. If she asked, he would wait. He wanted her first time to be perfect. "I love you too."

He poured the wine. They skoaled each other as they sat shoeless on the sofa, making jokes about their dinner. Eventually, Rika put down her glass and curled her legs up. A.C. put his arm around her and drew her close. Rika's shoulders tightened, then relaxed when he whispered, "Rika." He kissed her as he slowly began to unbutton her sweater. "I promise to be gentle."

CHAPTER 70

Four days later, Kjell and Haugland met Kjelstrup at a weathered fishing hut owned by A.C.'s family. It was a blustery, gray day. They huddled around the peat stove. While Haugland tended the fire, Kjell talked to A.C. about the extent of the arrests in Trondheim and surrounding areas. "I want to shore up security," Kjell said.

They talked behind Haugland's back about life in general. "Security isn't the only thing I'm worried about, A.C. The fishing's just not good enough. I'm going to have to let Jens go."

A.C. was shocked. "Poor dumb bastard. How will he make out?"

Haugland's cheeks burned, the humiliation digging deep into him. He moved closer to the fire.

Kjell sighed. "I think he'll be all right. I hope. The Deaf Church in Oslo's going to place him. After the war he can come back. I'd take him any day."

***

Kjell and Haugland took off for the Haraldsens' an hour later. Kjell sat in the captain's seat in the *Otta's* wheelhouse.

Haugland was quiet, musing over Kjelstrup's words. "*Poor dumb bastard.*" He remembered his humiliation. He supposed he shouldn't fault Kjelstrup's ignorance, but it did make him angry.

Is this what his *Onkel* Kris felt? When would people learn and understand?

Haugland looked outside, seeking something to focus on there. The fishing boat rolled along under sail and engine power so he had to brace himself often.

"You all right, Jens? You're quiet."

"I'm all right. Long day."

"I thought it might be A.C.'s words. He didn't mean anything."

"*Nei*, most people don't."

They arrived at Sig's island not long after a waning moon had risen. They were greeted on the icy dock by Holger and his son Ulstein and unloaded by lantern light. The buildings beyond loomed like black boxes.

"*God kveld*," the poet said heartily. "It's good to see you."

"Where's everybody?" Kjell wondered.

"In the store. They're all anxious to see you."

Inside, the entire Haraldsen family— sons, daughters, and grandchildren— crowded around the table in the corner, including Arne Finn, Sig's deaf nephew. They clapped when Kjell and Haugland came in. Haugland was pleased to see Sverre looking well. The color was back in his face.

"Well" *Fru* Haraldsen beamed. "We are so happy to see you both. *Vær så snill.* Come in and sit while I get coffee and anything else I can find." She got up and winked at everyone. "You sit here, Jens." When he hesitated, she told him not to be silly. She put a hand on his shoulder. "Sit, Jens. I'll be right back."

While they waited, the men caught up on news in general. With the women there, they wouldn't talk business. Suddenly, they hushed when *Fru* Haraldsen returned. Haugland had his back to her, but when Holger's son Ulstein reached up to turn down the lantern, he wondered what the hell was going on. There was a rustling behind him, a glow of light and a multi-layered cake covered with cream and preserved peaches and bristling with candles was placed in front of him.

"*Han skål leve*, Jens!" Sig grinned. With Arne signing, everyone started singing,

"*Han skål leve, han skål leve, han skål leve, han skål leve aldri dø.*"

Puzzled, Haugland turned to Kjell. You know this? he signed.

"*Nei*, but enjoy," Kjell chuckled. "It's apparently your birthday."

It is, Haugland thought, *according to my forged pass. How did they know?*

Suddenly the whole table began to shake as the men pounded it with the flats of their hands to "å dica, dica, dic re la la, hurrah, hurrah, hurrah for ho, hurrah, hurrah."

Astrid Haraldsen and Andrina Paal were laughing helplessly, leaning into each other as they stood beside the table. The Haraldsen men seemed to enjoy the surprise on Haugland too, pounding the table like schoolboys and making the cake platter bounce so hard *Fru* Haraldsen grabbed it firmly by its sides. Still laughing and chattering, the family finally quieted down, patting Haugland on his shoulders and wishing him well.

Tusen takk, he signed, touched by their affection for him. How get cream and sugar?

"Our cow and a good friend on Hitra," Sig answered over the din of conversation. He smiled warmly at him. "*Hans skål leve*, Jens! Blow out your candles. Make a wish!"

I wish you will be safe.

At ten, the womenfolk went upstairs. *Fru* Haraldsen left behind a fresh pot of coffee. The men brought out pipes and cigarettes. The talk turned serious as they discussed their future together. Haugland had information to share with them.

"First, the Russians have entered Nordmarka. Kirkenes has been liberated."

"Wonderful," Sig said.

"*Ja*, it is, but there have also been reports of devastation by the retreating German army."

Haugland shifted on his wood chair. "There have been arrests. Sivorg has been hit heavily. Rinnan has found ways into some other areas of the resistance." He reminded them of the boat from Frøya that left for the Shetlands last spring and how Rinnan had arranged it. "A.C. Kjelstrup's brother was on it. That incident has ingratiated people on Frøya to his agents. With Vikna out of the way, Rinnan may be concentrating there."

"People would have noticed strangers," Magnus said. "I trade on Frøya all the time. I've heard of nothing unusual."

"These are good people you've might have known for years, who have strong *jøssing* feelings. They believe they are doing good, may even have been sanctioned by legitimate groups, but working unwittingly for Rinnan nonetheless. Their very faith in what they are doing makes them dangerous. That's what led to the arrests of Sivorg members in Trondheim. We must take care."

He opened up his rucksack and took out an envelope. They had already seen his sketch of Sorting, but this time he had something new. "It's taken months, but this is Rinnan."

It was a haunting photograph. Coatless and wearing a dark shirt, Rinnan was looking into the camera, but it seemed that he looked directly into the viewer's heart. Set deep under a heavy brow and high forehead, his eyes stared out with a hypnotizing intensity. His irises were light— but they seemed dark and unsettling. A sensitive mouth made him almost handsome.

"He looks like the *Draugen*," Ulstein said under his breath.

"Then beware," Holger said passing the picture on. "Pray God, he never looks at us."

"I want to thank you for all your help getting the new line set up," Haugland said quietly as they passed the photo around. "My place just south of here is secured. I'm leaving soon."

The men took this additional information soberly. Sig said it was for the best.

"We still will support you, Jens" Holger said.

"*Takk*. The Shetland Bus will continue to deliver to the area, but there is additional work that I'll be handling. I'd like your input on it."

They talked for another hour. By the time they were ready to go, Haugland was satisfied the group was strong and tight. It would hold.

Haugland and Kjell spent the night and stayed for most of the unhurried day that followed, then loaded the *Otta* for Hitra where they would check in with the radioman. As they prepared to leave, the family gathered one last time in the store to say good-bye. Last minute conversations were wrapped up. Andrina Paal stood with Kjell, her arm slipped through his. They had talked most of the morning and it seemed to have done her some good. Her strawberry blonde hair was combed back and she was dressed in a flattering patterned dress.

Eventually, Haugland and Kjell gathered up their gear and headed outside to the docks with members of the family trailing beside them in brisk afternoon air. A few minutes later, the *Otta* was underway.

While Kjell maneuvered the boat out into the channel, Haugland stood at the stern and watched the group recede. There was a friendly wail from Kjell's siren and then they were off.

Standing on the dock, Sig and his family members waved good-bye. As they receded, the sun covered them, the small bare island and its buildings with glittering gold pollen, blocking out their forms.

Good-bye, thought Haugland. And it was.

In a few weeks, most of them would be dead.

CHAPTER 71

There were only a few lights on in the vestibule of the University of Oslo library. From where *Sturmbannführer* Martin Koeller stood, the large mural in front of him looked unearthly in the gloom. Painted some eleven years ago, he was told, it was a modernistic vision of the *Yggdrasill*, the giant ash tree from Scandinavian mythology. All things rested on it, as its branches spread all over the world and reached to the sky. He was no scholar, but he knew quite a bit about the old tales and could hold sway at many of the drawing room gatherings of SS personnel where such supernatural discussions often took place. For an antichurch organization, the SS had acquired near mystical teachings that bordered on the religious. The SS wove the ancient themes of Odin and Thor into the pseudo runes on their uniforms and their politics of race. It amused him sometimes.

"Have you been waiting long, sir?" *Oberscharfürer* Franz Gebhardt came out of the dark and stood next to him.

"*Nein*. Where are you taking me?" Koeller tugged on his wool greatcoat.

"To the personnel office across the square. They're opening it up for us. I found some pictures you might want to see. It's been almost a year since the student riots here."

"Very well."

Across the snow-covered square a gray-haired man dressed in a well-worn shirt and sweater met them at the door to his office. His gold spectacles glimmered in the soft lamplight.

"This is Professor Karlsson," Gebhardt said. "He's seen the sketch of the schoolteacher."

Koeller nodded at him. "You found something?"

"Just some possibilities. *Bitte*, be seated," Karlsson said in excellent German. A series of photographs lay on his desk.

Koeller went through the photographs quickly. "He's not here. Do you have others?"

"These were the men on the staff from 1936 to 1941 that matched your sketch."

"Perhaps his hair was dyed."

Karlsson went to some large volumes on a bookcase. The results were the same.

"What about teaching assistants and other supporting personnel?" Gebhardt asked.

"What I have are here in the annuals."

"What are these?" Koeller pointed to a box of framed pictures on the floor.

"Old sports photographs, past teams and the like. Many of these athletes refused to participate so they were removed from the hallway displays. Frankly, I don't know what to do with them. Occasionally, Gestapo headquarters will ask for them. Maybe I should send the whole group over. I understand similar photographs fingered some agitators a couple of months ago."

Koeller picked up one of the framed photographs. It looked like countless other pictures of sport teams no one would remember five years from now unless one was fanatic: the stiff pose of muscular youth, the camaraderie of the golden moment. He found nothing. Picking up several others, he was about to put them back when something caught his eye in one of the photos.

"What team is this? Soccer?"

Karlsson came over and looked. "*Ja*. That's a special university squad that went abroad before the war. Says 1938 in the corner."

Koeller stared at the face. There was something about the young man who stood second in from the left in the front row. His arms were crossed behind his back and his head was uncovered. Dark hair and light eyes. There were only thirteen young men in the picture so it was a close-up shot of the group. Behind his wire-rimmed glasses, the schoolteacher had light eyes.

"Do you know anyone on this team?"

"Well, I don't normally pay attention, but they were outstanding. Later they got a bad reputation for refusing to join the reorganized sports groups." Karlsson craned his neck and recited a few names.

"Who's that?" Koeller interrupted, pointing to his source of interest.

Karlsson adjusted his glasses and stared. "My, I'd forgotten. The professor's son."

"Who?"

"Jens Nils Haugland. Professor of geology and department head since the 1920s until his death in the fall of 1940. He created quite a controversy when he demanded the order to fill university departments with NS folk be rescinded. He was very vocal and eventually arrested."

Koeller looked thoughtfully at the picture. It fit. Professor's son. He grew excited. "And him? The soccer player?"

"Let's see. Haugland. Tore Kristian Haugland."

"I think he's our schoolteacher. What do you know about him?" he asked Karlsson.

"I believe his studies were in languages and literature. What is he wanted for?"

"Sabotage."

"Well, there should be records on the professor at Gestapo headquarters or police headquarters. Perhaps the son."

Or not, Koeller thought. For the first time, he felt the schoolteacher was an agent.If he was an agent, someone might tamper with records to protect him. Still it was worth a look. The schoolteacher was no longer a myth but a living entity. He had a family and a past. If nothing else, good detective work and interviews would flesh him out.

He looked at Gebhardt whose face was frozen somewhere between apprehension and hope. "Well done, Franz. Go to Møllergata 19 now. Let me know what you find."

***

"Say the name again."

"Ryper." The man groaned through his tortured lips, the name barely a whisper.

"He said 'Ryper,' Chief," Birger Strom answered.

Rinnan came out of the shadows along the wall of the Cloister and looked at the man now slumped and barely holding his position on the stool. His back and backside had been flogged so hard that he could only sit for a short time before shifting from one buttock to the other. He stank of blood, sweat and acrid urine. Rinnan pushed his head. "He brought arms?"

"It's… only… a… name… I heard." Spittle bobbled at the edge of his dry lips. "I don't know anything else."

Rinnan signaled and a *totenschlager* descended on the man's back. The man screamed and twisted as it caught his flesh, then dragged down. The man moaned, then began to sway and croak incoherently. "*Vær så snill.* I never met him."

"Who is he?" Rinnan waved Karl Dolmen over. Strom picked up a smoking soldering iron. The luckless man began to weep.

"He is the leader of them all. From the Shetlands."

"Give the man some water," Rinnan said. "And Birger, you go south down the coast."

***

Haugland climbed the trail toward his cabin and once shielded among the trees turned on his flashlight. Behind him an old moon retreated behind a night cloud. The walls of the fjord loomed. Back from Sig's only a few hours, he felt like he had been gone from Fjellstad for weeks. Kjell said he felt likewise.

"It's those arrests in Trondheim," Kjell said. "I can feel it in the air."

"That's why I'm leaving," Haugland answered.

Haugland followed the beam of light around to the back of his cabin, just to check. The woodshed seemed fine, the chopping block untouched. He splashed the light around the rough building and on the ground and started to the front on the other side of the cabin. Halfway down he discovered a disturbance in the pine needles in the path.

Squatting down, he splayed the light closer and discovered an unfamiliar tread. From the way pine needles lay over it, it had been made recently. Cautiously, he moved to the window. When he went on trips, he always left the blackout curtain up so anyone coming by would see the innocence of the place. But that wasn't his only security. He shined the light through to the corner by the front door. To his dismay, the fishing pole was out of place. *Visitor.*

As he stepped into the cabin, the fishing pole fell down. He grabbed it and put in the corner. He lit the lantern on his table and checked its level of fuel. A slight drop. Whoever the intruder was, he had the audacity to light it. Haugland raised the light and searched the room. His visitor had made a clean sweep of the rugged cabin, but had not been able to avoid some traps Haugland had set up for such searches. A sewing thread across the back door frame and the door. Broken. Fish lures on his bookshelf in a certain order. No longer. Yet the intruder must have taken his time.

He was sure it was Sorting. He must not think the least of the man, but credit him with intelligence and cunning. Because he was Rinnan's man, he would be ruthless. All the more reason to leave.

He sighed, looked around the room. Sorting must have discovered something.

Twenty minutes later, he was at Kjell's back door.

"Jens." Kjell wore a flannel robe over pajamas. His hair was tousled. "What's wrong?"

Haugland stepped into the kitchen. You alone? he signed.

Kjell waved him over to the table. "*Ja.* I'm quite alone."

"Good." Haugland unbuttoned his coat. "I've had company while we were gone. I wonder if you did too. Anything out of place?"

"Not that I know of. Who?"

"Sorting. I'm sure of it. We should look around."

"All right, but at this hour I can barely keep my eyes open."

They searched the house, but found nothing. Haugland still wasn't satisfied. "He's been here. I know it."

"What do you think he was looking for at the cabin?"

"I'm not sure. I think he still believes who I say I am, but something has shifted. At least the W/T was undisturbed." Haugland thought of something. "Let's check the basement again."

Downstairs, Kjell turned on the sole light hanging in the middle of the bone-chilling space. It had the scent of old leather shoes, moss and something Haugland couldn't put his finger on. Kjell had organized the space in an orderly fashion: shelves filled with old fishing equipment and paint. Old pieces of furniture neatly arranged. Over in a corner against the stone wall, an old desk stood out. Kjell showed him the desk and the maps again, then went off to look around the potato bins. Haugland crouched down and began to work his fingers along the stones down to the floor, then over to the desk. He felt blindly around its back. Behind one of the legs, he touched something soft. Carefully, he dragged it into the light. In his hand was a smashed cigarette butt. He held the butt up to Kjell.

"Rika wasn't smoking on you, was she?"

"Where the devil did that come from?"

"Sorting. Everyone smokes pipes around here, except him." He sniffed it. "Not ration tobacco. This is good quality and commercial made." He put it on the desk and picked up a chart tube. "What's in this?"

"The German battery map you gave me last summer." Kjell's face turned pale under the glaring light. He slid the maps out and looked through them carefully. "Thank God. It's still sandwiched in. I believe no one has looked at it."

"What about the others?"

"They are ordinary sea charts, something I'm allowed to have."

Haugland smoothed his hand over the desk and noticed a burned spot on the wood. "He laid it here for a moment. Bastard." He stood up. "All right. We've been warned now. I'm going back out to the cabin and get some rest. In the morning, I'll get ready to leave. Solheim sent me a letter from the national Deaf Church with an invitation to go to Oslo. All the other paperwork including my travel permit is in place. In the meantime, burn that German map. We don't need it anymore."

A coal popped in the upstairs parlor stove like a gunshot. Both men started.

"Steady," Haugland said, though his nerves were frayed.

CHAPTER 72

Max Schiller tromped into the Tourist Hotel, mindful his boots were shaking the wood floor of the lobby as he led the other officers and aides in. He put down his leather valise with a thump at the hotel desk and rang the bell under the nose of an anxious Foss.

It's good to be back, he thought. Once this little affair is over, I can really enjoy my assignment here on a more permanent basis.

"*Oberleutnant* Schiller. How good to see you again," Foss said.

Schiller gave the little Nazi a curt nod. *I'm here to have a good time*, he thought, *not to listen to a lecture on the virtues of the* Vaterland, *you prick.*

The Schiller heard enough crap from the others around him and although he could "*Heil Hitler*" like the best of them, lately he held his tongue on his shifting views. It was dangerous. He found people like Foss difficult. Having once been caught up in the euphoria of the early years of the Third Reich, even stirred by Hitler's speeches, the last two months of the war soured him and he no longer believed. Germany was lost and he saw little future for himself. He would ride out the rest of the war in the backwaters of Norway. He hoped.

"Gentlemen," Foss said. "Your rooms are ready." With a flick of his hand, he sent his staff scattering to help with baggage, some of it belonging to two women who accompanied them. There was a spasm of laughter and giggling, followed by the tramping of steel boots as the party banged its way up to the rooms.

Schiller decided to delay going to his room and went to search for something to eat.

There was no one in the dining room, although the tables were set. The lobby was equally deserted. He thought of going down to the *konditori*, when he heard a commotion in the kitchen. It was his superior officer's voice.

"You there! Did you hear me?"

Silence followed.

"Damned insolence!" Kaufman barked. "Answer the lady!"

Still no response.

"Damned Norwegian pretending he doesn't understand."

Curious, Schiller pushed his way through the swinging doors into the kitchen. To his left across the room, a tall, dark-haired young man stood looking out a curtained window. He appeared oblivious to the colonel behind him seething to the boiling point. It was only when a spoon slipped out of his hand and fell to the floor did he seem to realize there were others in the room. Rising up with the spoon he seemed surprised to see the colonel and his lady—quite drunk Schiller noted—standing across the way from him.

"What's the hell's wrong with you?" Kaufman roared in heavily-accented Norwegian. He was an older man in his early sixties with close-cropped gray hair and an ample build that tested his field-gray uniform's seams.

The Norwegian stared at him and the woman.

"Speak up." Kaufman asked.

Nei. The Norwegian tapped his ears and made a series of flat sounds in his mouth.

"The devil... He's very stupid or… I want him arrested. Have him beaten."

"Problem, sir?' Schiller interrupted as he recognized this Norwegian—Anna's hired hand. "He means no harm, whatever he's done, sir. He can't hear you. He's a deaf-mute. I believe he works here." Schiller came around them and nodding at the woman continued to address the colonel. If you want to talk to him, you have to get his attention first."

"Humpf..."

Schiller studied Hansen. Except for a brief glimpse at the hotel some time ago, Schiller hadn't seen Hansen since the night he had gone to the Arneson home and saw him lying so ill in the dim windowless room. He remembered how pale and feverish he had been. How he had struggled for breath. He didn't look poorly now. In fact he looked quite fit.

"*He has done work for me. He is very kind.*"

He remembered too the look on Anna Fromme's face when she learned that Hansen had pneumonia. As if he mattered to her. Schiller wondered how he'd get out of this.

Hansen reached carefully into his overalls and offered a notebook and pencil to Kaufman and noticing Schiller, to him.

"Why don't you go into the dining room, sir," Schiller said. "I'll take care of things here. Foss or the cook has to be around. I'll see to lunch."

The colonel glared at the Norwegian, as if he wasn't sure if he hadn't been slighted. "All right. Come Gretchen, we'll go in."

"May I stay a moment? A drink of water, *bitte*. I'll come shortly." The young woman played with the colonel's collar and made some motions to straighten it, rubbing her breasts against his chest. The colonel patted her shoulder indulgently and left. She kissed the air back. As soon as he was gone, however, she descended on Schiller and put an arm through his.

"*Na, schöner Mann.* Honestly, Maxie. You keep leaving me with him. Come see me."

Schiller removed her arm. "Not now. Be a good girl and get your drink and leave." He flushed when he remembered that Hansen was still waiting.

"I don't know how." She slurred her words. "But... perhaps this man does." Her lips curled up in a drunken smile. "My... he's quite a nice looking man…"

"He's not your type. I don't think he'll understand."

To Schiller's disbelief, she staggered toward the deaf-mute and planted herself in front of him. To balance herself she grabbed one of his arms. Hansen pulled back.

"Oh, Maxie, I think he's shy. Don't be shy."

"Gretchen!"

"I… want a glass of water." She pantomimed drinking out of a glass to Hansen. "*Takk.* Do I say *takk*?" she asked turning back to Schiller, swaying precariously.

You idiot, Schiller thought. You make us look like fools. He watched Hansen push her hand away and go to the cupboard over the kneading table. Taking down a glass he filled it with water for her. His mouth hovered on distaste.

"*Takk*," she said. She drank, then brushed her breasts against Hansen, nearly falling over.

"Stop it, Gretchen," Schiller said. He felt sick to his stomach. He waved his hand at

Hansen. "You can go."

"*Nein*," the woman whimpered. "I like him." She grabbed Hansen's arm and to Schiller's revulsion, promptly threw up on the deaf-mute's shirt.

"Gretchen! *Komm doch, mein Spatz.* You've impressed him enough!"

CHAPTER 73

At Ella's, Haugland showered, working the stench of the German woman's puke off his skin. Once he was dressed, he went downstairs with his ration card to pick up some bakery items from the *konditori* before going out. He was anxious to get away. The small group of officers at the hotel had brought a patrol of about fifteen well-armed soldiers for what purpose he didn't know. Right now they were perched on the seawall in front of the building. Standing by the window in the shop, he observed them for a moment, while keeping an eye on the weather. A storm front was coming in, bringing with it their first real taste of winter's snow. Though there was snow up on the *fjell*, up to now down here there had been only occasional flurries that didn't stay or snowfall that melted a few hours later in the day leaving clean roads and little patches on the ground. The soldiers pointed to the sullen afternoon sky and made comments about it.

Ella's helper, Bette, came over and stood by Haugland. Tapping his arm, she looked nervously toward the soldiers. "Do you have your papers, Jens?"

Ja.

"Good. If they bother you when you go to the office, I'll come out."

Takk. Haugland turned his attention outside. A stranger walked down the wharf by Kjell's warehouse. He was a fisherman by dress, wearing the clothes naturally, but his gait wasn't quite right. Curious, he touched Bette's arm and pointed to the man.

Know him? Haugland nodded at the stranger.

"Oh, *ja.* He came in just yesterday afternoon. Has some boat trouble, so Ole Sorenson is going to fix it. He's been staying on his boat. He seems nice. He had breakfast here this morning. He says he's from Namsos, but he sounds like he's more from Trondheim." Bette nodded at the man who was now alongside the resting soldiers. He was tall with an athletic build. Haugland wondered what she was thinking. She reportedly liked Sorting.

"*Frøken* Olsen." Ella appeared to restore order. "*Herr* Kolberg is waiting for his coffee."

The girl curtsied, hustling off into the *konditori.*

Ella shook her head. "That girl. Her head is in the clouds these days. I don't know what to make of it." She smiled at Haugland. "Never mind. It's a business problem."

The doorbell jingled and the stranger came in. He bowed politely to Ella, giving Haugland a quizzical look before passing up into the tearoom.

"New customer," Ella said. "I best go before Bette gets all dreamy-eyed. Really, her father should have married her off long before this."

Good idea, he signed.

Outside, Haugland paused on the doorstep while he put on his gloves. The air was moist and cold. The pale gray sky felt closed in and thick, but beyond the mouth of the fjord, it appeared strangely pink and flat. There was snow coming all right.

The wind snapped at the lines on the boats in front of him. Looking down the wharf, Haugland saw the familiar figure of Bugge walking with some of the older local fishermen. These days, he knew, Bugge saw less of Sorting. Financially, Bugge could no longer pay for an extra man and had finally given up going out into the Trondheimsleia to fish. Instead, he stayed close to his fishing grounds and hoped the need for cash wouldn't arise. He sold what fish he had to the Germans or the hotel when he needed to. This was a sobering turn of events, but it made his dismissal as Kjell's hired man more believable.

The soldiers along the seawall were standing up now and assembling their gear. Haugland glanced up the road to the top of the ridge looking for Schiller. Once again, he wondered why the soldiers were here. There was no strategic reason for them being in the village. Had the Gestapo in Kristiansund N. tipped someone here? Anna had said Schiller thought soldiers would come only at the request of the Gestapo.

Stuffing his hands in his pockets, he stepped down and strolled to the frozen trail that led up from the seawall to the ridge behind Ella's building. Halfway up, he stopped to look back at the soldiers, looking for signs of any communication with an outside man. Could it be that stranger? Something wasn't right.

You're becoming paranoid, he thought and began to dismiss his feelings when he saw Sorting coming down the ridge road over by the warehouse. At the edge of the wharf, Sorting stopped and waited for Bugge and the group of fishermen. Briefly, they exchanged some words then Bugge and the group went on into the *konditori*. Sorting walked over the seawall. While avoiding the soldiers' gaze, at the same time Sorting seemed to be looking for someone. He pretended to look out over the seawall, but he held his shoulders too taut. Warily, he took a cigarette out and began to light it.

Instinctively, Haugland drew back out of Sorting's range without losing sight of him.

A few moments later the soldiers started toward to the *konditori.* A mix of young and older men, they all ignored Sorting, except for one who asked for a light. They exchanged a few words, then the soldiers stomped into the store.

Haugland didn't miss what happened next. As the soldiers went in, the stranger came out and it seemed that he and Sorting bumped into each other. Haugland knew it was a ruse. The stranger put something into Sorting's pocket and made a faint acknowledgment before the two men separated. So they were together.

The stranger stepped down and walked out on the wharf. Sorting, after finishing up his cigarette, went inside. It had all happened in less than a second, but Haugland knew Fjellstad was no longer safe. If the man was a Rinnan agent, the pressure was on. Making sure that he hadn't been seen, he quietly climbed up to the ridge and made straight for Grimstad's home, hoping that he was there.

"Jens," Grimstad said, answering the door himself.

Where lady?

"Oh, it's perfectly safe to talk. My housekeeper is gone. What's wrong?"

"That stranger that came in yesterday with boat troubles," Haugland said as they passed down the hall to the study. "I just saw him hand something to Sorting. What do you know about him?"

"Only that he has engine trouble. Ole's been working on his motor."

"Fasting talk to him?"

"Once to look at his papers."

Haugland ran his fingers through his hair.

"Who do you think he is, Jens?"

"Rinnan agent. Just don't know what they have in mind."

"God... you think Sorting knows something?"

"Maybe. I'm getting out as soon as the weather clears." He looked at the doctor. "You need to make plans to shut everything down here. Kjell has done that too."

"Will you be close by?"

"I'll be on the coast where I'll run the line to at least Christmas, but with the Allies bogged down and Rinnan trying to penetrate resistance groups, the whole area between Kristiansund N. and Trondheim is vulnerable."

"Will you need me?"

"You're always needed, Hans, but unless you have to, just stay put. I can get the messages some other way. Even though the cutout is secure in Trondheim, I may suspend it for now. Did you know there was another round of arrests in Trondheim a few days ago?"

"*Nei.*"

"All the more need to be careful. There was a *razzia* down south too."

The men stopped and listened. The doctor took out a pad and wrote a prescription for his throat. "Take it with you. Maybe you'll need it later. I can also pack a box of medicine for you to keep for your people. Just in case."

They talked softly for a few minutes more. Haugland buttoned up his coat.

"Influenza's going around again," Grimstad said. "I think it's the thin, worn-out clothing and the lack of fats. I treated one of the soldiers this very morning along with Lisel Fromme."

Lisel. Haugland said nothing. He mustn't give himself away. He looked at a clock on the desk. It was dark now. The thought of going to his cold cabin wasn't very appealing, but he needed to compose a message for the W/T, then wait. With the troops here, he was leery of sending anything. Instinct told him not to. Instinct told him not to see Anna either.

"Why don't you stay, Jens? You look beat."

"*Tusen takk*, but I can't wait." He put on his cap. "*God kveld.*"

Minutes later Haugland was on the fjord road. The temperature continued to drop and there were occasional snow flurries. Winter loomed with an oppressive weight. As he trudged along in the dark and cold, he felt it push down on him.

He was leaving. Never had his urge for self-preservation been so high. He put his fingers around the gun in his pocket. Neither was his desire. He whispered her name: Anna.

CHAPTER 74

"*Fru* Fromme," the young soldier said in German. "Compliments of *Oberleutnant* Schiller. He sends his best wishes."

On the other side of the screen door a soldier barely out of his teens stood in the outside light holding a bouquet of flowers. They were slightly wilted from an obvious long trip, but to have appeared here in late November, Anna thought, was short of a miracle. Once, before the war, airlines brought fragrant cargoes up from North Africa. The German officers, she supposed, probably found ways to get around that, another sign of their arrogance.

Anna peered around him. Another equally young soldier waited by two motorcycles.

"*Bitte*," the soldier said. "Take them before they freeze. I think he'd kill me if they die."

"I won't let him kill you. Is there a message?"

The boy mumbled, "He wishes," to see you at your convenience."

"It is not convenient.Tell him that my daughter's ill and remind him of his gentleman's agreement."

The boy snapped his heels. He was so young and the inferior field gray cloth of his uniform didn't fit him very well. The *Wermacht* must be slipping in standards, she thought. Factories were being blown up and raw materials were becoming scarce. When Anna took the flowers, he stepped back and gave her a "*Heil Hitler*."

Anna didn't respond.

She found a tall jar and set the flowers in it. She really hadn't wanted to accept them but thought that might cause more problems than it was worth if she didn't.

She wished Schiller hadn't returned. She could never make him out and in her heart just didn't want to put in him in the "bad" category because he was a soldier. Yet she knew she couldn't permit any association with him. Not even give him a hope. She sensed more than ever she must keep whatever activity Jens did with his friend Kjell absolutely safe and with the soldiers here that would be difficult.

She heard the motorcycles start up and go past her house. When the *stue* was silent again, she listened for Lisel. She had been feverish all day. Anna had to fetch the doctor. Since Grimstad left, her coughing had quieted down and she was resting now. It had been a tiring day and in fact just before the soldiers had shown up, Anna had been lying down on the bed with her.

She brought the flowers to the table, then lifted the blackout curtain. It was pitch black outside, although the sky hinted at severe weather. In the village, they had been talking of snow. She lowered the curtain and looked at her wood bin. Perhaps she should go out now and replenish it before the snow struck. She didn't doubt the villagers' word.

She put on a coat over her wool dress and rubber boots and went outside to the woodshed. The wood that Jens had stacked and split for her was piled neatly. She helped herself to an armload in the frigid night air then jumped when she heard a sound from the meadow.

"*Hallo?*" she asked into the dark, clutching the wood against her pounding chest. She squinted through the mist. Had there been other soldiers? The thought frightened her, but the figure that came through was only Jens carrying skis and poles.

Jens! Over the past weeks their friendship had grown beyond a platonic relationship. There was genuine affection now, a deepening of feelings they both shared, but never acted upon. Sometimes that was a relief to her, but when he was gone, she missed him terribly.

You want wood?

"*Ja*," she nodded. Jens put his skis against the house wall. Anna started for the door. Behind her, she could hear him stacking a load of his own into his arms and suddenly she was very happy.

Inside, he worked quickly, stacking the wood into her bin. When he straightened up, his cheeks were red and his whole face was alive. How Lisel? he signed. Friend say sick.

"She'll be all right," Anna said. "Just a few more days of rest."

Good. Out came the notebook and pencil. Why soldiers here?

"You saw them?" Anna shifted with unease. "Schiller has returned and I'm afraid he will not stop bothering me." She pointed to the flowers on the table. "He has brought me flowers at God knows what expense. How will I convince him I don't want to see him?"

You find way, A-N-N-A. He reached into his coat pocket and brought out a small paper bag. When she smelled it, she laughed. It was English cocoa.

She put on her teapot. Hansen disappeared, his coat and scarf tossed on the sofa. She laid out some cups and waited for his return. A short time later, he came out of the bedroom hallway.

Lisel sleeping, he signed. He moved his fingertips from his shoulders out. *Angel*.

"She is an angel. I couldn't ask for a better child. Even as an infant she was easy, so happy, but I hate this occupation does to children. Was she awake?"

She took my hand, he motioned. She sleep now. He seemed preoccupied despite his interest in Lisel. She was going to ask if his friends were all right when he bent down to check on the stove. When he stood up again he accidentally brushed her shoulder. Instantly, she felt tense. He rubbed his fist against his chest. Sorry.

"It's all right."

I missed you.

They laughed awkwardly. It had been a long time since she had experienced any sort of adult companionship, and she wondered about him. Had he ever had a girlfriend? It had never occurred to her before. It didn't matter. They were acutely aware of each other. He wants me, she thought, and briefly felt panic. The only man she'd known was Einar. She was relieved when the kettle whistled.

While she fixed the precious chocolate. Jens sat on the rug by the stove. He began to work on a puzzle strewn on the floor.

Anna brought a tray and set it down on the floor beside him. She patted his leg to get his attention and he reached over for his mug. They skoaled each other, then drank.

"There's a hole in your sock. Do you see it?"

He looked at the long wool sock he had pulled up to his knickers. There was a hole on the calf. You fix? He motioned. His eyes looked mischievous.

"Sure. I can knit you a new pair. I have lots of wool yarn now." What color you like? she signed.

What color? He shrugged. Maybe red.

"I have *hvitmaure*—bedstraw. It's supposed to make a red. I've been collecting the roots since July. I can make red socks or maybe socks with red stripes."

You make… reindeer? Trolls with big feet?

"*Nei!*" she laughed, batting his arm.

For over an hour they sat on the rug and talked, looking at pictures in magazines or talking about anything that came into their heads including the soldiers, what each knew about the war and the hope for an end at Christmas. They drained their cups and Anna went for more.

They worked on the puzzle and eventually had a race to see who would finish their section first. Working on their knees, they jostled each other for the pieces and he ended up spilling one of the mugs of chocolate.

"Jens," Anna laughed. "You're worse than Lisel…" She went to the bathroom to get a sponge. She checked on Lisel, then stepped back out. Jens was dabbing up the spill with a rag of his own from his coat, his head bent down in concentration. As usual, he seemed to have everything under control.

She looked at him tenderly and thought, Jens not Einar. With Einar, it was almost an instantaneous feeling of love. With you, it has been trust. But I care for you too and more. At times, though, she was afraid. He had an unquiet power about him. With Jens, she thought she was looking at two different people.

She came back into the room with the sponge and went through the motions of wiping the already spotless floor. He finally turned and smiled. Coming over he sat down by the tray and poured half of his chocolate into her empty mug.

She sat down next to him. He leaned against the chair closest to the stove.

"Is it snowing yet?" she asked.

Ja, he motioned. Big snow.

Winter's come again and I'm still here. But I had my summer. She smiled at him. He had saved it. His presence had made the difference.

They talked quietly for a bit. Drinking the rest of his chocolate, he put his mug on the tray. He took hers when she was done and when his fingers brushed against hers, she felt a jolt as close to electricity as she could imagine. He must have felt it too. Like her he tried to ignore it. She busied herself in the puzzle, he drew himself up cross-legged and toyed with one of his pieces. She wasn't making any progress, sitting so close to him. He leaned over and put his piece next to hers. It fit.

He straightened up, brushing her shoulder. He turned and looked straight into her eyes then hesitating briefly, reached over and brushed her hair away from her face. She sat very still, hardly breathing, managing a smile when he leaned over and kissed her. He began to stroke her shoulders and kiss the hollow of her neck. *I have forgotten how smooth and soft a man's face could feel after shaving, how wonderful a man could smell*, she thought.

He stroked her hair with the back of his hand, looking for permission to go on. She smiled at him shyly. He pulled her to him and kissed her with increasing passion, then forcibly pushing the tray out of the way with his foot rolled her gently to the floor. Lying on his left side on the rug, he held her in his arms and looked at her.

You beautiful, he signed. I want you.

"I know," she said weakly, looking up at him. Her heart pounded when he kissed her forehead and mouth, but it was not as wild as the confusion she felt. He pressed her lips harder and for the first time, she kissed him back. Encouraged, he stroked her throat and chin with his fingers then ran his hand down across her breast. She gasped and arched her back.

"Jens," she murmured, thinking how odd he wouldn't hear the most intimate sounds of love.

He removed his hand and waited. She smiled sweetly at him, but she was uneasy. He lowered his head and kissed her on her throat, then one-handed, began to unbutton the front of her dress. She began to tremble, her lips parted. She felt like she was dissolving, but suddenly it was too much. She sat up abruptly, banging his face and pushed him away.

"I'm sorry," she said, her back to him and leaned over, trying to put herself back together. Then she remembered that he wouldn't have heard, so turned. "I'm sorry, Jens. I can't. *Vær så snill.* Forgive me." She felt cold.

He sat up. Reaching over to the chair behind him, he pulled down a crocheted afghan. He put it around her, gently tying the ends in front of her unbuttoned dress. He kissed her lightly on her forehead. It felt like fire, but anything he did from now on would feel that way. At that instant she knew she loved him very much. But she was afraid.

He got up and offered her his hand. She stood, still clutching the afghan. Snow hard, he signed. I go.

Dully, she watched him. *He's ignoring what's passed between us*, she thought. *How could he do it? I've humiliated him.*

He headed out to the entryway. Anna buttoned her dress. By the time she went to the back door, he was dressed and organizing his ski equipment. He pursed his lips when he saw her.

He is regretting everything, she thought.

Taking a flashlight out of his pocket, he opened the door. Anna came over and turned on the back light. Outside the snow was falling heavily, the flakes as big as goose down. Several inches had fallen already making hummocks out of the uneven places in the barnyard.

"God natt, A-N-N-A." His face was impassive, telling her nothing, but she knew she had hurt him. What could she say?

She put her hand on his sleeve. "Jens." Her voice trailed away.

My fault, he signed. Stupid. He leaned over and kissed her quickly. A moment later he was gone, carrying his skis on his shoulder and balancing his flashlight and poles in his other hand. He disappeared around the corner, the flashlight's glow a faint circle in the thickly falling snow. Then he disappeared.

For a moment, Anna stood in stunned silence as she played the whole scene over and over in her mind. Why had she panicked? Was it out of loyalty to Einar? It *was* hard not to think of him, to wonder how he would feel. She would never do anything to sully her memory of him and what they had. Was there some social constraint? Or was it the fear of being loved again but by someone so totally different?

Suddenly, nothing mattered more than the lonely figure going home.

Wearing only house shoes, she flung open the back door and took off after him in the blinding snow. In the dark onslaught somewhere on the driveway, she saw the flashlight laying at ground level. Had he fallen? She slipped in the snow nearly losing her footing, but as she came closer, she realized that he had laid the flashlight on the ground and was putting on his skis.

"Jens," she shouted as she touched his shoulder.

He stood up and shined the light on her.

"Come back, Jens. Vær så *snill.* I don't want you to go."

He smiled at her and held the light so she could see his right hand.

I stupid. I wrong, he signed.

"*Nei*, you weren't Jens. Come. We'll talk about it."

He put a finger on his lips. *Nei.* He reached out and touched her cold cheek. She couldn't see his face very well, but she understood. He didn't want to talk.

A blast of wind threw a flurry of snowflakes at her, making her shiver. He undid his coat and put it around her shoulders. She stood like an errant little girl while he buttoned it. When he finished, he took her arm and tugged her toward the house.

***

They went back silently, Anna leading the way with the flashlight. Haugland glided along behind her. There wasn't quite the right amount of snow for the skis, but he was too upset to take them off now. He watched her slim form in front of him backlit by the flashlight and swore for being so reckless. He had misjudged her feelings for him. Now he'd lost everything.

The back door was open, filtering yellow light through the falling snowflakes onto the carpet of snow. She went inside and disappeared. He quickly undid the leather straps on his skis and went in after her. He had no intention of staying except to make sure she was all right and get his coat. He walked into the *stue* and found her standing in front of the woodstove. She turned when he came by her.

"*Takk.*" She returned his coat to him.

He folded it over his arm, then noticed her stocking feet.

Your socks wet. Take off.

She sat down on a chair and took them off, arranging them mechanically on the low stone hearth. She was so listless that he became genuinely alarmed. You stay. I make tea, he signed and left her. Rummaging through her cupboard he found a tin of tea and was preparing to measure it in her teapot when he noticed she was gone.

What a mess I've made of things, he thought. Where he pushed the tray away to lay down with her, the puzzle had been broken up and scattered.

Restless, he paced up and down the room. For a brief, confused moment he seriously considered telling her who he was, to get everything finally out in the open. That was, of course, impossible. To tell her the truth would only endanger her and endanger the village. The less anyone knew of his mission here, the better their chances if they should be arrested and questioned.

After another long moment, he went over to the nearest window. He lifted up the curtain to check on the storm and saw the snowflakes had become smaller, but were falling thicker. They'd get several more inches tonight.

A noise came from the hallway, but he didn't move. Anna came to him and stood beside him, waiting for him to turn. When he did, he was stunned.

She had changed out of the dress and had put on a light blue quilted silk robe. Her golden hair was combed and flowing above her shoulders with a ribbon to hold it away from her face. She didn't look dull and listless now, but was bright as though she had made a decision and would follow through. She seemed at peace with herself and her face glowed.

"Is it still snowing hard, Jens?"

Ja. Very hard.

"I'm glad," she answered. "Now you'll have to stay."

When he was a little slow on her meaning, she took one of his hands and pressed it against her breast. She had nothing on underneath.

Friend, she signed, then brushed a hand on his cheek.

Haugland's mouth dropped, but she closed it with a kiss.

***

So Jens made love to her on the bed she had lain with Einar, on the bed where Lisel was born. And a place that had been dead, a place she thought would never be alive again, revived, filling her with a happiness she had forgotten. She was loved again. Finally her doubts about Jens left her. When he finally entered her, they gasped with the pleasure it gave them. It was the only sound he made, but it did not matter.

Jens, dear Jens.

Once they rested and with legs and arms entwined. He lazily stroked her shoulder and breasts with his fingertips, making little swirls that gave her goose bumps of pleasure. Her hair spilled next to his face. He grinned at her, his eyes twinkling and she laughed. It didn't matter he didn't speak. She stroked his dark head and kissed him deep before laying her head back down on the pillow next to him. Their breath touched in the cool, candlelit room like a warm fog, but under the *dyne*, the heat was searing as they waited. Finally, he traced the line of her body from her hip to ankle with his foot, then lifted her and pulled her tight against him. He found his way into her again, gently thrusting and teasing her with each stroke until she came.

Later, she lay with her head on his shoulder and traced his breastbone with a finger. She was as silent as he was, but she knew he was content.

I see it in your eyes, she thought.

He closed them and rested, his breathing regular. She watched his chest rise and fall and wondered if he felt the same: that in the dying world, there could still be this thing called love.

She began to drift, but opened her eyes when she felt him stir. He was on the edge of the bed. In the candlelight his bare shoulders and chest looked golden, his hair was like coal.

She touched him on his shoulder. "What is it?"

He handed the notebook to her. I will be gone fishing for a while, she read.

"Will I see you soon?"

He moved his hands in front of his face and chest. *Nei.* Sorry.

She lay back down on her pillow, crossing her arms over her breasts. He pulled the *dyne* higher up on her, then stroked her cheek gently.

A-N-N-A. You beautiful. I want stay forever. He paused, then making fists, crossed his arms. L-O-V-E, he fingerspelled. I love you. He pointed to her. You understand?

Anna understood, but his declaration hit her harder than she thought it would. It frightened her and made her feel safe at the same time.

"Jens, don't go."

He put a finger on her lips. Not now. Say nothing. I not care. He slipped back into bed and let her snuggle against the hollow of his shoulder. He felt warm and solid. He kissed her full on her mouth, then holding her hand on his chest, closed his eyes. The room became silent. Soon he was asleep. Outside the snowstorm raged, but it never broke the peace and comfort Anna felt.

She drifted, then finally dozed, the memory of a kiss on her cheek. The candle sputtered and went out. Only when she was awakened by Gubben purring in her face and kneading the pillow next to her, did she know that Jens had truly left.

She hid her face in the cat's fur and wept in joy and in sorrow.

CHAPTER 75

It was snowing again when Haugland started back to his cabin. It rushed down in a shower of flakes and wind that obscured his way but moving by memory and aided by a faint glow caused by the pouring snow Haugland found the entrance to the brambles. He stopped to shoulder his skis and poles and looked back up at Anna's farmhouse. Having acted on his passion for her, he found his feeling of elation was rapidly being replaced by one of regret.

I shouldn't have done it, he thought. No matter how wonderful, it hadn't been in her best interest. With the patrol in village, he had to go and soon, but without telling her anything. "I'll come back somehow," he said out loud. "I promise."

He brushed snowflakes from his eyebrows and slogged his way through the snowy thicket and came out back of the woodshed. He started to descend, then stopped. There was light seeping out from the blackout curtain. Someone was inside. Laying down the skis, he took out his pistol and crept down. At the door, he put his ear against the frame, listening for any sound or conversation coming through the crack. To his surprise, he heard Tommy Renvik and Petter Stagg speaking to someone else. At this hour? Were they in trouble?

Their sudden appearance didn't concern him, but who was other party? Alarmed, he felt inside his coat and brought out a heavy silencer from a pocket sewn just for it and prepared to put it on. Suddenly, he heard laughter.

"Cousin, you've got to be kidding."

"*Nei*, Helmer, I'm not. They shot a reindeer, but all they wanted were its innards. They cooked them up, but when someone spilled them on the floor, they panicked. They ate them right there. Said it gave them strength."

"Commandos," Tommy said. "They're all nuts." The men started laughing again.

Haugland took a deep breath and testing the door, yanked it open. There was an immediate scramble to all corners of the room.

"Well," Haugland said. "This is a fine way to start the morning. What the hell's going on?"

Tommy, Helmer and to Haugland's surprise, Petter, slinked back to the center of the cabin, lowering their weapons.

"Where have you been?" Tommy asked.

"Out." He nodded at Helmer. "I see you've met Petter."

"*Ja*." Helmer smiled at his cousin. "Proud of him too. A fisherman in Milorg."

Suddenly, Haugland was aware they weren't alone. Sitting behind his bed were three bedraggled young men. Haugland's mouth went dry. "Who are they?"

Tommy put his Sten gun on the table. "There was a crash on the *fjell* the other night not far from my hut. A SOE RAF drop gone wrong. They're the only survivors."

One of the flyers looked up. His face was cut and the sleeve on his leather bomber jacket torn. His brown hair was matted. Next to him was a flyer, his legs out straight. He was not moving.

"Where's the plane now?" Haugland said in English.

"Under a head of snow," the stranger said with an American accent. "And last night's fall. Thank God you speak English. I wasn't sure if I was getting through."

"What's your name?" Haugland asked the American.

"John Trumball." The man's mouth tightened as he gave his rank and serial number. Trumball nodded to the man on the floor. "That's Eddie Conway. He's Canadian."

"And these two?"

Trumball gave Haugland the names Graves and Ekberg, all American.

Haugland crouched down in front of the Canadian. The side of his knit shirt under the opened jacket was bloodstained. He lifted it up, revealing a hurriedly made bandage, stained with dried blood.

"How did you get him down?"

"Sled," Tommy answered. "There was no way to export east or south. I had to come here. Can you get them out?"

Haugland switched back to Norwegian. "*Ja*, but it will be dangerous. There are not only troops in the village, but someone who came in a few days ago with a possible DRT. Sorting is working with him."

"God help us all," Helmer spat. "Obviously, we can't leave from the village, but I know a path. Not used much and a bit tricky, but you can pass along the fjord wall without being seen."

"Really? Do you know it Petter?" Haugland had a plan forming in his mind. When Petter said he did, Haugland laid out his idea. While he skied out to send a message, Helmer would go into the village and find Grimstad. He would tell him there was an emergency and they would have to go to a farmstead beyond the fjord mouth. Helmer would take him in his boat. If the soldiers should challenge them that would be their story. They would meet Tommy, Petter and the airmen out at the channel. It would take several hours. "I'm not going. It's imperative I stay here. They are sure to search for the W/T. Where's Kjell?"

"Either in the warehouse or at the *konditori.*"

"He's to stay put. I think he's being watched."

***

The *konditori* was open, its lone light spilling onto the snowy ground in front of it. The early morning fishing community was up by habit, though they hadn't much to do. Sorting sat at the window when Dr. Grimstad came in. They acknowledged each other with a nod, then the doctor sat down with Ella Bjornson. Sorting wondered what they were talking about. The doctor intrigued him. He was the one person who could move easily throughout the district but never seemed to do anything else but keep to his calls. Since the arrival of the troops he had been busy with looking after cases of flu that arrived with them. Foss said soldiers too sick to stay at the schoolhouse cluttered the hotel. Another patrol was ordered.

Sorting shook his head. The patrols messed up his work. He stared out the window, frowning at the weather. Everything seemed to be coming apart.

On the wharf he saw Birger Strom walk up toward the *konditori.* Since his arrival he had pretty much stuck to the boat until the freeze hit, then had to seek a room up at the hotel. In his rucksack he carried a small portable DRT, but the direction finder had been silent. No wireless radio signals sent. Maybe it was the weather. From the looks of Strom as he hunkered down against the wind, he appeared to be in a hurry, but more from wanting to get out of the frigid air. When he came into the shop, the little bell jangled loudly. Sorting looked down at his coffee. Only when Strom stomped his feet on the stair before entering the tearoom, did he venture a look. There was a triumphant look in Strom's eyes.

He tried to pry the sides of a metal cigarette case open with his cold fingers. When he couldn't, Sorting offered to help.

"*Takk.*" Birger offered him a cigarette. Sorting chose one and took a slim roll of paper with it. After thanking him for his generosity, he settled back in his chair. "Care to join me?"

"*Nei, takk.*" Birger held up an old detective novel. He bowed and then moved on.

It was a well-acted scenario. Feeling secure, Sorting lit his cigarette and next to his plate, unrolled the note. It said simply:

"Signal confirmed. Location within fjord valley confines. Approximately five miles away. Will act accordingly."

Sorting took a drag and slid the paper under the plate. He would retrieve it when he left, but for now, who was making that signal? He should have brought the DRT in earlier, but who thought a courier line started here? Was his code name Ryper? And how did they reach him?

The answer, of course, was simple. Hansen. Dumb, unfortunate Hansen.

Behind the counter, there was movement as Bette came into the tearoom. She briefly looked at Sorting with lowered eyes and a faint smile before she went to the table where Bjornson and Grimstad sat.

"*Herr Doktor*," she said. Someone is here to see you. You can come to the back."

The chair scraped as Grimstad got up. He was gone for a few minutes then returned.

"I have to go," he apologized to Ella. "I'll be gone for a while." He gathered up his coat and gloves and left the *konditori* without a nod for Sorting as he passed. He seemed preoccupied. Outside the window, Sorting watched the doctor go up the hill with his medical bag. When Sorting turned around, he caught Bjornson staring at him. She got up and went upstairs to her apartment.

Now what in the hell had that been all about? He looked over at Strom and hoped he would take the cue to get back to his room so they could move on this.

***

A couple of hours after skiing out to send his message, Haugland was back at his cabin. He unpacked the W/F from his rucksack and after secreting it away in the stump, went inside. Trumball was sitting on the bed next to the other airmen. Haugland was relieved to see Eddie awake. He held a bowl of pottage in his shaking hands.

"How'd it go?" Tommy closed his rucksack set on the table and buckled the strap.

"I got a message off. Export will be waiting." He took off his snow-covered wool cap and hung it over a chair post. "You'll need to move fast. The Krauts will go to where I sent the signal. Is everyone ready?"

"I'm ready." Petter stood up. "I'll show them the way."

***

Kjell went behind the curtain to Ella's kitchen in the *konditori* and found her rolling out dough. He went to a side curtain and turning off the light, discreetly lifted the blackout curtain. It was dark, the frigid air hanging like fog around the water and the buildings, but he could see what he thought he had seen. Sorting. He was coming down the road from the hotel. A faint glow signaled the path of his flashlight.

Kjell carefully put the curtain down. "Ella. We've got a problem." He told her about the airmen, and how they would get out. Ella took the information calmly as she always did.

"This is bad trouble. Worse than the dead German. Have you seen Sheriff Fasting?" he asked.

"Not since around two this afternoon. He came for his usual *spekemat.* What can I do?"

Kjell could have kissed her. "I'm going to tell you something very secret, but I think you of all people should know. For the last several months there has been someone in the area using a transmitter to talk to London. I can't tell you who that person is, but I think Sorting may have figured it out. I'm worried he's finally discovered where it is and worse, who it is. If I'm wrong, there's still the possibility that he knows about Jens's role in getting the boys away last summer."

Ella looked stunned, but composed herself. "When will Jens get back?"

"I don't know. He's following my directions on where to go—my contacts in export."

"Is he expected at the Hotel?"

"*Nei.* He's quit."

"Quit?"

"*Ja*, Ella, it's just in time. The Deaf Church offered him a place in Oslo. Since he'll have a small salary, it is better that he goes." When Kjell saw the sad look in her eyes, he tried to reassure her. "He has promised to return when things are better. I'd like that very much. Now, I think he should go immediately. If Sorting *has* found out."

"Don't worry, Ella. I'll cover for him if questions are asked." She rested her hand on his arm. "I have already warned the rest of the committee about Sorting and his friend. It'll work out. The village is blameless."

CHAPTER 76

Haugland stayed at his cabin for most of the day, preparing to leave, thinking about Anna and Petter and Tommy leading the airmen out to the fjord mouth. Petter estimated a two hour walk if the Canadian could handle it. After that, it was up to Helmer to get past the soldiers on the wharf. Grimstad's presence was the key.

In the late afternoon, he skied down to Kjell's house. Haugland knocked the snow off his boots on the steps and came in. Kjell was in his kitchen making potato hash. The room was warm, the window steamy.

"Jens."

You alone?

"Ja, I'm alone."

"Good," Haugland said. "Any word about the airmen?"

Kjell put the hash in a bowl. "Not a word. I'd give them more time. Grimstad has free travel and can be gone as long as he needs. With the influenza, there are no soldiers out. Heard a new unit has been sent in to reinforce those who are sick. It's turned into quite an epidemic."

"A godsend for us," Haugland said as he leaned against the sink. "I'm sure only so many are able to go out in this continuing blast of Nordic cold."

"It gives us time, the thing we need most."

"Everything is set. I'm leaving," Haugland said. "Can Helmer take me out tomorrow?"

"*Ja*. If there're no restrictions. You ought to see Ella, before you go. She won't like you leaving like this, no matter the reason." Kjell sat down and spooned hash onto a plate.

"You tell her about my supposed job in Oslo?"

"*Ja*. More than a couple of people know." Kjell hesitated. "But I also told her about the airmen and the possibility of an agent in the area. That's all I said. I thought it best."

"That's fine. At this point I need all the ears and eyes I can gather. She's tough. Before I forget, tell A.C. Kjelstrup to lay low. Don't know how the arrests in Trondheim affect him."

"Why don't you stay here, Jens?"

"I can't. I'm packed, but I've got to call London some time tonight."

"Not before you eat something." Kjell put a plate in front of him.

Back at his cabin, Haugland hid his skis and the W/T and fiddled with the remainder of his meager possessions. He would leave his fishing pole and books with Ella. His clothes were in a borrowed valise and would go out on Helmer Stagg's boat. He stacked the remainder of his things on the floor. The dishes and bedding belonged to Magnuson and would be left as he found them. Satisfied all was ready, he pondered about the last thing he needed to do: see Anna.

He'd been thinking about her all day. At first he had planned to go without seeing her again, but he couldn't bring himself to just leaving her. It was wrong. But it was equally wrong not to tell her who he was. Miserable, he extinguished the lantern and went up to see her.

CHAPTER 77

Anna woke abruptly to tapping on her bedroom window. When the taps became playful, she slipped out of bed in the dark and carefully lifted the blackout curtain. It was Jens. Standing in the pale light created by the gently falling snow, he rubbed the frosted window with his hand and pointed to the back door. She threw a shawl over her white flannel nightgown and hurried down the hall.

"Jens!" She turned on the light. His bare head and heavy wool sweater were covered with snow and his face was pink from the cold. "It's late!" I sleep, she signed.

I not. I think of you.

"I thought you were gone. Marthe said you were working for the Staggs."

Finished. Please come in?

"Of course, you can. Oh, how I've missed you." She wasn't sure if he'd gotten every word, but reaching out to him she pulled him inside. His hands were cold, but his lips weren't. He kissed her softly on her mouth, then pulled her into his arms.

"Come by the fire, Jens and get warm." She pulled back. His closeness was disturbing. She was no longer sleepy. "Your hair is full of snow. Your clothes too." She tried to sound matter-of-fact, but all she could think of was how worn her nightgown was. She was acutely aware how thin a barrier it was between them, how her breasts pushed against his sweater.

At the woodstove, she showed him a lightweight *dyne* that was draped over the chair. "If you want to dry out, put that on," she said before going down the hall to her bedroom.

I get shirt for you, she motioned.

Bring me slippers. With red flowers.

When she came back into the room, he stood barefooted and half-naked in his wool knickers with the *dyne* wrapped around his shoulders. His hair was wet. He ran his fingers through it several times to shake the water out. He didn't see her until she touched his arm.

"You're still wet, Jens. You'll catch cold."

Come inside. You make me warm.

He drew her close to him and wrapped the *dyne* around them both. Grinning, he kissed her. She smiled when he locked her in his arms.

His skin was cool and there were little bumps around his flat nipples. Playfully rubbing his muscular chest, she put her arms around his neck and kissed him on his mouth.

"I love you," Anna said.

I love you, he signed, his fingers moving with great tenderness. The look in his eyes was haunting. I love you forever. You believe me?

He made a little sound, then leaned down and kissed her, pulling her tight against his hard body. He moved his hands down her back and caressing her, pushed deeper into her mouth. His fingers followed the line of her spine. She felt herself letting go of all inhibitions because she loved and trusted him. When he slowly gathered the nightgown above her waist exposing her naked buttocks and belly, she raised a leg and leaned against him. Kissing her hard, he laid a hand between her thighs and touched her with his fingers. Anna gasped. The heat under the comforter was intense. They were so eager for each other, his desire as powerful as her own was.

"Jens," she said stroking his cheek. "Make love to me."

They lay on the floor wrapped in the *dyne*, thinking they were the only lovers in world to feel this way. They nuzzled and stroked each other, then gently, he pulled her astride him in their tight cocoon. Anna moaned when he entered her, then squeezed and sucked her breast. It was a sensual assault. Engulfed in pleasure, his passion almost overwhelmed her. It was as if he was trying to tell her something he couldn't express in words or sign. In the end they created their own dialogue and were one. Later they dozed, their moist bodies entwined.

***

Haugland lay in the *dyne* with Anna snuggled tight against his side. He couldn't completely sleep, afraid to make some noise or mistake. He stroked her hair absentmindedly in the faint light from the attic stairs. She was everything he ever wanted physically in a woman. Yet he was miserable. He was leaving and he couldn't tell her. How could he show her his love was genuine and that he wouldn't abandon her or Lisel? He felt wretched and wondered if she could see through him. He'd made sure that she didn't become pregnant, but could he prevent breaking her heart? I'll come back, he promised.

He checked his watch. He had to send a late message to London and then get the last of his things ready. Then he would leave Fjellstad. He grazed his lips over her breasts and throat. She stirred and opened her eyes.

"Hmmm?"

I go now, he signed. He hoped he didn't show the shame he felt. He tried to sit up, but he was tangled in the *dyne*. Anna laughed as she tried to find the opening in their cocoon, but when she couldn't, he signed: You make trap.

He felt a surge of emotion as sharp as electric current when she laid a hand on his bare thigh. It was as if she could hold him back from leaving. For a moment she did.

A-N-N-A, he thumped her name on his chest. Stop. You make me crazy

"I hope so." She stroked his head.

Eventually, they untangled. As Anna turned on the lights, Haugland didn't miss one last look of every gracious line of her body before she put her nightgown back on. He dressed quietly. Anna disappeared, coming back with a blue coat.

"This was Einar's. You can borrow it." She helped him put it on, securing every button carefully.

Beauty, he signed. My love real. Remember.

She kissed him. "Be careful. The soldiers are everywhere now."

There was one last kiss and then he was gone.

***

Anna couldn't sleep after he left. She felt incredibly alive and vibrant, recalling vividly how he had made love to her. She glanced at the clock on the wall behind the woodstove. It was nearly five in the morning. Jens had been gone almost an hour. Outside, it was pitch-black and snowing she supposed. She lifted up the blackout curtain, and saw to her surprise, lights bobbing on the snow-covered driveway. Frightened, she drew back carefully, leaving a crack to follow the group's progress up to the back of her house.

Soldiers? At this hour? She counted to ten to compose herself, then fled to her bedroom to retrieve her bathrobe. She was calm when she opened the door. A group of German soldiers was outside, dressed in heavy wool coats and whitewashed helmets, suitable for the snow that was falling steadily around them.

"Our apologies, *Frau* Fromme," a youthful-looking sergeant said in German. "*Oberleutnant* Schiller sends his regrets for disturbing you, but it is orders."

"Is something wrong?" Anna answered in German. "It's so early."

"We're searching for a transmitter. Someone used it yesterday."

"Have you searched the rest of the fjord road?" Anna was beginning to be afraid for Jens.

"Not yet," said the soldier, "but we're split up. Every place will be covered." He apologized again. Standing at attention, he gave her a "*Heil Hitler*."

Anna managed to murmur something back. The patrol backed off and headed out to the logging road. The snow was falling heavily now. By the time they started up into the trees, she could not see them in the dark. She listened carefully for their muffled passing, then closed the door.

Looking into the dim kitchen, she felt growing concern. *I must warn Jens.*

Hurriedly, she searched for her warmest clothes. There was no sound from Lisel's room. She was curled up in her *dyne*, thankfully, sound asleep. It would probably be all right to slip away. If she could see Jens briefly, she could get back before Lisel woke up or worse, before the patrol returned.

The snow was falling fairly steadily now. Staring out toward where the meadow should be, she tried to calculate the best way to go without leaving any suspicious footprints in the snow. There couldn't be a connection between her house and Jens's cabin. She decided to go a little lower below the house as though she were searching for pine boughs. Jens's cabin was below a hill, she imagined, and if she came out above it, she might be able to hide her path through the pine trees and the snow-laden brambles. Hopefully, the rapidly falling snow would take care of everything else.

She forced her way to the edge of the brambles and found to her relief a sort of path a few yards down. In summer, it probably wouldn't have been noticeable, but it was something deer and other animals seemed to use. The snow had defined its entry and exit on the other side of its twisted thorny length. When she felt safe, she turned on the flashlight.

She worked her way through more brush. Eventually, the stand of pine thinned out and she could see her way to what might be a roof in the dim light made by the snow's glow. A yellow light was coming from the other side. Jens must be outside. She moved closer. Above the swish of the falling snow, she heard a steady clicking sound.

She turned off the flashlight and tiptoed down the slippery path. About halfway she stopped to get her balance. Seeking better traction, she moved over to the side in the dead, low-lying growth and saw that she could see clearly into the back of the cabin. Outside a small shed she had seen in the gloom there was a lantern and beside it, a chopping block. She stepped down a bit more to the left and saw Jens.

Jens had his back to her and bent over some contraption was lost in deep concentration as his fingers tapped out the clicking noise she had heard earlier. On his ears was a headset, similar to one her brother had used many years ago with his crystal radio set. Like a jolt her mind grasped the truth. When he moved one of his hands to adjust its position on his ears, she felt the exquisite knife of betrayal.

He had lied to her. Everything about him was a lie. His deafness, his identity, his very soul. It was so stunning and hurtful that she lost her footing. In one unceremonious swoop, she landed on her rear and slid down to the frozen ground below.

Hansen's reaction was swift. Before she could even move, he had turned and trained a gun into the dark. He threw the earphones away, rolling toward the cabin wall, then scrambling into the gloom beyond the lantern's light.

For what seemed a long time neither one moved. Anna began to get cold and finally stood up. Instead of being scared, she felt a stir of anger.

"Jens. I know you're there. You can at least have the decency to come out."

Silence, long and drawn out. Then movement. Hansen stood up and came into the lantern light. His face was serious, but instead of looking at her, he went back to the radio. He put down the gun. Picking up the headset, sat down and resumed signaling for one short burst, then put down the earphones. He fussed with a long flat wire and took it down. Silently, Anna watched him securing everything and then at long last turn to her.

He sighed softly. "I didn't mean to hurt you." He spoke in a strong masculine voice that surprised her.

Norwegian, she thought. From the Oslo area by his accent. "But you have. Most cruelly. You've made a fool of me. You've taken my heart. You're not the person I thought you were. Did you find pleasure in that? Am I the German whore everyone wants me to be?"

"Anna. *Nei*."

"How foolish I must seem to you. So easy. I believed you, had such empathy for you. You were my most precious friend. I told you my deepest secrets. I let you make love to me! Did you enjoy that? Did you?" In anger, she picked up some snow and threw it at him.

"Anna."

"Who are you?" she demanded.

"Someone who loves you."

"Am I so *naive*? What kind of woman do you think I am? I don't throw myself at men. I loved my husband. I believed who you said you were!"

"I know. You're a kind, caring person. I love you for that."

"You talk of love! You make me feel cheap!"

Hansen moved closer to her, his face contorted in what appeared to be grief. "Anna. I've wanted to tell you, but it's been so dangerous."

She laughed bitterly, then looked at the chopping block now closed and with an axe in place. She swallowed, remembering why she had come. Her anger dissipated. Of course the radio transmitter meant he was in contact with the Allies. If so, he was doing something potentially more deadly as the work Einar had done. Maybe worse.

"Oh, God... You are the one they are looking for."

"Who's looking?" Hansen's face became still.

"The soldiers. There's a patrol out right now making a sweep of the area. They plan to come here. They were at my house about fifteen minutes ago. They said that someone sent a signal yesterday."

"*Takk*, for the warning. I'll make sure everything's secured. You'd best go back."

She nodded weakly. The anger she felt now seemed unimportant, but when he came closer to her, she dreaded him touching her. It would only confirm his manipulation.

He didn't touch her. Instead, he just said, "Anna."

She saw the distress in his eyes, but she still shook with anger. Maybe she would let him be miserable for a while. "I didn't know how they would treat you, but obviously, you can take care of yourself."

"Anna... Don't tell anyone about this." He motioned to the stump now hiding the radio.

She nodded her head numbly, swallowing. Her mouth tasted sour. "You said things had become dangerous. Did you know about the soldiers?"

"The house-to-house search? *Nei*. There are other worries. I'm going to have to leave."

Briefly, her anger flared up again. He wouldn't have told her about that either. Yet there was a sadness in his eyes that she decided was real. *My love real. Remember.*

"Would you have stayed in the district?"

"I can't say."

"Of course." She hugged her arms, rubbing them. "I'll go now. Lisel is alone. The soldiers may come back."

"Anna. I *do* love you. And I will find a way to stay in touch."

Her eyes suddenly filled. This was all too much to take in. "Good-bye," she said. She started to go back toward the little trail she had slid down, avoiding his gaze. From near the front of the cabin, a man shouted something unmistakably German. Soldiers were coming up the hill. "Jens!" she whispered.

"I know. I hear them." He looked about the shed and the chopping block. "There's no time to run. They'll find you." Stunned, she watched his thoughts race across his face, then darken. "You'll have to get in the woodshed. There's a small space to cram into. I'll cover you up." He moved swiftly toward the shed door, and motioned for her to come. Taking her hand, he led her into the corner. It was freezing and smelled of pungent split wood. He laid a canvas tarp over her, but before he hid her face he said, "No matter what happens, no matter what you hear, don't come out. I'll let you know if it's safe. Or—once it's quiet and they're gone, come out. I have to protect the W/T. can't let them find it and question me."

Numbly, she nodded, then bit her lip. "Jens."

He kissed her for reassurance. "Piece of cake," he said in English, further confounding her. "I've got to hide your tracks."

He hid his gun in the small stack of wood next to her and went out of the shed, closing the door behind him. The snow crunched under his boots and soon she could hear the sound of wood as he tossed some on the ground, then the axe as he began to split wood at the block.

The soldiers rushed up to the cabin, the sound of their boots seeming to pour around its sides. They creaked of rifles, haversacks and metal helmets. "Halt!" one of the men shouted, angrily.

Hansen didn't stop. From inside the shed Anna heard a thud. Had someone struck him? The voices rose in anger, followed by a mocking command. Someone ordered Jens to show his papers. He must have gone into the cabin, for there was a pause, then more jeering. Someone kicked over a metal pan inside the cabin.

"*Dumkopf!*" They were shouting at Jens in German and broken Norwegian, and from the sound of it, pushing him around. She wanted to scream at them, to warn them away. She wanted his gun, to excise the Germans that were a part of her. Why didn't he defend himself?

One of the men began to laugh. Had Jens written something in his notebook? He was trying to explain himself, but all he got were kicks and jeers.

"Enough." The voice sounded authoritative. "His papers say he's deaf and dumb. I don't think *Oberleutnant* Schiller will like this."

"I found some books," another voice said. "American titles."

There was silence, then a lecture in baby talk to Jens, explaining that such books weren't allowed. "All right. Now show him what I mean, but that's all," the voice with authority said. There was some struggling, the sound of blows being delivered, yet remarkably, except for a single grunt, stoic silence from Jens.

Something heavy fell to the ground. The boots crunched off, leaving a deathly silence filtering through the hiss of falling snow. She waited for several more minutes, then pulled down the tarp.

Silence. Eerie and forlorn, then a groan.

Jens? She pushed off the canvas and scrambled out carefully. Stealing to the door, she peeked through a slit between the boards. The lantern was still going, but she couldn't see him. She leaned her ear to the crack and listened. Nothing. Feeling safe, she opened the door.

The cabin door was open, shedding light over the shed's wall and hill behind it. It was still dark beyond the lantern's reach. The snow was churned up, and wood from the woodpile had been thrown about. She squinted through the falling flakes. With a sinking heart, she located what she thought was a boot at the edge of the light.

"Jens!" She tumbled toward the inert form. Turning him over, she cradled his bloody head in her lap.

He was bleeding freely from his scalp. His eyes were half closed as if he had been stunned, but after a moment, he began to stir. Bringing his cold, red hands to his midsection, he drew his legs up in the snow as though in considerable pain.

"Christ," he groaned, trying to sit up.

"Don't go so fast," Anna soothed. "They're gone. Just rest for a moment."

"Not in your lap. I'm about to lose breakfast." He rolled to his side and coughed, but nothing came up. He tried to sit up. "Can't stay out here in the snow."

"Then I'll help you inside. Don't rush." She put her hands under his arms and helped him struggle to his feet.

He swayed, clutching his stomach. "Did they move the chopping block?" he asked.

"*Nei*. It looks the same."

He sighed deeply. "Good."

Moments later she had him inside and sitting on the bed. Stepping over broken furniture and crockware, she located his teakettle and put water on the stove, then after listening carefully to any sign of the patrol, closed the front and back doors. She found a towel, his bucket of spring water and a pan. Removing his coat, she placed him against the wall, which he did without protesting. Soon she was stanching the wound and cleaning him up. Giving him a clean cloth to hold against the cut while she poured hot water into a pan, she then daubed the edges of the cut carefully with a cloth of her own.

"When I saw you on the ground, I was so frightened for you. So angry at them.Why did they beat you? Because of the books?"

"They didn't take kindly to my manner of public speaking nor my taste in literature."

Anna looked away, trying to avoid his eyes. Hansen reached over and took her hand.

"It's all right. They didn't find the most important thing. If they had, I'd be facing more than a beating. Thanks to you warning me, everything's safe."

"I only came because I was afraid for you."

"Not because you love me?"

"You used that love. I don't even know who you are."

"I'm the same person, Anna. All the things we've shared, the books, the time together, that was real. My love is real. Making love with you was real." He reached out and turned her face toward him. "God, I love you, but don't you see how dangerous this is? I couldn't live with myself if the Gestapo made a connection to you and Lisel. That's why I didn't tell you the truth."

Anna pulled back. It was very hard to take this all in. "I don't know your name."

"Jens is a good name. It was my father's."

"Are you with the British?"

"Do you want me to say that?"

"I would like to know what I am dealing with here."

"I work with the British. That I will say."

Anna swallowed hard and hugged her arms. Noticing she still had the bloody cloth in her hands, she put it into the pan of water and then turned around and put the metal basin on the table. Searching there for a clean cloth for his head, she went on, "All this time doing illegal work for them. Why you pretended to be..." She couldn't finish, but she had the courage to look at him.

"*Ja*. And why I'm going. It's no longer safe. There have been arrests in Trondheim that have bearing on my work." Hansen clutched his stomach and grimaced when he tried to change his position. "I'm all right. My stomach got hammered. I'm a bit seasick."

Anna smiled faintly. She was beginning to adjust to him. He was the same, but he was also different. More and more like the lion in the springhouse. She wondered if that was his true self. He had a quick, intelligent wit that was self-deprecating and she suspected that he was highly educated. He spoke English. It was odd but she was calm after the fright with the soldiers. Maybe he was the same person.

She looked at his eyes. They were light with little sparkles in them. Unbidden, an image came to her of him holding her in his arms under the *dyne* and she relived the passion and heat as their moist, naked bodies worked as one. How maddeningly tender his lips and hands had been. How strong and powerful his body. Uncomfortable, she tried to concentrate on something else.

"Are you a fisherman?" Anna asked. "I believe that you could be, but I think not. Your accent. You're from the south. You sound educated. Are you?"

"I fish. I've been to the university. What are you going to do with that clean cloth?"

"I'm going to patch up your head."

"I think it's best if it's left uncovered. I'll have Grimstad look at it."

He leaned back and gingerly rubbed the back of his neck. "You'd better go. I'll clean up."

"Are you sure you'll be able to?"

"*Ja*."

"Will I see you? Or are you really going?"

"I'm going, Anna. Probably sometime today, unless there's restriction on travel. What else did the soldiers say to you?"

"They said a signal was sent yesterday. They were looking because it was the best time."

"They seem to favor five a.m. arrests. They were talking about Schiller too."

Anna looked aghast. “You understood them?

Ja, he signed. He looked straight at her. “*Ich liebe dich*,” he said. “I love you.”

Anna didn’t know what to say. She stood up in front of him thinking she would step back, but he reached out and put his hands on her waist. Drawing her close, he looked up at her.

“Wait for me. I won’t be far away and I’ll look after your interests. Yours and Lisel’s. When capitulation comes, I’ll speak for you.”

She smiled down at him and without thinking stroked his hair on the opposite side from the wound. “And then?”

Grunting, he lifted himself off the bed so he stood over her. For a brief moment he swayed then seemed to shake the dizziness off. She put a hand on his arm to steady him.

“I’ll take you away from here.” He smiled softly. “I know what I’ve done has been a sham to you, but your kind consideration of me as a simple human being, a deaf-mute, touched me deeply. It’s one of the reasons I fell in love with you.” He rubbed her hand. “I want you to know that this has been no wartime affair for me. I love you and Lisel both and will always look after you.”

“Even if I’m half-German?”

He lifted her chin and kissed her lightly on her lips. Forgive me, he signed. I care for you. I love you.

I… love… you, she signed back.

Who said love was never unspoken?

***

Outside, Anna prepared to leave the way she had come. The snow was still falling heavily. It looked as though it would continue the rest of the day. As they passed outside, he looked at the stump.

What’s wrong?” Anna asked.

“I’m just worried about it. I sent London an interruption code.”

“Is that important?”

“*Ja*, London will think the radio compromised if I don’t send back in the next forty minutes but the Germans must have the latest signal pinpointed. I want to take it up the valley, but I can’t come back in the village with the W/T. Yet I must. I was going to ship it out of here.”

“Then let me do it.”

Haugland stared at her. It had never occurred to him she would become involved.

“Send your message, then bring your W/T to my house. I can hide it in the dairy, move it where you want. I could even mail it.” She suddenly brightened. "I could have it packaged and have Schiller stamp it for me. No one would question me and once it's sealed, open it. I could send it to some place that you want by the mailboat."

Haugland shook his head. "*Nei*, Anna."

"I could do it. The hardest part is yours. I could do it, Jens." She touched his hand.

He protested again. After considering it further, he finally relented. He looked at his watch. "Three hours to sunrise. If it continues to snow, the day will be dark. I can make good time on skis and cover several miles in a short while, make a short signal, then come back. If they're searching for the radio with a DRT, they'd go in that direction and take the heat off in this area until I'm gone."

Going back into the cabin to the wall under the window, he loosened up a floorboard and retrieved his skis. Since an incident several years ago, when German soldiers stole every pair of skis in a village during a *razzia*, he'd always hidden his. Now he was grateful for the inconvenience. Feeling better, but fighting a headache, he dressed in a white canvas coat and cap, then emptied his rucksack.

"You should go, Anna," he said. "I'll leave immediately. Wait with Lisel. If you should have company, I'll wait until it is safe. After I bring you the W/T, go down into the village. There may be trouble later today if the Germans are looking for it."

"All right," she said quietly.

"Under no circumstances can it fall into German hands. There are too many lives at stake. The few must sacrifice for the greater good."

"I understand."

He came over to her and kissed her hard. Be careful, she signed, then he left.

CHAPTER 78

Hansen was careful. After skiing out deep into the valley and sending his message, he brought the W/T to Anna. She took even more of a risk. She placed it inside her sewing machine box and took it down to Schiller to have it stamped with his seal of the German *Reich*. Her knees shaking, she found him in the hotel dining room eating his supper.

"Anna Fromme. How good to see you," he said in Norwegian. He rose to greet her, wiping his mouth on his napkin. "*Vær så snill.* Sit."

She took off her gloves. "I only came to ask a favor. I have a box in the lobby. I was hoping you might stamp it so it could go out on the mailboat tonight. It's a sewing machine."

"Sewing machine? So domestic, so feminine," he said. "Of course, I'll stamp it for you." He snapped his fingers and asked for his stamp. A soldier set her sewing machine box on the table.

Carefully, she lifted back the folds of the box top, exposing the gray metal case of a German-made sewing machine. "It's a clunky old thing, but when it runs, it works well. I'm having it repaired. All it needs is to be sealed and the box stamped. Can you do it?"

"Of course. My pleasure. Are you sure you want to send it south? Is there no one here?"

"*Tusen takk*. I've already made arrangements. I'll have it back soon."

"All right." He closed up the flaps and taped it. When it was sealed, she gave him a label. By the time it was addressed, a soldier came back with the stamp. Schiller filled out some forms and taped them to the box. He banged a Reich eagle over all its sides.

"There," he said. "Finished. Now you will stay to chat. It's oppressive around here."

Carefully, Anna sat down. Schiller pushed away his food. He began to talk about the snow and of home before the war. It was a dreamy time Germany: hikes in the mountains; lace curtains in windows and lovely red geraniums.

Anna shuddered. Behind that facade, there was rot. She doubted if she could ever go back to Germany. She thought of Einar, dead. Jens lying in the snow with his scalp split open. Maybe I'm guilty too, to have them both come to this. It isn't just the Nazis. It's the looking away. The lace curtains and the flowers. Everyone looked away and then it was too late.

She tried her best to be pleasant, but she was uncomfortable. She sensed tension in the hotel as soldiers passed in and out of the lobby. It *was* oppressive. "*Vær så snill*, may I go? I have to get my daughter. She's with the cook."

She fumbled for her coat, but Schiller insisted on helping her. He stood very close to her, his breath soft on her neck, his fingers a little too hesitant to release the cloth. She finished buttoning the coat herself and found her gloves and scarf.

"I wish that we could be great friends and more." Schiller reached out and touched her cheek. Anna froze. "You are so beautiful. So very charming. I have never met anyone quite like you."

Suddenly he pulled her to him and clamped his mouth down on hers. He clasped her hair, holding her in his arms. He displayed his need intensely. Shocked, Anna twisted away.

Schiller put up his hands, his face red. "I'm so sorry. So sorry. Please forgive me," he said in quiet desperation. "It's that I have a hope. There isn't another man?"

"Only my husband. I will always love him." Anna put her scarf in place, hoping he didn't see her hands shaking. "I thank you for the favor, but after this, I cannot see you anymore. I must always think of my daughter. I can't allow anything to jeopardize her standing in the village. I'm sorry because I think you are a decent man, *Oberst* Maxe Schiller. If things were different, we could be friends."

Anna took the box and slipped out to the kitchen, hoping no one had seen him kiss her. But someone had and word went out.

Tyskertøs. German cozy.

CHAPTER 79

Haugland carefully pulled back the lace curtain at the bedroom window over the *konditori* and looked down at the wharf in the rapidly dying light. He watched as a heavily stamped box was hand-carried onto the mailboat and set down into a storage bin along with other mail. A hatch was shut down on it and then locked.

So she had done it. A sense of relief and pride swept over him. What a brave thing to do.

For the first time in a very long time, he felt a sense of love and connection with someone other than comrades who had populated his life for over four and half years. Some had been female too, but Anna was different. He loved her deeply. This simple, dangerous act strengthened his bond to her. But unlike the others, the act declared her love for him. She didn't have to do it.

I'm going to marry her, he thought. Yet the idea of the future was unsettling. It meant surviving despite increasing odds. It meant taking the same chances while acutely knowing each chance could be his last and he'd never see her again. It was a painful reality, but he had broken his rule by falling in love. Others depended on him and they would have to come first.

He looked to the end of the wharf. A small fishing boat had arrived, under a hooded light. It was hard to make out details, but he was sure it was Helmer Stagg's. *Where have you been, Stagg and Grimstad?* He was anxious to see them not only for their account but for Grimstad to check the wound on his head. It throbbed. He had been applying an ice bag all day.

He let the curtain drop at the sound from out in the hall and for the moment he not only felt for his gun, but the pill he had begun to carry with him at all times. That was the other reality. He mustn't be taken.

"Jens?" Ella opened the door behind him. Bright light illuminated the window and wall. Haugland turned toward her. She was dressed for church, but her face didn't reflect her usual pleasure in that. "There's trouble, Jens. Kjell wanted you to know. He thinks you'll be safe here."

What happen?

"They're looking for a wireless transmitter. The soldiers have been ordered to bring ten men to the warehouse for questioning. Kjell is one of them."

Haugland felt the hair on the back of his neck rise. When?

"He was told to go up on the main road." From outside there was shouting. Ella hurried to the window to peer out. "Dear Lord. Already..." She gripped one of his arms.

Down below they could see a group of men being herded onto the wharf and down to the entrance of the warehouse. In what looked like typical German overkill, one of the soldiers had a dog that pulled at its leash with a menace.

"Oh, God, there's Pastor Helvig and the schoolmaster Stagg. Jan Sorenson, Kjell..." She put a hand over her mouth.

Haugland knew all of them. He caught a glimpse of his friend as he went into the warehouse. *And I brought you to this,* Haugland thought.

"Kjell wants you to stay here, Jens. He fears they will ask about the boys last summer." She signed some words for him and he acknowledged he understood. "You can have the bed here for the night."

I not sleep.

"Neither will I, but it's yours anyway. Ella steeled herself. "I have some fish hash and potatoes for you."

Vær så snill, he signed. I want wait at window. He was restless. Kind as she was, he couldn't play this role with her much longer. He didn't want to be in the apartment. He didn't want to be in any part of the village.

As soon as she left, Haugland turned back to the window. A little drama was unfolding by the seawall. It was a relief to see Helmer Stagg and Grimstad back from their trip, but they were in a heated discussion with a soldier who kept gesturing toward the warehouse. He strained to listen when the German started to shout and push. Grimstad was equally charged, swinging his medical bag and pointing up the road to the ridge. Speaking in excellent German, he told the soldier of his medical emergency hours earlier and why he was needed up in the village.

Haugland groaned. *Don't get arrested.* His prayer was answered when Schiller suddenly showed up with another officer. He appeared upset, barking at the soldier. Then it was over. Sending the soldier back into the warehouse, he spoke a few words to Grimstad then bowed. The doctor took off, tugging on Helmer's arm.

The waterfront became quiet. Though only four-thirty in the afternoon, it was totally pitch-black out except for a hooded light mounted on a pole next to the seawall. Underneath were two soldiers. Haugland stared at the soldiers and knew he could do nothing for any of the men.

Out in the living room, the door opened and closed as Ella went down into the shop and *konditori*. He hoped he hadn't offended her. It was very difficult now pretending to be at everyone's mercy, needing protection when he was capable of taking care of himself. The urge to speak and tell her what was really going on had been overwhelming, but it was best she didn't know who he really was. She could be questioned.

Haugland pulled a wood chair to the window. He took his gun from his jacket and checked the clip. He fingered the pill in the little fob pocket of his pants. He closed his eyes and in his mind saw his own end. He must remember that. It must always be before him.

The office door to Kjell's warehouse opened and closed as two men stepped out. One of them was Schiller, the other a man Haugland hadn't seen before, but Gestapo for sure. They stood briefly in the muffled light flooding out over them, then Schiller took off. The soldiers stood at attention as he passed by and held the pose long after under the other German's eye.

Two men came down to the seawall and the soldiers stopped them to check their papers and passes. It was the mailboat skipper and his mate. There was some exchange of words, then they were permitted to board. The boat started up and after casting off, moved out onto the inky black water. Haugland heard them go passively, each chug of the motor taking the W/T further away from the village. The resistance would pick it up and hide for safekeeping.

For two hours he sat and watched until his backside ached. He could see and hear everything through the single paned glass window. Soldiers came and went. Then, sometime around ten at night, a soldier came over to get food. As soon as Ella left, Haugland put on his heavy winter coat and crept down the back kitchen stairs to the ground below.

It was very cold. Pulling up his collar, Haugland got his bearings. The back of the building rested close to the ridge, Ella's second story apartment roof peeking above it on its northern end. The stairs, however, were just opposite the snowy trail that led up to the top. He sprinted up the trail to the field on top and over to the safety of the bare trees that bordered the schoolhouse lane. Further down was Helmer Stagg's darkened house. When he felt it was safe, he dashed across the icy road and around to the back. At the kitchen door, he knocked lightly. He was relieved when the fisherman answered.

"Jens! You gave me a start. Come in. *Doktor* Grimstad is here."

Haugland slipped in and unbuttoned his coat. The kitchen was warm, making his cheeks tingle. Grimstad sat by the woodstove with a medical book in his lap. When he saw Haugland he nearly dropped it.

"Jens. I was wondering how we'd get in touch with you."

"I saw you have that tussle with the soldier. Is everything all right? How are the airmen?"

"They're handed off. Had no trouble getting Helmer's boat through controls, but Petter and your friend Tommy had a devil of a time getting the airmen out to the channel. The Canadian was in bad shape. Slowed them up by several hours. I did what I could with the wound. They're away."

For the first time, Grimstad noticed Haugland's wound. "What happened to you?"

"Got roughed up by some soldiers looking for the W/T."

"Let me look, Jens." Grimstad put aside his book and took up his medical bag.

Fifteen minutes later, Haugland had a cleaned wound and two stitches. All the time Grimstad worked, they talked about the men in the warehouse and what they should do. Haugland told him the W/T was gone, no longer a threat. As soon as it was safe, he would leave for good.

"What if the soldiers come for you?" Helmer looked worried.

Haugland pinched the pill in his pocket and shrugged. "I'll deal with it if that happens. I only regret is that Kjell will be fair game, especially if they continued to hold him."

"Would you like some tea?" Grimstad asked, like everything was normal.

"*Takk*. I have to get back. Ella will fret if she finds me gone. He paused. "Hans, you should prepare a rucksack and skis and be ready to go at a moment's notice. Do think you could brave the *fjell*? I'll draw a map to where to find Tommy." He made a quick sketch in his notebook.

Grimstad took the sheet. "As a boy, I went there often. With restrictions since the war, not so much. I think I could find my way across. Even in the snow. *Ja*, I can see the way to go."

Haugland looked at Helmer. "You too. Chances are, you won't be connected, but I want you to be ready." He put away his notebook. "Pray God, it won't come to that."

"It doesn't matter, Jens," Helmer said. "I've been proud to help. Don't you forget that."

"Go on back, Jens," Grimstad said. "If you have to bolt today, we'll understand. You must save yourself. With the war's end so near, our country can't afford to lose good people."

Haugland stood with his hand on the doorknob. In a way, he expected them to say that and knew they meant it, but how hard to walk away and leave them. All they wanted to do was to help, but neither really guessed how unmerciful the power that opposed them was. They were thinking only of the Germans. Haugland thought of Rinnan and was afraid for them. He stepped out into the frigid night air, wondering if he would ever see them again.

He put on his gloves and stepping onto the snowy road started back the way he came. Suddenly, a light shone on him. He froze as a group of soldiers approached dressed in their white winter gear. The gun in his pocket felt exposed. He wondered about his pill.

"Attention," a soldier said in broken Norwegian. "You stay stop."

Haugland stopped, stilling his instinct to bolt as the group crunched their way across the snow. Its leader shined the flashlight in his face. He looked away then thought better of it.

"I know him," one of the soldiers said in German. He made a circle around his ear. "*Gehörlos. Taub.*" At least they knew he was supposedly deaf. Dumb. Or crazy.

He took out his medical pass and pointed to the new stitches on his head, praying they wouldn't pat him down. He signed his anxiety.

The lead soldier adjusted his rifle and read the pass. Another twisted his head to see the stitches, bombarding him with the light again. "Hmph. Where stay? Cabin?"

He played dumb. A soldier responded with a kick, sending him sprawling into the snow facedown. They laughed as he got to his feet, his coat caked with powdery ice. One more push and they sent him on his way, but he was free. He did not look back.

***

During the night, a strong wind blew up, knocking out a power line to the Tourist Hotel and the buildings on the waterfront. It took hours to have it restored. The men at the warehouse stayed in darkness until six in the morning, when a weary Schiller came down and gave orders to let the men return to their homes. Trondheim had decided that since the signal had come only once from the village, it had been a ruse. Its source was out in the valley, miles away. The patrols would concentrate there. The men were released having been subjected to little or no mistreatment.

***

Sorting was in the *landhandel* when he heard that Hansen was leaving.

"For where?" he asked as he took his purchases off the counter.

Fru Riess shrugged. "I don't know."

Curious, Sorting went down to the waterfront. He came in time to see a small party exit the *konditori.* In the group were Kjell Arneson, Ella Bjornson, Pastor Helvig, and the schoolmaster Stagg. A few others followed. Hansen was dressed in his Sunday suit and carrying a valise.

"Where's he going?" Sorting asked a fisherman near the seawall.

"Oslo. I heard Jens will work and learn a new trade. The Deaf Church has arranged it."

Stunned, Sorting watched the group walk across the snow-cleared path to the wharf. This was unexpected. He had heard Hansen had quit at the Hotel. Like Bugge, Arneson was having trouble paying bills. Sorting never expected the deaf-mute to leave. They were a team. Hansen was a courier to the undefined group here. Why would he leave?

Sorting looked at the valise and thought Hansen was carrying something illegal. A W/T could fit in it. He watched for the soldiers who had continued to patrol the waterfront, but they only asked Hansen for his travel papers. Hansen's friends stood around him, some of them interpreting for him.

When the mailboat arrived, Hansen picked up the valise. To everyone's surprise, including Hansen's, it flopped open, spilling shirts, socks, and travel kit onto the icy boards of the wharf. As people rushed to help, Sorting saw to his disappointment that there was nothing illegal at all. Certainly no W/T. The clothing was stuffed back in while humorous comments were made. By the time everything was set back in place and closed up, the boat was nearly alongside them. The good-byes began.

They're taking it hard, Sorting thought. Ella Bjornson was usually an unemotional bitch, but there were tears in her eyes. Arneson was a bit subdued. Only the pastor seemed to be holding up well, shaking Hansen's hand and wishing him the very best. "Write as soon as you are settled. We're so glad you're able to make this change."

Hansen climbed down and stood at the boat's stern. When he was settled, the boat's motor started up. As the boat's siren sounded, Sorting came over to the edge of the wharf and watched as the boat pulled away.

"Good-bye," Bjornson said, signing some gibberish Sorting would never understand.

Hansen signed something back. He raised his hand at them and then looked straight at Sorting and smiled. Just a little bit.

CHAPTER 80

Knocking quickly, A.C. Kjelstrup looked carefully up and down the third floor hallway. From inside, he could hear a rustling, then the latch was turned and the door opened against its chain. On the other side was Freyda Olsen. Brushing her pale hair back off her forehead with her hands, she pulled her silk kimono tight around her voluptuous body and smiled sweetly at him.

"Ragnar. What are you doing here? I had no idea you were in Trondheim."

She undid the chain and invited him into the apartment. Freyda Olsen was an exotic creature, a woman who transcended the drab life of the occupation. She always looked provocative, always smelled of fine perfume that wafted around her like a light summer cloud. He couldn't see her working in an office.

She closed the door and padded barefoot to the kitchen. Her toenails, he noticed, were polished a bright red color. He wondered if she had any clothes on underneath.

"Help yourself to the telephone, Ragnar. It's by the sofa. Rika is probably going to lunch in about forty minutes. I'm going to get dressed. I have the day off." She left him and closed the door to her bedroom. A short time later he could hear water running in a bathtub.

Quickly, he made his call, surveying the apartment while he waited. He hadn't been here since the night he spent with Rika. Since then, it had gone through a sparkling transformation as its tenant prepared for Christmas. A small tree had been trimmed with ornaments and foil angels.

On the coffee table, next to a bowl of pinecones, were little wooden Christmas *nissen*, clever little trolls dressed in red coats and caps. Elsewhere, there were other bright and cheerful decorations. Kjelstrup couldn't believe Christmas was only ten days away. The most festive time in Norway was blurred and distant.

It took a couple of minutes to get through to Rika. They agreed to meet at the cathedral. They hadn't seen each other in nearly six weeks—although they had written to each other constantly. After he hung up, instead of elation, Kjelstrup felt edgy and irritable. Maybe it wasn't such a good idea to see her.

They went to dinner at a small hotel restaurant where they talked about their wedding plans for St. John's Day. Kjell had given them his permission to marry.While A.C. shared Rika's joy, he kept drumming his fingers on the table, looking furtively into corners of the room.

"A.C.? Is this something you really want? Please tell me."

He kissed her hand. "Of course. I love you. Don't ever forget that." He leaned over the cloth-draped table. "Just bear with me. I can't come into Trondheim for a while. Capitulation isn't going to come by Christmas after all." He gave her a tight smile, then paid the bill.

Outside, the streets were pitch-black, the city lights out. No light strayed from windows. They groped their way down toward the bridge over the river Nid to Oya. They were close when they heard the tramp of boots. They couldn't turn back. Frightened, A. C. pushed her against the stone wall of the nearest building and began to kiss her roughly.

"Let them see us," he warned, "then we will walk through. It's our only chance." As the patrol came closer into sight, he hurriedly opened her coat and groped her body with his hands. He knew his mouth was hard and unfeeling; that the stones hurt her back. "Shh. Not a word."

A soldier shined his light on them and discovering their lover's plight, made a raucous, crude comment in German. Other soldiers joined him.

Finally, the soldier said "Go home," in Norwegian. "Unless the lady wants some additional company." His companions behind him began to titter as A.C. and Rika slipped away from the wall to pass them. Seeing he was lame, the comments became more graphic and echoed behind them.

Twenty minutes later, they were at Freyda's apartment. Rika burst into tears.

"I'm sorry. I had to do it," A.C. said. "Did I hurt you?"

"*Nei*, I'm not hurt. Just shaken. I thought for sure we'd be arrested, but I don't understand what's wrong. You've been jumpy even before the soldiers found us."

A.C. cleared his throat. "I'm being watched. Some people I know were arrested. I think I should get out to Sweden."

Rika gasped.

"Problem is, I'm not sure where to start." On the table was a wine bottle with a note from Freyda. She would be gone for the night. He felt nothing until Rika touched his shoulder.

"I know how."

"You?"

Rika turned him around. "I've been working with an export group for the past couple of months. I can make contact right away. If you're lucky you'll be out in forty-eight hours."

A.C. decided to open the wine. While he poured, he asked questions until he was satisfied about her organization's security. He smiled at her. "All right. I'll do it."

"Wonderful. It will be my Christmas present."

They talked about the occupation, the horrific new German assault on the continent, the way he might be taken over the border to Sweden. Somehow the name Ryper came up.

"Do you know him?" Rika asked. "He's the leader of the whole line out there in the islands. Paul has done work with him."

"I don't know a Ryper, Rika. Besides, it's best not to say."

"Well, Frode then. They're the same. Someday, I'm supposed to meet him."

"Frode? Where did you hear the name Frode?" He felt a sudden chill go down his back. That was Jens Hansen's code name. "It couldn't be Frode. Who told you that?"

"My cell leader. He's done work with him. What's wrong, A.C.?"

"Nothing. I'm just jumpy."

"For nothing, you've turned awfully pale. Oh, sweetheart, I want you out more than ever. I'm going to call first thing in the morning."

"All right," he said blankly, patting her arm. He put the wineglass down on the coffee table. *I've had too much to drink*, he thought. I'm misunderstanding everything I hear. She couldn't possibly know that name. Suddenly he was afraid. "Any chance you could go too?"

"I don't think there's room," Rika said. She took his hand. "The routes are dangerous for the guides as well as those being exported. They only take those with the greatest need."

"Meaning me."

"*Ja*. Oh, darling. I want you to go. I want you to be safe." Slipping her arm through his, she kissed him on his cheek, then his lips. Wanting her, he turned off the light.

After spending a bittersweet night together, they left at seven in the morning. Rika promised he could contact her in a few hours and get the details on where he would meet. He gave her a long, final kiss before stepping out, knowing this could be the last time they would spend together for a long time. He might not see her again for months.

Not long after they left, a door to an apartment across the hall opened up and a thin, brown-haired man stepped out cautiously. Looking carefully up and down the corridor, he walked lightly to Freyda's door and taking a key out, quickly unlocked it. Without bothering to turn on the lights, he went straight to the coffee table by the sofa and feeling with his long fingers along its main side, pushed in a hidden panel. Sliding it, he exposed a reel-to-reel recorder. He turned some buttons to rewind the tape, then removing it, slipped the reel into an inner pocket of his coat. He closed up the panel, locked Freyda's door and returned to his own apartment where he set up the tape and listened to it. A half-hour later, he was on the phone.

"We've got it, Chief. Kjelstrup knows something for sure."

"Good," said the voice on the other end. "Wait for Freyda's call. We'll allow them to meet one more time to avoid suspicion then pick him up within the next forty-eight hours."

CHAPTER 81

Anna pulled the *dyne* over Lisel's shoulders and checked for fever again. It was disappointing to have her sick again. She had hoped the last time was the end of it, but now she was becoming resigned to an entire winter of illness. Like the weather, it bore down on her. She smoothed the cloth, got up, and burst into tears.

The three weeks since Jens had left had been especially hard. People had calmed down since the arrest of the men, but the village wasn't the same. She felt real solidarity to resist the remaining *quislings* in Fjellstad. The villagers couldn't make war on the German soldiers but they could on the Fosses and Reisses of the world that played friend to them. They did it with snubs and silences grown deeper and more bitter since the arrest of the ten men.

Unfortunately, hostility toward her increased too, something *Doktor* Grimstad commented after he finished looking at Lisel. She knew why. Someone had seen Schiller kiss her. Any time a soldier went out the fjord road toward her house the gossip increased. *Tyskertøs*. German cozy. She was having an affair. She was spying for Schiller.

Anna brushed the tears streaming down her cheeks. She could tell herself it had been worth it. That she had shown courage she wished she had for Einar. Yet, she had no idea if it worked. There was no one to congratulate her and say well done, so she had to tell herself she had done the right thing for the one she loved. *Ja*, she did love Jens Hansen. For him she had to fight back alone against the latest round of insults without losing her dignity.

There was movement in the hall. Gubben came down, rubbing against the door frame.

"Gubben, you silly." She motioned for the cat to come, but it pirouetted away and then came back, sliding its body in time to its loud purr. "Gubben." It trotted away at a creak in the hall. Anna froze, crossing her arms over her breasts when a tall shadow stood in the doorway. "Oh, God. Jens!"

"Are you all right, Anna? I heard you were having trouble so I came." He stepped lightly to her side and helped her up.

"It's nothing," she said.

"But it is to me." He wiped her wet cheeks with his thumbs. "I can't stand you being mistreated. I wish I could change it." He pulled her to him so her hands rested against his chest. "How can I say, `Look, this woman is mine and she's as brave and loyal as the rest of you. She slipped a W/T out from under the Germans' noses.'"

"It's all right. The time will come."

"I wish to God it was now. For both your sakes." He smiled faintly at her. "You were very brave and I thank you."

"Then everything was worth it. The insults and the shame. Nothing happened with Schiller you know."

"I know."

She began weeping again. "You shouldn't be here, Jens. You'll get found out."

"Everything will be worth it." He followed her lips with a finger.

She waited expectantly for a kiss, but it didn't come on her mouth. It came on her wet eyes, sweet and sensuous. He crushed her to him, whispering, "Anna." The power of his passion took her breath away. Suddenly he stopped. Lisel was awake and looking at them.

"Mama?"

Anna slipped out of Hansen's arms and came over to the bed. "It's all right, Munchkin. It's Jens. He's come to see us." She looked back at him and Hansen nodded his head. "See?"

Lisel looked at him with fevered eyes but she seemed sleepy and distant. "Where's Gubben?" she asked in a little voice.

"In the hall. I'll get him." She started to leave, but Hansen was ahead of her and brought the cat back to the bed. Lisel tucked it under the *dyne* then said dreamily, "*Takk*, Pappa," and went back to sleep. Hansen stayed by her for a moment then turning off the light, stood up.

"I'm sorry, Jens."

"Oh, it's just as well she doesn't remember. It would be hard to explain. I hope that she'll get well soon." He turned. "Come into the *stue*, Anna. I need to talk to you."

By the stove, he opened his rucksack. He handed her an envelope.

"What is it?" Inside she found several forms and papers, one stamped with some insignia.

"They're for you to put in your box down in the dairy for safekeeping. If you continue to have trouble, take them to Grimstad and if he's unable to help, see Ella Bjornson. It shouldn't come into German or *quisling* hands, only people like Hans, Ella, and Kjell."

"She doesn't like me at all."

"She doesn't know you."

She looked at the papers. "This is an affidavit."

"*Ja*," he said. "The original's down near Kristiansund N. with the resistance. For safe keeping. It's a part of a longer legal document that absolves you of any wrongdoing in Lillehavn."

Anna gasped.

"I'm giving you these papers because you mustn't count on me. I realized that when I heard the gossip about you since I left. I may not be here for you when I promised that."

"You're leaving the district?"

He didn't answer and the emptiness of that struck at her. He was speaking of the possibility of his own death. He came closer to her.

"I love you. Remember that." He touched her arm. "I've been working south of here, but I'm going to Trondheim in a few days. It will be very dangerous. The arrest of the men here in Fjellstad three weeks ago was a part of a much larger crackdown throughout the region."

"Must you go?"

"*Ja*. The Germans counterattacked the Allies on the continent. A total surprise. The Americans are calling it the Battle of the Bulge. Despite this, our country must plan for a good outcome. More help is coming. I'll be meeting people about that. I'm not sure when I'll return here. Rinnan, the little man you saw at Lillehavn, has spies and associates everywhere. He may be looking for me." He returned to his rucksack and brought out some wrapped packages. He handed her the smallest one. "Something for you."

She removed the paper from the box. Inside was an ornate silver brooch with delicate appendages laying on a piece of old cotton padding.

"It's beautiful, Jens. *Tusen takk*."

"Do you like it?"

"*Ja*. It reminds me of a little village near Bergen where all the women dressed in traditional clothes—right out of the newsreels. I'll wear it for you."

He pinned it on the neck of her dress. "I love you, Anna Fromme," he murmured. Remember, he signed.

Assured Lisel would sleep for a while, they crept into Anna's bedroom where they made love and slept entwined until her alarm clock went off at one-thirty. Rising together, she helped him dress, then went outside with him. A new moon, only days old, hung low in the winter sky.

"I'll do my best to get back to you," he said. "I just don't know my next orders." They walked around to the side of the house that faced the woods opposite his former cabin, their boots scrunching in the snow. "Don't forget to cut a tree for Lisel and to put the packages under it. There are surprises for both of you."

Anna smiled, but her lips trembled. She couldn't tell if it was the cold or her sense of loss on his leaving. "Lisel already wants to make the porridge for the Christmas *nissen* she thinks lives in the barn. We're going to put it out Little Christmas Eve."

At the entrance to the path to the cabin, he took her hand and held it for a moment, then reluctantly backed away. The moon came out behind a cloud and lighting the frigid ground with pale silver light. When she tried to make out his features, she couldn't see them as he waved one last time.

That image would haunt her for months to come.

CHAPTER 82

A.C. Kjelstrup exported out on the evening of December19th. Meeting Rika near the Marketplace, they followed instructions given to her and went to an apartment in the Brattorgata section of the city. A middle-aged woman gave him papers and clothing.

"A taxi will take you to the bus station and put you on a bus to the country north of Trondheim. There someone from export will meet you and take you to the border. Good luck."

The bus trip took an hour. A.C. held Rika in his arms as they talked in low voices about their plans for the future and what that would bring. He still felt nervous, but more in control of his bowels than he had been a week ago when he first felt he was being watched

The bus pulled in at a stop outside a *bakeri,* closed for the night. Stepping out into the black, cold night air scented of pine trees and a half-frozen dirt, Rika and A.C. looked around for their ride. As soon as the bus pulled away, a black Ford two-door sedan came alongside.

A man rolled down the window. "*God kveld*, Sonja," he said to Rika.

A.C. peered into the darkened interior. "Paul? What happens now?"

"The first in a series of stops that will put you near the border. Then you'll go by skis."

Paul got out of the car. "You say your good-byes now," he told Rika. "You'll be going with me by another car back to Trondheim."

"When will I hear from A.C.?" She held his hand tightly.

"Be patient. It's hard to get word out of the refugee camps where he'll most likely end up. It might be several months. But we will certainly let you know he's over."

A.C. gave her one last kiss and a strong hug. "Wait for me, Rika," he said.

"I promise." She took his hand and held it until the car slowly drew away. "Good-bye."

***

The car went north then east for several miles through a deep forest track. On the dark road, the tall pines loomed over them, making A.C. feel closed in. He should have been happy, but he was still apprehensive. The driver, however, was an agreeable fellow and soon had his fears calmed.

At a junction in the road, the car slowed down and stopped.The driver explained that the furnace was acting up. He got out in the middle of the country lane and went back to check, leaving the car lights and engine on. A.C. rubbed his face and realized he hadn't shaved. He felt so tired. His leg hurt. He leaned back against the car seat and scrunching down, closed his eyes. He didn't hear the sound behind him until it was too late. By then the rag slammed down over his nose and mouth had begun its damage. The arm around his neck was like a vise. He took a breath and drew in chloroform, and on the third attempt to resist fell unconscious.

When he came to, A.C. was lying face-down on a cold concrete floor in the close, pitch-black space. Turning his aching head to find his bearings, he was struck by the smell of urine and mold. A narrow slit of light seeped out at the bottom of a door. His heart contracted. On the verge of panic, he tried to recall the last moments before he had passed out. He started to sit up when he heard the scuff of boots coming down a hallway, then voices speaking German.

Oh, God, he thought. This isn't happening. Rika! Maybe he was being hidden for some reason. Maybe something happened. Boot steps stopped outside the door. The key turned. He put his arm over his eyes to protect against the glare smashing into them as the metal door opened.

"Get up, gimp," a small man said in Norwegian in a low resonant voice. He wore the uniform of the German SD. Another uniformed man tapped a truncheon in the palm of his hand.

A.C. hopped to the door. His bad leg had gone to sleep and the resulting pain was tortuous. How mild that would seem in the hours that followed. Beaten and questioned about names and incidents, he was horrified to realize they knew a great deal about the organization out in the islands. And always the name Ryper and Frode to a tune of a whipping. Who the hell was Ryper? Why did they want to know about a stupid deaf-mute?

"We know about your boat coming into Trondheim," the German yelled in A.C.'s bloody face. "We know about the shipment of arms."

When he returned to his cell, A.C. knew he had been betrayed, knew he was in Trondheim at the notorious Mission Hotel. Rika was in danger too for she had returned with Paul. He cried out her name but tried to hold his tongue against the assault on his body and mind.

He slept and dreamed he was on a mountainous battlefield near Kvam where he had been wounded fighting the Germans. Nothing had been worse than his transport from the battlefield to a makeshift hospital further up the line. Nothing worse than the pain and delirium after the medical unit was captured by German soldiers. When he woke on his pallet in the cell, his leg was on fire but nothing prepared him for sadistic treatment that awaited him.

"Heavenly Father, A.C. screamed. "Save me." It no longer mattered to him that he cried like a helpless baby. He was beyond pain. Knowing he was completely without help, his resolve weakened as he sought an end to his agony. Delirious from injuries to his internal organs, the names of men from the islands slipped from his lips. Name by name the network was revealed. Ankers was Kjell Arneson. Frode was Jens Hansen.

CHAPTER 83

Sorting put down the receiver and looked around the *landhandel.* No one seemed to be curious about him making a call, but there was a noticeable chill between him and the fishermen he couldn't ignore. Since the holding of the ten men, people were down right giving him the cold shoulder. It was Birger, he thought. Somehow they saw a connection between the two of them and the troubles when the search was on for the transmitter.

Well, it doesn't matter now, he thought. It will be over in a matter of hours. The boats were coming and the Chief wanted him to stay until they came. Rinnan was pleased. The whole operation was now exposed thanks to his little scheme with Rika Arneson. Innocent and trusting, she had condemned her father and an organization up to fifty people. The *razzia* would strike simultaneously at Fjellstad and the island homes of Sig, Holger and Sig's other sons.

At the counter, some women were talking. They were dressed for the cold, drizzly weather that had hit that morning. Christmas, despite the decorations hanging around the cash register, seemed remote and insignificant.

"Are you done, *Herr* Sorting?" *Fru* Reiss asked. *Quisling* that she might be, he didn't feel any comradeship with her. He had never been interested in NS politics or Nazi platitudes. They were all windbags as far as he was concerned, only the German windbags had more air.

"*Ja, takk.* I'll take that package now, too," he said. He was aware the women were looking at him. He ignored them and left after paying. Outside it was dark. The temperature had dropped. Snow coming? He wouldn't go out to his hut—the Chief would want him to stay in. He thought of going out to see the widow, but it was too far out.

Suddenly, he thought of Bette. Her father, he had learned only last night, had gone to N. Frøya to see an aged aunt and would not be back until just before Christmas. Why not see her? He needed a dry, warm place to sleep in the village and he really didn't care if it was the sofa. She was quite taken with him, but he had never acted on her romance magazine fantasies. She might do him a favor, though. In the end, Sorting got what he wanted.

"Why, Odd," Bette said coyly, half covered by the door. "Of course you can stay. I'm so sorry about your stove pipe."

She led him down the hallway to the *stue*. It was a small room covered with pictures of Christ with the multitudes or Christ with little children. Velvet curtains smothered the only window. He took his cap off and smiled. Her blue eyes blinked back. He felt a strange flick of desire for her. "You're very kind," he said. "Your Pappa won't object?"

"Pappa is away. I'm a grown woman, don't you know."

"So you are," he smiled. Then in the oppressive atmosphere of her father's house, he seduced her, feigning his respect for her. He took the sofa with a *dyne* to keep him warm, preparing for a good night's sleep, but she stayed. One thing led to another. He soon had her half dressed and panting. "You are so lovely." He stroked a bare arm.

The girl blushed. Naive and inexperienced, she did whatever he wanted. When he was satiated, he slept, waiting in her deep feather bed for the boats to come.

CHAPTER 84

"Going to snow." Sig put down his hooded lantern by Magnus who was working on the generator for the dock lights. They had turned it off early last night to save their rationed fuel.

Magnus blew on his bare hands. "*Ja*. I can feel it in my bones. Let me give it a pull again, Father." He pulled hard on the starter line and the motor sputtered to life. The lights came on slowly, first hitting the wide boards of their small wharf, then the water beyond.

"What is that?" Magnus said standing up.

Sweeping out of the dark Nordic dawn came two German deep-sea motor cruisers heading straight for the landing. Soldiers crowded at the bows.

"Run, Father!" Magnus shouted.

"We cannot run," Sig said in resignation. "It's too late." Charging off the top of hill behind their barn and store, soldiers of the SD swept down toward them. As they circled the buildings, some soldiers broke down the doors and smashed windows with rifle butts. Some crammed their way inside the store. Others seized Sig and Magnus. Sig winced and tried to shake them off, but was rewarded with a slap to the side of his head.

"Move," a soldier said in broken Norwegian.

Sig moved, but not before he glimpsed the main boat docking and probing the wharf with its blinding eye of light. A tall blonde man stepped down and ordered more soldiers to fan out ahead of him. In minutes, Sig and Magnus were herded into the store where his grandson Einar and nephew Arne Finn were standing in their nightclothes

"Sit down, old man." The man threw him onto a box. The action hurt Sig's hip, but not as much as the racket up in the apartment where the women were just getting up. He could hear the sounds of soldiers rifling the cupboards and armoires for illegal material. A woman screamed.

My Andrina Paal, Sig thought and closed his eyes. With dread, Sig heard thudding noises as his daughter was taken into a back room. She screamed. An eerie silence followed. A few minutes later, a soldier displaying bright red scratches on his face came down with the radio.

The man began to yell at Sig. Birger Strom, Sig thought someone called him. It was hard to accept that one of his own countrymen could be so cruel. Even though this man had good working information on the roles he and his sons had played in delivering arms and agents, Sig said nothing. Two soldiers came forward to hold him, but he did not cry out when Strom roughed him up, staining his white hair with so much blood that it turned pink.

"Father!" Magnus shouted, but he was knocked back against the wall with a rifle butt.

"Bring everyone's paperwork here." Strom gloated when he learned Arne Finn was deaf. He pushed Finn onto the box and had him beaten. Sig still didn't say anything.

About an hour later, another cruiser arrived. Sig's heart sagged when he saw his son Holger, daughter-in-law and his grandchildren Ulstein and Astrid. There were also some Hitra men the Germans had swept up in the *razzia*. Once again the men were separated out and the women sent upstairs. Sig and Holger were moved from the store to his barn where they were questioned.

"Where are Ankers and Frode?" Strom shouted. "How long have you worked with them?"

In a well-orchestrated program of terror, each man was alternately moved back and forth between the barn and the store. On one occasion, proud *Fru* Haraldsen was ordered down for questioning, but she remained resolute. But no one gave way.

Sig dared to look at her as she was marched back to the store and gave her a thin smile.

Our all for Norway.

By noon, the *razzia* had risen to a fever pitch. At least, Sig thought it was noon. The sun had finally come up, a stale butter globe in a pasty sky hovering at winter angle. With deliberate malice the Germans sat him on barrel outside and paraded his dog and cat before him, then shot their heads off with a machine gun. The action made him jump. "*Gud*," he groaned through clenched teeth and turned away. Across the water smoke rose from his neighbor's barren island.

The soldiers threatened to kill their cow the same way, but their officer ordered a rope thrown around her horns. Then a soldier took Magnus's motorboat and hauled her off far from shore where he threw a net over her and watched her struggle and bawl until she drowned. Behind him, his daughter-in-law fell sobbing to the ground. Sig said nothing, but he grieved inwardly when the first of several fishing boats were taken out into the channel and blown up. He felt numb.

As men were brought from the island of Hitra and smaller skerries, they were put into the store, but eventually the men were loaded on a cruiser for Trondheim.

Sig looked back at his home as he was dragged up on deck. He knew he would never see it again. He spied *Fru* Haraldsen standing in the door. His hands were bound so he bowed stiffly to her. He wanted to cry, but he would not cry. Not on this day. He kept staring back even as he was pushed down below to the belly of the boat until he could not see his homestead anymore.

CHAPTER 85

Kjell sat up with a start. Had he heard something? Since his detainment three weeks ago, he didn't sleep well and often woke in the tight hours of early morning and walked around the house checking windows. He felt for his gun set in its holster and was reassured by its blunt stock. He was grateful Jens had given it to him. He listened to creak of the house against a low wind outside and decided things were normal. Slowly, he lowered his head back onto his pillow and thought of the herring season.

"Be ready," Hansen had warned.

Ready? He'd rather be ready to fish. He missed his girls, but his feelings of loneliness grew stronger after Jens left. It was extraordinary how Jens had impacted his life, how much like a son he had become. Kjell smiled in the dark. They had said good-bye only yesterday afternoon at the fishing hut where Hansen had moved his headquarters and continued to coordinate runs from the Shetlands. Sverre had come down to take him to Trondheim to meet with people from XU.

"I'll be back at the hut for Christmas," Hansen said, then was gone.

Kjell looked at the clock's dial glowing in the dark. 5:25. Perhaps it was the old habit of rising for the boats, but he decided to get up. He'd work around the house, might even take Ella's advice and put up some Christmas decorations. They were in some box the girls had put away. Ella had talked him into going to the church two weeks ago to celebrate a spontaneous St. Lucia's Day. The pastor thought it would do everyone good. In the church's darkened hall, the villagers gathered to watch the young daughters dressed in white and led by Ingrid Larsen with candles on her head, sing and tell the story of the saint. Kjell had been wet-eyed. Hadn't both his daughters done the same when they were young? When would he see them again?

He ate a small breakfast of canned herring and rye bread. He was restless and kept looking at his watch. Finally he decided to go out to the cabin. Hansen had asked him to make one final sweep then close it up. It was still night but he didn't expect to be hassled by a patrol.

Outside the snowy ground was hard and crunchy. Kjell cringed as he stepped carefully, but his neighbors were dead asleep under the waning moon. Even their dogs were silent. At the end of the schoolhouse lane he froze. A murky form emerged from the gloomy lane coming up from the waterfront. It was Helmer Stagg carrying a coil of rope on his shoulder.

"What are you doing up?" he asked in a low voice.

"Restless, I guess. You see Sorting? His boat never went out last night."

"Haven't a clue." Kjell looked over his shoulder. "What are you going to do now?"

"Not going to go back to bed," Helmer shrugged. "I miss fishing and hate doing nothing, so I thought I'd get ready for the herring season. I could use the money."

Kjell stamped his feet to get warmth in them. "I'm going out to Jens's cabin. You want to come? I have some English coffee he gave me. I'm going to make a pot while I work."

Helmer grinned. "Now that's a pleasant thought."

They slipped out to the cabin quietly. They were not in the village when the boats came.

CHAPTER 86

Anna woke at seven. Lisel curled up next to her deep in sleep. She was pleased Lisel's forehead felt cool. Finally. No fever. She dressed for the day. Out in the *stue* she put more wood into the stove. It was hard to believe that Little Christmas Eve was tomorrow night. She had cut a little tree for Lisel and put the packages Jens had given her on the table underneath. They had cut rye growing wild on the edge of the fields and made bouquets for the birds. Lisel had investigated the barn for signs of *nissen*. They would be ready as they ever would be.

At the window, she raised the curtain and looked out into the gloom of the mid-winter dawn. Dawn was still a ways off, but with a swelling moon in front of her she could see fairly well out into the fjord. On the porch, a sheaf of rye had blown down. She stepped out and picked up the sheaf. As she tied it back in place on the ornate wood railing, she looked down in the direction of Jens's cabin and to her surprise saw smoke rising above the trees.

Had he come back? He hadn't said anything about that but then she hadn't asked. He said he was going to Trondheim but he could have been telling her a half-truth. That somehow didn't bother her. She accepted him and what he did now. She watched the gray smoke drift up and she smiled. It would be nice if he was there, but that would be hoping too much. It was a new tenant. She hugged her arms and blew her breath out into the cold. The air was very damp. In the pale gray light, she could see little specks of snow falling. That reminded her of their first night together. So much had happened. *Jens. Be safe.*

She started back in, thinking about him in the most wonderful way, when suddenly, from the corner of her eye, something moved out on the water, like a winking light. Squinting, she peered into the moon-touched fjord and saw to her horror two large gray motor cruisers moving like arrows toward the wharf. She blinked and looked again. A sharp chill spread across her arms as the implication of the boats ran through her. Her eyes riveted to the rising smoke.

Jens! She must warn him or whoever was there. The worst possible thing was going to happen here. A *razzia*. It would make the troubles three weeks ago paltry compared to a raid like this because the SD would lead it and they would bring their own hardened troops. Her heart pounding, she tore back inside to her coat and boots. There was no time to speak to Lisel. She sprinted out the back door and down the hill to the path through the brambles and soon was on the trail down to the woodshed. How long ago that seemed!

When she came to the frozen bank, she stopped to catch her breath. The moonlight zigzagged down through the trees, leaving some areas in total dark. She descended carefully so not to slip as she had done the last time and carefully made her way to the back door. Inside she could hear someone moving around, but she didn't hear the person behind her until she was grabbed roughly by her hair and cap and slammed back into him.

"Bitch!" the man hissed. "What you are doing here?" He swung her around and pushed her hard against the wall, causing her to cry out. It was dark under the trees, but she could make out his face. He was a man in his twenties, someone she had seen on the docks. He grabbed her by the jaw and pushed her head back when she struggled.

She tried to move but he kept forcing her back against the hard logs of the cabin. His anger frightened her, but she did not lose her resolve. She kicked him on his ankle. The man yelled.

The door to the cabin swung open, its hard wood edge just missing her head.

"What the hell's going on?" the new man asked.

"Look who I caught snooping around." Her captor turned her head roughly toward the older fisherman. It was Jens's friend, Kjell Arneson. When he saw her, he froze.

"Anna Fromme?" He looked at her with unfriendly eyes and her heart sank. They would never believe her good intentions.

"*Vær så snill,*" she said through the tight clamp the man's hand made on her chin.

"Let her go, Helmer," Kjell said. Reluctantly the fisherman released her. "What are you doing here?" he barked.

"I've come to warn you. To warn Jens. The Gestapo's in the harbor. It's a *razzia*. Like Lillehavn. They will show no mercy until they have what they want."

"And what do they want?"

"They want Jens. And you... and all the ones that have helped him."

"What? Catch fish? They come for their quotas?" Helmer yelled. He put his face so close to hers she felt spit.

"*Vær så snill.* Go and you will see the boats. They will have troops and will be armed."

Kjell nodded to Helmer to go look at the fjord. After he left, Kjell stepped down close to her. "Why the concern, *Fru* Fromme? How did you know how to get here?"

"*Vær så snill.* I don't want to argue with you. I want to help you. Where is Jens? Has he gone to Trondheim? Tell me that he is away and safe."

Kjell started to say something when Helmer came rushing back. "God. The woman's right. E-Boats. Right in the harbor. They're unloading now."

Kjell murmured something under his breath. He looked at Anna as if he was recalling something. "Hansen is in Oslo. He went down over three weeks ago. I haven't heard from him since then."

"I have. I saw him this past Sunday."

"Saw?"

"Tell me he is gone and safe." When Kjell said he was both, Anna breathed a heavy sigh of relief. "*Gud er god.*"

"What did you do that for?" Helmer hissed.

"Because something's going on here I didn't see," Kjell answered.

Anna came away from the wall. "I wouldn't do anything to hurt him. He's my very dearest friend. The only person to believe me. I love him...." She laid a hand on her breast, imploring them to listen. She spoke directly to Kjell without fear now. "Let me help you. I know how Jens regards you. You can't go into the village. They will arrest and kill you."

Helmer glared at her. "Kjell."

"Let us hear what the lady proposes."

"I can hide you. They will not look long at my house. I have a hiding place in my cellar that's big enough for the two of you. You could hide for days if need be, until you could get away to the *fjell*."

"Really? You wouldn't tell your fine friends?" Helmer sneered. "Let's get away, Kjell."

"And do what with her? Won't she tell?"

"Take her into the woods and drop her off the ridge higher up."

"I don't think that would be in our best interest."

"Because she sleeps with the German officer?"

"Enough, Stagg. Leave the woman alone. Go out and see what's going on now." He said to Anna, "You, come inside." He took her by the arm, but was much gentler this time.

Anna stepped in ahead of him. The room had been cleaned up since the last time she had been here. The furniture had been pushed to the sides of the walls and bedding stacked on the bed frame. Kjell went over to the stove and shut it down.

When he finished, he looked at her. "How long have you been friends?"

"Since the summer," Anna said quietly. "After he came to work for me. It happened very gradually, then I saw Sorting for the first time. When Jens was so sick." She breathlessly told Kjell about Sorting's betrayal at Lillehavn. "I told Jens this and he believes me."

Kjell nodded. From outside, there came the heavy boots of Helmer running back.

"Christ, they're on the wharf. I can see soldiers running around. I think some are already on the schoolhouse road."

"There isn't any time, is there? We're going to have to trust this woman."

Anna was relieved. She smiled at him. "Oh, *tusen takk*. I will be so happy if I can do this for you. If only I could get in touch with *Doctor* Grimstad."

"You love him too?" Helmer growled.

"*Ja*, because he believes me and is my friend when everyone else isn't." She stopped. "Come quickly. It's starting to snow. If you come now, it will cover the tracks between this place and my house."

"Let me check the cabin one more time," Kjell said. "Don't want to leave anything. The fire's out the best I can do." He crossed the room to close the front door without locking it then headed out with Anna. "Close the door, will you Helmer? And bring that coffeepot," he said to a fuming Stagg.

Up in the house, Anna tiptoed into the kitchen and listened.

"Lisel is still asleep. I think that it will be best that she doesn't see you here. That way if the soldiers do come, she cannot say she saw anyone." She went to the space under the attic stairs and pushing aside a wicker laundry basket, exposed the trapdoor to the cellar. "This place is very old and I'm afraid cold. I will bring down food and things to keep you warm."

Kjell pulled up the door by its metal handle. Below the stairs descended into pitch-blackness. Anna gave him a flashlight and let him go first. Hesitantly, Helmer came down last.

"Here is the pantry. Do you see the back wall? There is a cave behind it."

She opened the door in the wall. The lantern was still on the nail where Hansen had hung it. She pulled matches from her pocket and lit it. "The door can be opened from the inside too, but I think I will put a small box in front of it to give it the appearance of a dead end."

Helmer came over and looked into the cave. "I don't think I can stand up in it. It's a trick, Kjell. We'll be trapped."

"We already are. She's right. We'd only be arrested. If we are to keep everyone else safe, then we must hide and get away when we can. You, Grimstad, and I are the only ones that really know about Jens. The rest only think of the missing boys."

"My grandfather..."

"The old schoolmaster can take care of himself. Don't you know that by now?"

Helmer looked sourly at Anna. "She's a stinking German like the others and a traitor. A stinking German whore."

"Enough, Helmer."

She stepped back. "You should get in it now. There is a rug over by the dairy. You can use it until I find a *dyne*."

Kjell retrieved the rug, an old scrap of Oriental design. "This is good. It's thick and warm and should cover us both."

"I'll bring your coffeepot," Anna said. "If you want, you can stay out of the cave, and leave the lantern on. I could signal you by banging a broom upstairs. Only the lantern might give yourselves away. The heat of the glass or its fumes. You can have the flashlight."

"Good point," Kjell said. "Tell me, how did you and Jens talk?"

"With his notebook at first, then... like this," I want to be your friend, she signed.

"Want to be your friend," he said. "You can sign."

"Jens taught me." I love him, she signed. "I know he works for the British. That he can speak." Backing away, she left them to the dark.

CHAPTER 87

"*Heil Hitler!*"

"*Heil Hitler*!" The young, athletic-looking aide standing in front of the Mission Hotel elevator greeted Martin Koeller and Franz Gebhardt, then directed them to follow him. They had just arrived in Trondheim.

"Is Flesch in?" Koeller asked, removing his gray gloves as they went down the hall.

"*Nein*. He's out of the city. But he has seen your report."

Koeller made a face. Ten hours on the train from Oslo. He was beat. "Where is he?"

"He's overseeing a major *razzia* on the coast. In the meantime, you're his guest. I think you'll find the room more than adequate." The aide opened a door to a well-appointed suite with silk carpets, maple wood furniture, paintings and velvet curtains. "Make yourself at home. There's an excellent staff here for meals and whatever else you need."

Koeller hid his frustration and said he would wait. "Are drinks possible?"

"You'll find what you need in the next room." He snapped his heels and bowed.

"Prig," Koeller muttered after the young man left. He marched into the next room of the suite and found a collection of bottles on a stand. "Make me a drink, Franz. *Bitte*."

Koeller refrained from snapping Gebhardt's head off. Since November sabotage activity had increased. Recently, three factories in Bergen had been blown up and threats on shipping around Oslo had increased. He wanted to finish his inquiry into the schoolteacher so that he could put his attention on that. It was the reason he had come north.

After uncovering information at Gestapo headquarters on the father, he took the picture of the son around Bergen. He had seen the schoolteacher's mother and took pictures and papers from her home. Armed with this new material they had uncovered the possibility of his involvement in espionage at the U-boat base. Someone thought his picture resembled a man who had worked there then disappeared after the death of a Norwegian in the pay of the Germans. No one had seen him since. Tore Haugland had to be an agent. It was a case they hoped to solve soon.

"What's taking you so long?" Koeller barked at him.

"Sorry, one of the bottles was low." Gebhardt handed over the mixed drink and when Koeller wasn't looking downed a drink of his own.

***

Haugland and Sverre arrived in Trondheim at five in the morning. After they secured the *Marje* near the fish market where Sverre planned to sell his catch, they ate a light meal and talked.

"I'm going to be gone all day,' Haugland said.

"No problem. It's been nearly two years since I've been in Trondheim. I'd like to see Nidros Cathedral. Maybe shop for Christmas. I saved some money for my wife and Bode."

"Let me add to that." Haugland opened his wallet. "See you at three." He said good-bye and disappeared into the early morning crowds. A half-hour later, it began to snow.

***

Rinnan was the first to get off the boats in Fjellstad. A large unit of armed soldiers of the SD followed him. Dressed in his SD second lieutenant's uniform, he didn't cut a stirring figure. As the soldiers fanned out over the waterfront and up the hill to the village in precise execution, however, it was apparent who was in charge. Moving swiftly, they struck at the office of Kjell Arneson and the *konditori*, speeding up toward the homes of Anders Stagg the schoolmaster, Arneson and *Doktor* Grimstad. Sorting had been thorough. He had provided a map.

Sorting was lying in bed when he heard sounds of boots tramping and voices yelling out on the schoolhouse road. Sitting up in the dim room, he looked down at the plump, naked body of Bette curled up next to him in the feather bed and wondered how he had done it. Her honey colored hair partially covered her face and shoulders, but he could see bruises on her neck. He remembered the weight of her breasts. Her bee-stung lips were inviting, but she was snoring now. Stupid country girl. She had thrown herself away so easily. He reached over to the side of bed and found his cigarettes. She had been entertaining, though. Too bad she hadn't been Fromme's widow. Now that would have been something. He lit a cigarette and took a drag, he deciding he would partially dress because the humiliation of the girl was his parting shot to the staid community. A community of peasants. He hated them like he hated all the tiny hamlets of the west and central Coast; like he hated the dismal logging town where he'd come from.

He picked at a piece of tobacco from the edge of his tongue. Outside he heard more shouting and then a scream. The soldiers were next door and then on the front door step pounding. He put on underwear and pants. Incredulously, the girl continued to sleep until there was the sound of glass breaking in the entryway.

"Odd?" The girl sat up like a shot, her little hands doing a poor job of covering herself. "Oh, God. What is going on? My Pappa? Ohhh. My Pappa has found out."

"It's not your stinking Pappa," Sorting put on his socks and shoes. Downstairs, the soldiers rushed into the rooms in the front and eventually finding the stairs, charged up in terrifying leaps. The house shook. Sorting got up and went over to the lace curtain. He tugged on the blind and watched it snap up, letting in the predawn light.

"Odd?"

Sorting said nothing, not even when four soldiers burst into the bedroom. She shrank against the headboard unable to utter a word, and tried to pull the coverlet up over herself.

Sorting flicked his ash on the floor. "You can have her."

"You Morkdal?" one of the soldiers asked.

"*Ja*." He snuffed out his butt on the wood night table. "You want to handcuff me? Might make things look better." He left his suspenders dangling, his fly and shirt open. A picture of hurriedness under embarrassing circumstances.

"All right," said the unit leader. "Anyone else in the house?"

"*Nei*. Her old man is gone on holiday. What a surprise."

While his hands were secured with handcuffs behind him, one of the soldiers went over to the bed and sat down beside Bette. Setting his helmet on the floor, he stroked her hair. Then he pulled down the coverlet. Bette began to weep.

"Odd!"

Sorting shrugged. "Let me know how it goes. We can compare notes." He went downstairs with two of the soldiers and was shoved out to the small crowd now in the lightly snow covered lane. Behind him the shopgirl began to scream.

***

As the light grew stronger, the *razzia* increased in intensity. All men age sixteen to sixty-five were ordered down to the Arneson warehouse. Some were picked out and sent over to the *konditori* and put under guard in the tearoom.

The women and children were sent to the church and locked in. Once the main part of the village was secured, the soldiers fanned out in confiscated vehicles or motorboats, going to pick up named individuals further out. It was a smooth, well-oiled operation but no one could find Kjell Arneson nor *Doktor* Grimstad. When Rinnan learned this, he flew into a rage because A.C. Kjelstrup had said Kjell Arneson was the main person in the whole operation. Sorting's reports confirmed it. No one seemed to know where he might be. Consulting with Sorting, an armed search party was sent out the fjord road to the cabin used by Jens Hansen in hopes that Arneson might be there. After he learned that Helmer Stagg—often seen in the company of Arneson— was also missing, soldiers were sent to tear apart their boats and look for contraband.

***

Anna stood at the window as motorcycles sped up the fjord road. The snow had continued to fall and sometimes the vehicles slipped. When they disappeared under the brow of her hill, she waited for them to come tearing up the driveway, but they didn't. Had they gone to the cabin? She ran to the hallway and grabbing her broom, banged the handle on the floor. If they weren't hidden now, the men should be.

"Mama?" Lisel padded over to her, rubbing her eyes. Her pink nightgown dragged on the wood floor. "What are you doing, Mama?"

"It's a game."

"Can I play?"

"*Nei.* Only mommies and daddies can. It's for Christmas."

Lisel looked at her solemnly, then laughed. "You look silly."

"It's a silly game. Come, Munchkin. Let's get dressed. We may have to go into the village."

"For presents?" Under the tree where there were presents. "Is this really from Jens?"

"*Ja*, Lisel, but you mustn't say anything to anyone. Not even *Tante* Marthe, even if she's your friend. It has to be a secret." Secret, she signed.

"All right, Mama." Lisel yawned, then scuffed down to her room.

Anna went back to the window. A truck was in her driveway. She smoothed her skirt and the Peter Pan collar at her throat. Pinned in the middle was the brooch Jens had given her and she touched it for courage. Courage for herself and her daughter. Courage for the men down below.

Anna answered the door before the small detachment had banged it down. In front of the group was someone she had seen with Schiller.

"This is the SD, *Frau* Fromme. They have instructions to look in every household. *Leutnant* Schiller thought it best you complied."

She drew back from the door. "*Vær så snill.* Let me get my daughter. The men can come in." She rushed down the hall, the sounds of the soldiers close behind. It was hard to keep calm. Had they not come the same way into her own home waiting for Einar to come back from his walk? Now as then, the soldiers moved systematically through the house climbing upstairs to the attic, pilfering the parlor, pulling things out of the linen closet in the bedroom hall. She stood in the *stue,* gently wrapping her arms around her daughter's shaking shoulders. Lisel drew back deeper when a soldier let out a whoop upon discovering the trapdoor to the dairy. Schiller's aide came over and asked if the dairy had electricity.

"It's not wired. You'll have to use a lantern."

Down in the dairy, the Germans fanned out knocking things over with their rifle butts. They investigated everything in the dairy and storage closets, then opened the door to the room that served as pantry. A soldier stepped in, going all the way to the back. He looked over the shelves that hid the door. Finding only stored flat bread and preserves, he announced that nothing was there and came out. The men milled around the room and then went back upstairs. Anna held back, trying hard not to show her relief. She wasn't naive to think that it was over. It was bone-chilling down here and could kill if Arneson and Stagg had to hide for any extended length of time. It could be days before they could get out. To her horror, she was told she had to go back with soldiers.

"All must be accounted for," the soldier said.

***

Rinnan gave schoolmaster Stagg and Pastor Helvig a heavy grilling at the *konditori*, but no one seemed to know where Kjell Arneson was. When a patrol coming back from the cabin said they found the remnants of a fire, another group of SD soldiers augmented by Schiller's own men went out to stumble around the snowy trails leading up to the *fjell.*

By noon, Rinnan was livid and hungry. He sent one of his men to the hotel kitchen, another to the church. "Bring me a woman," he said to Karl Dolmen, his second in command. Rinnan pointed to the German agent with him. "And one for Tauner."

Schiller came into the church with Dolmen and ten soldiers. Only two were from his unit, the only ones he could trust. The church, decorated for the Christmas season, was subdued and cold. No fire had been lit in the hall. In the pews over seventy hostages—women and young girls and a score of small children and babies—huddled together in fear. In the very back, Bette sobbed.

"Damn, it's freezing," Schiller said as he stepped onto the creaky floorboards. "Riker, Allman," he said to his men. "Go down and start the furnace."

When the soldiers were gone, he looked around for Anna. This was the most distasteful part of his assignment, but fearing difficulties for himself, he decided he'd better say nothing. He didn't trust this Rinnan and his man, Karl Dolmen. There was enough about both men to fear.

Awkwardly, he stood to the side and watched as Dolmen strolled up and down the front of the altar, asking each row to stand up when he told them to. After the third row stood up Dolmen stopped and stared at a pretty young girl not more than fifteen standing next to a heavyset middle-aged woman.

"You," Dolmen said, pointing to her. "Come here."

The girl stood rooted in a state of shock. Schiller recognized the woman next to her as the hotel's cook. *Marthe Larsen's daughter?* Some of the women muttered and shifted uneasily on their seats, but they could do nothing as the girl slipped out and stood trembling in the aisle.

"You'll do," Dolmen and nodded for the agent to take her. The girl blanched and appeared close to swooning. The cook began to sob.

"Now, another. You, sit down," he ordered the women in the row. "You," he pointed to the next, "Up."

Schiller cringed as Dolmen ranged his eyes over them falling at last on a woman who sat off to the side with her young daughter.

"You," he pointed and Anna stood up.

Nein, Schiller thought. Not Anna. The idea of her with that little bastard Rinnan made his stomach churn, but he was under orders to assist. His heart sank as she came forward to stand beside the Larsen girl. What happened next surprised him.

"Have you no shame?" he heard Anna say. "She's only a girl. Let me go alone. I will dine with your officer. Surely he would prefer a woman."

Dolmen licked his lips, then laughed. "All right," he said.

The girl began to shake. Anna put her arm around her shoulders. The room stilled. All the women in the sanctuary were looking at Anna. When the cook came up to get her daughter, her eyes were full of tears. Anna reassured her with a smile and touched her arm.

"*Vær så snill*. Keep Lisel safe for me. Your daughter for mine." Her eyes filled up too as she peeled her little girl's fingers off her skirt. "Go with *Tante*, Lisel. I'll be back soon."

She started toward her seat trying to ignore her daughter's wailing when Dolmen told her to stop. When she came back toward him, he slapped her. The blow's force made her fall against the row post. She grabbed onto it, covering her cheek with her other hand.

"You do what I say, not what you say," Dolmen shouted. "Do you understand me, bitch?"

Anna nodded. The women stayed frozen to their seats, their mouths clamped shut. They couldn't take their eyes off of her.

"I need another woman," Dolmen barked. "It will go easy for the rest if someone just volunteers. No one wants to make war on women."

There was a scuffling sound. "I'll go," Ella Bjornson said.

Dolmen looked at her. Schiller thought she wasn't such a bad choice. She had lost weight over the months he'd been coming here and looked even pretty with her turquoise eyes. He wondered if Dolmen saw her backbone of steel. She picked up her coat and joined Anna on the other side of the aisle.

Dolmen gave Schiller a nod and he came over. "We're ready to go."

Schiller announced to the women that they could go down into the basement to the fellowship hall. Food would be brought over. When Dolmen wasn't looking, he leaned toward Anna.

"What are you doing?" he whispered in German. "You shouldn't have talked so boldly. These men are not in the *Werhmacht*. They were lewd with the shopgirl." He looked around the room afraid the SD soldiers would see him.

Disgusted, she whispered back, "Look at yourself. Your association with these men makes you guilty as well."

"What about your daughter? Is this how a mother should act?"

"Marthe and Ingrid Larsen have cared for Lisel many times. These men have no right to terrorize the girl or any of us. Besides, I asked Marthe to watch my daughter." She stepped away from him. "As for the others, I don't care what any of them think."

***

Haugland spent the day outside of Trondheim with Axel and Mollenburg, a man from MI II in Stockholm. His new orders were to stay on the coast for now unless there was a poor outcome of the military action now called the Battle of the Bulge, which had begun six days before. The Germans had launched additional attacks in the last twenty-four hours that had the Americans and British forces reeling.

"There's total confusion in some of the fighting," Mollenburg said.

"But here in Norway we must go forward," Axel said. "There's a new XU station north of the Trondheimfjord. The Shetland Bus is going to bring help on the twenty-ninth." He gave Haugland the coordinates in case he could assist. "Be careful. *Ryper* is no longer secure."

Haugland returned to Trondheim alone in a furniture truck. Let off close to the fish market, he made his way down across the cold and slippery streets to the quay where the fishing boats were jammed next to each other. The streets were a weary gray as snow fell in fits and starts. He slowed down and looked for the *Marje*. When he spotted it among all the spars and wheelhouses, he was surprised to see Sverre on the boat.

Back early, he thought. In the late winter light, Haugland could make out the figure of a man in a long coat coming out of the wheelhouse. The man was looking down.

Haugland froze. It was not Sverre. The man standing on the quay next to the boat wsn't Sverre either. Cocking his head, he could hear German words pierce through the frigid air.

Christ! Were they inspectors of some sort? He knew they checked the registry of every boat coming to Trondheim in the *Norwegian Fishing Boat Register*. Haugland thought not. They were looking for something else. Slowly he stepped out of their line of sight toward a row of old stone building with a *konditori* in it. When he felt safe, he looked back. The men were still walking around the boat. To his dismay, a third man came out of the crew quarters where months ago Sverre had been knifed. The *Marje* was lost. Neither he nor Sverre could go back to it.

"Jens! Oh, do get him. He'll be so surprised!"

Haugland didn't dare turn. It was Rika Arneson. He didn't know whether to be ecstatic to have a way to get out or angry at the complication this would create. He'd have to explain why he was not in Oslo. Footsteps came up to him, a hand touched his shoulder.

"Jens, thank God. Did you see the Germans?" It was Sverre Haraldsen. Haugland turned with relief.

"They were here when I arrived around two-fifteen," Sverre said under his breath. "Found them approaching my boat. I didn't dare go closer. They're Gestapo. They were asking questions, then got on the *Marje* to stay. What the hell's going on?"

Haugland shrugged. He nodded in Rika's direction.

"I just ran into her. I couldn't very well explain why I was waiting here in the cold. I had to catch you, but I'm sorry she's seen you. I haven't seen her in a year or so. Pretty, isn't she?

Haugland looked back over to the fish market. Better go. One of the Germans was leaving.

Sverre and Haugland turned back to where Rika stood out of the cold. When she saw him, she waved a mittened hand at him. "Oh, Jens! How wonderful! Why didn't you have someone call me for you? Are you with Sverre? If you are, his manners are lacking."

Sorry, Haugland signed. He kissed her on her cheek. You look nice. Christmas look.

"*Tusen takk,* but I'm confused. I thought you were in Oslo."

Ja. I get pass. Come home for Christmas. He moved his hands smartly in the cold.

"Without saying hello? For shame. Oh, I wish I could go, but I haven't the money nor the time off. I haven't worked here long enough." She continued to chatter. She linked her arms through theirs. He watched politely, but his thoughts were riveted on the fish market.

"Rika, we need to go." Sverre pushed Haugland's elbow. "What about a quick treat?"

They found a *bakeri* a couple of blocks away and spent a few minutes with Rika. She had news about Kitty and stories about the city. The only time she appeared distracted was when Haugland asked about A.C. "He's well." She leaned over. "No one knows yet, but I'll tell you, Jens. A.C.'s asked to marry me. Pappa says it's all right. We're going to get married this summer."

Nice, Haugland signed.

Sverre got his attention. It was time to go.

They got up, and while Sverre paid the bill, Rika signed to Haugland. She was glad to have seen him. He helped her put on her coat then pointed to her. Do something for me.

"Sure, Jens. What is it?"

Not tell Pappa I here. Surprise. Tell no one.

"All right. I like surprises, especially Christmas surprises."

He smiled then leaned down and kissed her on the mouth. For the bride. I early.

Rika blushed. Sverre came back and signaled they better go. Outside, it had begun to snow. Haugland pulled his collar up around his neck. He gave Rika a final hug, set off up with Sverre hoping to get more distance between them and the fish market.

***

Rika wistfully watched them go, then crossed the street toward her trolley stop. About halfway up the wide block, a car began to follow her and eventually came up beside her. To her surprise she saw Paul sitting in the driver's seat. "*Hei*, Sonja. I thought that was you."

"You surprised me. I didn't expect to hear from you for a while."

"I know, but I have good news. Hop in. Say, who were your friends? The one you were wagging your hands at?"

"That was Jens, my…" She abruptly stopped and backtracked. She had promised not to say anything. "Paul, you stinker. You won't tell Ragnar, will you?"

"That you have another boyfriend? Not me. You can tell him yourself. Hop in, Sonja." He waited for her to get settled and close the door. "It's Ragnar. He's safely over. If you wish, you can write him a letter. He won't be able to respond for quite a while but mail does get to the camps."

"Do you know where he is?"

"Outside Stockholm. At one of the largest camps."

"Oh, Paul. That's so wonderful. You can't imagine."

"My Christmas present. Look, want to go home? There's a storm front moving in."

"Oh, that would be very nice. Do you mind if I get some things at the department store? For my hosts. Christmas Eve's two nights away and the stores won't be open tomorrow because it's Saturday."

"*Ja,* sure," Paul said. While she shopped, he made a phone call from a public phone booth. To the person on the other end, he said simply:

"Something's up. Radio the Chief and tell him that I just saw Kjell Arneson's man here in Trondheim. Then call Mission Hotel and ask for spot checks to be put up."

From the other end came a burst of excitement as the voice exclaimed that a boat belonging to one of the Haraldsen men had been identified at the fishing market. "It's registered to Sverre Haraldsen who's been missing." There was a pause, a garbled rush of air, then the voice got back on. "Special units will go out now." The voice asked for the location Paul had seen Arneson's man, then signed off. The hunt for Ryper was on.

CHAPTER 88

All the way down to the Tourist Hotel, Anna walked in silence with Ella Bjornson. Dolmen swaggered ahead of them. Signs of destruction were all around her—curtains waving like handkerchiefs out broken windows, furniture stacked outside on the snowy ground—but no signs of the villagers. Only soldiers under a sullen gray sky. Inside the hotel, they were led to the sitting room. The French doors were opened. Inside two men sat at a cloth draped table with silver candelabra in the center. "Go inside and sit," Dolmen said.

Anna obeyed, untying her wool headscarf as she stepped in. Only then did she fill with dread. Sitting with his back to the door was the tiny man who had arrested Einar so long ago. The other man was a German officer with red puffy jowls with tiny veins in them. She slid into a chair trying to avoid their eyes. Ella took the only other seat next to her.

For the next hour, they ate with the men, pretending it was a normal dinner party. Ella was cool, but polite. Anna kept talk to a minimum, eating with her best finishing school training, sitting erect, taking small bites. Outside the room, the hall hummed with activity. Rinnan's men came and went, sometimes bringing radio messages for him to read. The *razzia* had a much broader reach than just the village.

"What do you think we should do about the ladies at the church?"

Anna started. The German was looking at both of them. *Tauner? Was that his name?*

"Let them go home and if you have any decency, let us go now too," Ella said.

Rinnan said nothing, but the German sputtered. "Watch your step," he growled in poor Norwegian. "I beats you for that."

Tauner got up from the table and spoke to someone outside, then came back. He stuck his napkin down his collar and sat down. A few minutes later a *kake* dessert was brought in. As soon as the Norwegian waiter left, he went to the French doors and locked them. He pulled down the shades on the doors. "Would you like to see the women and children released?"

Neither woman answered, but Anna sensed something was going to happen whether they answered or not. She stole a glance at Ella. For once Ella looked back.

"Take off your sweaters and skirts."

"I will not," Ella Bjornson said. The German leaped up. He slapped her cheek. Ella gasped, but began to comply.

Trembling, Anna followed suit, sitting back down in her slip. She felt exposed and cold.

"*Gut*," the German said. "Now, you eat dessert." Anna took a small bite. Over her fork she looked at Rinnan. He did nothing except smoke and watch.

The German gave Anna his fork. "You. I need help eating my *kake*. Feed me."

Anna swallowed. She was aware of Ella stiffening next to her, but there was nothing she could do. They were in the same predicament. Anna cut a piece of the *kake* and put it in his mouth. It was like feeding Lisel when she was a baby. He got whip cream all over his mouth. He picked up his wineglass, toasted her, and then drained it. He patted his lap. "You come feed me."

"Must I? You'll get *kake* all over."

"You will sit." He patted his lap again.

Sick to her stomach, Anna complied, sitting sideways down on his knees, but he squeezed her rump and forced her to move closer. His breath was an overpowering mix of wine and spices; sweat reeked from under his arms. Bite by bite she fed him until he was done. She put the plate down. The room was so still, with only the sound of her breathing and footsteps in the hall. "May I go now?" Her voice sounded far off, like it was some else's.

"*Nein*. You are so beautiful, *meir Spatz.*" He sniffed a strand of her hair and stroked it. "Take down your straps and undo your brassiere."

Anna put a hand on her throat and flushed. She looked at Rinnan who continued to smoke and stare at her. His light eyes pierced through her. She said in High German. "I am a proper German woman. I am not a whore."

She pushed away from the officer, but he pulled her back and nipped her on her neck with his teeth. She held back her cry. He pawed her front and her strap. Anna slapped him.

"*Nei,* I'll do it." She took a deep breath and peeled the straps off her shoulders and pulled down the slip. When she was done she undid her brassiere. It cupped her for a moment then fell into her lap.

"Is she not beautiful, Rinnan?"

Anna stared straight ahead at the French doors as he squeezed one of her breasts, then kissed and fondled it with flabby lips and clammy hands. He pulled her against him and she could feel him harden.

One can endure these things, she thought as she kept her face away from him and looked past Rinnan to the door. She was glad Marthe's daughter was not here. He would have ruined her.

***

Anna returned home late that night. Coming into the freezing house, she told Lisel to go feed the cats. Numbed by exhaustion and cold, too tired to think, she listened for the truck as it backed out of the barnyard and headed down the driveway. Schiller had done it again. Setting out on the fjord road on her own in the dark, he had sent a truck to take her out.

Tyskertøs. The name hurt so much, but after today, she no longer cared. She was numb, devoid of any feeling one way or another.

A half-hour later, she had two fires roaring. Leftover soup was on the kitchen stove and the woodstove in the *stue* was popping. They ate quietly together, but halfway through the meal, Lisel fell asleep. Anna put aside her tray. She wrapped Lisel up in the *dyne* and carried her to her bedroom. When she was sure Lisel was asleep, Anna went down into the cellar.

"*Herr* Arneson?" she called out, terrified the men might be completely frozen or dangerously lethargic. The door to the storage room was closed. Shining a flashlight on it, she pushed it open and heard movement by the cave door. A second later, one of the men piled out.

"*Herr* Stagg? Where is *Herr* Arneson?"

Stagg glowered at her but it was halfhearted. He shivered uncontrollably.

"I'm here." Kjell stooped coming out of the door. He moved stiffly, rolling his shoulder to get out some ache. "What has happened? We heard explosions earlier."

"It's been a terrible day. I will tell you, but first you must come up by the kitchen fire. I have soup for you and toast."

In the *stue*, she piled blankets around their shoulders. When they were seated, she gave them heaping bowls of fish and potato chowder. Their hands shook when they held their soup bowls, but soon they were eating like the starved prisoners they had been all day.

Once they were settled, Anna sat by the fire. She felt worn-out and incapable of conversation. She took a skein of wool yarn and setting it on her winder, began to form a ball. The motion was soothing.

"Aren't you eating?" Kjell asked.

"I ate already. *Tusen takk*. It's nice to just sit here by the fire. It's been a long day."

Kjell smiled back at her, just a light smile but friendly. Stagg stayed quiet, slurping his soup. When he was done he put the tray on the counter by the sink and went over to the window.

Stagg lifted up the blackout curtain and swore. "Christ, there are fires in the village. Kjell, come and look at this. Jesus, those are boats in the fjord. And houses, on the schoolhouse road!"

Kjell stood up with his tray. Suddenly the truth flushed his face. "Those explosions. My house isn't it? They burned my house."

"*Ja*," Anna said quietly. "They blew it up with dynamite some time around four o'clock. We could see it from the church."

"And the boats? The *Otta* too?" Kjell asked flatly.

"I'm sorry ... I'm so sorry," she murmured.

"I'll bet you are." Stagg spat at her. "Why are we staying here Kjell? There's no point to it." He came close to her, his eyes full of hate.

"Shhh...! You'll wake the child," Kjell said. "Can't you see the woman's exhausted?"

Stagg muttered some apology under his breath, but did not look at her. He crossed his arms and hugged them close to his chest. Kjell put down his tray and joined Stagg at the window where they both stood locked in their own thoughts.

Anna felt helpless and ashamed the soldiers had destroyed the fishing boats. Just when every vessel was needed to bring in any catch. She didn't understand Germans any more.

While the men stayed at the window, Anna cleaned up and arranged the parlor for the men to sleep. Coming back, she started on the dishes. She put them in the hot soapy water, then stopped abruptly as a dizzy spell came over her. She gripped the counter edge for support.

"*Fru* Fromme? Are you all right?" Kjell asked. "You should let us do that." He brought his tray over. "It'll put some heat into our cold hands. Helmer does it all the time for his mother."

Anna smiled wearily at Kjell and absentmindedly wiped the front of her sweater causing it to pull down at the neck below her Peter Pan collar. Behind her, Kjell gasped. He put his hand on her shoulder. "There are bruises on your neck. What happened?"

"It's... all right."

"It's not all right. Where are the women and children?"

"We were in the church," she answered in a quiet voice." They allowed us to go home about an hour ago." Her response must have bothered Kjell.

"None of you were abused, were you?"

"*Nei*." She looked away sharply, trying to avoid his gaze and questions.

Kjell reached out and smoothed her hair away from her shoulders. Anna stood very still.

"There's a bite mark on the back of your neck. What happened, *datter*? You must tell me." Kjell's voice was so gentle Anna turned. All her attempts to hold herself together for the last six hours began to crack. She started to tremble. Her eyes filled with tears.

"Soldiers were sent to bring women down to the hotel. Ingrid Larsen was picked first, but I protested. I went in her place. *Fru* Bjornson went too." She twisted her fingers together.

"Is Ella all right?"

"*Fru* Bjornson? *Ja*, She's safe at home." *Gott*, she felt so tired. "That bite mark. Did he hurt you?"

"*Nei*," she said in a little voice. He was too drunk to hurt me." Anna put a hand on her throat, her fingers trembling. She rubbed the front of her sweater. She felt so filthy. "We were escorted back to the church. Later Marthe came with Lisel and sat with me. She is the first woman in the village to ever do that."

Kjell nodded to Stagg to start washing the dishes. "It is not necessary," Anna said.

"I think so." He gently pulled her to him. At first resisting, she gave in and resting her head on his chest, let him hold her. A little shudder ran through her. "I'll be all right."

"I know you'll be, *datter*."

Datter. Did he think of her like that now? He certainly held her like she was his own daughter. It comforted her as tears streamed down her cheeks. No one consoled her after Einar died.

He cleared his throat. "I'm sorry I didn't see. I found your box downstairs in the cave. There was an affidavit in it. It says you are absolved. I just don't understand why Jens didn't tell me. I'm going to make it up to you. You and Jens will get together again. Look," he said as he gave her a hug, "you sit and I'll make you some tea. How big is the *razzia,* do you think?"

Anna wiped her cheeks dry with her apron. "Widespread. It won't be safe to leave for days. I overheard the reports of patrols going out during the lunch. The leader didn't think you'd gotten away at all and might be somewhere in the village. That was why your house and boat were blown up. As a warning to the others and as a way to prevent you or friends from retrieving anything that would aide in your escape. The trails are being watched too."

She sat down at the table and told them more. She had overheard enough to know who was in the *konditori* being questioned. Stagg became more relaxed around her. After he finished the dishes, he stretched out his fingers and saying they felt better, waited on them.

The men went to sleep around eleven, curled on the floor in the parlor. Anna slept with Lisel. At six, Anna woke them quietly and sent them back down into the cellar with a thermos of hot coffee and extra blankets. She promised them hot food later and maybe a respite at noon, but at eight two trucks roared up to the garden, disembarking a load of *Wehrmacht* soldiers. Leading them was Schiller and a corporal from the SD.

"*Guten morgen*." He removed his peaked hat at her back door. "I have orders to occupy the farm. Your view's excellent for the search. We'll sleep in the barn."

"You're staying?" The thought horrified her.

"A word, Anna." He stepped into the entryway and said under his breath, "I heard what happened. That pig Tauner bragged about it at dinner. I'm so sorry. Please understand. If I hadn't insisted on coming here now, Tauner would be here instead. Nothing would stop him a second time." When Anna gasped, he hushed her. "Not a word. We'll both be in trouble. I'm your friend, *jo*?"

Anna nodded that she was.

"*Gutt.* Now let the men come in and set up. We'll try to disrupt you as little as possible. I don't think we'll be ordered to stay beyond a second day. The *razzia* is nearly wrapped up. Arrests elsewhere have been very successful. They have cornered a leader in Trondheim."

Schiller stepped out to issue orders. He didn't see Anna sink against the wall, didn't hear her faint cry of anguish.

It was happening all over again. Like the dark nightmare that came with Einar's arrest, as deep and smothering as *Morktiden*, the death head horde was searching. And as before, she knew there was no hope, no place to hide from the tightening storm. With the men in the cellar and soldiers on the farm she had no place to give way to her fear and grief. All she could do was wait and hope she could hold onto her sanity.

CHAPTER 89

As soon as they left Rika, Haugland and Sverre hightailed it. Avoiding Munkegata, which led straight from the fish market to Nidaros Cathedral, Haugland chose a route through the ancient city that would take them down to a contact in export. The first thing he wanted to do was to get Sverre out to Sweden. The *Marje* had been seized by the Gestapo too quickly, suggesting a more sinister problem he didn't care to share with Sverre right now. Haugland worried his earlier meeting with the XU chief had been monitored. What if he was followed? He felt on edge, but couldn't let Sverre see. He moved them along the broad, gloomy sidewalk without drawing attention, staying close to the stone and brick walls.

They were more than halfway down the block when Haugland heard sirens. Without a word, he grabbed Sverre's coat sleeve and dragged him onto a narrow cobbled street that ran between some ancient two and four story buildings. Once his eyes adjusted, he groped his way down the street to a crossing. Ahead, the street continued south between another mass of buildings. To his right, the street seemed to open up to a wider public area. For a moment he was unsure where to go when at the far end of this new space the blue lights of the police cars went by in the muted glow of the falling snow. Heading toward the Ravnkloa fish market, he thought.

"Let's keep going. I think there's a trolley down there."

They hustled along the nearly deserted street and came out onto a broad avenue.

"Where are we?" Sverre tucked his scarf around his neck.

"Still too close to the fish market."

A muffled bell clanged. A trolley appeared. Haugland stepped out and hailed it. They quickly found seats just in time to see a Black Maria heading the same direction as the police cars. Haugland picked up a newspaper and began reading. Sverre got the hint. He trimmed his fingernails. The trolley was packed with shoppers and workers going home for the weekend and the beginning of the Christmas holiday. Tomorrow night was Little Christmas

Eve, the twenty-third. The trolley traveled the length of the block then turned away from danger.

"Kongens Gate," the conductor said as the trolley made a stop. Haugland began to relax. He knew where they were now. When it reached Erling Skakkes Gate, Haugland pulled the bell and they got off. Two German soldiers got on, but paid them no notice.

No building lights or streetlights were on. With the snow beginning to fall heavily, visibility was poor. Haugland kept them moving at a steady pace, his eyes on the lookout for patrols that roamed the area this time of night. From a block away he heard a siren. They stepped into the safety of a doorway while he assessed its direction, moving when he felt it was safe. They cut across the snowy street and down a smaller one. To their left was a dairy. Beyond, was a large building set near the end of the block. At its back, he knocked on a door. A young girl answered.

"Is Willy in?" he asked.

She smiled and led them into a large space clattering with waddling bottles going through machines that filled and capped them. The beer smell gave Haugland a headache. Ducking under a conveyor belt, she led them into a quieter space outside a door. Knocking, she left them.

"*Ja*?" a thin, dark-haired man in his fifties answered.

"Willy," Haugland said. "I've come for my sugar ration."

The man acknowledged the joke and code words. The place had been a sugar refinery in the mid-1700s. He invited them in and closed the door, muting the clink of the machinery.

"We're running overtime for the Germans," he said, "so they'll drink themselves to death during the holidays. How can I help you?"

"I'm looking for immediate export of my friend here. Axel sent me."

"Ah, Axel. How's his mother?"

"His mother's fine, but his aunt's ill. She requires surgery."

Haugland quibbled back and forth with "Willy." At one point he looked at Sverre who looked spooked at their exchange. The ancient building creaked from the wind.

The man rubbed his bearded chin. "Let me make a phone call. But not here." He excused himself and stepped out a door behind his desk.

"You think something's really wrong, don't you?" Sverre said.

"*Ja*, unfortunately. It's too much of a coincidence about your boat."

"What's he doing?"

"Probably using a public phone. He'll be back." Haugland took out his pistol and checked it. Sverre took his cap off and stared at a calendar on the wall.

"I can't go home, can I? My wife... My son, Bode. He's only seventeen."

"*Nei*, Sverre. I'm sorry. You've got to go to Sweden. Your family will be looked after."

"Will you be coming?"

"*Nei.* Right now they're looking for you. You don't have any fishing fines do you?"

Sverre smiled. "Illegal nets, maybe."

Haugland chuckled. Sverre would be fine. He had grown to like him in the past few months and would miss him. From skeptic to colleague, he had served the group well.

Haugland explained how he'd be passed along until he was safely in Sweden. "I know someone who can get you situated. You can volunteer for the police camps if you wish."

Sverre pulled some keys out of his pocket. "I'm not going to see my *Marje* again, am I?"

"Be hopeful."

Willy came back. "Sorry to take so long. There's real trouble brewing. They shut the pay phones down. Had to use a phone in another building. Your ride's on its way. It'll be tricky, but I think we can get you out before the bridges are blocked. You coming too?"

"*Ja*, I'll see him off."

The brewer led them out the back door along a dim hallway. He listened at the door, then waved them out into the back street. It was dark and cold. The snow drifted down. "Your driver's name is Moestad. He'll get your friend out, then lay over a day."

"They'll go out a Selbu route?" Haugland asked.

"*Ja.* It's secure if you're worried, despite the problems the last two months."

There was little traffic on the snowy streets. Close to six o'clock, most people had found their way home. On a signal, Willy led them across the street to the corner. "No telling who's out now. There's definitely a search on." He looked at Haugland. "Axel says to stay low." Willy slipped a piece of paper to him. "Go to this address for help. He'll contact you as soon as possible."

Haugland pocketed the address then stared. Had he seen headlights? Over there, Haugland pointed to the corner. The brewer squinted. Seconds later, lights flickered again.

"Let's go," he said. They approached cautiously, Haugland looking around at all corners of the intersection. A truck rumbled by, its lights hooded and its tires muffled by the thick layer of snow on the roadway. Soon chains would be needed. They walked to a black Chevrolet sedan.

"Moestad. Here's your package. How does it look for getting over the bridge?"

"So far, nothing on the police radio. We'll sprint now."

Sverre got in. He looked pale and drawn. Haugland came up to him. "It's going to be all right. I'll get word to you as soon as possible." He whispered a name and password into his ear. "Ask when you get there." Haugland patted his shoulder. "It's been one hell of a fishing trip."

Sverre held onto his rucksack like a boy on his first day of school. He looked up at Haugland and flashed him the "V for Victory sign." Haugland waved them on. The car turned the corner and headed down toward the bridge. The men headed back across the snowy street.

"You going now?" Willy asked.

"*Ja*. I'll check in with Axel. *Tusen takk* for all your help."

After leaving the brewery, Haugland stopped briefly in a doorway to read the address by penlight, then set out again. The snow came down steadily, only to be stirred by a gusting wind." Holding onto his cap, it was hard to concentrate on his surroundings as he headed toward his contact near the river. He didn't see the hastily put up checkpoint until too late. Standing stock-still, he looked for some direction to hide, but the area to his left was wide open—a park of some sort—and to his right, people and cars bunched up by a school that was lined with a high iron fence. If he tried to climb it, he would be seen. If he crossed the street, he would be seen. He was trapped. He didn't have a new identity card, only the one he had brought into the harbor. He felt for his gun, preparing to shoot it out if necessary.

Two soldiers standing in front of a black van manned the spot check point. A lantern was hanging on the side mirror. Off to the side a third man watched over the whole proceedings. SD, Haugland thought. The number of vehicles and pedestrians was small, making it hard to be inconspicuous. He got his papers ready when suddenly a group of young children came skipping across the snowbound street. They went straight to the front of the line with little bags of candy and began to chat with the soldiers. Only it was a strange sort of conversation. They used their hands and spoke in odd voices. *God Jul.* The soldiers didn't know how to react. They didn't see the oldest child turn slightly and sign directly at Haugland. Go quick. Pastor Solheim in park.

While the children surrounded the soldiers and the SD man, Haugland backed off. When all three of the Germans looked safely distracted, he walked quickly across the street and into the cover of the snow-laden trees. Hiding behind a trunk, he caught his breath. The children were still there sharing their candy, but the agent had stepped away from the car and craning his neck.

Had he seen him bolt? Had he looked and found him gone?

After a time, the children withdrew and headed down to the corner some distance away. He knew where they were going now and grinned. *Hjemme for Døve,* the Home for the Deaf. Following them through the trees, he eventually came directly opposite the old edifice. Not too far in front of him, Solheim stepped out onto the sidewalk.

Go home now, he signed to the children. Good job. Like Christmas *nissen*, they scurried across the street and up the snowy stairs to the main door of the institution. When the door was shut, he turned and addressed the trees, his voice muffled by snowfall.

"It's safe to come out now, Ryper. Go in the side entrance. I'll meet you there."

Solheim crossed the street. When Haugland thought it safe, he darted across to the side entrance where he had come months ago. At the back, a light winked behind the kitchen blackout curtain. There was a turning of a key at the door and he was beckoned in.

"*God kveld.* You looked like you needed help," Solheim said.

"I did. That was a little too tight. *Takk.*"

Haugland stomped his snowy boots on a mat and stepped into the warm kitchen that smelled of cinnamon and other spices. It still had its polished look of an institutional kitchen, but the portrait of Jesus had a garland of gold Christmas foil around it. Solheim closed the door behind him. His cheeks were red above his clerical collar.

"You shouldn't be out this time of night. The patrols are always itchy when they go on duty for the first time."

"I don't think this has anything to do with itchiness. I think they are actively looking for a man who came into Trondheim with me. Worse, they're looking for me, too."

"What makes you think that?"

"He's part of my group. He brought me to Trondheim early this morning so I could meet with Axel. His boat's been confiscated, but after checking its registry, all hell broke loose."

"I heard sirens when I was walking back with the children."

The door to kitchen swung open. A girl barely into her teens came in. She was dressed in a pinafore over a red dress, with a large silk red ribbon in her fair hair. Her white wool hose bunched at her knees. When she saw Haugland, she smiled.

"Is this my rescuer?" he asked Solheim, careful to sign to her. The girl grinned broadly at Haugland. She seemed very interested to meet a young man who could sign.

"This is Ona. She's one of the students here at the school. She's very good with the younger children. I trust her with many responsibilities." Solheim's hands and fingers moved swiftly, but precisely. When he was done, Haugland signed hello.

"I mmm ver' happy t' met you," she voiced.

"Ona, I need to talk to this man," Solheim said. "Could you bring something for him to eat to the dining room?" He led Haugland out another door into the dining room where a tree had been set up on a side table and decorated with children's handmade ornaments.

"We can talk here. The children probably shouldn't see you, but Ona's all right. I'll set you up in the back room for the night and we'll see about getting in touch with some people."

"Maybe I shouldn't stay. I was on my way to meet a contact of Axel's down by the river. I think it's important security gets on this right away. Some of my people could be in danger."

Ona brought a tray and served them coffee. She put a sandwich in front of Haugland. He signed thanks and asked her about her studies. She chattered on in sign. After a bit, Solheim nodded at her to go. After Haugland gave her a wink, she slipped out smiling.

While Haugland ate, Solheim made a phone call. When he came back his face was grave. "Things *are* serious. The whole city's on alert for 'saboteurs.' All bridges and the port are closed. Anyone caught on the street will be arrested. Anyone who resists will be shot."

"Anyone specific?"

"Someone's going to check at Stapo headquarters. A *jøssing* in Mission Hotel will be contacted, but that will take longer to get back information. Want more coffee?"

"I'll get it myself." He started toward the kitchen door, when Ona came rushing in.

Soldiers! she signed. At the door! She waved her hands frantically. Solheim gently cupped them in his own to reassure her. He jerked at Haugland to go into the kitchen.

"You better stay low. I'll see what it's all about." He signed to Ona: Stay with friend.

As soon as Haugland slipped into the kitchen, Solheim went down to the lobby-like front room of the home. Standing just inside the door was an officer of the SD taking off his gray gloves. Behind him in the vestibule and outside were *Wehrmacht* soldiers, their greatcoats dusted with snowflakes. The housekeeper was doing her best to keep them at bay.

"Oh, *Herr* Solheim...These soldiers..."

"I have orders to search the building." The German waved the soldiers in.

"*Vær så snill.*" Solheim tried to slow them down. "What are you looking for?"

"A man. He escaped from a checkpoint a couple of blocks from here."

"Why would you look here? This is a home for deaf children and young adults."

"He could've slipped in here. He's very dangerous. He could hurt your children. How would they know he was here?"

"Please be considerate of them." Solheim reluctantly stepped aside. "*Fru* Andersson will go along with some of your soldiers so she can interpret for them. "I'll call a teacher down."

The German ignored him. The heavily armed soldiers split up, thundered through the building. Solheim ended up following a group back to the kitchen. At the door he paused, his mouth dry. How would he explain Haugland? All his years in the resistance came down to this. They could get shot. In the kitchen, however, there was no sign of him. Not even Ona.

While the soldiers threw open the cupboards and the doors to the dumbwaiter, Solheim followed the sound of someone outside scraping the snow away from the back doorsteps. It was Ona, calmly shoveling away the tracks Haugland had made to the door. The steps were already cleared and she had made it almost to the street sidewalk. Behind her the snow gently filled up the wet space. Smart girl. Where was Ryper? The tension was unbearable.

When the soldiers left the room, he followed them out through the dining room to the empty rooms at the back of the building. Throughout the home only the tramp of boots and the occasional German word could be heard.

In the end, they found nothing. Solheim was summoned to the main entrance.

"We're going now," the officer said. "Be sure to lock your doors." He stood at attention and clicked his heels. "I wish you all a Merry Christmas." He started to say more, but Ona, who had finished up her job, came through the heavy glass-paned door. She stomped her feet and brushed the snow off her coat. She made a sweet picture. The soldiers smiled and commented on her. "Enough," the officer said and left abruptly, the chastened soldiers closely behind.

When the last man was out, *Fru* Andersson closed the door and breathed a heavy sigh of relief. Solheim stood thoughtfully at the entrance. "Could you go upstairs? Make sure the children are all right, then get them dressed for bed. There will be vespers."

"And now Ona, what made you do such a crazy thing?" Solheim asked after *Fru* Andersson left.

Footprints bad.

"I know they're bad. Where's my friend?"

The girl laughed. Stuck. Giggling, she took him by the hand to the kitchen. See.

She pointed to the dumbwaiter and swung open the doors. Inside, all he could see was the cable and a note saying, "Broken. Please fix." Up, she signed and then he understood. Haugland was sitting on the dumbwaiter between floors. Solheim shut the doors, pushed a button to restart it and slowly the dumbwaiter descended. "I'm bringing you down," he said through the wall.

Inside, sitting on it all scrunched up, was Haugland, his gun ready to fire. In his left hand he gripped his pill. His face was grim. Although he looked comical, Solheim knew he had spent an hour of hell hiding there. But he was safe. For now.

***

Haugland spent the night sleeping in the same back room as he had done during the summer and despite a stiff back, slept fairly well. At eight, Solheim came in and roused him with a cup of coffee and hot food. While Haugland had been sleeping the early morning hours away, Solheim had made some more phone calls.

"I'm afraid there's bad news. It appears there's a major *razzia* being carried out on the islands and coast. Fjellstad's been part of it. Axel is on his way over to talk to you about it."

Shocked, Haugland sat up. "I should have had Kjell leave after the last incident."

"I'm sorry. You must, of course, realize that you can't stay in Norway now. You must get out. You are connected too highly in XU. You know too much."

"How will I get out? The city's closed off.'

"Axel is working on it right now." Solheim offered him the tray of coffee and food. "You should eat. You'll need your strength."

As it would turn out, Haugland would need more than food.

CHAPTER 90

The day after the *razzia*, Rinnan and the boats left Fjellstad for Trondheim, arriving in the city around eight in the evening. Onboard were several prisoners from the village including schoolmaster Stagg and Pastor Helvig. Ten in all, they were met at the docks and thrown into a black van for the ride to Vollan Prison where they would be culled for Gestapo headquarters and interrogations there. Unknown to them, several doors away were prisoners swept up in the *razzia* on Hitra, among them Sig Haraldsen and his sons.

While the prisoners were processed, Rinnan and his inner circle returned to Mission Hotel and met with *Kriminalsekretaer* Boesten and Gestapo head Flesch. Missing was Odd Sorting sent to wrap up some business near the northern tip of Hitra.

Rinnan was pleased. The illegal resistance organization had been broken. A unit had been left behind in Fjellstad to watch the trails to the *fjell* and the valley road to prevent Arneson's escape to coastal points. Pictures seized at his home would be published in the police gazette, *Polititidende*. He wouldn't get far.

Here, with the city under strict surveillance, Arneson's man Hansen wouldn't get far either.

Around nine, Rinnan drove to his elegant villa in the suburbs. He would spend the night with one of his mistresses. He was to be interrupted only for anything of real importance.

***

Haugland stayed all day at the *Hjemme for Døve*, hiding in the back rooms on the top floor. There he could look out a window onto the snowy park of trees and open fields and a building belonging to another school now in use by the Germans. Most of the children were gone for the coming holiday, but none of the remaining residents of the home saw him other than Ona who brought him food. At one o'clock, Axel and another man from Milorg showed up to see Haugland.

"We've been discussing the situation, Ryper," he said. "We believe we can get you out through the Danish Relief. The church has received a shipment of food from them which is to be taken to the countryside for distribution at Christmas. We'll arrange for you to be on one of the trucks. The Germans approved the paperwork two days ago and the men are just finishing up unloading the cargo from the ship in the harbor."

"The *Wehrmacht* commander is somewhat sympathetic to the Danish Relief, especially at Christmas. He should overrule the Gestapo. Once the trucks are out of the city, you'll be dropped off into the hands of a Milorg export group."

"You'll have to go to the trucks now," Axel said. "They're leaving tonight. You're going as a respectable elder from the church. Papers are being made up and anything else to aide in your export. MI IV in Stockholm knows you're coming."

"Takk." Haugland said, resigned now. *Get out. Save the others from a worse fate if he were caught.* He went over to the window and saw snow flurries. Down below, a group of children were playing in the snow, throwing snowballs at each other in the wheel they had tramped out in the deep powder. Their clothes looked bright in the gray and white landscape. There were no sounds from these children. Only the insults and chatter they flicked with their hands. "Can I get a bath?" he asked Solheim.

"Sure, I'll get you a towel. We'll take your picture when you're done."

"I'll need spectacles." To Solheim's surprise, Haugland quoted part of his catechism.

They couldn't leave until eight at night, due to some holdup in obtaining permission to leave, but Haugland dressed and waited. When the signal was given, Solheim led him down the backstairs where a car waited for them. The Milorg man from the morning sat in front.

"Go on," Solheim said. "Perhaps we'll meet again. At war's end."

Takk for help, Haugland signed. Moments later the car took off on the dark, sanded street.

The convoy of three trucks was held up for a couple of hours before the Germans allowed it to proceed over Elgeseter Bridge. It continued south through the suburb of Elgeseter. The fourth truck went over Bakke Bru into the older suburb of Rosenborg with its timbered dwellings through the industrial area of the town. Not far away were the pens for the U-boats that slipped out regularly to the Norwegian Sea. Slowly the truck made its way out of the area and north toward the towns and hamlets there. The road wasn't bad, but chains were needed for the ice and snow. The road followed the fjord and the railroad going north.

Haugland sat by the passenger door in front, his body taut and tired. The truckload of Milorg men had made it safely through the checkpoint. His new papers worked. The elders and church helpers who normally would be here were back in Trondheim, tied up in an apartment near the wharves where the trucks had been loaded. That had been done to protect the regular people who delivered the Danish Relief. Once Haugland was safely away, the missing people would be "discovered" and the "hijacking" uncovered. In this way, since none of the relief people had ties to the resistance, they would withstand any scrutiny by the Gestapo.

Outside the first village they came to, the truck pulled over to a roadside building serving as a bus stop. The men got out. A few minutes later, a car came up alongside them and they all piled in, leaving the truck locked up and the keys in the ignition. Pulling out into the deserted road, they continued on north. Ahead of them the road was curvy and narrow, rising up from the valley floor a little bit higher at each turn. The car's hooded lights stabbed the dark. Fortunately, the driver knew the area well. At the top of the rise, the road flattened out and the car picked up speed. The driver began to relax.

"We'll make good time now," the driver said. "Why not take off your collar? There is a sweater and a longshoreman's jacket for you."

"*Takk*," Haugland said and began to change.

For the next few miles they traveled with no difficulty until they hit a new grade on the forested lane and the driver shifted gears again.

Suddenly a German troop carrier pulled out from a side road on the right, causing the driver to swerve and lose control of the car.The car slid wildy across the snowy road and down the frozen embankment, slamming into a ditch. The driver was thrown against the windshield, while the men in the back were thrown partway over the front seat. They temporarily pinned Haugland against the door.

"What the Devil." A man screamed as he scrambled back into the back seat. "Do you see the flashlights? Get out. Get out."

"I see them," Haugland said. "Everyone for himself." He slammed against the passenger door and rolled out onto the snow, his gun ready. One of the men hanging over the front seat followed him and together they groped their way along the ditch toward safety. The driver wasn't so lucky. His door was jammed and coming out last, he was greeted by a rapid spit of gunfire shattering the windshield and killing him. The other man inside died hanging over the seat. Suddenly, the ditch and woods around them was filled with blinding light and the numbing clatter of machine guns. Haugland threw himself across a hummock of snow and tried to climb into the pine forest on the other side of the ditch.

The air was bitterly cold, the snow hard and icy. He could hear the sound of the Milorg man behind him breathing heavily, then a shout when soldiers with lights leaped down into the ditch in front of them. The man ran back. Haugland grabbed a branch above him and pulled himself up into a tree. A hand reached up to grab him, but he made it on top, then scrambled on his knees under the boughs. When the ghostly shape of a head appeared, he fired without thinking. The soldier fell back with a cry. Unable to get upright, Haugland dog-paddled his way through the deep snow looking for a way out. Behind him he could hear shouting and the bark of a dog as soldiers moved in the ditch where he went into the trees.

Getting too close.

His only hope was to get back on the road. He scrambled another twenty feet and then went to the edge of the hill and looked down. The soldier's lights were further down. Sliding down into the ditch, he grabbed for brush above him and swung himself on top.

Once up, he stared into the gloom across the road, taking a moment to catch his breath. It came away from his mouth in short blasts of steam. He removed his gloves. Reaching inside his pants pocket, he felt for the poison pill. He transferred it to his left hand and put the glove back on. They wanted him alive, but he knew the consequences of that. About fifty feet down was the truck, its lights staring off into the dark. Behind him were the voices of the soldiers as they crawled through the forest and along the ditch. If he had skis he would be long gone, but right now his only hope was the truck. The truck was idling and from what he could see, no one was near it. It would be a tremendous risk, but at this point alternatives were non-existent. Taking a deep breath, he dashed across the icy road gun in hand.

Hugging the steep bank running down to the truck, he stayed out of the light and made his way down. When he came up to the passenger side of the truck, he looked for any movement. Seeing no one, he opened the cab door and slid into the driver's seat. In one movement, he disengaged the brake and put the truck into gear. Hitting the accelerator, the truck roared to life. It jumped forward with a loud grinding sound and started up the road. Some of the soldiers scrambled up on the road and began firing at the truck.

"*Halt*!" one soldier shouted above the staccato firing of machine guns.

Others, appearing directly behind the truck, gave chase. Out of the corner of his eyes, Haugland saw two soldiers grab onto the passenger side of the cab. Another hung on the driver's side. He immediately slammed on his brakes to dislodge them, bouncing one on the passenger side off the edge of the truck's hood and hitting whoever else was behind. The heavy truck slid, but he was able to control it and move forward again as a soldier broke in on the passenger's side. Driving one-handed, Haugland raised his gun to fire, but the truck skidded on the ice, throwing the man on top of him. The soldier grabbed onto his arm, trying to pull him off the wheel, but Haugland threw his shoulder into the man's face with such force that the soldier flew across the cab. He shot him dead.

Too late. The driver's door opened. A soldier seized Haugland's head in a vise-like grip. Clawing at his attacker, his foot came off the accelerator as he counterattacked. He turned the steering wheel left and right to throw him off, but the soldier was too burly. His lock on his throat so tight that when they hit another patch of ice, he was jettisoned along with the soldier onto the frozen ground. Both were dazed. To Haugland's disadvantage, the man lay half across his legs. The truck eased forward, stopped and then rolled backwards into the trees on one side of the road, narrowly missing them.

Haugland scrambled to stand up, but several soldiers jumped him. For a desperate moment he was able to fight them off, but there were too many. Eventually they overpowered him. Holding him firmly to the ground, he was subdued by blows to his face. His helplessness enraged him. He tried one more time to thrash his way out, but he was trapped.

"*Gut*," said an officer coming up to him. "No move." He turned to a man in civilian clothes who came forward with a flashlight. "This the one?" the officer asked in German. The civilian shined it directly into his eyes and looked at his hair.

"*Ja*, that's him."

Haugland stared back at the men, trying to think of some way to get his glove off and get to the pill. If he behaved, they might let him sit up. He would play dumb and when he was able he would slip it into his mouth.

He lay on the cold ground, oblivious to its warmth-stealing power. He wasn't even aware of breathing. He focused on one thing: he must die. He must be very careful and follow their rules. Only they didn't have any.

The civilian reached into his greatcoat pocket and making sure Haugland's arms were pinned to the ground, clamped a cloth over his nose and mouth. It smelled sharp and sickly sweet. He choked as he struggled to twist and turn his head, but the cloth stayed. Haugland's struggles ceased.

CHAPTER 91

Solheim sat up suddenly in his bed at the *Hjemme for Døve* and turned on his lamp. The clock read three in the morning. Far off the sound of loud banging reverberated through the old building. Wondering if anyone else on the hearing staff heard it, he put on his robe to investigate. The banging suddenly stopped, but Solheim could hear someone racing up the stairs and running down the hall toward his room.

"Pastor Solheim," *Fru* Anderson called in a panicked voice, the flat of her hand beating the door. "It's the Gestapo. They want you to come down immediately. Dressed."

"Did they wake the children?" he asked.

"No one has stirred."

"Good. Tell them I'll be right down."

Coming hurriedly downstairs minutes later, Solheim came face to face with a small group of soldiers and an angry Gestapo officer who instantly ordered him outside into a waiting car. Solheim barely had time to grab his coat.

The assault of the frigid air on his lungs was nothing compared to this assault on his nerves, but he had to hope the German's show of aggression was designed only to terrorize him. He needed to stay calm, and get the facts. Since the *Obersturmführer* in the front seat wasn't about to tell him, Solheim sat in the back and spent the ride in gut-twisting silence.

The Gestapo Headquarters for Trondheim was located in a multi-storied stone edifice with a high-pitched roof. Elegant and grand, it had been a major hotel before the war. Adapted to its new use, it had gained an infamous reputation. The driver pulled up to the sanded sidewalk and parked.

The lieutenant got out and opened the door to the car. "Follow me please."

On the fifth floor, Solheim was ushered into a suite of rooms turned into an office. Nazi flags glared on both sides of an oak desk. An officer dressed in the black uniform of the SS greeted him with a sour face.

"You are a minister of the Evangelical Lutheran Church, are you not? The so-called Deaf Church? You can talk with your hands? I need your help. You will come with me."

The German gave Solheim no time to grasp his surroundings. They were off and immediately down to the elevator. If this was designed to intimidate him some more, it was having its effect.

And so they descended into Hell.

The first thing Solheim noticed was the smell. It wasn't much different from the prisons he had visited before, but this was the basement of a *hotel.* It was obvious that doors had been converted to metal ones for the sole purpose of detaining individuals. Sounds, faint but powerful and disturbing, the ravings of someone in pain, the stirrings of someone in sleep as a nightmare came true. Solheim's skin crawled, as though he were in the presence of the Fallen One. "The Lord is my shepherd," he whispered to himself.

An old man with hair in his ears led them down the narrow hall and the rough labyrinth under pipes, jangling his keys as he walked. The jailer unlocked the metal door to a large dreary room with a light covered by a metal hood hanging down over a chair. In the chair was a man sitting with his bare, sweaty back to him. From the light Solheim could see that the man had been beaten. As Solheim came closer, he saw that the man's hands were tied down at his side so he couldn't move.

Do unto others as you would have them...

Solheim's mouth became dry as it dawned on him who the prisoner was. Haugland. He felt the blood drain from his face.

The German gave him a bemused look. Two other men—one a half-naked brute of a man, the other as common as a hotel clerk—stood off to the side, waiting for orders.

"Do you know this man?" The German lifted the man's head up so Solheim could see the battered face.

He heard the cock crow as he looked straight at the man. "*Nei.* He must be from a different district."

"Will you talk with him? All he has done is use his hands and make strange noises. I want to know what he is saying."

"You think he is deaf?"

"You tell me."

Solheim looked at the beaten face with compassion. Whatever else, this was going to be the performance of his life. He tapped Haugland's arm gently.

Haugland didn't show any emotion but his eyes told Solheim to be wary. Ryper wasn't as disoriented as he looked.

"What did you say?" the German barked.

"I told him to pay attention. Untie his hands."

Signing quickly, he asked what had happened. Haugland told him everything. Where are the other trucks? Make sure everyone is safe.

"What you talking about?" the German growled.

Solheim felt the hair on the back of his neck rise as he formed his lie. "He doesn't understand why he was arrested. He says he became disoriented after the car crash. He didn't understand what the soldiers wanted. He thought he had been set upon by thieves."

"All right. Ask him his name."

Solheim signed the question and was surprised that Haugland fingerspelled Jens Hansen.

"He's says his name is Jens Hansen."

"Good. Now ask him where Kjell Arneson is. He is wanted."

I not know, Haugland signed. Which was the truth.

Before Solheim could finish, a man grabbed Haugland by his hair and slammed his head into his lap, then beat his back with a truncheon.

Haugland gasped from the pain initially, then let out a strangled cry that sounded high pitched and uncontrollable. Deaf speech. His face was drawn and covered with sweat. His left eye was bruised. He stared ahead gaining control of himself, swallowing.

"Was that necessary?" Solheim asked. "I can't talk to him if you do that."

The German raised an eyebrow. "I just wondered if you thought that was a real voice."

"He has vocal chords, for God's sake," Solheim said. "He just can't make speech."

"Then ask him where Kjell Arneson is. If he doesn't, he'll be beaten again and worse."

Solheim signed to him, but Haugland didn't talk about Arneson. Leave city. I here. They have what they want. No one look for you. But, go now!

And you?

I do what I have to do. I say nothing. Save yourself. Go Sweden. Call Boy Scout. Tell him say to mother, I love her. I never forgot her.

Solheim looked at him miserably, aware that the Germans were expecting some answer. They had been signing too long. But Haugland gave him some answers to say: Tell trolls I go Oslo. For school. I come home for Christmas surprise. Take boat to see friend. Friend at home.

Solheim passed this on to the Germans. The officer whom he now realized must be the *Kriminalsekretaer* frowned. "Ask him where Arneson would go if he wanted to leave."

Haugland indicated that he didn't know. Really. His friend lived in village, didn't travel much, but had friends out in the islands.

In three vicious punches to his head, Haugland was knocked off the chair onto the floor. One of the Germans grabbed him by the hair and held his head off the floor while another took a chain and whipped his back. The officer kicked him in the side repeatedly.

Helpless, Haugland writhed and groaned, but remarkably, still stayed in character. Solheim had no idea how long he could continue to do it.

"Stop!" Solheim cried. "He needs to see me to answer." He knelt down beside his prostrate friend, half expecting a kick in the side himself, but he became pastor to this prisoner and tended to him. To his great relief, the men stepped back, and he was left alone.

He turned Haugland over carefully. A little moan escaped from his swollen lips, but he was conscious. His face was battered near the left eye, a swelling quickly developing. Blood seeped out at the edge of his panting mouth. He opened his eyes slowly.

Go now. Leave me.

I get lawyer for you.

Not work. Go.

Maybe... they stop if you play dumb... completely.

They not care. Haugland gasped as he tried to move.

What can I do for you?

Get me pill. Haugland laughed harshly at that, his teeth etched with blood. Better.... you run. Warn others.

"That's enough, priest," the German warned.

Solheim stood up, watching helplessly as Haugland was roughly placed back on the chair. He hadn't passed out yet, but he was close. Blood from his left ear was dripping onto his muscular shoulder. Solheim thought that it was odd he noticed that. All the prayers on the earth wouldn't help. No bolt of lightning for the wicked. He couldn't do anything except wait for the German to tell him what to do next.

Solheim was there for over an hour, precariously answering the questions thrown at Haugland in such a way as to limit the abuse now viciously increasing each time he answered the wrong way. Sometime during the hour, a small, slender and dark man with intense eyes under a heavy brow walked into the room. Solheim immediately felt those eyes on him. They seemed to probe his very soul. It was Rinnan. He was sure of it.

After a time, the newcomer asked some questions of his own. He never showed himself to Haugland. He always stayed behind him.

Evidently, Rinnan knew a good deal about Fjellstad and the movement of arms and intelligence out in the islands. He knew of boats coming from the Shetlands. He asked Haugland who Ryper was. When Haugland didn't answer or was evasive, he was flogged with a whip or punched in the face.

Yet throughout the whole ordeal, Haugland held himself very well, sometimes on the edge of stubbornness or defiance. But always in character. He created a confusion, a wanting to cooperate in some way but never sure what they wanted from him. His signed answers were simple and logical, but limited by what a deaf man actually might know.

"Enough," Rinnan finally said. "Horst needs a rest." He nodded at the German interrogator, then gave some orders and left.

For a moment, Solheim didn't know what to do. When the Germans came over to Haugland, in an act of bravery which seemed to him like cowardice for being so late, he asked to talk to Haugland one more time.

"All right," the *Kriminalskretaer* said, leaving. "Help him get dressed."

Solheim helped Haugland struggle into his shirt and sweater. Haugland was in a lot of pain, barely able to raise his arms, but he didn't cry out, just as he hadn't during most of the session. Solheim buttoned the shirt, worried that it would stick into the cuts on his bleeding back.

Tusen takk, Haugland signed. His eyes looked so weary, but there was a sparkle there that shamed the priest. He smiled faintly at Solheim. Go in peace. But go fast.

Solheim laughed nervously. Anything more I do for you?

Haugland looked like he wanted to say something, but for the first time, he looked afraid. *Nei.* Nothing. He turned away.

Solheim tapped his arm. I sorry.

No need. I did my part. My all for Norway.

He looked straight at Solheim. Help yourself. If you can, help my friends. Now go.

"Get up," the German ordered, pushing on Haugland to move. "Leave," he told Solheim. The *Kriminalsekretaer* was waiting outside for him.

Solheim backed away and headed for the door. At the door, he turned back to say farewell. Haugland must have sensed it, for he looked up at him. Tall and erect, he didn't seem stooped or cowered by anything, but fiercely proud.

This is how I want to remember you. Solheim signed a blessing, then quickly left.

Solheim was out of Mission Hotel by five and home by a quarter to six. He declined a ride, wanting instead to breathe in the sharp cold air. He walked home in the predawn dark guided by the faint light reflected by the snow. He wasn't followed. By noon he had disappeared from Trondheim now free of restrictions and waiting for the Prince of Peace.

CHAPTER 92

"More sausage?" The staff waiter in a crisp white uniform waited patiently.

Martine Koeller looked up from his plate of poached eggs and smiled. Since he got up this morning, things had gone quite well. Gebhardt had flirted with a pretty *fraulein* in the Gestapo office, capturing a ten o'clock appointment with *Obersturmbannführer* Gerhard Flesch, Gestapo head for the region. Now all they had to do was wait for the secretary to come get them. First brunch.

"*Danke.*" The gentle strains of *Stille Nacht* made him feel homesick. This had always been a happy time of year for him. The Christmas music drifted through the SS officer dining room decorated with gold foil angels and silver tinsel. "Some for my aides here too."

The wait wasn't long. After consuming liberal amounts of poached eggs and sausage at a table gaily decorated for the season, they were given a few minutes to freshen up, then ushered into a room with high windows hung with red velvet curtains. Two officers of the SS waited behind a leather-topped oak table. While Gebhardt stayed to the back, Koeller stepped forward and saluted them smartly, stomping in place at the end of "*Heil Hitler*

Flesch nodded. "Why don't you sit? Some coffee, perhaps?"

"*Danke.*" Koeller sat down. "I heard there was a *razzia* on the coast. Excellent results?"

"*Danke schein.* It went very well indeed." Flesch smiled, one colleague to another. Now, about this schoolteacher in your report. He was fingered for the train sabotage last spring when Stapo head Martinsen was aboard?"

"*Ja*, and more." Koeller told of his recent findings about the man in Bergen.

"U-boats?" He had the attention of both officers now.

"Who the devil is he?"

"A very clever Norwegian agent too long out of our scrutiny," Koeller snapped his fingers at Gebhardt. He came forward with a file. Koeller took out the pictures of Haugland. The skier and the soccer player. Flesch stared at the team picture, his face puzzled, then took one look at the single picture of a young Haugland holding skis and wearing a Nordic sweater.

"*Mein Gott.* Boesten, look." He passed the photo to the *Kriminalsekretaer.* "How did you come into these?" Flesch asked.

"The team picture is from the university." Koeller pointed. "That photograph is from his mother's home in Bergen." His heart thumped. What he had was important.

"You have a name?" Flesch's eyes bulged.

"His name is Tore Haugland. He comes from a well-educated family. His father was a professor at the university in Oslo. He did studies in England. Speaks English fluently."

Flesch scanned the report. "His uncle is a defective, a deaf-mute." He rang a bell under his desk. A male secretary came in. "Call Lola and have him come here immediately."

"You find this useful? You have a possible lead?'

"You, sir, have provided us with some very worthwhile information. Most extraordinary."

Koeller stood up, feeling warm glow of pride. "I was doing my duty. You know him?"

"*Ja.* At the moment the criminal is in the basement of this building. You will come to dinner later? We're having a little Christmas Eve fete."

"I'd be honored."

***

Haugland stirred against the wall. He must have passed out again or dozed. He was sitting on the cold concrete floor, in the same position since he was first brought here in the morning, his right wrist handcuffed to a metal pipe. He hurt everywhere except for his fingers. They had to leave those alone so he could sign. He hadn't been allowed to drink water or go to the bathroom. He was aware of the metal pot over by the door, but he couldn't reach it, so he had relieved himself an hour ago not far from where he was. He knew that this was all a part of the dehumanization planning the Gestapo excelled at. He had had training lectures on it years ago, grisly reports of those who had gotten away to freedom in Sweden or England.

He leaned against the cold wall. His sense of humor must be turning macabre. A report of a woman physician imprisoned for some time in the early years popped into his mind. She had said torture and treatment of prisoners wasn't so bad, from what she'd seen. One could bear it. It was like the pain of childbirth.

"If this is childbirth, I'll be extra careful about getting a woman pregnant."

He thought of a baby being born. It was something he would never see.

He tried to conjure Anna's face. He'd like to have made a baby with her. Maybe a whole bevy of them. He tried to imagine her body looking pregnant, but all he could see was the slenderness, the special places he liked to touch. Wonderful.

He'd never see her again, either. She smiled at him and disappeared into the dark.

He shifted his weight gingerly, trying to rub some life into his legs. He should move around. Start some sort of physical program, to keep alert, to be able to respond to questioning.

He knew what was going to happen to him. He could be shot any time, but in the meantime he had to limit the interrogations that would wear him down. He had lives to protect.

He stopped and listened when footsteps echoed down the hallway. Some time before Flesch had come down with an officer in the SS. He looked familiar. Koeller. That was the name. "This the man?" Flesch had asked. Koeller said "*Ja*!" and left.

He braced himself when a key was turned and the metal door thrown open. The light from the hallway blinded him. A soldier in the SD unlocked the handcuffs, ordering him to get up. In the hallway were two heavily armed Norwegians dressed in ordinary clothes. The soldier handcuffed Haugland again, making him wince. He tried to relax, not to show fear, but he *was* afraid. Perhaps a firing squad waited for him.

They slammed a blindfold across his eyes. Helpless, he was led down the hall limping on a half-dead foot. He climbed a long flight of stairs and suddenly he was outside in the frigid bite of the night air. It was sweet, like freedom. Was it Christmas Eve or early morning on Christmas Day?

They shoved him into a rumbling car, barely clearing his head. Someone sat beside him, and the car took off. He listened for the sounds of the street under his feet. First cobblestone, then a different surface. He assumed he had been at Mission Hotel. Where was he going now? Vollan Prison? Falstad concentration camp? The people in the car gave him no clue.

Eventually, they stopped. The door was opened. Haugland was shoved up a sidewalk. Somewhere far off he heard a church bell toll one in the morning. His feet hit stairs and he stumbled. Hands grabbed him roughly and propelled him into some building then down a hall. He was stopped and the blindfold removed. To his surprise he found himself in a residence. Looking into a parlor, he saw a tree gaily decorated for the holiday. He also spied a large collection of medieval torture implements displayed on the wall. Haugland's mouth began to get even drier than it was. He was pushed toward a door that opened down into a basement.

"Move," a voice said behind him. He was walking better now so made his way down the stairs steadily, lowering his head as he did so. Halfway down he stopped. He was coming down into a spacious basement that apparently had been divided up into several different rooms.

The one in front of him had been a den of some sort. There were still bottles on the wall in an open display area and a number of large caskets. What really made his heart stop were the posters on the wall. One was supposedly of a man, created from a question mark, stating that the man who knows everything—can do everything and does everything. The second was more direct. It was a skeleton holding a scythe. Underneath, it read, "Welcome to the Party!"

Haugland's heart sagged. He had arrived at the Cloister and Rinnan was host.

CHAPTER 93

The soldiers left Anna's farm on Christmas Day, regrouping at the schoolhouse. They were still looking for Kjell Arneson and Helmer Stagg. Due to the holiday and new orders from the Gestapo in Trondheim, the soldiers were permitted to celebrate the season. As she watched them from her window, she could see smoldering smoke still rising from the ruins of Kjell's home near the schoolhouse. There were now five destroyed boats on the water.

She rolled down the blackout curtain. The soldiers had been in and out for two days. Having discovered her gramophone, they asked permission to take it to the barn where they played Christmas music. Anna didn't know whether to be outraged or amused at the lack of sensitivity. Though they had seen action in Finland only last winter and were hardened soldiers, they were barely out of their teens.

Some of them made ornaments for her little tree. Others kept the wood bin loaded and the kindling wood split even finer. They tried to make friends with Lisel and played with her cat. By Christmas Eve, Anna wished they would get out and stay out, but when they came to her door and sang to her, she wept softly at the first harmonious strains of *Est Ein Rose.* It was lovely and poignant and very confusing. She thanked them and withdrew, wondering if she could get through the next day thinking of Jens.

Schiller asked permission to stay. He had kept to himself and was often gone on duty, but he must have known she would never let him touch her again. When he tried to tell her of his distress about the boats being blown up and the houses destroyed, she was unmoved.

She let him drink tea while she wrapped some final presents she had made. Using butcher paper she had stamped with paint and a potato, she finished off the package with yarn she had spun and dyed. "Nice," he said looking like he wished there was one for him.

He left at nine in Ella Bjornson's commandeered car. As soon as he was gone, she locked the back door and hurriedly put together coffee and hot soup for a mission of mercy to the cellar for the first time in over twenty-four hours. She had to bring the men up. They couldn't endure the cold much longer without becoming sick, but it meant she'd have to take a risk with Lisel who was already asleep with her new doll—a beautiful one Jens had given her.

Going down with her flashlight, to her surprise, she found them over by the dairy door looking out its dirty frosted window.

"*God Kveld.*" Kjell and Helmer came out of the dark shivering.

She put a finger to her lips, then invited them to come up.

Upstairs, they found the table lit with a candle and hand-wrapped packages beside by two place settings. The fires in both stoves were roaring and cinnamon wafted out a teapot.

"Where's your daughter?" Kjell asked.

"In her bedroom. You can't stay down there anymore, *Herr* Arneson. You'll both get sick."

"What about soldiers?" Helmer asked.

"Gone back to the village. Schiller's gone too. They won't be back."

The men sat down like famished prisoners, visibly moved by her act of kindess.

"This is very kind. *Takk.*" Kjell held socks she had knit originally for Jens.

Helmer spoke with a full mouth. "What news do you have?"

"The boats left on the twenty-third. Some men from the SD are still around, but the *Wehrmacht* soldiers will continue the search."

"Why? Why leave so suddenly?" Kjell wondered.

"Schiller said the bulk of the arrests have been around Hitra and the islands there."

Kjell's face turned pale. "Sig," he murmured under his breath.

"There is something else," Anna said softly. "I didn't say before, but they searched in Trondheim. Schiller said they were looking for a leader connected to the coastal operations. He said he was trapped." When Kjell's head shot up, she knew he understood her fear. It was Jens.

Without a word, Anna took away their bowls and cups and cleaned up. Anything to change the subject, but Helmer came over. "I'll wash. Go talk to Kjell."

"Anna, come and sit." Kjell pulled out a chair.

Anna sat down. Wanting to avoid the subject of Jens, she talked about their escape. "Based on what Schiller says, I think in a couple of more days it will be safe for you to go. I have a complete set of skis and another set of skis, but no poles. They're hidden downstairs."

"Maybe we can make poles." Helmer held up soapy hands. "All we need are saplings and some leather. They could be made by the fire here."

"I can cut them," Anna said. "There are saplings in the woods. As for food, I have some ham left from a trade during summer." She also had Einar's rucksack upstairs in the attic and clothes that she'd never had the heart to give away. "I can go to the *landhandel* tomorrow, though soldiers might be monitoring certain purchases, but if we plan well, you can leave two days from now."

Kjell said, "Gud er god." Helmer agreed.

And I am no longer the Woman, the German whore, she thought.

***

Haugland opened his right eye and stared across the concrete floor. Lying on his side, his left arm stretched out above him. *Where was he?*

The chill of the floor seeped into his bare shoulder, forcing him to move. Immediately, his back exploded with pain as sharp as a knife, causing him to gasp and cry out. Then he remembered. He was handcuffed to a sink.

He bit his lip to stifle further outcry, his body shaking from the cold. *Had someone heard him?* Haugland stopped trembling and listened. Something was over there. When he tried to raise his head, he was rewarded with not only excruciating pain but the sickening sensation of blood oozing down his back to the floor as wounds tore open anew and bled.

"Who's there?" he whispered. He felt weak and light-headed. The almost non-stop punishment was taking its toll. Someone had not only linked him to the coastal operation, but his activities in the Bergen area two years ago. His spy work alone singled him out for a firing squad, but Rinnan wanted to know everything about his role with the Shetland Bus.

All pretenses about being Jens Hansen were beaten out of him. He never admitted it to them, but they knew his name was Haugland and to prove it, hit him so hard in the ear when he attempted to remain mute and sign that his left ear was damaged. Now he *was* deaf.

He had lost track of time. The faces changed, but everyone seemed to enjoy their work, Gestapo and Norwegian lackeys alike. Worst of all was Rinnan. *Sonderabteilung Lola* who hosted the party with an intensity that defied description.

Haugland turned over his left wrist. There were burns all over it made by a soldering iron during the last session. The Gestapo decided to try a new method, although an old trick. Apparently, the Hitra fishermen had been giving the Germans a hard time. No one talked. Gestapo head Flesch selected one of them to come to the Cloister to watch Haugland being beaten and tortured. To his surprise, the poet Holger Haraldsen came, showing signs of mistreatment himself. When their eyes met, each man knew what must be done. When no one was looking, Haugland signed, Be strong. And then, very quickly, Sverre safe in Sweden.

It was all that passed between them, but Haugland knew this bit of news would comfort him and his father. It was the only comfort. Even after witnessing Haugland being burned and knocked senseless, the fisherman refused to cooperate. Not even the threat of execution made them speak.

Haugland thought he heard a stirring again. It was hard to tell with his damaged ear. Then a pungent smell hit his nose. Suddenly a rat scurried along the wall, stopping to sniff. It sat up, its tiny paws quivering. Instinctively, he pulled back, wondering if he should kick at it to go away. It got down on all fours and looked around, then scurried away.

From somewhere out in the main room came the sound of footsteps coming down the stairs, making Haugland's heart contract involuntarily. It was going to start all over again. He looked at his wrists and wondered if there was a way to cut them.

He lay with his head flat on the floor, trying to control his shivering. The shoes scuffed the pine board floor, sounding hollow as they reached the concrete. They stopped beside him.

Sorting squatted down next to him looking at Haugland curiously, like he was determining what sort of fish or fowl he was. He examined Haugland's wrist handcuffed above him, then suddenly rolled Haugland toward his stomach.

Haugland stifled a cry of agony.

"Is this what you want? Sorting asked. "It doesn't have to be this way. I can speak for you. I admire your intelligent campaign, but it's over and now you have to carry the brunt of it."

He turned on the tap and filled a cup. Gently lifting Haugland's head, he offered him some water. Haugland didn't want to accept, but his mouth was so dry, his swollen lips splitting, so he couldn't refuse. When he'd had enough, Sorting put it away, then laid a clean flannel shirt over Haugland's torso. Its warmth soothed him.

Sorting lit a cigarette. "Being stubborn won't accomplish anything. The end is pretty obvious, but the journey… that can be altered. You don't have to suffer anymore. I'll see to it. Just cooperate a little bit."

Haugland said nothing.

"The Chief knows everything about you. The case is pretty solid. He'd just liked to clear up the matter of the arms. A bunch of boxes isn't worth it. He'll kill you." He grabbed Haugland on his chin. "Believe me, I've seen him do it. He takes his time. I think you should think about it, because he doesn't like you. You're taking too long."

Sorting nudged Haugland, enough to make him gasp. He opened his eye.

"He's unpredictable. Last year, a man was brought here from Lillehavn. He died in a room not far from here. When we found him he was as stiff as a board. We couldn't get him into a coffin. The Chief had him chopped up so he would fit."

Haugland swallowed, his stomach in revolt. Sorting was talking about Einar Fromme. He was sure of it.

"Listen to me Hans—Haugland— the Chief will get what he wants. He wants to know how to get in touch with Arneson and where the boxes are buried. We know they're around here with more out in the islands. Say anything, I'll get him to stop."

Haugland's stomach rebelled. Maybe he drank too much water. Suddenly, he rolled over and threw up on Sorting's knee.

"Fuck!" Sorting scrambled back, slamming the handcuffed arm viciously.

Haugland cried out, then hushed, not wanting to give Sorting anymore satisfaction.

Above him, Sorting washed off his pants. "I'll ignore that accident. Remember what I said."

It was tempting. It would be so easy to do it—and then he could sleep. He remembered it when Rinnan returned with Birger Strom and Karl Dolmen. Together they lifted him up naked onto the stool. When he didn't answer their question, they took him over to a metal door on one of the cloister rooms and placing his left hand flat on it, took a hammer to it.

Bones crunching, Haugland began to pass out, but Strom wasn't done. Strom seized and twisted it behind him. Dolmen removed the nails of the damaged fingers with pliers. Not able to respond with anything other than heartrending cries hurled deep from his chest, Haugland found darkness, thinking of an old saying: "On the gallows, the first night is the worse."

But this had to be the fifth.

***

The same day Sorting came to the Cloister, Kjell Arneson and Helmer Stagg slipped out of Fjellstad.

Without suspicion Anna had been able to round up gloves, matches and other items useful on the *fjell.* Rummaging through Einar's old clothing, she added to what Kjell and Helmer already wore. She cut saplings and found an old harness strap for Helmer to make poles for the second pair of skis. And when all that was accomplished, she knitted caps, found food, and cooked.

Lisel couldn't be kept out of the *stue* for long. When told they were friends of Jens, she became a willing helper. It was one more secret that she'd have to be trusted with. It was a heavy responsibility for a little girl taught not to lie.

Around three as the sun set, the men put together their belongings for the final time. Assembling their rucksacks at the door, they waited while Anna went out with her skis and went up and down the hill criss-crossing it with tracks so that when they took off, it would be as though someone had been playing. When she came back in, Kjell put on his rucksack and the cap she had made him in record time. Helmer followed suit. He looked like he wanted to say something to Anna, but instead put his head down and went outside.

"He hasn't forgotten his manners," Kjell apologized. "He's embarrassed about what he said about you. He wanted me to say something, but I think he should speak for himself."

"I forgive him. I only hope he'll remember me kindly when I need it the most." She watched him put on his gloves. "There's no chance I will see you again is there?"

"What can I say? I have no idea of where I'm going myself but I will speak for you, Anna Fromme. I'll see the proper authorities know what you've done. Even if I'm not in Norway."

"And Jens?"

He put his gloved hand gently on her arm. "Oh *datter,*" he said in a quiet voice. "If only I knew." He embraced her hard, his fears showing, then kissed on her cheek. "God bless you and keep you safe. Now if we don't get out of here, we'll never be able to make a break for it. No matter what happens, you have my eternal thanks."

***

In the long mirror, Koeller adjusted his uniform. "What do you think?" he asked Gebhardt. They'd be going to see Flesch in just a few moments and he wanted to look perfect.

"You look fine, sir," his aide answered.

Koeller had enjoyed the holiday here after all and was looking forward to concluding his business. It was a remarkable stroke of luck that the very man he was seeking had been in the Gestapo's hands the past few days. Now the matter of the sabotage on the train could be wrapped up and perhaps the investigation of von Weber concluded as well. Trondheim was not only pleased with this major coup of capturing this agent, but Victoria Terrasse in Oslo as well. A job well done. Except for one small problem.

Oslo wanted to interrogate the agent, but he wasn't in Flesch's hands. He was in Rinnan's. He wouldn't be turned over until Rinnan was done with him. *How could a local Norwegian turncoat have such power?* Koeller wondered. He hoped to find out more about the progress of the interrogations. It had been nearly a week since the agent's arrest.

They took the elevator up to the main office. Someone from Flesch's personal staff greeted them. "There's been a change in plans," he said. "Flesch is unavailable, but *bitte, Kriminalskretaer* Boesten will meet with you."

The officer took them down to the next floor and ushered them into a spacious room.

"What's happened?" Koeller tried to hide his disappointment.

"Your schoolteacher has broken. Flesch is on his way over to Lola's operational headquarters right now. We'll have what we want."

The *Kriminalsekretaer* apologized with a curt bow. "It's a complicated case. It depends on the final outcome of the interrogations. We'll let you know as soon as possible."

He would let Koeller know, but when he did, it wouldn't be what Koeller wanted to hear: the prisoner couldn't be transferred because the prisoner was dead.

CHAPTER 94

Haugland lay face down on the cold floor. He could sense footsteps coming before he heard them, filling him with a listless dread. In one sense, it frightened him; in another, it just brought him closer to what he desired most. His ordeal had gone beyond anything fathomable. To face another session was too much. He was sometimes delirious and out of his head, the posters of the skeleton and question mark man dancing before him.

Once he hallucinated and saw his deaf uncle. Dressed in clothes from a concentration camp, the old man sat down beside him and warned him in sign about the *Draugen*. He mustn't look.

But Haugland had looked.

Onkel Kris told him to be still and not talk to the trolls. He'd be turned to stone.

But he had spoken.

He couldn't concentrate and keep track of things. On a couple of occasions, they tricked him into speaking English. Afraid that the names of Tommy, Lars, and captains on the Shetland Bus would spill out, Haugland recited the poetry of Dunne and Tennyson. When they realized what he was doing, they stripped him and suspended him upside down between two wine caskets and whipped him on his buttocks until he couldn't sit. His scrotum was swollen. His hand was pounded again until the fingers became infected, swelling to twice their normal size.

In the end, he suffered everything and finally didn't care. He sought release, but too weak to even lift his head to bash it against a wall, he had to find another way.

During a lucid moment, he became aware of their knowledge of the scheduled Shetland Bus coming to the area around Namsos. Alarmed, his muddled brain began to formulate a plan that would save it and at the same time give him the final release he sought.

"Stop," he said just as they were about to hit him again. "The… boat. I know about… that boat." Through torn lips that caught on his teeth he told them he'd talk, but only to Sorting.

Immediately, he was left alone. Someone brought him gruel and attempted to feed him, but it only made him sick. Exhausted, he drifted and fell into a troubled, semi-conscious sleep only to be wakened when Sorting came back.

Rinnan's men half-dragged Haugland to the main room with the posters, but he couldn't sit so they let him curl against the wall. At the little man's signal, everyone left except Sorting.

"I assumed you have been thinking things over." Sorting crouched down beside him. "What is it that you want?"

Haugland raised his head. He had no idea of time, but knew he had deteriorated and was very ill. When he spoke, his swollen lips made speech difficult. "You said you... would hel' me."

Sorting pulled up a stool and lit a cigarette. "*Ja...*"

"Hel' me. I'll tell about the boats. Your coordinates are wrong."

"How would you know that?"

"Because I met wi' someone… with XU. I'll take… you to the exact spot. Tell you… what to… radio... if you want them to come in."

Sorting rubbed his lips with his cigarette hand. "And what do *you* want?"

"Release me. Don't let them bring me back here. "*Vær så snill...* I can't stand it anymore."

Haugland put as much emotion into his words as his strength could allow and hoped to stay conscious long enough to get the message of warning off. He'd give them wrong coordinates and stall their return. He wasn't strong enough to kill himself, but maybe they'd throw him overboard. He closed his eye briefly.

"I'll ask the Chief. He gives final approval." Sorting took Haugland's damaged hand turning it back and forth. Haugland sucked his breath in. His bloated eye welled up.

"Pity," Sorting said before shoving it back.

Rinnan agreed. Set up against the wall, Haugland described an elaborate scenario. His knowledge of the operation of the Shetland Bus helped him to invent something that sounded real enough without damage to its operation. He promised Rinnan the correct frequency when they got out, but would write the message before they left.

"Why don't you do it now?"

When Haugland finished writing, Rinnan said, "You're wise to cooperate. We've had knowledge of your operation for some time. For months I've had someone from your village help us in uncovering every facet of the operation."

Haugland looked at Sorting.

"It wasn't my man here. It was a woman."

Haugland's head rang. He wasn't sure he heard him right, but there was a strange smile on Rinnan's lips and the others like they knew an obscene secret.

"Woman?"

"*Ja*. Someone very close to you. She's very beautiful. You've known her for months."

"I know… no woman..." Haugland's eyebrows crinkled. It was such an effort to think.

"So close and you didn't know. Probably screwed her." The men laughed, taunting him.

In his confusion, a horrible idea began to form. *A woman. Someone close to him. Someone he cared about.* An image formed through the haze of pain: beautiful Anna spinning wool out in a sunny meadow. A breeze caressed her face and hair. Then he thought of Schiller and the money under the floorboards of her bedroom. The sky went black. Feeling betrayed, not wanting to believe, he stared at them. Rinnan gave no name, only lewd comments about her.

"You trusted just like I trust you… but it'd be wrong if you should lie to me. That would disappoint me. Trust is such a special thing." Rinnan leaned in, smiling wickedly. "I'd like to impress on you what would happen if you lied. Let's call it my seal of approval."

On signal, Dolmen and Strom grabbed him and pushed him to the floor. When he couldn't struggle anymore, they pulled his pants down. Held in a vise, he looked helplessly to Sorting. The man shrugged and did nothing. Rinnan brought over a hot brand.

"You're mine," Rinnan said as he rammed it onto Haugland's hip. The skin seared and smoked.

Haugland jerked and screamed, "Jesus!"

It was more a prayer than a curse. By the time Rinnan removed the white-hot brand, leaving a medium-sized blistering, swastika, Haugland passed out.

***

Rinnan quickly ordered an E-boat. Naval command was notified and a number of heavily-armed ships diverted to meet them at the mouth of Trondheimfjord for a journey out to the islands.

"The boat's expected around eleven at night," he said. "I want to be in position long before."

They carried Haugland onboard wrapped in a heavy wool blanket and set him inside on the bridge. He wore only pants, a tattered shirt, and socks. When he regained consciousness, no one bothered him since he was too weak to move. He lay on the metal deck in the blanket with his knees drawn up to his chest, his hair matted and caked with sweat and blood. A couple of hours after they left, Sorting found him in a stupor and incoherent.

"I kept my part of the bargain," Sorting demanded. "Give me the exact coordinates and the frequency." He had to work to get Haugland awake and stay focused. Finally, he was able to get him to sit up, ignoring the man's suffering as he tried to comply.

Haugland asked for a piece of paper. His bloodied fingers made blots as he wrote the information down. When he was finished, he weakly lay the pencil beside him.

"It's done, you bastard... Now leave me alone." Haugland closed his eyes and painfully rolled himself into the blanket. It was the last thing Sorting heard him say. He lost consciousness after that, finally becoming comatose.

***

They never saw the boat. Haugland had apparently warned the submarine chaser off with some sort of interruption code. When the Chief realized the trick, he flew into a rage. Finding Haugland unconscious on the floor of the bridge, he had Dolmen beat him anyway, then taken down below decks to a storage locker and thrown in. He *would* return with them to Trondheim.

They smuggled Haugland back to the Cloister where Rinnan had more plans for him. He was dragged feet first down the stairs to the den, his head banging on the stairs and left in the blanket on the floor. Several hours later, Dolmen and Sorting found him still in the same position. Further attempts to revive him were fruitless. It was apparent Haugland wouldn't last much longer. His pulse was weak and his coloring pasty. With Rinnan present, the men decided he'd be disposed of by hanging then taken out to a forest twenty miles north of the town. They checked his pockets for any identification and his shirt and tags removed. Dolmen tied Haugland's hands behind him with a rope and made a noose ready, but Rinnan was still angry and kicking Haugland in the side, said they'd wait until morning.

Sorting rose early for breakfast. He found Rinnan still seething over being duped.

"He still alive?" Rinnan growled when Sorting came into the eating area.

"I don't know."

"Go check."

Haugland was slumped on the floor on his stomach and bound, a grotesque figure in the half-light of the basement. His face was swollen and there was widespread infection in his fingers and on his tattered, bloody back. Sorting listened for breathing. It was so faint that for a moment he thought the prisoner was dead, but he found a weak pulse. Sorting pulled the blanket over the stinking body so he didn't have to look at it.

"He's alive, but I don't think he's going to revive. His breathing's almost nil." Sorting spoke carefully, not sure of Rinnan's reaction. "What do you want done? I can get Birger to help me string him up."

"Never mind about that. I've got a call out past Sona. There was a disturbance I want to look into. We'll take him with us and dispose of him there in the forest nearby."

Rinnan's eyes flashed. "He outsmarted you, Sorting, but between you and Freyda, we got most of the damn organization. We'll crack the Hitra men soon enough. Perhaps even find Kjell Arneson."

They wrapped Haugland tight in a blanket and laid him on a rubber pad on the back seat of Rinnan's Studebaker. Riding out to the Stjordalen, a major valley and thoroughfare to Sweden, Rinnan interrogated a group of farmers thought to be aiding refugees from the POW camps for Yugoslavs. When he was done, the party of cars left. They were anxious to get back. There was not only a New Year's Eve party to go to but reports that a major snowstorm was moving in.

About five miles south of the village, the Studebaker stopped. Rinnan issued orders for the remaining cars to go on ahead. He had his driver turn his car up an old logging road. By now the light was growing dim and the snow falling steadily. The car went back until it stopped at the foot of a landslide. Rinnan ordered Sorting and Dolmen to bring Haugland out. Uncovering his face, he appeared to be dead. There was no pulse and the skin was cold. Together they carried him down into a ravine and pushed him up under some brambles.

They came back up but Rinnan became agitated. "Shoot him."

Dolmen obeyed, firing his revolver down into the bushes. Everyone piled back into the car and after turning around, they left, leaving the body to the snow and frigid winter wind.

CHAPTER 95

Six days after the New Year, Anna went into the *landhandel.* To her surprise, she found a letter for her. Going back, she stopped halfway out on the road. There had been a thaw and some of the boats left for fishing. It made her think of Kjell Arneson. It had been ten days since she had sent him on his way with Helmer Stagg. She supposed, though, that if there wasn't any news about them that was good, just as she supposed that the lack of news meant things were all right for Jens.

On one of the rocks above the scree that flowed down to the rocky beach, she stopped and sat down to read the letter. She had no idea who'd written it. It was postmarked in Molde. She knew no one in Molde. Opening it up, she found a typewritten, strangely worded message that read:

> *Arrived safe at Mother's. Please look in the dairy for lost sweater. Inside box. Be strong. Sad news. Love has died and won't be home when freedom soars. Ignore talk. So sorry.*
>
> *Signed, Otta.*

The signature was hand-written. She didn't understand what it meant until she realized that *Otta* was the name of Kjell's boat and then too swiftly the message became clear.

Love has died. He was speaking of Jens. Jens was dead. He wouldn't be coming home after the war. Kjell wanted her to know that while he was personally safe, Jens was gone. She was to ignore how the authorities said he'd died. She put the note down in her lap and stared out over the water, feeling at first numb and then pain as sharp as a knife.

Dead. She'd never see him again. Her lips began to tremble as she bit back tears, then she choked as the sobs rumbled out of her from deep inside. It wasn't fair. *Why him?* And why dear God, did she have to go through this pain again? To lose someone she loved all over again after gaining a new love and trust and feelings of tenderness. In her despair, she crunched the letter in her hand and brought it to her lips, then rocked and rocked until she was all rung out of tears.

A gull flew overhead and startled her with its cry. Standing up, she watched the bird sink and glide out over the water then charge away on some errand. Its confidence was inspiring. *I should be like that*, she thought. That was something *he* wanted for her.

Back at the house, Anna took out the letter she had stuffed into her pocket and studied the words. Sweater in the Dairy. Inside box. Now why would he say that? She decided to go look. Taking a flashlight, she told Lisel she was going to the dairy for a moment. She could come if she liked.

"Are the men still there?"

"*Nei*, Munchkin. They're gone." Anna waited for her to decide, but when she stayed back, went down on her own. It was cold in the cellar. She remembered how the men came to her when she brought food. Shivering, their hands and fingers crippled by the cold. Shining the flashlight about the bone-chilling space, an image came to her of Jens lying dead somewhere, his body gray and stiff as stone. Cold as the water in the fjord, as cold as snow. The image was so lonely that she began to weep again, her tears feeling hot in the chilled air.

She went into the cave and brought out the box. Sitting on a chair out in the dairy, she shined the light on the contents inside. There was no sweater, but on top of her letters, photos and affidavit, there was a note attached to an envelope. She assumed the note was in Kjell's handwriting. It said:

> *Jens will kill me, but I think you should let Ella know what happened. When things are more settled, take the note in the envolope to her. She will recognize my handwriting and believe you. She is a fair woman and can help. As for Jens, he is as honest a person as I ever met. He is well educated but he has good common sense to see things clearly about people. Some day he will make a great fisherman. God bless and keep you."*

Anna laughed through her tears. Friend. She signed it, gathering strength from its very meaning.

***

Two days later, while cleaning out the steamer trunk upstairs in the attic, she discovered a photograph wedged in the back of one of the pullout drawers. It was a picture of two young men and a boy joking around at some lake. One of them was Einar and the sight of him so much younger than when she first met him was delightful. He was so handsome and alive.

The blonde man next to him she didn't know. The boy was a teenager with dark hair and light eyes. Eyes that danced. As he looked at her across the distance of time, she knew that it was Jens. That he had known Einar and didn't tell her was shocking, but it was also oddly comforting.

Einar hadn't left her. He had sent a friend.

Book 4

Det vil helst gå godt.
Everything will work out all right.
—Norwegian saying

CHAPTER 96

Norway, 1945

The young man on the bed was on his side, still as death, the only sign of life the soft jagged breathing from his mouth. For more than a week, he had lain unconscious, first racked by fever, then an appalling listlessness that had disintegrated into a state of abnormal quiet as he feebly fought back against the effects of his injuries.

The past ten days had been pure hell for Hans Gunnerson. Ever since finding the man alive in the snow, the old logger had fought to save his life with every trick and skill he knew, cajoling the little spark of life along like a man coaxing a flame from tinder to wood. But after he had him stabilized from a second round of fever and chills, he knew his injuries were too insidious. Three days after finding him, he donned his skis and went to see the village doctor.

"Oskar's gone to see a case of bronchitis," Britta Torholm, the doctor's wife, told him. "You can visit, if you like."

"*Takk.*" Gunnerson warmed himself kitchen, but became increasingly impatient.

"What's wrong?" she finally asked after thirty minutes of his smoldering edginess.

"I must go back. I can't wait any longer. Tell Oskar that I need to see him as soon as possible." He paused, and then muttered. "*Nei.* I can't do that. He's gone until tomorrow, right?"

"*Ja.*"

"Then *you* must come. God forgive me, but I need your surgical nursing skills. It's a matter of life and death. You mustn't tell anyone. Leave a note saying you'll be back tomorrow."

He gave her instructions on what to bring and how to meet him outside the village. Assembling his knapsack and skis, he left after she promised to go with him.

It was snowing heavily and growing dark when Britta Torholm and an anxious Gunnerson arrived at the cabin. Although he had filled her in on some details about his charge, he could see she wasn't prepared when she lifted up the blankets covering him.

"Oh, dear Lord." She leaned closer. "Is he gone?"

Gunnerson fell on his knees, feeling for a pulse. "Thank God," he choked.

"Let me, Hans. You're exhausted." Composing herself, she attended to the serious state of the man's injuries. Eventually, Gunnerson lay down, sleeping for the first time in three days.

The next day she returned to the village and came back with her husband, *Doctor* Oskar Torholm, and Jon Olsen, a member of the resistance from the next village.

"Who is he?" Olsen asked while the doctor examined him.

"I was hoping you might know. He wrote a name down, but it's not from around here." Gunnerson said. "Have there been any *razzias* lately?"

"There were some arrests before Christmas in Trondheim and rumors about a major *razzia* out in the islands, but I don't know. You sure it was Rinnan who put him there?"

Gunnerson glowered at him. "It was Rinnan."

"All right, but this is dangerous, Hans," Olsen said. "We'll assume this fellow is innocent, but if we are caught with him, we will be shot. Our friends and families will be shot."

"You may not have to worry about that." *Docktor* Torholm got up. "He should be hospitalized. but that would alert the state police and Gestapo so we must care for him here." He went to the sink and washed his hands. "Unless he's watched round-the-clock, he will die."

"I could do that, dear," Britta said. "I could announce I'm going on a `trip' south, but come back here until he's at least stable and hopefully conscious."

Torholm dried his hands. "I'll see about getting some medicine from the clinic. Should take a couple of days to get things set up.

"We'll get you some relief, Hans."

"In the meantime," Olsen said, "I'll put out some feelers."

***

The patient on the bed stirred and Gunnerson put his spoon down to watch him. The swelling on his face had gone down and under Torholm's care, there were signs of healing on his back as it changed from black to a mottled wine-purple color. The stitches had been removed from the numerous gashes on his back and the stubborn pockets of infection gone. There was even improvement in his mangled fingers and burn in his side. But he wouldn't wake.

"He may never, wake" the doctor said one evening. "You should prepare yourself for that, Hans. Perhaps it would be a kindness if he slipped away. He has suffered enough."

But Gunnerson couldn't admit defeat. The man had cheated Rinnan.

Torholm smuggled out an intravenous bottle and together they rigged a stand, but supplies and medicine were difficult to obtain as the war wound down. What they could give him was hit and miss. Forced feeding was sometimes necessary.

The man on the bed coughed. Gunnerson turned and was moved to see that at long last the gray eyes were opened and staring off into the space before him. He moved his bandaged hand closer to his face, but it disturbed the muscles in his shoulder and back.

He moaned in his throat like a wounded animal. The eyes closed, then opened again as if he were rationing all his strength. This time he made a concerted effort to look around. He seemed to focus on the wall of books going from floor to ceiling around the door, and then slept. An hour later, he woke again, moaning in pain. He stared blindly across the room.

For the rest of the day his patient drifted in and out. Sometimes he would open his eyes and stare vacantly into space, obviously in considerable pain. Other times he seemed more focused and responded to Gunnerson when he came over to him. During this time he would sometimes try to speak but his voice was so weak and whispery, he wasn't understood. Exhausted, he would drift off again. Sometimes, he would shape his fingers into patterns.

"Sweet boy," Britta murmured when she came back. "Do you think he's deaf?" She sat down and took his hand. Weakly he squeezed her hand back and holding on, fell asleep.

***

Tore was playing in a tree when he slipped and fell, landing on his back. It only knocked the wind out of him but when he rolled over to get up, his back began to split and tear like an old rotten curtain. It bled and bled and oh, God, it hurt so much. Lars said he was sorry and he called Onkel *Kris but he couldn't hear so he ran to their parents but Pappa couldn't come because he was dead. Mother came, though, and she soothed him with some magic words and lots of soup. He wanted to say he loved her and tell her he was sorry he couldn't call over the years, but he didn't dare talk because he might get into trouble with the trolls. She said she understood and sat down on a chair by the bed, looking at him lovingly with yellow eyes.*

In the warm stillness of the cabin, Haugland slowly came to consciousness and opened his eyes only to come face-to-face with that of a large gray cat with yellow eyes. Sitting opposite him on a chair, it regarded him in a drowsy way for a while. Satisfied that all was well it went to work washing a back leg. Haugland was drowsy himself. For a moment thought he was in his grandfather's cabin. They must have brought him here after the fall from the tree... *nei*. Puzzled by the silence of the room, he lifted his head from the pillow and discovered sound. He was deaf in his left ear. Was it the fall? He couldn't remember. Settling back into the sweet softness of the down pillow, he began to drift again when he heard something stir slightly behind him.

"Mother?" When there was no response, he tried to will his body to sit up. He was rewarded with excruciating pain in his back and shoulder. He felt like he had been stabbed with forks. "Christ," he cried out in a faint croak, then fell on his back in further agony.

There was movement and then a grizzled, white-haired man in a heavy wool sweater and pants was standing above him. The man gently got him on his side. The sensation of pain was odd: it was either in breath-shattering jolts or not at all. Had he been drugged?

Weakly, Haugland lay deeper on his side and studied the older man's face. It was both familiar and friendly but it wasn't his grandfather's. He was a stranger.

Like lightning, a memory cut through him. *Found you in the snow*. He shivered as he experienced the cold and then the icy hot searing of his flesh as the brand burned him.

His hand. He tried to move his hand up to his face but it felt heavy under the splints and bandages. Like a dead stone. Underneath the layers of gauze, the fingers were seeping.

A face came at him, thin and narrow, the high forehead stretching up into the black hair, then it began to dissolve in to a skeleton.

"Welcome to the party."

The macabre face smiled and then laughed. "There isn't anything I won't know."

The grinning mouth widened and the sea spilled out with a boat on it, running swift and smooth. It was so beautiful Haugland wanted to cry but first he had to warn it away. He blew on it and it shrank down to a toy boat he could hide in his pocket so the Draugen *wouldn't get it.*

"Son, are you all right?"

Haugland's mind stopped rambling. The images scattered and the man's face and voice clarified. He remembered that he was safe. That he knew the man.

"You've been floating in and out since yesterday." The man reached across and touched his forehead. He grunted, taking his hand away. "Hand hurt?"

Haugland watched his lips, then shook his head *nei*. He couldn't really tell. Maybe he didn't want to know. He tried to speak, but his throat was so sore and parched he could only get out a weak aspirant rush of sound that hurt him more.

"More snow is coming. Are you warm enough? I can add a *dyne* to the blankets."

Haugland realized for the first time that he was totally naked. He shivered, but not from feeling cold. It was a flashing image of being helpless and naked while being beaten. Did that happen? He thought he had fallen. The man pulled a *dyne* up from the bottom of the bed. The drowsiness was returning, but he wanted desperately to stay alert. The man was talking.

"... don't even know your name. You have a name, don't you?"

He wondered what he should say. This man had obviously saved his life, but he should be wary. Wasn't he supposed to be wary? He decided that he wouldn't give him his name, something he barely remembered himself. *For security*. But who had told him to do that?

He made a scribbling motion. The man brought him a pencil and paper. Haugland wrote some whispery letters that spelled "Per Clausen."

"Hmph. Per..." The man looked at the paper and at him, his eyebrows furrowing. Finally, he said, "I'm Hans Gunnerson." He smiled. "Glad to know you. How 'bout some soup?"

Gunnerson fed him, all the time giving him a running account of the last twelve days. Haugland was able to follow along, but the words meant nothing to him.

"Uh." Disjointed thoughts were threatening him again. His eyes felt hot and his left hand throbbed. It didn't help when the cat jumped on the bed and made its way over the top of his legs to his chest. It sniffed his bandage then drew back in distaste and shook its head before high stepping down on Haugland's other side where it made preparations to curl up. It seemed to waiver and hang in the air like an apparition. He closed his eyes and slept.

***

Haugland woke a couple of hours later to the sounds of arguing. He didn't float to consciousness this time, but awoke almost clear-headed. He found himself lying on his stomach.

"For God's sake, Hans, the resistance blew up the Jorstad Bridge north of Trondheim only hours ago. There were troops on that train. The Germans have patrols everywhere. They could come here. How will you explain him? Hide him. Take him away. We don't know who he is. He gave you two different names, didn't you say?"

"I can't do that and you know it, Jon. He's too weak. I'll have to take my chances here."

Haugland kept his eyes closed, but he recognized the type of man this other was: a man with responsibilities and a suspicious mind. He heard the footsteps come closer through his good ear and then the blankets were lifted, exposing his back and backside. It was embarrassing, but he wasn't in control here. The man grunted. What was wrong with his back?

Gunnerson came over. "In God's name, how could we let him go? Even move him to another site. Look at him. He's completely helpless. He can't sit, can't feed himself. Torholm says he'll have to be hospitalized for weeks once he's over."

"Then let's do two things. Have Britta make her return from her `trip' as soon as possible and let me question him as soon as he wakes up." The blankets were lowered and decency restored while the group sat down at the table. He lay quietly with his eyes closed. The medication had worn off leaving a hard edge of pain in his mangled hand and side.

He must have groaned because there was movement at the table, then quiet as he feigned sleep. His head pounded as he tried to put what little facts he had together.

He knew his name was Haugland. He was sure of it although beyond that he didn't know anything about himself or where he came from. And he wasn't sure about his first name. He kept thinking `Jens' but it didn't feel completely right. He had been found in the snow over twelve days ago. Had he fallen? Some skiing accident? *Nei*, his back.

The whip hand came down. "Welcome to the party, you'll tell us everything."

The intense eyes flashed and his back exploded in pain.

"See you, Jens." Another face, and weathered. Kind. Friend. "See you."

Someone came over and gently stroked his hot forehead. He moved his head and heard soothing words. An attractive middle-aged woman with dark blonde hair smiled at him. Did someone say Britta?

"He's awake. May I look at your hand?"

She undid the dressing, asking for scissors and warm water. "I'm going to check your fingers, but first we'll get you on your side again, all right? We'll do it quickly."

Once he was comfortable, she carefully cut through the last layer of gauze around his ring finger and exposed the entire hand. The purple-red flesh on the side of the ring finger strained against the stitches and was oozing matter. It wasn't long before perspiration beaded up on his lips under his unshaven whiskers. Yet he couldn't remember how he had hurt his hand.

A stranger dragged a chair alongside the bed. Gunnerson was close behind. Haugland glanced at the lean, brown-haired man and thought, *Milorg man.* But he didn't know why he thought that either. It had no meaning for him.

"This is Jon Olsen," Gunnerson said. "He's going to help us plan for your care. It's too dangerous to hide you. We're going to send you to Sweden."

Why? He was puzzled by their concern over the type of injuries he had.

The hand came down. He flinched. Horrific, disjointed images flicked across his mind. Something wasn't right. He had to be somewhere.

"So, when were you arrested?" Olsen asked.

Arrested? Was he in trouble with the police? "I don't know. Was I?"

The hand came down swinging the... the totenschlager.

"You don't remember?" The man leaned into his face.

"Jon," Gunnerson warned. "Please be careful."

Haugland felt his face drain of color. He tightly clenched the mattress's edge. "I... I... don't remember." He whimpered when she spread his fingers apart to examine the ring finger.

"Sorry." Britta wiped his damp hair off his brow.

Olsen continued. "We need to know something about you. Is there anyone we can contact?"

"*Nei*...no one. There...is... no one." Because I can't remember. Haugland frowned. That wasn't exactly true. It was hard to keep a thought, but sometimes he did see people and places and heard sounds like the rush of waves on rocks, the *tonka-tonka-tonka* of a boat. He had come from somewhere and was supposed to be somewhere. He had been doing something dangerous. Was running away.

Docktor Torholm came over and took his wife's seat and examined the hand gently. Gunnerson came and stood behind Torholm. Haugland raised his heat-swollen eyes to him.

"I'm going to lose my hand, aren't I?" he said faintly.

"Not if I can help it," Torholm answered. He carefully re-wrapped the hand, then touched Haugland's forehead. He said nothing, but Haugland could tell he was making a decision.

He watched the doctor talk to Britta and Gunnerson. Their motions seemed slow and exaggerated. He knew he was slipping away, burning with fever. He was aware of the woodstove popping and faintly, the lantern's hiss and then he was somewhere else, drifting, drifting, like on a boat. He saw a blonde man, robust and weathered, pick a fish out of a net, then look up.

"See you, Jens." Suddenly, he remembered the name and face and with that, a flood of images poured across his mind. "Kjell," he cried hoarsely.

For one brief moment he knew perfectly clear who he was and what he must do. Sweden. He had to get word to headquarters in Sweden. He signaled to the woman because he trusted her.

"Help me..." he whispered when she took his good hand and held it. "Help me."

"Shhh," she said, "You are going to be all right. You just have a fever."

"*Vær... så... snill.*" He weakly squeezed her hand for emphasis. "Listen. I'm Ryper. I want... to go home... to roost."

CHAPTER 97

In his small flat in Oslo, Lars sat with several other Milorg members discussing the *Hjemmefronten* s' training for liberation. J.C. Hauge, national Milorg head and friend, led the talk.

"The police camps are up to several thousand men," Hauge was saying, his shadow a stark black on the papered wall behind him. "Our three permanent bases and other camps are growing. All we have to do is stay ahead of the Gestapo and avoid detection."

Lars wondered what he was really thinking. They hadn't been identified yet, but there were prices on their heads.

For the past week Lars had worked like a fury, doing anything to keep his mind off the emptiness he felt. He had taken Tore's death hard. It had been bad losing his boyhood friend Einar Fromme, but he hadn't been prepared for this loss. Somehow, he always believed Tore would make it through. He would miss his dry wit. Thinking of his brother's scholarship and great potential as a writer and teacher, that loss would be felt by their country when the war was over. It would need him as well as his experiences in the special service he'd given in wartime.

Torrey... Their mother's pet name for him. A ridiculous image of him at three parading across the snow after the family cat in only his sagging woolen underwear crossed Lars's mind and he laughed softly to himself. Tore had been a spirited little boy and mischievous teenager, but had the sensitivity to things that mattered. Sometimes it was hard to believe that the boy who once in a lemming year collected nearly a dozen and put them in a cheese box in their sister's armoire at their grandfather's mountain cabin was the same young man who graduated from *gymnasium* with honors. And no one would forget the relationship between him and *Onkel* Kris. It was a bond formed early and never be broken even in death. Everyone in the family was charmed by it when he was little, moved by the intensity when he was older, but only Lars knew the depth of his feelings. Often it had been easier to talk to his uncle than his own father who was busy or away with little time for his youngest son. *Onkel* Kris had in some ways been his father.

Hauge looked at him from across the table. You all right? he mouthed.

Lars hunted for his pipe. *Hell, no*, He wasn't all right and he wondered if he'd ever be. *Tore, forgive me. You never had a chance. Not with Rinnan.* Feeling his throat grow tight, Lars hastily lit his pipe. The thought of Tore suffering...

'You want to comment, Erling?" Hauge asked, using his code name.

"*Nei.* It pretty much matches what we worked out. I think we can close now."

There were some last minute instructions from Hauge, then the small group dispersed from the flat except for Lars and Hauge. Hauge stacked up papers. "Any plans for the evening? We can get dinner." When Lars shook his head, Hauge sighed. "Dammit, Lars, I've the mind to send you east."

"Rather finish up some loose ends here."

"Let security do it. They'll get to the bottom of your brother's arrest and murder."

Hauge started to say something else when the phone in the living room rang three times, then stopped. A few seconds later it rang again. It was for Lars. He stepped over to the phone and listened soberly to the message. When he was done, he slowly put down the phone.

"What's up?" Hauge asked.

"Cryptic message from my aide. I'm to meet a contact at the Deaf Church. If you don't mind, I'll call my driver and go now."

Fifteen minutes later, Lars was in a vehicle sporting its State Police sticker, insuring access to city streets without hassle. A quick dart across town and he was in the church.

It was dim inside the Deaf Church, but he knew his way to the sanctuary's front. It had been some time since he had come here, yet it provoked strong memories, especially of Tore. Before the war, his brother had come here with their uncle many times. Conrad Bonnevie-Svendsen was the pastor here. Lars stood by the railing and looked at the large painting of Christ on the white wall. His face was full of compassion, but Lars resisted His assurances of comfort, feeling dead and empty inside. A sledgehammer couldn't break the rock wall around his heart.

Several minutes passed, and he began to get restless and wary. He would leave. He started down the aisle when a side door opened sending a patch of light across the pews. A young fair-haired woman stood there. She motioned for him to follow her. The pastor was waiting.

Down a dark hallway, she came to an office door. Inside the simply furnished, wood-paneled room Conrad Bonnevie-Svendsen stood. Lars hadn't seen him in a year, but though he was like a member of the family, his genuine graciousness and humility disarmed Lars every time he saw him. As minister for the deaf, Conrad was tirelessly dedicated, but Lars was one of the few who knew that Conrad was also a member of the KK—the Cordinating Committee that directed the civilian resistance and managed matters concerning the churches, homes, schools, and underground press.

"Lars, forgive me. I just arrived." He moved aside some papers. The bookshelves behind him were filled with religious texts. Turning to the girl, he signed a few words. Smiling, she left.

"She helps out in the parish office and does a few other unofficial things." Conrad didn't elaborate, but looked at Lars a bit bemused. "So, would you like some tea?"

Nei, thought Lars, *I'd like a drink*.

"It's been a couple of hard months, hasn't it? Yet we're still here." The pastor set a kettle on a hot plate, then put some tea into a ceramic tea pot. 'Sit, sit. He placed two cups on the desk, then went on." I also heard from Solheim, my colleague in Trondheim. He's safely away in Stockholm."

A knot hardened in Lars's stomach. Solheim had made it over. Tore hadn't. He looked away and stared at a cross on the wall behind Conrad. His eyes began to sting.

"Lars, sit down. The last thing I want is to put you through the meat grinder, but I know about Tore, Lars—his arrest and murder—and I share your grief. But *vær så snill*, sit down."

Lars sat down, not caring to remove his coat.

Clasping his hands, Conrad took on a pastoral air, one of compassion and understanding. "Solheim sent a message asking to contact you immediately. It goes like this: Two days ago the British Legation in Stockholm received a coded message. It read: 'Ryper wants to go home to roost,' the roost, of course, being Sweden."

Lars gasped. "Tore..."

"Exactly. This, of course, has to be validated. London was notified. Someone will make the identification. According to the report, the man's gravely injured."

Lars felt sick. "Is it a trick?" His feelings dangled between hope and suspicion.

"It could be a ruse, but his description matches."

Lars started to get up. "I think I should go."

"Not with Sor-Trøndelag in such an uproar over the train bridge. There's a massive search under way right now and to keep people in line, the killings have begun. Thirty-eight men were executed the other day in Trondheim as a result. *Nei*, MI IV will handle it. They'll send someone who can identify him. They're doing it now."

Conrad looked at Lars with compassion. "I'm sure you'll be allowed to go over and see him." He reached over and laid his hand on Lars's arm. "Why don't we pray?"

CHAPTER 98

Anna gave her scarf one more tug and went into the *konditori*. It had been a week since receiving Kjell Arneson's letter. Three weeks since the *razzia*. Feelings still ran high with some villagers still imprisoned. The little bell rang, but the tearoom was nearly empty of customers, except for one couple.

"What do you want?" Ella Bjornson glowered from behind the cash register. She nodded at the couple who got up and vacated the room leaving them alone.

Anna laid an envelope on the counter. When Ella saw Kjell's handwriting, she stepped back, drawing her cardigan sweater tight around her body.

"He's safe. He got away," Anna whispered. "Both he and Helmer Stagg,"

Ella turned very pale. She could not hide the confused hope on her face. For the first time since she'd met Ella, Anna discerned a soft spot, a gentleness. She loved Kjell Arneson.

"How could you know?"

Anna simply told the truth: how she found them and hid them. When she finished Ella asked, "Why would you do that? Why would they go?"

"Because I'd never want anyone to go through what happened to me in Lillehavn. And because of Jens." She pushed the letter toward Ella. "Kjell sent a note to me last week and wrote that he put this in the cellar before he left."

Ella read it. When she was finished, she put it in her apron pocket. For several moments neither woman said anything. Finally, Ella spoke in a quiet voice.

"Kjell writes how you saved him from the soldiers and says that you have an affidavit from Jens exonerating you. He also speaks of Jens. And that you loved him...." Ella swallowed. "I don't understand, but then you were brave in the church. I don't know what to believe." She shook her head slowly, tears at her eyes. "Kjell says we have suffered long enough. That we must be vigilant, but be careful not to be so swayed by the injustices against us nor believe the rumors. He says it's the best kind of courage."

She ran her hand over her pocket, smoothing the material. "Kjell's right, of course. It's easy to call someone collaborator or *tyskertøs*. It's another to stand up and count that person as a friend in the face of suspicion and hate. You will need a friend, and since he has asked, I will try."

Ella seemed to be swallowing her pride and bitter distrust. She gave Anna's shoulder a hesitant squeeze and walked over to the window. She crossed her arms and stared out over the forest of masts and destroyed boats in front of the *konditori.*

"So it was Jens. I loved that young man. I will miss him as long as I live," she in a pinched voice. "And so will everyone else in our little village. We will always be proud he came to stay with us here. We will always call him son."

"Even with the *razzia*?"

"Because of the *razzia*. He helped us do our part."

CHAPTER 99

Hans Gunnerson stood by the window and gazed at the tall, snow-laden pines that lined the bowl. Beyond, the sky was blue, the winter sun bright. Sunshine flooded into his cabin and hit the chimney of the kerosene lamp on the table, scattering a hundred blinding diamond shapes on the walls.

Things had moved quickly over the past two days. The disjointed message their injured charge had desperately wanted to pass onto him was sent but only after they tried to figure out what it meant. There was no help from the young man who had lapsed again into semi-consciousness. Jon Olsen could only guess, but intrigued, sent it by courier to Milorg headquarters in Sweden where Olsen had a connection.

The old man turned away and looked at Per. Or was it Jens? He'd had a rough time that in the end had forced Torholm to make a decision he'd hoped not to make, but if the young man was ever to regain enough strength to make the grueling trek over, it had to be done. Now he was recovering, sleeping under what sedatives they could get for him. *What a mess.* Gunnerson prayed that he could be identified so they could work quickly to get him safely out. The woods were becoming too dangerous since the train sabotage, but hopefully his export was close at hand. Hopefully, because they had heard back almost immediately—not from Stockholm—but London and with an interest that surprised them all. They began to wonder who the half-dead man was.

Something moved against Gunnerson's legs, startling him. It was his cat. He reached down. "*Hei*, Samers. Unloved and neglected aren't you?" He cradled it in his arms, rubbing its chin. "When Olsen comes, he'll bring you a fish." And an agent who could identify Per Clausen.

A movement from the bed distracted him, but when Samers stiffened, Gunnerson looked back out the window and saw two figures coming up into the bowl on skis. It was Jon Olsen and another man completely dressed in white. His heart thumping, he went out to meet them.

***

When they glided into the small clearing, Tommy Renvik had small hope for what he would find. Since receiving orders from London, he had been in constant motion going by skis to car and back to skis again as he passed through Milorg and resistance contacts. By the time he met Jon Olsen outside of Trondheim, he was nearly exhausted, but could not let down his guard. German soldiers were everywhere as they searched for the saboteurs who blew up the Jorstad train bridge. They terrorized the town and even out here in the forest he feared their heavy hand. He hoped to get this over with and retreat.

The door to the hut opened and a man in his late sixties stepped out and waved. Tommy acknowledged him with a tense smile, then stooped to undo his leather bindings. When the older man invited him in, Tommy held out his hand.

"London sent me." He stepped into the little hut, flicking his eyes across the room to the bundle on the bed, dreading what he had to do. Olsen followed him in.

Gunnerson took his canvas knapsack and parka. "You can have all the time you want."

Taking a deep breath, Tommy walked over to the bed. "God," his voice cracked.

It was Haugland. Barely alive. Lying on his stomach with only his head visible, he appeared shrunken and disheveled. His pale skin was pinched tight over his cheekbones and under the growth of beard. Where it was visible, there was bruising around an eye and the side of his head. Even the thick hair had changed, lying dull and lifeless against his skull. His eyes were closed and a heavily bandaged left hand drawn up to his opened mouth—like a little boy in sleep. His hand shaking, Tommy gently lifted the visible eyelid just to be sure. Gray eye.

"He's sedated," Gunnerson said. "He's coming out of surgery earlier this morning. He should be waking shortly. I'm afraid one of his fingers had to be amputated."

Tommy lifted the blankets off the shoulders and back, exposing hideous wounds on Haugland's body. The blood in his face drained. "Shit." Shaken, he looked away.

"You need a drink." Gunnerson guided him to the table just opposite the bed. Olsen took a seat to the side. Rummaging around on his food shelf, Gunnerson found a bottle of whiskey and poured.

Tommy downed it quickly. Gasping, he set the shot glass out for more, but drank only half. He kept shaking his head. "I've seen things, but not this." He waved his hand at the bed.

"My friend is too vibrant and active to be crippled." Tommy looked up. "Is he?"

"*Doktor* Torholm says his hand needs more surgery, but proper care will bring a fairly good recovery. Our concern now is the journey. He's very weak. The trip over the mountains could kill him." Gunnerson cleared his throat. "He's lost hearing in his left ear."

"You're kidding." Tommy wiped his mouth and looked over at the bed. "We've known each other a long time, such as it is in wartime, but we've survived."

"A friendship cemented during the worst of times," Gunnerson said softly, "will last forever." He cleared his throat. "Yet, he might not remember you. He's been confused."

"Jesus," Tommy said under his breath and downed the remaining whiskey.

"Tell me," Olsen said. "Who is your friend? Why is London so interested?"

Tommy paused. London had cleared Olsen and Gunnerson for any remarks he might tell them, but he still chose his words carefully. "He's a top agent sent over eleven months ago by High Command in London. He disappeared three weeks ago and was presumed dead. They'll be relieved, as I am." Tommy's voice strained but he stayed composed.

Gunnerson's eyes seemed to moisten. "Any others involved? Was it a sweep?"

"It's a bad affair. His network was exposed and many people arrested. Ten of them, mostly fishermen, were executed just a few days ago along with twenty-eight others in reprisal for the train bridge sabotage. The rest are either at Falstad or on their way to Grini. There was talk of sending some directly to Germany. Someone betrayed them."

Haugland groaned. Everyone turned to look at him. Eyes closed, he lifted his head and turning it toward the wall, he lay quietly.

"The doctor wants him to rest a bit more before he is moved, but with the sabotage we'll have to move soon. A very difficult export. We can't afford to make any mistakes."

***

When Haugland woke, he was lying on his stomach facing the wall. For a moment he lay there, listening to the sounds around him with his good ear. It was bright in the cabin. The sunlight hit the walls in square patches, sometimes shimmering as the trees moved outside.

Chunk! Someone was outside chopping wood. It made him think of food and his shrunken stomach growled. Gingerly moving his shoulders, he made the agonizing shift to his other side to look into the room. He must have let out a groan, for something moved near the window. To his surprise, he saw a familiar figure.

"Tommy... is that... you?"

"Aye," Tommy answered in English. "I've come to get you out." He sat down by him. "Thank God you're alive. We gave you up for dead weeks ago."

Lying deep in the pillows, Haugland nodded his head, but overcome with emotion from all the things he was remembering, he began to weep silently. Ashamed, he turned his face into the pillows, then remembered that he shouldn't. He wouldn't be able to hear. So he lay like a helpless infant as the tears rolled down his cheeks and from his beard onto the bedding.

Dead. They're all dead, he thought, and in one horrific vision saw the *Hitra* sinking from countless German shells. "The boat!" He took Tommy's hand as he reached out.

"Shh... Haugland, it got away. They got your warning message."

"My fault. All my people..."

"Nothing's your fault. God, what you've been through. Please. Rest," he soothed.

The blanket slid off Haugland's shoulder, snagging on a large raw patch of healing skin. He grimaced. "Damn... I'm falling apart."

"You have reason to feel that way. The bloody bastards beat the shit out of you. Gunnerson says you've come a long way. No riding *fjordings* for a while."

Haugland's eyes went unfocused as he remembered the Cloister. He sank into the pillow. "I can't hear out of my left ear."

"I know. Gunnerson told me. Said you were hit pretty hard on the side of the head."

Haugland looked at his hand for the first time and saw the ring finger was missing two joints and the middle finger was braced. "Damn..."

"I'm sorry. They couldn't save it. You would have lost your hand. I've brought some penicillin and that should get rid of the infection that's left." He gently put the blanket in place.

Haugland bit his lip and looked away, but he couldn't stop the slow roll of tears, so he closed his eyes and began to drift. He was soon fast asleep.

The second time Haugland woke, Tommy was writing at the table. It looked cold outside.

"Tommy," he said clearly in English. "It really is you. I thought I was dreaming."

"I'm here. Have been all along."

On his side, Haugland shifted his weight, trying to rest higher up on his shoulder. For the first time in a long time he smiled as thought of rescue became real. "What time is it?"

"Two-thirty in the afternoon. You've slept quite a while. Probably the anesthesia."

"Where's Gunnerson?"

"He's gone to the village to look in on the progress of a sled that's being built for you."

"How'd you find me?"

"FO IV in London. They got your coded message."

He was hesitant to ask anything else, not trusting the yo-yo stability of his emotions but he did remember. Quite a bit now. FO IV sounded familiar. "Does my brother know?"

"Lars will know within twenty-four hours. I promise. Look, are you cold? Hungry?"

Haugland bit his lip. "No. I think I want to sit up, though."

Gritting his teeth, Haugland sat up, leaning weakly against Tommy. He felt dizzy. Sweat broke out on his forehead. The slightest movement put pressure on the tender cuts recently held together by stitches. "I keep dreaming my back is made of rotten cloth. It tears when I sit up."

"I think you're stronger than that. In fact, I know you are." Tommy's voice became thick. "You're going to get through this, Tore. When you get out, we'll get you proper hospital care. You'll be safe and secure for the duration of the war. Eat, sleep, whatever you want."

"I don't really want to go," he said distantly, as images came to him. He suddenly recalled Holger Haraldsen at the Cloister and how they had been pressed for answers. "I need to know about my people. We were… compromised. The Gestapo knew minute details." He clutched Tommy's hand, remembering Holger with blood streaming from his nose. He began to feel cold.

"Lie down again. You're starting to shake." Tommy awkwardly pulled a flannel blanket around Haugland's bare shoulders. When he was settled back down, he covered him up more.

"Where's Kjell? Is he safe?" Haugland asked hoarsely.

"Kjell, Helmer Stagg and *Doktor* Grimstad are all with me in a mountain hideout south of Fjellstad. Solheim's safe in Sweden."

"And the others?"

"Oh, shit. Wait until you're stronger and security has it figured out."

Haugland took a deep breath. "I can't wait. I need to know the truth."

Tommy shifted uncomfortably on his chair. In a flat voice he told what he knew: the *razzia* on Sig Haraldsen's home and his sons; the near simultaneous *razzia* on Fjellstad. Tommy gave him a hard, unflinching litany of names. "About forty in all were taken area-wide initially."

"Where's Sig now? His sons? Kjelstrup?"

"Christ," Tommy groaned. "I'm sorry. This is killing me. Kjelstrup disappeared but Milorg thinks he might have been killed at Mission Hotel. As for the others, Sig, Holger and Magnus and seven others were executed in reprisal for the train sabotage north of Trondheim a few days ago. Their names were published in the papers and over the radio."

Haugland let out a soft cry of anguish. He thought he was prepared for this additional horror perpetuated on people whose names he'd only recently begun to remember, but he wasn't and it took away what little reserve of strength he had recovered.

Sig! He saw the face so clearly, the stern white-haired old man as unforgiving as the rocky skerries he loved. He saw the homes violated, the fishing boats burned and what vestige of pride stripped away. He'd loved that old man and his family, had been so happy at their home. He sank into the pillows, resting precariously on his ravaged back. "Did Rinnan find the arms?"

"No, they died without saying a word. I'm sorry." Tommy's lips were moving, but Haugland didn't hear him. Unbidden, an image came to him.

A woman. A beautiful woman with golden hair who turned and welcomed him with a warm smile, moving her hands in sign. Her hair floated around her like an angel. Anna.

He touched her and then they were naked, making love under a dyne *and he thought he would burst from the ache for her, the desperate need for her. The sheer physical joy of loving her was almost overwhelming, but suddenly she was standing away from him and he was sitting on a stool with blood dripping down his back. All around him were the faces he feared and hated the most. They were laughing. "A woman from the village. Someone you trust."*

It was the final humiliation and in remembering his helplessness and despair, he curled up into a ball, straining his healing wounds. Anna. He remembered her now and the fear that she had betrayed him. *"A woman from the village."* The words were like poison, making him sick.

"Scarlett. Haugland!" He was aware of being touched, of someone wiping his acrid-tasting mouth and then he saw Tommy.

"Jesus... You scared me, Haugland."

The stench of watery vomit hit his nose and he realized he had thrown up. Tommy was wiping him and the bedding clean.

"My fault," he heard himself say. Sometimes with only one ear drum, his voice seemed to reverberate in his head. "My fault."

"You keep saying that. God, what a dope me talking to you about this. Don't do this to yourself. Nothing's your fault. You were compromised, Haugland. Compromised!" He wiped Haugland's face dry. "Let security take care of it. When you're in Sweden, MI IV will talk to you."

"They said there was a woman in the village helping them," Haugland said faintly. "They made fun of the fact that I knew her. If it's true, I'm responsible for the *razzias*."

"And who do you think this woman is?"

"Anna Fromme." He looked at Tommy with guilt he knew was as translucent as his feelings of love. "I let passion get the best of my common sense and mission."

Tommy sat up sharply. "You think Anna Fromme betrayed you? No wonder you're sick. I'd be too if I thought the woman I loved betrayed me."

Tommy patted his arm. "I know about you and Anna Fromme. Kjell told me."

"Kjell?" Haugland stared.

"She saved his life." Tommy recounted everything to him. "Hid them in a secret cave."

The hiding place. He suddenly saw it and remembered. "Anna." He shivered.

"You're still cold. I'm going to get you some clothes, but first I'm going to pump up the fire." Tommy pulled the blankets higher on his shoulders. Their warmth made him sleepy.

"Why didn't you tell me about her? I've never known you to keep a secret."

How should he answer? It was becoming hard to think and he felt weak. He was only just remembering, but he knew he loved this woman. Desired her.

He rubbed his temple listlessly. "Would you have trusted me? Honestly, I'm having trouble thinking. Too much, too fast." Haugland's eyes filled with tears. One got away and rolled down his thin face. He inched his way down in the blankets on the verge of sleep again.

"Why did you think it was her?"

Cloister. "Rinnan said it was a woman I knew who was working for him. Implied I slept with her. That's all I remember. Does anyone know how she is?"

"I really don't know. When Kjell and Helmer got to us, we hightailed it. I did hear Kjell say something had upset her, but she was dealing with it."

Haugland struggled to sit back up.

"Scarlett, take it easy. I'll look into it right away. Please rest." He clasped his good hand. "I hope to God we're out of here soon. The hills are thick with German patrols, but I promise you, I'll go all the way with you. If MI IV allows, I'll stay until you're settled in Sweden."

"I'd appreciate that." Haugland became quiet, rubbing his temple with his good hand. He lay back weakly in the pillows feeling as pale as the linen he lay against, his lips bloodless.

"What was the last thing you remember?" Tommy asked.

He struggled to remember. "A boat. I told them I would show them where the *Hitra* would be coming." Haugland's voice became a whisper. "I must have gone out. Don't remember."

"You have no idea how you ended up in the mountains?"

"No," he said tightly. Tears loomed again. "I don't know." He looked off, his voice hushed. "Fromme died there. In the Cloister."

"Who?" Tommy asked.

"Einar Fromme died in one of the side rooms. Sorting told me. He was chopped up, Tommy. Like cordwood. Then thrown away." He tried to block the image, but he couldn't. "How can I tell Anna that her husband died that way? What am I going to tell my brother?"

He stopped rubbing his forehead and let the hand rest palm out exposing the wounds on the underside of his wrist. Haugland knew Tommy was staring at them. He looked decidedly green.

"I don't know," Tommy finally answered. "Maybe nothing should be said. There's been enough suffering." He gave Haugland a strained smile. "Let me help you dress."

After he was settled, Tommy sat back down. "Why don't you sleep? I'll look into supper."

Haugland closed his eyes. He knew what little strength he had left mustn't be wasted. It would be barely enough for the trek ahead. Not just avoiding German patrols. Strapped to a sled, he would be at the mercy of the elements. Suddenly, he wanted very much to live.

An image of Anna appeared. She was clutching flowers from the steep meadow alongside the woods where they had picnicked long ago. The sun caught her hair. She looked at him and smiling sweetly, took his crippled hand. "I love you," she said, kissing him on the mouth. A feeling of tenderness and desire swelled up in his chest, but before he could touch her, the image dissolved and he saw Fjellstad behind her in the dead of winter, the austere smoke curling out from blown-up houses and fishing boats.

"Tommy. Promise me, you'll help her. Find out what's happened to her if it's possible."

"I said I would. Now rest. We'll talk later."

Half asleep, Haugland murmured, "I love her..."

***

Fromme and Haugland. One dead, one barely alive. Both treated hideously.

Tommy sat precariously in his chair, watching the shattered figure on the bed. Haugland lay deep in the pillows, a shadow of his former self, his damaged hand set high on his chest. Tommy cringed to see his face once so alive and vibrant now haggard and in pain. He kept seeing the wounds and burns.

The stench of the bed unsettled him. Finally his stomach couldn't take it anymore. He shot up from his chair and fled to the outside where he threw up the hot, yellow contents from his heaving stomach onto the snow. He closed the door and stayed outside in the frigid air.

Jesus Christ, he thought. How the hell am I going to pull this off? How on earth would the export team drag a sled across the frozen *fjell* through subzero temperatures and possible blizzards and—avoid patrols? The Germans were getting desperate and were employing radical members of the *Hird* to guard the passes. Haugland's health was fragile. Could he stand the stress of a dangerous trek that could last several days out in the cold?

And his promise. How could he do that? How would he find out about the woman? Rinnan had destroyed the resistance in Fjellstad. It might take months to safely reestablish contact. By then would they see the war's end and their country free? Or would it go on as the Nazi made a last ditch effort against the rest of the world here in Fortress Norway? He wasn't sure if she mattered in the scheme of things—except to Haugland. She mattered to him.

And maybe she matters to me, he thought.

Maybe this is where the healing begins. She needed protection. She was in danger not only from forces seeking justice for Lillehavn but the Gestapo and SD as well. For no other reason than being Haugland's woman, he finally decided he'd do it.

Tommy turned at a sound behind him, thinking it was Haugland calling for him, but it was only the cat meowing. He decided he'd go catch some sleep himself, then he'd press to leave as soon as possible. The woods were too dangerous. He could feel it in the biting air.

He kicked the snow with his boots, covering up the mess by the side of the steps. Behind him in the snow-laden forest, a hawk let out a cry. Thinking trouble, his hand went to his pistol. He searched the trees for movement. Eventually he relaxed and looking up followed the raptor's lazy circle as it passed out of the bowl of trees into the rapidly fading sky.

Freedom, thought Tommy. It's free.

For some reason it reminded him of their coming dash across the border and most of all his friend. Not necessarily a sentimental or emotional man, he was moved by the bird's uncaring flight, then was suddenly seized with an overwhelming panic that after all he'd been through, Haugland wouldn't make it. It was so obscene a thought he vowed that no matter what happened, his friend would at least get over into Sweden.

"God," he prayed. "Help him hold on. Don't let him die before he's free."

***

They left for Sweden sooner than Tommy thought. He had been inside for only a minute, when Gunnerson and Olsen came tearing into the clearing.

"We've got to move," Gunnerson said as he leaned his skis against the cabin and staggered inside. "A troop carrier just showed up in the village."

"Where's the sled?" Tommy grabbed his parka and Sten gun.

"Right outside. *Doktor* Torholm had the good sense to move it last night to a farmstead not far from here. It's ready to go as well as the export team. They were alerted this morning." He looked at Haugland sleeping on the bed. "We'll have to wake him and bundle him up. We'll take him to a place northeast of here. A truck will take us closer to the border."

"Is the village in danger?"

"We have no idea why the troops are there. Could just be for food at the *konditori*. Fortunately, Britta and the doctor are out on medical rounds. At least that's the story."

Tommy looked at Haugland. His stomach was still sour. Now it had a knot.

***

Ten hours later, in the dead of night, they moved Haugland for the second and final time from a *seter* hut in which they had been hiding to a truck loaded with cellulose. Heavily bundled into a sleeping bag, Gunnerson helped strap him back onto the sled and hauled him down through the forest to the main road. Loaded onto the farm truck's back behind the bales, Gunnerson sat on the floor beside him along with Torholm and Tommy.

Gunnerson felt old and beat up. Since rushing him out of the cabin to a safer point, Per seemed to have worsened— a prospect that saddened him. After weeks of trying to keep him going, he seemed to have lost what energy he gained since becoming conscious. Torholm had warned Gunnerson of this possibility, but he didn't want to believe.

***

The truck headed off toward the border, but despite the fear of patrols and checkpoints, they saw none. Eventually, Gunnerson felt the truck slow down. He peeked outside the canvas cover and saw a break in the snowbound forest. They turned onto a snowy road going higher into the mountains, the truck rocking and jarring as it climbed. He put a hand on Per to encourage him as the truck pulled over. With Tommy's help Gunnerson unloaded the sled onto the snow. Per had taken the ride in silent agony, but now would be exposed to the frigid air for hours. Jon Olsen and Britta joined them from the cab.

It was bitter cold. The woods were pitch-black, but the sky overhead was hung with a field of stars and a pale winter moon. While the doctor examined Per, Gunnerson listened to Olsen's final instructions. Gunnerson would go home. Torholm and Britta would return to the village at first light while he and Tommy would rendezvous with the members of an export group who would take the sled over the pass into Sweden.

Little was said. Each came forward to say good-bye. All kept a brave front, sobered by the doctor's concern earlier that Per was too weak. *Doktor* Torholm didn't blame them for trying because it was preferable to having him fall back into the Gestapo's hands, but it was hard to see a successful outcome. All they could do was make him comfortable and pray for the best.

Gunnerson crouched down by the sled, setting a lantern on the snow and without explanation put a worn ski jumping medal into Per's sleeping bag. "It was my son's," he said. "I'd appreciate it if you would take it over."

"He's dead, isn't he?"

"*Ja*." Gunnerson paused then went on. "He got caught up in illegal work early on in the occupation. I didn't know how serious it was until he was arrested. Some students in the sports clubs in Trondheim were running a courier line over the Swedish border. He was exposed by one of Rinnan's agents and shot after three brutal days at Mission Hotel."

Gunnerson smiled faintly and hoped the man understood why he had fought so desperately to nurse him back to health. "Stay well," Gunnerson said. "It'll be our little joke on Rinnan. Nils, yours, and mine."

Gunnerson stepped back and watched Tommy come out of the moonlit gloom. He was carrying skis and poles, ready to start out. Gunnerson knew they would have to pull Per up through the forest until they broke out on the barren *fjell*.

"Ready, Scarlett?"

Haugland nodded wanly. He looked at Gunnerson one last time.

"If I can, I'll come back when Norway is liberated. We'll spend some time together."

"I think that would be fine." Not knowing what else to say, Gunnerson stuffed his gloved hands into his pockets. Olsen came around to the front of the sled and picked up one of the heavy ropes while Tommy adjusted the Sten gun strapped across his back.

Tommy nodded at Gunnerson and they stepped away from the sled.

"*Tusen takk* for what you have done,"Tommy said in a low voice. "Please thank the others. We'll get a message to you as soon as we can, but there might be a delay. In no way do we want to alert the Germans or Rinnan's agents that he might still be alive. That could put you in danger. I'll send word even if... complications... should arise."

Gunnerson clapped him on the shoulder. "Have faith. He's stronger than you think. What are a few more mountains? He's already been through the worst of them."

Tommy nodded his appreciation. "Be careful driving back. Display those emergency vehicle papers I got you if you have to. And stay quiet. No inquiries. We'll do the contacting."

In a few moments they were ready. Tommy came to the front of the sled and picking up a rope, put it over his left shoulder, balancing his skis and poles on his right. He nodded to Olsen and they moved off dragging the sled behind them.

Gunnerson watched them work their way into the forest. Almost immediately they were swallowed up by the cold gloom. The last thing he could see was the sled taking a bump and having to be tugged at. He couldn't see the face of the man on it, only a shape, but it wasn't necessary. He would never forget it. Yet he wondered if he'd ever see Per again.

CHAPTER 100

Anna put on her rubber boots and coat. Picking up the shovel against the entryway wall, joined Lisel in the garden. The April thaw had resumed. A snowstorm's bounty five days ago was already gone and the snow level on the mountains and high meadows had rolled back again. The air was still very cool, but there was a softness to it now. As the days grew longer, spring became entrenched and with it, a longing for peace.

It had been three months since Jens had died, the rumor officially confirmed by Schiller the day after she had received Kjell's note. Schiller had come to question her.

"He's an imposter," he said flatly. "A wanted criminal. Not deaf at all. He was shot during an escape from transport to a prison in the south."

When Anna gasped, he said, "It's not common knowledge. I've seen it in a report."

Anna said nothing. She felt Schiller study her, but he couldn't guess how hard she took it; how his words destroyed her last vestige of hope. Schiller had been posted to the village since the *razzia,* a reminder to the village of what had happened and a warning to future thoughts of resistance. With the mayor arrested, civilian matters were often left in Schiller's hands. To give him credit, he tried to act fairly, but he was a lonely figure, totally without friends. Since February, he would ask to visit once or twice a month,. She allowed it because she found it useful to garner any outside news she could pass on to Ella.

Three months she endured.

Anna took the shovel and plunged it into the wet earth. Amazingly, it was workable to the point of turning over several inches of soil. The soil was muddy and clumpy but it felt good to work it. All around her there were projects to do, but the garden was the most tangible. Though she had taken Jens's death very hard, each passing day she had found she could cope better. Finally, Anna felt she could forge a future for herself and Lisel.

Into the garden she could plant her little seeds of hope for the long light summer. She could lay the groundwork for what she knew would be the difficult time that was coming.

"Mama?"

Anna looked up. A truck was climbing up the muddy driveway to the farmhouse, its gears grating. It was most likely Schiller. The village had known since the twenty-fourth that the soldiers would withdraw. They weren't needed anymore in such a remote place. They were needed to fight in their homeland.

The small truck ground its gears up to the garden and stopped. Schiller got out. He looked Prussian again with his greatcoat and full military uniform. He tucked his hat under his arm.

"*God dag*," he said in Norwegian, mindful to do that. "Pity two pretty young ladies have to get all mucked up. I didn't realize that it was that time of year already, but I guess it is."

"There's always work on a farm," she replied.

"You're honestly going to stay here? The villagers will hurt you."

"You speak as though it is all over." Anna pushed her hair back off her forehead.

Schiller looked hurriedly over his shoulder. "Not so loud. Talk is dangerous. Many on the general staff in the *Wehrmacht* think the *Reich* will survive in Norway. The coast and mountains can be easily guarded. We have nearly a quarter million in troops and coastal artillery."

Anna gripped her shovel. It frightened her to think of the war going on and on. She changed the subject. "Where are you being transferred to?"

"To Oslo and over, though there's a bit of a bottleneck getting troops out. I have no hope for my own hometown. I think the Russians have taken Leipzig. They are very near Berlin."

Anna shivered. It wasn't the chilly air. It was her father and her brother Willy. She had no idea where they were. It had been over eight months since she had last heard from either of them.

He patted his coat front, his gloved fingers restless. "Are you sure you want to stay? I could arrange transport for the both of you, at least to Oslo. I could ask when I go to Trondheim."

"*Ja*. I will stay." Anna remembered the village after the *razzia*. After Jens's true identity became known, the Germans burned ten boats and blew up several homes. Anyone associated with him was punished in some way, but it only pushed resentment deeper into the psyche of the village and hardened their resolve. It hardened hers too.

She picked up her shovel and headed for the barn. Schiller followed her. Inside she hung up her shovel up on the wall.

"I still don't understand why you are staying." Schiller said.

She faced him. "I know you are trying to be kind, but I would never go with you. You are my enemy. My husband's enemy. I'll never forgive for what happened to him. Or for what happened here. These are good, decent people. It was wrong to destroy their homes and livelihood. This is my home too."

Schiller looked crestfallen. "I didn't want to do it. I didn't want any of this, but I was under orders. The SD troops did most of it." He walked over to a window. Through it, Anna could see the high meadow. There was the hint of new life in the trees there. "That Hansen. What was he to you?"

Startled, Anna quickly suppressed her emotions. "He only came to log. I didn't know him very well."

"You never guessed his identity?" He turned toward her.

"*Nei*," she answered in a small voice. "He wasn't here for long. Why do you ask?"

"Because it was so senseless. What was his point? He didn't have a chance, you know. After he was arrested, it was a moot question whether he lived. He didn't die escaping. He was killed long before by that Norwegian Rinnan."

Anna turned away, the blood draining from her face. Schiller's voice seemed far away.

"I think that is the thing I'll remember the most. How strong everyone was here. How they held themselves together." He sighed. "I'm sorry. I didn't want to leave like this. I didn't come here to talk about him. I just wanted to say good-bye."

He came over to her. She stiffened so her shoulders wouldn't shake. Had he guessed her true feelings? He lifted up her chin. It was dim in the barn. She prayed he couldn't see her face.

"If I may, I'd like to write. Just to see how you are. Maybe that way you will think kindly of me. If I'm lucky, I won't have to go over." He stroked her cheek, then took her hand and kissed it. "*Auf Wiedersehen, meir Spatz.* I will always care for you."

Anna didn't follow him out. She listened as the truck's motor revved up. She heard the truck turn around, then head down the hill. The motor whined when it hit the bottom, then picked up as it went down the fjord road. In the light spring air, she could hear it go a long way. When she couldn't hear it anymore, she still stood quiet in the gloomy, cold space of the barn with her eyes closed. *He didn't have a chance.*

The words hurt her so much, opening up the raw wound again. It made Jens's last, desperate situation all the more ugly and hopeless. All this time she had suppressed the images of him hurt, of being tortured, of lying somewhere in fear and pain, dying. Now they revived.

She walked over to the window and leaned against its dirty frame. The sun was coming out. Up on the high meadow, she could see the edge of the woods where Jens had walked out looking for her and Lisel when they had the picnic long ago last summer. She remembered how the light breeze had lifted his dark hair off his forehead. How he stood with his hands on his hips, his shirt open at the chest, then the surprise as he talked to himself with his hands. *Her lion in the springhouse.*

She began to weep, saying under her breath over and over again, “I’ll remember you, I’ll remember.” She promised to always remember him that way, in the summer and in the light.

CHAPTER 101

"Rika, how good to see you." Freyda looked around the half full *bakeri* tearoom, then flopped down beside her. "It's been ages."

"It's been only two weeks, Freyda, but it does seem like a long time." Rika looked down at her cup and frowned. She must stop getting all serious and downcast. She was here to enjoy girl talk. She didn't do it much anymore. Not since the *razzia* on her village. Damage and punitive measures were extensive and lifelong friends and neighbors arrested. Most shocking was the destruction of her childhood home and her father's boat.

"I ordered pastries. Shall I get them now?" Freyda's voice bubbled.

Rika smiled at Freyda. It *was* good to see her. They always had a good time together.

Freyda came back with pastries. "They are so expensive, but worth it. You look like you need cheering up."

Rika sighed. "I don't mean to be so glum. It's just that I'm worried."

"About your father?" Freyda leaned over the little corner table. "You still haven't heard?"

"*Nei*," she whispered. "It's A.C. I'm worried about him. It's been four months since he was exported out. Surely, I would have heard from him by now.'

Freyda took her fork and daintily cut a portion off her pastry. "Not necessarily," she answered carefully. "The camps may not be able to get letters out. Maybe the Swedish Red Cross has no access to where he is."

"But that's what has me worried. I got a letter from my sister Kitty today. It came through the Red Cross."

"Your sister?"

"*Ja*," Rika answered. "My father somehow arranged for her to get out. She's been in Sweden since just before New Year's."

Freyda paused just slightly, her mouth full, then resumed chewing. "How extraordinary."

"I thought so too. I had no idea."

"Well, you had no idea of what your father was doing. You should be very proud."

"I am, but at what cost. Our home, our business, our dear friends. He loved the *Otta*—that's our boat—was our boat. He must be in torment to think it gone." Rika put her fork down ignoring her food. "But that's not what I'm worried about. I can accept not knowing where my father is, because I believe that he's doing some good somewhere and isn't allowed to contact me. It's A.C. If I can hear from Kitty, I should be able to hear from him!" Rika looked away, her eyes beginning to glisten.

Freyda wiped her mouth with her cloth napkin. "Rika…"

"Something's wrong. What if he got caught on the pass? Or froze from the cold going over?"

"Rika," soothed Freyda. "He's all right. Paul said he got over. It's probably something else." She gave a list of reasons. "Look, I'll have Paul look into it."

"Could you do that? Oh, Freyda, that would be wonderful. Everything's loosening up, I hear. There are releasing Norwegians and Danes from the concentration camps on the continent, letting them travel to Sweden. Some day our men will come to free us. The end must be near. It has to be!"

"It'll be wonderful won't it? I'd like to be able to buy a new dress and stockings. That's the first thing I'll do when capitulation comes."

"Freyda!" laughed Rika. "You're always thinking of the practical side."

"What else can a girl do?"

***

A little while later, the girls separated. Freyda took a trolley and got off near the cathedral. At the post office a few blocks away, she waited outside looking at posters tacked to a board. Like many an April day, the weather was unsettled. It was chilly and bright. Freyda wouldn't be surprised if it snowed. She straightened up her short coat and smoothed out the skirt to her dress, acknowledging the look of a man going into the building. He had flicked his eyes over her. She knew she looked good. Only she wished she could wear stockings instead of little socks. She stared at the papers on the board then instinctively slapped the hand that goosed her from behind. Thinking the man had come back, she prepared her verbal assault on his character then giggled when she got nuzzled on her neck. It was Odd. "You're late."

"I'm early. You're late. I've been watching you for hours."

"And what did you see?"

"Something unprintable. Come on, there's a flat not far from here."

A couple of blocks away, he let her into a third floor apartment. Inside, it was dim. Sorting went over to the window and lifted up the blinds. Across the broad space he could see a dentist's office above a dress shop. Someone was getting his teeth cleaned. Lighting a cigarette he watched the street. Behind him Freyda's dress rustled. "It's not very warm in here," she said.

"See if the furnace goes on. If not, I'll light the stove in the kitchen. It might be disconnected." He smiled at her knowingly. "Right now, come here. It's been days since I've seen you."

Changing his cigarette to his left hand, he pulled her to him and kissed her on her mouth. His right hand unbuttoned her dress front. "Hmm, beautiful." He pinched her nipple hard enough through the lacey front of her slip to make her gasp. "I hate it when I go away. Too bad we've got to work." He gave her a peck on the forehead and removed his hand. "Check that thermostat."

He took a drag. "What did that Arneson girl have to say?"

"You saw her?"

"*Ja*. I told you I was watching. If that man had talked to you, I would have punched him."

"He said nothing, Odd."

"*Ja*, but he was looking."

She came back, gathering her hair up on top of her head to pin. Her dress was still open, her breasts straining under the slip as she reached up. Sorting felt his groin swell. He changed the subject. "I was talking about the Arneson girl. She hear from her father yet?" He gazed at her with a half smile. She ignored him. If she drove him crazy, so what?

"*Nei*. She tells me the same thing every time. She doesn't know."

"I wonder where he is. Dropped completely out of sight. No description came up in any of the camps in Sweden. He's got to still be here in Norway. What else did she say?"

Freyda finished her hair, then began to button up her dress. "The usual bits of information gathered through her contacts. A potential problem might be brewing. She keeps asking about A.C. Kjelstrup."

"Why?"

"Well, for one, she's heard from her sister in Sweden. She apparently got out of the country in December. Rika's wondering why she can't hear from Kjelstrup."

"Because he's deader than a doornail. When we took Hansen out to sea to intercept the boat, we took Kjelstrup's body out in a coffin and dropped him overboard." He squashed his cigarette on the sill. "Just stall her. We'll act like we're looking. In meantime, work on her. Arneson's got to still be in this country."

He took a drag and grinned at her. "Got any plans for tonight?"

"Not here. It's too cold."

"We'll go to Brattorgata. The Chief's not using it tonight. It has a nice bed."

"Are you going out again in the next few days?"

"*Ja*. When I come back, we'll talk. I think it's time to get out."

"The end is coming?"

"I think it's inevitable. You should start packing your bags."

"I'll take only the best."

***

The bed at Brattorgata was nice, but some time during the night, Sorting woke up in a cold sweat. It wasn't the usual nightmare of Einar Fromme down in the Cloister. It was a new one.

Out in the forest the deep snow had begun to thaw, uncovering a moldering body wrapped in a blanket. Under the brambles a putrid, mangled hand poked out of the rotten material. Its fingers began to move.

CHAPTER 102

The snow didn't surprise Anna. It was the men on the hill skiing down toward the barn. Dressed in white coats with ski caps and knickers, in the developing twilight, they looked like phantoms. Only when they were up close did she see they were heavily armed. She put a hand to her throat. She knew instinctively who they were—soldiers from the resistance. The cause Einar and Jens had died for.

There were five of them. The leader glided up to the end of the barn and stopped. Anna realized then he was quite young. A school boy, but by the way he carried himself, a man. And somehow familiar. From Fjellstad?

"Anna Fromme? May I have a word with you? *Vær så snill.*" He coasted in close. Stopping, he fiddled with his poles and gloves. "We have orders to take you with us."

She dropped her basket of wood. "Go with you?" Anna could barely get her words out.

He slid closer. He fished into his pocket and took out a medium-sized fishhook, holding it out to her like an offering.

"Oh." Anna bit her lip to hold back sudden tears as she accepted it. The hook. A symbol as intimate as a ring. "You knew Jens?"

"He was my friend. He saved my life once." The young soldier adjusted the rifle on his back, then signaled for the others to spread out. Bringing his attention back to Anna, he watched her clutch the hook against her breast. "Where is your daughter?" he asked. "It's important."

Anna hesitated. "In the village. This is her day to stay with friends."

"So she won't be back tonight?"

Again, she hesitated. Behind the young man, one of the soldiers was positioned at the end of the house, his strange rifle ready.

"*Fru* Fromme," he said gently, "I'm not here to harm you. I'm here to protect you. Word has come of how you helped Kjell Arneson and my cousin, Helmer Stagg, escape last winter."

Anna put her hands to her mouth. "Helmer's your cousin?"

"*Ja.* My name is Petter Stagg. My instructions are to take you with us to see someone in our group. He wishes to assist you. Will your daughter stay in?"

Anna nodded cautiously. Her knees felt weak.

"Good. It's about a two-hour journey. We've brought skis for you and will help you. If we leave now, we'll get there by ten tonight. You'll stay a few hours, then we'll bring you back."

He removed his cap and ran his fingers through his hair. It was cut short, except the top. The movement reminded her of Jens.

She hugged her arms, holding the hook so tight in her fist it cut her. When she opened her hand, it began to bleed. The man took the hook, pulled out a handkerchief from his coat and gently tied it around her hand. He wiped the hook clean with his coat sleeve and gave it back. "There," he said shyly. "My name is Petter. I would be honored to help you."

Inside the house, Anna changed into ski clothes. When she came back into the *stue* she found Petter standing at the window. "Is the patrol still around?" he asked.

"Schiller and his men left two days ago. But Foss has been named mayor. It isn't safe. Everyone's suspicious, afraid to talk. During the last thaw, an Allied plane was uncovered high in the *fjell* above the northern meadow. Sheriff Fasting is asking questions."

"I can imagine. Nerves, I'm sure are frayed. The end is very near, yet no one knows how the Germans will behave when they are asked to lay down their arms. Did you know Holland was liberated on the 19th?" Craning his neck, he looked down toward the village.

"I heard a rumor. If you are looking for Kjell's house, it is gone. Over by that space."

From where they stood, any remains were too far off, hidden by the other homes standing around the vacant lot like vigilant mourners. In the harbor, the carcass of a boat tugged at its anchor in the fast-approaching twilight.

"Did you know Jens well?"

"He helped me get away last summer during the AT mobilization. I saw him several times after that." His mouth tightened. "I was told you were close. I'm very sorry for what happened, that he's not here to see the end. He's a hero and he'll always be remembered."

***

And I'll remember this, Anna thought when they reached the *fjell* where an early moonrise greeted them, bringing light for the rest of their way. The moon illuminated the jagged snow-covered mountains on either side of them and turned the *fjell* into wide expanse of translucent white. They urged Anna forward in the middle of their line until she got into the familiar rhythm of skis. They kept a relentless pace, the landscape becoming wilder with large hummocks of snow, broken up by brush or naked dwarf trees in snow-clogged gullies. Suddenly coming around one particularly tall tower of snow, they came upon a cluster of huts glimmering like boxes caked with frost.

"We're here." Petter glided up to the first hut and unstrapped his skis. A door opened, the yellow light of a lantern shooting out across the snow. In the door frame, a tall, stockily built man stood with a Sten gun. His cheeks had a ruddy complexion, his hair reddish. He came out with a blanket on his arm and closing the door issued some orders to the other men before dismissing them. "Anna Fromme. Is everything all right?"

Anna couldn't answer. She was cold, but also bewildered, and worse, afraid. She began to shiver uncontrollably. *Why was she really here?* This stranger knew her name.

"Allow me." He put the blanket over her shoulders, bunching it around her neck. "Petter, you can go in with the men. I'll take her to the other hut."

He helped her remove her skis then told her to follow him. He was so military in his posture that her pounding heart kept time to his deliberate steps as they crossed the deep snow to a one room hut.

He opened the door to a one room hut. "*Vær så snill*," he said softly. "There is someone who wishes to see you."

The room inside was sparse. There had only a metal cot, some chairs, and a wood-burning stove made out of an oil drum. Its heat wafted out toward her. She sighed with relief then jumped when she realized a man crouched near it. He was a thin blonde man with broad shoulders, dressed in a military uniform of sorts. On his arm there was a band with the Norwegian flag. Then she saw his face. It was filled with an expression of hope and love and gray eyes that danced. She thought she was hallucinating. "Jens?"

Anna clapped her hands over her mouth, her limbs suddenly gone cold. "Jens?" The face beamed and swayed before her, then she blacked out.

When she came to, she was lying on a musty straw mattress. An unzipped sleeping bag covered her. A fire crackled not far away. "Anna."

Opening her eyes, she turned her head and looked into those of Hansen. He was sitting next to her on the floor, his face full of concern. This was a dream after her long trek. He wasn't real. She smiled and reached out to his face. His hair and eyebrows were the color of straw.

"I'm sorry I scared you," he said. "I wasn't thinking. No one must know I'm here."

Dreamily, she said it was all right and touched his cheek. It felt warm; the little stubble on the cheek rough like sandpaper, but it was real. She looked into the gray eyes as they flared up with lights that revealed the deepest love. Suddenly, her head cleared and she saw him for the first time. "Oh, Jens. It is you. I thought you were dead."

"I'm alive," he whispered, then kissed her hand.

"Jens… *Mein Gott.*" She threw her arms around his neck and crushed him to her, kissing his neck. He felt so thin. It made her sob, but he was real.

He stroked her head and rocked her, whispering her name. A shudder passed through him. There was nothing else to say. Only the power of holding on. He was alive.

After a while, she drew back. At the edge of his left eye there a little scar, a rose pink as it continued to heal. Another by his lip on the same side disappeared when he smiled at her.

"Where have you been?" she whispered. "They told us you were dead. Kjell wrote and said so. Schiller said so."

Hansen cocked his head at her. "That's because they didn't know anything else at the time. The authorities still believe it." He tensed up. "I've been in Sweden."

"Sweden? Then you got away? You weren't arrested?"

The look that flicked across his face lasted for only a few seconds, but she saw the pain—and briefly—fear. He placed his right hand on her shoulder, rubbing it gently as though he needed to believe that she was real too. "*Nei,*" he said in a whisper. "I didn't get away." He looked at the stove. She decided she shouldn't pursue this any further for now.

Anna touched his hair. It was still thick, but the color was all wrong. She traced one of his eyebrows. "Your hair," she said. "Your eyebrows. You look like Sonja Henie."

Hansen laughed—a real chuckle that made his eyes twinkle. "Those Swedish hairdressers." He took her hand and kissed it, stroking each finger with his own. He smiled. "How about some hot chocolate to warm you up?"

"That sounds wonderful, but what you must think of me. Did I faint?" She eased her feet onto the floor and stood up. He had removed her boots so she was in her wool socks.

"You were out only a second, I assure you." He went over to the oil barrel stove. A coffeepot was set on an iron shelf bolted onto the top. He prepared a mug of cocoa for her without using his left hand. He kept it stuffed in a pocket in his knickers. He made a second mug.

Anna took the one he offered. They stood very close. She'd forgotten how tall he was, how he disturbed her when he was next to her, even the special way he smelled. She laughed to think that sometimes it had been the smell of fish, but that had never mattered. She remembered the way it was when he had stayed the first time. The clean smell from bathing and shaving. She touched his cheek. It was so amazing. So unreal.

He motioned for her to drink her hot chocolate. In that instant she saw his left hand was damaged. Before he could tuck it away, she took it in her hand and turned it palm up, then down.

"Oh, Jens," she murmured. The ring finger was missing, the skin of its stub neatly pulled over the bone. The tip of the middle finger jagged out of line as though the hand of someone drawing it had slipped. The hand seemed as bent as a garden rake.

"Jens," she whispered. "They hurt you." She took his hand and pressed it to her cheek. "I'm all right." He withdrew his hand. "I'm fine." He swallowed and turned away.

"I love you," she said. It was the only thing she could say. She put away her cocoa and took his hand again. "I love you."

"I know. That saved me."

"You're in danger, aren't you? Why else would you dye your hair? Why did you come? Why didn't you stay where you were safe?"

"Because the resistance lost so many people in intelligence over winter. They needed me, and I needed to see you."

"Jens."

He looked her straight in the eye. "Not Jens. My name is Tore Haugland. I should have told you. Anna, I knew…"

"Shh. Enough. You've been through so much." She took both his hands. "Whatever else you have to say, you can say later." She paused. "And if it is about Einar, I know. I found a picture in the attic after the *razzia*. You knew him as a boy. That gave me great comfort when I thought you dead."

Hansen's face flushed, his eyes glistened. "Anna."

"You're alive. I thought I'd never see you again. *Tusen takk*, for believing me."

Hansen smiled faintly. "I thought I'd never see you again either." *Takk* for be my friend, he signed. My love.

She met him halfway in a kiss nothing more than a seal of friendship. The fire popped. He fidgeted, then got up and toyed with the fire, ignoring her awakening feeling of desire. Anna felt his shyness again and wondered what was wrong. "Where will you go now?"

"I'll be here for another day, then I'm going to Trondheim. We're setting up a new radio station. It isn't strenuous," he reassured her. "The war will be over very soon. Northern Holland was just liberated. Berlin will fall any day now. We've sent the *Wehrmacht* here in Norway our assurance there'll be no more sabotage. The Germans outnumber us ten to one— nearly a quarter million in number—but when they surrender, our units will be as professional as their soldiers."

"But it's still dangerous, isn't it? What if you're caught?"

"I won't be taken. I've seen to that. I couldn't go through it again." His voice was flat and uncompromising. "I have passports and visas for you and Lisel for America. I want you to get out and go where you can start a new life. Germany's done for. There's no going back."

"And Norway?"

"We've been stripped of everything." He frowned. "There's something else, Anna. I have an account in London. It's payment for my services. I've built a small fund of several thousand pounds. I've left a will in Stockholm with the British Legation. It's in your name. It's modest, but I want you to have it. To ease your way if something should happen to me."

Anna's face fell. "That's it? There's no hope?"

"There's always hope. I've certainly learned that in the past four months. By all rights I should be dead." He closed the makeshift door to the stove and stretched his back. He grew quiet again and she knew not to ask anymore.

Distance stirred between them, something he seemed to want. She couldn't understand why. There was no doubt in her mind about his feelings for her. But he was awkward around her for some reason. Had something been done to him he couldn't tell her?

"Do you want more cocoa?" he asked.

"*Vær så god.*" She watched his hands while he poured. The underside of the wrist on the other hand had also been burned. She wondered what else they had done to him. She touched his arm. He leaned down, kissing her gently on her lips, but that was all. "You're so thin."

"I'm doing all right. My stamina's the most important thing right now and I have that. I'll gain the weight back in time. Do you want to lie down and rest before you go back?"

"If you'll lie with me."

His eyes became and haunted. "Anna." He said it so faintly she barely heard him.

"Don't you want to? I want to," Anna said. "I want you to hold me and make love to me. I want to know that we're all right. After all this time."

"We're all right. I care for you so much." He brushed a tendril of hair back off her ear.

She put a hand on his shoulder and felt him freeze. "What is it, Jens? Did they hurt you?"

When he realized what she was asking, he laughed harshly and pulled away. "There's nothing wrong with my anatomy."

His eyes began to well up. She'd seldom seen a man cry except her father when her mother died. Or Einar when Lisel was born. What she saw on Hansen's face wasn't sorrow. It was shame and humiliation. The idea was astonishing. He had always been strong and she had relied on him, needed him in so many ways. Now it was the other way around. He needed her.

He traced her mouth with a finger. "I do want you very much. But I don't know. I'm such a mess." He spoke in a hushed voice. "You must understand. They tortured and beat me within an inch of my life. Often, there were times when I wished I was dead."

"Jens, are you ashamed of what I'll see?"

Hansen sighed, a shaky sound that came from deep inside his chest. "*Ja.*"

She took his crippled hand and kissed the stub gently, then lay the hand on her breast, holding it there tenderly. "Look at me. I will always love you. Always. And when you make love with me, your body will be strong and whole. I will never look away."

To prove it, she turned the hand over and pushed back his sleeve so the burn scars showed. She kissed them. She felt him tremble. *How could anyone so strong tremble?*

She pulled his woolen jersey from out of his knickers and pushed it up so she could touch his bare chest. She'd never been this forward, but she loved him so. She kissed him on his chest then put her arms around him under the shirt in the back. To her shock, she felt webs of raised scars everywhere. She forced herself to be strong. Ignoring them, she kissed his mouth. He made a little sound in his throat.

A tear came down and touched her lips. She could taste the salt in it when she pulled away. She stroked the strange yellow hair. His face looked so sad, the pain in his eyes so deep. He began to weep steadily and she wondered if he'd ever cried after his ordeal. She stoked the back of his head when he laid it down on her shoulder. He began to sob quietly, stifling it as if he were in pain, then shaking, suddenly began to collapse.

"I gave them nothing. Nothing," she heard him say.

She quickly sought out the low stool before they both ended up on the floor and let him fold into her lap. He curled up around her feet and putting his hands on her waist, laid his head against her stomach. He was crying hard now, his body wracked in pain and she rocked him until he was quiet. For a long, long time, he stayed silent with his head in her lap.

It was still in the cabin. Only the sound of the fire and her hand as she stroked his head. Outside, the wind seemed to have picked up but other than that she could hear nothing else. Eventually he began to stir. He removed his crippled hand from her waist and ran it slowly up and down the outline of her hip and thigh. He moved his head away from where her wool pants were soaked with his tears, then looked up. Smiling, her lips met his in a tender kiss.

They made love on the bed with half their clothes on. Under the sleeping bag, she sought only to please him. She knew he would never be the same, but she could help make him whole in a new way and believe in himself again. What he had gone through was too awful for someone else to fully understand, but he had survived it. When he finally turned, they came together in a joining of familiarity and peace, a slow, tender dance.

When they finished, they lay in each others' arms and told stories about each other, but mostly he talked about himself before the war and his family: *Onkel* Kris, the Deaf Church and the people he knew. He talked about Einar and shared stories about him that made her laugh.

They lay side to side, their bare legs entwined.

"I was always getting in trouble with them. I was eight years younger, and a pest, I'm afraid. We use to go my grandmother's in Bergen during the summer—that's where I first met Einar. The Frommes had raspberry bushes at the back of their property. Einar and Lars liked to go out there to sit on the grass and eat and talk. Many times I hid in the bushes and listened into their discussions, which at that time of their lives was usually about girls. Once I slipped a rubber snake into Einar's pack. He thought it was reindeer sausage until he pulled it out."

Anna laughed. "I love you, Jens Hansen."

"Tore."

"Jens. You will always be Jens." She snuggled against him.

"All right." He held her close. "You're so warm. I was so cold going over, but don't remember much. Just remember cold." He went on to tell about being hospitalized for weeks; the painful nights and days of his recovery. As he spoke, he opened up and she knew that he would be all right in time.

"After the war, I'll take you to Bergen to see my mother."

"Will she accept me?"

He stroked her cheek. "My mother is a woman of both compassion and conviction. You've nothing to fear. Will you wait for me?"

"*Ja*."

"Ten minutes," someone yelled in English.

"All right," Hansen called back. "That's us," he said to her. "Time to go."

They dressed quickly and quietly. When the knock came again, Anna had her boots and coat back on, Hansen his uniform. He opened the door and let Tommy in. Neither man said anything, but an understanding passed between them.

"Anna, this is Tommy. Tommy, Anna."

They shook hands. She settled back into Hansen's arms.

"I'm sorry to break this up," Tommy said, "but the time. If we're to get you back…"

"I'm ready," said Anna. "Will I have the same escort?"

"New bunch. Everyone wants in. You'll go by sled this time." He nodded for Haugland to say his good-bye, then left.

Hansen gave her shoulder a squeeze. "I'm sorry, but you can't be missed. The village."

"I know." Anna leaned into him, fighting back tears, "but it's hard to bear."

She stayed quiet while he buttoned her coat up tighter, and pulled up the collar. "Oh, I forgot about this," she said. She took out the fishhook. "Petter gave it to me."

"I thought it would make you come with him more easily," Hansen said quietly, "though he didn't understand why Tommy wanted him to take it. Did you guess it was me?"

"*Nei.* They said you were dead. But the hook told me Petter was a friend of yours." She put it into Haugland's good hand. "I want you to have it. A token of my love."

"True love." Hansen leaned down and kissed her on her mouth. "*Takk.*" He straightened up slowly, looking thoughtful. "I want to marry you, Anna Fromme. I want to adopt Lisel, but no matter what happens, remember me."

Her heart pounded at the thought he was going back into danger. That it could be the last time she saw him. "Oh, Jens." She choked on her words. "I'll always remember."

He closed the hook in his good fist. "*Takk.* That gives me hope. You're the only reason I came back. The only reason."

CHAPTER 103

After Anna left, Haugland slept for two more hours. Since arriving from Sweden days ago he had been pushing himself and he felt it. His hand became stiff when he was tired and it ached frequently. His back hurt if he exerted himself. He wasn't supposed to be running around on the *fjell* yet. Headquarters in Sweden wanted him to stay close to Trondheim. He was to be an intelligence agent, not an operational one charging around the countryside with commandos. He wasn't physically ready.

He woke to Tommy pounding on the hut's heavy door. "Are you decent, Scarlett?"

"I'm looking for a match." He felt around for the match tube and lit a lantern. By then Tommy was inside, carrying a coffeepot and a tray of hot food. "What's up?"

"We're moving to a safe house. There has been a *razzia* in Trondheim. Rinnan caught an agent named Froyland. Some in XU have been arrested."

Haugland sat up. "When will it end? Germans are dying in Berlin and here they just go on and on, smashing Sivorg and Milorg groups."

"Soon." Tommy put the tray down on a stool. It contained a ration meal straight from an air drop.

Haugland tried to keep his voice calm. The mere mention of Rinnan's name paralyzed him. He hid his hearing loss, but this was the other piece he fought to keep hidden: the daytime nightmares and jittered feelings of approaching danger. Rinnan had left more than scars on his back. He threw aside the sleeping bag and dressed. "Is Anna safe? When's the escort due in?"

"I expect them back any time. Eat fast. I'd like to get you out of here quickly."

"This the place where Kjell and Grimstad are holed up?" In theory, he knew where it was. Tommy had described the ancient mountain farmstead as set back deep in the mountains, difficult to reach even in summer. Kjell had been secure there since New Year's, acting as liaison between resistance folk coming from the south and Tommy's mountain unit.

"Our home away from home." Tommy saluted him and went out.

***

They took off at a steady clip, heading south under a low overcast sky. There were seven in the party, all trusted members of Tommy's inner group. For an hour they moved along by twos, their skis and poles working in fluid unison. Haugland, already tested just getting to Tommy's main encampment, put his mind to it and kept pace. Once in a while, they would stop and someone would take readings from a compass. Others searched the wild *fjell* with binoculars looking for German patrols or NS groups that regularly searched for illegal units. In their winter whites, the enemy blended into their surroundings.

After a time they descended to snowy hills with forests and open fields. On a rise, Tommy stopped and tugged at a glove. He signaled for one of his men to split off and survey the area around them on the *fjell.* "We're getting there, Scarlett. There are many who are anxious to see you. Kjell's been beside himself since he knew you were alive and coming back."

"I'm anxious to see him too." Haugland blinked when something touched an eyelash. He looked up. Snowflakes descended in lazy zig-zags. "Looks like we're in for weather."

Tommy stabbed a pole into the snow. "Good. It'll give cover. Where's Paulsen?"

The group of young men scanned the *fjell* around them. There was no sign of him.

"Maybe he's taking a leak," someone laughed.

"Bloody hell," Tommy said. "I told him to take a look."

Suddenly, the Milorg man appeared back in their range, skating his skis across the snow, waving his poles like a demon. "Patrol!" Paulsen shouted.

In an instant, Tommy unslung his Sten gun. Haugland froze, but Tommy pushed him. "Move. Follow me."

It was a mad run. Automatic fire blossomed behind them, strafing the snow and causing it to explode like frozen white powder. Someone cried out in pain, but as they tore past a clump of dwarf birch, they turned smoothly, their skis sounding like the bow of a ship cutting through water. Behind them the gunfire continued, so they hunkered down, their poles under their arms, fighting to increase the distance between them and the soldiers. Tommy signaled to break up. "Follow me," he shouted to Haugland. "The others know their way around the hills." Tommy's words whipped away as he peeled off, and led their flight down toward.

At the bottom of the hill, the area leveled and Tommy changed his rhythm to a new tempo as they turned to a pathway leading south. From far off, came the occasional sound of gunfire, but once their stride was established, they began to make good time and the sounds got further away. As they traveled, the sky became increasingly cloudy. The temperature plunged. Soon the first taste of snow began to drift down on them.

They stopped for a brief rest, to Haugland's relief. He leaned hard on his poles, his back aching. "Obviously, we're not taking the quick way home."

"Sorry. Had to lead them away. You okay?" Tommy searched his pockets and brought out some chocolate and raisins "Try this."

Haugland took the pieces gratefully. "I'm managing. Sorry I'm not up to par yet."

"I'll back you. We'll meet with the lads eventually, but you do look beat." Tommy took a bite of his chocolate piece and looked at the snow falling now more heavily. "Hope the bloody Germans freeze."

They left moments later, this time climbing up a steep rise covered with birches wallowing in deep snow. Ahead was open *fjell* with mountains rising above them. At the top, Haugland took out his binoculars and through the falling snow studied the ridges around them. They looked clear, so he turned his attention to a small stand of birch and pine and was about to dismiss them, when his eye caught something smooth and white behind the light curtain of snow flakes. Too late he realized it was the whitewashed helmet cover of a German soldier. Before they even heard the crack of the rifles, Tommy cried out in pain and slumped forward on his ski poles.

"Go! Go!" yelled Haugland, urging Tommy to move. Grabbing his friend's arm, he physically moved him forward. Tommy responded as though he was coming out of a daze. They dug their poles into the snow and burst across the open field. Behind them shots went around them as soldiers took up the chase. Up the hill they charged as fast as their burning lungs and skis could take them. At the top, Haugland turned and shot at one of the Germans, striking him down. Haugland caught up with Tommy on the other side who signaled for him to make a turn just as two soldiers came up over the rise. Halfway up the next hill Tommy faltered.

"Which way?" Haugland shouted. Snow was falling heavily. Visibility was poor. Finally, he made the decision for them. When they reached the top, he guided them down over an edge into a forest. Finding some sort of a trail, he went several hundred feet weaving in and out the trees before slipping down over another edge and stopped. Without disturbing the snow on it, he pulled Tommy under a large pine and undid the other man's skis. Inside, the ground lay thick with frozen needles, but it was wide enough for two men to sit and stretch out their legs. Above him the branches of the tree were large and majestic, swooping clear down to the ground. Snow covered them like thick cotton batting, but from his vantage point, Haugland could see up into the trees. He laid out their Sten guns. After removing his own skis, he tended to his friend.

Tommy had been hit in the side, two bullets going from the back through to the front where one was still apparently lodged. The other had traveled down toward the thigh and out. He was bleeding freely, but fortunately, Tommy's heavy coat and sweater had contained the blood, leaving no trail on the ground. Haugland worked quickly and found whatever he had in his rucksack for stanching the blood. He tried to make Tommy comfortable. Above the swish of the snow, he strained to listen, but found it difficult with only his one good ear. The other was useless in the slight wind. Once Tommy was comfortable, he sat and waited for the Germans he knew would come.

It was very still. Only the pines and the hush of the snow. Tommy stirred and put out his hand to Haugland. He became agitated.

"My pill. Scarlett. In my coat."

Haugland patted his arm. "You won't need it." He kept his voice low.

"Please." Tommy's breath came in short pants. He looked pasty. "Save yourself. I won't make it. It's so cold."

Haugland put out a hand to hush him. Above them he saw just in time the white covered legs of a soldier as he cautiously glided down through the trees. He held his breath, but the heavy snow-laden branches hid them better than he hoped. The increased snowfall helped too. Another soldier joined him and they talked. Haugland cocked his head, listening for each word. Apparently, they were from a larger patrol making a sweep of the area, but the snow was making them nervous. They wanted to get off the *fjell.* They talked for a while, then deciding to join their comrades, made their way back up through the trees.

For a long time Haugland waited, gripping his pistol tightly. Finally convinced that the soldiers were gone, he left their hiding place. All around him there was nothing but the falling snow and heavy silence of the forest.

Scrambling back in under the dry cover of the tree, he scratched the ground for stones and laid them side by side until he had a twelve inch square. He set out the Primus stove he always carried on top. He pulled out Tommy's sleeping bag from his rucksack and helped Tommy into it. Zipping him up, Haugland told him he was going to look around.

"Stay tight. I'll be back shortly." Shouldering his Sten gun, he moved quietly up through the trees in search of the soldiers. The snow was deep in some places, but by staying close to the trees, he was able to go back up to the open field where he had cut off. At the top of the rise, he cautiously came forward and lay down upon the snow. Taking out his binoculars he panned the open *fjell* and the woods around it. The whole area was gray and socked in by falling snow. A light wind whipped it up, stinging Haugland's face. There was nothing out there.

Cautiously he returned to the shelter, careful not to make new tracks. When he crawled back into the dry space he discovered Tommy slumped over on his side. Panicked he had chosen to end his life, Haugland scrambled over to him only to discover he had passed out. A pill was tightly clenched in his gloved hand. Shaking him, he revived Tommy for a moment. He looked at Haugland with fevered eyes. "What's new?" he whispered.

"They're gone, but we might have to hole up here for the night with the storm."

"I don't think I can make it."

"No. I'm going to make you make it. I owe you for my life."

He lit the paraffin underneath the Primus stove. Once it was going, he melted snow in his tin cup and made a bouillon soup, keeping Tommy engaged in conversation. After feeding him,Tommy drifted. Haugland was tempted to sleep himself, but with the snow falling heavily now, he knew the storm would take them both if he wasn't alert. So he talked and told him of his fears when he first woke to see him at the Gunnerson cabin.

The Primus stove made the space warm. Haugland took care it did not melt the snow on the tree. He still worried about detection. Tommy eventually fell asleep. He checked the pad to make sure the bleeding had stopped and watched him for signs of lethargy. His situation was tricky, but Haugland hoped once the snow let up, he could devise a sled of some sort with the skis and continue the trek south. He had a general idea of where he should be heading and with his compass could get across. If he was lucky, he'd run into Tommy's men who by now would be concerned. He leaned his back against the trunk of the tree and closed his eyes. His shoulders and upper back throbbed, as though the scars were rebelling against any exertion. He knew he must conserve his strength. He fought the urge to sleep.

Suddenly not too far off came the crack of automatic gunfire followed by an equally strong volley of return fire. He crawled to the edge of the tree's heavy canopy and poked his head out. Above him and to his left, the sounds appeared to be coming closer. They sounded like German arms followed by Sten guns. A resistance unit?

Buoyed with hope, he grabbed his Sten gun and pistol and crawled back up to the trail. He made his way up to the ridge through the trees, arriving in time to see four German soldiers charging down the hill with a pack of men in white parkas in pursuit. Throwing himself on the snowbank, he took aim at the first soldier and fired. The big man's legs buckled, throwing him into the next man. Both went down in a jumble of skis and poles. The remaining soldiers swerved around them, heading for the trees. The Milorg men continued pursuit, some stopping to take two downed men prisoner, the rest firing at the fleeing Germans. One of the soldiers yelped and slipped but was able to make it to the stand. The other followed close behind.

Haugland moved in closer and joined the firefight. Outnumbered eight to one, the Germans gave up and walked out with their hands up. Haugland stood up and staggered over to the party of Home Force soldiers.

One of the men recognized him and called out to him.

"Jens," he shouted. "Is it really you? Was that a fight or what?" It was Helmer Stagg, his face flushed from the excitement. The others were men from Tommy's encampment.

"Tommy's been shot," Haugland said then exhausted from the cold and the strain of the past several hours, collapsed against Helmer.

***

"Jens?"

Haugland pursed his lips. Who was that?

He opened his eyes. Above him was a pine ceiling decorated with a rosemalling pattern of red roses and blue beasts entwined, moving to the flicker of a candle lantern. For a moment he panicked and thinking he was back in Gunnerson's cabin, braced for the first wave of pain he was sure to come. He raised his hand and was surprised to see that it was not bandaged, just looking like the foot of a chicken after slaughter.

"Jens."

Haugland turned his head. It was Kjell Arneson. His face looked strained, but his eyes were warm and welcoming.

"I thought you'd sleep your life away."

Haugland lifted his head. "Where am I?" He lay on a bed with a bolster and a *dyne* with covers woven with hand-dyed yarns. He was undressed.

"The farmhouse of Ola Torkelson. Our headquarters since January. They brought you and Tommy here a couple of days ago. You were out of it. Hans Grimstad says exhaustion and the cold."

"Tommy!" Haugland sat upright.

Kjell put his hands gently on Haugland's bare shoulders to steady him.

"It's all right. He's in the next room. Yesterday wasn't his favorite day, but he's going to be all right. Grimstad even has him sitting up." Kjell patted his arm then shook it affectionately. "Jens. Never in my wildest dreams. I thought I lost you forever, my dear friend."

Kjell seemed to have something caught in his throat. "Forgive me. Tommy told me you were alive only three days ago. Just before he met you up at the encampment. It's been a bit difficult." Tears sprang into his eyes, but he worked hard to keep them in check. "Sorry. I can't believe what they did to you. But you're alive. There wasn't a day I didn't mourn you."

Haugland gripped Kjell's hand. For a moment neither spoke. Eventually, he let go.

"So Grimstad's here. Who else from Fjellstad?"

"Petter and Helmer Stagg. That's all"

Haugland rested his hands on his drawn-up knees and signed for his clothes on Kjell's chair. "About all of us who's left. I think of Sig and all his fine sons. The men of Hitra. All gone."

"But don't ever think they regretted it, Jens. I know Sig. The life of a fisherman is a hard life but nothing galls him more than having someone come in and tell him what to do. The Haraldsens hated the Germans and the NS. They made their choice to join us. I didn't twist their arms."

Haugland still felt guilty. "What day is it?"

"April 29th." Kjell gave him his shirt and long underwear.

"I'm so sorry about your home and boat, Kjell. So senseless."

"It doesn't matter. They can be replaced." Kjell cleared his throat. "From what Tommy said about finding you back in January, you look better than I hoped. You're well?"

"FO IV wanted me flown to London for further doctoring, but I didn't want to go."

"Why the devil not, Jens? Why didn't you where your health was concerned?"

Finished pulling on his long underwear, Haugland swung his aching legs over to the side of the bed and slipped his arms into the top. The knitted wool raked against the scars on his back.

"Because they'd never let me come back to Norway. At least in Sweden, I could wear them down, though I had to be hidden the whole time for fear of Gestapo spies in Stockholm. When I felt better, I worked for the British Legation. Then, I got this opportunity."

He pulled his sweater over his head. "Got something for you from Sweden." He pointed to his rucksack by the bed. Once in hand, he gave Kjell a letter.

"Why, it's from Kitty." Kjell caressed the envelope.

Haugland finished dressing while Kjell read, then went to the room's only window. The sun glanced off the icicles hanging from under the eaves. Out across the *tun* of the old traditional farm he could see the farmer come out with a pail of milk. *Now that would be a treat.* Behind him, Kjell folded the letter and replaced it in its envelope.

"*Tusen takk* for getting this to me. She sounds homesick, but the family she's with is nice." He tucked it into his wool shirt pocket. "I wish I could see her. Rika too. Just to let them know I'm all right. We're so close to the end."

Haugland leaned against the window. "Sorry. It's not possible. But you knew that."

Suddenly, Haugland was aware of music from a radio coming from somewhere off, then a muffled voice of an announcer speaking. "Tommy's really all right?"

"*Ja, ja.* Says he has the luck of a Viking. Everyone from Tommy's unit is here, by the way. Ivar is here. His group is joining ours."

A cheer shook the house. Haugland dropped his arms. "What the hell was that?"

There was a commotion down below. Then, someone came running upstairs and along the hallway. The door flew open. Helmer braced the frame. "Big news," he panted. "Hitler is dead. He killed himself today. The news just came on the BBC."

Haugland felt a chill down his arms. "Have they surrendered?"

"Not yet, though the Allies are pressing. Radio says Dönitz is *Fuhrer*. Himmler's out."

"And where the hell are we? Where is Norway?" After five brutal years, it was hard to take in.

CHAPTER 104

On May 3rd, Tore Haugland and Kjell Arneson left the mountain farmstead and moved to the Trondheim area. There they met up with a resistance group who took them to a cabin hidden in the forested, hilly Bymarka area outside the city. A collection of old holiday cabins sheltered by tall pine trees, the area was heavily guarded. From the moment they arrived, Haugland felt an unsettled presence in the camp. Hitler might be dead, but Norway was more vulnerable than ever. The fear of Rinnan and the Gestapo making inroads into the illegal organizations was very high. News of recent arrests in the city gave Haugland a headache, but he had orders like the others to wait for word from the continent.

On his second evening there, he returned to the cabin to find Axel waiting for him. He was head of the local Milorg, an organization that continued to stay tight and out of the hands of Rinnan and the Gestapo. One of its few failures had been Haugland's capture. When he came in, a small group of hardened men rose to salute him. Haugland was deeply moved.

He cleared his throat. "Gentlemen," He knew that after they were surprised on the road, some from their unit took their lives in trying to safeguard him. He had been captured anyway.

"*God kveld*," Axel said. "It's an understatement to say how good it is to see you. Word of your death, like that of Lazarus, seems to have been premature."

"It's good to see you too. And I thank you all." He looked around. "Where's Kjell?"

Axel came over to the table. "He's out with Knudsen. Picking his brain about sea mines." On the other side of the table was a man wearing round wired glasses and a trim wool jacket—in total contrast to the Milorg men in knickers and sweaters. Axel was quick to introduce him. "This is Ola Borstad. He's security in Trondheim."

Borstad stood up. "Enormous pleasure to meet you. Your work has been vital."

Haugland flushed, wondering what the man wanted with him. Borstad had spread photographs around the table.

"I realize you have only recently returned to Norway after a difficult time. With just days to the end we have prayed for, we are compiling testimony against all *quislings* and in particular, Henry Oliver Rinnan. You are one of the few survivors of his heinous Cloister. We're hoping you'll testify when he comes to trial."

Borstad's words hit Haugland like a punch. He never thought he'd be asked. An image he always kept at bay stabbed at him. *The skeleton.* His back and hand began to hurt.

Borstad moved the pictures around. "For now, simple identification will help. Know them?" There were women as well as men in the pile of photographs. Haugland looked at the ones closest to him and saw a photograph of Karl Dolmen, Rinnan's main interrogator.

Despite the *Hjemmefronten*'s call for "Dignity, calmness, and discipline," Haugland wondered, are they really planning to try this man? Along with Birger Strom, he had been one of the most vicious during his interrogations. Haugland became uncomfortably warm.

Patience, he told himself. I'll get through this. He thought of Einar. "I know him. That's Karl Dolmen." He found photographs of Birger Strom and Odd Sorting. *The whip hand came down.*

"Were they in the Cloister when you were interrogated?" Borstad asked.

A headache formed behind Haugland's left eye "*Ja*, they were there. I can remember things... but… lately..." He looked sharply at the other men. "It's not really something I want to remember. I have gaps... I was out of it..."

"Do you think you could remember specific things?" Borstad leaned over the table a little too close for Haugland. "Things they did as individuals to you?"

"*Ja*..." Haugland's voice trailed off. Axel looked at him sympathetically.

"Good. That would be helpful. Now is there anyone else?'

Haugland listlessly pointed out some others, mentioning Gerhard Flesch, the Gestapo head in Trondheim. He avoided the shots of Rinnan. He walked away from the table to a small window by the door. Outside, it was sunny and warm. The birches and the maples were beginning to show some pale green among the pines.

"We have been able to piece together what happened to you before and after your arrest," Borstad went on. Haugland wondered if he had been a prosecutor before the war because he was so damned persistent. "Flesch might have sent you to a firing squad as Jens Hansen, but files were introduced on Christmas Eve Day by Martin Koeller of the Gestapo in Oslo. The files he brought were quite extensive. You were exposed as an English trained agent."

Haugland's stomach contracted. Koeller. Had he been responsible for his going to the Cloister? He had been transferred from Mission Hotel Christmas Eve. That he remembered. Their attack on him had been immediate and brutal. They knew his name was Haugland, not Hansen. Suddenly, he had a terrible thought. Did Koeller know Anna's whereabouts?

"Tell me," he asked sharply. "Did Koeller ever travel to Fjellstad? Since December?"

Borstad looked at Axel. "As far we know, *nei*. In fact, Koeller was in Trondheim only a few days then left before New Years."

Haugland's head throbbed. There was still the von Weber connection to Anna. "Didn't he ask for my transfer to Oslo, to V.T.? Didn't he want me for something?"

Borstad shrugged. "The request was apparently made, but Rinnan wouldn't allow it. At some time, Koeller must have been told you were dead and he lost interest, although he may have had other concerns. You seem worried. Any particular reason why?"

Haugland moved away from the window, trying to bring himself to make a difficult decision. He looked at Axel. He trusted him. "Could I talk to you outside?"

Haugland nodded to the others and led the way outside to a stand of pine trees. There he told Axel everything about Anna Fromme's secret American background, von Weber's role with the resistance, Einar's part in Milorg and how he had died at the Cloister. Cut in pieces and disposed of.

"Incredible. An American." Axel rubbed the blonde stubble on his cheek.

"I'll testify if you'll give me your word to protect her if anything should happen to me. *Promise* to never let her know how Einar Fromme died. At all costs keep the details secret should his killers come to trial. It would tear her apart."

"I'll see it done." Axel shook Haugland's hand solemnly. "I promise." When they came back into the cabin, Borstad was putting away the photographs. He looked up hopefully.

"I'll do it," Haugland said softly. He stuffed his hands into his wool pants, staring blankly at the remaining pictures on the table. One of them was a pretty woman with an oval face and fair hair. She had a full figure accentuated by her light colored sweater, her arm around Sorting.

"Who's that?" he asked.

"Freyda Olsen," Borstad said. "Sorting's mistress. They've been together for about three and a half years. She's done a variety of work for Rinnan's group, mostly of the hostess type. She was identified about two months ago by someone who went to her flat."

Haugland sifted absentmindedly through the small batch. He froze. An awful vision floated before his eyes, something so terrible he thought he was imagining it.

A woman from the village. Someone close to you.

He wanted to cry out because it not only had caused him unimaginable suffering, but also had set the whole ugly chain of *razzias* on its merciless course. And yet the worst was yet to come. If Kjell found out, it would kill him. Beneath a photograph of Sorting and his woman, was one of Freyda Olsen and Rika Arneson in a park, arms locked together in friendship.

Haugland picked up the photograph. "When was this taken?"

"A couple of weeks ago. The woman with the Olsen girl hasn't been identified yet, but she's been with her before. Do you know her?"

"*Nei.*" Even as he lied, he knew he had discovered the truth. Rika was the negative agent. *Poor Rika. Poor everyone.* She had progressed far beyond the H-7 painted on rocks on the fjord cliffs. She had gone to Trondheim to get a job and a new life. Somewhere along the way she was introduced to this Olsen girl. Had Sorting planned that from the start? And Kjelstrup? Did he know she was doing some illegal work? Had he come to her for help and got trapped by Rinnan? Haugland's mouth was dry.

Everything made sense. At Christmas, Rika had seen him in Trondheim with Sverre. Kjelstrup was already in the hands of the Gestapo. Did Rika innocently tell someone about their meeting, someone who in reality worked with Rinnan? Where was she now? She was still dangerous, believing she was working with legitimate people.

"I'm going to go back into town now," Borstad was saying. "I greatly admire you, sir. It will take a different kind of courage to do this." He put the last of the photographs into his briefcase.

"May I have that picture of the two women? I'd like to show it around."

Borstad gave him the photograph with Freyda and Rika together. Haugland pocketed it carefully. "Do you honestly believe you will catch Rinnan and bring him to trial?"

"We're trying to stay abreast of his movements as much as possible."

Borstad seemed very sure of himself. Haugland thought he probably was a good security officer but found himself saying, "You do better than that. Rinnan does the unexpected, sometimes recklessly. He'll bolt."

Borstad looked astonished. "To Sweden? He'd be returned. It's not an understatement to say that after Quisling, he's our country's most notorious criminal."

"He won't go to Sweden. He'll go to Russia."

***

Axel stayed behind with Haugland. "Are you all right? You seemed distracted."

"*Nei*, I'm fine." Haugland stretched the fingers on his bad hand. Of course, he wasn't fine. He couldn't get the thought of Rika as a negative agent out of his head.

"Well, maybe this. If we put a unit together to track Rinnan, you want to be a part of it?"

Haugland clenched his hand into a fist. "Absolutely."

"Excellent. It'll help us identify some of his people too." He smiled at him. "You're quite remarkable, Ryper. Against the odds, you managed to survive."

"I'm not sure it's survival. It was more the matter of luck which I had no control over."

"*Nei*. You're incredibly tough. A survivor."

"Look. I appreciate you, Axel. Your organization is superb. Just don't analyze me or make up legends about me." He looked out the window.

"This woman. This German… American... you really care for her, don't you?"

"Do you find it so strange?"

"War's strange. You're a solid man, but how do you think this'll be after capitulation?"

Haugland stared straight at him, thinking of Rika. "I don't really care. Nothing ever looks like it's supposed to be. Strong men cry, ugly women become beauty queens. Especially in war."

"She must be some woman."

"She's a *jøssing*." Haugland got up. He couldn't stand sitting for lengths of time. Not when he was being grilled and Axel was grilling him.

He went to the open door. At a cabin further away, he could see the uniformed men who watched the place at all times. He raised his good hand to them, then cocked his head to listen to some small birds flitting in the birches close by. After the difficult winter in Sweden, it was hard to believe spring had returned and he was back in Norway. He wanted the war over, but until the Germans surrendered the war continued.

"Look, I'm sorry. I didn't mean to press." Axel's voice was gentle as he came next to Haugland. "I gave my word, Haugland. I'll see she's looked after, though I don't think it's necessary. Somehow I think no matter what happens you'll come out of it fine."

Haugland brushed his hand against his jacket, feeling the photograph. The two young women looked so carefree and happy, but he believed he was right. It was an illusion. Rika had been duped and had caused untold suffering. He kept thinking of Koeller and Anna, of Rika and Kjell. One part of him was worried for Anna, the other sickened by the growing dread he felt. He must stop the girl before she did any more damage, even if it would grieve Kjell.

Axel put his cap on his head and prepared to leave.

"Axel. Wait a minute. I *am* distracted. Something's wrong."

Haugland told him everything. "God willing, you can warn your contacts as soon as possible. I want to send runners to Tommy's encampment too."

But he didn't count on Kjell. Just as he finished explaining his discovery about Rika, he heard the scrape of boots at the door. Kjell was standing there, his eyes full of tears.

"Jens, is this true?"

Haugland rose up. "*Ja*, I think it's true. Security has photographs here. And something I was told at the Cloister makes sense now. *A woman I knew*. Sorting got to Rika through his mistress."

Kjell's face was ashen. "The *razzias.* Sig. All my friends. Gone." His shoulders began to shake. "Oh, God. Rika. What will happen to her?"

Haugland went to his friend and put a hand on his arm, feeling his grief as if it were his own. "Let me handle it. I'll find the right channels. She thought she was doing some good, but she got involved with a cell run by Rinnan. I promise the bastard will pay."

CHAPTER 105

Lars looked across the square. He hunkered against the freezing rain skittering across the cobblestones with loud pings and decided to make a run for it. Turning up his collar, he adjusted his cap, then dashed out. He hadn't planned on going out, but circumstances made it necessary. Hitler might be dead, the Devil take him, but the terror in Norway continued. As an aide to Hauge, he was in extreme danger. There was a price on his head.

Since January the resistance had been hard-pressed. Key people both in Sivorg and Milorg had been exposed and sometimes captured by the Gestapo and the State Police. Others fled to Sweden, including Conrad Bonnevie-Svendsen. Word had come that someone had identified him as the leader of the illegal national conference held at the Olso Home for the Deaf last summer. Lars personally got him exported because he was in extreme danger. Losing Conrad was a blow to morale and the central organization.

There were hopeful signs, Lars thought. There was good cooperation now between Milorg's central staff, the Milorg districts, and Norwegian and British military authorities in London. Now with May five days old and Germany's cities in ruin, they waited. The *Hjemmefronten* leadership was holed up in an apartment in the west end of Oslo, the secretariat scattered around the city for safety, while senior German officers in Norway made up their minds about surrendering. There apparently was strong disagreement among them, but yesterday the German civil and military leaders were summoned from Norway *and* Denmark to see the new *Fuhrer* Dönitz. Lars thought German forces—250,000 in Norway—were being used to bargain the best possible terms for Germany.

Lars made it to the middle of the square, then slowed down. It wouldn't do to rush about, even in the rain. The streets weren't exactly plush with people. Spying an opening in one of the buildings in front of him, he sought shelter. He slipped under the stone archway and collected himself for the walk up to the bus stop to his flat further up the street, only to stiffen when a young woman passed by with a newspaper over her head. Suddenly, she turned back.

"Erling?" she said above the rustle of the freezing rain.

Lars pulled her into the opening and looked carefully around. Karin was one of many women who worked as couriers in the city. With so many checkpoints these days in the streets, she performed fearlessly, delivering important documents to and from meetings. Stuffing them into her bra and girdle, some of these papers had been vital material all the way from London. Only recently had the Gestapo begun to make personal searches of women at the checkpoints.

"What are you doing out this time of night?" he asked.

"To warn you. You can't go home. Someone tried to arrest your landlady. She's safe." She put a hand on his arm. You didn't have any papers at your place, did you?"

"*Nei*, I didn't." He looked out across the square and then suddenly pulled her into his arms when he saw someone coming toward them. He held her close like they were lovers, but his hand crept inside his coat to his revolver. The girl stroked his face and continued until a man passed by. "You've got to hide," she said.

They caught a bus out to the outskirts of town where he could stay low for a while. He was very jumpy. Only hours before, J. C. Hauge had been released from Stapo headquarters where he had been taken after a furnace violation on his car. Miraculously, no one there knew he was the national head of Milorg. If they had… It was too unnerving for Lars to contemplate. He watched the streets from the rain-splattered window as they passed through the city and he noted that there were not only more controls than he had ever remembered, but groups of men from the Hird—sometimes as many as twelve and he knew that they were armed now. Karin, sensing his tenseness, hugged the arm she had in her clasp. He hugged her back. Eventually, he reached his stop and rang the bell.

"*God kveld*," he said, then got off.

It was dark out now, the streets deserted and sinister as the blackout curtains pulled down over lifeless windows. Stuffing his hands into his pockets, he leaned into the weather, heading for a safe house a block away. The bus passed him but he didn't look up as his mind was on other things. Avoiding a large puddle, he listened as a dog barked not far off then slowed down as he became aware of someone on the street just ahead of him. Looking up, he saw a small group of young men. Even in the dark, he could make out the Hird uniforms as they came toward him. It was too late to run back.

"*Heil Hitler!*" he said as they crossed the street and passed him.

"*Heil Hitler!*"

He continued on, the hair on the nape of his neck prickling. If he could just reach the door of the apartment building without attracting further attention.

Slow down, he said to himself. Stay calm even if your knees are liquid.

He climbed the steps and came within the safety of the entrance, when suddenly one of the men called out for him to come back. Instantly, he bolted for the inside, tearing down the hallway to the back and out into a muddy alley. On the other side he could hear shouting and then a shrill whistle. Taking out his revolver, he went up to the top of the alley bordered on both sides by low-rise buildings and sporadic fencing. He was almost clear of the block when he realized that he was trapped. Coming down toward him from the street were two men apparently from the same group Drawing weapons, they moved quickly toward him.

"Halt!" someone yelled.

"What's wrong?" Lars asked in German, hoping to confuse them. When he was nearly up to them, he coolly opened fire. One of the Hirdsmen went down immediately, but the other fired rapidly at Lars before he too fell face down onto the icy, muddy lane. Lars felt bullets brush past him, but he didn't stop moving once both men were down. Dashing across the street, he bolted up the alley on the other side just as the Hirdsmen came out of the apartment building and discovered their comrades. The chase was on in earnest now. Lars ran halfway up the next alley, then hoping that the darkness would help his cover, went back through a building and out on the street a block above the safe house flat. There was a large group now, charging around the apartment building. Without streetlights, it was hard to make out the number. He strained to see if any vehicles had joined the chase. To his relief, none.

Lars hugged the wall of the building and headed north. He was feeling lightheaded. His upper chest and left arm were numb. To his surprise, he discovered he was bleeding. Realizing that he was in real difficulty now, he continued on, wondering where to go. The rain continued as full darkness fell. Fearing dogs, he tried desperately to remember the location of a neighborhood creek where he could lose his scent. His mind raced, but he knew he was slowing down. Each step he took seemed harder to manage. He checked his gun by feel to see if any bullets were left. He might need one for himself. He was barely aware of someone coming toward him along the sidewalk until she was almost on top of him.

"Karin," he said then sagged onto her shoulder.

***

Someone equally in distress was Martin Koeller. He felt the deepest betrayal when he heard the shocking news Hitler had killed himself. As it began to sink in, however, he saw that it was done to spare the German people from final humiliation as there had been in Italy when Mussolini and his mistress had been killed and publicly displayed

The *Fuhrer* had been noble.

But now what?

The halls of Victoria Terrasse were subdued. There was still hope Norway would hold. Troops and other personnel were willing. Discipline was being maintained. But as May slowly unfolded, Koeller felt a personal crisis bordering on despair. It was ending. On May 4 a rumor circulated that capitulation was not far off. The next day when it appeared to be coming true, Koeller began to withdraw from the others and spend more time in his office alone and drinking. Unlike his superior Fehlis, Koeller had no particular notions of how he should conduct himself. Nothing mattered anymore. By six that night, he was soused.

He could hear his secretary and Gebhardt whispering outside his office door and see behind their wooden faces whenever he came out. At eight, he told his pretty secretary to go home. If she still had a home. A former resident might claim his or her old flat back. Weeping, she said good-bye and that was the end of that.

"You too, Gebhardt," Koeller said to his aide. "You've done well."

"Will I see you in the morning, sir?"

Koeller didn't respond directly. "Look after yourself. Don't resist the occupying forces."

Gebhardt bit his lip and swallowed.

"Do you understand me?"

"*Ja*," Gebhardt said in a disheartened voice. He saluted Koeller and left. As soon as his aide was gone, Koeller went into his office and locked the door. He went over to his window and looked out into the pleasant spring evening, then closed the curtains out of habit. When they were set, he got out the last bottle of his whiskey and poured a glass. He went over to the file cabinet. Opening it up, he began throwing files into his metal wastebasket.

When it was full, he lit a match and for the next hour and a half, burned his files. No one came, no one asked questions. When the files were completely reduced to ashes he went to the file cabinet one last time and took out a shabby old envelope and shook it out on the desk. He poured one more whiskey and sat down.

Koeller spread the photos out across the desk. He took a drink. Picking up the picture of the woman he had coveted since he first found it, stroked the photo with his finger. He especially liked the picture, but with the schoolteacher dead in Trondheim and von Weber non-compliant, he had never found out where Anna von Schauffer lived, so she became an ideal to him. He raised his glass to her, then downed the remainder of the whiskey. The taste was good in his mouth. It numbed his tongue and throat, spreading warmth through him. He looked at her and smiled, then threw all the photos into an ashtray on his desk, except hers. Tearing off the portion with the man, he put hers in his jacket pocket. He sprinkled the photos with the whiskey and lit a match. When they were consumed, he took his revolver and put it in his mouth.

No one heard the shot.

The lights were off at Victoria Terrasse.

CHAPTER 106

It was well into the evening of the same day when Rika received callers at the Nissen home. Summoned from her room where she had been packing, she found a man and woman talking to Bea in the parlor. They sat on an old sofa by a low table.

"We've been talking about the news, Rika. Isn't it wonderful?" Bea was wearing a little paper Norwegian flag on her blouse. "Capitulation is coming in to us in days, perhaps hours!"

Rika didn't answer. She looked at her guests and shuddered. They were strangers, but she sensed they were from the resistance. How far she had come. It had been ten months since A.C. first climbed the hill to the Nissen home, limping into the garden and setting her down the path to illegal work. Now she felt old and tired.

"*God kveld, Frøken* Arneson," the woman said. Like the man, she wore outdated clothes. Dark, sober-faced blondes, they almost looked like brother and sister. "A new day is coming. I understand you're packing. You going somewhere?"

"Home. I'm quitting my job. I want to find my father."

"Excellent." The man turned to Bea. "May we have a word with *Frøken* Arneson alone?"

"All right. I'll make some tea."

After Bea left, the man shut the French door. "We have been trying to reach you for some time."

"Who are you? You never said." Rika felt a growing apprehension.

"We're from security in the resistance. I'm *Herr* Omdahl and this is *Frøken* Moeja."

The man reassured Rika with some names from the ration coupon group A.C. Kjelstrup had first set her up with. The woman was friendly. Rika began to relax.

"But why do you want to see me? Isn't it still dangerous? I've heard all kinds of rumors."

"It's more dangerous not to." The man cleared his throat again. "*Vær så snill,* sit down. I want to show you some photographs." He opened his briefcase and brought out a packet of photos. The woman handed the first one to Rika.

"Why, that's Odd Sorting. He was a fisherman in my village last summer."

"Sorting' is one of his names. He's also known as Odd Morkdal or Ake Morkdal."

Rika gasped. "He's an agent?"

"In a matter of speaking. Tell me, did you know of your father's export activities?"

"Export? My father was in Export? *Nei*."

The man seemed to have the answer he wanted. The woman took over.

"What was your relationship with Andrew Kjelstrup?"

"A.C.?" Rika fiddled with a button. How did this stranger know? "He's my friend."

The woman leaned in. Rika noticed she had tiny tear in her cardigan. "When was the last time you saw him?"

"Before Christmas. Why?" A terrible tension grew in her. She felt the blood drain from her face. "Oh, my God, he's dead isn't he? Did he die in the Swedish camps?"

They didn't answer. Omdahl laid down a picture of Freyda Olsen. "Tell us about her."

Rika's voice was small. "She's a friend from my office building."

The woman put down a picture of Freyda and Sorting together. Freyda was sitting in his lap with her arms around his neck. Sorting had a hand on her breast. Rika startled.

"Did you ever see them together?" the man asked.

"*Nei*. They're lovers?"

He laid down other pictures. One of Paul, another man she worked with.

"I know them," Rika said. *A.C.!* God, she was afraid.

"Did you ever hear of the agent provocateur, Henry Oliver Rinnan?"

"Everyone has."

"Could you describe him?"

"*Nei*. Who has seen him?"

"You have."

"Me?" She laughed, a tight little laugh. "Whatever for? He's an enemy of the worst kind. Are you accusing me of disloyalty?"

"*Nei*," the woman said. She smoothed the printed fabric of her dress and folded her hands in her lap before speaking. "But you do know him. You've been working for him for months."

"Never!" Rika jumped up from her seat. "My God. What are you saying?"

"*Frøken* Arneson. We're not a jury. We're not here to judge you. We want to help you if we can. You could be in great danger."

"You *are* judging. Who are you, really?"

The woman stood up. "You must listen. Don't you want justice for him?"

"Justice?"

"Kjelstrup is dead, *Frøken* Arneson."

"Dead..." Rika put her hand to her throat. Her pulse under her fingers pounded like fury. She felt light-headed. She trembled.

The man laid down the final picture. Rika swallowed. "That's Olav Whist. My superior."

"That's Rinnan."

"*Nei…*" Rika sank down like a falling rock into the padded chair. Her stomach churned.

The man began telling her what they knew about Kjelstrup. As he spoke, she knew that he was telling the truth. Her fears about A.C. had been real. She couldn't bear to look at them.

"Sorting is an agent for Rinnan. Freyda Olsen is also a part of the organization. It was carefully planned. Rinnan needed someone with ties to Fjellstad. Sorting set you up through Freyda. You've been working for Rinnan since the end of the summer."

"*Nei*!"

"They arrested Kjelstrup a week before Christmas," the woman said. "The *razzias* hit Fjellstad and the islands around Hitra. The raids destroyed an active group involved with the smuggling of arms and agents into this country. Your father was a vital component of it as well as a man you knew as Jens Hansen. In fact, Hansen was a British-trained agent and led it."

"Jens?" Rika looked up. "But he's a deaf-mute."

"He's a very good agent. He's not deaf or mute."

"Where is my father?"

"He's safe."

Rika sighed, her voice wobbling. She hugged her arms. "And Jens?"

She remembered his teasing, the fun they had together. An image of him off-loading crates from her father's boat came to her. She had gone to thank him for the salmon for her going-away party. She sensed toughness then. *Oh, dear Lord, it was so long ago.*

"He was caught."

Rika rubbed her forehead to ease the headache about to crush her. "Is he—dead?"

"*Nei*. He was tortured, but he had incredibly good luck and was rescued. He's one of the few survivors from the *razzias* who were key people."

"Thank God." She murmured it so softly they leaned in to hear her. She clutched her stomach trying to get control of it, but eventually couldn't help herself. *A.C.!*

She stumbled over to a wastebasket and threw up. The woman leaped up to help, but Rika wrestled away. She began to wail.

"Rika! My dear, what's wrong?" Bea Nissen burst through the doors and rushed to Rika. "What's going on?" She told the woman "You get a towel from the kitchen." She pulled Rika close. "Rika, dear."

Bea's voice only made Rika feel worse. The talk behind her grew dim. She felt as though she was moving through a dream. The next thing she knew Bea was cleaning her up, telling the woman called Greta she could stay. The couple seemed to be insisting on it.

The man picked up his hat. "Believe me when I say that we have her interest at heart." He bowed politely and left.

Bea prepared a hot bath and helped Rika undress. When she was settled in the tub, Bea added some bath salts. "I've been saving them from before the war. Don't they smell nice?" She laid a towel on a stool next to her. "Now I'll show *Frøken* Moeja where she'll sleep."

Rika nodded her head numbly and lowered her body deeper into the water. She stayed that way even when Bea came by the bathroom a couple of times and peeked in. Lying against the high porcelain back, her head just sticking out of the hot water, Rika stared into the mist rising up. Her hair was wet and scraggly. Tears rolled down her pale cheeks. "Rika dear," Bea said softly, but Rika didn't answer.

Finally Bea left. Bea had been as close as a mother to her in the last year and Rika loved her. How could she look her in the face? She had been duped. And Freyda. Rika was sure the friendship was real. She put her hands over her eyes. What was real? Hansen wasn't real. A British agent? It was crazy. Just like the images she saw of A.C. lying dead somewhere.

"I killed him!" she whimpered into the steaming room. The sound was hollow, just like she felt. How could she look at her father?

And Jens. Dear Jens. He had been like the brother she had always wanted.

Tortured. She knew what that meant. How could she ever look at him again? What could she say? I'm sorry? All she wanted was to do something for her village, for her country. A.C. had shown the way. Why hadn't she seen through Freyda and the others?

She shuddered. *Rinnan.* The little man who looked like a boy. His high forehead and eyes seemed to float through the steam like an evil spirit. Why hadn't she seen? She began to weep again thinking of A.C. He had trusted her. She had put him in that car.

She wiped her mouth, stirring up the hot water around her. Bea was right. It did feel good. It would be so nice just to stay here and keep the water running hot. The steam was thick like fog and floating close to her face, caressed her like a kiss. She wanted to stay in the steam and hot water and never come out to face anyone. She sobbed and hugged her arms, turning her body in the tub's deep water. She wanted to be with A.C. She laid her cheek on the side of the tub and stared at the soap rack. It took a moment to distinguish it, then it took form through the steam....

A razor.

CHAPTER 107

It was just after midnight on May 6 when Rinnan summoned a tight-knit group of men to the Cloister. Sorting was among them. In the parlor the Chief outlined what he had learned from high Gestapo contacts in Oslo and underground sources in Trondheim.

"Now that Germany's capitulated on the continent, it could happen here any time. That will bring into the open thousands of well-armed and highly-trained militiamen."

You're not kidding, Sorting thought. Rinnan didn't add that despite their own siege of terror on illegal groups in Trøndelag and Møre for years, in the end, they hadn't destroyed the underground. In Trondheim, Milorg was still strong. Despite the *razzia* just days ago on a radio group attached to XU, Rinnan hadn't been able to identify its leader in the district.

"It's time to go," Rinnan said. "We're going to Russia, through Sweden and Finland. I'll put our services to good use."

Sorting knew it wasn't an egotistical dream. Rinnan had been in touch with agents through the Soviet Legation in Stockholm for several years. He would bring them damaging information about the Germans and Norwegians to use in the aftermath of the war. The Germans thought him an anti-Communist, but to the Soviets, Rinnan always insisted he was a devoted follower. He would become a member of the KGB.

Sorting wasn't sure what to do. He couldn't stay in Norway—he didn't want to get shot—but he was reluctant about leaving. Not before he found Freyda.

Where are you? It had been a couple of days since he'd seen her. He loved her, but she'd become so skittish. It didn't help that she was fond of Rika Arneson. In the face of this genuine friendship, Sorting worried she would spill everything she knew about Kjelstrup to the girl, putting them both in danger.

The room filled with the stink of dread crammed into a closed space.

"I have commandeered four limousines," Rinnan droned on, "all with good strong motors. We'll head for the Swedish border as far as the cars can go then on by foot. We'll pack now and leave within the next few hours. Any questions?"

There were none.

Rinnan dismissed them. Out in the hall, Sorting decided if he couldn't find Freyda in the next hour, he'd leave her to take her chances, which he felt were not too bad. Once he got in place over there, he would send for her, although Russia wasn't his idea of a good place to be. Maybe he could go somewhere else. He started to go out the door when Dolmen came over.

"*Hei*, Sorting. The Chief wants to see you privately. It's important."

Sorting came back into the parlor where Rinnan was smoking a cigarette. He smiled wanly when Sorting came into the room and indicated that he should shut the door.

"What's up?" Sorting looked for any danger signs in the Chief. They had only just returned from a *razzia* out on the coast, coming back to learn the state of things in Germany and the country here.

"We'll be taking the hostages out later this morning. I want you to go check on them."

"This the one you interrogated this morning?"

"*Ja*. Why don't you go down now? I'll be down in a minute."

"All right."

Some of the men were bringing files out into the hall to take downstairs. They would be burning papers for a while. One of the men looked at Sorting funny and he wondered why. He went around them, heading over to the door to the basement. Taking his usual big breath, he went down.

There was nothing in the main room where the posters still hung on the wall, but there were signs of the morning's activities on the pine floor. Blood. The man had been severely flailed. Sorting wondered what condition he was in for travel. He doubted Rinnan would take him very far. There was a woman too.

He started for the dark spaces that served as cells, when he heard someone stirring in the laundry room. He thought it was the female hostage, but when he came into the dim light, he realized he knew that silky head, that turn of the shoulder. It was Freyda, sitting up against the laundry tub, her hair and clothing disheveled. Abject fear overtook him.

Sorting was a hard man and had done his share of dirty work, but nothing prepared him for this unspeakable evil. He looked to see if they were alone.

"Freyda," he whispered to her. "What happened?"

She opened her swollen eyes, turned her battered face to him. She smiled when she saw him. She reached out with her unchained hand.

"Oh, Odd..." Her blouse was torn, exposing her brassiere and slip. He could see that her breasts were bruised. "I've been waiting for you." she gasped. "I've been waiting for so long." She made a little sound in her throat and tried to lean against him. "I didn't mean to make him mad. I only wanted..."

"Make who mad?"

"The Chief. He can get so angry..." Her voice was pinched like a little girl's.

"What did you do, Freyda?"

"I kept waiting for you at the apartment, but you didn't come. I was afraid you'd leave me. I didn't want to be left alone. I thought if I talked to someone, maybe things would all right."

She leaned against his shoulder. He put his arms around her. She wasn't making any sense, but he knew she was in danger. He held her close, stroking her hair. Her voluptuous body suddenly felt small and frail. "Freyda..."

"My, what a touching scene. Lovers on a grand scale," Rinnan said behind him.

Sorting closed his eyes, terrified for her. He was deeply shocked at how much he loved her. His arms began to tremble. He gave a final squeeze, rising to face Rinnan. Freyda whimpered, reaching out to him as he stood up, but Sorting stepped away.

"What you do think of her now, Sorting? What should the price of loyalty be?"

"I don't know what you are talking about."

"She's gone over. She's been speaking to people she has no business dealing with. She's a traitor. And after all that's been done for her. What do you think about that, Sorting?"

The hair on the back of his neck stiffened. Behind Rinnan stood Karl Dolmen. Neither man had any qualms about cold-blooded murder. Sorting had seen equal treatment meted for illegal worker and gang member alike. He could easily make a mistake and end up on the floor of the basement too. Yet he couldn't just let her go.

"She means nothing to you, Henry," he answered carefully. It was a great risk using Rinnan's first name, but he hoped to invoke the time before the war when they had been friends, not Chief and subordinate. "But she means something to me. Let her go. She can do no harm. It's not much different than from what we planned. Or if you wish, leave her here for them to find. But I do ask this."

Dolmen snorted. "You're a fool, Sorting."

"What if I made you lie down with her? End it here?" Rinnan asked. Sorting blanched. He had seen Rinnan's extreme cruelty only days ago. He wasn't well-disposed toward lovers. He was warped.

Sorting took a breath, then thought, what the hell. It was either this or a firing squad. Maybe this would be easier. "Then do it quickly," he heard himself say.

Rinnan looked straight at him and as if he planned it, took out a bottle of chloroform and his gun. "How will this do?"

Sorting swallowed. He felt Freyda's hand brush his pant leg like a futile moth wing. "All right." He began taking off his clothes. They would die together. He undid his tie and took off his jacket, then began taking off his clothes. Below, Freyda wept softly. Rinnan watched him for a few moments, then suddenly told him to stop.

"Enough. You've made your point. Bring in the prisoner from the back room and get him ready to go."

"And Freyda?"

"She can stay here." Rinnan stooped down and lifted up her chin. "Say nothing."

"I won't. I promise."

"Good girl. You were always my favorite. Go back to Harran. Become a housewife and have lots of babies. Say good-bye to her, Sorting, then tend to business."

Rinnan backed off. He jerked his head at Dolmen to follow him and left. He made no mention of giving Sorting the key to the handcuffs.

Sorting took out a handkerchief. Wetting it from water in the laundry tub he gently wiped his lover's face. She sat very still against the metal leg of the tub, keeping her eyes on him the whole time. Finally, she reached out to him and took his hand.

"You really do love me."

"*Ja*, I do, Freyda. I can't stay though."

"I know. I don't want you to get caught."

"If I can, I'll try to reach you. Perhaps get you out."

"You've been good to me, Odd. I've had a wonderful time."

"Will you go back to Harran?"

"Not if I can help it." Her swollen mouth gave him a lopsided smile. "You've taught me about the better things."

"Listen," he said. "I don't want you with anyone else."

"I'll make no promises, but I'll wait. Maybe after things calm down." She smoothed his hair and then began to put on his tie one handed.

It was too much for him. Seizing her, he kissed her hard, disregarding her bruised lips. She moaned a little, but kissed him back with equal desperation. Sorting looked behind him. Finding the basement deserted, he folded her in his arms and rocked her not far from where Haugland lay so close to death only months before.

CHAPTER 108

On May 6, Germany capitulated in Holland, Denmark, and northwest Germany. The *Hjemmefronten* and other illegal organizations waited to see if General Bohme, the German commander-in-chief in Norway, would comply with orders from Dönitz, the new *Furhrer*.

In anticipation, Haugland was given orders to go north of Trondheim and wait. Worried about Kjell, he was determined to bring him along. Kjell had been subdued since finding out about Rika. He kept to himself in their cabin and avoided the other men, even though they didn't know why. Haugland found him sitting in front of the wood-burning stove, warming his hands. The sun hadn't reached here yet.

"Are you sure you want me to go?" Kjell looked solemn.

"Nothing's changed, Kjell. I need you. You're my partner in all this."

Kjell blinked back tears. "You're very generous, Jens, after what happened to you."

"You are my friend. Rika's family. Get your rucksack. We're leaving in a half hour."

They skirted the city and under tight security, were taken to a rural hideaway to the north.

Axel greeted them at the farmhouse door. "Do you feel the tension?"

"*Ja*," Kjell said. "I can almost taste it."

"That's because this morning Bohemia capitulated. Someone thought they meant that bastard commander of German Armed Forces in Norway, Böheme, had too. Now that the name confusion's sorted out we're waiting for word, *any* word that it's going to be over." Axel led them into a place dimmed by curtains pulled across high windows and full of men engaged in illegal activity. Some were cleaning Sten guns, some packing rucksacks. Others were studying maps and making lists.

Kjell shouldered his rucksack. "Why must Norway be last?"

"Patience," Axel said. "Some of the lads want the German forces to start laying their arms down now, but we must wait until *they* have word. The Americans and Brits are sending in troops to help handle them when they do." He led Kjell and Haugland into a *stue*, its long windows covered too.

"What about our mountain units?" Haugland put his rucksack down.

"Not here yet. We can't arrest anyone because we can't spare our local Home Forces. The special units for the electrical plants and other facilities haven't been called into the city either. But they'll help in the release of political prisoners and in Falstad concentration camp."

Throughout the day men came and went, bringing military intelligence and news from Trondheim or from Stockholm and London via a radio hidden up in the hills. While Haugland assessed, Kjell worked on plans protecting the harbor and naval craft. It was nearly impossible to sleep, but at one in the morning, Haugland lay down on the floor in his sleeping bag and slept until seven.

He sat up, stiff and hungry. "Any word on capitulation?"

"*Nei*," a man sitting on the sofa said. "But the Milorg units are on full alert."

Haugland went in search of Kjell. He found him eating cheese and flat bread in the kitchen of the old farmhouse.

"Did you sleep last night?" Haugland asked.

"Not very well. I can't stand being so close to Rika and not being able to see her."

"I've asked security to speak to her—for her protection as much as damage control. When it's safe, we'll go find her."

"Will they arrest her?" Kjell's eyes were red, his cheeks dotted with blond stubble.

"*Nei*, Kjell. Don't trouble yourself. If and when formal inquiries are made, I'll stand with her." Haugland rubbed the stump of his finger on his left hand, stretching his fingers by making each finger touch the thumb.

Kjell sniffed. "I don't think I'll ever forgive myself for what happened to you."

Haugland sighed. "Dear friend, don't do this to yourself. You protected and hid me in plain sight all those months. At great risk to you and your girls. It's not your fault."

He opened the back door. Outside, he could barely hear the sharp chirps of little birds flitting from branch to branch in the birch and maple trees sprouting new leaves. The air smelled sweet with a pinch of pungent wood smoke. Somewhere a sheep bawled. The sunlight hit his hair. He rubbed his head, wondering if his roots were showing. Carefully, he slipped his crippled hand into his jacket pocket as he leaned against the door.

"Restless?" Kjell cleared his throat behind him.

"Like hell. I think I'll take a bike and go out for a bit."

"How about a bike ride down to the city, Ryper?" Axel said as he came into the kitchen.

"What's up?"

"Rumors. Thought I'd check them out. Someone wants to see you anyway."

Haugland looked at Kjell. "Want to come?"

Kjell smiled and put on his cap. Haugland was pleased he acted like his old self.

They crammed into a canvas-backed truck with four others, pulling their bicycles in after them. They sat on the metal seat and checked their pistols, not sure if they would use them.

"Where to?" Haugland asked.

"Elgeseter. It's as close as I want to get."

In Elgeseter, they tried to coast down the main street in two's and three's, but bicycles were everywhere, clogging up their route. There was a palpable tension as sweet as the warm spring air as men and women full of raw hope rode in one direction toward the River Nid and the Elgeseter bridge into Trondheim. There were German soldiers on the tree-lined street, but they kept to themselves in small silent groups reluctant to show they were waiting too.

At the next block, Axel left the main street and took a side lane that headed toward the grounds of the Technical Institute. There, Haugland knew, members of XU were gathered in readiness should Norway's fortune go either way, but Axel changed direction again and cutting across the back of some grounds, he brought Haugland and Kjell up to the back of the Deaf Church. He laid down his bicycle near a heavy wood door and knocked. A middle-aged man in a worn wool suit poked his head out. He looked cautiously at the group and then beyond them. Satisfied, he opened the door. "*Velkommen.* Come. There is *ersatz* upstairs."

"*Takk.*" Axel made quick introductions. "This is *Herr* Landvik, an elder at the church." Landvik looked at Haugland for a brief moment, then away as if embarrassed.

"Any news?" Axel asked as the elder started up the stone stairs.

"We're all waiting," Clausen said.

At the top, he led them into a small, sparse room under a long angled roof. "*Vær så snill.* Make yourselves at home while I get the coffee."

At the other end of the room, a man standing at a window turned. "Ryper!"

"Solheim, you're back." Haugland grinned with pleasure.

"Indeed." The pastor bounded over. He shook his hand until he grimaced. "You're looking well, Ryper. Disgusting hairdo, though. You ought to be run out of town."

Haugland laughed. "Kjell Arneson, this is Pastor Harold Solheim, my cutout here. He's been in northern Norway helping in the liberated areas. When did you get back?"

"Just yesterday. A bit of a risk, I realize, but necessary." Solheim shook Kjell's hand. "I've heard a lot about you. Good work, Arneson."

"*Takk*," Kjell said modestly.

Landvik brought in the *ersatz* coffee, then left. The men sat down on the worn furniture. They would sit there all morning long, listening to the stream of news that came from men making their quiet appearances. Some of them were associated with Milorg or XU. Others were ordinary people from the church office.

The day dragged on past noon with no change, then suddenly, just after one, there was a loud noise in the stairwell as someone rushed up the stairs. It was Landvik.

"Praise God," he said, his hands clasped in prayer. "It's over. The BBC just announced it. Capitulation was agreed upon early this morning. We are free, free!"

As if on cue, they could hear shouting outside. Haugland and Kjell went to the window.

People were pouring into the side street, heading for Elgeseter Gate. A man waved a handmade Norwegian flag back and forth. Haugland's throat tightened as more people appeared, waving flags, ringing the bells on their bicycles. Others linked arms or hugged. A woman began to sing the national anthem, her pure voice rising up like a bell. Others joined her.

Haugland felt his eyes sting and fill with tears. He blinked them away. All his pain and fears rewarded. *My all for Norway.* Out of nightmare, the dream of liberation came true, but he felt an urgency to move. They had to get Rinnan. He grabbed Axel by the arm.

"We've got to go now," he said with a thick voice.

"I'll call a car," Axel said. "We'll go immediately." They started for the hallway door.

"What are you talking about?" Kjell asked.

"Rinnan," Haugland said. "The Home Forces are not to mobilize yet, but Axel's had a watch on both residences and the Cloister since yesterday afternoon. Just in case."

"You're going back there?"

"*Ja.* It's been my plan all along." Haugland turned to Solheim. "Would you be so kind to come with me?"

"*Ja,* sure, Ryper. Any way that I can help.'

"Can I go?" Kjell asked.

"Of course, I was hoping you would. I just thought you might want to stay and call Rika."

"I'll be ready to go in just a moment. I'll call the Nissens now.'

But there was no answer.

***

A short time later they arrived at the house at 46 Jonsvannsveien a quiet area surrounded by trees and modest houses. Barbed wire curled along its boundaries. *This is the Cloister?* Haugland thought.

He stared. He'd never seen the house's exterior because he had been blindfolded. Out in front some armed men wearing hastily assembled armbands with Norwegian flags were gathered. Some wore the knickers and jackets of Milorg, but others looked like they had rushed out of their workplaces or offices. One of them saw Axel leaning out of the car window and trotted down.

"We're too late, Axel," the man said, shouldering his Sten gun against his body.

"Too late? What do you mean?"

"He's gone. The Cloister's been abandoned, the other residences too."

"Rinnan's gone?" Axel shouted. "He was supposed to be watched." He slammed his hands on the steering wheel. "Damn." He got out of the car, avoiding Haugland.

While Axel ranted and gave orders to put out an all-country alert, Haugland sat in the car feeling numb and uneasy. Finally, he got out.

A small crowd of residents gathered on the road, whispering and craning their necks to see the men going up into the house. The conversation around him implied that the house had always looked a little imposing after barbed wire had been put around it and people going in and out at odd hours, but people were surprised that the notorious Henry Oliver Rinnan had used it.

Axel led the way through the group of Milorg men who stood on the sidewalk and porch. Haugland, Solheim and Arneson followed. Axel spoke to a Milorg man at the door. They talked for some time, then both looked at Haugland.

"All right." The man opened the door.

For just a moment, Haugland hesitated. Inside the hallway was dim. Going ahead, their guide turned on a light. In one of the side rooms, some Milorg men were going through boxes, carefully putting their contents on the floor. Another room lit by a floor lamp they pulled books off shelves, sniffed decanters.

Axel stepped in. "You remember this room? It's the parlor, I gather."

"Vaguely. I was blindfolded. They took it off in the hall, then pushed me along."

They stared at the instruments of medieval torture hung on the wall.

"Jens," Kjell said. "Is this the door?"

Haugland came back into the hall. To his left was an ordinary wood door, one that could open into a bedroom or bath.

"The Cloister. Is it down there?" Axel asked.

"*Ja*," Haugland took a short breath to clear his lungs. He felt warm.

"I'll go first," Axel said.

Solheim went next. Haugland was left to his own devices, but he didn't blame them. He came last. Axel opened the door, flicked on a light and descended slowly into hell.

No one knew what to expect, least of all Haugland. All he had were his fractured memories, but when the dank smell of neglected plumbing and musty cupboards struck his nose and he saw the pine floor and the emptiness of the main room, they hit anew like sharp boning knives. His head began to ache with voices from a dream of delirium.

Welcome to the party! The name! You will say the name! Who is Ryper?

In some ways the room was as he remembered it except that it was smaller. The posters that terrorized his dreams for months seemed forlorn and drab. The collection of bottles was still on the shelves. Large wine caskets were stacked in the corner. Haugland moved away from the others, afraid his emotions were too close to the surface.

Axel came next to him. "Is this the chief room for interrogating?"

"*Ja.* I was here most of the time. As much as I can remember."

He pointed to a stool with fresh signs of blood. The other men in the group looked at Haugland and shifted their weight like awkward schoolboys. Kjell blanched.

I know, Haugland thought. *It's hard to imagine.*

More Milorg men came down. After pausing to take the scene in, they began a through search of the basement and its individual rooms.

"There's a large pool of blood on the floor by the sink," someone called from the laundry room. "It appears to be recent." The man crouched down. "There was a body here. And look. Some hair." He lifted up a strand of flaxen hair long enough to have come from a woman.

"Rinnan's become careless," Solheim said.

Haugland backed off toward the stairs. There he noticed a silk scarf bunched against the wall. Curious, he lifted it up. One end was blood-stained, but the scarf's flower pattern was still clean and familiar. Suddenly he remembered where he knew it. Freyda Olsen was wearing the same scarf in the picture in his pocket. He wondered if it was hers. Carefully, he stuffed the scarf into his pants pocket.

"Best leave everything there until it's inspected." Axel motioned for them to spread out.

They looked around, but no body was found. They did find some implements used in torture on the pine floor behind a wine casket.

"Again, let's leave things as they are," Axel said solemnly. "This is for legitimate police work here. Will you see that the rooms are sealed off?" he asked one of the Milorg men.

Kjell came and stood by Haugland.

"You all right?" he asked.

"I'm all right," Haugland said. "Really. I felt worse before I came down." Haugland looked around. "Rinnan. I wonder where the bastard is. Where's Sorting?"

They didn't get their answer until two days later.

In the meantime, Kjell's world came crashing down.

***

Trudging back upstairs, the group reassembled in Rinnan's parlor, but Haugland needed to get some air and went outside. Kjell stayed back to call the Nissens.

"Any luck? Haugland asked when he came out.

"Can't get through." Kjell frowned. "I'm going out to the Nissens. Can you come, Jens?"

"Give me an hour or so. I'll see if Axel can you get a car."

An hour later, Haugland located the Nissen house. The front door was ajar, but no one answered when he knocked. Cautiously, he took out his pistol. Inside the dark hallway, the faint sound of sobbing floated like a disembodied ghost. He followed it.

In the parlor, Kjell sat in a chair next to a wooden coffin. As Haugland approached, the hair on the back of his neck rose. His heart felt like it would pound its way out of his chest. He knew instantly Rika was lying there.

She lay in a fresh blue dress, holding some violets in her hands. She looked like she was asleep, taking a nap on her lunch break. Haugland lifted one of the long sleeves. Under the cuffs, there were slashes on her wrist.

Kjell looked up. "Jens?"

"I'm so sorry. I don't know what to say. She was a good girl. Always kind to me."

Kjell put his hands over his eyes. "If only she had talked to you. "

Haugland squeezed his friend's shoulder. "How could we know?

"There were visitors last night," Kjell said in a monotone. "They told Rika A.C. was dead. Bea Nissen said she got very upset. After the man left, she went upstairs and...."

"Who is helping you with the arrangements?"

"Thomas and Bea. I'm afraid I'm not much use at the moment. The funeral is tomorrow."

For the girl who wanted to do something, Haugland thought.

Against the great excitement of liberation, they buried Rika outside Trondheim at a small country church. The funeral was poorly attended. As they gathered around the open grave, Solheim said some words and offered what condolences he could, then left the mourners to their pain. Only a few of

Rika's local friends showed up from the office, their black clothes incongruous against the flags of celebration. The whole episode was kept quiet.

Haugland watched Kjell helplessly, knowing that this was something he would have to work through, just as he had to work through what had happened to him in the Cloister.

After the funeral, he left Kjell in the care of the Nissens. He returned to business with XU and MI IV and the hunt for Rinnan. When he was not at the Technical Institute, he was at *Hjemme for Døve* where he spent the night. Several times, he tried to reach Anna in Fjellstad, but the phone lines were down. The country was still unsettled and there was fear of sabotage.

Was she safe? The thought of her alone in the fishing village made him restless, but duty came first.

On May 9, the first British and American forces began landing in Norway, mostly in the Oslo area, but in Bergen and Trondheim as well. Troops from the OSS made up of Norwegian-Americans arrived from Sweden in Trondheim, swelling the number of military men to several thousand. Since the order to mobilize on the night of the 7th, the men had been moving out of the *fjells* and forests into the cities. They were well armed—although not always in uniform—and they were trained.

Haugland stood on the front steps of the *Hjemme for Døve* and watched as Trondheim celebrated. Bright red Norwegian flags with their blue and white crosses hung from the windows and people danced in the streets. *Fru* Andersson the housekeeper stood next to him weeping from time to time into her apron. She wasn't quite sure what to think of him now that she realized he could speak and hear, but her joy over the liberation of Vollan Prison and the Falstad concentration camp could not be contained. She seized his arm and wept on his sleeve. Haugland gave her arm a pat. The long years had been especially hard on the women.

Someone tugged at his coat. It was the girl Ona.

Germans all gone, he signed. Safe now. Ona gave him a big smile.

Back inside Haugland made several attempts to reach Anna by phone. Each time the call failed to go through, his anxiety for her increased. He pushed away his fears by working on his gear.

At *mid-dag* Axel showed up in the kitchen where Haugland was cleaning his Sten gun.

"We got a lucky break. We've found Rinnan's location."

Haugland sat up with a snap. "You're kidding. How?"

"Rinnan and his men took hostages with him—a man named Caperson and a woman. The man escaped, poor fellow. Tortured and beaten within an inch of his life. But he got away and alerted some *jøssings*. Before he collapsed, he gave Rinnan's location."

"Where's that?'

"Near the Swedish border. Snowstorm caught them. They had to turn back for shelter."

"Now what?" Haugland asked.

"Join the search party. There is a newly mobilized Milorg group in Levanger." Axel grinned. "I'll take you there."

Haugland's face must have betrayed his conflicted feelings of anxiety and resolve.

"You can always say no."

"*Nei*. I'll see it through."

Axel clapped a hand on Haugland's shoulder. "I hope it brings you peace."

Haugland stood up. "I'm not looking for peace. I'm looking for justice. Our country was turned inside out by people like Rinnan. Men thought to be heroes become foes. Look at Frøya. The man they trusted to run a secret radio unit for the past few months and raised the flag on capitulation day turned out to be Rinnan's own brother."

Haugland picked up his gun. "I'm going to find Rinnan and his gang. Then I go home."

CHAPTER 109

The old German troop carrier groaned and growled as it lurched along the snowy mountain road. Hours ago the way had been slick, but now sharp-edged ice crystals covered it. At the wide forest's edge, the truck stopped. Out of its back, a dozen heavily armed men dressed in British Army uniforms with a Norwegian flag on the sleeve climbed down. One of them was Haugland.

Once on the ground, he laid down his skis and strapped them on. Joining him was Lasse Vang, the Trondheim group leader with whom Haugland had words with last summer after the arms delivery into Trondheim. Since their last meeting, Vang had become humble. Capitulation had taken much longer than he had argued.

"Is it true Rinnan's somewhere out there under a pine bough shelter?" Vang asked.

"That's what Caperson said." Haugland slipped his boot onto his ski. "Pray the woman survives. We'll learn more when we meet the main search party."

Haugland finished the last strap. Standing up with his poles, he awkwardly adjusted his wool beret. Outside in the cold mountain air for just a moment, his damaged hand already felt stiff. He looked across the gray landscape and watched the snow drift lightly down, feeling like he had just climbed out of bed.

Vang followed Haugland's line of sight across the open snow-covered meadow to the massive white mountains rising before them. Behind them was Skjaker Valley where there were farms and forest. "So they're out there. Right near the border."

"A blizzard turned them back. Caperson said they traveled by car for two days until there was no road, then went on foot. Twelve miles from Sweden." Haugland turned to watch the group leader signal for them to come together. It was time to go hunting.

A few hours later, they skied into a mountain farmstead where they were met by the Milorg search party from Levanger. Heavily-armed, the party emerged from the cowshed starved for news and cigarettes.

"*Velkommen*," their leader said "You Hansen?"

"*Ja*. How did you know?"

"Axel gave me your description. Come in and get warm. We have a stove inside."

Haugland was led into a low-lying structure smelling of cows and sheep. A couple of the men sat on benches next to a potbelly stove whittling or drinking tea.

"I'm Anson Oyen."

Haugland removed his glove and shook his hand. "Glad to meet you. I understand you met Caperson."

"*Ja,* poor fellow. Close to a nervous breakdown and in considerable pain, but he gave us a description of the other hostage, *Fru* Holm."

"Is it true he was branded?"

"*Ja*. Terrible. Rinnan is a monster."

"*Nei,* he's the Devil himself."

Oyen looked at him with sudden curiosity.

Haugland gave him a rueful smile. "I was at the Cloister. Mostly intact."

"Good God, you're Ryper, the agent from the coast." Oyen took off his beret, nodding respectfully. "Make yourself at home."

At the stove, they talked for several minutes about Rinnan and his party. "I'm looking for a man," Haugland said. "Stocky with blonde hair. Goes by the name of Sorting or Morkdal."

"Don't know who's with Rinnan. Won't know until we catch up with them."

"Catching up" was delayed, however. To Haugland's great disappointment, a blizzard struck and trapped them for nearly three days. When the wind died down, they strapped on their skis and set out to find Rinnan in the barren *fjell* above them.

***

There were no tracks. The blizzard had wiped the *fjell* clean.

"No worry," Oyen said to the group of thirty men as they rested on their skis. "Rinnan has to be around here somewhere. No one could have survived the storm without shelter. We'll look for Rinnan and his gang in the summer cabins around that mountain over there. Look for smoke from the chimneys. They're the only ones up here. First, we'll make smaller groups."

Haugland stayed with Oyen's unit. Dressed in white parkas, they carefully combed the area, skiing silently from open *fjell* to forest stands of pine and spruce and back out into slushy open tracks of land. After several hours, they finally came upon a small cabin set back among tall pine trees, emitting smoke.

Immediately, Oyen signaled his men to spread out, but before they got into position gunfire erupted from the cabin. "Run!"

The frozen ground exploded in front of them, sending up shards of dirt and snow into their faces. A bullet whizzed past Haugland's head. Behind him someone yelped. Stabbing his poles into the ground, Haugland skated for cover.

In the safety of the trees, they returned fire for the first time, making their way into position as Oyen directed them. Setting a vicious crossfire on the cabin, they nearly tore it apart. Tingling glass and jagged wood splinters sailed in every direction, the doors and windows disintegrating under the merciless fire. Gray, acrid smoke drifted across the yard as thick as the smoke from the chimney. Soon a makeshift white flag waved at them through the destroyed door.

"Watch it," Oyen said. "Jorgeson. Sorem. Cover me. Ryper, you coming?"

Haugland slid forward on his skis, his Sten gun pointed at the shattered door frame. Men were starting to come out of the cabin, some of them coughing. Then a woman appeared. One of Oyen's men helped her away while Oyen ordered the prisoners to put their hands on their heads.

Haugland pointed with his gun. "There he is. That's Rinnan."

Dressed in tweed knickers, heavy sweater and a wool jacket, Rinnan stepped out, looking like someone who had been caught in bad weather without his rain gear on a hunting holiday. His unshaven face looked haggard. At the moment, he was not the figure of power he had been for so long. Haugland had forgotten how small he was, but then he had been sitting on a stool eye-to-eye with the monster most of the time. His stomach tightened at the memory. Cautiously, the Milorg men came forward, motioning the men with their guns to form a group. Haugland searched each face. Sorting was not among them.

From the side, Haugland watched Rinnan dispassionately as they searched him for weapons and suicide pills. It was strangely unsettling, almost anticlimatic. Haugland had expected a fiercer fight.

"Do you know the others?" Oyen asked Haugland.

"That one. Birger Strom." He went back to watching Rinnan. The little monster was almost jovial as they handcuffed him, chatting with his captors. Surely, he knew there was a nation-wide hunt for him since capitulation. His cars had radios. The bile in Haugland's stomach rose higher and burned.

Once the men were secured and *Fru* Holm looked after, they prepared to return to Levanger where Rinnan and his gang would be transported to Trondheim. The snow had stopped and where they stood, a thaw had created a swampy mix of water and heavy snow all over the terrain. Haugland didn't look forward to going back.

Rinnan continued to play court with his gang members and guards despite his handcuffed hands. Asking for a cigarette, one of the *Milorg* men obliged. Rinnan joked as it was lit for him and placed between his lips. He leaned his head back to take a drag.

Haugland closed his eyes. Rinnan had done that at the Cloister then smashed the burning cigarette into his broken, bleeding hand.

Welcome to the party. There isn't anything I won't know.

Despite the chilly mountain air, Haugland felt his face grow hot. The bile in his throat rose higher and seared his throat.

After a while, Rinnan realized Haugland was staring at him. Despite his new hair color, something must have struck Rinnan. "What do you want?" His mouth worked around the cigarette.

"I want you for murder."

Rinnan choked on the cigarette, but kept it between his teeth. "Do I know you?"

"You should. You left a few messages on my back last Christmas."

Rinnan's face clouded. "I don't know what you're talking about."

"Oh, I think you do. I think you can remember every little detail that went on in the Cloister. The people you tortured, the woman you stripped and hung, the man you cut up into pieces because he wouldn't fit into a box." Haugland spat the words out, his voice rising.

Rinnan said nothing, but he avoided Haugland's gaze. He turned away.

Haugland took two leaps. "Don't you turn away, you bastard." He grabbed Rinnan by the arm. His hand went more than halfway around. *And for once I tower over you*, he thought.

"You take a good look. You branded me and left me for dead."

"I don't know who the devil you are." Rinnan shrugged Haugland off, but Haugland grabbed him again. His gloved fingers dug into Rinnan's arm.

"I'm Ryper, the SIS agent from Fjellstad."

"Ryp…." Rinnan's face seemed to collapse losing all its color. His cigarette, teetering on the edge of his lips, fell onto the slush. Haugland ground the butt deep into the mud with his boot.

Rinnan's jaw began to twitch. "You can't threaten me." He jerked his shackled arm away and backed off, but Haugland kept coming until Rinnan was forced back against the dismal group of handcuffed men. For once he looked for the safety of the Milorg men. Oyen caught his eye and prepared to intervene.

"It's no threat," Haugland snarled. "You can hold court all you want here, but you can't hide behind the Germans any more. You can't inflict fear or bully good, decent people. You will be judged for the murder of the men of Ålesund and the *razzia* on the good people of Fjellstad. You will be judged for the murder of my brother, Per Haugland, Einar Fromme and the Haraldsen men. You will remember them all when they take you out and blast you to hell!"

"You're raving mad. It's all lies."

"Not lies. I'm going to testify against you and tell what happened in the Cloister." He balled his hands into fists.

"Oyen," Rinnan called out.

Haugland stepped back, his hands up. "It's all right," he said. "He's all yours." He started to leave then sharply turned around. "Where's Sorting?"

"I wouldn't know."

"Never mind. I'll find him. I just want to see the look on his face when I tell him that his woman is dead and you killed her. Her body was found in an abandoned car outside the city."

"Shut up!"

"He'll sing."

Without warning, Rinnan charged Haugland despite his handcuffs. "Shut up!"

Before Oyen and a couple of Milorg men could intervene, Haugland grabbed Rinnan by the collar, and lifting him off the ground stuffed his beret into his mouth.

"You're a sick banty rooster, Rinnan," Haugland yelled. "That's all you are." Dropping him, he punched him twice. The little man went sprawling into the mud and snow.

"Enough!" Oyen shouted. "He must come to trial." He threw himself between Haugland and Rinnan. Another man restrained Haugland by the arms.

He pulled away. "Don't worry, Oyen. He's all yours. I'd like to take a couple of your men with me. I want to find Odd Sorting. He's responsible for the *razzia* in Fjellstad."

"All right. I'll give you Jorgeson. He grew up around here. He can pick the others." Oyen whistled to a tall lanky man and motioned him over. Haugland snapped up his beret and stepped over Rinnan. Underneath him, the little man struggled to a sitting position and swore as men lifted him to his feet. Already his eyes were swelling up shut, the side of his face one large bruise. He twisted out of his captors' grasp, yelling at the top of his lungs.

Haugland didn't bother to turn. "Rot in hell, you devil," he spat, walking away with his skis on his shoulder.

***

Haugland caught up with the other two units in the late afternoon. They had run down more of Rinnan's gunmen, bringing the total to seventeen. Sorting was nowhere to be found.

"I got the idea," the Milorg leader of the second unit said, "after talking to this crowd the man you are looking for broke away with another. Might be trying to get to the border again."

He waved his hand at the group of newly captured men standing in a circle with their hands on top of their heads, waiting their turn to be handcuffed and taken away.

"Sorry lot," he said. "They didn't appreciate the news you brought about Rinnan. I've put a watch on them so they don't do away with themselves. It's the explicit wish of the *Hjemmefronten* that they all come to trial."

"Has the area been thoroughly searched?" Haugland studied the frozen land around him.

"Had a pretty fierce fight before you showed up. After they surrendered, the hut was pretty well cleaned out." The man was unshaven, looking like he hadn't slept since liberation.

"I thought I saw another cabin above this one when I came in. Was it checked?"

"*Nei*. We came in from over there."

"Sorting's got to be close. Rinnan had them split into smaller groups, but they couldn't move after the blizzard hit."

"Well, if you lads are going up, you can take a couple of my men too."

The second hut was situated on a heavily forested hill of pine and birch. Going up on either side were two snowy trails. One came in from the right of the cabin, the other straight up. Avoiding the latter, the men broke off and worked their way silently through boot-deep snow. Leaving his skis behind, Haugland went to the far right, trying to find a way to approach the hut from above. Soon he was separated from the others.

The woods were quiet. A slight breeze caressed the soft needles of the pine trees, giving an aura of suspense. Haugland gained the top, turning to listen. Down below he could see one of his companions moving cautiously through the stand. Further to his right, the other Levanger man moved into position and waited. Directly below was the hut, a summer cabin with a stovepipe sticking out of the snow-covered roof, wood stacked at the back door. The windows were uncovered, but gave no clue as to who was inside.

Leaning against a tree, Haugland removed his glove to scratch the stump of his finger. Behind him, the top of the hill was flat for a couple of hundred feet, the forest of thin pine trees and birch going further back to yet another hill and deeper snow. He cocked his head for better hearing. A bird darted out from a bush behind him, the sound of its frantic feathered flight nearly lost to him. Suddenly gunfire erupted with a tremendous roar down below. Someone screamed. Seconds later the guns of the *Milorg* men exploded, automatic fire tearing into the wood walls of the cabin. He watched for movement at the back of the cabin. Whoever was inside couldn't take the numbing gunfire too long.

He nearly missed movement at the corner of his left eye. From out of a clump of young straight-as-arrows pines, something dashed back into the deeper recesses of the thick stand. In a single fluid motion, Haugland brought his Sten gun around to bear on the gray-blue blur as it disappeared into the late afternoon gloom of the forest. The gun bucked but his quarry got away. Unable to grip the gun properly with his damaged hand, he flung the glove off.

Haugland dived into the safety of a clump of trees as a single revolver returned fire. It glanced off a tree trunk near him, flinging pungent splinters at his chest. He twisted around to the other side of the pine and waited. Further off he could hear movement, but unless he cocked his good ear, it was hard to distinguish it over the gunfight below. When he thought it safe, he moved forward to his right, using the trees for protection.

The thawed snow underneath his feet was icy. Ahead of him a shadow moved back between the pines. Instinctively, Haugland flattened himself against the trunk of a large birch, just in time to avoid a single shot whizzing past his face. He took a deep breath. Rolling around it to his left, he fired into the direction of the shooter. The Sten gun's staccato report was loud even to his poor ear, but its barrel felt cold in his exposed hand. When gunfire was sparingly returned, Haugland pulled back to wait, blowing on his fingers to warm them.

Two more shots fired. He's low on ammunition, Haugland thought. He got a glimpse of a man in gray and dark blue clothes as he darted for the next hill. On his head was a skier's cap, but underneath the hair was straw blonde. It was Sorting. Haugland was certain.

"Sorting!" Haugland called out. "Give it up. We have Rinnan."

As he talked, Haugland moved forward slightly, mentally checking the clip in the gun. He would have to fend Sorting off without assistance for a bit, but the gunfire had stopped below.

"Your hostage got away. Both of them made it."

Haugland got a glimpse of blue and fired rapidly, freezing against the nearest trunk when bullets came strafing back at him in rapid succession.

"You won't be able to do that long."

"Go fuck yourself, whoever you are."

"I'm Jens Hansen. I've come back." Haugland spurted forward. Firing above Sorting's head, he forced him to change his direction just as he was starting to leap up on some rocks. Sorting fired three times, his aim going wild. Faintly, Haugland heard the clicking sound of an empty gun.

"Damn!" Sorting charged the rocks once more but Haugland fired above him, stopping him in his tracks. Backing down, he threw away the gun.

"Hands up! On your head!"

Sorting came down and stopped. His face was pink from the cold. A beard of gold prickling his skin, Sorting looked tired and haggard.

"Keep you hands in sight," Haugland ordered. He tucked the Sten gun under his arm, keeping aim while he searched his pockets with his left hand for his handcuffs. All the time he kept his gaze on Sorting whose expression went from disdain to disbelief.

"Christ… Hansen? You were as dead as a field stone. I put you there myself. How'd you do it?"

"Does that gall you? I hope so because I'll never tell."

Haugland ordered Sorting to put his hands together in front of his chest. Haugland noticed he smelled of stale alcohol and sweat.

"You were beaten to a pulp, Hansen. You were out over two days. You lay there like a piece of stinking meat. We finally dumped you."

Haugland said nothing, staying focused. He slapped the first cuff on Sorting's right wrist and snapped it closed. "Why don't you shut up."

"Do you remember?" Sorting continued. "Dolmen liked working on you. Thrilled him."

"Dolmen's dead. Shot himself."

"You do remember. Strom beat you. He was good with the whip. Liked how it sliced a man's back open."

"We have Strom. Hold still, Sorting."

"Your hand looks terrible. Does it work?"

Haugland flinched, his mouth tightening at the corners. He grabbed onto Sorting's right wrist with his bad hand, but in one motion Sorting tore his hand out of his grasp and swung the free end of the cuff at Haugland's face. It struck him on the side of his eye. He jerked his head away but when Sorting tried to seize the Sten gun, he swung it at Sorting's side. The light mechanism went off. Sorting still grabbed the gun.

Like two stags, they twisted against each other in the semi-frozen mud. Haugland couldn't get Sorting's hands off the barrel. Gradually, he tired, his bad hand stiff from the cold. Exerting himself one last time, he pushed hard against Sorting, nearly gaining the gun when they hit a patch of ice. They both crashed to the ground, the gun flying against a tree and bouncing to the ground. They rolled and tumbled back up again.

"Fuck!" Sorting pushed away, going for the gun. Haugland swung him into a tree, but went down with him. They fought and rolled on the thawing earth, their clothes gathering mud and pine needles. They broke off and faced each other again.

Between breaths, Haugland pointed out the silence from below. "It's over, Sorting. Give it up."

"Forget it." Sorting sounded equally winded. "You know who got you, Hansen? Arneson's daughter. Kjelstrup was screwing her. She was working for Rinnan. Exported Kjelstrup out right to Mission Hotel. How do you like that?"

Haugland said nothing. He could see the Sten gun and mentally noted the distance. He waited for Sorting to attack again, but was unprepared when Sorting hurled a heavy stick at his bad hand. It hit him like a club, making him cry out in agony. As he staggered back, Sorting seized him by his throat and knocked him to the ground.

Straddling him, Sorting seized Haugland's head and repeatedly pounded it into the cold slush. Haugland twisted his body to dislodge him. When that didn't work, he grabbed a handful of snow and rubbed it on Sorting's face. It made Sorting loosen the grip on his throat.

Without a word Haugland grabbed Sorting's coat and brought up his knee full force into the small of the man's back. In one flip, Sorting was over his head, crashing into a small birch tree. While Sorting struggled to his feet, Haugland scrambled across the icy ground. Reaching the Sten gun, he fired, hitting Sorting three times in the shoulder and arm. Screaming, the man fell back against the tree and was still. Haugland limped over, covering Sorting with the gun.

The man's head was down. Blood blossomed on his sweater and coat. When he stirred, Haugland aimed the gun at Sorting's head. For a long black moment, he thought about his brother Per, Einar, and the five lost years of his life. He brushed the trigger, knowing how sensitive it was. He paused, the longest pause in the long years of struggle he had ever taken, then slowly lowered the weapon as a heavy weariness swept over him. Weariness from battle, weariness from pretending to be someone else.

Conscious now, Sorting stared at him in disdain. "You can't do it, can you?"

"*Nei*, you're not worth it." Haugland pulled back. He felt light-headed and disconnected.

Behind him, the Levanger men rushed up and trained their guns on Sorting. Someone from Oyen's unit knelt to tend his wound.

Haugland grabbed one of the men by his jacket. "Why bother? Let him bleed out."

The man patted Haugland's shoulder in sympathy. "You know the orders—we have to take them back alive."

Haugland didn't answer. His breath came out in slow pants of steam.

Someone gave him a canteen. Another brought his beret and glove. Haugland put the glove on gently. His hand throbbed, but the pain would settle down after a while. The weariness continued to spread through him. He felt like a sleepwalker. Time to go.

Sorting groaned. Still propped up against the tree, his blood-soaked jacket was opened. Hands pressed a scarf into his shoulder. It looked bad, but Haugland didn't care. He started to leave when he remembered the silk scarf he had found in the Cloister.

"Recognize this?" He dangled it over Sorting. It had a dark stain on one end of it. Dropping it, it floated down to Sorting's chest.

Sorting clutched the scarf. "Where did you get this?"

"Ask Rinnan. I don't think they'll shoot you, Sorting, but you'll spend a long time remembering the one thing that you really did care about. Maybe that's justice."

"Where'd you get this?"

"You know the place. Your chamber of horrors. Rinnan killed her there."

Haugland turned and walked away, ignoring Sorting's howling calls.

"Freyda! What the devil have you done with her?"

Haugland shouted back, "Ask Rinnan." He shouldered his Sten gun and signaled to the Levanger men.

"Where are you going?" someone asked.

"Home. I'm going home."

CHAPTER 110

On May 17, Tore Haugland returned with Kjell Arneson to Fjellstad. Kjell drove a German truck Haugland commandeered in Trondheim. Helmer, Petter Stagg and his father and the other *på skauen* boys, Karl and Arne, were crowded in the back.

"Nervous?" Kjell swerved around a pothole full of last night's rain.

Haugland cocked his head. "*Ja*, for sure. I feel I've been away for years." He rolled down the passenger window and let warm air into the cab. Ahead he could see the steep sides of the fjord rising like blue-green wings above the fields and woods.

"I do, too. Afraid to see what's left of my house."

Haugland looked away, rubbing the stump of his finger. Ruin and sorrow amidst the joy. The Norwegian Police Corps had come into the country on May 11. Crown Prince Olav returned from exile in England on the following day. The concentration camps had been liberated, the pitiful POWs from Russia, Yugoslavia and Poland freed. Those who had aided the Germans or had been NS officials and party members were arrested. Norway was exhausted, half-starved and broke, but they were all free. Including his brother Lars, hospitalized in Oslo with a serious wound, but reunited with his wife and son.

And now he was coming back to Fjellstad. *To Anna.* He had no idea of her whereabouts.

In the five days since he fought Sorting in the mountains and snow, he had pushed for this moment, anxious and fearful. Some *quislings* in Fjellstad had cut the phone lines and blown up a number of poles. That ended all communication. With materials so scarce, it would stay that way for some time. It had been weeks since he had last seen her and he was rife with uncertainty and desire, hallmarks of a more adolescent love. Kjell found it humorous, so unlike the person he'd shown himself to be the past year, but he was terrified that after all he'd been through, some silly little disaster would happen and he'd get killed now. He would never see Anna again.

He took the fishhook Anna had given him from his uniform jacket and rolled the smooth end between his fingers. Yet he had gone out with the party to get Rinnan and Sorting. Sometimes he felt guilty leaving her for that.

As they crossed the last bridge outside the village, Haugland could see Norwegian flags everywhere, their bright colors snapping in the breeze off roofs and makeshift poles. The main road was muddy, as usual, and everywhere, the trees and flowers were blooming. Radios blared. Nothing could be more spring-like than this sense of freedom.

Kjell drove past the outlying buildings then stopped. "Sure you don't want to come into the village first? So many people will want to see you, Jens."

"I told Anna weeks ago I'd meet her at the house. She'll be waiting there." He got out of the cab and shouldered his leather rucksack. "I'll see you as soon as I can." He shut the door, adjusting his beret as he walked to the back of the truck.

Helmer Stagg stuck his head out of the canvas top and grinned. "Can't wait, can you?"

Haugland felt absurd. "Would you? Besides I need to practice my speech for the villagers. I don't know what to say to them." Haugland nodded toward the water and laughed. "Come think of it, they've never heard me speak. I might disappoint them. I'm not Charles Boyer."

"Whatever you say, they will listen. They are just proud of you, that's all. We all are. Anna will make sure you're presentable. Ask her to fix your hair. Your roots are showing."

Haugland pulled at his hair. "*Ja.* See you." He waved his friend off and began to jog the narrow country road toward the forested hills above the fjord road. Behind him, the truck started up, running smoothly on the gas he pilfered in Trondheim. Another skill he had learned.

It had been more than a year since he hiked this way to his hidden radio after the Germans searched the village for contraband. A lifetime away of deceit and danger. It felt strange, unnatural not to be looking over his shoulder or careful of speaking in this place. And what of his future? Except for his desire to marry Anna and take her and Lisel away, he had no idea if he would continue his old life and go back to the university or start over. Maybe go to America where Anna had relatives.

He kept jogging. Once he passed the last farmhouse and headed up into the trees, he looked back into the village. The German troop carrier had attracted attention as soon as it was in the village proper. People were out of their houses running alongside it, some of the children waving flags. When it stopped at the ridge the crowd surged toward it. For a moment, he wondered if they had heard about Rika. Unable to discern faces the size of summer grain, Haugland took out his binoculars and focused on the truck.

Haugland chuckled. To his relief, the villagers greeted them all with joy. Some of Kjell's fishing friends were hanging on the running board shouting at him to come out. Behind them, their wives and daughters laughed and wept. In the back, Petter, Helmer, and the other men got out. When Kjell stepped down, he was nearly flattened against the truck's cab in a heartfelt crush. Ella plowed her way through the crowd. To his surprise, Kjell kissed and hugged her tight to the laughter of everyone around him. *Well done, dear friend,* he thought.

He stepped into the trees. He had his own welcome waiting for him.

Ducking under the branches of the birches and pines, he worked his way through the thick stand. He started down a path showered with pine needles that would put him on the far side of Anna's main pasture. The farmhouse was blocked by the forested hill that went up to the logged-out area, but he looked for telltale signs of wood smoke from the chimney. When he saw none, he moved down toward the fjord for a better view, then stopped in horror.

The house was gone.

Uncomprehending, he squinted against the warm spring sun, staring across the pasture and the trees that lined the garden. It wasn't there.

He began to run, his voice crying out in anguish. It wasn't true. She had to be safe. He charged across the wet meadow, his boots slipping on the green grass.

"Anna!" he yelled, his words whipping away from his mouth. He clutched his chest with his damaged hand and ran like a crazed man until his lungs burned. At the garden's edge, he vaulted over the fence.

The barn was still there, old and in need of repair more than ever. The springhouse and the other outbuildings were intact. But the house! The upper structure and roof were gone. The rest of the house was a charred ruin, the walls, the beams and uprights standing like a burned-out skeleton. Only the ancient stone foundation of the dairy and basement remained untouched.

His nightmare of the village on fire returned to him, but this time, Anna was trapped in the *stue,* her mouth a soundless "o" as she pounded at the fiery window.

"Think, think," he muttered, trying to remain calm. He knew the phone lines had gone out on the day of liberation. Someone jimmy-rigged a phone connection miles out on the valley road by the lake. A new sheriff was on his way, someone in the resistance all the years, and trained for peace.

Where was Anna? What had happened to her?

The fire, he could tell, had spread quickly. She could have been easily trapped. Like a blind man, he walked down to dairy looking for clues. At the back, some of the beams were lying like giant pick-up sticks where the windows and wall had been, the beautiful view destroyed. On the ground in front of the foundation, glass was scattered, evidence of the intense heat of the fire. The windows had blown out.

"Anna!" he cried. "I'm sorry. I should have come sooner."

He wiped his sleeve across his eyes. Then the anger came. It was Rinnan's fault. He had taken someone else Haugland loved. His most precious one. He choked back his tears. Taking out the fishhook, he squeezed it in his fist until the barb cut him.

Miserable, he closed his eyes, too drained and heartsick to think. His damaged hand throbbed, his back burned along its maze of scars. A breeze from the fjord caressed his face, bringing with it the smells of the inland sea and wood smoke. Smoke? Opening his eyes, he looked in the direction of his old cabin.

A little trickle of smoke rose above the trees. Was Magnuson clearing and rebuilding the blown-up cabin? Jogging down to the path in the brambles, he made his way through to the pines.

The front of the cabin had collapsed, causing the sod roof to cave in at the front door, but at the back and sides, most of the walls were still standing, supporting the beams at an acute angle. Miraculously, the stovepipe seemed to be functional. It looked deserted, but someone *was* there. Quietly, afraid to say anything, to hope anything, he looked inside.

She was sitting by the woodstove on a stool, digging at the torn-up floor with a stick. A sweater was draped over the shoulders of her cotton spring dress. Her gold hair was combed back and held with barrettes. She turned sharply when she heard him.

"Jens!" she shouted as she ran to him.

He crushed her in his arms for fear she wasn't real. "God, I was so afraid," he whispered as he rocked her. "I thought you were dead."

"I'm all right." She pulled back and lifted up his chin. "The chimney caught on fire and went right to the roof. I couldn't stop it, so I ran with Lisel. For five days we've been staying in the village with Ella."

I safe, she signed. And now with you.

"What have we here?" Anna opened up his fingers.

Traces of blood followed the lines in the palm of his hand. "My promise to you."

He said it with conviction. After all the years of danger and intrigue, he didn't have to lie or hide his motivation anymore. He could finally be his true self.

Det vil helst gaa godt. Everything will work out all right.

Her lips felt soft as she took the hook from his hand.

AUTHOR NOTES

An action film about skiers in the snow during World War II and a couple of books on wartime Norway led to ideas for THE JØSSING AFFAIR, but a declassified book for spies bound for Norway found on a university bookshelf framed and brought the novel to life. Personal interviews with survivors of the occupation of Norway and a lot of sheep cheese provided more story and appreciation for this nearly forgotten piece of history.

The stories of those who fought back against the Germans in Norway are epic in nature. The Shetland Bus, a SOE-run organization made up of mostly Norwegian fishermen, ran arms and agents between the Shetland Islands and occupied Norway. Conrad Bonnevie-Svendsen, the minister for the deaf in Norway, was a leading figure in the resistance. And Henry Oliver Rinnan, a man barely five feet tall, led a sadistic organization that disemboweled resistance cells all over central Norway where the story takes place. After Quisling, he was Norway's top war criminal.

To learn more, there are a number of books and websites to consider. Some are classics:

The Shetland Bus. David Howarth.
Blood on the Midnight Sun. Hans Christian &Per Klem
Report from 24. Gunnar Sonstedby.
9 Lives Before Thirty. Max Magnus.
Hvem Var Henry Rinnan? Per Hansson

Websites:
Tore Eggan's amazing collection of photos, many taken by German soldiers from occupied Norway http://krigsbilder.net/coppermine/
Home Front Museum, Oslo. http://forsvaretsmuseer.no/Hjemmefrontmuseet

ABOUT THE AUTHOR

J.L. Oakley grew up in Pittsburgh, Pennsylvania. After college, she worked her way west to the Hawaiian Islands. While going to school there, she met her future husband and for a time they lived on the Big Island. They moved to the Pacific Northwest where they raised three sons.

A award-winning author, Oakley writes historical fiction that spans the mid-19th century to WW II with characters standing up for something in their own time and place. Her writing has been recognized with a 2013 Bellingham WA Mayor's Arts Award, the 2013 Chanticleer Grand Prize, the 2014 First Place Chaucer Award and the 2015 WILLA Silver Award. Recently, she began writing mysteries. Saddle Road and Coconut Islands, Lei Crime Kindle World novellas, are best sellers.

When not writing, Oakley demonstrates 19th century folkways at national parks and museums, and presents history workshops to school-age students. Good times!

To find her work, go to http://www.amazon.com/J.L.-Oakley/e/B004CF0W0W

Her website and blog: https://historyweaver.wordpress.com

Twitter: @jloakley

Made in the
USA
Lexington, KY